The Lanterns of the King of Galilee

Ibrahim Nasrallah

The Lanterns of the King of Galilee

Translated by
Nancy Roberts

The American University in Cairo Press
Cairo   New York

First published in 2014 by
The American University in Cairo Press
113 Sharia Kasr el Aini, Cairo, Egypt
www.aucpress.com

Exclusive distribution outside Egypt and North America by I.B.Tauris & Co Ltd., 6 Salem Road,
London, W2 4BU

Dar el Kutub No. 23472/13
ISBN 978 977 416 666 2

Dar el Kutub Cataloging-in-Publication Data

Nasrallah, Ibrahim
        The Lanterns of the King of Galilee: A Palestinian Novel / Ibrahim
    Nasrallah—Cairo: The American University in Cairo Press, 2014
        p.   cm.
        ISBN: 978 977 416 666 2
        1. English Fiction
        823

1 2 3 4 5   18 17 16 15 14

Designed by Shehab Abdallah
Printed in the United States

To Mai Nasrallah, Ali Nasrallah,
and the Arab Spring witnessed by their generation,
I dedicate this new journey
in search of deeper roots

Contents

Acknowledgments

Special thanks go to the following friends and colleagues: Dr. Ziyad al-Zu'bi for his assistance in locating a number of manuscripts and for the numerous discussions we had on the topic of this novel; Dr. Juni Mansur for his help in procuring manuscripts and oral testimonies, as well as every new piece of information being published on the time period I was researching; researcher and critic Elias Nasrallah for his rich, insightful, and detailed observations on many of the novel's events; Dr. Jabbur Khuri who, in a loving gesture that took me totally by surprise, made a tour in which he photographed many of the fortresses and other places where the events of this novel are set; Muna Darwaza for her observations and comments, and for translating various materials dealing with the period in which Daher lived from English into Arabic; Hanna al-Hajj; Ghazi Mas'ud; and finally, Dr. Muhammad Abd al-Qadir for the careful observations he offered from start to finish.

Author's Note

In the eighteenth century, on the shores of Lake Tiberias among the mountains of Galilee, an ordinary man began his journey toward the greatest aim anyone could hope to achieve in those days, namely, the liberation of his land and establishment of an autonomous Arab state in Palestine. In so doing, he was destined to challenge the rule of the most powerful state in the world at that time, the Ottoman Empire, which had extended its sway over the continents of Europe, Asia, and Africa. The man's name was Daher al-Umar al-Zaydani (1689–1775).

While researching sources for my novel *Time of White Horses*, I happened across various short studies of Daher al-Umar al-Zaydani. However, they weren't exhaustive enough to give me a complete picture of this historical figure and his grand liberation scheme. Then one day in December 1997, at the opening of an art exhibit in Amman, Jordan, I met engineer Ziyad Abu al-Saud, who gave me a book entitled *Daher al-Umar: A Book on the History of Galilee in Particular, and the Lands of Syria in General* by Tawfiq Mu'ammar al-Muhami. When I read the book, I did so with the idea of drawing on it for *Time of White Horses*, and some of the events it recounted made a powerful impression on me. I also thought of writing a play some day based on the book's contents.

In fact, however, none of the events recounted in al-Muhami's book appeared in *Time of White Horses*, nor did I ever write the play I had in mind. What happened was even better: Daher al-Umar began to steal ever so gradually into my inner being, taking shape in his own time.

I was afraid at first that if I attempted a novel about such a major historical figure, I would find myself unduly restricted in what I could say. However, after reading two biographies of Daher al-Umar, one by Mikhail Niqula al-Sabbagh *(Tarikh Daher al-Umar)* and the other by Abbud al-Sabbagh *(al-Rawd al-zahir fi tarikh Daher)*, I began to feel more confident about the prospect. When I finished my study of this man and began forming my own vision of him, I thought: Why not travel back to the eighteenth century and live there for a while? It's an opportunity that might not present itself again! Why not learn how to be free even when writing about a historical figure of the stature of Daher al-Umar al-Zaydani? And that is what I did.

What saddens me now is that I didn't come to know this great man earlier in my life. And what saddens me even more is that he remains virtually unknown to a large sector of the population, both in Palestine and elsewhere. This matchless character has long been worthy of the attention of novelists and film and television producers, who could have made him a luminous part of our popular consciousness and the ongoing struggle of the people who have populated and given life to the land of Palestine. I'm certain that if we had made Daher al-Umar's acquaintance before, we would be the better for it!

Unfortunately, many people are ignorant of what Daher achieved toward establishing an autonomous Arab homeland in Palestine. Ironically, it was this very homeland that later fell prey to the Zionist onslaught that wrested it from its owners by means of myths, tanks, and collusion, both external and internal, claiming that it was "a land without a people for a people without a land" when, in fact, it was a land teeming with life!

Given the stature of Daher al-Umar al-Zaydani, or the "King of Galilee"—as he came to be known during the middle phase of his liberation struggle before his influence extended beyond Galilee—the experience of writing this novel was exceptionally difficult, and laid on my shoulders a huge weight of responsibility. However, I emerged from the experience a changed man. I feel as though the time I spent with Daher al-Umar rearranged my soul and laid a wonderful new foundation for my identity, enabling me to trace the roots that go so deep into the land of Palestine: Arab Palestine; the Palestine of beauty, tolerance, and the willingness to embrace the other, accepting his or her difference and respecting this difference in all its forms; the Palestine of cultural, spiritual, and human richness; the Palestine that aspires to all that is free, lovely, and good. If I have any hope, it is that those who read this novel will relive all the feelings I experienced in the course of writing it, and when that happens I'm sure they'll sense how much better they've become.

And now for a few necessary remarks:

— The two biographies of Daher's life together come to a mere hundred pages, and contain occasional discrepancies. Hence, given the brevity of these accounts and the points on which they diverge, I found it necessary to overlook or rewrite some events, as well as to add events that would help create a narrative world that went beyond literal factuality. It was also necessary to create additional characters in order to establish a novelistic structure that could do justice to this rich and lengthy historical period.

— The dramatic course of the novel required me to move a few events up and to delay others in keeping with the logic of the narrative.

— Despite its overall faithfulness to the facts, this work does not purport to be fully accurate in the information it presents. Rather, it relies primarily on the power of reality and imagination as they combine to communicate the essence of events and characters.

Translator's Note

The body of water from which the Jordan River arises has two names: the Sea of Galilee and Lake Tiberias. The novelist refers to it most often as "the lake."

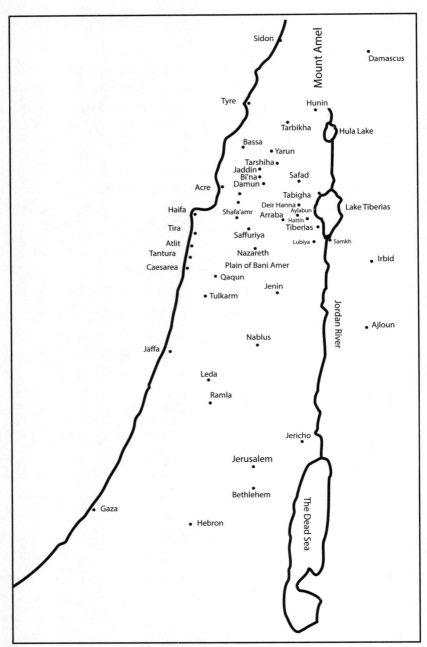

Map of Palestine in the eighteenth century

What you believe doesn't matter to me.
What matters to me is what you do with your belief!

Lake Tiberias

Daher opened his eyes one morning
to find his brothers standing over his head.
If it hadn't been for the fact that their swords
were in their sheaths,
he would have thought they were about to kill him!
"So, are you going to sleep through the night and
leave us in this state of confusion?"
Saad wanted to know.
Daher rubbed his eyes with the back of his right hand.
"Have you arrived at a solution?" he asked.
"No, we haven't," said Saleh.
"Oh yes we have!" Saad contradicted him.
"Tonight we'll light the lanterns!"

In that spacious room four lanterns shone.
The wind was still, and there was nothing but the sound of breaths,
breaths coming from distant lungs
that didn't belong to the four statue-like bodies.
The waves rolling in from Lake Tiberias and striking the wall of the
house had the impact of a roaring sea.
Each of them sat staring into the
flame of the lantern before him,
certain that he was staring into his own fate.

The Enormous Shadow and
the Barefoot Woman

The road to the cemetery one winter's day was the beginning of their journey. The brothers buried their father, Umar al-Zaydani, in silence, each of them stealing glances at the others. At the same time, people were watching every move being made by the eldest brother, Saad al-Umar.

The father's departure had come as no surprise. He had died after a protracted, enervating illness, which had given him time to choose one of his sons as his successor. However, the four brothers, who alone were aware of their father's wishes, kept them well concealed.

A powerful wind blew up and scattered the dirt that had been brought up from deep in the earth. Daher, the youngest of the four, began thinking about how far that winter's rain had soaked into the ground, and was surprised to find that the water that had come pouring down hadn't reached any deeper than it had.

Everyone gathered around the grave managed to hold back their tears, with the exception of Bishr, a boy who stood crying some distance away. Daher gestured to him to come forward. With timid steps, he approached until he was standing in front of Daher. Patting him on the shoulder, Daher looked skyward as though he wanted to say something.

As Saad nudged him out of his reverie, he saw the corpse they'd been carrying descend placidly beyond the line the winter rain had reached, which was near the grave's dry base, and onto the whiteness of its shroud fell warm drops of rain.

Daher didn't know whether the stillness he sensed was the serenity of a body that had been released from all its burdens, or of a soul at peace knowing that there were sons capable of managing the idyllic little town's affairs now that its multazim had passed away.[1]

---

1 The multazim was an individual appointed by the Ottoman state through a decision by the governor or vizier to collect the taxes imposed on peasants and others, and to deliver them to the state after deducting his own share.

Throughout the forty-day wake, they could only think about two things. The first was the deadly sorrow that had afflicted their sister Shamma, now married to a cousin who was multazim in the town of Damun. And the second was the question of who would carry on their father's work. Winds blew, rains fell, the sun rose, and frost cropped the heads of the trees and singed their leaves. Yet none of that could assuage the pain of their sorrow over a father who had left them with memories so sweet that they nearly forgot he had died.

Safe beneath his enormous shadow, they had been able to carry on with their lives without the state being able to see them, call them to account, or pursue them if necessary to collect the taxes that two years of drought had prevented them from paying in full. Thanks to their father, they'd been able to keep themselves beyond the reach of the governors and viziers.

With its fertile plains, Tiberias was the ideal place for raising cotton and grain and for salting fish for export to both local and foreign markets. However, even its abundant water and fertile soil weren't enough to satisfy the state, which was a master at devising new ways of imposing taxes and inventing new names for them.

"You're the best person to take our father's place," Saad said to Yusuf. "You were closer than any of us to the details of his work, and you knew the most about what he did and did not pay the state."

Yusuf rejected the idea. "I didn't know any more than you all did," he said. "Besides, you're the eldest, and everyone relates to you as the future multazim. But if you don't want the post, I'll waive it in favor of my brother Saleh!"

Daher observed his brothers' conversation as though they were people speaking in the distance whose voices he couldn't hear. The matter was of no concern to him, since he was sure that, being the youngest, he was the last person who would occur to them. After all, he was only sixteen years old.

Suddenly he heard someone say, "Daher, I say! Daher's the person for the job! He's the youngest, it's true. But he knows quite a bit."

For a moment Daher thought Saleh must be talking about someone else by the same name, so he said nothing. Then he saw his brothers looking over at him, waiting to hear what he had to say.

"Are you talking about me?" he asked.

"And how many brothers do we have by the name of Daher?"

"What will people say?" he objected. "There's only one person who can take my father's place, and that's you, Saad! Neither I, nor Yusuf, nor Saleh is fit for the job."

Daher spoke sternly, as though he were issuing a command. He had his father's voice, his father's features, and the same piercing, confident look in his eyes. He was a thin, short boy with a fair round face tinted with roses, thick eyebrows, a small mouth, and thin lips. His hands and fingers were noticeably long, his hair black, and beneath his straight nose rested a faint moustache.

"I don't want the state to know my name," Saad said.

"And why should the state know *my* name?" Daher wanted to know.

"You're the youngest!"

"Yes, I am! Which means that many years from now, after we've all lived to a ripe old age, I'll be the last one to become multazim in Tiberias!"

The others fell silent. Then they got up and walked off. In fact, it seemed they were never coming back, as though they'd left Tiberias forever.

Daher stayed alone in the house with Najma.

"They'll be back," she told him. "But they're not going to change their minds!"

She gathered up the hem of her robe and, with her lovely, delicate features and her eyes wide as saucers, she launched her frame into the air like an ash tree and left the room.

Daher watched her as she flitted barefoot about the house. She would have been willing to give up anything, with one exception: walking around barefoot. This habit of hers had caused numerous problems between her and Umar al-Zaydani. However, whenever it came up she would always say the same thing: "Every time I feel the earth isn't touching my feet, I start to wobble and nearly fall!"

Najma occupied a place that was unique to her among both the women of Tiberias and the members of Umar al-Zaydani's household. Daher called her Ummi (Mother). Saad called her Amti (Paternal Aunt), and Saleh and Yusuf called her Khalti (Maternal Aunt). And Shamma, the eldest of the children, called her Ukhti (Sister) whenever she came to visit. As for Umar al-Zaydani, whenever he saw her or wanted anything from her, he would beam, and she would respond to his unspoken request as though his name for her were Ibtisamti (My Smile)!

"I'll refuse. I'll refuse again," Daher said to Najma.

"I'm going to tell you something, and I want you to consider it well. You're the only one who can manage Tiberias's affairs. I say this because I know you. Believe me!"

"It's as though you agree with them!"

"If there's anyone on earth I can agree with, it's you, Daher! And if you were my son, you'd believe me."

"I *am* your son, and you're my mother. You know that!"

"No. Your mother is Halima, the white mare standing over there. She's looking at us the way she looked at you that day so long ago. And for some reason, I get the feeling she's listening to us now!"

Daher looked over to where Najma was pointing, and sure enough, Halima stood gazing at him with wide, teary eyes filled with pride as if to say, "You've grown up!"

A Distant Day and
a Defeated Sword

Clutching his infant son Daher with trembling hands, Umar al-Zaydani walked to the end of the large enclosure. Then, standing in a solitary spot along the high stone wall that surrounded the house, he said, "Please don't die. You've got something of her scent in you that none of my other sons has. In fact, you've got all of it. Don't die!"

As Najma watched Umar al-Zaydani, who was in torment over the loss of his wife and the death that hovered nearby, she wanted to snatch the newborn away. She couldn't say a thing. Her greatest wish was that she could hold the baby to her breast and suckle him, though she knew that no matter how she might long for such a thing, her longing wouldn't give him a single drop of milk.

Najma's eyes met Umar al-Zaydani's, and she slapped her chest. She slapped it with all her strength, then squeezed it with her fingers as though she wanted to rip it out of her body.

Umar walked over to her, bent down, and handed her the baby. As he did so, he caressed her hair with a sorrowful tenderness.

"Lord, isn't there a woman on earth whose milk he would accept?"

"Take him to Nazareth, to Safad, to Acre. Take him anywhere. He's bound to accept some woman's breast in the end and start to nurse."

"This little piece of flesh wouldn't survive the journey, Najma. You take him. I don't want him to die in my arms. Please, just hold him. Love him. Love him with whatever light he has left."

No sooner had she taken the baby into her arms than Umar unsheathed his sword and began screaming, "Where are you? Where are you hiding? I'm going to rip you to shreds!"

Najma started to cry. "Fear God!" she pleaded.

But he kept spinning around them, shouting, "You won't be able to touch him as long as I'm around! Now come closer. Show me your face. I'll rip you to shreds! I'll relieve the whole universe of you!"

He brandished his sword, slicing the air, tearing mercilessly at the darkness of the sunset. "Where are you? Would you dare come near this piece of flesh? Where's your nerve, Death? Come on, face me!"

For long hours Umar made circles around himself until he didn't know where he was any more. However, he never forgot what it was that he was fighting, defying.

One thing brought him back to his senses: the soft whinnying of Halima, his white mare. With a muted, sorrowful neigh, she had turned in their direction. How many times had she neighed before they finally noticed? Before they noticed the little foal thrusting her head between her mother's back legs to nurse?

The white mare gave her daughter a nudge. The foal moved away, then went back to circling around her mother in an attempt to find her nipple again.

A light went on in Najma's head. She stood up. Umar's hand had frozen in midair, exhausted, and everything about him seemed prepared to receive his enemy's fatal thrust.

Najma took the sword out of his hand. Then she drew him toward her and gave him his newborn son.

She went inside without a word, and came back carrying a clay bowl. When the white mare saw her, she neighed even more, as if to hurry her up. Once she was next to the mare, Najma bent down and grasped her teat with a hand that had never milked a horse before. It was a hand afraid of everything, a terrified hand that didn't know what a mare would do if she found herself being milked like a ewe or a cow. The mare cast her an encouraging glance, and it seemed to Najma that she was nodding her head, pleased with what was taking place.

The milk was as limpid as a little moon in her hands. She walked past Umar and into the house. He took his sword and planted it in the ground. Then, holding his newborn son in his arms, he followed Najma toward their last hope.

To everyone's surprise, the baby's appetite exploded. Just when they expected him to screw up his nose and shut his mouth tightly—the way he had in response to every woman who had tried to nurse him—he began running the tip of his little blue tongue over his lips. The aroma of Halima's milk was too powerful to resist. When he'd finished it, Umar al-Zaydani started to get up to bring more. But Najma reached out and pressed his knee, and he sat back down.

When at last the baby went to sleep, they sat gazing prayerfully into that tiny face, their gaze penetrating its lids to the eyes that had yet to decide what color they would be.

From that day on, Najma began looking at all God's creatures in a new way.

After the nights of insomnia the likes of which they wouldn't have wished on an enemy, Najma, Umar, and Umar's children were woken the next morning out of a sound sleep. To the baby's voice they awoke, one after another, as though they were dead and life were summoning them anew. They sat up one by one, staring in the direction of the sound. It was alive, as alive as life itself. At that same moment they heard Halima neigh. It was the same neigh they'd heard for the first time the day before, and they turned toward it as though it were visible.

Najma picked up the bowl. Then she went to the corner, washed the bowl out well, and left the house. Joyful, Halima's neigh grew louder. As Najma approached, the mother prodded her little foal with her foot and she moved away, making room for Najma to milk her.

Najma walked up to the beautiful white head illumined by sympathetic eyes. She kissed the mare's forehead and patted her neck. Her hand caressed the taut body with a downward motion until it came to the teat. Then she bent down and her fingers began ever so gently squeezing and releasing.

Umar watched Najma quietly, and before she'd finished what she was doing, he cast a glance at his sword planted in the ground. He stepped toward it and pulled it out. Then, looking skyward, he said, "Only You understand what I did. You alone, and no one else. Forgive me!"

A Broad Plain and
Gazelles on the Run

Najma thought back on the night when Umar al-Zaydani had noticed that Daher was missing. He'd made inquiries about Daher, but he was nowhere to be found. Then, two days later, someone had come and told him, "Someone's seen him in Bi'na!"

"What on earth is he doing in Bi'na when the vizier of Sidon is besieging it?"

Three years of drought had left the plains of Bi'na, Arraba, Jaddin, Damun, Tarshiha, and the surrounding villages nothing but colorless, lifeless expanses. The springs had dried up, and the fact that the olive trees had managed to keep their dry leaves seemed nothing short of a miracle. It was even said that if they hadn't been described in the Qur'an as "blessed," not a single leaf would have remained on their branches!

The birds had fled, and the deer that had once filled the countryside were gone, having seen the voracious looks in people's eyes as they came after them in mad pursuit.

Even the widest and most fertile of plains, with all the verdure stored in its memory, couldn't have endured three harsh years like these, and people longed not only for a drop of rain, but for a mere drop of dew.

The vizier of Sidon sent word that he'd waited longer than he could afford to, and that, unless they paid what they owed, he would come out with his army and collect by force the money due the state. They knew he was capable of carrying out his threat. They also knew that if he did, he would steal what remained of the meager provisions they always kept stored away for such circumstances.

In the course of those three years they had slaughtered most of their livestock. Some had even slaughtered their horses when they saw them on the verge of starvation.

Before the vizier's army reached the villages near Bi'na, news of his march on Acre, Haifa, Jaffa, Nablus, and Jerusalem had spread, and as soon as they had gotten wind of the approaching storm, some of the peo-

11

ple of Bi'na had fled in search of safe haven, leaving their homes empty. Meanwhile, Hussein, Bi'na's chief elder, had set out with his townsmen and volunteers from the surrounding villages to meet the vizier's army and block its way between Bassa and Tarshiha.

They managed to surprise the vizier's army, which was routed and turned back. Before long, however, the routed army made a wild rush on them, displaying a strength the villagers hadn't seen before. They retreated toward Bi'na, which had been well fortified since the earliest times. Before reaching the town and shutting its gate securely behind them, Sheikh Hussein sent some men out asking the people of nearby villages and towns to come and help defend Bi'na.

Meanwhile, the vizier regrouped his forces and set up camp on the Jaddin plain in preparation for a major battle.

Horror stories had come from villages in the Bekaa Valley, where homes had been looted, more than three hundred women had been raped after being chased through the orchards, and entire villages had been burned to the ground. And as if this weren't enough, the governors and viziers had turned a blind eye to these atrocities in order to appease their soldiers, who were strangers in those parts.

When Daher heard Sheikh Hussein's plea for help one day, he'd jumped on his horse and headed for Bi'na, certain that his father had gone there before him. In fact, however, his father hadn't heard Sheikh Hussein's call for help until after the town was already surrounded, and by the time he attempted to reach the town, the situation of those trying to penetrate the blockade was far worse than that of the people under siege.

A solid, lasting friendship bound Umar al-Zaydani to Sheikh Hussein. Daher remembered Sheikh Hussein's visits to them in Tiberias and his own friendship with his son Abbas, who was in love with the lake. Whenever they visited them in Tiberias, the first thing Abbas would do was try to persuade his father to leave Bi'na and come live in Tiberias.

Sheikh Hussein would laugh and say, "Leave Bi'na? That would be difficult, Abbas! But if it's all right with Sheikh Umar, you can spend the week here with your friend."

Sheikh Umar would welcome the idea every time. Then one week would stretch into two, especially in the winter, since Daher would always argue his case, saying, "What's Abbas going to do with himself there in Galilee's cold?"

Abbas was keen on fishing, but Daher loved to hunt ducks on dry land.

As he thought back on those days, he could see Abbas's face and hear Sheikh Hussein's resounding, jolly laugh—a belly laugh that came from the heart and diffused through the air. Daher had never heard one like it before. Of all the men Daher had ever known or would ever come to know, Sheikh Hussein was the only one who could infect others with such joy that all the men near him were either smiling or laughing as though they were discovering their hearts for the first time.

Whoever came out of his diwan laughing would say in a loud voice, "O God, let it bring good!" The reason for this was that they were afraid of laughter, and when they caught themselves laughing so much they saw it as an evil omen. It was as though they thought their share of this world was nothing but sorrow.

Daher reached Bi'na's gate shortly before midafternoon. Gazing out at the short, skinny boy, the men stationed along its wall asked him his name. "Daher," he replied. When they asked him about his acquaintances in Bi'na, he said, "Abbas." "Abbas who?" they asked. "Abbas the son of Sheikh Hussein," he said, surprised. "So what brings you here?" they wanted to know.

"I want to fight with you," Daher replied.

"Whose son are you?"

"I'm Daher al-Umar al-Zaydani."

"Go back to your family, son. You'll be of more use to them there than you'll be to us here."

Just then the men on the wall shouted, "The army's arrived!"

Chaos broke out, and they scrambled to secure the gate with more wooden beams.

The angry vizier had given them no forewarning. He'd made his decision to bring the town down on their heads.

He set up his cannons and began pounding the town with shells.

Night fell, and his cannons carried on with their work with such intensity that the residents of Acre, eighteen kilometers to the west, could hear the explosions quite clearly.

The following day the bombardment continued, but to everyone's amazement the walls of the town stood firm. By the seventh day, the

13

vizier realized he would need more shells, so he sent people to bring some from Sidon.

As for those inside, they realized that the vizier, who hadn't given them the chance to fire a single bullet or shoot a single arrow in the direction of his forces, wasn't going to retreat until he had leveled their town to the ground.

Behind the army the vizier set up a huge, gaudy pavilion which, in its peacock-like pomposity, was alien to everything on the surrounding plain, and spent the day issuing orders to kill all the fleeing villagers his soldiers brought him.

He asked them all a single question: "Are you going to pay the taxes you owe?"

He had no need to ask such a question, of course, as he sat looking at their emaciated frames and tattered garb.

At a nod of his head, the soldiers would lead the villagers away from the tents and, next to a low stone wall that surrounded one of the lifeless orchards, shoot them dead.

The Wild Chase and
the Chased Boy

When Daher had been gone for three days, Halima started to neigh. On the fourth day she started neighing and crying, and by the fifth day she was crying in silence.

Najma took the mare's wan face, which had taken on the color of ashes, into her hands and tried to calm her. The heartbreaking thing was that the mare was calm—unbearably calm. Najma wished Halima would start neighing again, become agitated, and paw the air with her hooves. But she didn't.

After a five-day absence, Daher's father came home exhausted and hopeless. When he brought his horse into the stable, the white horse raised her head and looked over at him. He couldn't bear to look her in the eye. Najma took him by the hand and led him out of the stable. From time to time she would look back to make sure they were a safe distance away, certain that the white mare would understand anything Umar said.

"Where is Daher?" she asked him.

He made no reply.

Najma burst into tears. "Has something happened to him?" He reached out and gently caressed her hair.

For some reason Umar was sure he would never see Daher again. As if he were trying to prepare everyone for the pain to come, he replied, "I don't know, Najma. I couldn't get near the town. All you can hear there is the sound of explosions, and all you can see is fire and smoke. The last thing the vizier wants is to see them alive."

Najma took her head in her hands. Then she began pounding it with her fists. As she was about to fall, he put his arm around her shoulder.

"Thank God Shamma isn't here. Thank God she's off in Damun!"

What was happening in the yard just a few meters from the stable door was too momentous to be concealed. Distressed, the white mare started neighing again, turning this way and that.

Umar al-Zaydani took Najma by the hand and brought her up the three steps that led to the raised patio in front of the house. By the time they reached the doorstep, Saad, Yusuf, and Saleh had arrived.

Gripped by a sense of helplessness, the men who met in the diwan spent the entire evening in silence as though they were at a wake, and when one of them got up to leave, the others got up and followed him out.

Umar was sitting at the head of the diwan, and his son Saad sat alone across from him. Patting the cushion beside him, Umar gestured to his son to come sit next to him. Saad got up, traversed the sorrow-drenched space between them, and took a seat beside his father.

"You're the eldest of your brothers, Saad, so you're entitled to have me speak to you frankly and consult with you."

It was the first time he had ever spoken to his son in this way. It was a big moment, a proud moment that every son waits for. But Saad was so weighed down with sorrow that he didn't realize the significance of what his father had just said.

"I'm thinking of going back there again tomorrow, Saad. I can't just sit here waiting for my son's ashes."

"Let me go this time."

"Saad, it's taken everything out of me to wait for just one. So imagine what it would do to me to have to wait for two! This way, at least I'll have the comfort of knowing that you're here when I'm near Bi'na. If I know you're safe, maybe I can extinguish some of my worry over your brother who's there under fire."

Just before Deir Hanna came into sight, Umar al-Zaydani saw the vizier's horsemen chasing peasants across the plain and firing at them in a wild hunting scene.

Stunned by the screams and cries for help, he hid in an olive grove.

From the back of his horse, a policeman was aiming his musket at a fleeing boy. Sure the boy was a goner, Umar al-Zaydani drew his pistol and waited. The boy came rushing past him, and when the policeman was ten steps away from Umar's hiding place, he sensed that someone was lying in wait for him. He turned and saw a dark eye staring at him. It was the eye of a pistol, which spewed forth all the fire inside and sent it raging through the policeman's chest. Silence fell. Umar al-Zaydani looked around him. Everything was quiet. He saw the boy running away and caught up with him. Realizing that he didn't stand a chance, the boy was about to fall. However, Umar al-Zaydani reached down, snatched him up as he ran, and hoisted him onto the back of his horse.

A few moments later the boy found himself on the back of a horse in front of a rider who seemed to have come out of nowhere. He turned around and Umar said to him, "It's all right. God has destined you for a new life!"

When Umar al-Zaydani caught a glimpse of Lake Tiberias shimmering in the scorching noonday sun, he realized he'd gotten far enough away to be able to catch his breath and find out from the boy what had been happening back where they had come from.

The boy said, "More than five hundred horsemen came to help Bi'na, but the army killed them all. They surrounded them and wiped them out. Only a few people managed to get away, and I was one of them."

"And what on earth would have made you go there?" Umar al-Zaydani bellowed. "What could a boy your age do?"

The boy became flustered. Realizing how harsh he had been, Umar patted his shoulder.

"Bless you, son. Bless you. But really, what brought you here?"

"It's a long story, Uncle. The story of what happened to me, my family, and my cousin."

"And what is this story?"

"It's long, Uncle. Really long!"

"Well, then," said Umar, "I'll leave you here and head back."

"Where are you going, Uncle?"

"To Bi'na."

"No, Uncle! I won't let you go. You can't imagine what's going on there. No, Uncle. There's nothing there but death! I won't let you go back even if you kill me. This life of mine that you saved, nobody has more right to it than you do!"

The sound of the explosions grew louder, and from time to time they would hear the sounds of gunshots and cries coming from a distance. "You'll come with me to Tiberias, then," Umar said.

"All right, I'll come with you, Uncle!"

When they reached the entrance to Tiberias, the boy said, "I thank you, Uncle, but I have to go now. My cousin is waiting for me. She has

17

nobody but me in this world, and I have nobody but her. I don't want to leave her there worrying. Goodbye, then."

"You haven't told me your name, young man."

"My name is Bishr, Uncle. Goodbye."

The boy shook Umar's hand and waved to him as he walked away. Umar gazed thoughtfully at the boy's slight frame and tattered robe. Suddenly he called out, "Wait, Bishr!"

After the boy had come back to where Umar stood, he reached out and placed the horse's reins in his uncertain hand. "You're going to need this, Bishr."

"No, Uncle. You save my life, and then you give me your horse too? Bishr could never accept that!"

"I'm just returning the favor you did me, Bishr!"

"Favor? What did Bishr do for you, Uncle?"

"Though he didn't know it, Bishr was headed for Bi'na to save my son!"

"Your son is there, Uncle?"

Umar al-Zaydani nodded.

"That means your son is braver than Bishr, and faster too, Uncle! What's his name?"

"His name is Daher. Now don't waste another minute. And since you don't want the horse, I'll just lend it to you, and my sword along with it. This way there'll be a chance I'll see you again."

"You're strapping Bishr with a debt he could never repay, Uncle."

"Listen, Bishr. Don't you love that cousin of yours? Didn't you tell me you were all she had left, and that she was all you had left? If you care about her, Bishr, then take the horse and the sword and go. By getting to her faster you'll be able to relieve the torment of her waiting. Or do you want to make her suffer more?"

Bishr came forward and gave Umar al-Zaydani a tight squeeze, wishing he didn't have to leave him.

"Bishr will never forget this kindness of yours, Uncle."

"Go, Bishr. Don't keep her waiting any longer. Go."

Bishr jumped on the horse's back, surprising Umar al-Zaydani with his skill. Confused, the horse made a couple of circles around himself, since the way home had suddenly changed, as had the rider on his back! Then he stopped and just stood there, stone still. Umar al-Zaydani came up to him and patted his back. Then he gently slapped the horse's haunches, and the horse took off running.

Gunfire and Flying Insults

All the vizier's calculations had gone the way of the wind. First he'd run out of cannon shells for a second time, without having been able to make a single breach in the wall. Then came a heat wave that decimated the area's already scorched crops. Hence, he suddenly faced a second problem: water.

Everything fell still. Acre's heart trembled with fright, Safad and the surrounding region were stupefied, and the silence that filled the houses in the renegade villages grew all the heavier.

Might the vizier have broken Bi'na?

Bi'na caught its breath, and its defenders ascended its walls again to repel the attacks being launched by the Janissaries' and Moroccan mercenaries' foot soldiers and horsemen.

Sheikh Hussein looked for Daher, but didn't find him. When he asked about him, he was told that he was staying on the walls.

He sent some of his men to look for him, and one of them found him on the large bridge over the city gate. "Come forward!" Daher shouted defiantly at the enemy soldiers. From time to time he would shoot an arrow, and before the arrow had reached its target, he would follow it with an insult that pierced the attackers' ears more forcefully than his arrowheads pierced their shields.

With difficulty, the soldier who had found him managed to bring him back. When Daher saw Sheikh Hussein, he ran up to him and embraced him warmly. "You're going to defeat them, Sheikh. Don't worry!"

Sheikh Hussein stood pondering the boy. Then he laughed. He laughed the way he always laughed, and joy spread infectiously to everyone there.

"I called for you to tell you to be careful, Daher, and to watch out for your friend Abbas."

"Don't worry, Sheikh Hussein. Abbas and I have agreed that he should stay on the other side of the wall. There aren't as many attacks there!"

Sheikh Hussein, who knew that the calm that had spread would be followed by an even more severe storm, patted him on the back and told him to go join his friend on the other side of the wall, and stay there with him.

Daher turned and headed back to the gate.

Ammunition and provisions were dwindling at such a worrisome rate that the people of Bi'na had begun contenting themselves with dates, and whereas at an earlier time they had had enough dough to fill large pots, they now prepared it in small copper vessels, and every egg they came across was more precious than gold.

As people were gathered for prayer in the town mosque at noon on the third Friday since the siege had begun, cannon shells came raining down again, shaking the walls with a terrible force and falling into the streets and alleyways. Those worshiping in the mosque cut their prayers short and spread out in search of shelter from the cinders and flames.

Even as the siege entered its fifth week, Sheikh Hussein was confident that Bi'na would endure, since he knew its walls. He also knew, as did everyone else in the city, that the vizier would show them no mercy if they were defeated. It had been many years since a city had borne up for so long under such a full-scale attack. Ottoman governors and viziers weren't accustomed to returning defeated from battle and, with the exception of a few cases in which a governor had been so thoroughly shamed that he paid for his defeat by losing his position, Ottoman armies advanced on the villages to crush them, and to teach them and other cities to show the governors the proper respect.

Daher went back to hopping around on the wall, and when he sensed that his insults weren't bothering the soldiers any more, he began insulting the vizier himself. He called him every name in the book, at the top of his lungs.

With his own ears the vizier heard the insults, which were bound to reach him in those evening hours between one volley and the next.

"Whoever brings me that boy's head, I'll give him whatever he asks," the vizier announced, pointing with his stubby forefinger toward the wall.

The siege had so thoroughly enervated the village that food had to be prepared in new ways. A woman would take a small amount of flour in her headscarf. Then she would place it carefully in a mihmas—a small, long-handled metal pan used to roast coffee. After making certain that not even a speck of flour was still clinging to her scarf, she would add a bit of water and begin stirring the mixture until it had cooked thoroughly over the fire. Then she would distribute the resulting "loaf" equally among the members of her family.

It was a lesson the people had learned from the Bedouins, whose situations often required them to resort to measures more dire than this.

During the long, hungry nights they would poke fun at their plight. Someone would chant:

> We swear we're telling you right.
> We cooked sparrows' legs every night!
> We invited viziers
> From Istanbul and Tangiers,
> But they soon disappeared from our sight!

Then someone would respond with the same sarcastic levity:

> Good food of all kinds I savor,
> Though not all meet with my favor.
> I can't bear white bread,
> Roast beef pains my head,
> And stuffed chicken makes me quaver!

The vizier met with his troop commanders and informed them that the siege had gone on too long.

"Are we going to withdraw as if nothing happened?"

"No," replied the vizier, "we'll negotiate their surrender. In a few days we have to join the jarda,[2] and we can't afford to leave a situation like this hanging. If we do, we'll be a laughingstock from Damascus to Mecca!"

"And how will we convince them to surrender?" asked one of his commanders.

---

2 The word 'jarda' was used in Ottoman times to refer to zwieback and other dry foods that were sent to the pilgrims on their way back from the Hijaz to the Levant in view of the fact that, after traveling such a long way, their food supplies would have run low. 'Jarda' then came to be applied to the pilgrim supply caravan that transported these supplemental provisions.

"We'll offer them safety in return for surrendering, and we'll agree to postpone collection of the taxes they owe the state until next year," the vizier replied.

On the thirty-fifth day, the bombardment came to a halt. A soldier on horseback approached the city gate carrying a white flag. He kept advancing until he was a short distance away. Then he grasped his bow, raised it into the air, and drew the string. Those watching from atop the wall knew the arrow had to bear a message.

The arrow soared through the air and landed inside the gate. As Sheikh Hussein gestured for them to bring it to him, he eyed the soldier, who turned and went back to where he had come from.

He untied the black silk thread that had been wrapped around the letter, tossed it aside, and began to read. Then he folded it up.

As he cast a distant glance at the army that surrounded him and at the imposing pavilion, he felt as though he were looking the vizier, who stood at the pavilion's entrance, straight in the eye. He glanced at the town—its streets, the ruins of its houses, and its hastily dug graves—and took a deep breath.

The mutual war of attrition had come to an end, and all that remained now was to see which side would be the first to give up.

Most of the townspeople rejected the terms of the surrender and demanded that a letter be sent back to the vizier saying, "Lift the siege and leave!"

No one had been waiting to hear Daher's opinion. However, he announced his support for the majority view. He was full of zeal, and ready to fly like a cannon shell.

With Sheikh Hussein standing beside him, one of the men waved a red flag. The enemy soldiers saw it, and within moments one of them was advancing toward the wall.

They knew what would be written in the message from the color of the flag.

When the soldier came closer, the arrow bearing the message was shot. It fell directly in front of him. It came so close, in fact, that his horse shied.

The soldier dismounted and pulled the arrow out of the parched ground. Before he went back to join his fellow soldiers, he heard another insult from Daher's lips, one that was aimed at the army and the vizier together.

In the distance, the vizier said, "There's nothing I want more right now than that ———'s head!"

His army commanders exchanged glances. It was the most vulgar epithet they'd ever heard him utter.

By the time the soldier returned to him, the vizier had already given a signal for the bombardment to resume. He read the message, rolled it up into a ball, and flung it to the ground. Then he trampled it to shreds.

Daher only uttered one statement. However, Sheikh Hussein pretended not to have heard it.

Daher said, "It's time for the jarda to set out, and the vizier will have to go meet it. I don't think he sent his message just because he wants us to surrender. He sent it so that he can go join the jarda before it sets out from Damascus in a few days' time."

A matter such as this was no secret to anyone in Bi'na. Nevertheless, they miscalculated, and after several days of wild bombardment that went on night and day, Sheikh Hussein decided to surrender.

On the morning of the fortieth day, one of the men made his way carefully to the top of the city gate and raised a white flag. The cannons fell silent. When Daher saw the flag, he rushed over and lowered it again. Looking imploringly at Sheikh Hussein, he said, "Please, Father, don't surrender! They'll be leaving in just a few days!"

At a signal from Sheikh Hussein, the man raised the flag again and began waving it.

Down below, a man said ruefully to the sheikh, "I'm afraid that boy is right."

Air, Darkness, and
the Lantern's Flame

As death roamed Bi'na's streets that night, Daher lay awake thinking about what the vizier was going to do to him. Even if he pardoned everyone else, he would never pardon him after the way he'd insulted him.

He knew that, with the town set to surrender the following day, the vizier's soldiers would be sleeping soundly. However, attempting to escape over the walls would still present a major risk.

Shortly before daybreak, Daher heard a faint knock on the door. For a moment the face of his friend Abbas flashed through his mind. He opened the door, and to his surprise he was met by a strange woman. Before he had a chance to speak, she asked him the very question he had spent the entire night asking himself:

"Do you know what awaits you, brave young man?"

"Yes, I do: the blow of a sword that will send my head flying!"

"Follow me, then. Perhaps I can deliver you from this unjust vizier."

"I'll take my friend Abbas with me, then!"

"Don't worry about Abbas. The vizier wants your head, not his," she said, and pulled him along by the hand.

"Wait a minute," he said. He put on his shoes, picked up his sword and bow, and followed her.

At length they came to a house along the wall. She opened its door and went in. Daher was puzzled. What was she doing taking him from house to house?

Noticing his puzzlement, she said to him, "Don't stop like that. You'll expose us. Follow me."

He went back to following her as she led the way. Without wasting a moment, she bent down and began trying to move a large chest next to the wall. As she worked, she turned and said to him, "Don't just stand there. Give me a hand!"

Together they moved the chest away from the wall and, to his surprise, he was met by a pitch-black passageway that seemed to have no end.

"Go through this tunnel," she said. "When you come to the end of it, you'll find yourself in an olive grove. Make sure no one sees you. This tunnel is here to save your life and the lives of others. When you're sure it's safe to proceed, keep going till you're home again. Farewell."

And with that she handed him a small lantern.

He crawled for a long time through an expanse whose bleakness was dissipated by nothing but the lantern's flame. From time to time his head would collide with its ceiling or one of its sides. However, the tunnel kept extending before him, as though it were an endless journey toward the center of the earth, not toward its surface!

Some time later—he didn't know how long—the tunnel ended with a harsh blow to his forehead, which started to bleed. The lantern fell out of his hand, but he managed quickly to right it again, and he thanked God it hadn't gone out.

Looking behind him, he saw nothing but a solid mass of darkness. He reached up and ran his hand over the roof at the tunnel's end, and realized that there were several small wooden beams directly above it. Setting the lantern to one side, he brought his shoulders up against the beams and began gently pushing them outward. He saw a faint, ashen ray filtering gently down, accompanied by a thin stream of dirt. He took a deep breath and pricked his ears, trying to pick up some sound coming from outside.

Everything was still.

He straightened further. A pale dawn light rushed into the tunnel's exit, while thick clods of dirt streamed down and nearly put out the lantern. Once again he paused, trying to pick up some sound.

All was still.

By this time his head was outside the tunnel. After making certain the area was clear, he slipped out between the beams, one of which left a gash in his back. He came out.

Bloodied, dirty, and exhausted, what he needed most was air, and he filled his lungs with it: a first time, a second time . . . a tenth time.

He put everything back the way it had been, making sure the tunnel's exit was well hidden. He ran his hands over the ground again and backed cautiously away from the tunnel opening on all fours. As he retreated he erased his tracks, until he reached the low stone wall surrounding the olive grove. He stole a glance around him, searching for some sign of where he was. He saw Bi'na in the distance, and the vizier's soldiers dancing for joy around it in the knowledge that it would be surrendering in just a few hours.

He would have to begin the second phase of his escape before sunup. So he planned out his course to ensure he wouldn't be seen. Then he set off.

The fatigue and hunger that had eaten away at his body for forty days brought him down at last, and he collapsed under a large oak tree.

What he feared most was that someone who had heard about the prize the vizier had announced would recognize him, chop off his head, and take it to that pavilion with the gilded columns.

He woke with a start to find a peasant eyeing him in the blazing noonday sun.

The news of Bi'na's surrender had spread. The vizier had made certain of this, because he wanted it to precede him to Sidon, Safad, Damascus, Acre, Haifa, Jaffa, Nazareth, and Tiberias.

"What did you do to make you so tired? I've been next to you for the past two hours, and you didn't realize it," said the man.

"I'm a stranger in these parts, and I traveled a long way before getting here."

"Tell me the truth about yourself, and if you've come from Bi'na, reassure me."

Daher fixed his gaze on the ground, trying to hide his eyes. "Its people surrendered this morning, Father."

"I heard that they had, but I didn't believe it," the peasant said, and began to weep bitterly.

"Do you have brothers and sisters or other relatives there?"

"No, I don't. But I'm crying over that boy, Daher al-Umar. When we heard about the bounty the vizier put on his head, we knew nobody would be able to speak for him. After all, he said so many terrible things about the vizier that the vizier would never pardon him. If only I could meet this Daher before the vizier gets hold of him!"

"I'm Daher, Father!" Daher blurted out without thinking.

"What did you say?" the peasant asked, not having taken in what he had just heard.

"I said, 'I'm Daher, Father.'"

Then the peasant began weeping even more bitterly.

"Father, you're shedding more tears now than you were a little while ago."

"They're tears of joy, son. Tears of joy!"

After gathering his wits, the peasant got up and looked around the place, and when he was sure the coast was clear, he said to Daher, "Come, follow me. There's a safe place I can take you to."

The Half Dead and
Their Peculiar Mission

The town's gates were opened and out came the people of Bi'na, their headscarves and kaffiyehs around their necks, the devastation behind them revealing the cruelty of the days they had endured.

Bi'na's chief elder was in the lead, followed by the town's men, wounded fighters, and boys. Behind them walked the elderly, the women, and the children. Gazing at the townsfolk, Sheikh Hussein whispered to himself, "What a ruinous journey war is. Death dogs us at every step, and after it's all over it looks around for some new reason to finish us off!"

The villagers were so exhausted that death might well have wondered to itself, "Why not mow down the rest of them with a single blow?" As though he had overheard that savage whisper, the vizier of Sidon called out in a loud voice, "First, Bi'na's chief elder and his family!"

His beard soiled and his small eyes streaked with red, Sheikh Hussein came forward so sorrowfully one would have thought he'd never laughed before. As the soldiers began dragging him and his family away, the townspeople realized that the surrender agreement wasn't worth the paper it had been written on.

The vizier raised his hand, signaling for the execution to be carried out. Taking care not to let anyone notice, Abbas clung to his father. He clung to him as if in search of some point through which he could go back inside him: inside his flesh, his bones, his seed.

"Since you aren't going to keep any of your promises, I have one request to make," Sheikh Hussein said to the vizier.

"And what is that?" the vizier asked him.

"For us to be facing Bi'na when we're shot."

The vizier stroked his beard, took a few steps, and stopped.

"After what you did to me and my army, I can't grant you more than half your wish."

He raised his right forefinger. "Let their faces be toward Bi'na, then," he said to his soldiers. "But you'll have to gouge their eyes out first!"

In due course the vizier's carriage moved out, adorned with three horse tails,[3] and the army marched behind him. Meanwhile, in the distance, Bi'na's plain lay filled with corpses.

However, the vizier decided not to return to Sidon until he'd laid his hands on that boy and impaled him! When at last he learned his name—Daher al-Umar—he was incensed to discover that he was none other than the son of Umar al-Zaydani, the multazim of Tiberias, which was under his authority!

So he set out for Tiberias at the head of an army that had one mission: to impale the boy. However, when he reached Deir Hanna he received a command to turn back, because the pilgrim supply caravan was about to set out. He realized then that time had hemmed him in, since the caravan's journey would be a long one. First they would be required to gather up provisions needed by the pilgrims: rusks, oil, rice, barley, broad beans, fodder, ropes, and clothing. Then they would need to meet up with the pilgrims' return caravan, which was located three days' journey from Medina and twenty-two days' journey from Damascus. In short, it promised to be a taxing sojourn that would take fifty days going and coming.

The vizier stopped and looked eastward toward Tiberias. Then, as though he wanted to ensure he wouldn't go back on his oath, he swore to his soldiers at the top of his lungs, "So help me God, if I return safely from this journey, I'll wipe out the memory of this Daher!" He repeated himself twice more to be certain that everyone had heard him.

When news of the vizier's oath reached Tiberias, Umar al-Zaydani turned to his son and boomed, "What kind of life does a boy like you have to look forward to now that he's crossed a vizier?"

However, things were to move in a different direction, a direction people would only discern much later.

---

3 Ottoman officials' ranks were known by the number of horse tails they displayed on their carriages and standards. The Sanjak Bey, an Ottoman official next in importance to the governor (wali), had the rank of pasha, and decorated his carriage with a single horse's tail beneath a crescent moon, which was the symbol of the Ottoman Empire. The vizier's rank was symbolized by three horse tails, and the grand vizier (prime minister) by five. As for the sultan, he would raise a standard bearing seven or nine horse tails during wartime. When Ottoman officials were removed from their posts, their standards were taken from them.

The Night of Waiting and
the Four Lanterns

Daher opened his eyes one morning to find his brothers standing over his head. If it hadn't been for the fact that their swords were in their sheaths, he would have thought they were about to kill him!

"So, are you going to sleep through the night and leave us in this state of confusion?" Saad wanted to know.

Daher rubbed his eyes with the back of his right hand.

"Have you arrived at a solution?" he asked.

"No, we haven't," said Saleh.

"Oh, yes, we have!" Saad contradicted him. "Tonight we'll light the lanterns!"

The villagers knew that the Ottoman Empire fattened its multazims the way they fattened sheep for slaughter. The empire gave them a free hand to collect the taxes due the state and turned a blind eye to whatever they extracted unjustly from the peasantry. Then, when it was certain that what they were collecting far exceeded what they were paying the state, it would send someone to get rid of them and seize everything they had.

But Umar al-Zaydani wasn't that sort of person. He realized that the most important thing he could do to protect Tiberias and its people was to pay what he owed to the state and not give it a chance to pounce on him in its greed.

Saad, Yusuf, and Saleh looked around them and saw the multazims, including even the more God-fearing and contented among them, getting wealthier and wealthier. After all, there's no limit to the greed born of power.

"If we could convince Daher to be our front, we could do whatever we wanted without anyone trying to grab what we have. After all, he's just a kid," said Yusuf.

"I don't think you do him justice. Daher is young, that's true. But he's no weakling, and you know that," said Saleh.

"There's only one solution: the lanterns," Saad concluded.

"But you'd better be careful," said Saleh. "If you're thinking of trying to pull the wool over his eyes, he'll never fall for it."

They were waiting in the front room of their father's house when Najma came in carrying four lanterns on a large tray. She set the tray before them and sat down to watch.

None of them dared ask her to leave the room.

After handing Saleh a wick, she watched him like a hawk as he cut it into four equal pieces. When he had finished, he held them out and showed them to her so she could make sure he had done it correctly.

Squinting, she scrutinized the four small wicks. After giving a nod of approval, she held them in her hand, leaving one end showing, and each of the brothers drew one for himself.

Before long the wicks had been placed in the lanterns.

She exited in the midst of their silence. Then she came back in and crossed the room carrying a long stick. Its end was covered with a piece of cotton dipped in oil, its flame dancing back and forth and emitting a stream of thick smoke.

She extended the torch to Saad, who lit a twig in his hand. She did the same for Yusuf, then Saleh, then Daher. At last she gave them a signal, and they lit their lanterns at the same moment.

Then she took her torch and left the room, since she knew it would be a long time before the first flame went out.

The first half hour passed as though the lanterns had been lit only moments before. Any of them could look at any of his brothers without fear, since the lanterns were still at their brightest.

Saad reached up twice and fiddled with his little beard with an odd complacence. With his small eyes and his narrow forehead, Saad appeared to be the calmest of them all. As for Daher, he was somewhere else, seeing what was in front of him, yet not seeing it. Suddenly he heard Najma's voice saying, "You're the only one who can manage Tiberias's affairs. I say this because I know you. Believe me."

Daher turned in the direction of the voice, but saw no one.

31

The lantern-lighting ritual was a last resort for people who disagreed over some question that touched on matters of life and death, and the number of parties to the disagreement determined how many lanterns would be lit. The person whose lantern went out first was believed to be the one destined to live the shortest life, and he would be chosen for the most difficult task.

As midnight approached, everything changed. All eyes were fixed on the flames dancing before them, as no one could see through the lanterns' clay bases to know how much oil they had left in them. Their eyes grew weary, darkness surrounded them, and the rays turned so sharp that they burned through to the backs of their heads.

They became more and more fearful, knowing that the outcome would be decisive and that once it became apparent, there would be nothing they could do to change it.

Daher lifted his eyes and looked at his brothers. Their features had changed, as if they weren't themselves any longer. At some moment along the way the brothers were gripped by a strange sense that they were playing a game that summed up their entire lives. It was a sense that the issue went beyond allowing fate to choose one of them to do the work of a multazim, and had turned into a moment of farewell to the one who would die first, and to the ones who would follow him.

A cold, biting fear wrung their hearts, and they felt death peering over their shoulders in a way they never had before.

When the flame in front of Daher began to sputter, their spirits trembled with a curious ambivalence, at once savage and hopeless. Then his flame began burning steadily again. In fact, it seemed brighter than any of the others, and again they didn't know how to feel!

"Is Daher going to die before we do? He hasn't lived yet!" Saleh whispered to himself. He seemed prepared at that moment to snuff out his own flame with his fingers. However, his flame also started to sputter and seemed about to merge with the darkness, and he felt his heart leap out of his chest. He forgot all about Daher's flame, his eyes fixed on his own.

Najma picked up her abaya, wrapped it around herself, and left barefoot, as was her custom. When she looked in the direction of the room where the men were, nothing reached her but the coldness of silence, which intensified the night's chill. In the outer courtyard she could see a small puddle of water now turned to ice, the ice that took Tiberias by surprise once every few years.

Halima neighed. Her neigh sounded like a prayer, sending a shudder through Najma's heart. She crossed the courtyard and went over to her. She kissed her forehead and whispered reassuring words in her ear.

She stayed there next to the mare for so long that she started to feel her feet turning to slabs of ice. With difficulty she plucked them off the ground, then patted Halima on the neck and went back to her room.

The four lanterns were breathing their last, and the four brothers were about to discover the order in which they would bid farewell to this world.

The flame of Daher's lantern tilted and straightened again. Then its head fell into the darkness.

He raised his head.

The others looked half dead.

"The game's over," he said, "and you all win!"

However, their silence told him that they wanted to know the entire result. They also wanted to know when they were going to die, and each brother's death had been transformed into a clock chime announcing the death of the one to follow him.

Daher quietly turned his back to them, leaving the lanterns behind him to breathe their last.

For some reason all he could think about was what he was going to do the next day.

Light had begun stealing in from outside as though it were stealing in for them alone. At last they got up and patted him on the shoulder on their way to the door.

As they left, Saad asked him, "Don't you want to know whose lantern went out after yours? And whose lantern went out after that? And whose lantern went out last?"

He remained silent. But when, reassured by his silence, Saad said, "The second lantern to go out was—" Daher interjected in a voice that sounded remarkably like their father's, "If you can catch up with somebody walking, don't run after him!"

Saad said nothing. They left, sensing that the boy had changed completely.

Hearing their steps moving away, Najma came out. She took Daher by the hand and led him toward his room. She brought him to his bed and straightened his pillow. He lay down quietly, wearily.

You're the only one who can manage Tiberias's affairs. I say this because I know you. Believe me! As she moved away, he felt as though he could hear her saying these words.

He lifted his head and asked, "Did you say something?"

"Go to sleep now. There's a lot we can say later on."

After he woke up and ate his breakfast—at noon—Najma stood looking at him as though she'd just remembered something she shouldn't have forgotten. Then she said, "Follow me!"

Daher quickly realized what it was that she had forgotten, and got up.

She led him to a wide-open space where horses were raced. She looked behind her and found him taking off his shoes. She smiled. She waited for him to come up beside her. She closed her eyes, and he closed his. Then they went walking barefoot across the open area. Daher was preoccupied with thinking back on the first time she had brought him to this place, but every time he remembered it, he was distracted by memories of some other time that had preceded it.

As though she were reading his mind, she said, "You took your first steps here. It was the best spot in all of Tiberias for you to walk barefoot, since it was full of horses! But don't try to recover what's past. It's all inside of you now. What you need now is to walk over this ground and feel it. You need to feel all the horses that have run over it. You need to take them both in: the land and the horses!"

At length, she shook him. He opened his eyes. "That's enough!" she said. "I don't want you to turn into a horse, or even a mountain. You've got a long road ahead of you!"

And He Said to Them,
"I'm Not Going to Die Today!"

one of them was happy about what the lanterns had said.

It seemed as though Daher were a mere breeze blowing through.

He gazed at them, his dark greenish-brown eyes open wide, and they felt as though his presence among them promised to be nothing but a long day of farewell.

Nevertheless, he greeted them the way he always did: as though the lanterns hadn't yet been lit, as though the lanterns hadn't yet gone out.

He disappeared briefly, and when he came back he was winding a cotton scarf around his head and wrapping himself in a thick brown goat-hair mantle.

As they looked on in silence, he jumped onto his horse's back. Then he turned to them and uttered a statement that made their torment all the worse: "Don't worry. I'm not going to die today!"

He rode north, leaving Tiberias behind. Then he headed northwest before circling back to the east, toward Tabigha. As he surveyed the town from a distance, it was completely calm apart from delicate wisps of gray smoke rising from its ovens and stoves.

The air was redolent with the fragrance of lemon and orange trees, so he took a breath that cleansed his spirit. Seeing a thick stand of oleander bushes surrounded by reeds up ahead, he rode around it.

He knew his way perfectly.

After a two-hour journey he saw Bishr—the orphan skinny as a reed—waving to him. Bishr took off running barefoot in his direction as though he were receiving the tribe's chief elder rather than just a friend.

They embraced. When he asked Daher how he was, Daher didn't speak.

"You're not yourself today!" Bishr said. He waited for Daher to say something, but he remained silent.

They sat down, separated by nothing but the head of the horse that had insinuated itself between them in search of a bit of warmth.

"I want you to teach me how to fight with a sword and a spear," Daher began. "I want you to teach me to fight with all the weapons people use today."

"I'd be happy to," said Bishr. "How many times have I told you that it isn't fitting for someone who rides a horse to be anything less than a knight?"

Bishr jumped up nimbly, in his hand a large staff. "Here's my sword. Let's find you a sword like it."

"I've got a sword," Daher said. He opened his mantle and pulled the sword gingerly from its scabbard.

"Bishr fights you with a staff and you fight him with a sword . . . how is that?"

"You're my teacher today, and I'm your student. Your staff knows more about fighting than my sword does."

"But my neck doesn't know what my staff does. So be careful!"

Daher flung aside his mantle, which landed on the horse's back, and charged. He charged as though someone else, not his friend, were in front of him. Bishr received the frenzied blows with dexterity. Then with the staff he aimed a blow at Daher's back that sent him sprawling to the ground.

Drawing his hand out of the stiff, damp grass, Daher charged again, this time even more fiercely.

"You didn't come to learn today. You came to kill an enemy! But you'd better be careful, since the person you're fighting is me!" Bishr said, panting and leaping from a boulder onto a branch.

Suddenly Daher drew himself up straight and stood motionless. "Where are you?" he asked.

"Anger's blinded you," said Bishr. "I'm behind you!"

But Daher didn't seem to hear what Bishr had said.

"Where are you?" he shouted again. Then he began slicing the air with his sword, making that sound you only hear when metal passes through an invisible body.

Bishr sat down and watched him until he fell to the ground exhausted.

He came up to him. "Maybe you've killed the one you wanted to kill. But I've got to teach you how to defend yourself so that you won't die too!"

Wordless, Saad, Yusuf, and Saleh sat in front of their house's high gate, indifferent to the drizzling rain that made them all the more miserable as they thought back on what had happened.

Najma flitted about barefoot nearby, as though she didn't have a care in the world. Glancing over at them, she saw them hunched over as though they were waiting for an executioner's sword to fall on their necks.

She smiled, hands on her hips, and said, "I don't suppose you ate at Saad's house. Your breakfast is ready!"

She went inside, where several warm loaves of bread, olive oil, olives, white cheese, and seven boiled eggs lay on the straw mat.

The three men didn't budge.

She picked up an egg, tapped it gently on the ground, and began peeling it.

In the far corner of the courtyard a cock crowed, and a white mare neighed.

On Unexpected Gifts

Daher would never forget the way Bishr looked the first time he saw him.

Bishr had approached from a distance on the back of a horse that Daher recognized as belonging to his family. When Daher turned to look at his father, he found him smiling with an unspeakable bliss.

They were in a field of theirs—next to the lake—that had been planted in vegetables. As Bishr came closer, Daher's astonishment doubled. Bishr was carrying his father's sword, too! Within a few moments Daher realized the secret behind the horse's absence and the disappearance of the sword, matters about which his father had long held his tongue.

Noticing his son's bewilderment, Umar al-Zaydani turned to him and whispered, "I'll tell you everything. But now we need to receive our honored guest."

"Our guest?"

"Yes, Daher, our guest."

Before he reached them, Bishr leapt off the horse and went running toward Umar al-Zaydani. No sooner had he reached him than he wrapped him in a powerful embrace. Daher felt all the more bewildered as he saw his father embracing this strange boy in a way he had never embraced him, his own son!

"Thank God you got here safely, Bishr!"

"May God grant you safety, Uncle."

"We've missed you, Bishr."

"Is Bishr that late, Uncle?"

"No, Bishr, you aren't late. Someone like you would never be late!"

"Thank God. The whole time Bishr was worried that he might be late. But he was tired, Uncle. And to be honest, Bishr looked for a present to bring you, but he didn't have anything. So he decided that the best present he could offer you would be to come back and be like a son to you. So, I'm Bishr's present to you, Uncle. I hope you'll accept it!"

"And could there be a better present than to have a son like you, and like Daher?" asked Umar al-Zaydani, pointing to his son.

Bishr reached out and warmly shook the flustered Daher's hand.

"Do you know who this is, Daher?"

"It's Bishr! I heard his name."

"He's a lot more than that, Daher. He's the boy who marched to Bi'na to rescue you. Did you know that?"

"To rescue me?"

"Yes, when you were under siege there, Bishr was coming to help you."

"May God preserve him. But I didn't see him there!"

"That's a long story. In any case, I'll leave you with Bishr and go on ahead of you to the house to see about getting the guest's lunch ready."

"And why a guest's lunch? Didn't we agree that you've accepted me as a son, Uncle?"

"Sons eat too, don't they? Besides, now that you're my son, you've got to stop calling me Uncle!"

"Oh, that's right. Why didn't Bishr notice that?"

The thing Daher noticed was that the Bishr he had seen on horseback was different from the Bishr who was walking beside him. He had turned into nothing but a good-natured boy. But his intelligence was unmistakable.

"I know you don't know about what happened to me near Bi'na, but I'll tell you everything," Bishr said.

The morning hours crept sluggishly toward a midday that they obviously had no desire to reach, since it promised to be one of those unbearable summer days. The two of them strolled along the shore. The air was as still as the lake, which lay glistening like an enormous diamond. The fish leaping out of the water produced sweet little plopping sounds that grew more and less frequent by turns, and whenever a fish jumped, it left delicate white circles on the lake's vast blue surface.

Bishr didn't stop talking. Everything about him talked: his hands, his feet, his head, his thick hair, his braids, and his luminous eyes.

Daher loved him, and for a moment Bishr's face merged with the face of his friend Abbas. Tears nearly escaped from his eyes. Noticing this, Bishr asked him, "A sad memory?"

"Sad once upon a time, but happy now that you're here, Bishr."

Daher took a deep breath and sent the tears back where they'd come from.

"Which do you like best, Bishr: fishing, or hunting?"

"Bishr likes hunting. Besides—and don't be angry with me, Daher—fishing is for lazy people who don't like to have to move around to earn their keep! Now don't tell me you like fishing!"

"No, I don't like it. I don't remember catching a single fish in all my life. But I hunt other things in the lake besides fish. The lake is my land!"

"Your land? Bishr doesn't understand what you're saying, Daher. Are you testing me? How could water be land? Does it have things in it besides fish?"

"Yes, it does, Bishr."

"You *are* testing me, then, and Bishr doesn't know what you're getting at."

"I hunt ducks, Bishr. Daher hunts ducks! And even though he hunts them in the water, he has to move around now and then. He lies in ambush, he sneaks up behind them, he pounces, and he swims, too."

"You got me, Daher. You got me!"

Bishr spent three days in the home of Umar al-Zaydani, during which time Daher didn't go anywhere. When the day came for him to be on his way, Umar said to him, "You brought us a big present, Bishr. So how can we give you a present big enough to do yours justice?"

"I've already received your present, Father. You've given me a brother—Daher!"

Umar al-Zaydani came up to him and gave him a warm hug. Then, reaching out and drawing Daher toward him, he held both of them close. As he let go of them, he said, "Don't be gone long, Bishr."

"How could Bishr stay away now that he's found you, Father?"

Even so, this was his last encounter with Umar al-Zaydani. When Bishr arrived in Tiberias at noon one day after a long absence, he saw a funeral procession leaving Umar al-Zaydani's house. His heart tightened as he realized what had happened. When he looked for Umar al-Zaydani among the funeral goers and didn't see him, he walked behind the funeral procession, crying. Once at the cemetery, he stood at a distance, looking on at the motionless corpse silently preparing itself to return to the soil.

A Feeble Glow in a Dark Night

Four days later Daher returned. Seeing him approaching from a distance, his brothers rushed out to meet him on horseback in the midst of a driving rain. Once alongside them, he continued his precipitous advance toward the house, and they followed.

By the time he reached the gate, the white mare's neigh was rending the thick sheets of rain and illuminating the place like gentle lightning. Najma heard her and smiled. She rose calmly and headed for the door, then opened it and stood there waiting. Daher dismounted. Najma's smile broadened. He went over to the corner of the enclosure and tied his horse next to the white mare, who turned tenderly toward him as though she were a foal and he were her mother. He patted her neck, looked into her big, worried eyes, and kissed her forehead. Then he knelt and kissed her right foreleg. "I know you must have been worried. I'm sorry!"[4]

The white mare shook her head and her mane went flying in all directions. As he walked away, she watched him approaching Najma, who received him with a warm embrace.

When his brothers arrived, he was sitting in the front room of the house with Najma seated beside him.

"You worried about me, I know! But you can set your minds at rest now. This evening let's write a letter to the vizier of Sidon informing him of what we've decided to do, and let's call the imam, the town judge, the mufti, and the prison warden as witnesses."

They gathered in the house's large diwan and signed a request that Daher be appointed as his father's successor to the post of multazim. In it they described him in glowing terms as a "fine, intrepid, astute, trustworthy young man with high aspirations and impeccable manners."

After the imam had finished reading aloud what they had written

---

4 It is said that Daher was the first person ever to kiss a horse's foot in a show of respect.

about Daher's character, Daher chuckled in spite of himself. They all turned and looked at him disapprovingly. However, their glances were repelled by his own steady gaze, his smile now a frown.

"I laughed because the vizier of Sidon would never accept a man with a character like that. What he wants is some niggardly coward who knows just how to lick his boots whenever he comes to collect taxes for the state! He wouldn't want somebody who was sharp enough to outsmart the state, or honest enough not to rob the people!" Daher said.

"What should we write, then?" asked the judge. "It's the custom for us to open our letters with preambles like this."

Turning to the prison warden, Daher asked, "Aren't you with me on this?"

To their consternation, the prison warden, discomfited, averted his gaze from Daher's and said, "I agree with you. Yes, I agree with you!"

"The state itself supports me! Don't you see? Leave the letter the way it is, but remove everything that has to do with my character. Let's tell the vizier of Sidon what he wants to hear: that I'm 'loyal to the state and determined to preserve its wealth and its rights over the people no matter what it costs them'!"

They signed the letter and it was stamped by the judge, the imam, the prison warden, and the mufti.

At that moment Najma came in with supper: a large copper tray filled with rice and meat.

Saleh jumped up, took it out of her hands, and placed it before them.

Pleased at what she saw, she said, "Show me the letter."

Saad handed her the letter. She took it and pondered it briefly. Before giving it back, she said, "God willing, you'll gather some day to write a letter appointing him multazim for all of Galilee!"

They knew that no one could possibly make light of anything Najma said. So, half-smiling, they simply nodded in silence.

"Bon appétit, and welcome! Now, help yourselves," she said, and left.

The imam and the judge, who were known for being the most avid meat eaters on the whole lakeshore, were in an especially good mood after seeing the huge repast.

Looking over the tray groaning with food, the judge chose the best piece of meat and set it aside for Najma. This was a way of showing

respect for the hostess, who had slaved for hours in the kitchen to prepare the meal being served to the guests.[5]

The imam and the judge ate so freely you would have thought they
were all by themselves. Eventually, nothing remained but a single piece
of meat atop the rice in the very center. Not wasting a moment, the
judge reached out and dug some rice out from under it. The piece of
meat tottered, then fell in front of him. In order to disguise what he had
done, he said with a chuckle, "The food was so happy to see me, it came
forward straightaway!"

To which the imam replied in a witty riposte, "You dug so deep
under the foundation, you knew it would have to give way!"

As for Daher, he laughed till he cried.

Night had fallen early, and the few lanterns hanging in the street emitted
a feeble glow. Light gusts of wind caused their wicks to flicker repeatedly, though the weather seemed warmer than it had during the day.

Generally no one noticed street lanterns unless they'd gone out.
However, Saad, Yusuf, and Saleh gazed fearfully at the little dancing
flames as though they were looking at their own lanterns: the lanterns
that had gone out on that fateful night, submerging their questions in
cruel darkness after coming up against answers still crueler.

---

5 If a guest failed to make this gesture, it was the custom for the hostess, in a kind of
symbolic punishment for his lack of consideration, not to send anyone at the conclusion
of the meal to pour water over his hands.

The Poet and the Shadows
of East and West

Daher had disappeared again. However, his disappearance was no longer worrisome to anyone, since they knew he would be back eventually.

And he did come back.

Upon his return he was different: he looked taller and more robust, and he seemed to have a greater appetite for life than before.

"Aren't you afraid of the death that's lying in wait for you?" Saad asked him.

"I am. I'm really afraid. But if I live as long as Tarafa ibn al-Abd[6] did, I will have done him one better!"

"Is all you hope for to reach the age of twenty-five?" Saleh asked him fearfully.

"And is that so little to hope for? Make it twenty-six, then. After all, there are people who say he died when he was twenty-six. But you're forgetting something important, namely, that the person who killed him couldn't confine him to the grave. His murderer died, but Tarafa is still alive to this day!"

"You aren't afraid, then?" Yusuf asked him.

"Afraid of what?"

---

6 Tarafa ibn al-Abd was born in around 543 CE in present-day Bahrain to parents of noble lineage, and his ancestry laid the foundation for his rare poetic ability. His grandfather, his paternal uncles al-Muraqqash al-Asghar and al-Muraqqash al-Akbar, and his maternal uncle al-Mutalammis were all poets. Tarafa was a young man when his father died, and his paternal uncles provided for him. Nevertheless, he spent a wild and profligate youth. After he satirized the king of Hira, Amr ibn Hind (died c. 568–69), the king gave Tarafa and his maternal uncle al-Mutalammis sealed letters, which he led them to believe contained rewards, and sent them with the letters to Dadrafuz Ghushnasban, the Persian governor of Bahrain's southern shores. According to one account, al-Muta-lammis opened his letter, discovered its contents (which ordered the Persian governor to behead him on arrival), and escaped, whereas Tarafa refused to open his letter and, as a consequence, met his end. He was killed by Dadrafuz Ghushnasban on orders of King Amr ibn Hind, who had given him written instructions in the letter he had sent with Tarafa, saying, "When the bearer of this missive of mine reaches you, behead him." It is said that Tarafa was in his mid-twenties when he was killed.

"Of death!" Saad shouted in his face.

"I *am* afraid of death. But the fact that my lantern went out before yours can't possibly frighten me. I'll do my best to drive death out of Tiberias, and maybe some day I'll be able to drive it farther away than that!"

Then he turned to leave.

"Where are you going?" Saad asked.

"To face something that frightens me more at the moment: my tutor's wrath!"

Roaming the streets of Tiberias at dusk was a custom close to Daher's heart. Even on a winter's day like this one, he enjoyed watching the clamor of the city die down as people departed for their respective villages or returned to Tiberias from the fields and distant cities.

A fisherman on the shore of Lake Tiberias had slung down his day's catch onto a large straw plate. One of the fish was still alive and struggling. Daher came up to the fisherman and stood looking thoughtfully at the fish. "How much is the fish going for today?" he asked him.

"Ten for a piaster," the salesman replied.

"And how much do you want for this live one?"

"A quarter piaster. As you can see, it's the biggest."

Daher grabbed the fish and threw it into the water.

"What are you doing? That's the biggest fish I've caught in a month!"

"Is this how much it costs?"

The fisherman reached out and took the quarter piaster, his eyes glued to the water. When he turned to look back at Daher, he was gone.

He walked down the road with light steps, filled with an exuberance whose source he couldn't identify. When he got to Saad's house he cast a glance skyward. The gray clouds that had filled the sky were receding, while a wispy one on the horizon sought in vain to eclipse what remained of the sun's glow.

He knocked on the door and heard Saad inviting him in.

Saad's house, one of the largest in Tiberias, had a spacious courtyard shaded by two towering palm trees, and a staircase leading to an upper story from which you could see the lake more clearly than you could from any other house.

As he was about to cross the threshold, Daher was surprised to find that Saad had a guest. He greeted the man respectfully, trying to remember where he might have seen him before.

"This is my brother, Daher," Saad said to the man.

"You've never seen me before, Daher! I'm Sheikh Abd al-Ghaffar al-Shuwayki from Damascus. I'd heard so much about your father that I decided to come to Tiberias to make his acquaintance. But death reached him before I did, may he rest in peace!"

Sheikh al-Shuwayki fell silent for a bit. Then he said to Daher, "It seems you're coming from your tutor's house. Nobody would be toting all those books around otherwise!"

"That's right."

"What is his name?"

"Sheikh Abd al-Qadir al-Hafnawi."

Al-Shuwayki nodded. "Have you memorized the book of God, son?"

"Yes, sir."

"And what parts of it did you like?"

"I liked all of it. But the verse that impressed itself most on my heart is the one that says, 'Say: "O God! Lord of Power and Rule, Thou givest power to whom Thou pleasest, and Thou strippest off power from whom Thou pleasest; Thou endowest with honour whom Thou pleasest, and Thou bringest low whom Thou pleasest. In Thy hand is all good. Verily over all things Thou hast power."'"

"And what poetry have you memorized?"

"I've memorized some of every type."

"And what type did you like the most?"

"My favorite verses are the ones by al-Mutanabbi:

> Let it be known in Egypt, Iraq, and Syria
> That I am a man with a noble heart,
> That I have been faithful and resisted the foe
> And raged against those who rage.
> Not all who profess loyalty are loyal,
> Nor are all who suffer disgrace graced with dignity.
> Should someone be ignorant of his own faults,
> Others will see in him what he sees not.

Sheikh al-Shuwayki nodded. "Have you read books on history?" he asked Daher.

"Yes, I have."

"And which of them did you find to be the best?"

"The nicest were the ones about Abu Muslim al-Khurasani[7] in the east, and about Abu Abdullah al-Shi'i in the west."[8]

Sheikh al-Shuwayki sat up straight and looked at Daher for such a long time that Daher and Saad thought he must be trying to think of another question to ask. But no further questions were forthcoming. After his prolonged silence, he gestured to Daher to come closer. Daher leaned down toward him and he whispered something in his ear.

Daher nodded. Then he asked their permission to be on his way.

Tiberias's main gate was about to close when Daher heard a man atop the wall shout, "Don't close the gate! The Nablus caravan has arrived!"

Two men, each armed with a sword and a musket, reopened the gate, and life pulsed anew in the city's main thoroughfare as merchants, would-be buyers, and young boys thronged toward the caravan.

Daher made a wide circuit around the city, ending at its northern tower. Then he came around again, watching the lamplighter as he commenced his work. Daher followed him closely until he had finished lighting the last lantern.

Before reaching home, he heard the white mare's neigh, and he smiled.

Saad insisted on escorting Sheikh al-Shuwayki to the outskirts of Tiberias. As he bade him farewell there, he loosened the reins of the mule that had been tied to his horse's saddle and tied them to the saddle of al-Shuwayki's horse.

"What is this?" al-Shuwayki objected in astonishment.

---

7   Abu Muslim al-Khurasani (died c. 755 CE), otherwise known as Abd al-Rahman ibn Muslim or Abd al-Rahman ibn Uthman ibn Yasar al-Khurasani, was an extraordinary man of whom peculiar accounts have been related. It is said, for example, that he traveled on the back of a donkey all the way from Damascus to Khurasan (a historically Persian province that covered parts of modern-day Iran, Afghanistan, and the central Asian states of Uzbekistan, Turkmenistan, and Tajikistan) before coming to rule it nine years later, and that he returned with huge battalions to overturn the Umayyad state and establish another.

8   Al-Hussein ibn Ahmad ibn Muhammad ibn Zakariya al-Sanaai (d. 911), otherwise known as Abu Abdallah al-Shi'i, was known by the title al-Mu'allim, the Teacher. Known for his astuteness and courage, Abu Abdallah al-Shi'i was an inhabitant of Sanaa, Yemen, from which location his surname is derived. He helped pave the way for the establishment of the Fatimid state, whose doctrines he propagated in North Africa.

"This is some of what you may need along the way. And take my advice: beware of the Bedouins, since all they do is loot and steal."

"Don't worry. From here to Damascus they're all my friends."

Al-Shuwayki shook Saad's hand warmly and set out. Before he disappeared around the bend beyond the lemon grove at the bottom of the foothill, he stopped his horse, obliging the mule to halt with them. He turned and saw Saad waving to him.

"Saad!"

"Yes, sir?"

"Watch out for your brother Daher!"

From where he stood at the top of the hill, Saad thought about what al-Shuwayki had said, and about the lanterns. He didn't know whether he should believe the lanterns, or al-Shuwayki and the certainty he saw in his aunt Najma. If he hadn't known what a great love she harbored for Daher, he would have suspected that she was happy Daher would be leaving soon!

A Gray Stallion with Kohl-lined Eyes

B ishr was alone in the desert one day when he saw a rider approaching. He picked up a stick and stood watching him. The man was approaching at a trot on the back of a gray horse with kohl-lined eyes. Before he reached him he called out, "Are you Bishr?"

Bishr nodded. "Yes, I am. But you haven't told me who you are."

"Pardon me. I'm Muhammad Mikhlid of the Bani Saqr tribe."

When Bishr saw the rider smile, he loosened his grip on the stick slightly. The man continued his approach.

"If only I had a horse like that!" Bishr whispered to himself.

The horseman's smile broadened, and when he dismounted in front of Bishr he said, "This horse, as well as fifty she-camels, will be yours if you grant me my request."

"And who said I wanted a horse like that?" asked Bishr, taken aback.

"A look of love can't be hidden, young man. Hearts have a way of exposing themselves. Didn't you know that?"

Bishr was silent. "And what is your request?"

"I've been told that you have an orphaned paternal cousin, and I want to marry her."

"You want Ghazala?" asked Bishr in alarm.

"Well, yes, if that's the name of the girl I'm speaking of!"

Bishr was silent again, feeling as though he had just received the blow he'd dreaded all his life.

"So what do you say? I see the cat's got your tongue!"

Bishr thought back on that distant day when horsemen had attacked their campgrounds, sparing no one but the children.

"I don't have anything to say," he replied. "I'll have to consult with my cousin!"

"So be it. I'll come back to see you again in two days. Does that give you enough time?"

Bishr nodded sadly and watched the horse gallop away, hoping he would never see it again!

Bishr sat wordlessly across from Ghazala.

"You've got something to say, Bishr!"

"Yes, I do, Ghazala. But it's difficult for Bishr to speak."

"I'm your cousin, and you're all I have. Speak, Bishr. I'm listening. And whatever you want is what will be."

They heard the neighing of mares in the distance, and Bishr continued to hesitate.

"Speak. How could Bishr not tell me what's in his heart? If the matter has to do with you, your secret is safe with me, and if it has to do with me, then—"

"It has to do with you, Ghazala," he interrupted. "A horseman came to me today and spoke with me about you. But I couldn't tell him anything!"

"Since it had to do with me, you should have spoken with him. Aren't you my paternal cousin, Bishr?"

"He wants you as his wife, Ghazala! He wants you as his wife! He said your dowry would be his thoroughbred stallion and fifty she-camels!"

"And what did you tell him?"

"I told him I'd consult with you about it."

"And what do you want from me?"

"Your opinion, Ghazala."

Ghazala got up and made two circuits around her tent. As she walked, Bishr followed her, if not with his eyes, then with his ears.

Then she came and stood next to him without saying a word.

"So what do you say?" he asked her anxiously.

"Cousin," she said, "this is a dish I could eat, or not eat, and it would be all the same to me."

"Is that what you have to say, cousin?"

"That's what I have to say."

For two whole days Bishr wandered aimlessly over the plains, and for the first time in his life he felt he was about to go blind. The ewes would disappear behind boulders and in the tall grass along the bank of the river where it met the lake, and when they reappeared, he knew they might have been vulnerable to attack by wolves, leopards, or even the bears that people encountered from time to time in those parts.

"What if I told you her dowry would be two stallions like this one and a hundred she-camels?" the horseman asked him.

"I'd tell you what I told you before: that I'll consult with her."

The man jumped on the back of his horse.

"I'll be back at this time tomorrow," he said as he rode away.

Bishr gathered his ewes and returned to camp.

He passed Ghazala's tent, hoping she wouldn't see him so that when the horseman returned the following day he could tell him he hadn't seen her. But he was out of luck.

When she saw him, she called out, "Bishr!"

He stopped, while the ewes continued on their way to Sheikh Fawwaz's house.

"You have something to say, Bishr. Tell me what it is. I'm listening!"

"He'll give you two stallions and a hundred she-camels!"

"And what did you tell him?"

"The same thing I told him the first time." He fell silent before adding, "So what do you think?"

"As I told you before, cousin, this is a dish I could eat, or not eat, and it would be all the same to me!"

And he was all the more confused.

A Story about Love
and Madness

In the wee hours of the morning Daher heard a knock on the court-yard gate. When he got up and opened the door to his room, he saw Najma in the darkness, heading toward the source of the sound.

"Don't open the gate," he said. "I'm coming."

But before he could catch up with her, she had opened it.

Before her stood a young man on the verge of collapse. "I'm Bishr," he said to her.

She heard a cry of disapproval from behind her. "Bishr? What on earth brings you here at this hour of the night?"

"Are you going to spend the night interrogating the guest at the door, Daher?"

"Come in, Bishr. I apologize. But what would bring you here at . . . ?"

"Didn't you hear me, Daher? Since when do we ask a guest why he's come until he's been here for three days?"

"But he's my friend, Mother!"

"And he's my guest now, just as he was your father's guest—may he rest in peace. So don't ask him any questions."

And in fact, they had no need to ask him anything after that. He started to talk of his own accord, his body wracked with what seemed like a thousand fevers. He related everything that had happened with him and his cousin, up to the last thing she'd said to him.

Najma nodded and said, "Bishr, you didn't have to say all that in order for me to know what's tearing you up." She fell silent, picked up a mantle, and draped it over Bishr, whose eyes had turned into wells of darkness.

"I'll leave you with Daher, since he knows a lot of stories like yours! And if his stories don't help you, I'll tell you some of my own tomorrow."

They sat in silence, the flame of the lantern swaying before them. They gazed at it, not knowing whose flame it was.

At last Daher spoke. As he spoke, he noticed the flame burning more brightly. A distant hope passed fleetingly through his heart. "If this story of mine doesn't help you, we'll have to wait for my mother Najma's," Daher said.

Bishr fixed his eyes on Daher's lips, waiting for his first word the way someone who's been cast into a well looks for a patch of light above, dreaming of the rope he hopes will dangle down to rescue him.

"I'm going to tell you a story from olden times. Are you listening?"

Bishr, who had been lost in thought, said with a start, "I'm listening! I'm listening!"

"Long ago, before there were people on Earth, virtues and vices roamed the world together. One day, to relieve their boredom, Madness suggested that they play a game. He called it hide-and-go-seek. You know it, right?

"Well, they all liked the idea, and Madness cried, 'I want to start! I want to start! It was my idea, so I'll be the one to close my eyes and count, and you all have to hide!' He leaned his elbows against a tree and started counting: 'One . . . two . . . three . . .' while the virtues and vices went looking for places to hide.

"Gentleness found a place for herself on the moon, Treachery hid in the mud, and Hope slipped in between the clouds. Dishonesty said aloud to himself, 'I'll hide under the rocks,' and Longing dove to the bottom of Lake Tiberias. Meanwhile, Madness kept counting: '. . . seventy-nine . . . eighty . . . eighty-one . . . .' Eventually all the virtues and vices finished hiding—all, that is, except Love who, as usual, didn't know how to make a decision! Consequently, he didn't know where to hide. That should come as no surprise to anybody, of course, since we all know how hard it is to hide love!

"Madness kept counting: '. . . ninety-five . . . ninety-six . . . .' When he'd counted to a hundred, Love jumped into a rosebush and hid there. Madness opened his eyes and began his search, shouting, 'Ready or not, here I come!'

"Sloth was the first to be discovered, since he hadn't gone to the trouble of hiding himself! Then Madness found Gentleness hiding on the moon. He found Hope, too, and Longing ran out of breath and came up from the bottom of the lake.

"Well, Bishr, Madness ended up finding all of them, one after another, except for Love. He kept looking until he was so frustrated that he nearly gave up. Just then, Envy came up and whispered in his ear, 'Love is hiding in the rosebush!'

"So Madness plucked a thorn as big as a spearhead and began poking around in the rosebush. He didn't stop until he heard a sound of weeping that would have broken your heart. Then Love came out with his hands over his eyes and blood seeping out from between his fingers. 'Oh, my God, what have I done?' Madness cried out in remorse. 'What can I do to make you see again?'

"'You'll never be able to restore my sight,' Love replied. 'Never!'

"A pall of sadness lay over everything for days. Then one morning Madness came and said to Love, 'I want to correct my mistake. Help me!' 'Are you sure?' Love asked. 'No matter what I ask of you?' 'I'll do anything you want,' Madness assured him. Love bowed his head. Then, after a long silence he said, 'Be my guide!'

"'Who, me?'

"'Yes, you!'

"And that's the way things have been ever since: Love roams the Earth blind, with Madness leading the way. So, what do you think?"

"What do I think about what?" asked Bishr.

"Your love is obvious, Bishr, however blind you happen to be. But where's the madness to lead the way?"

"And what am I supposed to do?"

"What are you supposed to do? Do you still not understand what your cousin said? She wants *you*, Bishr!"

"And what can I say to her?"

"Don't worry. I'll tell you everything."

Don't Go Looking for
Somebody Who's in Love

When Daher opened his eyes on that chilly morning, he didn't find Bishr. He headed for the door and looked outside. The wind had driven away all the clouds in the sky, but the sun wasn't up yet.

He heard the white mare neigh.

He took a step back, picked up his mantle, and went out.

The courtyard gate's wooden latch was open. He pushed the gate open and looked down the road in both directions. Tiberias was waking up. From a distance came the sound of roosters crowing and words that were difficult to make out. He heard the sound of a riding animal's hooves, and turned to find a woman on a donkey holding a large bunch of radishes.

"Good morning, Daher!" Najma's voice came from behind him, and the radish vendor's voice from in front of him.

"Good morning."

The radish vendor rode away with her wares, and he turned to face Najma.

"You seem to be looking for something."

"Actually, I'm looking for a dear friend who spent the night in my house, and who's gone this morning."

"Don't go looking for somebody who's in love. Until he's found himself, you won't be able to find him either!"

Daher stood pondering her.

"Why are you looking at me that way?" she asked him.

"You know, Mother, I want to you tell you something, and I hope you won't be angry with me."

"I think I know what it is even before you say it. I can see it in your eyes."

"What is it, then?"

"Say it, and if it's what I'm thinking, I'll tell you!"

"I think you need a husband. What do you say?"

"Who, me? And why would I need a husband? Do you think I'm going to live to be twenty-five?"

Daher laughed. He knew she was about to turn thirty-five.

"And why are you laughing?"

"Oh, nothing. I was just going to ask you if that was what you thought I was going to say."

"And how should I know whether it was or not!"

The white mare neighed again, and Daher walked over to her. He stroked her neck and kissed her forehead, and she licked his face as usual.

"You'll always be her baby, Daher. How many foals has Halima brought into this world? Lots of them! And she's forgotten them all. But for the last sixteen years she's gone on doing the same thing with you. She neighs whenever she picks up your scent, and she licks your face as though she'd given birth to you just moments ago."

Najma took Daher by the hand and led him back inside. Halima neighed. "After all these years, she still gets jealous of me! What will she do when some pretty girl comes along and takes you away from both of us?"

Najma looked into the distance, not to see a place, but to see a time that would never return.

Halima neighed.

Having discovered his hands and knees at last, Daher went crawling toward the source of the sound. Naked except for a piece of white cotton fabric wrapped around his waist and his backside, he crawled past the big rugs in front of the house toward the stairs leading down to the courtyard. He looked at the stairs, not knowing what to do. Then he reached out with one hand, and before he touched the edge of the top step, he found himself tumbling to the bottom of the staircase. He cried. By the time he found his knees again, he was covered with dirt. He rubbed his eyes with the back of his hand, causing his face to disappear behind a layer of soil. When the mare neighed again, he swallowed his tears.

The mare nodded in a signal for him to come closer. He began crawling faster in her direction, indifferent to the clods of dirt and pebbles that began pricking his hands and legs.

After passing under the wooden crossbeam that closed off the entrance to the small stable, he sat directly in front of the mare and peered up into her face.

She bent down and began licking him all over, which sent him into gales of laughter.

Standing at the door to his room, his father saw him. "Najma, Najma!" he called out softly. When she came up to him, he pointed with his head to the stable.

Najma made a move to rush out and get him away from the mare. But Umar al-Zaydani grabbed her hand and held her back.

For a long time they stood watching the mare as she labored with the diligence of a mother bathing her newborn. At last she raised her head and whinnied, as though to announce that she had finished her task.

Umar and Najma approached quietly and sat down on the ground a few meters away from the baby, who sat there serenely, his tiny body glistening with the mare's saliva. His father smiled at him and called him to come. Najma did the same. Saad, Yusuf, and Saleh stood behind them calling him also. But all he did was sit there nodding and laughing without budging from his place.

Najma moved cautiously in his direction. He tried to flee into the stable, but she caught him. The moment they moved away from the white mare, he started to cry. He struggled to free himself from her grip, wanting to go back.

And from that day onward they would see the same scene repeat itself time and time again.

Fear and the Strange Rider's Horse

B ishr stood before Ghazala and said, "Where would I get a hundred she-camels and two stallions?"

He felt calm and reassured, sensing that it was Daher and not
himself who was speaking. After all, wasn't it Daher who had coached
him to say what he had just said?

"And what would I do with a hundred she-camels and two stallions
now that I'm in grief?" Ghazala wanted to know.

"What is it that grieves you, cousin?"

"What grieves me is that you saw the man who came to ask for my
hand, but you haven't seen yourself yet!"

"And what do I need to do in order to see myself?"

"You need to dare to see *me*, cousin."

"I do."

"Who else worries about me the way you do? And who else worries
about you the way I do? Isn't it enough for me to know how women
gloat over me behind my back? I can see it in their eyes."

"What can I do to relieve you of this?"

"Marry me, cousin!"

"But I don't have anything to offer you, Ghazala!"

"What if I told you that if you do what I tell you, you'll have everything?"

"I'll do whatever you say, cousin."

"All I want from you now is one thing: for you to open your tent door
wide while some of the girls and I go get firewood."

"Is that all you have to say, cousin?"

"And would you want me to say more, Bishr?"

That evening Bishr went out into the desert and sat waiting atop a huge
boulder.

It wasn't long before the rider on the horse with kohl-lined eyes
appeared.

"Tell me your news, Bishr!"

"My cousin doesn't want she-camels or horses."

"Tell me what she does want, and I'll bring it."

"My cousin wants her cousin to be her husband."

"She wants *you*?"

"Yes, she wants me."

The rider took a deep breath. Then he turned his horse to leave. As Bishr watched him ride away, he suddenly saw him stop and begin riding back. He came up to where Bishr stood and dismounted. He reached for his musket and drew it out of the saddlebag with the deftness of a well-trained horseman. He looked into Bishr's eyes, which suddenly froze.

Puzzlement

They could never know for certain what Daher was thinking.

Saad asked Najma, "What's going on in Daher's head, Aunt?"

"All I know is what I know about him," she said.

When he asked Saleh the same question, he replied, "He's his usual taciturn self. I don't know whether he's gotten less that way since he became multazim, or more!"

Saad asked Yusuf the same question, and he said, "That's Daher for you. You can't find out what happened with him yesterday. So how do you expect to find out what he's going to do tomorrow?"

"We'll meet tonight at my house," Saad told them.

"Are you going to invite Daher?"

"I don't know."

Fear Again

The sun began to set, and the first stinging breezes started to blow. Another cloudless night, and another frost that would envelop everything.

Ghazala looked into the distance. She waited for him, but he didn't return. She began to worry about what might have happened to him. After all, he was out there alone. But she remembered that he'd always been brave. He was the only one who'd been able to take her hand on that day so long ago when both his family and hers had been killed. He'd hidden with her among the reeds, and when the flames began consuming the dry plants, he'd taken a goatskin flask and blown it up. Then, after instructing her to hold on to it, he'd helped her cross over to the other side of the river.

The girls had asked her why she needed so much firewood, but she had made no reply. She thanked God that she hadn't replied. She thanked God that she'd kept her excitement to herself and hidden it away because, if the news of her upcoming marriage had gotten out, it would have scattered her thoughts.

But he didn't come back. Without noticing what she was saying, she began murmuring to herself:

> O cousin of mine out yonder,
> Did your enemy come, or your friend?
> If the enemy, I'll give my life for you,
> Stand by you till the end!

The sun went down, and for a moment Ghazala felt as though she'd seen it for the last time. The night closed in on the wadi from all sides: a harsh night hard as granite.

"What are you doing out here at night?" The voice of Sheikh Fawwaz came to her from a distance.

"Bishr, my cousin, isn't back yet."

"And since when have you worried about Bishr?"

"He's my cousin, Sheikh, and you know how dear he is to me."

"Go back into your tent, Ghazala. Tonight's cold is different from the nights past. Bishr is like our son, and we worry about him as much as you do. If he isn't back soon, I'll go out and look for him myself."

So she went back inside her tent, but she left her heart at the door.

A Snuffed-out Lantern
and Hot Tears

Two hours later Ghazala heard a horse's hooves. Her heart sank. But then she remembered that the dogs hadn't barked. She rushed toward the tent door and peered into the darkness. She saw a riderless horse approaching. She couldn't see Bishr's minute body, which was hardly noticeable alongside the large creature.

Before she knew it, Ghazala found herself walking toward the horse. She would take two steps forward and one step back. The horse came closer, and in its towering shadow she finally saw Bishr.

"Whose horse is that, Bishr? Did you marry me off against my will? What did I tell you? What am I going to do with the firewood over there? Shall I set a fire and throw myself into it?"

Bishr knew he was a goner. Catching his breath with difficulty, he said to the horseman, "You've come back with good intentions, I hope!"

"With nothing but good intentions. That's how my people have taught me to be."

He handed the horse's reins to Bishr. "This is your wedding present, Bishr. I hope you'll accept it!"

The force of the surprise tied Bishr's tongue. It froze his whole body, in fact. The rider came up to him and placed the reins between Bishr's stiff fingers. Then he patted him on the shoulder and withdrew.

Bishr watched him for a long time until he disappeared from view, and when he heard the horse's neigh, he knew for certain that he wasn't dreaming. He stared at the reins in his hand, not knowing what to do or say. Should he mount the horse or walk beside it? Finally he decided to walk beside it. The burden of poverty under which he labored pulled him downward, planting his feet on the ground and keeping them there. It hemmed him in so completely that, although he'd mounted many horses in his lifetime—to wash them or water them at the river—he couldn't bring himself to mount a horse that was his own!

63

"This horse is our wedding present, Ghazala."

"And who might give us a horse?" asked Ghazala.

"The one who came to ask me for your hand."

She took a deep breath, then exhaled all her cares.

"He's a noble man," she said. "But why did you come back on foot now that you own a horse, Bishr?"

"Cousin, you know that somebody like Bishr would never mount a horse when he's surrounded by Sheikh Fawwaz's tents!"

"Have you forgotten that you rode a horse that belonged to Sheikh Umar al-Zaydani? Listen, Bishr. Listen to me well: You're going to go half an hour's journey from this campground. If in that half hour you don't find the strength to return on that horse's back, then you'll find the strength to stay away from me for the rest of your life. After all, there are plenty of other places to live in this world God made!"

Bishr stood there listening to her. Ghazala had become another girl, a girl he'd never known before. She was as powerful and stern as Sheikh Fawwaz's wife—more so, in fact!

She pointed silently into the opaque night that lay beyond him. He turned with the horse and left, walking alongside it.

"Get on your horse, Bishr!" she shouted.

As she watched him depart, her eyes filled with hot tears that streamed down her cheeks, sweeping away the hope that had budded inside her.

She turned and walked back toward the light that emanated from her tent. Before she pulled the tent flap shut, she reached up and snuffed out the lantern that hung from the tent post. She snuffed it out as though she were shattering it.

The Guards and Talk of Death

Yusuf said, "It was a game we played so that Daher would believe it, and we ended up believing it ourselves."

Saad gathered his small beard between his fingers and said, "It was a game until we actually played it, but now it's a reality. You've all heard about it, and you know it tells the truth."

"If that's true, then why are we meeting?"

"We're meeting for an important reason. If Daher is going to die before we do, then we've got to do everything we can to protect him," replied Saad.

"Protect him from what?" asked Yusuf.

"From death," replied Saad curtly.

"And who can prevent death, Saad?" Yusuf asked.

"Nobody can, and I know that. But our father kept Daher from dying that day. He'd seen death hovering around them, wanting to snatch his newborn son away, so he fought it, and defeated it."

"But our father wasn't able to prevent his own death, Saad!" interjected Saleh ruefully.

"That's just the point. You can protect someone you love from dying, possibly because death senses all the love you feel for the other person. But you can't protect yourself from it, since death picks up the scent of ego that it knows so well!"

"I seem to be the only one who doesn't get what you all are saying. Unlike you, I've never been a disciple of Sheikh al-Hafnawi. You should never have gotten us involved in that game, Saad," Saleh objected.

"If you want to know what's really happening, you should never leave Daher alone again."

"I suppose he's just like us, and is thinking the same thing we are. He told me he'd bought a live fish for a quarter piaster, and instead of taking it home, threw it back in the water!"

"And what's that supposed to mean?" Yusuf wanted to know.

"He's redeeming himself. What else would an act like that mean?"

"But someone who redeems himself offers a sacrifice. In other words, he slaughters an animal, but Daher did just the opposite!"

"I don't know why we've come together if we're just going to end up more confused than ever," Yusuf commented.

"But we've agreed to protect Daher, haven't we?" asked Saleh.

"Did we need to come here in order to make that sort of decision? As long as we're brothers, it goes without saying that every one of us would defend the others. Or are we going to have three more meetings, so that in each one we can decide that we're going to defend one of us?" quipped Yusuf sarcastically.

"For some reason I have a feeling Daher is the one who's going to be protecting *us*! Whenever I remember the fear that came over us after the vizier of Sidon threatened to cut his head off, I nearly go mad. But in the end we received news we would never have expected!" Saleh said.

"That was God's blessing on our father. Can you imagine how brokenhearted he would have been if he'd died before having his mind set at rest about Daher? But that's all over and done with now. That particular death retreated. But there are a thousand deaths a person can die."

They fell silent for a long time.

In the light of the lantern on the broad windowsill, Saad gazed into his two brothers' faces, and they gazed into his. And to their astonishment, they found that the heads on their shoulders had been replaced by three lanterns with three flames aflutter.

Dancing on the Lakeshore

Yusuf and Saleh left the meeting, and Saad sat down alone. His wife called him to supper several times, but he didn't hear her, even when she came and stood at the door just a few steps away. She sensed that he wasn't there. He was so absent that she couldn't see him, nor could he see her. So she retreated without another word.

During those days Umar al-Zaydani was distracted, searching in vain for a solution to Daher's problem. He thought of sending him east, to Irbid or Ajloun, where he could hide until God provided him with some way out. However, he also knew that if the vizier came and didn't find Daher, he would cut off *his* head, and all his sons' heads as well. Umar al-Zaydani knew no one would be able to stop the vizier after what he had done to Bi'na's chief elder and his family.

He was constantly on the watch for news from the pilgrimage caravan. When there was no one to bring reports, he would sit down and draw a line on the ground. Beside it he would write dates and place-names, estimating the distances the caravan had covered on its fifty-day journey: "Today they reached Qatrana," he would say. "Today they reached Hasa," or "Today they spent the night on the outskirts of Ma'an."

In the end he decided to sell everything and, taking whatever he could carry, flee Tiberias with his family.

Then he waited.

He drew another line and traced the progress of the returning caravan. As he saw it approach Damascus, he could feel his son's head tottering on his shoulders.

What baffled him was that Daher paid no heed to the vizier's threat. In fact, he seemed to have forgotten all about it!

"Isn't he afraid?" his father wondered aloud. "Doesn't he realize what the vizier's threat means?"

But to Daher, who dreamed every night about Sheikh Hussein and Abbas with their empty eye sockets, nothing mattered any more. As far he was concerned, there was no difference between death and revenge. In fact, he went so far as to make plans to go to Sidon and look for an opportunity to attack the vizier as soon as he reached the city. As he saw it, this was the best way he had of protecting himself and his family, even if he had to pay for it with his life.

On the lakeshore atop the boulder he loved—"his" boulder—he picked up a piece of chalky stone and sketched the caravan's route both going and coming, without knowing that his father was doing the very same thing.

Umar al-Zaydani had grown thin, and Daher was filled with a desolation that deepened and intensified, his rage mingling bitterly with his despair.

Ultimately, Umar al-Zaydani felt he had no choice but to sell his property, as the pilgrimage caravan was about to enter Damascus. But before he had sold the last item, he received news he could hardly believe: the vizier of Sidon had been removed from his post.

Umar al-Zaydani leapt into the air, brandishing his sword, laughing and crying. Then he ran toward the lake and waded in up to his neck. After coming back to shore, he began to dance. Then he tossed his sword in the air and watched it come down again and plant itself in the ground.

Suddenly he decided to look for Daher, and realized he would probably find him on top of the boulder.

When he was about to reach the boulder, he leapt off his horse, leaving it free to roam, and made his way through the reeds.

"Daher! Daher!" he called.

There was no answer.

He pushed onward until the boulder was in sight. Daher wasn't there. Even so, he kept running all the way to the boulder. He looked out toward the water, thinking that Daher might have gone for a swim.

He didn't see him. The water was still.

He glanced down at the boulder and saw two lines. When he realized he was standing on top of them, he stepped back. He looked at them again, and found to his astonishment that they were lines representing the caravan's trip to and from Mecca with dates written clearly beside the names of the cities and villages.

Daher had disappeared.

They looked for him, but he was nowhere to be found.

His brothers fanned out in all directions, only to return feeling even more hopeless.

Umar al-Zaydani took comfort in the knowledge that, now that the vizier had been removed from his post, he would have a thousand things to think about before Daher even crossed his mind. He knew the vizier would have to move quickly to protect his money and property before the new vizier found some excuse to seize them for himself. He might also need to take measures to protect himself, since everyone knew what enmity existed between the outgoing and incoming viziers and how they had vied for power over the vilayet of Sidon.

"But where did that Daher go?"

On his way to Sidon Daher passed through Bi'na, and the minute he arrived he sensed something peculiar. People were dancing in the streets as though there were a wedding, and singing and women's ululations filled the air like colorful birds:

> The bloody tyrant has gone the way tyrants always do,
> No matter how they wound us, no matter what they do.
> We'll never forget Bi'na, its injustice ever new
> With the blood of the innocents on its gate.
>
> The bloody tyrant has gone, O Lord—never bring him back!
> Bring him to his knees, O Lord—cut him no slack!
> He robbed me of my loved ones, turned my future black,
> When he descended on Bi'na like cruel fate.

Daher stood there confused. Recognizing him, people rushed over and embraced him, and before he could ask what was going on, they began congratulating him on the vizier's removal.

At the graves of Sheikh Hussein and his family, in the cemetery that had abruptly expanded when confronted so suddenly with so many deaths, Daher stood reciting the Fatiha. He closed his eyes, and when he opened them he found himself back in Tiberias.

His arrival brought back the moment of joy Umar al-Zaydani had experienced on the lakeshore, and he relived it by dancing in front of his mare.

The celebrations went on for three days. Umar al-Zaydani slaughtered half his flock of sheep and half his cattle, and banquets were served morning, noon, and night.

When, on the evening of the third day, he came home and informed Najma that the celebrations would go on for an entire week, she took his hand and squeezed it.

"Three days are enough for us to congratulate each other on what happened," she said.

"Do you really think so?"

"Yes, Sheikh. Quite enough!"

Cities of Light, Cities of Darkness

U mar al-Zaydani's death in the middle of winter left his sons some time to put their affairs in order. Summer was still far away, and the first tasks involved in collecting taxes for the state wouldn't begin until mid-June. If they succeeded in the tax collection, they would succeed in planting their feet more deeply in Tiberias's soil. Otherwise, the first summer wind would pick them up and carry them off like the chaff that went flying over the threshing floors.

Like everyone else in Tiberias, Saad knew that the summer winds that year might be especially merciless, since Sidon's new vizier, like every vizier new to his post, was certain to strike a violent blow against any attempts at tax evasion in order to assert his authority from the start. In so doing, he would convince the state that it had made no mistake in its decision to appoint him.

Saad decided to revive the evening gatherings that had once filled Sheikh Umar al-Zaydani's diwan with life, and there was no better occasion for starting them off than the arrival of Sheikh Saadun, the most renowned storyteller in the country.

Wrapping him in an embrace, Saad told him that he'd sent him a messenger when he learned of his arrival in Safad.

Sheikh Saadun said, "And would I need a messenger to bring me here after learning that your father had passed away, may he rest in peace?"

"So you heard the news? It really is a small world!"

Daher made a point of being the last person to arrive that night. Everyone was there: his brothers, the judge, the imam, the prison warden, his teacher Sheikh al-Hafnawi, and Sheikh Saadun. He came through the outer gate on his mare, and dismounted at the diwan entrance.

It was clear to everyone that Daher had thought of everything before his arrival. His father's sword hung from his waist, and his father's pistol with its wooden grip inlaid with ivory and brass was suspended from his belt. His olive-green cloak embroidered with fine orange thread opened to reveal a honey-colored cotton tunic, and he had wrapped his head several times in a honey-colored silk muffler that concealed a white cotton skullcap.

After greeting those present, he walked over to Sheikh Saadun, who was seated in the center of the gathering beside his brother Saad. He embraced the sheikh warmly, and then turned to salute the men seated to the right and left with a lifted hand. At that moment Saad realized what was going on in Daher's mind. As though an invisible hand had begun distancing him from Sheikh Saadun, Saad found his body moving away against his will, clearing a space for Daher so that Sheikh Saadun would be to his left and Saad to his right.

From that moment on, everything that had been ambiguous became clear as day. Sheikh Saadun sensed this when Daher turned to him and said, "We're all ears, Sheikh! Where will you start?"

So Sheikh Saadun began: "Once upon a time there was a city that was surrounded on two sides by mountains, and on two sides by plains. It could have been like any other city, since it was located in the middle of the world. As a matter of fact, however, it was different from any other city on earth. Ask me why!"

"Why?" his listeners thundered.

"Because the people who lived there couldn't see each other the way people normally can. There was no sun to light up their days, and there were no stars to light up their nights. They couldn't see either themselves or anybody else unless they lit lanterns or fires. So when they looked around at night, their eyes glistened like fireflies. But as you all know—may God give you long lives—that wasn't enough to pump life into their cities!"

He continued: "At night, as in the day, the men, women, and children would walk around like shadows, running their hands over the walls and doors of their houses, and you could hear their shadows rubbing up against each other like bats' wings! As for colors, they were a peculiar mixture, of which all you could see in the end was black. They had no distinct name for color. And if you ask me about the weather there, well, it was cold all the time, and the only thing you could hear was the chattering of their teeth!

"People knew, of course, that the sun, moon, and stars existed, since people from the cities of light would sometimes pass through when they'd lost their way, thinking that night had suddenly fallen. They didn't know they'd crossed the boundaries into a city afflicted with darkness. However, when they started bumping into people and hearing words of apology, they would realize soon enough that they were passing through a country where there were people like them. The people passing through would talk about the blue sky, the vast blue sea, colorful birds, and women's long tresses, which were sometimes dark and sometimes light; they would talk about the flowers that bloomed in the spring, the trees that towered above them, and children frolicking in soft green grass.

"One day the king who ruled in those parts said to his wife, 'This is unjust! How is it that the sun, stars, grass, and beautiful colors are there for everyone else, while we have no share in them?' The queen wasn't of royal lineage, but had come from a household of goodhearted peasants who knew the wise saying that I know and that all of you know too: 'Whoever seeks will find!' So the queen said to her husband, 'We've lived here for many years. We were born here and our mothers and fathers lived and died here. With them, we've waited for the sun to come to us, but it never has. So there's only one thing we can do: we have to go looking for the sun and stars and ask them to come to us the way they come to everyone else!'

"The king—God bless you all—was impressed by his wife's point of view, and said, 'I'm going to announce that I intend to give my sister in marriage to whoever can persuade the sun and stars to light up our city!' After fumbling about for her husband's hand, the queen squeezed it in the dark and said, 'I hope to God that we find that man, and that he wins your sister's approval!'

"'As do I,' said the king, 'since we shan't give her in marriage against her will, even in return for the sun and the stars!'

"When, the following day, the king's sister heard of her brother's plan, she agreed to it. So his men spread out in the dark, loudly proclaiming the king's decision.

"Now, you all have a good evening, and we'll finish the story tomorrow!"

Voices of protest went up. "Don't leave us hanging, Sheikh Saadun!"

"The story won't be a story unless you're waiting to hear the rest of it with bated breath!"

His listeners peered into each other's faces, wanting to make sure they weren't living in the city Sheikh Saadun had told them about. The prison warden said to the man next to him, "I don't seem to be able to see you very well!"

"And how would you expect to see me, when you're the one who shuts us up in the dark when you want to, and brings us out when you want to?"

They all laughed.

"The guests' dinner, Jum'a!" shouted Daher.

On their way back, Daher, Saad, Yusuf, and Saleh rode along in silence. In the distance they could make out a horse's shadow against the wall of their father's house. It wasn't until they'd come closer, however, that they saw the slight figure on the horse's back.

"Bishr?" Daher called out. "What brings you here at this time of the night?"

"Pardon me," Bishr replied. "Aunt Najma told me you were in the diwan, but I didn't dare go out there."

"You're my friend, Bishr, and nobody has more right than you do to be by my side!" Daher could sense his brothers exchanging glances in the dark.

"Whose horse is that?" Daher asked.

"It belongs to the horseman who came to me about marrying Ghazala."

The weight of the shadows on Daher's shoulders suddenly doubled.

"Did you sell your cousin for a horse, Bishr?" he asked angrily. "How dare you come to me bringing news like that? Hadn't we agreed on what you needed to do? Even if I receive you, I don't think Najma ever will again."

"But it isn't what you think, Daher!"

"Do you mean you're the one who's going to marry her?"

Bishr nodded. "But it's no easy story."

"You're scaring me, man. With mysterious talk like that, you make this night even darker than it already is!"

". . ."

"Come in!"

Saad bade them farewell and headed for his house. However, they didn't see his hand clearly enough to know whether he had waved or whether they had just imagined it.

Before riding away, Bishr said, "I have something to talk to you about tomorrow, Daher." His voice sounded dry, and deep as a hole in the dark.

Halima neighed as they approached the gate. Once inside, Daher grasped the reins of his guest's horse and led it to the stable, whence his voice carried clearly across the yard as he spoke to her. "How are you today?" he asked her. "I know I've kept you waiting. Anyway, I wish you could have been there with me to hear the story. What do you I say I take you with me to the diwan tomorrow?"

Bishr stood there watching the scene in disbelief. But the biggest surprise was when Daher knelt in front of her and kissed her right front foot.

"What did you do out there just now?" Bishr wanted to know. "Did you kiss the horse's foot? Or am I imagining things?"

"No, you're not imagining things, Bishr. That's my mother!"

"Your mother!"

"How could I have forgotten to tell you about that? I'll tell you all about it tonight."

Yusuf and Saleh went to their room, while Daher took his guest to the larger room that he would be sharing with him for the night as hospitality required.

When Daher learned that for days Bishr hadn't dared to go back to his cousin after she had asked him to enter the campground on his horse's back rather than walking beside it, he suddenly forgot all the traditions of hospitality and shouted, "And what do you lack in order to be her man? Tell me! You're her paternal cousin, and whether other people know it or not, I happen to know that you're a courageous horseman who's mastered the art of fighting better than anybody I've ever known. Didn't I choose you as my trainer when I wanted to learn to fight? With your staff alone you're able to repel an enemy, human or beast. How much better a fighter you'll be, then, now that you have a horse! You can sleep here tonight, but know this: you won't be my friend any longer, and I won't let you darken my door ever again, if you break the heart of that girl who's waiting for you and put her to shame!"

Daher got up, and before he left, in total disregard for the rules of hospitality, he mustered all his breath and blew out the lantern.

"If you want to see the world, Bishr, you're going to have to light your own lantern!"

Bishr stood at the door to Ghazala's tent, which had been battered night after long night by bitter cold winds.

"I didn't hear any hoofbeats, Bishr. Have you come to see me on foot again?"

Bishr turned and jumped on the horse's back, and she could hear its hoofbeats growing fainter and fainter as he rode away.

He kept riding until he sensed that he had covered the distance she wanted him to.

Hearing the hoofbeats again, Ghazala got up and walked toward the door of the tent. The sun was rising blood-red behind him, and for a moment she felt as though he were emerging from its very center, being born, and that she should reach out like a midwife to bring him into the world.

That same afternoon, Ghazala brought all the firewood she'd collected and placed it in front of Bishr's tent. When she had finished, she said to him, "Now you go and do all the things I've told you to!"

Handing him a lit torch, she said, "This is for your wedding fire, Bishr. Light it!"

He took the torch out of her hand and inserted it among the branches. Going to the other side of the heap of firewood, he inserted it again. The fire slowly began consuming the branches until they were all in flames.

Bishr gave the torch back to her, and she handed him a white banner, saying, "Now finish what you started, Bishr."

The sun hadn't gone down yet when Ghazala heard a din approaching from a distance. Little by little there appeared what she had always hoped to see: Bishr was driving his collection of gifts in her direction, the air filled with the bleating of sheep, the neighing of horses, and the bellowing of camels.[9]

That evening, singing rang out and circles of dancers formed. Peo-

---

9 It was a Bedouin custom for someone who wished to ask for a woman's hand in marriage to make the rounds of his people's tents, and the tents of friendly neighboring tribes, carrying a white banner as a way of inviting them to his engagement ceremony. Whenever he passed a tent, its owner would come out and present him with a ewe, a she-camel, or a horse. Since the tribesmen knew of Bishr's poverty, they showered him with gifts in a typical show of generosity toward the needy.

ple's bodies were aflame, flying rapturously like sparks around the bonfire, which they stoked with firewood whenever it asked for more.

And Ghazala's heart was filled with rising suns.

A Lantern Bigger Than a Sun

On the other side of Tiberias, something was happening: something entirely different. Saad had spent the previous night in the dark, like a piece of charcoal whose features had fused with a dense night that appeared to have no end.

He didn't need to see the lantern go out again in front of him to realize what had happened. He thought: *We started the game. But Daher took it and, more quickly than anyone could have imagined, directed it to his own ends. I should have known that Daher would never be content to be in my shadow, crawling along beside me and behind me wherever I go. He agreed in silence to the terms of the game, and now he's making us agree in silence to its outcome—in front of everyone, with everyone as witness.*

The question of death no longer kept Saad awake at night. In fact, he had put it entirely out of his mind. He thought: *For him to die before I do, for me to die before he does, or for all of us to die—all of that means nothing, compared to what he's done. He's decided that since we've burdened him with everything, he'll make himself into everything. Do you suppose Najma put him up to it? No, no, it couldn't have been Najma. Maybe it was the judge, or the imam, or his teacher, Sheikh al-Hafnawi? Or maybe they've all egged him on!*

Saad spent his day cursing everything, realizing that Daher had tied his hands and that he was helpless to do a thing, since any dispute that arose now was bound to tear the family apart and rob them of the one legacy their father had left them: the post of multazim.

By nightfall he was about to explode, and the summons he received through Jum'a was all he needed to take him over the edge.

"Sheikh Daher is waiting for you in the house, and he wants all of you to go to the diwan together," Jum'a announced.

"Get out of my face!" Saad screamed. "Get out!"

Saad's wife came out flabbergasted, and Jum'a froze in place, terrified. It was the first time anyone in Umar al-Zaydani's family had shouted at Jum'a since the day he set foot in their diwan, since he lit his first fire in the diwan courtyard, since the first cup of coffee he had served them.

Seeing Jum'a standing there statue-like, Saad realized what he had done. He took a deep breath and said, "I apologize, Jum'a. I was thinking about something else, something that has me very upset."

Within a few moments Jum'a found his feet again and turned to leave. "Tell him I'll be there shortly," Saad instructed him.

Deeply distressed, Jum'a felt like an orphan. He started crying, and cried the whole way to where Daher was without realizing he was crying. People who knew him asked him, "What's wrong, Jum'a?" But he didn't hear them. He just left them in their confusion and went on crying. "Has somebody died, Jum'a?" someone would ask. But he went on his way weeping. When he got to the house, Daher saw him. But when he asked him, "What's happened, Jum'a?" he just kept crying.

Daher shook him. He shook him again, and got his attention. "Why are you crying, Jum'a?" he asked.

"Who, me?" he replied. "I'm not crying!"

Daher told him to go wash his face. When he came back, Daher asked, "Has something happened? Has someone hurt you?"

Jum'a shook his head and said, "My master Saad will be here shortly!"

"Since when do you call him 'my master Saad'? Never has anyone in this household been called such a thing. You're free, just as he and I are. I don't want to hear you say that ever again!"

Without a word Jum'a withdrew, and Daher turned to find Yusuf, Najma, and Saleh staring at him.

"If someone wants to be a sheikh, Daher, he needs to choose his friends well," Saad said to him, realizing that he couldn't discuss the step Daher had taken to make himself into a family elder.

"What do you mean, Saad?"

"I'm talking about Bishr. It won't do for Sheikh Fawwaz to be my guest while Bishr the shepherd is your guest and friend!"

"Is that what's bothering you, Saad? Or is there something else you don't want to say directly? Saad, you insulted Jum'a this evening. I know you did even though he didn't say a word about what had happened. And now you're insulting me by insulting my friend. I'll have you know, Saad, that Bishr is his own master even though he's a shepherd, and that he has more courage, decency, and integrity than the scores of sheikhs, multazims, and emirs who fill this land from Tiberias to Damascus, from Damascus to Beirut, and from Beirut to Cairo! I hope you'll forget what you just said, Saad, because if you don't, it means that you intend to insult not only me, but Umar al-Zaydani, who considered Bishr one of his own sons. The poor loved Umar al-Zaydani in life, and wept over him in death. That was because he didn't collect taxes in order to line his pockets with the sweat of their brows, but rather to preserve their dignity and give them something the empire could never take away from them. All I ask of you, Saad, is that you not force me to choose between your sheikh and my poor man, because if I do have to choose, I'll choose Bishr in spite of my love for Sheikh Fawwaz!"

"What I meant was that he should at least come looking more presentable when he knocks at your door."

"I know Bishr, Saad, and it won't be long before you see him at my door looking the way you hope to see my friends looking!"

When they were a short distance from the diwan, they saw the largest crowd they'd seen for a long time. People filled the courtyard and blocked the outer entrance. When Jum'a cried, "Sheikh Daher has arrived!" the crowd divided to create a narrow corridor leading to the diwan entrance.

Everyone there had prepared himself for a long night, with a heavy cloak and something to cover his head and neck.

When Daher came in with his sword and pistol strapped to his waist, everyone stood up. He greeted them and said with a laugh, "It looks as though all of Tiberias is here tonight, Sheikh Saadun!" He shook his hand warmly. Then he shook hands with the judge, the imam, the mufti, and the prison warden, who cleared a space for him and his brothers to sit down.

"You kept us waiting, Sheikh Daher," the judge said.

"That way, you'll be all the more anxious to see me!" quipped Daher.

"Well, you've made us anxious enough!"

"But where did all these people come from?" Daher asked.

"It seems that everyone who was here last night went out and told his family and friends what he'd heard. And this is the result."

Daher nodded, and Sheikh Saadun addressed him and everyone else present, saying, "We won't leave you in the cold any longer!"

Then, to stir up his listeners, he asked the judge, "Where were we, Your Honor?"

Voices chimed in eagerly, indicating the point where he had left off.

That night marked the threshold between two eras. But, like his three brothers, Saad had no idea of the mighty wind in whose path Daher would find himself quaking within a few weeks' time.

Monday Night and the Prince's Wedding

On her wedding day, Ghazala had no mother to receive a young camel in compensation for having breastfed her daughter, and she had no paternal uncle to receive several camels in return for agreeing to marry her to someone other than his son.

As for Bishr, he wasn't obliged to present her paternal cousin with a ewe in return for marrying his tribeswoman and taking her somewhere far away. Nor was he obliged to buy clothing for her maternal uncle to wear when he went to fetch the bride from her tent. Poor man that he was, he had no slave to give a few piasters to for leading the bride's camel. Nor did he have dogs to guard his tent—dogs that would be honored on such an occasion by being served a young donkey that had been slaughtered especially for them.

The Bedouin believed that Mondays and Fridays carried a special blessing, and it was their custom to marry on one of these two days. Hence, they waited until the last Monday in April, which brought them a warm night with a full moon.

One bright noonday before the wedding, Sheikh Daher and his brothers headed north. The weather was splendid, and the sun was bathing the earth in a gentle light. The mountains and plains were blanketed in red anemones and daisies, and the trees were in full bloom. To their right stretched Lake Tiberias, and they could see teal ducks taking off joyously over the water.

Daher said, "There's nothing more beautiful in my opinion than an autumn or spring day!"

Glimpsing Daher and his brothers from a distance, Bishr leapt onto his horse and took off in their direction. By the time he reached them, they had dismounted.

When Bishr embraced Daher, it seemed he didn't want to let go of him. "It's as if you're afraid the bride will take you away from your friend!" Saleh commented.

"I don't think so!" Bishr replied. "Ghazala isn't the type that would deprive her husband of his brothers."

As a wedding gift, Daher and his brothers had brought a Damascene sword they had bought for a thousand piasters. Holding it gently in his upraised palms, Daher presented it to Bishr in front of Sheikh Fawwaz.

"It seems Ghazala and the two of you agreed on this beforehand!" Bishr whispered in his ear.

"The staff days are gone for good!" Daher whispered back.

Bishr's wedding would have been fit for a prince. The tragedy that he and his paternal cousin had suffered lingered in the hearts of all who knew their story. Consequently, everyone had become "family." Horses raced, horsemen held fencing matches, and shots were fired in the air in celebration. When Sheikh Fawwaz's shepherd came to inform him that his mare had given birth to a filly, he stood up and announced the news joyfully to all. Then, in a gesture no one had anticipated, he presented the filly to Bishr as a gift.

Night fell and the wedding party broke up. Alone with his wife, Bishr began to undress.

"What are you doing, Bishr?" she asked him.

Taken aback, he said, "What am I doing? I want to sleep!"

"You won't be sleeping tonight, Bishr!"

"What else can we do on a night like this, cousin?"

"Rest! Just rest! In a few hours the sun will be up. I want you to take half the livestock you received as gifts and sell it in Tiberias or Safad. Then in the late afternoon, the sun will take you by the hand and bring you home!"

"And what will I do with the money, cousin?"

"You'll buy a goat-hair tent with four posts."

"And what else?"

"You'll buy things for making and serving coffee. As for the rugs and the saddle blankets, leave those to me."

"Why should we buy all these things when we don't need them, cousin?"

"I'll tell you when you get back!"

A few weeks later, Ghazala saw Sheikh Fawwaz going out on a raid. She looked for Bishr among the men and didn't find him. Furious, she headed quickly back to their tent and found him asleep. She shook him awake.

"Why are you sleeping, Bishr?"

"And what else is a newly wed husband supposed to be doing?"

"Don't you know, cousin? The men have gone out on a raid!"

"Has Bishr ever gone out on a raid before? Has anybody ever asked him to do that?"

"The new Bishr isn't the same as the old one, cousin. The new Bishr has a sword instead of a staff, a thoroughbred horse instead of a donkey, and a filly that was given to him by Sheikh Fawwaz himself! Now you get on your horse and catch up with them!"

"What if they tell me to come home?"

"Don't do it, Bishr. I know they'll tell you that you're an orphan and that you don't have any family. They'll tell you to come back and that they'll bring you your share. But don't you dare do what they say. You stay with them. And when they come back, I don't want to see you in the rear."

"Where should Bishr ride then, cousin?"

"You put your horse in the front row. After all, he's fast as a racehorse, and nobody can keep up with him. And remember that when you drive the booty home, you're not to ride with the slaves."

"Whom should I ride with, then?"

"With the horsemen, cousin. With the horsemen! And don't forget: when you approach our campgrounds, you're to ride ahead of everyone else, holding your spear crosswise in front of you."

"What else?"

"Leave the rest to me, cousin. Now go with God's blessing. And remember what I've told you."

Sparrows' Wings, and Sparrows' Milk, Too

W hen the tax collector arrived in Tiberias one hot afternoon in July, Daher had made the first of the decisions that would define his relationship with the Ottoman Empire. He had decided to pay all the money it claimed he owed.

Saad opposed his brother's decision. As for Yusuf and Saleh, they were of two minds on the matter, since both sides had arguments in their favor.

"There's no need for us to pay all the taxes we owe them this year," Saad insisted. "We should keep some money back in case we need it in the days to come. After all, no one knows what the future holds!"

"I'm going to give them everything that's theirs," replied Daher. "I don't want them to be able to hold anything against us, especially in view of the fact that this is the first year since our father died."

After they'd argued all night without either of them budging from his position, Saleh said, "Let's try going with Daher's opinion and see what happens."

Agitated, Saad asked Yusuf, "What do you think, Yusuf?" But he said nothing.

Najma sat listening, pretending to be busy mending a dress. After the others had left, she asked Daher, "Why didn't you listen to Saad?"

"For one reason only, Mother. I don't want to see any of the government's employees or soldiers here more than once a year!"

The tax collector stayed in Tiberias for seven long days, in the course of which he made inquiries, investigated, roamed the harvested fields, and scrutinized the crop over and over in search of evidence that they were concealing part of it. He even sent out spies, but the conclusion was always the same: this was the entire crop.

Disgruntled, he demanded things over and above the tax: a lamb, which his soldiers led away, a calf, and a jar of honey. He even took a rug from one of the houses.

Daher watched in silence, and when Saad asked him to intervene, he said, "Let him do as he pleases. Let's help him commit whatever mistakes he wants to. We might need them later on!"

When the judge, the imam, and other men of Tiberias came to the diwan that evening angry and shouting, he repeated what he'd said to Saad.

They left angrier than ever.

On the last morning of the tax collector's visit, Daher handed him the last piaster of the state's taxes. But instead of bidding him farewell, the tax collector said, "I want enough food for our journey to Sidon. It will be a long one."

That was when Daher issued orders for him to be arrested along with his men.

The men of Tiberias, who had been hoping for a moment like this, surrounded them, bound them, and led them to prison.

When the prison warden tried to object, Daher whispered in his ear, "If you refuse, I'll lock you up with them!"

The prison warden nodded in resignation.

"There's only one thing I ask of you: to honor them and give them whatever they want, even if they ask you for sparrows' milk. I said milk, mind you, not wings! Because if they escape, I'll put you in their place!"

That evening Daher summoned the prison warden, who came promptly. "How are your guests faring?" he asked him.

"As per your instructions," he said.

"Sit down," Daher commanded.

He sat down.

Presently, the judge, the imam, the mufti, Saad, Yusuf, and Saleh arrived with a number of Tiberias's leading men.

"I've called you together for one reason: I want us to write a letter to the vizier of Sidon informing him of everything that's happened. We'll tell him how we paid all the taxes we owed the state, and how we said nothing about what the tax collector and his soldiers did. And we'll tell him that they went to such extremes that we had no choice but to imprison them."

Three days later a letter arrived from the vizier of Sidon, in which he commended Daher for his commitment to paying what he owed, including taxes that had been delinquent, and promised to punish the tax collector for everything he had done.

The following morning Daher sent the money to the vizier, but kept the tax collector and those with him in prison till after noon.

Daher went to the prison himself, opened the door, and let them out. "We hope we've shown you the proper hospitality and provided everything you needed!" he said.

"Yes, you have," replied the tax collector irritably.

"In any case, the money we owed the state has already been sent to Sidon."

"And our horses?"

"Your horses are ready and saddled for you so that you won't be delayed."

Daher had left the livestock and other things they had collected for themselves in the stable. When the tax collector instructed his soldiers to gather them up and follow him, Daher told him irately, "I told you we'd already sent the tax money this morning!"

Realizing that he had better make a speedy departure, the tax collector prodded his horse and took off, followed by his soldiers.

Your Dreams Are
the Things You Do

The ground beneath her feet was shaking. Ghazala listened, and knew that they'd returned. She left her tent and stood in the middle of the tent-lined road. She didn't have to search long for Bishr. She saw him approaching ahead of the other horsemen. He was carrying his spear crosswise, his braids loosened, and in his eyes the look of a tiger.

Blocking their path, Ghazala called out, "Sheikh! Sheikh!"

Women's ululations filled the air, and happy children scampered about among the returning steeds.

"What is it, Ghazala?"

"Sheikh Fawwaz—may God protect you!—we would like lunch to be served in Bishr's house. Don't refuse the request of a woman who won't take no for an answer!"

The riders stopped and dismounted.

After they had eaten lunch in Bishr's four-post tent and drunk their coffee, they began dividing the spoils.

Their customs dictated that one share would go to those who had taken part in winning the spoils, one share to the leading horsemen, and one share to the family who hosted the returning raiders.

When they divided the spoils, Bishr received the largest share, and he couldn't believe his eyes. From that time on he was among the wealthiest men in the tribe.

The gathering dispersed and the clamor died down.

At siesta time, Ghazala turned to Bishr and said, "You need a little sleep now, cousin."

"A little? I'd say I need a lot!"

"No, cousin. Someone with your status doesn't need much sleep, since his dreams are the things he does!"

A Long Road and
a Tethered Horse

There was nothing Daher adored more than duck hunting. An hour spent on the shores of Lake Tiberias was enough to cleanse him of any anger or sorrow that might be clinging to his soul. So that was where he would go whenever he felt the need.

He took Halima, the white mare, and tied her to his horse's saddle. Then he set out at a leisurely pace, bearing in mind that she wasn't as strong as she used to be. It was her outing as much as it was his. When he reached the lake, he untied her and let her run free. He thought he was the one watching her. In fact, however, she didn't wander far, and was keen to make sure he stayed put so that she could keep an eye on him!

He sat down in his favorite spot between two towering palm trees, on a flat boulder being lapped gently by the waves. The first thing he did after getting there was to check on the fish. He took a large round of pita bread out of his pocket, tore off part of it, and threw it into the water.

He didn't have to wait long, since Lake Tiberias was filled with fish. One fish came rushing to the surface, followed by scores of others. He tossed another chunk in, and the scene changed. The piece of bread bobbed up and down as though it were on the back of a large wave. As he sat there watching, the white mare crept up behind him, and when she saw the fish she whinnied gently in what sounded like a chuckle. Eventually all the fish disappeared except for a small one that hadn't been able to grab a bite in the earlier rush. It hovered near the surface, searching in vain for at least one nibble. Daher tossed it a little piece and watched it hurriedly gobble it down before the swarm came back.

He watched it swim away, then lay down on the rock and stared motionless into the sky. The white mare moved away slightly and stood there watching him. At length he sat up again and gazed for some time out into the lake. By the time he got up, he felt rested and renewed.

He patted the mare's neck, kissed her forehead, and whispered, "Let's go."

As he rode along on the back of his stallion, he felt as though he were riding a wave from shore to shore, his body a mast, his cloak a sail. However, the pleasant sensation vanished abruptly when he heard a woman's wounded scream coming from the lemon grove.

He brought the horse to a sudden halt and tried to identify the source of the sound, which seemed to be coming from all directions. He prodded the horse and it began going in circles. Seeing that the white mare was hindering the stallion's movement, he loosened her reins from the stallion's saddle and took off in search of the source of the sound. The plea for help grew more intense and anguished, and his consternation deepened.

Seeing that it would be difficult to make his way through the grove on horseback, he dismounted. Then suddenly the voice was gone, as though it had fallen into a bottomless well, and he heard a man's indistinct mutterings. He began running, not knowing whether he was running in the right direction or not. He stumbled, and the lemon trees' thorns bloodied his hands as he moved the branches out of the way. Suddenly he found himself before a man who had one hand clapped over a woman's mouth and the other on a sword, which he brandished in Daher's face.

The man realized that the person before him was Daher al-Umar, in the flesh. However, he considered the fact of having been exposed more intolerable than any act of madness he might commit. So, removing his hand from the woman's mouth, he advanced toward Daher. Her clothing in tatters, the woman began covering herself in a frenzy, not knowing which part of herself to conceal first.

The two men fenced, sparks flying when their swords clashed. The woman crawled behind a tree and cowered, trembling. The look of terror in her eyes robbed Daher of his senses, and he found himself attacking the man without a thought for anything else. The man's sword swung forcefully toward Daher's neck. Daher leaned forward and delivered a blow that pierced him through. The man reeled. The sword in Daher's hand, and the life that remained in his opponent, had propelled him onward. Yet, as the man tottered, Daher didn't know what to do. He had just killed someone, and he didn't know whether he ought to pull the sword out or leave it in place forever.

Time froze. The lemon trees froze. The air went still and dry, neither entering his lungs nor leaving it. Still also were the eyes of the woman, who seemed to have expired as she stared into an unknown fate, her hands, her feet, and her spirit bound by an unseen force.

Daher felt something flowing down over his hand. When he mustered the courage to look, he saw a thick, blackish liquid covering the fist in which he gripped his sword. He pulled the sword out quickly, and the man collapsed before him. He was dead.

Daher bent down and rubbed his hands in the dirt a couple of times. He stood up, then bent down and rubbed them in the dirt again. He came slowly up to the woman, being careful not to look at her.

"Did he violate you?" he asked.

"No," she replied.

"Thank God. Whose wife are you?"

"I'm the grove owner's daughter," she said with difficulty.

He took off his cloak and, with his back to her, handed it to her. Then he walked over to the man's corpse. After she'd covered herself with the cloak, he looked over at her.

"What is your name?" he asked.

"Haniya."

A tall, pretty girl no more than seventeen years old, she had large eyes whose color Daher couldn't distinguish, so muted was it by the terror that had her in its grip.

"Do you know who I am, Haniya?"

She nodded.

"I was angry on your account, Haniya. So do you promise to keep my secret?"

She nodded again.

"I'd like to hear you say it, Haniya."

"I promise."

"You go now, and I'll look for a place nearby to bury him."

The girl stumbled away. He watched her until she disappeared. Then he rolled up the sleeves of his robe and tied his kaffiyeh around his forehead. He walked over to the corpse and looked around. He could hear the girl's footsteps as she made her way back home. He crouched and scanned the area under the trees, then straightened up again. Grasping the two swords with his left hand, he closed the fingers of his right hand around the dead man's wrist and began dragging him away.

As he stood crying in front of the white mare, she wiped his face with her tongue for the first time in many years. He calmed down a bit.

"But I've killed someone!" he told her miserably.

Halima nickered and walked before him toward his mount. He tugged on her reins and began heading for home, not realizing what a long road now lay ahead of him.

Meanwhile, the approaching night loomed dark and eerie.

The Shepherd's New Path

Bishr woke up early.

"So, you're awake!" Ghazala said. "And what are you going to do now?"

"I'm going to take the sheep and goats to the valley to graze."

"That isn't why I asked you to get up early!"

"And what is Bishr supposed to do if he doesn't graze the sheep and the goats, cousin?"

"He's supposed to look for a shepherd to graze them for him."

"How am I supposed to have a shepherd when I'm a shepherd myself? Besides, I wouldn't trust my livestock with anybody else!"

"The Bishr that once was doesn't exist any more, cousin!"

"He doesn't exist any more?"

"No, he doesn't. The new Bishr is a chieftain of his tribe."

"Who, me, cousin?"

"Yes, you, Bishr. You and I are of noble birth, and if our families hadn't died, we would still enjoy positions of prominence. All we've lacked are wealth and livestock. And now you're a rich man."

"But I'm an orphan like you."

"If someone has high aspirations, Bishr, those high aspirations are his mother, his father, and his tribe. Don't worry. I'm with you!"

Strange, the things Ghazala was saying. After all, how could Bishr become a chieftain in a world filled with chieftains?

He looked for a shepherd from among his tribesmen, but no one was willing to work for him. "What would people say about me?" one of them would say. "That I'm a shepherd who works for a shepherd?"

However, it wasn't difficult for him to find a shepherd elsewhere. So he brought one from another tribe and gave him his old tent.

"You see? Finding a shepherd is easy as can be! What I want you to do now, Bishr, is to honor this shepherd and take good care of him. Give him what no other shepherd in this tribe receives. You're going to give him one-tenth of your flock's newborns, and a she-camel of his own."

"Why should I do that? I worked my whole life as a shepherd, and nobody gave me anything!"

"Do what I tell you, Bishr, and everybody who refused to work for you will regret it sorely!"

"And what is Bishr going to do with himself now that somebody else is grazing his sheep and goats for him?"

"I'll tell you!"

Ghazala had thought about all this long before. Day after day she'd built up her future status in her mind to the point where she thought of herself as a woman of influence in her tribe. She didn't deny what Sheikh Fawwaz had done for her and Bishr. However, Sheikh Fawwaz knew that his one-time reluctance to do his duty had besmirched his honor. He had always been an ally of her tribe, and he realized that his failure on that day long ago to lend them a helping hand was the reason for the storm of death that had ravaged her people. This, at any rate, was what people whispered to each other.

A noble man asks no reward for his nobility. His reward is the sense of pride and satisfaction he receives from being noble.

This was how Ghazala thought.

And the noble man is the one who reaches out to restore those who have suffered the vicissitudes of fate to their rightful places.

Sheikh Daher, You Forgot This!

Evening had fallen, and Daher stood hesitantly at the entrance to the diwan. He saw horses in the courtyard, one of which he recognized as belonging to Emir Qa'dan of the Saqr tribe. But before he had a chance to retreat, he heard his brother Saad calling him from inside.

Daher didn't know what to do, or what he would say if he had to face them. So he retreated.

Sensing that something was amiss, Saad excused himself and came out.

Daher took him aside and told him what had happened. Saad looked around in terror.

"Someone who's shed blood can't hide, Daher. If the people of Tiberias learn that we have their blood on our hands, how will we able to maintain any standing among them from now on?" Saad demanded.

"I swear to God, if you'd seen what I saw, you would have done worse. Could I let some lecher rape a girl while I stood there and watched? I wouldn't be Umar al-Zaydani's son if I'd done a thing like that. And believe me: if I hadn't killed him, you'd be standing here with someone else, who'd come to bring you news of my death!"

"Your death? That's all we need now! Go in the house ahead of me, and I'll follow you."

By sunset of that day, much had changed. Daher walked home despondent, dragging a despondent stallion who was dragging an even more despondent mare, and wishing the earth would open up and swallow him.

He didn't know how he made it back to Najma, whose heart quaked at the sight of him. She'd never seen him so broken before. He took a few steps in her direction and froze. She waited for him to come closer, but he didn't. He stared at the ground, and from time to time would stare at his hands as though he held the slain man in his arms.

She walked toward him, past the raised platform and across the large courtyard, and before saying a thing she took him in her arms.

Daher wept silently. Then he pushed her gently away and turned his back to her, taking care not to let her see his tears.

"I'll be back soon," he said, and left.

Emir Qaʻdan and those with him noticed that the Saad who had left their gathering was not the Saad who had returned. He was silent, his eyes darting to and fro as though they couldn't find anything to settle on.

"You're not the Saad I know!" commented Emir Qaʻdan.

"What?"

"I said, 'You're not the Saad I know'!"

It was then that Saad realized that he had as much of a problem as his brother did, since the worst thing that could happen would be for Emir Qaʻdan and those with him to feel unwelcome!

Having made his decision, he said to the men in attendance, "Would you allow me and Emir Qaʻdan to have a few moments alone?"

They exchanged glances and nodded, more baffled than their leader.

When Saad leaned against Emir Qaʻdan's mare, the emir realized that something momentous was afoot.

"Say what's on your mind, Saad. I'm listening, and I won't abandon you even if the sultan himself has declared himself your enemy!"

Saad repeated everything he'd heard from Daher while Emir Qaʻdan nodded thoughtfully, in search of a solution even before Saad had finished speaking.

"If you want, Saad, you'll have ten thousand cavalrymen at your door tomorrow morning, and they and I will be ready to lay down our lives for you."

"That isn't what I was getting at. I can't bear to think about how I'll face the people of Tiberias if they learn of the matter!"

"In that case, I have only one thing to tell you: our campgrounds in Galilee are just as fertile as Tiberias. Besides this, the weather there is more moderate and there's more trade. So go get your family ready, and come with us now."

"That wouldn't be easy," replied Saad. "We have lands, houses, and all sorts of interests to maintain here. We couldn't leave the country just like that. If we did, the people who don't know what happened would find out about it, since people would have plenty to say about Umar's sons, who packed up and left everything without even saying goodbye!"

"You've got to act before the matter becomes public, Saad. By the time our three-day stay has ended, you need to have sold all your property and be ready to come with us. If people ask you about it, say, 'We're going with our friends of the Saqr tribe to Safad. It's more fertile than Tiberias, and we'll have a lot of work there.'"

Saad nodded in approval of the emir's plan, and they went back inside.

Without knowing it, Daher found himself back in the place where he had buried the slain man's body. He was weeping bitterly, and the water of the lake echoed his sobs. A wolf howled in the distant mountains, and dogs barked. When he came back, he found Najma, Saad, Yusuf, and Saleh waiting for him.

There was no solution left to them but to leave.

Daher said, "Let's stay here. I'll tell people what happened, and we'll let the judges and the elders rule between us."

"But Daher, whether the ruling is in our favor or not, people will never look at us in the same way again."

"We're the chieftains of Tiberias now, Aunt Najma. So why should we run away like this?" Yusuf protested.

"You *were* its chieftains!" Najma replied. "But now, nothing stands higher than that shed blood."

"So then, let's stay and not tell anyone, Mother!"

"But you'll never be the same again, Daher. How will you be able to walk over the spot where you hid the man you killed? You'll go on tripping over that body wherever you set foot. His grave will go on drawing you back till it breaks you, and you won't be yourself any more. We have no choice but to accept the solution Saad agreed to with Emir Qa'dan."

People gathered to bid them farewell. Emir Qa'dan and his men were in the lead, and behind them marched Saad, his wife and children, his brothers, Najma, Jum'a, the white mare and their other horses, and a few mules carrying their clothes and household goods.

Daher did his best to appear composed. However, the moment of leave-taking itself was painful enough to justify all the sorrow written on people's faces.

Everyone who had gathered waved goodbye.

At that moment, a girl's face emerged from the crowd. She was crying, but her tears couldn't conceal her beauty. Daher's heart fluttered in a way it had never fluttered before. Was it fear? Or was there something else that he felt but couldn't explain?

Before they set off, a boy came running after them with a bundle in his hands. "Sheikh Daher!" he cried. "You forgot this! You forgot this!"

Daher stopped and rode back toward the boy. Before he reached him, he was sure he knew what the bundle contained. He realized that the girl was returning his cloak. He looked back at the crowd, and all he could see of it was a single hand waving to him.

Two Horses at a Single Trough

Within a few weeks, Bishr's tent was being sought out by visitors from all parts. Word had spread about the orphan boy who, with his orphaned cousin, had forged his way to a position of prominence in the tribe.

Sheikh Fawwaz observed this development with concern as he saw guests flocking to Bishr's house, every one of them trying to see if he might be some relation of his.

One sweltering midsummer night, Bishr recognized Sheikh Fawwaz's lanky frame approaching from a distance, and jumped up to welcome him. Sheikh Fawwaz declined Bishr's invitation to come in.

"I have something to say to you," he announced, "but it can't be said in your house."

Ghazala observed what was happening in silence. In the distance she could see Sheikh Fawwaz talking and talking. Now and then a word would reach her hearing, but she couldn't make out what was being said.

"Maybe they're planning a raid for tomorrow!" she thought proudly.

She continued to watch them, suppressing her anger over the fact that Bishr hadn't said a single word. All she could see was his head nodding from time to time in the dim light.

Not long afterward, the two men passed wordlessly in front of her tent. Sheikh Fawwaz saw her. However, he kept going without bidding Bishr farewell, and without greeting her.

Bishr stood before her without saying a word.

She asked him, "Why are you tongue-tied, cousin? What did Sheikh Fawwaz say to you?"

"Two horses can't feed from the same trough!"

"He wants us to leave, then! And what did you say to him?"

"I told him what he wanted to hear: that by sundown three days from now, we'd be gone."

"Will you go to Tiberias, to your friend Daher al-Umar, and arrange to move there?"

"They'll say that Bishr left the Bedouins to go live near peasants and farmers!"

"You won't find a place more spacious than Sheikh Daher's heart. As for the one who bears the shame of having driven you out of his campgrounds, he has no right to criticize you no matter where you go, even if you're forced to work as a fisherman!"

Bishr returned from Tiberias more downcast than he had been before he went. The news that Daher al-Umar and his brothers had left hit him like a thunderbolt.

"What would have led the town's multazim to pick up and leave that way? Might somebody have asked him to leave, too?" Ghazala asked. "And where did he go?" she added.

"To the area around Safad, with the Saqr tribe."

And the world looked even grimmer.

Summons from Afar

T he village of Arraba stole their hearts the moment they laid eyes
on it. It was a piece of heaven surrounded by forests, and its
broad plain overflowed with God's blessings.

They bought a spacious, multiroom house with a diwan and a stable
that reminded them of their house in Tiberias. Even before the people
of the village and its environs had finished welcoming them, they had
opened their own house to guests and, thanks to the wealth at their disposal, they outdid their new neighbors' generosity.

As their fame spread, people flocked to see them, and as the story
of Daher's tenure as multazim in Tiberias receded into the past, Saad
regained his former prestige.

Meanwhile, Daher's sense of guilt continued to mount. He was
haunted by the blood he had shed, which had driven his family from
their home and deprived them of their former standing and possessions.

Although Saad had reoccupied his father's position, he wasn't happy
knowing that his stature had only been enhanced because they had lost
their positions as multazims and because they were standing, as it were,
atop Daher's tragedy. Nor had the night of the lanterns lost its grip on
him. Even when he was occupied with other things, it would pass fleetingly through his mind's eye and he would see their flames flickering
endlessly, like the finger of fate drawn sword-like in his face. And if he
had mentioned it to his brothers, they would have confessed to having
similar thoughts.

Daher hadn't forgotten that final farewell to the most beautiful place he
had ever seen, and while the lovely Arraba appeared to be a fair replace-
ment, the lake itself remained his dream.

Daher would sit for long hours in front of the bundle the boy had
brought him, and when he looked into the distance, all he could see was
that hand waving to him, the hand that would go on waving eternally.

He suspected there was a cloak inside the bundle. However, he didn't know whether it was his own cloak—the one he had thrown over the girl's nakedness—or a different one.

One night he decided to take the plunge and undo the two tight knots that held the bundle together.

Was his hand trembling? Maybe. He himself didn't know for certain.

With difficulty he untied the first knot. He took a deep breath and stopped, hesitant: Should he untie the other one or not?

In the end he made the decision that he had put off for days. His fingers went to work gently undoing the knot. He wanted that old cloak of his, and at the same time he didn't want it! Before he'd managed to decide how he felt, he saw it. It was his old cloak, after all. However, what he hadn't anticipated was the fragrance that came pouring out of it, filling his nostrils with a sweetness he had never known before.

He tried to recall what fragrance it was, but couldn't. It was a peculiar mélange.

He picked it up gently and sniffed it. When he did so, he felt something strange happening to him. He felt his body slipping away from him and coming out of its hiding places. The fragrance rang forgotten bells inside him. He brought the bundle closer to his nose. Then, in spite of himself, he opened it and felt something fall out. He turned to see what it was. It was a smaller, snow-white bundle. He was uncertain at first whether to bend down and pick it up or to answer the call of the cloak, which seemed to be struggling to release itself from his grip and wrap itself around his body. Eventually he put on the cloak, and the moment he did so he was overwhelmed by a kind of intoxication.

What had the girl put in it to take control of him this way? He was perplexed. If he hadn't seen her waving to him, he would have suspected that someone had filled the cloak with this mad, overpowering fragrance in order to kill him with ecstasy!

It was a long time before he regained his senses. When he came back to the present, he remembered the white bundle and bent down to pick it up.

He was afraid of something, something more powerful and penetrating than the cloak.

He ran his fingers over the smaller bundle, but couldn't guess what it contained. His fingers moved up and down over something inside that seemed to be wound into rings. He set the bundle gently down and sat staring at it.

What could she have sent besides his cloak? What could she have sent beyond that fragrance that he would remember till his dying day?

Daher wasn't one of those people who wait forever before they act. On the contrary, he was more prone to take his common sense by surprise and act before he thought. His fingers went to work, and before he had opened the bundle, the fragrance burst out again like a fountain, bombarding him with its magic.

In his hands he found a thick, tight braid, black as night.

He laid it out flat. It reached from his elbow to the tip of his hand.

Then the fragrance began pouring out again: shaking him and embracing him, pushing him away and drawing him near, stirring up memories and wiping them out. Had she gone to the lake on that moonlit night before their departure? Had she gone out before "girls' Thursday"[10] and picked all the lemon blossoms she could get her hands on, and other blossoms too? Had she gone to the shore and scattered the flowers over the water, waited until the water and the flowers were saturated with starlight, then washed her hair in them? Had she washed her hair in the sky, the earth, and the sea, then sent what she had sent?

Suddenly he got up, strode across the yard, and took off on his stallion.

The white mare looked at him and neighed. He didn't hear her. She neighed again. He didn't hear her. Then he was gone.

Najma came up to her and loosened her halter as she patted her on her neck.

Before he began his final descent into Tiberias, he felt as though he could hear her neighing more and more loudly. The last thing he would have thought of doing was to look behind him. Yet in spite of himself he turned, and what should he see but Halima, galloping after him.

He stopped, frozen in place, until she caught up with him and began rubbing her sweat-drenched head against his leg. He looked into the distance and saw a soft mist enveloping the lake. He wished he could go one step farther. He wished his stallion could take him all the way there in spite of everything. But he turned back.

When he arrived, Najma was standing at the gate waiting for him.

He came in, followed by the white mare. Najma patted the mare's neck as if to say "Thank you!"

---

10 An annual rite engaged in by unmarried young women on the lakeshore in the belief that, by washing their hair in the lake's starlit waters, they would improve their chances of marrying.

103

A Smile as Broad as the Day Is Long

Najma waited for Daher to come tell her what was going on in his mind. He didn't come. She kept waiting.

He was making circles around himself like a madman who wants to bite his own earlobe, but ends up biting nothing but dry air and an impossible hope.

He took the braid out, then gently put it back. He ran his hands over it and sat looking at it. He thought: *The white mare was right. That's a place you can never go back to, Daher. It's off limits. The beauty that's there can't erase the effects of the blood that was shed. Don't go there, Daher. Don't go. Don't go near the blood you shed ever again, and don't go back to the beauty you saw at the scene of the crime. The blood may be stronger, so strong that it obliterates the beauty, and obliterates you along with it. Don't go any closer than you already have. If you do, you're liable to be burned by a soul who won't allow you to defeat him again now that you've robbed him of what he wanted.*

Was it his own voice or Najma's that he heard reproaching him, forbidding him, restraining him, bringing him back to his senses?

"You know, Daher, that she's pledged herself to you. When she cut off her braid and sent it to you, she was making you a promise and giving you her life. Unlike some women here might have done, she didn't take the vow by placing her hand on her braid while looking you in the eye. Her oath was more far-reaching than that. It was an oath of the sort that's rarely taken on this earth. You know this, Daher. But every time you embrace her, you'll find blood on your hands, and every time you go sailing in her waters, it will drown you. Think about this well, Daher. You granted her a new life, an opportunity to carry on with the life she had lived before: as pristine as she had been, and free to choose whom she would give herself to, just as she had been. Salute her from where you are, Daher, and tell her loud and clear: 'Even love couldn't bear a burden like this for more than a fleeting moment in a fleeting dream!'"

Najma stood on the terrace outside her upper room as though she knew what was going on. Daher passed by, and when she glanced down at him she saw him as a little boy no more than six years old. She sighed.

Shortly before dawn, Daher knocked on Saad's door. He knocked hard. Saad started, terrified, only able to think of one thing: that the slain man's relatives had come to avenge his death!

He nudged his trembling wife gently into the corner, drew his pistol, and loaded it hurriedly in the lantern's sallow light.

"Who is it?" he called out.

As he stood there, the lantern's flame wavered, its shadow dancing on the wall. The knocking continued, more vigorous than before.

"Who is it?" he repeated.

He came warily up to the door. With his left hand, he took down the sword that hung on the wall, and unsheathed it, sending forth a shrill clang as though he'd beheaded the night.

He quickly opened the door and, finger on the trigger, aimed the pistol steadily at the body that stood outside. But by the time Daher shouted, "What's wrong with you? It's me!" Saad had recognized him.

Without turning around, Saad drew in his breath and said to his wife, "It's Daher! It's Daher! Don't worry!"

Najma was still on the terrace observing what was taking place when she heard Daher utter the statement she had been waiting for:

"I want to leave on the first caravan to Damascus!"

"And why shouldn't you go to Damascus? In fact, why didn't you go there in the first place?" Saad replied.

Najma's smile illumined the terrace like a flash of daylight, and she turned to go back inside.

Suddenly she was overcome with drowsiness, and the angels of slumber alit on her eyelids.

The Caravan Leader's Little Secrets

From a distance they glimpsed Damascus, which they hoped to reach before sundown when it closed its gates. The huge mountain behind the city loomed like a great giant protecting its back and pointing south. Daher's heart was aflutter as the travelers began congratulating one another on their safe arrival.

The caravan leader, a friend of the Zaydani family and of Umar al-Zaydani in particular, grasped Daher's hand and said to him, "I'm going to show you something you've never seen before!"

Saad had left him with instructions to take good care of Daher, saying, "He's your special charge!"

The night of the lanterns had begun losing some of its impact. However, some eerie aspect of it had lingered in Saad's heart. It was the instinctive fear of the inscrutable, and the question: What if the lanterns were telling the truth?

Saad had no doubts about the caravan leader's concern to protect his brother. Nevertheless, wanting to make certain that all would be well, he reminded Daher to take the pistol and sword with him. In spite of everything that had happened, none of Daher's brothers, least of all Saad, had the heart to demand that he return their father's sword. It was as though they all recognized that the sword had found its rightful place in Daher's hand.

No major difficulties had attended the journey. They had proceeded northward until Safad, with its terraced houses and towering citadel, came into view on their right. Then they veered eastward across a valley that could well have been named the Valley of Figs, given all the fig trees that grew there. In the hills above them appeared the remains of a Crusader castle, ancient walls, and fortifications enveloped in a lonely silence. As the caravan ascended, they saw a vast expanse that seemed to extend into infinity.

They spent the night and the following morning and early afternoon in a large caravanserai atop a hill. An enormous structure reminiscent of a fortress, the caravanserai sported eight towers that provided a view of things one could never have imagined down below, and anyone climbing them felt he had sprouted wings.

The caravan leader took Daher by the hand and began leading him from tower to tower. As Daher looked across the foothills covered with oak, terebinth, and carob trees, it horrified him to think how far he was from the earth below.

"Don't look down. Look over there," said the caravan leader as his index finger drew a broad arc that took in half the horizon.

As the two men stood there in silence, the caravan leader stole an occasional glance at Daher's face, which registered a curious mix of emotions.

"Is this whole country ours?" Daher asked him.

"You know it is. Why do you ask?" the caravan leader queried.

"I've been asking myself this question ever since the Bi'na massacre. Whenever I open my eyes I see Sheikh Hussein's face, and whenever I close them I see the face of his son Abbas."

"God have mercy on them."

It was difficult for people to move from place to place unless they traveled in caravans or under the protection of Bedouin chiefs, who would send their men out as guards for wayfarers and pilgrims, and who received wages in return for the protection they provided. Consequently, every traveler realized that his life would be in danger unless he filled his pouch with sufficient funds to placate the tribes through whose lands he would be passing, and who turned over their charges one to another as they passed from one territory to the next. Every journey thus required both protection money and money for expenses, both of which travelers needed to have ready before the herald's cry announcing the caravan's departure. However, although traveling with a caravan was preferable, caravans occasionally came in for devastating attacks in which their entire cargo was looted because, when times were hard, the Bedouins sometimes decided that what the caravans were carrying was worth more than the few piasters they could have earned by protecting them.

The caravanserai consisted of several halls and storehouses, as well as boarding rooms for travelers. In the center of it was a spring, the water from which collected in a large pool surrounded by masterfully formed rocks.

One also encountered Syrian traders, both big and small, who flocked to it every Sunday night. The caravan leader had plotted the course of his journey with precision to ensure that they would reach the caravanserai on Sunday evening and spend the following day selling their merchandise, which included cotton, soap, wheat, sesame seeds, and jars of honey. Thousands of people came together there.

One night Daher saw another side to the caravan leader's personality. A robust man approaching seventy, with a taut physique, eagle eyes, and a black beard that still lacked even a speck of gray, he was fond of song and dance, and Daher concluded without difficulty that his periodic trips to his room had a single purpose: to down a slug of the liquor he always carried with him.

The nightly gathering around a large fire went on until the early hours of the morning, and when the partygoers dispersed, their laughter would continue to echo through the place, filling it with merriment.

Daher watched the fire until it went out. Then he went to bed.

The doors of the caravanserai opened in the morning to receive a huge influx of local merchants and residents laden with wares to sell. Men came driving horses and livestock, while women drove donkeys bearing baskets of eggs and chickens suspended by their legs.

People came peddling raisins, figs, apples, lemons, and red grapes. Jewelry, clothing, and shoe vendors, cloth merchants, saddlers, and farriers all called out, inviting people to purchase their wares or services.

Daher had never seen a market like this: teeming with life and merriment, and filled with laughter and protracted negotiations over the price of a donkey, a gazelle, a baby leopard, or a cubit of silk fabric imported from India. Donkeys brayed, horses neighed, dogs barked, and hens clucked, and before he knew it the time had passed and people had begun gathering their things and leaving the caravanserai so as to reach their homes by sundown.

The Night and the Lanterns

The caravan leader shook Daher's hand in front of the Damascus gate, and they agreed to meet in the same place in seven days' time. Then, as Daher was leaving, the caravan leader's voice followed him, saying, "Wait!"

Daher stopped his horse, turned, and began riding back toward him. "I forgot to tell you that the first thing you should do is buy a lantern. In a while it will be dark. Light it and make sure it doesn't go out. Otherwise you'll land yourself in trouble you could do without!"

"What kind of trouble?" Daher asked.

"There have been lots of thefts and attacks on people's property of late. Some have even been murdered. So the vizier of Damascus has issued an edict whereby anyone who walks the streets at night without a lantern will be considered in violation of the law, a robber lying in wait for his next victim! The last time I came here I got into quite a bit of trouble. I ventured out at night not knowing anything about the edict, and if it weren't for the fact that the judge and the city's leading merchant were friends of mine, I would have rotted in jail! So be careful. You're in Damascus now, not Tiberias."

Damascus was another world, a world bustling with activity: soldiers scouring the faces of passersby in search of easy prey, women clad in colorful attire, and girls with pretty faces who insisted on their right not to wear the headscarf the way their mothers did.

He bought a lantern and led his horse down the streets in search of Sheikh Abd al-Ghaffar al-Shuwayki's house. He didn't expect to have any difficulty finding the house: after all, who didn't know al-Shuwayki, one of the most famous teachers in all of Damascus?

Captivated by the city's magic, he was torn between going straight to his destination and lingering in the streets to see more. He was stunned by the invitations of the women of the night, who stood on street corners with painted faces and garish, sheer garb, luring male passersby of all ages with their charms. The soldiers would tease them as they passed, while the older men would turn their heads, uttering prayers for God's forgiveness.

He walked along dazed, as though in a dream, until one of the women woke him out of his reverie with a pat on the shoulder. "Since you've bought a lantern, handsome, you'd better light it. The better for us to see your good looks with, and for you to see ours!"

Flustered, he turned into a greengrocer's shop that sold spices and asked the shop owner to light his lantern for him.

The man brought out a wooden stick, lit the end of it from his own lantern, and handed it to Daher.

"So, Damascus," Daher said to himself, "whoever hasn't seen you hasn't seen the world!"

Hardly had he finished speaking when he heard a loud rushing noise from above and saw something hit the street in front of him with a huge thud. His horse shied, and took two terrified steps back. People began shouting and pushing each other out of the way in an attempt to reach the spot where the body had fallen. As for Daher, he stared dazed at the corpse that lay before him, blood gushing out of its eyes and ears and its skull split in two.

"He threw himself off the minaret!" he heard someone wail.

The burning wick in Daher's lantern quivered, and he wished it would go out so that he wouldn't have to see what he saw.

The Things You Never See
Anywhere but in Damascus

Daher stood before her feeling awkward. He heard a voice saying, "This is Nafisa, the one I told you about." She was the most beautiful girl he had ever seen, a girl the likes of whom he hadn't thought existed on earth.

He wasn't supposed to cast more than a single glance, but he couldn't keep his eyes off her. The last thing he'd expected was to find his soul mate, just like that, in someone so beautiful.

How could I have lived my life thus far without that radiant face, those big green eyes, and that figure tall and lissome as an ash tree?

He wanted to say, "I agree." He wanted to shout, "I agree, and then some! And I'm ready to give you whatever you ask!"

However, protocol dictated that he write to his brother Saad requesting his permission.

No one could have known what awaited Daher in Damascus. But had Najma known? She had been the happiest one in the family when, after giving him a farewell embrace, she pushed him gently away, saying, "Go. Damascus is waiting for you. All of Damascus is waiting for you! The most beautiful things there are waiting for you!"

The white mare neighed faintly. The passage of time had begun tearing at her flesh with more ferocity than any wolf could have done.

Before he left, Najma said to him, "Bring back a present for Halima that's worthy of her. She deserves that, and so do I!"

He stood in front of the Damascus gate waiting for the caravan that would be returning to Arraba.

He watched the lamplighters putting out the street lanterns as the first threads of dawn became visible and people began gathering at the Damascus gate to sell their wares and bid farewell to family and friends. He saw the clerks that one always found at city gates preparing for a

111

long day of work. After bringing out inkwells made from animal horns and placing them atop small, short-legged wooden tables, they began cutting pieces of paper into useful sizes, and with their sharp knives they honed the tips of reeds and placed them side by side, since one never knew when a reed tip might break.

As the sun rose, its rays began penetrating the veil of the early morning mist. Daher looked inside the city gate and saw people pouring into the streets. However, he saw neither the caravan leader nor the caravan. He thought: *Maybe he spent last night at a caravanserai with some girl. After all, he seems to be in good enough health!*

The caravan leader had hinted of such things on their way to Damascus, and later had spoken of them frankly: "In Damascus you can take off your clothes and dance if you feel like it, without anybody disapproving. If it weren't for the fact that I didn't want to make Saad angry, I wouldn't have let you stay in a sheikh's house! What will Damascus mean to a young man like you if he goes to sleep and wakes up in a house of learning, and comes home with nothing to remember Damascus by but the knowledge he gained there?"

He reached into his pocket and brought out a small bag containing a mixture of almonds, walnuts, and raisins. Taking some in his palm, he held it out to Daher, saying, "Here. This will come in handy for you if you change your mind!"

Daher ate some of the mixture and chuckled as the caravan leader whinnied like a stud, saying, "Damascus, here I come!"

Then he turned to Daher and said, "Do you see that jar of honey?"

Daher nodded.

"I've never been to Damascus without it!"

The caravan leader was late in arriving, and as Daher looked around for him, others were full of anxious questions.

Eventually he appeared, strutting between a pair of stunning beauties who had come to see him off. When he saw people waiting for him, he gave each of them some money and they turned to leave. He sent them off with one of his stud-like whinnies, and they ran away laughing. But by the time he reached the gate, he'd turned into another man, as serious and stern as a commander on his way to battle, and began barking out orders right and left.

When he had finished making arrangements for the caravan's departure, he came up to Daher, shook his hand warmly, and said, "I've heard your news!"

"How could you have heard my news when we haven't met up?"

"Daher," he said chidingly, "there's no better way to learn the secrets of Damascus's notables than to be in the company of a beautiful girl. You get my drift?"

"I do."

"In any case, give me the letter."

"And how did you know there was a letter?"

"Daher, my dear nephew, I've spent my life traveling from city to city, so I can tell the difference between arrivals and departures, between people seeing somebody off and people receiving a newcomer."

Daher gave him the letter and he tucked it into his breast pocket. "Is there something you'd like to tell Saad that you were embarrassed to mention in the letter?"

After some hesitation, Daher said, "Tell him not to take too long getting a reply back to me!"

"You're in love, son! Praise be to God, who revives hearts with beautiful women the way He fills the earth with people, the day with sunshine, and the night with the moon and the stars!"

He embraced him.

Then his features changed once again, and he went back to giving orders.

Daher watched him walk away. Then he glanced over at the clerk and saw a woman, who had concealed three-fourths of her face with her headscarf, dictating a letter. When she heard the herald announcing the caravan's departure for Aleppo, she urged the clerk to write faster.

States of the Heart

Sharif Muhammad al-Husseini stepped aside with Abd al-Ghaffar al-Shuwayki and asked him about his guest, in whose honor a large banquet had been hosted and attended by a number of the city's notables. Al-Shuwayki told him everything he knew about Daher and about his first encounter with him in Tiberias. He told him about Daher's perspicacity and intelligence, and concluded by saying, "When I saw him, I wished he were my own son, and he's been on my mind almost continuously ever since. When I saw him again recently, my old feeling was confirmed. But why are you asking me all these questions?"

"Because I'd like to know everything about the person I'm thinking of marrying my daughter to!"

"Your daughter?"

"Yes! As you can see, time isn't going to sit waiting for us on the doorstep if we're late. So, what do you think?"

"If I had a daughter, I would have married him to her before you did!"

"But you know it's hard for me as a father to broach the subject with him."

"Don't worry. I'll sound him out."

When Daher heard Sheikh al-Shuwayki ask him why he hadn't married yet, the face of the girl on the shore of Lake Tiberias filled his mind's eye. Hoping to soften the question, al-Shuwayki said to him teasingly, "Or maybe you'd rather get engaged when I'm not around!"

The sheikh sensed the sorrow that had stolen the sparkle from Daher's eyes.

"Tell me who she is, and if I don't marry her to you, then I'm not Abd al-Ghaffar al-Shuwayki!"

Daher thought for a bit. Then he said, "If there were someone, I would have asked you to do that."

"But the sadness in your eyes can't be hidden!"

"It's an old sadness, and the time may have come for me to get over it." He said this without realizing that one doesn't decide such things for oneself.

The caravans hadn't been delayed. However, he could hardly bear to wait any longer.

Two weeks later he received the letter. He opened it, and there he found them: the very words he had expected, together with the money he would need to cover the wedding expenses.

When Sheikh al-Shuwayki relayed the news to Sharif al-Husseini, he lifted his hands heavenward in thanksgiving. "So then," he said, "let's get on with the wedding preparations. And let it be the wedding an only daughter like mine deserves!"

"Daher has only one request."

"Now that he's a member of the family, he can ask for whatever he wishes."

"His request is that you allow him to pay all the wedding expenses."

"That's too much for him! You know how costly that will be."

"That is his request. It's his brother Saad's request as well."

"He's a noble young man. So be it, then. I wouldn't want to deprive him of something that would help him win people's esteem."

Daher was more willing than other suitors might have been to honor the bride's father's request that they stay in Damascus. Doing so would cleanse his soul and, if he did decide some day to go back to Arraba, he would return there a new man.

Daher's father-in-law had been dwindling away. But from the time he saw the joy that now glowed in his daughter's eyes, he had realized that he could close his own eyes and depart in peace.

Damascus and the
Summons from Afar

The time they'd spent in Damascus seemed far away. It hung suspended on the last breaths Nafisa's father had breathed, and on his body, which had begun slipping through their fingers. When nothing had remained but a finger's hold and wan looks, Daher realized that once the man was gone, there would be nothing left to keep them in Syria.

Within a year Nafisa's father was gone, leaving his sole heiress more than either she or Daher could ever have imagined.

After her grief had subsided, Nafisa said to Daher, "I'm going to register everything in your name now. After all, what am I going to do with all this wealth? My father was right about you, and I think he's looking down on us now with joy in his heart."

"Everything's going to stay just the way it is, and I'm not touching a single piaster of yours. However, I do have one request."

"May all your wishes come true."

Daher had never spoken to her about going back to Arraba. But something happening inside him had prompted him to raise the issue. Was the Damascus that had so dazzled him when he first saw it beginning to push him away, now that he'd seen what he had seen?

"Now that your father is gone, you have no one left in Syria. As for me, all my family is in Palestine. So my request is that we go live there. The news I'm receiving from there makes me feel I should be with them. If you don't want to come with me, you can stay here in Damascus, and I'll go back myself and come see you now and then."

She shot him a glance filled with reproach, and was about to cry.

"I hope I didn't hurt you by what I said," said Daher.

"Al-Husseini's daughter wouldn't let her man go back home alone. Wherever you go, I go. I'm not going to leave you at the mercy of the roads and highway robbers, and I won't just sit here worried sick about you when you're on your way here or after I see you off at the Damascus gate!"

Palestine was ridden with fear, insecurity, and the tyranny of the multazims. As for Damascus, it remained ensconced inside its walls, and the vizier's Mamluks could easily seize whomever they wanted and order them bound and imprisoned so that they could take whatever money or property their mood happened to dictate. If a man so seized was unable to pay, his family members would redeem him, knowing that if it weren't for the ransom they provided, their relative would never see the light of day.[11] Nafisa had known that she might find herself in a position like this some day. Daher was a stranger to the city, and her father and protector was gone. Consequently, there would have been nothing easier than for those with evil intentions to notice Daher's aloneness and for her to lose him, and thus lose everything.

Damascus was a place where blood could be shed with impunity. The vizier and his soldiers, who descended from cities near and far, weren't the only source of danger. After the wave of price hikes that had swept through the land and brought people to the brink of starvation, looting became widespread. As the vizier and his commanders looted the rich, the vizier was carrying out sentences against those who stole from the poor. On the evening of October 20, 1715, orders were issued for a thief to be hanged in front of the Umayyad Mosque and for a pickpocket's hand to be amputated after he was caught stealing from the imam of the Arudak Mosque west of Salihiya. People would walk past shops, unable to consume any of the merchandise they saw with anything but their eyes. The price of an uqiya of clarified butter had risen to five and a half masriyas, a rotl of rice cost sixteen masriyas, a mudd of barley cost eight masriyas, a rotl of white bread sold for twelve masriyas, a rotl of cake sold for fourteen masriyas, a rotl of brown bread went for five masriyas, a rotl of local meat sold for thirty masriyas, a rotl of sheep's rump for a piaster, and eggs sold two for a masriya. And as the month of Ramadan began, the price of fruits and vegetables went through the roof. Whereas before Ramadan you could buy a hundred zucchinis for a masriya, you

---

11   The city of Damascus was divided into two classes, rulers and ruled, the distinction between which the state was keen to perpetuate. The ruling class consisted of governors, judges, muftis, and army officers. As for the ruled, they included both townsfolk and the peasantry, who were left free by the state to organize themselves into artisans' guilds. However, it was their duty to sustain the ruling class by filling their pockets with money through the payment of taxes and fines, in return for which they were subjected to oppression and cruel abuse.

could only buy forty-five for the same price during Ramadan. One rotl of eggplant, which had once sold for a masriya, had doubled in price. As for meat, there wasn't any, and all because of the vilayet's failure to exercise proper oversight!

The last remaining source of protection was the presence of Sheikh Abd al-Ghaffar al-Shuwayki, who introduced Daher to a number of merchants in Damascus so as to facilitate his work with them.

Saad's funds had begun to dwindle. It was as though he had sworn to spend them all on hospitality! It was true, of course, that his generosity had earned him and the family an enviable and much-needed position in and around Arraba. However, Saad, his two brothers, and Najma knew that even if they had owned a well full of money, it would have run out in the end.

Saad sent word to Daher asking him to send him merchandise from Damascus, especially the handcrafted copper and wood items so renowned for their excellence, and he in turn began sending wheat, cotton, sesame, and salted fish from Lake Tiberias.

In this way the family began to catch its breath.

Daher then sent word to Saad informing him that he would be coming to Arraba, and promising to arrange matters of trade between Damascus and Arraba to Saad's satisfaction by choosing someone suitable to replace him. The decision took Saad by surprise. In fact, it hit him like a lightning bolt.

Deep down, though, he realized that things were moving in a new direction in and around Arraba, and that even if they succeeded in their business, they wouldn't be businessmen forever. Hence, he dispatched a missive to Daher consisting of four words: "We'll be expecting you."

The Second Bloodshed

Najma spent the whole day in her upper room watching the northern horizon, anticipating the sight of the blessed cloud of dust that would herald the arrival of Daher and his bride.

Not wanting to arrive unexpectedly, Daher had sent news of his approach with the caravan leader three weeks earlier. Because the caravan was scheduled to arrive precisely on Thursday, any delay would require those expecting the caravan to go out and check on it.

And the caravan was, in fact, delayed. Somewhere between Abisiya and Na'ima it was attacked by a band of more than sixty Bedouin horsemen. The caravan had been traveling through an open area, to its left an old stone quarry and to its right a series of low stone walls bordering a large olive grove, when it was suddenly charged by the attackers.

The caravan leader and his men knew which spots were most dangerous, and this spot in particular was a source of concern. Consequently, his men readied themselves without anyone noticing, and without receiving any orders to do so. But since the enemy is the one who determines an attack's time and place, it's always bound to come as a surprise.

The raiders managed from the start to split the caravan in two. This had been their plan, since it would scatter the force of those defending the caravan, thereby enabling some of the raiders to steal away with the fleeing camels, mules, and horses while others kept up the attack.

The travelers needed no invitation to join in the fighting. In a situation like this, one instinctively defends himself, his property, and his family regardless of whether he may be inclined to defend anyone else. Daher looked over and saw the caravan leader clashing with three of the raiders. He was spinning like a whirlwind, and no one who saw him would have believed that he was nearly seventy years old! Brandishing his father's sword, Daher went on the offensive, and when one of the raiders saw him approaching, he rushed madly in Daher's direction. Daher could easily have killed him. However, an old memory shot through his body like a knife, prompting him to strike his assailant with the flat edge of his sword, though with sufficient force to knock the man off his horse.

The attacker, who scrambled frantically in search of the sword that had fallen out of his hand, realized that the person who had delivered the blow hadn't intended to kill him, since if he had, he could have done so without difficulty.

Daher left the felled man where he was and headed toward another assailant, who realized only at the last moment that someone was attacking him. Daher could easily have turned and cut off his head. Instead, he delivered a blow just powerful enough to send him flying through the air until, at some length, he landed unconscious on the ground. He didn't move. However, Daher was confident that if he was dead, it was the force of his fall that had killed him.

The caravan leader charged at the last horseman, who turned and fled. When the leader saw one of the two horsemen who had fallen get back on his horse and ride away, he looked over at Daher without saying a thing. Then he and Daher went in pursuit of the raiders who had scattered in flight.

When the other horseman who had fallen to the ground sensed that the caravan leader's men were busy chasing the other raiders, he got up in search of his sword. Before he got to it, a boy from the caravan saw him and rushed at him with a heavy stick. But it was too late. The raider delivered a fatal blow to the boy's heart as he stood there transfixed, staring at the tip of the sword that ran him through.

The raider drew his sword out of the boy's body and brandished it in front of the women, who, rushing at him in a frenzy, managed to wound him, then overpowered him and killed him.

All the raiders managed to get away with were two she-camels and three mules. The caravan leader asked Daher to stop pursuing them, but Daher wouldn't listen.

Knowing that the Bedouins designated certain men to set up ambushes for their pursuers, the caravan leader followed Daher. Not long after the two men began pursuing the raiders together, Daher changed course. As though he were fleeing from them rather than running after them, he disappeared over a hill.

When the caravan leader looked behind him, he saw his caravan in a state of such miserable disarray that you would have thought he'd been defeated. His men and others in the caravan were doing their best to control the agitated animals, and much of the cargo lay scattered over a huge area.

His mother's agonized weeping and prayers did no good, and the boy's life was snuffed out like a candle. A number of women and men had been wounded, but none of them fatally.

When the caravan leader and his men returned, Nafisa looked for Daher but didn't find him. Breaking away from the group, she went running around in search of him.

"He's fine!" the caravan leader shouted.

"How can you say he's fine when he isn't with you?" she asked woefully.

Not finding the words he needed to set her mind at rest, the caravan leader scanned the horizon in search of some hope that might appear in the distance. Fortunately, he didn't have to wait long before he saw a she-camel on her way back to them. He also saw the three stolen mules. But there was no sign of Daher. The caravan leader waited, his heart and Nafisa's pinned to a single point on the horizon. But still, no Daher.

Followed by five of his men, the caravan leader prodded his horse and headed out toward the returning animals.

Unable to find her tears, Nafisa was paralyzed with terror, which turned her into a cracked statue on that bloodied spot between Damascus and Arraba.

One day long before this she had said to Daher, "If it isn't in God's plan for me to have a son, then you'll be my son, my husband, my father, and my whole family!"

Yet it continued to grieve her that her father had died without having heard her make that most coveted happy announcement: "I'm pregnant!"

The months had passed slowly, wearing down her delicate body like a great millstone, yet without any sign of some approaching joy. The blood that had first flowed at the same unchanging intervals began flowing nonstop, with one menses following on another without respite until her body turned into a fountain. Every night she would dream that it was sweeping her away, and Daher would wake up to find her clinging to him with both hands and crying, "I'm going to drown, Daher! I'm going to drown!"

But she didn't tell him anything about the river of blood.

One day Sheikh al-Shuwayki asked Daher, "Are things all right with you? I mean, is *everything* all right?"

"Yes! This is just what God has planned for us!"

Meanwhile, Nafisa's aunt asked her, "Is your husband all right? As a man, I mean?"

Nafisa nodded.

"And how about you?" she probed.

"I've got a river of blood that runs nonstop!"

"That happens sometimes," she said with a nod. "Let's wait and see what happens."

But nothing happened. There was nothing inside her but a resounding emptiness that spun round and round in search of a drop of life, a drop that, to her, would have meant life itself.

"Don't you worry!" Daher said to her.

She wept. Wiping away her tears with his thumbs as he held her face in his hands, he said, "Remember that I loved you from the moment I saw you. And nothing in the world will ever change that."

"I'd dreamed that God would give me a child by you. At least one. I know how badly my father suffered. He always dreamed of having a son, not just so that it could be said that he had a son, but so that he could give me a brother!"

"I'll be that brother, just as I'll be your father and your husband, Nafisa!"

"And you'll be my son, Daher. I'll pamper you like no mother has ever pampered and loved her son!"

Daher had yet to appear, and the caravan leader and his men had moved farther out. They and their horses had disappeared in the hills, and all was silent. They went in circles, bearing in mind that there were other directions from which he might appear.

But there was no sign of him.

Suddenly, in the distance, the caravan leader saw Daher fighting the raiders with a madness the likes of which he had never witnessed before. He spun, dodged, pounced, and retreated, not allowing them to close in on him, and by the time they caught up with him, the raiders had fled.

Daher reached for the reins of the last stolen she-camel. Terrified by the clamor around her, she began pounding the earth with her hooves.

She swung her head back and forth, shooing away the fear that surrounded her the way she might shoo away an obnoxious fly on a hot day.

Once he had her reins in his hand, Daher came up to her with soothing whispers. The she-camel looked at him and, with a look of recognition in her eyes, following him willingly.

"Would you die for a she-camel, Daher? To hell with her! You're more important than she is!"

"No, sir. The she-camel wasn't the issue!"

The wailing reached them before they got back to the caravan. Shuddering with dread, Daher goaded his horse and rode on ahead, leaving the she-camel's reins in the hands of the caravan leader.

Once back at the caravan site, he jumped off his horse and made his way with difficulty among the weepers, and there he saw the boy's lifeless body in his mother's arms.

"Who killed him?" he asked.

But before they had finished answering, Daher felt the earth start to spin.

The caravan leader grabbed hold of him, sensing he was about to fall. "What's wrong?" he asked.

Daher turned and, looking him straight in the eye, said, "Never again will I allow people to be killed this way. Never again will I let anyone steal so much as a date from me or anyone else!"

From that day onward a new feeling took up residence in Daher's being. The burden of the blood he had shed years before, and that had weighed so heavily on his heart, had suddenly been lifted by the blood of this boy, for whose death he would feel responsible as long as he lived. And in a fleeting moment he realized that if he had it to do over again, he would kill that man on the shore of Lake Tiberias just as he had the first time.

However, the present has a way of erasing the past, and the days to come were preparing another test for him, one that he could never have imagined.

Equine Epiphany

Nafisa's body was still racked with anxiety even after Daher had come back to her safely, even when she was about to hold him in her arms. After all, in waiting for him she had been awaiting all her loved ones at once: husband, father, son.

With the passing of the moments that hung suspended from Death's fingers, the image of the husband and the father had disappeared, and nothing remained but the image of the son. However, a powerful gaze from his deep eyes brought her back to her senses. Perhaps it was the nearness of their arrival in Arraba that had kept her from taking him in her arms. What Nafisa didn't know was how much he too needed such an embrace.

Sheikh Hussein's face fluttered before him like a bird, and Abbas's sightless eyes grew wider and wider. He had tried desperately to forget the day when Sheikh Hussein and Abbas had had their eyes put out, wanting to protect himself from the deadly sorrow he felt for having left them behind. But he couldn't.

As soon as Daher had crossed the threshold and embraced Najma, Saad, Yusuf, and Saleh, he took off for the stable. He was longing to hear the white mare's neigh. But he didn't.

When he came in and saw her, he was shocked at her condition. She was emaciated, and for a moment it seemed that she didn't even recognize him. He walked over to her, his heart filled with a strange fear, and when he was two meters away she raised her head and gazed at him with weary, reproachful eyes. She tried to neigh, but nothing came out but a rattle that bore no resemblance to the lusty neigh of times gone by.

He took her face in his hands and began stroking her forehead. "God, how she's aged!" He looked back and found them looking at him, aware of the sorrow wringing his heart.

A heavy, hot tear was about to fall. He struggled to hold it back, but it kept pulling him downward until he found himself on his knees before her.

In a matchless moment, he took her right front hoof and lifted it. She responded with difficulty. Even though she needed all four legs more than ever, she surrendered it to him, struggling not to fall.

Could she have possibly surrendered it to anyone else?

As they looked on sadly, Nafisa understood what he had once said to her about his mother, the white mare.

It was a long time before he rose. She shook her head as if to rid her body of all the years that clung to it. Then she began licking his forehead as if to say, "God bless you!"

He kissed her forehead again and, as he turned to leave, she let forth the same throaty rattle. Turning to the others, he said, "Bring me my mattress. I'm going to spend the night here!"

They withdrew without a word. For a moment Nafisa felt an acute discomfort. However, the feeling dissipated when she looked into their faces and saw no sign of disapproval.

Not long thereafter he saw Nafisa come back carrying a mattress. It surprised and delighted him to see that she had brought it herself. But the biggest surprise was the request that followed: "Would you two allow me to be your guest tonight?"

Daher wept.

As soon as the door closed behind them, Nafisa found herself drawing close to him and taking him in her arms. Ever since the battle, Nafisa had needed nothing more than to hold him. And now that he had seen the state his mother was in, his own need for closeness had multiplied several times over.

If she hadn't taken the initiative, would he have asked her to do such a thing? When he came back from the shore of Lake Tiberias trailed by the curse of the first life he had ever taken, he would rather have been killed himself than shed blood ever again. But he had resisted the urge to ask Najma to hold him.

Najma had said, "Horses have a dignity about them that human beings are incapable of comprehending. Horses grieve, but don't let on. They hurt, but without breaking, Daher. It's as though what passed from the white mare to you wasn't just her milk. But you need to remember that in the end you're a human being, not a horse!"

Daher had thought back on all the stories his family had told about him, about death, about his father and the way he had dueled with death the way a man duels with another man. He thought back on the first neigh he had ever heard. He thought back on the taste of the milk that he had gone on drinking without realizing that the milk was drinking him, too. He recalled how, even when he was more than five years old, he would go running after the white mare in hopes of nursing directly from her. He had once said to Najma, "Nobody can separate my body from hers, or my spirit from hers. Just as I exist inside my body, so does this white mare!"

"Daher," she'd replied, "you need something that will make the human in you prevail over the horse. Having them both inside you at once is going to make you miserable. It might even kill you."

"Or maybe it's what will give me life, Mother. Maybe it's what will give me life!"

Animal Friday and
the Forest Path

Happily, Daher and his bride had arrived in Arraba just in time for the "Animal Friday" celebrations.

When Nafisa opened her bedroom window overlooking the courtyard, she was met by a sight she had heard about for years, but had never witnessed.

Najma and Saad's wife were busy decorating the animals of the household with reddish-brown clay, in what appeared to be a celebration of her arrival.

The white mare, worn out though she was, seemed pleased with her new color, and the cows even more so. The sheep and goats seemed in a hurry to scamper happily off as though they had been waiting for this day, their day, for a long time. Meanwhile, the children busied themselves decorating the hens and the chicks and painting the pigeons' wings and tails, then letting them fly off.

In the sky and on land, Arraba was a lovely sight thanks to the delight that went hopping about in every household, street, and barnyard and the festive atmosphere that hovered about the houses. It was a wonderful day: A day when the animals were certain to be aware of everything that was happening. A day when, after being bathed and dyed, they were left free to come and go as they pleased. A day when no one dared slaughter any of them, use them to transport anything, or even make use of their milk, which, instead of being consumed in their owners' households, was distributed among the poor.

It was the animals' annual holiday.

The white mare made the rounds of the courtyard as though she were waiting for something. Sensing this, Daher went over to her, took hold of her bead-festooned halter, and led her out to the nearby meadow.

He made a point of walking next to her, cheek to cheek. From time to time he would look over at her and think about all the time that had passed. He looked heavenward, wishing horses could live longer than they did, that they could live as long as human beings or even longer. But then he thought of how she would suffer if he passed away before her. He could barely forgive himself for being away from her in Damascus, and he wondered whether she had aged so much simply because she was nearing the end of her lifespan, or on account of his absence.

The white mare seemed content, and he felt some strength returning to her body. They entered a large stand of pine trees. When she heard the sparrows singing, she lifted her head in search of the source of the sound, looking about in wonder like a little child.

Shortly before midafternoon he brought her back to the house, where the children shared in the excitement of the goats leaping in the air and the pigeons fluttering above.

From a distance he could see Nafisa gazing wordlessly out her window at Saad's two sons. As he approached the house, she moved hurriedly away from the window, only to reappear at the door.

With that lovely broad smile of hers that revealed the most beautiful teeth he had ever seen, she came up to him and, without saying a word, reached up and stroked the white mare's neck and colored forelock. Then they walked her into the stable.

"Memories are the only things that enable people to overcome time," said Najma. "Through memories people confirm to themselves that they don't just pass through this life without a trace."

The day went by quickly the way holidays and happy times always do, leaving behind pleasant memories that hover in the air like translucent birds invisible to the eye.

Shortly before dawn they heard the horses neighing and a loud clamor in the stable. They dressed quickly and rushed out, certain that someone was trying to steal the animals. Then they heard a wounded scream—Najma's scream. Before they got there, they saw her coming out of the stable, her hair disheveled and a dazed look in her eyes. Then they realized what had happened.

She held Daher tight and whispered to him, "She died with the dust of the road on her feet. God have mercy on her." Then she looked upward and said something, as though she were whispering in Heaven's ear.

The Seaside Paradise

It has come to my hearing,
sisters and brothers,
that according to some people,
these things are happening to us
because Daher refuses to be anything less than a hero!
The worst idea anyone ever had was to be a war hero.
There are a thousand other ways to be a true hero.
This war was imposed on us,
and we aren't fighting in order to be heroes.
Rather, we're fighting in order to be human.
God Almighty has honored human beings, saying,
"Now, indeed, We have conferred dignity on the children of
Adam."
All we want is to be human.
My dream is for you all to be heroes after this siege is over.
Heroism means building your country in safety,
planting your trees in safety,
and not being afraid for your children because they are free from
danger. Every man will be a hero when he can roam the streets
however he pleases, without anyone harassing him,
insulting his dignity, stealing his children's daily bread,
or encroaching on his freedom.
I dream of the day when a woman can walk alone
through the city or the countryside
and be honored and respected by all in the knowledge that
she is a heroine, flanked by the spirits of hundreds
of heroines and heroes.
I want every one of my people, from Lake Tiberias to the Sea of
Acre,
to be a fearless hero.
True heroism means for you
to be so safe
that no other kind of heroism is required.

Nights of Terror and
the Blue Princess

Daher collared the tax collector who had been sent to Arraba by Muhammad Pasha, governor of Sidon.

"I didn't hear you!" he growled. "What did you say you wanted?"

"I want money for the trip back to Sidon!"

"And since when do you get that from the people of Arraba? Do you work for them, or for the state?"

"For the state."

"So, then, you're taking what doesn't belong to you." Using all his strength, Daher shoved him to the ground.

The soldiers who had escorted the tax collector drew their weapons.

"You'll all die if you don't put those down!" Daher bellowed.

The people observing the scene were visibly frightened, and the soldiers and the tax collector lying in the dirt wore looks of stunned surprise. No one before this had ever dared disobey or insult a tax collector or multazim. As for Daher, stories of the things he had done in Tiberias had preceded him to Arraba.

"Take them to jail, Saad. Then we'll decide what to do with them."

Sensing that Daher was reversing their roles once again, Saad grew uneasy. He saw the four lanterns burning and burning, their flames flickering and flickering.

Daher had picked up the game where it had left off, and Saad could see that things were going to be different now.

They led away the tax collector and the soldiers, who had put down their weapons.

"Treat them well," Daher told them, "even though they don't deserve it."

The slain boy's face hovered in Daher's mind, the caravan awash in tears writhed in its pain, the rapist's hands closed around Haniya's neck in the lemon grove on the shore of Lake Tiberias, and Sheikh Hussein and his son Abbas peered at him with eyes like bottomless wells.

Had he been looking for a moment like this? He had no answer for such a question. However, the moment had come, and it had come forcefully. It had melted him down in its cruel flames and thrust that tax collector into his face to see what he would do.

That night was one of the most terrifying Arraba had ever lived through. The townsfolk realized that by doing what he had done, Daher would be the cause of their destruction one and all. The moment the governor of Sidon heard about what had happened to his tax collector, he would march out personally at the head of his army to bring Arraba down on their heads. However, there were many who felt that the time had come for them to stand up in the face of the unbearable injustice they had endured for so long. The tax collector had gone too far this time, and had confiscated everything that struck his fancy. On the pretext of helping to support the state's war efforts, he had seized horses, mules, donkeys, and chickens. He had even helped himself to rugs and mattresses in people's homes. No one had dared ask him the simple question: "What does the army want with the mat I sleep on?" And, as if this weren't enough, he had ordered a number of houses evacuated so that his men could spend the night there. He'd reserved an entire house for each pair of soldiers, his sole purpose being, of course, to force the villagers to pay him in return for ordering the soldiers out of their homes so that they could come live in them again.

July's sun disappeared over the horizon, dragging its river of fire behind it.

"Is it true that you're going to Sidon?" Nafisa asked him.

"There's nowhere else I might go tomorrow!"

"You do what you did to that tax collector, and then you go to Sidon of your own accord?"

"That's the best thing I could possibly do before the news reaches the governor!"

Nafisa felt silent. As for Saad, he was furious. "You're digging your own grave! Do you realize that?"

"I'm now the age Tarafa ibn al-Abd was when he died, and we'll see whether I outlive him or not. If I don't, I'll be passing on to another existence. But I can't carry on the way I have been, Saad. Gone are the days when we waited for the lanterns to go out. The Ottoman authorities have left us no choice but to light them, then light them again, whether we're dead or alive! The time that's past, Saad, wasn't our own lifetime. It was simply the time they had granted us to go on working for them like a herd of pack animals. During that time they didn't give us so much as a single day of our own. They never gave us a day like the one we give our animals once a year: a day when none of them can be slaughtered, a day when they can run free, fly free, and delight in being alive!"

Daher fell silent for a while. Then he continued: "Tomorrow I'll take the tax collector with me, but I'll leave his soldiers here until I get back."

"You talk about coming back after all you've done? Do you realize the significance of what's happened? A lot of people here in Arraba are about to throw us out of town! And don't forget, Daher, that this is their town, and that we're still guests here!"

"This whole country is yours and mine, Saad, just as much as it's theirs. This country belongs to whoever has the guts to defend it. As for cowards, they have no country. Their only country is cowardice. They're free to go there right now if they like, and if they do, good riddance!"

Najma stole softly to his room and opened the door. He was asleep next to Nafisa. She stood there pondering him for a while. Then she bent down and shook him gently. He woke up. She took him by the hand and led him toward the door. He looked over at his shoes, but realized he wouldn't be needing them. He stepped over the threshold. The roosters hadn't woken yet. Najma headed down to Arraba's meadow, and he followed, feeling strangely placid.

"There's something you need to say to this earth before you go see the governor, and there's something she needs to say to you."

He closed his eyes, and she closed hers. Then they began walking barefoot back and forth across the meadow.

Finally Najma placed her hand on his shoulder and said, "Let's go back now."

The moment Daher opened his eyes, Nafisa reached out to touch him, and she felt as though her hand were stroking a mountain.

Wakeful and apprehensive, the people of Arraba kept their eyes on the northern horizon, knowing it might yield any number of possibilities. Saad was the most fearful of all, since it was his own brother who had seized the soldiers and the tax collector and led them away like a herd of livestock, indifferent to the power these men wielded and the lofty standing of the governor and the empire he represented.

Daher had heard from many people about the governor's dream of acquiring a certain blue-gray mare that belonged to the Saqr tribe, his repeated attempts to buy her from them, and their steadfast refusal to sell her.

He turned in the direction of Bani Saqr's campgrounds and kept going until he found himself in front of the tent of their emir, Sheikh Rashid al-Jabr. Behind him were a number of Arraba's men, as well as the tax collector, who was smugly confident that as soon as they reached Sidon, the governor would kill Daher and all his escorts. His confidence was evident in the ominous sneer on his face, which bespoke a certainty that he would personally collect their dead bodies the way he had collected their money.

In front of the tent, which had been erected in a spacious open area in order to be seen by all, a long spear had been planted in the ground as a sign of power and authority.

Emir Rashid listened to Daher at length. As he did so, he regarded him thoughtfully. For some reason Daher reminded him of his own youth, and more. He had the same eyes, the same demeanor, the same bushy eyebrows and broad forehead, and as Daher spoke, he repeatedly felt as though he were sitting with himself, with the young man he had once been.

He said, "God knows what a special place you and the whole Zaydani family have in our hearts, Daher, and no one could be happier than we are that you've come to live among us. But the request you're making is a difficult one."

"It might have been difficult if I'd made the request of someone other than Emir Rashid al-Jabr! But rest assured—may God grant you length of days—that Daher al-Umar couldn't possibly have asked such a thing of anyone but you!"

The emir held his head in his hands and, without looking at Daher, said, "You win, Daher. You win!"

After a few charged moments, he clapped his hands and said, "Bring the blue princess."

When they brought the mare, Daher knew that Emir Rashid was relinquishing to him the most beautiful thing on earth.

135

He gasped. "I didn't know she was this beautiful!" he said. "I couldn't possibly take a horse like this from you even if it meant saving my life and the lives of everyone in Arraba!"

"I've given her to you, Daher, and Sheikh Rashid al-Jabr isn't someone who goes back on a promise. I would have liked you and your men to be my guests for three days. But since that won't be possible, I have only one wish: that what you receive in return will be far greater than what you're going there for!"

When the tax collector saw the blue mare tied to the saddle of Daher's horse, the smile on his face vanished, and if he had thought it a prudent choice to flee, he would have found an opportune moment and disappeared forever.

She glided over the terrain light as a cloud, her feet barely touching the ground, and she was so blue that whenever they reached the top of a hill, she blended with the sky. Every now and then Daher would glance over at her, certain that she was too precious to be given to any man on the face of the earth. As they approached the outskirts of Sidon, he thought: *I'd rather be butchered alive than give her up to this governor!*

Daher knew that all the governors put together were nothing but a single greedy ruler whose sole aim in life was to swallow up every city, village, mountain, plain, and valley that crossed his path. And he knew that not one of them deserved even the eyes of this exquisite blue princess.

Having glimpsed the horse before he glimpsed her escorts, the governor came running toward her, forgetting all his titles. He hopped and skipped around her, unable to touch the dream that had suddenly materialized before him. Daher could hear Emir Rashid al-Jabr's voice echoing: *I have only one wish: that what you receive in return will be far greater than what you're going there for!* And he swore to himself that he would make the state's soldiers, multazims, viziers, and sultans pay for her dearly.

A Fountain of Beauty
at Sidon's Door

When Daher returned with his men, all of Arraba came out to receive them. Some came running for joy over his homecoming, and some for joy over Arraba's well-being. The mere fact that he had come back alive meant that things had come to an auspicious conclusion.

His brothers' lanterns, which had flickered before their eyes, burned brightly again as they saw the new life that had been ordained for them.

Seeing the blood return to their pallid cheeks, Najma said, "Didn't I tell you last night that he could run like a horse and that nobody would be able to catch up with him?"

All that mattered to the governor was to receive the taxes people owed the state, and Daher had given him a promise, saying, "The taxes we owe will be paid in full, as I won't deduct a thing for myself as multazim. What's more, I'll deliver them to you personally every year."

Muhammad Pasha hadn't known such bliss since the day he was decorated with two horse tails on the occasion of his receiving the title of pasha, and he wasn't prepared to let it be ruined on account of some tax collector about whom Daher had had nothing good to say, especially when the man's greed was leading people to believe that the cruelty and injustice they were suffering were caused by the state!

However, the pasha was brought back to earth by the request Daher then made: "Since you've agreed to appoint me as your multazim in Arraba, all I ask is that the state's soldiers stop coming to the village, for any reason whatsoever!"

"And what does that mean? Do you want to be exempted from having to obey the empire?"

"Quite the contrary, Pasha. What we want is to be under the empire's rule, but without it needing to send soldiers to ensure our obedience. We know His Excellency the Sultan needs them to fight real battles beyond the empire's borders!"

"You offer far more than is asked of you, Daher, and that worries me."

"You know the values we live by, Pasha. As far as we're concerned, obedience to the empire is as important as obedience to God and one's parents."

The governor looked down, then looked up again, trying to discern what kind of person he was dealing with. He still wasn't certain.

Suddenly he barked, "Be gone with you before I change my mind— before I forget you were the one who brought me this filly!"

Muhammad Pasha gazed longingly at her as his stable hand took her reins and let her make circles around him like a fountain of beauty.

The Lesser of Two Evils

Things went precisely as Daher had planned, and the governor's soldiers disappeared entirely, as though Arraba and its environs were off limits to them. Even Arraba's meadows and plains could feel it, and to those who lived there the land seemed more expansive and the sky higher.

People's dignity became the most important thing, and their rights a red line that no one dared cross. Things had changed so radically, they felt as though they had been born again. And once the multazims and sheikhs of the region learned of Daher's direct ties with the governor of Sidon and the privileges he now enjoyed, they began to avoid coming near him or Arraba.[12]

As for the tribe of Bani Saqr, no one could predict when or where their sword of terror might strike next. The undisputed masters of raiding, looting, and pillaging, their swords hung like a shadow over the length and breadth of the land, and people no longer dared even leave their homes. Weary of Bani Saqr's reign of terror, the people rose up in protest, and Muhammad Pasha was obliged to give a free hand to Ibn Madhi, chief elder of Nablus, who was more loyal to the empire than the empire itself. Ibn Madhi then began launching one attack after another on Bani Saqr until he had worn them down.

Bani Saqr's days turned as black as their nights. Faced with Ibn Madhi's never-ending attacks, they went in search of a solution, and their emir, Rashid al-Jabr, had no choice but to settle the matter. He said to his men, "You know that the empire treats us unjustly. It takes more than a quarter of what we earn by the sweat of our brows. Then, when we're forced to take to the road to

---

12 The tyranny of Ahmad, sheikh of Jaddin, lay like a pall not only over Jaddin, but over Safad, Abu Sinan, and Deir Hanna as well. His rival Ibn Madhi, fortified within the Sanur castle, went raging through Nazareth and surrounding villages, the Plain of Bani Amer, Haifa, and Tantura. Meanwhile, Muhammad Pasha's power extended to every corner of his vilayet.

feed our children, they send someone to wage war on us! I've given the matter a great deal of thought, and I've reached a conclusion that I hate even more than I know you will. We have two options: either we pack up our tents and leave this land far behind, or we find someone here to serve as our head and protector. In view of the influence and generosity for which the Zaydanis are known, not to mention the love we know they have for us, I can't think of anyone better to seek out for help. Besides, we were the ones who brought them here from Tiberias, and we've been of help to them. Now they've become the multazims for Arraba, and they've won the hearts of its people and the neighboring villages."

Emir Qa'dan sensed that they were about to enter a new era. However, he realized that the paths before them were closing off, and that unless they moved quickly, the deluge embodied in Ibn Madhi and his hordes would sweep them away. As for Daher, he was observing events from a distance, unable to determine whose territory the flood would strike in the end.

One cold evening in December, the emirs of Bani Saqr, Daher and his brothers, and a number of Arraba's leading men met in the Zaydanis' diwan. As a cutting, dry wind blew outside, Emir Rashid al-Jabr searched for a way to open the conversation that wouldn't make him appear to be in a position of weakness.

They discussed Arraba's situation, which had become more and more untenable due to the fact that some day the governor of Sidon was bound to be removed unexpectedly from his post and they would find themselves without protection. They reminded themselves of the governors of Damascus, the largest of the Ottoman vilayets, who were sometimes removed from their posts less than a year after being appointed. In fact, many of them had lasted less than six months, with the result that over a period of forty years, Damascus had had approximately forty different governors.

All these things worried Daher. However, he didn't let on. Instead he looked at a distant point on the horizon that beckoned him onward.

Emir Rashid al-Jabr interrupted the men's conflicting thoughts—thoughts searching in vain for a moment of tranquility.

"Good evening," he greeted them.

"Good evening," they intoned.

"I'd like to raise an issue for your consideration."

"Go ahead, Emir Rashid."

"This is my spear," he said. Grasping the spear, he added, "I want this spear of mine to stand upright in soil that's hard as granite. So tell me, what should I do?"

"That's impossible!" Saad objected.

"We bore a hole in the rock and set it in the hole!" said Yusuf.

One of Arraba's elders commented, "I don't think the emir is talking about his spear. He's talking about something bigger than that."

"That's correct," replied Emir Rashid. "But let's assume for the time being that I do mean the actual spear."

Daher quickly realized that Emir Rashid had instructed those with him to remain silent, since they sat waiting patiently for the Zaydani brothers and the men of Arraba in attendance to make a reply. As Daher let the others try their luck at an answer, the question, serious though it was, turned into something resembling the riddles told during nocturnal social gatherings. In the end everyone ran out of ideas, and Emir Rashid al-Jabr said, "My question seems to be quite difficult. But I haven't heard anything from Sheikh Daher!"

Daher took a deep breath. He looked over at Emir Rashid for a moment as the others sat waiting to hear what he would say. Daher looked up and saw the torrent about to sweep Bani Saqr away.

"What are you looking at, Sheikh Daher?"

"I'm looking at what I see here."

"But you're looking into the distance. Or are my eyes deceiving me?"

"You're right, Emir Rashid. But what's in the distance has arrived."

"You know the answer to my question, then."

"It's easy, Emir Rashid."

"Well, then, I'm waiting for your answer along with all the other good folks gathered here."

"Come and plant your spear in front of me, Emir Rashid."

Emir Rashid reached out and placed the spear upright in front of Daher, who was seated beside him. Daher grasped the spear, placing his hand above Emir Rashid's.

"Now what?" asked Emir Rashid.

"The spear is standing upright, just the way you wanted it to be. After all, horsemen's forearms are harder than granite, Emir Rashid!"

Emir Rashid looked over at Daher and said, "Well, I have to confess that I've come to you for help."

After returning from his consultation with the men of Arraba, Emir Rashid met alone with Bani Saqr's emirs and elders.

"What do you think of what happened?" he asked.

"We'll do whatever you think is best, Emir Rashid."

Looking into their faces, he shook his head and said, "I'm in awe of this man. But what disturbs me is that he put his hand over mine, as if to tell us that he rules over us and that we can't oppose him. But that's all right. Send someone to Arraba to inform him that we agree to his being our leader, before I change my mind."

On that cold, cloudy December day, the sun rose on a new era unlike any that had preceded it.

Nafisa's Sorrows and
the Return of the Past

In Nafisa, Najma found something more precious than a daughter, and in Najma, Nafisa found something greater than a mother.

Nafisa wondered whether it was right to wish that someone could be one's mother or father. However, she almost wished Najma were her own mother. She remembered quite a bit about her mother, Zayn. However, the things she remembered were what had kept her close to her father. She was certain that if her mother had been alive, she wouldn't have approved of her marriage to Daher.

Zayn had come from a large family. However, she hadn't inherited the sort of endearing modesty that elevates people's souls. Her husband was descended from a noble family, and despite the troubles she caused him, he had continued at her side until her dying day. A headstrong woman, she would have been willing to spend everything they had on some dress or piece of jewelry that had caught her eye, and hardly had she been married a week when she began hosting one soiree after another.

Zayn never tired of putting on appearances. Knowing this, the coterie of Damascene socialites who'd attached themselves to her outdid themselves extolling houses in which they had never set foot, or women they had heard of in Aleppo, Sidon, and Cairo, but had never met. She began vying with the phantoms of distant women, intent on proving that she was the most generous woman on the face of the earth.

But nothing caused greater consternation to her family and husband than her reaction to Nafisa's birth. When Nafisa was born she cried, "I'm not somebody who has girls!" She was so furious that if she could have sent her back to where she came from, she would have.

As for Sheikh al-Husseini, the minute he saw the newborn he exclaimed, "What a durra nafisa—what a precious little pearl!" Thereupon he'd decided to name her either Durra (Pearl), or Nafisa (Precious).

Less than a month later, Zayn threw a huge party to celebrate having recovered her svelte figure after her nine months of pregnancy.

Stranger still was the fact that as time passed, her guests included none of the women who had come to congratulate her on her daughter's birth or sent her a present for the occasion. And when her siblings and parents asked to see the baby girl, she would become enraged, as though they were reproaching her or reminding her of a scandal.

This hatred for Nafisa on her mother's part was transformed into an overwhelming affection for her on the part of her maternal aunts and uncles. As far as her father was concerned, she was royalty, the sun that lit up the household.

Nafisa didn't know whether the reason she had no brothers or sisters was that her mother hadn't wanted to repeat the experience for fear of having another daughter, or whether her father had developed such an aversion to his wife that he didn't want to have any more children by her.

In their huge Damascene home, which, with its many rooms, rivaled the most sumptuous governor's mansion, Nafisa lived with her wet nurse, who then became her nanny. In the meantime, Zayn's family came to anticipate, and without the least rancor, that any day al-Husseini might send her home to them. To their surprise, however, he never did.

When they broached the matter with him directly, he said, "Don't talk to me about the members of my own household!"

A year later, al-Husseini's father-in-law brought him a fair-skinned concubine.

As al-Husseini looked at the girl, he realized that she had the most beautiful face he'd seen in his life. Clad in a lavender silk dress with a blue shawl over her shoulders, she looked like a mermaid.

"If you don't accept her, I'll take my daughter!" the father announced.

"I'll accept her! But I'm afraid I might wrong her by letting her live in this household."

"Be stubborn if you want to. But you won't be able to close your eyes to a beauty like this living under the same roof with you!"

For a long time Nafisa thought of her nanny as her mother. She was puzzled at the woman who lived in their house, who threw endless parties, and who didn't bother to reply when she said "Good morning" or "Good evening" if their paths happened to cross. When Nafisa was eleven years old, she woke up one morning to the sound of a painful scream.

"What's happened?" she asked.

No one answered her. But several hours later she learned that Zayn had died.

It struck her as odd that no one grieved over the woman's death, but if it hadn't been for the sanctity people feel obliged to accord the deceased, al-Husseini's family would have gone out to the Faradis Cemetery that day in celebration rather than in mourning.

"I didn't feel sad, Auntie Najma, until the day I found out that my nanny wasn't my real mother! When they told me that the woman who'd died was my mother, I was miserable. I felt as though, without their knowing it, they'd killed my real mother—my wet nurse and nanny—before my very eyes. They might as well have torn me away from her and thrown me into that dark grave where they'd buried the woman who was supposedly my real mother.

"It was less than a month before my father was able to smile again, and not just in front of me! The house itself, with its jasmine and carnations, started to smile at me too. I could sit beside the pond in the center of the inner courtyard, put my feet in the water, and swing them back and forth, I was so happy, and the concubine turned into a butterfly that would go flitting around me and my father without being afraid."

"If only you were my mother, Auntie Najma!"

"I *am* your mother, and your mother-in-law too. If Daher hadn't brought you back from Damascus, I would have gone looking for you myself, and I would have recognized you right away!"

"And how would you have recognized me without having seen me before?"

"When Najma tells you she would have recognized you, you have to believe her!"

Nafisa fell silent for a while. Then, with a couple of tears trickling down her cheeks, she said, "I wish I could have had a daughter so that I could love her the way you love me, and the way my mother didn't!"

The New Door

T en days after the Bani Saqr had joined the Zaydanis with Daher as their leader, they held a meeting. They knew that time was of the essence, with more people being killed at the hands of the empire and its collaborators with every passing day.

Daher was aware of the ordeal the Bani Saqr had endured, and he realized that although you might be victorious today, you can't count on victory being yours tomorrow. He knew he had set his foot on a path from which there was no retreat.

They agreed that Emir Rashid al-Jabr and his men would encamp on the grassland between Acre and Nazareth and establish a hold there, and that Daher would lead the Zaydanis back to Tiberias.

All they needed now was some event that would justify their next step, and everyone saw Daher as the only person capable of discerning what that event would be.

Nafisa rejected the idea of staying in Arraba. "I came here with you from Damascus, and you're not going to go off without me to Tiberias!"

As for Najma, she had made up her mind what she was going to do, and no one would have dared oppose any decision she made.

When Daher and Nafisa were alone, he said to her, "Don't worry. You won't be staying in Arraba."

"I'll get myself ready to leave, then."

"Get yourself ready to go to Nazareth."

"Nazareth!"

"Yes, Nazareth. I know you well, Nafisa, and if it weren't for the fact that my mother Najma is here, I would have sent you back to Damascus. I can see that you're alone here. So, since I don't want you to be so far from me, I'm going to send you to Nazareth and arrange for your stay there. There are many women from Damascus there that you can get to know. Besides, Nazareth has a different atmosphere from Arraba, and I think you'll be quite happy there."

"How could I be, when you're in Tiberias and I'm in Nazareth?"

"This will only be temporary, and I want to make sure you're all right. We're in the process of opening a new door now, and we're not certain what lies behind it!"

Nafisa cried, but she had no choice but to agree.

The Approaching Solution

Arraba gave them such a tearful farewell one would have thought they would never see them again.

Before their departure Daher sent Nafisa to Nazareth, escorted by his brother Saleh, some of his men, and some men from Bani Saqr. As Najma embraced her, she whispered in her ear, "Don't worry about a thing. We'll be meeting again soon."

As always, it amazed Nafisa to see how confident Najma was of her promises.

Saad went ahead of them to Tiberias, where he bought the diwan they had sold when they left. However, when he learned that the man who had been living in their old house had died just two weeks earlier, he refrained from offering to buy it. Instead he went to offer his condolences to the man's family, and before leaving left two bags of coins on the windowsill, each containing five hundred piasters.

Purchasing other houses presented no difficulty, since he was prepared to pay whatever their owners asked, and then some. Prior to Daher's arrival, Saad hosted a large banquet to which he invited the city's mufti, imam, and judge. As they reminisced wistfully about the good old days, the mufti, the imam, and the judge told Saad how they'd been wronged by the local multazim, who showed little mercy to anyone who couldn't pay everything he owed. Rather, the degree of compassion he showed was directly proportionate to the amount of money he was able to extract from people's pockets. So, at their request, he didn't invite the multazim to the banquet.

The morning after the banquet, a man came up to Saad and asked him about Sheikh Daher. Saad replied that Daher was in Arraba. However, before Saad could say another word, the man turned to leave. Saad had been about to tell him that Daher was due to arrive in Tiberias that very day, or possibly the next. As the man walked away, Saad asked, "Why do you ask?"

"I need something from him," the man replied.

Hoping to establish a foothold in Tiberias, Daher had spent the days previous looking for a reason to come back to the city. Little did he know that the reason would be waiting for him halfway there.

After reaching Aylabun, he went down toward Hattin, a village on the northern slopes of a double hill surrounded by plains filled with olive and fruit trees. Enormous cactuses formed walls that were impassable to human and beast alike, and fire-resistant as well. Daher cast a glance at the Horns of Hattin: the stark, twin-peaked volcano toward which the Crusader armies had once retreated before Saladin's forces.[13] Little did those armies' commanders know that after leaving the springs of Turin behind, and being unable to reach the springs at Hattin to replenish their forces there, they had doomed themselves to die of thirst even though the springs were only a stone's throw away.

Daher slowed his mount and looked thoughtfully around him.

Everyone who had ever passed through there had sworn he could hear war cries, the neighing of horses, and the clashing of swords.

On the plains of Hattin, the man found himself face to face with Daher and his caravan. He had come out alone without a thought for whether he lived or died.

He greeted them and said, "Where are you coming from?"

"From Arraba," Daher replied. "Is that where you're headed?"

"Yes, as a matter of fact. It's my last hope. If it closes its door to me, I'll have nowhere else to turn!"

"Take it easy, brother! What is it that Arraba might have to offer you?"

"Rather, say: What might Sheikh Daher have to offer? Everyone I spoke with in Tiberias indicated that the only person who could get me out of the situation I'm in is Daher al-Umar."

"And what do you want him to do for you?" Daher asked.

"Pardon me, good man, but I don't have time to spare talking when my son is in prison there."

---

13 At the renowned Battle of Hattin, which took place in 1187 CE, the Muslim army led by Salah al-Din al-Ayyubi (Saladin) defeated the Crusader army, an event that enabled him to advance through Galilee and free the remainder of Palestine from the Crusaders' grip.

"I assure you you're not wasting your time, sir, since the person you're speaking to is Daher al-Umar."

The man was disconcerted.

Daher dismounted. Then, sensing that the man would rather not speak in the presence of other people, he took him by the hand and led him away from the caravan.

They sat down at a distance, and whenever the man spoke, he would look around warily for fear someone might have heard him.

The man's son Jurays was a farmer who hadn't been able to pay everything he owed the multazim. The multazim had summoned him and told him, "Don't worry about a thing, Jurays. I'll cover the amount you owe, and you can pay me back later. What do you say?"

Incredulous, Jurays had accepted the offer. Several days later, the multazim sent him word, saying, "You'll have to pay the interest on the money I lent you."

Jurays was beside himself: "So now he's demanding interest? Why didn't he tell me that from the beginning?"

But it wasn't the money the multazim was after. After seeing Jurays's wife, he had made up his mind to make her his by any means possible, and when the opportunity arose he seized it.

When she learned of the matter, the wife cropped her hair and smeared her face with soot. Not content with this, she waited for an opportune moment and stole to the top of the wall of Tiberias intending to throw herself down, only to have others prevent her at the last moment. This had happened twice, in fact.

"I want her, alive or dead!" vowed the multazim.

Finally the multazim had Jurays shackled and thrown in prison, where he starved him and prevented his father and young children from visiting him. He said, "There's only one person who can remove his shackles and bring him food before he dies: his wife!"

As for the wife, she would rather have died a thousand deaths than agree to such a thing.

"We've got to hurry!" cried Daher.

"Let's go, then, sir!" replied the distraught father. "There's no time to lose."

The caravan continued on its way to Pigeon Valley, so called because of the large numbers of pigeons that nested in the crevices of the boulders that dotted the terrain. There was something eerie and frightening about the rocky valley, despite the sense of tranquility produced by the rustling of the birds' wings as they took off in flight whenever they sensed an unfamiliar movement. The stillness was deepened all the more by the gentle purl of a brook that flowed from a point southeast of Aylabun and passed through the valley before emptying into Lake Tiberias.

No sooner had Daher arrived with his men than he headed for the diwan and issued his first order: "Bring me that multazim."

The multazim was standing in front of a jail cell, negotiating with a number of peasants over what they would pay him in return for their release, when suddenly a number of armed men burst in. He shot them a contemptuous look and went on with his business.

Daher's men waited for him to finish. When he lagged, a huge hand unexpectedly seized him by the neck and dragged him toward the exit.

As he struggled to free himself from the iron grip, other hands reached out and pulled him along with still greater force, then picked him up by his arms and legs. He shouted for his soldiers to intervene, only to find them bound and gagged in front of the jail entrance. Daher's men carried him from the jail to the door of the diwan as passersby looked on in amazement.

There would be many happy times to come. However, the people of Tiberias dated numerous events thereafter by that auspicious day. On that day, which marked the end of that multazim's reign of terror, they'd witnessed things they had never imagined they would see with their own eyes.

"Have mercy on me!" cried the multazim when he found himself face to face for the first time with the young sheikh, and with Jurays's father standing at his side.

"Put him down," commanded Daher.

They let go of him, sending him tumbling to the ground with a thud. He crawled up to Daher.

"Have mercy on me, Sheikh!" he begged.

"Tie him to that palm tree, take the keys from him, and release all the prisoners."

"I'll release them myself, sir. Let me go, and I promise you I'll release them myself!"

"It's too late for that now. Those men shouldn't have been in jail in the first place."

151

Turning to the elderly man by his side, he said, "Go with my men and take your son home. Then bring him and his wife back here before sundown."

All of Tiberias gathered in front of the jail. People embraced their once-imprisoned loved ones, and singing could be heard in the prison yard:

> Daher, my brother, the crown on my head,
> Sword of silver, glinting like a diamond,
> The day you returned, you restored my life,
> Made the sun to rise, never to set.
>
> Daher, my uncle, my father, my brother,
> Vein of gold glistening in my blood,
> None but you relieved my affliction
> When in Tiberias once more we met.

Jurays's wife didn't believe her husband and father-in-law when they told her what had happened. They asked her to wash her face and get dressed, since evening was falling and Daher was waiting for them. But she refused to change her appearance until she'd seen the multazim bound with her own eyes.

She approached uncertainly, taking two steps forward and one step back. At last she found herself in front of the diwan, and with her weary, sorrow-laden eyes, she saw the multazim bound to the trunk of a palm tree. As he attempted to break loose, she retreated in fear. Then she sensed something stirring behind her. Realizing that all of Tiberias was there, she became even more flustered.

Daher came out of the diwan, having shed the heavy clothing he'd been wearing upon his arrival that morning due to the warmth that engulfed Tiberias at that time of day. He gestured for her to come toward him. As she approached, she squeezed her husband's hand with one hand and her father-in-law's with the other.

"I asked you to come so that you could see for yourself what's become of this godless miser, and to set your mind at rest."

He handed her a whip and said, "Flog him."

She took the whip and stared at it half-absently.

"Go ahead," Daher said to her.

"Flog him! Flog him!" the people behind her shouted.

She came toward him, whip in hand. But she was afraid. Meanwhile, the crowd's voice came to her: "Flog him! Flog him!"

Suddenly she flung the whip down, to the angry objections of the people behind her. She looked down at her mud-spattered shoes. Thinking back on the repeated torments to which she had subjected herself in her attempts to escape from the multazim, she took off her right shoe and picked it up. She looked at the multazim.

"Have mercy on me, sister!" he pleaded.

With that, she took off the other shoe, bent down, and took it in her hand. Then she came toward him and, with all the strength she had, began beating him wildly with her shoes. Many of those present stood silently about her, not daring even to breathe, while others wept for joy.

After some time people felt raindrops falling, and their clothes began getting wet, but she kept beating him. Night fell, and she kept beating him. A timid moon peeked out from between a couple of clouds, and she kept beating him. And when the sun came up, she was still beating him.

Daher came up to her and took her hand, which still had enough energy stored up in it that she could have gone on beating the man till Judgment Day.

When she turned to look at him, she was no longer the miserable creature she had been, and all the ashes that had clung to her face had vanished.

"Take your wife home, Jurays," Daher said. Then, turning to his men, he said, "Untie the good-for-nothing, set him on a donkey facing backward, and make the rounds of Tiberias with him. When people have finished slapping him and calling him names, put him in jail and bring me the key."

The Tiny Man

While standing at the diwan entrance, Daher was surprised to see a slight figure perched atop a black horse.

His heart skipped a beat.

His sword unsheathed, the tiny man shouted, "Let's see that strength people say you have!"

Daher's hand moved calmly toward his sword—his father's sword—and with a movement swift as lightning drew it out of its scabbard.

Daher's men made ready for a clash, but he signaled to them to stand back.

"If you want to fight, I'm ready!" Daher told him. Then, without further ado, he swung his sword. The tiny man drew back, light as the wind, and attacked Daher.

They dueled for a long time, sweat pouring down their arms and faces and dripping into their eyes on that cold day. They joined in battle a second time, then disengaged. Sparks flew like the spray of the waves every time their swords clashed.

"You've made the grade, Sheikh Daher!" shouted the man with the tiny frame.

"Yes," Daher replied. "I've succeeded in dodging the edge of your sword, Bishr!"

Then they dismounted and embraced.

The Second Horse,
and the Guest's Guest

I want to know everything that's happened to you," Daher said.

"You know the beginning," replied Bishr, "and how Bishr became a rich man. You also know what happened to him when Sheikh Fawwaz told him that 'two horses can't feed from the same trough.' When he first said it, I thought he was talking about somebody else. 'That's right,' I told him. It hadn't occurred to me that I was the second horse! Then he said, 'So, then, when will you be leaving?' and I realized he was talking about me. I was so taken off guard, I just said, 'Right now, Sheikh. Right now!'

"'No, Bishr,' he said, 'you won't leave right now. I'll give you three days to put your affairs in order.' We didn't see each other again after that. The first thing I did was to come looking for you, since I couldn't think of anyone else to turn to. When I got to Tiberias, they told me the Zaydanis had left with Bani Saqr. I thought of joining you, but I was afraid that if I were your guest, I'd be a burden to the people who were hosting you. So Ghazala and I ended up living with a tribe in the south. But that didn't last long, since I had to leave them, too!"

"Again?"

"That's right, Sheikh. The emir's daughter fell in love with me!"

Bishr fell silent for a bit. Then he added, "You know, Bishr always used to think that if his cousin hadn't agreed to marry him, no other girl would have wanted him!"

"Why do you say that, Bishr? I swear to God, if my sister Shamma were your age and weren't married already, I would have married her to you."

"That's noble of you, Sheikh Daher. But that would be a lot different than for a girl to choose Bishr of her own accord!"

"You're about to drive me crazy, Bishr. What do you lack, anyway? You're chivalrous, brave, a superb equestrian, and rich to boot! Yet you go on talking about yourself this way."

"That's because I'm an orphan, Sheikh Daher! Or had you forgotten?"

"Well, Bishr, I'm an orphan like you now. I've got neither father nor mother!"

"Your case is different from mine, Sheikh Daher. I might be a brave warrior. And since I'm rich, I can be as generous to my guests as the best of men. But I'm still an orphan in the eyes of the tribe, and in the eyes of any woman I meet."

Daher took a deep breath, holding his anger in check and trying to overlook Bishr's incurable condition.

"So what happened then?"

"I told Ghazala that the emir's mother had come to me and said that if I didn't marry her daughter, she was going to elope with the first drifter that happened to pass through and cause them a scandal! Ghazala just said, 'Marry her, then!' 'But you're my wife,' I told her, 'and you're pregnant now with our first son!'"

"By the way, I forgot to tell you I'd become a father. The little one's name is Umar, and the older one I named Daher."

"What did you say?" Daher broke in, shaken with surprise.

"Daher. I told you I'd named him Daher, Sheikh!"

"But you hadn't told me!"

"Yes, I told you just a minute ago."

Daher took another deep breath and smiled. "Go on, Bishr," he said, "I have a feeling I'm going to hear about more strange things that could only happen to you!"

Just then one of Daher's men came up and said, "Emir Rashid al-Jabr's men are here, Sheikh Daher."

"I'll be there shortly." Then he turned back to Bishr, saying, "Go on, Bishr."

"Bishr can't go on when Emir Rashid's men are waiting. He'll tell you the rest of the story some other time. You go, Sheikh. It wouldn't be proper for you to keep folks like them waiting. God be with you."

"No, you'll stay right here, and you'll sit beside me, Bishr."

"Who, me? With Emir Rashid al-Jabr's men here?"

"Yes, you, Bishr. And you're going to stay from now on."

Crime and Punishment

Six days after the multazim and his men were arrested, Tiberias and its environs froze over, an occurrence that repeated itself every few years. The water nearest the lakeshore froze, and the earth around it turned hard as a rock.

The air was so frigid that if a sparrow flew out into it, it would fall like a stone.

"You have a job to do, Bishr," Daher announced.

"What's that, Sheikh Daher?"

"You're going to go out at the head of a force of my soldiers and release the multazim's men on condition that they not leave Tiberias for any reason. As for the multazim, leave him in jail until we've decided his case. And after you've finished this job, we'll talk about your next one."

When they opened the jail door and began releasing the soldiers, the multazim shouted an insult at Bishr. "Didn't I tell you they wouldn't dare keep us in jail for more than a week?"

In an unusual gesture, he stood up to watch his men leave, shaking his head threateningly the entire time.

But when he finally came up to the door himself, Bishr slammed it in his face. After retreating in alarm, he began spewing insults and threats again. "Don't you know who I am?" he bellowed.

"No, we don't. Who are you?" Bishr retorted, as though he had never seen him before.

"I'm the multazim! Just wait and see what I'll do to you when I get out!"

Daher gathered Tiberias's leading men, foremost among them the mufti, the imam, and the judge, along with Emir Qa'dan of Bani Saqr and other men of his tribe. They composed a letter to the governor of Sidon informing him of everything Tiberias's multazim had done and how Daher, multazim of Arraba, had intervened at the insistence of the people of Tiberias and the surrounding areas. They told the governor how this tyrannical multazim had insulted the empire, its governors, its viziers, and its pashas. Whenever he did anything he would say, "I'm doing this on orders from the governor of Sidon!" and some people had believed him even though the governor had nothing to do with his actions. And they concluded by mentioning how, within a week of the multazim's imprisonment, the people had begun enjoying peace of mind and safety for the first time in years.

"Therefore," they wrote, "the people of Tiberias request that you appoint Sheikh Daher as their multazim. Since he held this position at a previous time, he knows the people and they know him, and we are certain that he will do his utmost to protect the empire's interests by paying the city's taxes in a timely fashion just as he did before. It was at our request that he came to Tiberias and jailed its multazim in order to protect him from the people, who were so incensed over his greed and dishonesty that they nearly killed him. So avaricious was this man that he had begun taking a share of the people's money equal to that of the empire itself. Nevertheless, we know you to be innocent of this man's crimes!"

After the three men had signed the letter, Daher examined it and said, "Muhammad Pasha will never swallow this letter unless we spice it with a thoroughbred horse! You'll need to find a horse that will make him agree to our request before he even opens the letter."

"I've got the horse for you," Emir Qa'dan replied. "Have your messenger pass by to see our men in the meadow and deliver them the message I'll dictate to him."

Daher's messenger reached Sidon just as Muhammad Pasha had finished gathering his forces.

"Nothing's going to stop me now!" Muhammad Pasha cried. "Get ready, and we won't sleep until we've come back with Daher's head! Isn't Arraba enough for him? What more does he want? If he covets Tiberias, he'll come later demanding to be appointed multazim over Sidon!"

When, the next morning, Muhammad Pasha's forces were at the gates of Sidon preparing to set out, someone in the vanguard shouted, "There's a messenger from Tiberias!"

Muhammad Pasha looked into the distance, but all he could see was a blue stallion, approaching with a swinging gait as though it were walking on the clouds. The messenger vanished from before him, and nothing remained but the horse and the surrounding expanse that made it all the more beautiful.

"Wait here!" he said to his army commander, and rode out to receive this puff of wind, this wave, this cloud.

He circled the horse seven times, and for a moment he was about to jump down and embrace it. However, he restrained himself and shouted in the messenger's face, "What are you doing here?"

Without a word the messenger came up and handed him Daher's letter. He read it in haste, with one eye on the words before him and the other on the horse.

"Lead the horse in front of me. Hurry up now!"

He wanted to drink in all its beauty, keen not to lose a single moment of enjoyment. When he reached the city gate, he shouted, "Who's the numbskull that brought those earlier reports about Daher from Tiberias? Couldn't he have taken the time to understand everything that happened there?"

Then he returned to his mansion, followed by his army.

Things might have gone in another direction if that horse hadn't robbed Muhammad Pasha of his senses. A day later, the imprisoned multazim escaped after attacking and killing the person who had brought him his breakfast. However, one of his innumerable victims recognized him and cried, "The multazim is getting away! Catch him!"

The moment the people heard the man's cry, they blocked the multazim's path. His horse bolted, and before he knew it he was flat on the ground and covered with mud. Kicks rained down on him from all directions, with everyone hoping he would be the one to finish him off.

Then Daher shouted, "Leave him to me! There's a better way for him to die!"

People stepped back.

"I wouldn't have wanted to see you in this condition, especially out in this cold! But you're the one who tried to escape, and you're the one who placed yourself at your victims' mercy!"

"Protect me, Sheikh, and you'll have whatever you want!"

"Are you trying to bribe me, you scumbag?" Daher retorted.

Then, turning to Bishr, he said, "You and your soldiers take him to his house and search it thoroughly. Make sure you don't miss a single piaster he's got hidden away. If he doesn't come clean about all his hiding places, send word to me, since I've got an idea I think he'll like! Then gather up everything he's stolen and bring it to the diwan."

Having seen Daher bind him to a palm tree, jail him, then rescue him at the last moment when his life hung by a thread, the multazim was sure Daher meant what he was saying.

He walked ahead of them, willing to do anything just to save his skin.

They found money stashed in wardrobes, cupboards, mattresses, walls, and chests he had concealed under piles of dung. They extracted money from a tattered, nondescript donkey saddlebag, and from a hole in front of his doorstep that people had passed over for years without once suspecting that there were riches beneath their feet. They came across a number of Damascene horses, cows, and sheep, plus a baby bear in a cage, as well as a carpet, beautiful rugs, and a boat.

Bishr, who had suddenly turned into a tiger, asked, "Is there anything else?"

"No," the multazim said.

They took him to Daher in a public procession as all of Tiberias looked on in delight. When they reached the diwan, Daher demanded, "Tell me the truth. Do you have anything else that belongs to these people?"

Shivering with cold and fear, he replied, "No, I swear to God, Sheikh! No, I swear to God!"

"But you're still an outlaw," Daher rejoined. "There's something else left that's plain to see. If you don't go now and knock on the door of everyone you robbed and return the stolen merchandise personally, I'll let them take it from you."

"I swear I don't have anything else that belongs to them, Sheikh!"

"On the contrary: there's more left than you'll be able to give back to them!"

"What do you mean, Sheikh? Tell me what it is, and I'll give it back!"

"There's this excess flesh on your bones, which couldn't possibly have accumulated the way it has if you didn't eat too much. So are you going to start restoring people's rights, or shall I let them recover their shares out of these layers of fat?"

The multazim looked around and saw all eyes fixed on his body. It was as though everyone there suddenly saw him as the fattest man they had ever laid eyes on. Sensing this, he said, "I'll do whatever you want me to, Sheikh."

"We're in agreement, then! All of you go home now and wait for what belongs to you."

Some people said, "We'll take what's ours right here, and then go home."

"No," Daher told them, "he's going to return everything he took to the place from which he took it. This is what justice requires."

The gathering broke up and the people dispersed to their homes. Before they left, Daher shouted at the multazim, "And don't forget to go to the house of that woman you tried to rob of her honor!"

"I don't have anything to return to her, Sheikh. And you're my witnesses that I don't want the money I lent you."

"You're going to go knock on her door and ask her if you still owe her anything."

"I swear to God, anything would be easier than that, Sheikh!"

"All the money in the world wouldn't be enough to compensate that honorable woman for what you did to her."

The Tax Collector Swooned,
the Sun Went into Hiding

Daher couldn't have asked for a more ideal scenario: the story of Tiberias's multazim spread through all the villages in the region, providing people with a perfect revenge on the multazims in their own villages and the tax collectors with them. Even before Daher's messenger returned with an answer from the governor of Sidon, people began fleeing their villages as though the plague were on their heels. After making their way secretly to Tiberias, some took up residence there, and others asked Daher to take over their villages and drive their multazims out.

But the strangest event of all was the arrival in Tiberias of Miqdad, multazim of Tabigha, to request Daher's protection.

Many people had lost their money. However, Miqdad, the tallest man between the two seas, would gladly have parted with every piaster he owned if, in so doing, he could have persuaded the tax collector to spare the most beautiful, precious thing in his life.

The tax collector and a number of soldiers arrived in Tabigha one Thursday morning. The sun was shining, and warmth had spread its wings gently over everything. The travel party was making its way along the lakeshore when something earthshaking happened. Together with a number of friends, a beautiful girl came walking out of a green wooded area. Hardly had the tax collector caught a glimpse of her when he froze like a statue. Nevertheless, he managed to raise his hand in a command for everyone to stop until she and the others with her had passed. When she saw them, she concealed half her face before continuing on her way.

The tax collector watched her, his spirit clinging to her so tightly that, as she moved away, it stretched and stretched like a rubber band until it nearly broke.

When she disappeared around a bend beyond the trees a hundred meters from him, the tax collector's chest tightened, and he felt his spirit exiting his body.

"What's wrong?" one of the soldiers asked him.

He couldn't answer.

The soldier asked him again. But instead of replying, he fell like a stone off his horse's back.

The soldiers dismounted hurriedly and examined their leader, certain he was dead.

They felt his pulse. There was no sign of life. They brought a mirror and held it under his nostrils, and no moisture appeared on it. They tried to sit him upright, but he fell onto his right side like a limp rag.

They stretched him out on the ground and recited the Fatiha over his soul, all the while looking around, wondering how to deal with this crisis that had arisen so far from Sidon. Time passed heavily as they began thinking about how to get him back home.

The soldiers mused aloud over what had gone wrong:

"He couldn't have been exhausted, since the trip wasn't that strenuous."

"The sun hasn't been that hot!"

"He couldn't have been hungry, since we ate just a couple of hours ago."

"He wasn't sick, since he insisted on being in the lead."

"So what came over him?"

"It was that girl! That girl!" the tax collector cried. Spooked, the soldiers scattered in all directions. Finally one of them mustered the courage to come up to him. After expressing his relief at seeing that he was all right, he said, "What happened to you, sir? You fell off your horse all of a sudden!"

"Didn't you see what she did? She hit me in a vulnerable spot!"

"Who did, sir?"

"I told you: that girl!"

"What girl, sir?"

"The one who passed by here."

"Seven girls passed this way, sir. Which one of them do you mean?"

"That gorgeous one. Didn't you see her? She might have killed me without you even noticing! Are you soldiers or a bunch of nincompoops? Now where did she disappear to?"

Tabigha, a village as idyllic as the waters of Lake Tiberias, wouldn't have been large enough for anybody to disappear in. How much more impossible would it have been, then, for a blinding sun to disappear there?

The tax collector forgot about the crops, the empire, and its shares of this and that. He forgot all the plans he'd made to fleece the peasants as thoroughly as he could. He only had one purpose now: to find out whose daughter that girl was.

He wished he'd brought a larger force of soldiers with him. After all, taking a girl, who might also be someone's wife, from her home wouldn't be an easy matter. However, madness turned into an army under his command—an army that, for the sake of finding that girl, he ordered wherever he wished and with which he turned earth and sky upside down however he pleased.

Tabigha was so small that you could have searched all its houses in twenty minutes. He made the rounds of the village twenty times, but found nothing. He went through it in the early morning, at midmorning, at noon, in the afternoon, in the evening, at night, at dawn, and again in the early morning, but to no avail. He went back to the spot where he had seen her, also to no avail. He was like a straw being blown to and fro, and the people of the village watched him in bewilderment, not knowing what had come over him.

In the end he had no choice but to demand that the townsfolk congregate in the mosque courtyard.

Miqdad said to the tax collector, "Say what it is that you want, and I'll bring it to you."

The tax collector, certain that they would hide the thing he wanted, kept his lips sealed.

"I want them here, all of them: men, women, children, and elderly. I don't want you to leave anyone where he is, even if he's dead. If anyone among you has died, bring him here before you bury him!"

"You're making things difficult for me. Nothing like this has happened for a long time. This is what used to happen when the empire was looking for someone who had broken a law. So what can I say to people to persuade them to congregate here?"

"Just tell them to congregate, that's all."

"Give me until this evening to arrange things with them."

"All right. But if you don't bring them, I'll go get them myself."

Miqdad managed to take one of the tax collector's soldiers aside. At first the soldier refused to divulge any information. However, when he saw a bag of money emerge from Miqdad's pocket and settle in his palm, he began looking this way and that.

"Don't worry. There's nobody around," Miqdad told him.

Before Miqdad had a chance to ask what lay behind the tax collector's bizarre behavior, the soldier snatched the bag of money and said, "He's looking for a beautiful girl he saw beside the lake yesterday morning."

Miqdad went jaundiced. He didn't even notice that the soldier had disappeared. Realizing what a catastrophe had descended upon him, he took off running for home. The minute he arrived, he shouted, "Where's Badr al-Budur?"

"She's inside," replied his wife. She was the tallest woman in Tabigha, but when she stood next to Miqdad, she didn't even come up to his waist.

She watched him scornfully as he ducked to get into the next room.

"Worried about her? Why? Has somebody told you an ogre's going to eat her?"

Little did she know that there really was an ogre in town.

He took Badr al-Budur by the hand and began making circles around himself, not knowing where to hide her. He went outside and walked around the house, surveying the entire village from over the wall.

In his feverish circling, he realized that, by bringing her out, they would be discovered immediately. At that moment he felt as though the height that had once been a blessing had suddenly turned into a curse, and he wished desperately that he weren't so very tall.

"I'll crush that tax collector with a single blow. I'll smash him to smithereens!" he said to himself. And he could have done just that. However, he also knew that this wouldn't solve the problem, since then he would be sure to lose Badr al-Budur. Rather than her leaving him, he would have to leave her. Not only that, but one of the tax collector's soldiers might take her to the governor of Sidon as evidence of the crime he had committed!

He tried to think of someone he could trust who could take her far away until the tax collector and his men had left the village.

But then he felt even more fearful. "Whom could I possibly entrust her to?" he wondered.

He decided that the best course of action would be to hide her in the house. He fetched sacks of wheat and stacked them into a wall. Then, as his wife looked on, he hid Badr al-Budur behind it. Every time she asked him anything, he would roar like thunder and nearly knock her to the floor. After he had supplied Badr al-Budur with all she could possibly need in that cramped space by way of food, water, clothing, and blankets, she disappeared behind the wall of wheat.

Then he left the house.

"Do you feel better now?" his wife asked.

He didn't turn around. Sweat was pouring off his body like little streams running down a mountainside, and he smelled powerfully of a newly harvested field.

The tax collector searched frantically for the face that had occupied his head and taken possession of his thoughts. However, he didn't see it among the faces that filled the mosque courtyard.

"I said I wanted everybody!" he screamed.

Miqdad cast a meaningful look at the soldier he had spoken to. The soldier didn't understand exactly what the look meant. Miqdad was pleading with him and promising him more than what he had already given him, but the soldier saw it as nothing but a look of entreaty.

The soldier looked away from Miqdad, and that was when Miqdad felt the knife go in. However, by that time it was too late to get her out of the village.

The tax collector had no choice now but to use his last resort: to search all the houses in the village one by one.

He gave the order, and his soldiers rushed off to begin the search.

Three days later, after the village had been searched no fewer than thirty times, the soldier with whom Miqdad had spoken realized that his commander would hold them captive in the village forever unless the girl appeared.

"Sir," said the soldier with feigned innocence and serious mien, "we haven't searched the house of Miqdad, the multazim."

"And why would we do that? The multazim would never deceive us!" retorted the tax collector.

"I think we should search his house anyway. He may be the mult-azim. But he's still a subject of the empire, isn't he, sir?"

"Do you mean to say that Miqdad might deceive me?"

"He might, sir. He would have to if that girl you saw is his sister, his daughter, or his wife."

The tax collector stood up and looked around him. In the distance he glimpsed a towering Miqdad looking anxiously in all directions.

"To Miqdad's house!" he commanded.

Miqdad's giant frame loomed in front of the door. However, the sense that he was going to lose Badr al-Budur robbed him of all his power, transforming him into another man who bore no resemblance to the Miqdad with the towering frame and the superhuman strength.

At first he refused to get angry. Then he shrieked and raged.

"If you want to fight us, we'll fight. But I'd advise you to let the matter pass without incident," the tax collector said to him.

Miqdad stepped away. The soldiers went in and conducted a search while the tax collector kept an eye on Miqdad outside.

After a short while they came out again. "There's nothing!" one of them said.

Miqdad's features lit up.

"Search again," commanded the tax collector.

They went in and came out a second time.

The soldier who had revealed the secret to Miqdad became increasingly perplexed. "There's nothing, sir!"

Miqdad's features lit up still more.

"You stay out here with him. I'll go search myself," announced the tax collector.

He left the soldiers and went inside. A moment later they heard him shout, "Three of you come in here!"

Three of the soldiers rushed inside to find the tax collector standing in front of the wall of wheat and trying to penetrate it with his eyes.

As they departed, Miqdad trailed them for a long time, weeping and pleading with the tax collector. "Take everything I have. But give her back to me! Take my life, but bring her back to me!"

But the tax collector and his entourage moved farther and farther into the distance until they disappeared.

167

As people rejoiced over having been exempted from the annual tax in exchange for Miqdad's concubine, they could see Miqdad, his heart broken, running after the tax collector, and Badr al-Budur on a horse, struggling to free herself and come back.

When night fell, Miqdad was still standing in the road. Some time before dawn they mustered the courage to approach him, and when someone took his hand, he followed him back home like a little child.

One morning as Daher was looking into the distance, he beheld a sight unlike any he had ever seen before: a palm tree mounted on a horse.

Startled, he stood there watching until Miqdad's features came into view.

Miqdad stopped the horse. Then, as usual, he brought his feet to the ground, and the horse slipped out from under him as though it were passing under a bridge.

He said to Daher, "Would you be willing to offer your protection to a multazim?"

"If a multazim asks for my protection, first he'll spend three days as my guest. Then I'll say to him, 'Go back to your village, which needs you, while I need you there more than I need you here.'"

"But I hope you won't leave us alone there in Tabigha, Sheikh."

"Rest assured, we won't abandon you or Tabigha."

"But I have one special request, Sheikh."

"Consider it granted."

"I need you to help me get my heart back."

Daher listened to Miqdad's story. When he had finished, he said to him, "We hope the tax collector hasn't taken her so far away that we won't be able to catch up with them."

The Sweet Fragrances
of the Cosmos

A festive atmosphere spread through Tiberias as the girls set out for the lake that Thursday evening carrying large quantities of flowers, their laughter rising heavenward like a colorful fountain of delight.

Daher searched the eastern horizon and found the moon, bashful as a winter sun. With something from the distant past stirring in his spirit, he ascended the city wall. Down below on the lakeshore, the girls looked like swans flapping their wings and diffusing an unspeakable joy.

As the sun set and the moon rose in the sky, they began throwing the flowers into the water. Within an hour, night had fallen completely, the stars had come out, and the sound of their singing began rising and falling like a swing suspended from ropes descending from the sky. They sang:

> O hair of mine, this night is yours.
> Flutter, fly away, and I'll follow.
> His face bright, my beloved will come running
> When you smite him with Cupid's arrow.
>
> O hair of mine, my sorrowing dower
> With your vibrant, dazzling sheen,
> Summon my beloved and he'll hear you
> From Aleppo, or from Jenin!

It was one of Tiberias's loveliest rituals.

Daher searched in vain for a certain swan. When he noticed what he was doing, he averted his gaze. Standing atop the wall on this particular occasion had opened wounds in his heart that he thought had been healed.

169

After a fitful sleep, he went early the next morning to the diwan, where he found Bishr waiting for him. They drank coffee together and ate dates, which Jum'a had brought in such abundance that Daher said to him, "Get those dates out of here before we finish them off!"

After Jum'a had left, he turned to Bishr and said, "I need you now, Bishr."

"Sheikh Daher needs Bishr? How is that?"

"You, Bishr, are going to be responsible for forming two brigades, one from the people of Tiberias, and the other from the Bedouins."

"Me?"

"Yes, you. Who better than you to train my soldiers? After all, you trained me once. Or have you forgotten, Bishr?"

"No, I haven't forgotten. But now you're more skilled than I am."

"No, I'm not. It's just that you don't want to believe that you're more skilled than I am. Or maybe you're just trying to flatter me!"

"But you really are better than Bishr now, Sheikh!"

"So, you don't want to believe you're the better of the two of us. Enough of that, then! We've agreed that you'll be responsible for forming the two brigades, right?"

"Right. But you know, Sheikh? To this day I feel like a little orphan boy."

At that moment Daher realized that if he wanted Bishr to be a courageous man, he had to put him on the back of a horse, and if he wanted him to be Bishr the orphan boy, he had to bring him down to the ground or strip him of his weapon, be it a sword or a staff.

"Bishr," he said, "children were made to make the world beautiful, and adults were made to change it."

"So where do I fit, Sheikh? Which category do I belong to?"

"You belong to both, Bishr. But now let's get back to that story of yours. I'm anxious to hear what happened to you!"

Daher's thoughts roamed. He began thinking about the fact that even after many years of marriage, Nafisa had never borne him a child, though they had resorted to every remedy they could think of.

At that moment one of Daher's men came in with a bundle in his hands.

"What's this?" Daher asked.

"A woman whose features I couldn't make out came and gave this to me. She said, 'This is for Sheikh Daher!'"

Daher took the bundle and placed it in front of him. Before opening it, he felt what was inside it. It exuded the familiar fragrance that still clung to his spirit.

When he untied the two knots, he found a carefully folded cloak. He pressed it gently with his fingers and felt the same firm round mass.

His heart pounded violently.

"Bishr requests your permission to be on his way, Sheikh."

"Goodbye, Bishr. Goodbye," he said solemnly.

When he found himself alone after nightfall, he carefully unfolded the cloak to reveal a snow-white bundle like the one he had seen once before. Filled with trepidation, he ran his fingers over it. Then he untied its two knots. Curled up around itself like a little child, the braid that lay before him exuded all the sweet fragrances of the cosmos.

He stood for a long time holding it in his hand. Suddenly he noticed that the flame of the lantern was about to go out. He took a deep breath and blew it out.

Secrets That Can't Be
Entrusted Even to Paper

T he sun rose, promising a day that would be more than warm.

People had gathered at the Tiberias gate, some to bid others farewell, and some to receive arriving travelers. The imam sat writing letters for people, both men and women. If a man wrote a letter to his family, it would be addressed to his son, not to his wife, even if the son in question was still an infant, whereas wives wrote to their husbands directly. As for merchants, the imam would pass by their places of business to write the letters they dictated. He did the same for some of the city's wealthy and notables.

Imam Abdullah, who had grayed completely by the time he was in his mid-forties, knew everyone's secrets. He kept them to himself, and would never have divulged them even to his wife. He often suffered and even wept as people dictated heartbreaking letters to him, revealing secrets that could hardly be entrusted even to a piece of paper. He would come home grief-stricken, and on many occasions would ascend the minaret and issue the call to prayer as though he wanted to deliver their messages straight to God in a plea for divine mercy and grace.

Aware of this, his wife would utter the phrase he had come to know so well: "God help them!" and he would repeat after her, "God help them!" But never once had she asked him what he knew.

The multazim had tried to find out some people's secrets, and whether they mentioned his name in their letters to relatives and acquaintances. He had attempted to glean information about the nature and size of merchants' business deals, and the prices of the merchandise they imported and exported. But Imam Abdullah would stop him short with a stony look. When one day the multazim went too far, the imam asked him, "Wouldn't you like to know how many supplications they make to the Almighty every day so that you can take a fourth of them in taxes? Or would you be satisfied with the number of times they bow in worship and the number of times they come to the mosque, a place I haven't seen you in once since you came to this town?"

One day, when the morning hours had already turned hot as high noon, the imam began to fret. Several days had passed since Daher's messenger had set out for Sidon, and he had yet to return. His mind worked overtime, his thoughts going this way and that. He thought: *After finding out what happened to his multazim, maybe the governor imprisoned Daher's messenger, or even had him hanged! Maybe he's on his way to Tiberias at the head of an army, and plans to bring the city down on our heads. Maybe he's planning to hang everyone who signed that letter by their eyelashes from the city gates? I know that what the multazim did was unforgivable. Even so, what Daher did to him might well have been the worst insult anyone has inflicted on a man of state for the last two hundred years or more, and I don't think he'll ever be forgiven for what he did. He should have contented himself with Arraba rather than coming to take over Tiberias, too! And on top of all that, he comes with Bani Saqr, who've terrorized people both in Galilee and elsewhere with their constant raids! The governor will say: Abdullah, how could you, an imam, bear false witness? On the other hand, I didn't exactly bear false witness. All I did was sign what Daher had dictated. And my situation might not be as bad as that of the mufti and the judge. Even so, I'm afraid the governor is going to make the three of us a laughingstock by parading us through the market with our beards tied together!*

"Where have you wandered off to, Abdullah? You seem distracted. What's on your mind?"

He turned and found the judge standing in front of him. "I've been standing here all this time and you haven't even seen me. You must be thinking about something really worrisome!"

"I'm thinking about the three of us with our beards tied together!"

"About what?"

"Never mind. It's nothing!"

"But you said something about our beards? Is something wrong with our beards?"

"They seem to have gotten a bit long, don't you think?"

The judge ran his fingers down to the tip of his beard and said, "Maybe you're right!"

Suddenly the judge cried, "Look, Abdullah! There's the news we've been waiting for: Daher's messenger is back!"

Forgetting his dignity, the judge took off running toward the approaching travelers. When Imam Abdullah saw how overjoyed the other man was, he knew for certain that his friend had been even more frightened than he was.

173

A One-Man Army

D aher was afraid no one would respond to his plea. After all, why would anyone choose to join such brigades when the fate of Tiberias was still uncertain? However, he didn't want to lose any time.

The first person to arrive at the diwan was Jurays, the man whose wife Daher had defended from the former multazim. "I felt it would be a shame for anyone else to come register his name before me," Jurays explained. Daher welcomed him.

An hour went by, but no one else came. Daher came up to Bishr, who was mounted on his horse, and said to him, "You've got a one-man brigade, Bishr. What are you going to do with it?"

"I'll occupy Istanbul if you'd like, Sheikh Daher!"[14]

"Well then, don't get off your horse until I tell you to!"

"I didn't think you'd really want Bishr to occupy Istanbul, Sheikh. Bishr was only joking!"

"But I'm serious, Bishr!"

Daher looked at him. Then he burst out laughing, and so did Bishr.

As they dried their tears, Daher said, "Never mind Istanbul for the moment. We don't want to wear out your army on foreign expeditions just yet!"

"As for Bishr, he's promised you now, and Bishr doesn't go back on his promises!"

"Go back on it, Bishr. Go back on it!"

They heard a commotion. When they turned to see what it was, they saw a large party of men advancing toward them.

"Why did they take so long to get here?" Bishr asked.

---

14 The name Istanbul derives from the Greek *istimbolin*, meaning 'in the city' or 'to the city.' The city has also been referred to as Islambul, meaning 'city of Islam' or 'city of peace.' This appellation appeared shortly after the Ottoman conquest of the city in 1453 in affirmation of the city's role as capital of the Islamic Ottoman Empire, and has been attributed to Sultan Mehmet II. The first use of the word 'Islambul' on coinage took place between 1703 and 1730 CE during the reign of Sultan Ahmad III.

Jurays replied, "Sheikh Daher's men asked them to assemble in front of the mosque first so that they could all come together. I couldn't stand to wait, though, so I came before they did."

Daher turned to Bishr and said, "I don't want to see your feet on the ground unless you and I are alone, Bishr. Understood?"

"Yes, sir."

Bishr began to say something, but thought better of it when he saw Jurays staring at him. Understanding what Jurays must be thinking, Daher came up to him and whispered in his ear, "You, unlike him, can do all the things that need to be done without having to stay on horseback!"

During the following weeks, which passed with lightning speed, Bishr proved himself to be the finest trainer an army could wish to have. With what seemed to be a touch of magic, he managed to transform the farmers' shovels, sticks, and winnowing forks into swords.

Standing before the peasants who had fled from the multazims in their villages, Daher shouted, "Let the men from Samkh come forward!"

They stepped forward. Turning to Bishr, Daher said, "Your responsibility is to take them back to their homes. Then arrest the multazim in Samkh and bring him to me."

"But we want to stay here!" shouted more than one voice.

"Your land and your houses want you there. I intend to be the multazim for Samkh just as I am for Tiberias."

"Let the men of Majdal come forward."

They stepped forward, and Daher gave his brother Yusuf the same instructions he had given to Bishr.

In this way Daher's soldiers were deployed south, north, and west, returning people to their villages and bringing the villages' multazims back to Tiberias in shackles.

"Who will go with us, then?" the people of Hattin whispered among themselves.

"I will!" Daher said.

From the high tower at the corner of the city wall, Daher stood pondering Tiberias and the surrounding area. The landscape was tranquil as far as the eye could see. Three years after his arrival in Tiberias—the best three years the city had seen in a long while—he knew the time had come for another step.

175

City of a Thousand Lanterns

The walls of Tiberias rose higher with every passing day until the city became an impregnable fortress. Daher issued orders for the gate to be changed, keen to ensure that it was no less secure than the gate of Damascus itself. The Damascus gate was something to which he had devoted a good deal of thought, and he sensed what a source of pride it was to everyone in the city: its governor, its judge, its merchants, its soldiers, weak and strong, poor and rich, and even its women of the night. In the eyes of bakers, lamplighters, confectioners, and sword makers alike, Damascus's gate and its high wall were symbols of strength and of the city's impregnability.

He ordered towers built, and they rose in every direction. Tiberias had become another city: a beautiful new city. For the first time, people were exempted from the burden of paying for the street lanterns in front of their houses, since Daher had sent to Damascus for a thousand lanterns and appointed a number of lamplighters whose sole responsibility was to ensure that not a single lantern went out between sunset and sunrise. Whoever saw Tiberias from a distance was enchanted by the oasis of shimmering lights. Hence, while the lake was the source of Tiberias's magic by day, once the sun had set Tiberias itself turned into a lake of light.

Daher was in need of more muskets and gunpowder. As for cannons, they were the last thing on his mind, since he knew well what problems he would face if he set them up on the city walls.

Abdullah Pasha al-Aydinli, governor of Damascus, rose to his feet and shouted, "Why didn't you tell me about this? If he's raised the walls and fortified the city in this way, he must be thinking about something no one has ever thought about before!"

"However," replied the daftardar,[15] "since the time he became multazim

---

15 The term 'daftardar' is composed of the words 'dar,' a Persian word meaning 'owner' or 'master,' and 'daftar,' a word of Greek origin derived from the term 'diphtheria,' which referred to the animal skin on which writing was done. The term 'daftardar' entered the Arabic language long ago as a reference to the government official responsible for public records and state archives.

over Tiberias, he's done everything required of him."

"In fact," he added, "I don't recall our disputing with him over a single piaster! Of all the multazims in Palestine, he's the most trustworthy. Besides, people don't complain about him, which is exactly what we want, since unrest only causes the empire to lose money and men!"

"I know that. But can anyone explain to me why he's raised the city walls, built towers, and armed his soldiers?"

"Fear of attacks by the Bedouins! That's what he says, at any rate."

"And you believe him? How could he possibly be afraid of the Bedouins when he's entered into an alliance with the most powerful force among them: the Bani Saqr tribe? And why haven't you said anything? How has he managed to distract you, and even blind you, by acting trustworthily in connection with the state taxes?"

"But he's been doing this for years without giving us any cause to worry."

"That was when he was in Arraba. Wasn't he multazim in Arraba? But haven't you thought about why he left Arraba and went to Tiberias?"

"His brother Saad stayed in Arraba, and he also pays everything he owes in a timely fashion."

"But no one has answered my question: Why has he gone to Tiberias?"

"Because people there were complaining about its multazim."

"Rather, he's gone there because it's the place he can most easily fortify, and it's farthest from the empire's reach. That's why he's gone there."

On that sweltering midsummer day in Damascus, Abdullah Pasha did a lot of thinking. He turned to his men, making a point, as was his custom, of looking every one of them straight in the eye. Then he said, "The time has come to bring Tiberias into submission."

"But it hasn't rebelled!" objected the daftardar.

"It's rebelled more than you think!"

After a brief silence he said, "I want you to get Bani Saqr to terminate their alliance with this man. Use the carrot or the stick. Do whatever it takes."

177

A War of Letters and a Storm of Fire

The news Yusuf had brought descended on Daher's head like a lightning bolt: Bani Saqr had taken Saleh captive.

"How did that happen?"

"We came unexpectedly upon a group of them attacking a caravan headed for Tiberias. We skirmished with them, and then another group suddenly appeared. We tried to retreat, but Saleh didn't make it."

Daher turned away from his brother Yusuf as though he didn't want to see him. Yusuf and those with him left, not knowing where they had found the strength to face Daher with the news. Daher thought about all possible scenarios. However, the cruelest of these didn't cross his mind. He recalled the last conversation he had had with Saleh, which had taken place that morning.

"As soon as the next new moon appears, I'm going to marry you off, Saleh."

"Marry me off? It's enough that you, Yusuf, and Saad have married. Do we all have to marry?"

Daher chuckled. "I'll answer that question when you get back!"

When they chose Daher as their leader, Bani Saqr had agreed to his demand that they bring their raids to a halt and enter into a mutual defense alliance with him. For his part, he had promised to allot them a share of his wealth sufficient for their needs, just as he allotted a share of it to pay taxes to the empire.

Emir Rashid al-Jabr had agreed to all of this.

"All your time will be yours now," Daher had said. "You'll be free to raise your children, graze your livestock, and buy and sell them as you need to."

Emir Rashid al-Jabr, who had voiced his approval of the arrangement twice, had seemed quite pleased with the agreement, since it promised to protect his tribespeople and their children from the woes of warfare.

After Daher and his brother Saad left Bani Saqr's campgrounds, Saad said to him, "You gave them more than you'd give your own family!"

"I know, Saad. I know! But if we want this country to be a true country, we have to get them off the highways. If people go on living in fear of this tribe's attacks, they won't feel that their possessions or their families are safe from harm. I want people to feel settled on their own land, Saad. I want them to be planted alongside the trees they've planted. If the people who till the land thrive, the land will thrive too."

"Well, you granted them concessions fit for a sultan, and I'm afraid even that won't help."

"What *will* help, then, Saad? To let them go on attacking people while I look on? To let them tear down everything I build and break every heart I win? I cherish every moment of tranquility people experience between Lake Tiberias and Arraba. I also need some tranquility myself, and I crave it more than they crave the money I'll be giving them!"

"One of these days you'll find yourself at war with them again."

"I know, Saad. But what I need right now is to be able to build."

Daher's plan turned out to be so successful in the beginning that Saad wished he hadn't said what he'd said to him that day. However, later events served to confirm his fears.

Bani Saqr's attacks began increasing with every passing day. At first Emir Rashid al-Jabr said, "The people launching the attacks aren't our men. They're from other tribes claiming to belong to Bani Saqr in order to ruin the good relations between us!"

Daher said nothing until he caught a number of Bani Saqr's men in the act. After giving the matter some thought, he decided to return them safely to Emir Rashid al-Jabr without a word.

Daher instructed his men to escort them home.

"Don't you want to send some message to the emir?" Saleh asked him.

"These captives *are* the message, Saleh. Nothing I might say would speak more eloquently than their safe return!"

"Are you honoring the emir by sending them back unharmed, or are you threatening him?"

"We'll wait and see how he interprets the message, Saleh. We'll wait and see."

179

When Bani Saqr began launching raids again, Daher decided to form armed brigades to protect the roads, and assigned Yusuf, Saleh, Bishr, Jurays, and others to command them.

The next message Emir Rashid received came in the form of five of his men slain. He tried to ascertain whether Daher had killed them in battle or after they had been taken captive. Some said they'd been killed on the battlefield, while others claimed to have seen them alive in captivity.

Emir Rashid then gathered a force so large that none of Daher's brigades would be able to defeat it, and led it out himself.

A number of Bani Saqr's men were sent out first to serve as a decoy. As they came rushing at the caravan, a number of Daher's men clashed with them. The two forces initially appeared to be equal in strength and number. But this situation didn't last long, as the fighters from Bani Saqr who had been lying in wait then launched a second, devastating surprise attack.

Yusuf and his men managed to retreat from the battlefield, leaving Saleh vulnerable to capture. Although he knew Saleh well, Rashid al-Jabr failed to realize at first what a prize had fallen into his hands.

Daher awaited his brother's return. He waited and waited, not imagining for a moment what had actually happened. When fear began to creep into his heart, he sent a message to Emir Rashid saying, "You've only waited this long because you want an exorbitant price for Saleh's head. So name your price."

Rashid al-Jabr replied to Daher's messenger, saying, "What I'm asking is greater than anything Daher might pay. Besides, someone richer than him has already bought him! This is what you can tell Daher when you go back to him."

The messenger returned with these words, words that terror had etched into his heart.

"So that's how it is. He's sold Saleh! If he's sold Saleh to someone who has more money than I do, let it be known to him that Daher alone owns Bani Saqr!"

Emir Rashid knew that if he wanted to deliver himself from the empire's wrath—a wrath that had grown more and more fearsome on account of Bani Saqr's raids in the past and their subsequent alliance with Daher—then Saleh was the best gift he could send to the governor of Damascus.

The news struck like a thunderbolt: the governor of Damascus had hanged Saleh.

Saleh's body had swung to and fro for a frightfully long time. He had twitched and convulsed, his bound feet searching desperately for something as solid as the air that had turned to stone in his lungs. Finding none, they fell into the darkness of eternity. About to suffocate, Daher woke up breathless, searching for a lungful of air.

"Let's teach Emir Rashid how many heads from Bani Saqr it takes to equal my brother Saleh's."

This was all Daher had to say as he swept through Bani Saqr's campgrounds like a storm of fire.

The attack was swift and sudden.

The first thing Daher did was attack Emir Rashid's tent. He bent down and pulled up the spear planted in front of its door, broke it, and flung it some distance away. It went flying through the air, and the moment it touched the ground, his soldiers rushed like a whirlwind into Bani Saqr's campgrounds.

In those bloody dawn hours, heads went flying in all directions before they could open their eyes to see what was happening.

Death descended like a stony cloud as broad as the sky, crushing everything beneath it.

Like the passing of a scythe through a bundle of grain stalks, the attack was quickly over. Daher told his fighting men, "We'll pass through their camp without stopping and come out the other side. I don't want a battle."

A stunned silence went wandering among the scattered corpses, the tents ripped to shreds, and the eyes that gaped, unbelieving, at what lay before them. A baby boy cried and a woman screamed at him to be quiet, not because he was crying, but because she hadn't yet been able to do what he was doing. As though they had lost their feet, the tribespeople just sat there staring in horror at the scene before them.

Two hours later, a woman realized what had happened. She screamed, and the entire plain filled with wails.

Back into the Labyrinth

ow we'll receive people's condolences," Daher announced.

People came in throngs from every direction, until it seemed there were as many horses in Tiberias as there were grains of sand along its lake. Then they vanished as though a storm wind had blown up and carried them away.

Throughout the days of the wake, Daher noticed something peculiar: whenever he looked over at his brothers Yusuf and Saad, he found them staring at him.

The silence between them was a vast dark space that not even a thousand lanterns could have illumined. Yet his brothers' glances made their way through the air and came to rest on his shoulder like some exotic bird.

Their eyes were opened wide as though they wanted to see something there could be no doubt about, a single fact they could believe. Instead, the night had swallowed up the day the way endless darkness swallows up the flame of a lantern. Everything had grown heavy, and the earth and their spirits closed in on their steps.

They shook hands as though they had never met before, and as though they would never meet again. The presence they felt wasn't only that of grief, nor of Saleh's spirit. Rather, they felt a multitude of spirits spinning about like a palm tree that had been uprooted by a whirlwind.

Suddenly, as Saad made his way to Arraba, he no longer wanted to be associated with anything in his past. He wanted to be free from everything: from the night, from the lanterns, from his brothers. When he reached home, he shouted at his wife to bring him three lanterns. When she was slow to respond, he shouted again.

She came in and placed the three lanterns in front of him. After emptying them into a small container, he poured some oil into the first lantern. Then he poured the same amount into the second and the third.

Since all of them needed to be lit simultaneously, he called for his wife and one of his sons. After each of them took a lantern, they lit them all at the same moment. Then he asked them to leave and close the door behind them.

The first lantern was his, the second was Yusuf's, and the third was Daher's. He stared at the three flames, which burned brightly without a care for anything but their delight in their ability to dispel the sea of darkness.

As night began to fall, he thought: *Why does night approach even though it knows it's going to end up dead on daylight's doorstep?*

For the first time Saad realized that each daytime is besieged by two nights, which close in on it from both directions at once so that they can swallow up all the secrets it's brought to light.

He wished the flames would start to flicker. Instead, they were as confident as three daytimes that no darkness could overcome.

Somewhere in the distance, Yusuf sat looking at three other lanterns. The darkness closed in on him from behind, while the lanterns before him emitted three beams that were as dazzling as they were vulnerable. There in that vast room, Yusuf seemed to shrivel up every time his lantern flame sputtered.

As Najma passed in front of the closed door, the light shone brightly through the crack beneath it as though there were a fire ablaze inside.

Forgetting herself, she stood there in silence, watching. When she heard the door behind her open and close, she came out of her reverie. She turned and saw Daher approaching. He was about to ask her why she was standing there alone in the middle of the night when he glimpsed the burning light emanating from under the door.

"So Yusuf's gone back to lighting our lanterns?" he asked.

Najma nodded.

He found himself looking involuntarily toward the mountains behind which Arraba lay hidden. Had he seen a light dancing, or had he just imagined it?

Taking her by the hand, he said, "I need sleep like I've never needed it before, Mother."

As she came away from the door with him, they were trailed by the light escaping from the crack beneath the door.

Najma woke before sunrise. The night lay in the courtyard in meek surrender, ready to accept whatever would happen to it within the coming hour.

She looked over at the door and saw a quivering light that grew fainter and fainter.

Suddenly it went out. She expected the door to open and Yusuf to come out. But he didn't.

Daher came up to her, light as a spirit, and squeezed her hand.

When Saad's wife woke, Saad wasn't beside her. She went outside and found him sitting on the doorstep. She wanted to ask him something, but he placed his finger on his lips in a signal for her not to utter a word.

Seeing all that night in his eyes, she went back inside.

After midday, Yusuf finally emerged, his eyes red and encircled by more than one night. As he passed Daher and Najma, he suddenly stopped and looked into Daher's face. He was about to say something, but thought better of it at the last moment.

He mounted his horse and left.

Saad and Yusuf sat in silence. Each of them wanted to begin the conversation, but neither of them dared say what was on his mind.

Finally Yusuf said to Saad, "I'd like to close my eyes for a while. Maybe I'll be able to sleep."

"You won't," Saad replied.

The Difficult Mission
and Fodder for the State

T he days passed heavily in Tiberias. The cruelty of the revenge
that had been inflicted couldn't ward off the specter of fear, since
everyone knew that Bani Saqr were, in the end, Bani Saqr, and
that they wouldn't let the recent bloodshed go unrequited.

However, everything passed without incident.

Their raids came to an end, and Daher managed to annex still more
villages to his realm of jurisdiction.

Emir Rashid awaited the arrival of his reward from Damascus. It was
late in coming. Just as he was about to give up hope, a battalion of soldiers sent by the governor of Sidon arrived.

Emir Rashid received them enthusiastically, searching in their hands
for his gift. However, he found none. He looked for it in their mouths,
but they remained closed.

The soldiers made the rounds of the camp the way they usually did.
They counted up the cows, the horses, and the camels the way they
usually did, and on the last day they informed the emir how much he
owed in taxes.

Emir Rashid was dumbfounded.

"Is that my reward?" he asked, incredulous. "I show you my loyalty
and send you the head of my enemy's brother, and this is all I get in
return?"

"You sent a gift, sir. And to our knowledge, generous folk don't
expect gifts in return for their gifts."

"So that's the way it is?"

"Unless you have some other perspective to offer!"

"No, you've spoken truly. You've spoken truly!"

He left them in his guesthouse and, without delay, told his men,
"Give them the fodder the state demands!"

The sultan's messenger reached Damascus from Istanbul bearing a decree removing Abdullah Pasha from his post, and on Thursday, the eighth of Ramadan, Sulayman Pasha commenced his duties as governor of Damascus. He entered the city without fanfare from the direction of Salihiya, and when the city's notables, clerks, and muftis learned of his arrival, they hurriedly came out to receive him.

When the news reached Tiberias, Daher realized there was no time to lose.

Watfa', Emir Qa'dan's mother, took four spears, planted them in the ground, and draped her cloak over them. When Emir Rashid, just back from a raid, saw her, he approached and asked her what had prompted her to do what she'd done. She made no reply. He pressed her, which was precisely what she was after. Rather than have to go present her demand to the emir himself, she wanted everyone to see her and feel her anger. With men circling around her in astonishment, she spoke about the way Bani Saqr had been scattered and weakened and what Emir Rashid had done to Saleh. She hadn't forgotten the seriousness of what Daher had done. However, she pointed to the goodness of Daher's heart and the need for Bani Saqr to speak to him and win his approval, and to pledge to put the past behind them and restore their former alliance.

Emir Rashid refused. "Do you expect me to be reconciled to him after what he did to us?"

"Yes, you're going to forgive him. You were the first to commit a wrong, and the worst offender is always the one who offended first. You'll write to him what I tell you to!"

Three days later, a messenger sent by Emir Rashid reached Tiberias with a letter for Daher.

This was the last thing anyone in Tiberias would have expected.

Daher read the letter. Then he took a deep breath and said to the messenger, "They're welcome to come."

Daher handed the letter to his brother Yusuf. Yusuf read it, but said nothing.

"What's happening, Sheikh?" asked the judge.

After looking over at Daher and hearing no reply, Yusuf handed the letter to the judge. The judge read it, but said nothing.

"Can anyone explain to us what's happening here?" exclaimed the imam. "What does the letter say?"

The judge handed the letter to the imam. The letter was then passed around among everyone present until it came to rest again in Daher's hands.

Everyone in the diwan sat staring at everyone else without saying a word.

After everyone but Daher had left the diwan, Yusuf remained seated. Daher gave him a long look, then sat down again.

"What is it that you want to say, Yusuf?"

"Are you prepared to receive Bani Saqr when they have our brother's blood on their hands?"

"You should look first at our hands, which are covered with their blood!"

Yusuf made no reply.

"I know Bani Saqr are bound to be my enemies. But when they ask to be my allies again, I have to agree."

"And what obliges you to do that, Sheikh?" Yusuf asked, doing his best to keep his anger in check.

"What matters most, Yusuf! What matters most!"

"And could anything matter more than your brother's blood?"

"There will always be something that matters more than our brother's blood, and more than our own blood: this land, Yusuf. This land!"

Daher took a deep breath. Then he said, "Let us receive them more graciously than we've ever received anyone before."

Today, Yesterday,
and Tomorrow

"I miss little Daher and Umar, Bishr. I want to see them!"

"And they want to see their grandfather."

"What grandfather?"

"You! You're their grandfather, Sheikh Daher!"

"How can I be their grandfather when I'm only two or three years older than you, Bishr?"

"You're our sheikh, Sheikh Daher. And as long as that's the case, you're a lot older than Bishr!"

"So be it, then. Now take me to them!"

"How can Bishr take you to them just like that? We've got to get ready for a visit like this, Sheikh!"

"Bishr, you just told me I was their grandfather and turned me into an old man, which I can forgive you for. But for you to tell me that you have to get ready for a visit from me—*that* I can't forgive! Is this the way a grandfather visits his grandchildren's house?"

"No, it isn't. You're right, Sheikh. So let's get going."

They mounted their horses and set off.

When Najma had been alone with Daher the night before, she had said to him, "Be honest with me now. Is the problem with you, or with Nafisa?"

"Believe me, Mother, there's nothing wrong with me."

"Everything's all right with you as a man?"

"Do I seem less than a man to you?"

"No, of course not. But I had to ask. I asked Nafisa the same question and she told me the problem was with her. But I didn't believe her. She loves you, Daher!"

"And that's what causes me such torment."

"You need a son, Daher. You also need a woman. So it makes no sense for you to be here and for her to be in Nazareth. I know you insist on her being there. But your occasional visits to her aren't enough."

"You know I wouldn't break her heart by taking another wife."

"We're not getting anywhere, then. All this talk has been for nothing!"

Tiberias looked tranquil, pristine, and powerful on that bright autumn day. The scent of the lake wafted through the streets, prompting house-holders to open their windows wide.

Bishr sat perched hawk-like atop his horse. His sparse beard had grown out slightly and turned a bit gray. Daher's beard, though graying like Bishr's, was bushy, and his moustache was long and thick.

Glancing over at Bishr, Daher saw a new person. *How horses have changed that boy,* he thought, *and how much more they're going to change him!*

Daher had often thought of Bishr as his son rather than as his friend. He was so innocent and pure, he could have lived and died a little boy. At the same time, Daher realized that innocence and purity alone wouldn't enable him to meet life's challenges.

Bishr was his son who would have to grow up and become a man. But there was also Ghazala, a delicate yet stern woman who deserved to be nothing less than a queen. When Ghazala saw Daher for the first time in Tiberias, she said to him, "No harm can come to Bishr as long as he's with you, Sheikh Daher. So now I can stop worrying about him and pay attention to the children!"

Daher stopped in front of a small grocer's shop. As the shop owner rushed out to greet him, Daher gestured to him as if to say, "I'll be right there!"

Seeing Bishr start to dismount, Daher came up to him and said, "What did I tell you?" He sat up straight again in the saddle and began surveying the city with the eyes of a hawk.

Daher bought Bishr's boys some sweets and Damascus-made jellies that had become popular in Tiberias, Nazareth, and elsewhere.

"Let's be going," he said to Bishr.

Invitations from Afar

Daher couldn't allow himself to go to the lake. Hence, he contented himself with gazing at it from the top of the wall as he oversaw his various construction projects. One day he stood for a long time in the southern tower, lost in thought. Even his beloved boulder hadn't afforded him such a panoramic view. Nevertheless, he continued to see in it a throne for his soul that he dared not try to reclaim.

What he feared most was that he might go to the shore and, in spite of himself, begin looking for that grave. He had been largely freed from the burden of the blood he'd once shed at that spot. Even so, he was afraid he might go and find that girl without her braids!

When he received the second cloak, he didn't know what to do with it. It was as though he'd forgotten that cloaks were simply made to be worn.

He sat pondering it. He suspected that it possessed some extraordinary power, since it seemed to struggle to free itself from his grip so that it could wear *him*. Was it because of the way it smelled? Perhaps. He sniffed it at length in the darkness after putting out the lantern. It was the first time he'd realized that the sense of smell is only perfected in the dark, where vision is excluded, allowing the nose to take over for the eyes.

Daher was almost certain that she'd put it on before sending it. Or maybe she'd wrapped herself in it. On the other hand, the scent of the braid alone might have been sufficient to saturate the cloak with all those invitations from afar, with all those words that had never been spoken.

That night when he'd come home, he had felt afraid. It was as though he had expected Nafisa to be there waiting for him. He knew, of course, that she would have been able to sense what lay hidden in a new cloak that had been brought into her house by frightened hands. However, the person he encountered there was Najma, who surprised him the next morning with the words, "Whether you hide it or not, it's wearing you!"

Daher was taken aback. He knew that Najma's intuitive capacities were even sharper than her eyesight. As old age began bowing others' backs, topping their heads with hoary crowns, she had gone on standing straight as a palm tree.

"Go get married, Daher."

"Whom should I marry?"

"Anyone you wish—anyone, that is, except the girl who sent you the cloak. You've still got a long road ahead of you that you won't be able to travel if you're tethered to a peg driven deep into the shore of Lake Tiberias."

"We've had this conversation before, and the subject is closed. I've told you: I won't break Nafisa's heart by taking another wife."

"Nafisa is coming, Daher."

"Coming where?"

"Here. To Tiberias."

"But I haven't sent for her."

"I haven't sent for her either, but believe me, she's coming!"

"When?"

"I don't know. Maybe today, tomorrow, day after tomorrow. But she's coming."

Daher picked up the cloak the way one picks up a baby and began making circles around himself, not knowing whether to throw it in the lake together with the two braids, or what. He folded it and placed the two braids inside it. Then he spread out the brown muffler that had been wrapped around his head and placed everything on top of it. He gathered it up, tied it with a firm knot, and called out, "Yusuf! Hide this for me with your things! I don't want anyone to see it. And if I ask you for it some day, don't give it to me even if I beg you."

"If you don't want it, then why should you hide it with my things, Sheikh? Just burn it!"

"There are things that mustn't be consumed by fire, Yusuf, and this is one of them."

Daher hoped the second braid would be the last. He wondered whether he would recognize her if he happened to see her on the streets of Tiberias after so long. He couldn't say for sure. At the same time, he feared that he might find himself face to face with her some day without being able to remember what she looked like.

It was a clear day, and Daher stood looking out at the lake until he thought he could see Samkh on the lake's southernmost edge. When he looked back at the shore, he saw fishermen returning from their night's work. He descended the wall and came up to them. It gave him pleasure to buy fish from them when they came back to shore in the mornings. They gathered along the beach near the remains of an old wall and emptied their baskets.

There were huge quantities of fish: Tiberian tilapia, which people referred to as St. Peter's fish, carp, bolti, a good number of Zill's tilapia, Galilean tilapia, orange roughy, and tiny fish the size of sardines.

"I know what you want, Sheikh Daher," one of the fisherman said.

"So you know just what to do!"

"Will this be enough, or shall I add some more?"

"Add a few more. We have company coming today. Now, tell me: How much will that be? And I don't want to have the same conversation we've had so many times before. You say, 'This is my gift to you!' and I say, 'This is what you've earned to take home to your children.'"

"Sheikh Daher, you've given us a bit of heaven on earth, and you want us to make you pay for a few fish?"

"Here we go again! Didn't I tell you?"

"All right, then, two piasters will do. Or is that too much?"

"I told you, this is what you've earned to take home to your children. Don't deprive them of their share. Here are four piasters."

"But that's too much, Sheikh. Much too much!"

"Don't forget that the empire is one of your children, and it's going to gobble up one of those four piasters. Isn't that so?"

"Believe me, Sheikh, I save up more for the empire than I do for any of my children!"

"Be patient. It won't be much longer."

A Shamefaced Little Girl Picking at Her Food

When she saw the quantity of fish Daher had brought, Najma smiled and said, "I was afraid you didn't believe me any more."

"And who wouldn't believe Najma? But haven't you seen anything else you'd like to tell me about?"

"When I do, I'll let you know! Right now, though, all I see is that pile of fish you've brought home. I'm going to make the best sayyadiya anybody's tasted this side of the lake!"

"Why don't you let someone else cook, Mother?"

"You know what, Sheikh? I love your modesty and lack of pretense. It shows in the house you live in, the clothes you wear, and the way you speak. So don't deprive me of the best thing about you!"

Najma tried to postpone the meal for as long as she could. She would pop in to see Daher and Yusuf from time to time, saying, "Just a little while and it'll be done!" After the "little while" had passed she would come back and say something like, "Why didn't you think to invite Bishr and his family, Daher? They love sayyadiya!"

"Don't worry," Daher replied. "Nothing's too hard for Ghazala. I ate it at their house once."

"But it isn't like the sayyadiya I make!"

"Nobody could compete with your cooking, Mother. I'll back that statement up with ten fingerprints, not just one!"

"And why would you need to put your fingerprints on it when you could write the document yourself and sign it?"

Daher chuckled, but his chuckle died away as the thought of Saleh's absence flitted through his mind.

There was a touch of gaiety in everything Najma said. However, she only allowed it to show in front of Daher and his brothers. If even a hen passed by as she was about to say something droll, she would shoo it away, and keep her words to herself until after it was gone.

She had no choice in the end but to serve the food.

While the others dug in, starving, she picked at her food like a shame-faced little child.

"I know she'll be here. You eat now."

"So you still believe what I said?" she asked him.

"And whom could I believe more than I believe you, Mother?"

"Believe your desire to have a son!"

"Here we go again, Mother! Do you want me to leave the table?"

"No! I'll eat with you, and you won't finish before I do."

"You embarrassed me yesterday, Nafisa! How could you have been late?" Najma asked in mock reproach.

"I didn't know we had an appointment to keep! Did someone tell you I was coming, Auntie?"

"No, no one told me. My heart was saying you'd be here yesterday, but you arrived today instead."

"What matters is that she's here," said Daher.

"We passed through Arraba, and your brother Saad insisted that we spend the night at his house, since the six-hour journey from Nazareth to Tiberias isn't easy!" Nafisa explained.

"So that's why! Saad was the reason. He's always the reason! I'm just sorry you missed the sayyadiya I'd fixed for you yesterday, and since it's nearly afternoon, it's too late in the day to buy more fish. But that's all right. I'll make it for you tomorrow."

"Well, that depends on Sheikh Daher. If he agrees to the request I've come to make, we'll eat. If not, things will be different!" Nafisa declared as she stepped inside.

"Do you know what she's come for?" Daher asked Najma.

"Believe me: even if I knew—and I don't—I wouldn't tell you, since I would never come between a man and his wife! Why don't you ask her yourself?"

"I won't ask her until after I've come back from Jaddin."

The Ruse

When a number of elders from the villages surrounding Jaddin came to Tiberias seeking Daher's help, he looked behind him. It was as if he felt someone pushing him to take the next step. Safad suddenly passed before his mind's eye with its impregnable, towering ancient fortresses, many of which dated back to Crusader times. He paused, gazing at the Jaddin fortress that had withstood onslaughts by so many before him. The mountainous region in southern Lebanon known as Mount Amel also passed through his mind.

Feeling that he had already made sufficient use of the injustices people were suffering to justify his expanding influence, he tried to think of a pretext to attack Jaddin other than the fact that these elders had sought him out. But he found none.

A few days after the elders of Jaddin had departed, Yusuf stormed in and announced, "Some of our servants have run away!"

Bishr and a number of other men mounted their horses to go out and bring them back.

"Let them go," Daher told them. "No matter how far away they get, they'll still be in my hand!"

Everyone knew what the elders of Jaddin had done. They also knew that Ahmad al-Hussein, the feudal lord who wielded control over the fortress, had flown into a rage when he learned that they had sought Daher's assistance, and had punished them by ordering them to pay twice their usual taxes.

The runaway servants had sought refuge in the Jaddin castle, and Daher sent a politely worded letter to Ahmad al-Hussein, requesting that he send them back. He refused. When Daher sent another letter, Ahmad al-Hussein replied with a message reviling Daher and threatening to extirpate him from God's land.

Daher began by marshalling a force of fifteen hundred men from in and around Tiberias. The force also included men belonging to

Bani Saqr, who were eager to win Daher's approval. After giving them the training they would need to storm the fortress, Daher sent Ahmad al-Hussein a message no less fearsome than the one he'd received from him. The message infuriated Ahmad al-Hussein so thoroughly that, had he not known how difficult it would be to march on Tiberias without permission from the empire, he would have set out forthwith and attacked the city.

In the space of two days the governor of Sidon received two letters. The first was from Sheikh Ahmad al-Hussein, who had written requesting the pasha's permission to wage war on Daher, and the second, from Daher, was a duplicate of the first.

After giving the matter some thought, the pasha gathered his men and asked them how to resolve the conundrum. Some of them suggested that he go out against both of them to teach them a lesson. Others suggested that he wage war only on Daher, who, from the time he set foot in Tiberias, had spread his influence as widely as he could. Still others suggested that the pasha send someone out to make peace between the two men, since wars always made it more difficult for the empire to collect the taxes people owed.

The pasha listened without speaking to everything his advisors had to say. Then he got up and cried, "Call the stenographer!" There entered a young man with a comely appearance and a delicate manner who took his place at a table inlaid with colorful mother-of-pearl. With an elegant flourish he spread out his papers, and with a flourish even more elegant, unsheathed his pen. Then he turned his gaze courteously toward the pasha as if to say, "I'm ready, sir!"

In the first letter, which was addressed to Sheikh Ahmad al-Hussein, the pasha instructed the recipient to wage war on "this Daher" and to teach him a lesson. Then he told the stenographer, "Address the second letter to Daher al-Umar," and headed for the door. The stenographer followed the pasha out, saying, "And what shall I say to him, Your Excellency?"

Casting a sweeping glance at his men, the pasha said, "The same things we said to Ahmad al-Hussein!"

The stenographer stood there motionless, amazed that he was being asked to write the very same letter to two opponents.

"When you've finished the letters, bring them to me for my signature," the pasha instructed him. Then he left.

Ahmad al-Hussein was so delighted with the letter that he read it aloud. Daher was no less delighted with the missive addressed to him.

The two armies moved quickly.

"This is your first war, Bishr. Let's return from it victorious. If we're defeated, we'll have no hope of waging another one for a long time."

"Victory will be ours, God willing, Sheikh."

When Daher's army reached Bi'na, he felt an ache inside. The distance separating him from events of the past suddenly collapsed, and he found himself saying over and over, "God have mercy on them!" It was as though the town's chief elder, his son Abbas, and the rest of his family had been slain only moments before.

Daher wondered: *Is it a coincidence that I'm waging this war before their very eyes?*

With the Jaddin fortress before him and Bi'na's victims behind him, he could feel their gazes burning holes in his back.

Sheikh Ahmad al-Hussein saw Daher as nothing but a petty rival he could crush without being obliged to seek refuge in the fortress that surrounded the entire village of Jaddin.

"He's come of his own accord, asking for us to defeat him! So show him no mercy! Will they last an hour against us?"

"Not even half an hour!" shouted his soldiers excitedly.

"Will they last an hour against us?"

"Not even half an hour!" his soldiers roared.

"Less than half an hour it will be, then. We've taken a vow!"

He gave the signal to set out, and they poured through the huge gate like a raging stream.

"We've come here to achieve victory and nothing less!" Daher addressed his soldiers in a resounding voice. "Men such as you, who know the meaning of justice, won't allow their mothers, their sisters, their fathers, their brothers, and their children to go on living under tyranny. Many of you have come complaining to me about the injustice you've suffered at the hands of your multazims, and I've come to your aid. Now it's time for you to come to the aid of the people of Jaddin and surrounding villages who have appealed to us for protection. Every morsel of bread snatched away from others in this land is a morsel taken from you, and every handful of wheat or sesame stolen from these people has been stolen from you. We refuse to return to our wives, our daughters, and our sisters to tell them that we were less than men. From the moment we stepped outside Tiberias, we swore that injustice and degradation would have no place where we set our feet, that fear would have no place where our hearts beat, that ugliness would have no place where we cast our eyes, and that human dignity would no longer be trampled where we wield our swords and exercise our wills. Let us return to our homes free men, having made this plain a place of justice and security!"

Daher turned and looked at the army that filled the plain on the other side. Then he raised his sword and said, "Onward now, to teach them the meaning of justice!"

Daher took off on his horse, and his men charged after him, the plain convulsing beneath them. Gazelles began fleeing and birds fluttered away at the army's approach. Meanwhile, from the other side, Ahmad al-Hussein was advancing with all his might to keep his promise to his soldiers.

It was no easy battle. Half an hour passed. An hour passed. As still another hour passed, spears and swords dripped with blood beneath the noonday sun, which halted in the middle of the sky, not knowing which way to go in the face of such horror. Heads and arms flew, and the air whistled through bodies riddled with wounds. Bullets found their way easily to their prey, which went flying through the air off horses' backs, shaking the earth beneath them like huge stones.

As the battle entered its third hour, the two armies merged into a single mass and time ground to a halt, moving neither back nor forward.

As for Bishr, he was like a bumblebee, twirling deftly this way and that and attacking in all directions. When he glimpsed Ahmad al-Hussein in his ornate attire, he made his way over to him, his sword fluttering like a fan and mowing down whoever blocked his path.

Ahmad al-Hussein, surprised by this half-naked soldier with a body so small that the slightest breeze might have blown him away, lunged at him. But when their swords met, everything changed. Al-Hussein realized that he was up against a formidable foe. They engaged in two rounds so fleeting that al-Husseini's soldiers had no opportunity to intervene. Then al-Hussein made a failed strike that sent his sword flying, and before he could recover it from the bloodstained air, Bishr's sword was sinking into his chest.

Bishr quickly withdrew the sword and swung it again at his neck. However, the move was blocked by a host of drawn blades. The next moment everything was over. Al-Hussein's body fell limp onto his horse's neck and a cry rang out, shaking the entire plain: "Ahmad al-Hussein is dead! Ahmad al-Hussein is dead!"

Silence prevailed, and time took its first step away from the lake of blood.

Jaddin's army scattered, and its remaining soldiers began to withdraw. Realizing that if he didn't reach the city gate with his men before his opponents did, he'd face a major problem, Daher ordered the fortress occupied without delay.

Though many had been killed on both sides, the number of Daher's soldiers multiplied with the victory that had been won. He feared that the people of Jaddin would close the city gate, leaving the two armies to fight to the last man. This didn't happen, however, since the people of Jaddin felt no less wronged than the people of the surrounding villages, and when the first defeated soldier arrived back at the fortress, he found those inside the walls cheering, "Long live Daher!"

That day saw the birth of a new era that was destined for a long life.

Daher refused to meet with the elders of Jaddin in Ahmad al-Hussein's sumptuous home.

"This house belonged to him and his family," he said, "and I won't set foot inside a household that's suffered the loss of its head."

After promising them fair treatment and protection against anyone who might seek to oppress them and rob them of their hard-earned sustenance, he gathered with the village elders in a house not far from Ahmad al-Hussein's mansion.

As he spoke, one of the elders broke in, "This is what we would have expected from you, Sheikh Daher. Besides, you should know that this war isn't one we chose ourselves. It was waged against you on orders from the governor of Sidon!"

"Rather, it was waged against *you* on his orders!"

The elder reached into his pocket and brought out a letter. "Here, Sheikh Daher. Read this. It seems you'll have to see it before you'll believe us."

Nonplussed, Daher produced the letter the governor of Sidon had written to him and spread it out before them.

There was a stunned silence.

"If I were you, Daher, I'd march on Sidon right now and kill that bloody pasha myself," his brother Yusuf said.

Thinking about what Yusuf had said, Daher looked into the distance as though the walls had disappeared from before him.

"It seems you didn't hear me, Sheikh Daher."

"I heard you, Yusuf. I heard you. But I have something else in mind."

To Yusuf's amazement, Daher summoned his stenographer and dictated a letter to the governor of Sidon, informing him that he had seized Jaddin and pledging to pay all the taxes the city owed the empire without delay. He promised that, like Tiberias, Jaddin would be obedient to both the governor and the sultan. After signing and stamping the letter, he said, "Let a messenger set out with it tomorrow morning. But before he leaves let him come to see me. I want to give him a gift to take to His Excellency the pasha."

With the defeated soldiers standing in a long queue, Bishr came up to Daher. Before he uttered a word, Daher embraced him and said, "Today was your day, Bishr. Now, what did you come to tell me?"

"The captives are ready," Bishr said.

"Have you treated them with respect?"

"Absolutely, Sheikh."

"During the battle I noticed a dark-skinned young man who fought me with amazing skill. Do you know which one I'm talking about?"

"No I don't, Sheikh. Maybe you'll recognize him when you see him."

"Let's be going. We don't want to leave them standing in this hot sun and make them feel all the more defeated."

"You're worried about their feelings when they were all prepared to kill you?"

"You were prepared to kill them too, Bishr! Why do you remember that they were prepared to kill me, but forget that I was prepared to kill them? Don't defeat someone twice, Bishr. The first time you defeat him, he understands that you've defeated him as a soldier, but the second time you defeat him as a human being, and that, he'll never forgive you for!"

Before he reached the long queue, Daher recognized the young man and came up to him. This was the valiant warrior he had asked Bishr about.

Daher nodded and said to him, "You fought bravely. I can attest to that! What's your name?"

"My name is Ahmad al-Dankizli, my lord."

"If you want us to get along, then don't call me 'my lord.' I don't like lords one bit!"

"What should I call you, then?" he asked hesitantly.

"'Sheikh.' Call me 'Sheikh Daher.'"

"Very well, Sheikh."

"Where are you from?"

"Morocco."

"You know, Ahmad, that I didn't come here to wage war on you."

"I know that, Sheikh. But in order to be true to my leader, I had to wage war on you!"

"And that's no fault of yours, Ahmad. But now your leader is dead, and I bear witness that you defended him and fought for him as no other soldier did."

"God knows I gave it everything I had."

"In recognition of your bravery, I'm going to propose something to you, Ahmad. It's a proposal I wouldn't have made if it weren't for your obvious loyalty to your leader."

"What might that be, Sheikh?"

"I propose that you choose some of the other Moroccan fighters here and form a brigade that will be under your command. Later you can also choose men from in and around Tiberias. I want to have a standing army, and I want you to be its commander. So, what do you say?"

"If someone treats me, a former enemy, with this much respect, he's bound to treat me with even greater respect now that I'm on his side. I agree to your proposal, Sheikh, and I promise to be your right-hand man as long as I live."

"Very well, then, Ahmad. You can get started right away. You'll be responsible for these prisoners. Decide which ones you want to serve in your brigade, and which ones you want to release."

As the two men walked away, Bishr said to him, "Couldn't you have tested his loyalty before putting a sword in his hand again, Sheikh?"

"We haven't got time to put people to the test, Bishr. Besides, haven't you noticed that the worst disappointments sometimes come from the people you've tested the most?"

Daher turned and looked back at the dark-skinned soldier, who had set about his task at once, and smiled. Little did he know what role this young man was destined to play in his life!

Before leaving Jaddin, Daher left explicit instructions that no one was to lay hands on its slain sheikh's wealth or possessions, and that his family should receive a regular pension in keeping with their status in the community. Then he asked Yusuf to bring him the servants who had fled.

"Will you have them killed, Sheikh?"

"On the contrary, I'm going to reward them. After all, they're the ones whose loyalty decided this battle!"

Daher gazed at Tiberias from a distance, captivated by the sight of it. Remembering that Nafisa was waiting for him in the city, he prodded his horse, wondering what ulterior motive had brought her there.

An Easier Request,
and a More Difficult One

I 've come with two requests, Sheikh Daher. One's in my hand, and one's in my heart. Which should I start with?"

"You always make choices so hard for me, Nafisa! Start with whichever one you want, but preferably with the easier one."

"All right, then, I'll start with the easier one," she said. She reached under the cushion she was sitting on, brought out some papers, and handed them to him.

Daher took them, looking at her quizzically.

"What are these?" he asked.

"Read them and you'll see."

He unfolded the papers and began reading them. As he read, he nodded. He set the first paper aside and kept reading, nodding the entire time. He handed them to Najma and she began reading, but she didn't nod as he had. Rather, she approached the task like someone who downs an entire pitcher of water in a single gulp.

When she had finished, she looked at Daher.

"Did you say this was the easy request?" Daher asked Nafisa.

"Yes, this is the easy one."

"For me to march on Nazareth and declare myself its multazim?"

"That's right. The letter I brought you is from the notables of the city, both Muslims and Christians. They can no longer bear the way their multazims and the sheikhs of Nablus oppress them. When sheikhs from Nablus buy things from residents of Nazareth, they make them feel as though they're doing them a favor if they pay what the merchandise is worth. And sometimes they don't pay at all! They might just say, 'I'll pay you for it during the next season,' and the people of Nazareth don't dare question them."

"But I still don't know what they're going to say in Sidon and Damascus about my becoming multazim in Jaddin!"

"In any case, this is what they're asking. They promise to be your army, and I believe them. I saw some of them when they brought me the letter after hearing that I was coming to see you."

"And the second request?"

"You still haven't given me your reply to the first!" Nafisa exclaimed.

"What do you think, Mother?"

"I can see you there already! As far as I'm concerned, it's simply a question of whether you'll do it now or later."

"So you agree to the idea?"

"I know you've come a long way, and I know you're not going to stop."

"There wouldn't be any point to what I've done so far if I stopped."

"So I say: go there, take it over, and become its new multazim."

"Now!" added Nafisa.

"No, not now. I always say, 'If you can get somewhere walking, don't run!'"

Daher fell silent for a long time as though he were planning things out in his head. Then he said, "Now we come to the second request. I just hope you won't reach under the cushion and bring out a letter like this from the people of Istanbul!" And he laughed.

"Now that you've agreed to the first request, the second one shouldn't be difficult," Nafisa said.

"I'm listening."

Despite her best efforts not to, Nafisa looked over at Najma. Then she took a deep breath and said, "I want you to get married!" There followed an entire minute of silence like none that household had ever witnessed before.

"Is this your idea or my mother's?" Daher wanted to know.

"It was my idea," Nafisa insisted. "In fact, I arranged everything myself before I came!"

"I don't understand."

"I've found you a bride in Nazareth."

"You?"

"Yes, me! That's better than your having to go look for one yourself."

"But I don't want to get married!"

"You may not need another wife. But you do need children, and so do I. So, since God hasn't enabled me to have any myself, you'll have to father them with someone else so that they can be my children too. It's something I have the right to ask of you!"

"Have you spoken with her family?"

"Even if I hadn't, I would know this was what they wanted. You can't imagine what a special place you have in the hearts of the people of Nazareth. You've seen them yourself, Sheikh, and you know how much they love you."

"Let me think about it."

"What's there to think about?" Najma interjected. Then she added, "Within moments you'd drawn up a plan to take over Nazareth, and now you say you can't decide whether to get married?"

"You agree with Nafisa, then?"

"I wouldn't have wanted to have to side with her on an issue like this, since she's my daughter. But now that she's made the decision on her own, I support her, since you're my child too!"

"And have you forgotten that lantern of mine that went out? Who's going to raise them if something happens to me?"

"Daher, I realize you're not my biological son. However, I did raise you. For years you've been close as close can be to this heart of mine, and I understand you well. So, for my sake, dear heart, don't go back to talking about the lanterns!"

"All right, then."

"So you agree? How could you agree so easily?" cried Nafisa in mock anger.

"Come on now!" Daher protested.

"Nafisa," Najma reminded her, "don't forget that you're the one who opened this door, so you've got to be prepared for anything—not just the gentle breezes, but the storm winds too."

"You're scaring me, Mother! You're going to make me change my mind!"

"But Daher isn't going to change his mind now. You planted the seed, and within moments it's grown into a tree. Isn't that right, Daher?"

He made no reply.

"Whatever happens," said Nafisa, "nothing would make me happier than to see your children in my arms. That's why I needed to choose the bride myself, because I want her to feel that her children are my children too. And now: what will you write to the people of Nazareth?"

The Difficult Request,
and the Still More Difficult One

A nd now," said Daher to al-Dankizli as he sat beside him, his eye on his soldiers in the field, "it's time to take care of something we've ignored for too long!"

"You're frightening me, Sheikh! Has something happened?"

"A lot has happened, Ahmad. And I regret to inform you that you haven't noticed!"

"Me? I was born with eyes all over my body, Sheikh!"

"And that's what concerns me, because you still haven't seen what you ought to see with all those eyes of yours."

"Tell me what it is, Sheikh, and you'll see that I do see."

"What good would that do, if you haven't seen what you ought to see on your own? I've beaten you to it, even though all I have is these two eyes in my head!"

"Allow me to disagree with you for the first time, Sheikh Daher. I have yet to meet anyone whose eyes are inside of him the way yours are. So it doesn't surprise me that you would have so much insight when all we have is eyesight."

"In any case, Ahmad, I won't keep you guessing: I want to find you a wife!"

"Find me a wife?"

"That's right!"

"But I have a concubine who's precious to me, and since the first time I saw her I've had eyes for no one else."

"So that's the secret behind your blindness! You've seen her more than you should! Marry her, then, if you love her that much. You haven't told me her name."

"The moment I saw her, I named her Amira—Princess. So, as you might have guessed, I *have* proposed to her."

"Do you mean she refused?"

"Yes, she refused!"

"Strange! But you're commander of an army now. My army! So I don't think she would refuse if you proposed to her again."

"I did, as soon as we got to Tiberias."

"So give her a choice: either she marries you, or you marry someone else."

"Both these choices would be hard, for me and for her. If she still refused to marry me, I don't know what I'd do."

"If it came to that, the Solver of All Problems would show you the solution. But I don't think she'll refuse again."

"If you don't mind my asking, Sheikh: Why are you so adamant about this?"

"Because I want to see your children. I want them to plant you here among us forever. I want you to feel that this country is your country, which in fact it is. I want you to feel that you have family and friends here, and for your sons to have friends, wives, and children of their own in this country. No matter how large an army becomes, Ahmad, it can never be a family, and no matter how high one's rank and lofty one's mansions, they can never shelter you the way a household can."

As the sun's red disk descended behind a thick cloud, soldiers filled the plain, horses galloped, and horsemen practiced their maneuvers. But the scene was charged with silence. However captivated he might be by such a sight, Ahmad al-Dankizli could no longer see anything in it but a masterfully done still life. It was nothing but a vast open space embodying an old memory.

The Silence Within

He thought about all the ways he could avoid hurting Nafisa's feelings: keeping the wedding as simple and discreet as possible, for example, and spiriting the bride away from Nazareth to Arraba, then to Tiberias.

But Nafisa would have none of it. "I want you to spend at least a week in my house. Otherwise I will have gotten everything ready for nothing! I don't want anyone to think that you're running away from me with your bride! I want people to know that this is happening with my knowledge and approval. So please, don't hurt me by leaving for Tiberias like this."

"Nafisa," Daher pleaded, "I can't spend my wedding night with you in the next room. How could I?"

"This is all I'm asking, Daher."

"You're making things hard for me, and for yourself as well."

"No, it won't be hard for me. If it were going to be hard, I wouldn't have gone and chosen Badriya specially to be your new bride."

One evening Badriya arrived at Nafisa's house mounted on a mare.

Nafisa led the procession, clutching the mare's reins and singing a song Najma had taught her:

> Joy has made this house into two.
> It's caused my eyes to see hope anew.
> Badriya, there's none lovelier than you,
> My soul mate till the end!
>
> From Tiberias to the sea in the west
> You're matchless, my dear, you're the best.
> Your name outshines all the rest,
> My guiding star and friend!

Hearing nothing behind her, Nafisa turned and found Daher raising his hand in a request for silence.

"Why aren't you singing?" she asked, and began repeating the ditty.

Stepping forward, Daher took the mare's reins in one hand and Nafisa's right hand in the other. Then they entered the gate, followed by Najma, Saad's wife, Ghazala, and Daher's sister Shamma.

Barefoot as usual, Najma began dancing about in front of him like a little girl. He had thought of asking her to put on some shoes, at least for this occasion, but had decided to save his breath!

That night, as he had expected, all he could get himself to do was to lift the veil that concealed his bride's face, since he felt as though his entire being were in Nafisa's room.

Badriya was beautiful, and at least ten years his junior. He reached out and caressed her face, then gestured to her to go sit on the bed. Timidly observing the trajectory of his hand, she went and sat so close to the edge of the bed that she nearly fell off.

It was the first time Daher had seen this bed. He couldn't recall seeing anything like it before. It was so huge, a groom might have lost his bride in it! However, he was sure that Nafisa, who had had it brought all the way from Damascus and had made a point of showing it off to the neighbor ladies, wouldn't have wanted such a thing to happen.

Banishing all his thoughts as though they were another wall that had been erected between him and Nafisa's room, he listened for some sound. However, he encountered nothing but silence and the gaze of his bride, who knew what he was thinking, and who could sense that he was somewhere else.

Najma sat in the spacious courtyard under a heavily laden orange tree. Having received the last of the sun's rays, its fruits looked themselves like scores of enchanting little suns, and for a moment she feared that if she reached out and picked one of them, night would suddenly fall.

She heard a door shut. She turned. Without her noticing, Nafisa had gotten up from beside her and disappeared inside her room. From inside the other room, Daher heard a door close, and froze even more completely.

209

Nafisa wept in silence.

When Najma looked over at the room's closed door, she thought she saw tears gushing out from under it. She knew that this moment belonged to Nafisa alone, and that no one had the right to violate it with so much as a look or a question.

Night fell.

"You go find your children and husbands," Najma said to Shamma, Ghazala, and the bride's mother.

"And what about you, Auntie?" asked Ghazala.

"I should have brought some of Tiberias's warmth with me so that I could spend the night here under this tree. But don't worry. My bed's ready inside!"

When Daher came out, he went and knocked on Najma's door. Her voice came: "Do you think I'm a bride who shuts the door on herself till this hour of the morning? Come in!"

As Daher stood there pondering her, she said, "Why are you looking at me that way?"

"You know what, Mother? I'm going to tell you something, and I hope you won't be angry with me!"

"I think I know what you want to say. I can see it in your eyes!"

"What is it, then?"

"Say it, and if it's what I think it is, I'll tell you."

"I think you need a comfortable bed like the one in there!"

"Who, me? Why would I need a bed like that? Am I going to live to be forty?"

Daher laughed, knowing she was about to turn fifty.

"Why are you laughing?"

A Long Road, a Longer Night

The household was brightened by the news that Badriya was pregnant. For days on end, Najma's feet hardly touched the ground, and even when she was tired at day's end and sat knitting clothes for her grandchild on the way, she looked as though she were seated on a cushion of air.

Daher, on the other hand, was muted in his response to the joyful news.

To his relief, Najma discussed nothing with him and asked no questions. It's a miserable thing to have to explain to others something you can't explain even to yourself.

Badriya lacked nothing, as they say. She was perfect in nearly every way: her beauty, her quiet manner, her shyness, and her respect for everyone around her.

Yet she was distant.

More than once Daher had wondered whether she might be more approachable if she hadn't been chosen by Nafisa. He thought back on the pallor that had spread over Nafisa's face after they had married. There was a deep, dark sorrow about her now that no forced smile could conceal. It was an intense, overwhelming sadness that appeared in her features, then moved downward to flood her whole body.

Whenever Daher tried to approach her she would say to him, "Don't concern yourself with me. Go be with your wife. I just want to see your children before I die!"

"Before you die? What are you saying, Nafisa? Please, I don't want to hear you talk this way any more!"

"But I *am* going to die, Daher. If not today, then tomorrow, or the day after that!"

"Don't talk this way, Nafisa. How long has it been since I combed your hair? Come over here!"

Nafisa looked around in search of the comb. When she saw it, she bent down and picked it up off a wooden chest inlaid with mother-of-pearl. She came and sat down in front of him, surrendering her hair to him.

Nine months later Badriya gave birth to her first child. Little did she know that he would also be her last.

Daher gazed at the baby boy. He wanted to kiss him, but felt so awkward holding this tiny bundle of flesh that he handed him back to his mother.

"What will you name him?" Najma asked.

"Have you forgotten, Mother? We have seven days to decide."

It was the custom in those days for a child not to be named until he or she was seven days old. At that time the baby's hair would be cut. If it was a boy, two sheep would be slaughtered, and if it was a girl, a single sheep.

When Daher looked over at Badriya, he was surprised to see Nafisa's face instead. Disconcerted, he closed his eyes and opened them again. This time he saw Badriya holding her son.

Suddenly he said, "I'm going to call him Islibi!"

"What?" exclaimed Najma. "Didn't you just remind me a little while ago that we have seven days to decide?"

"Yes, I did, and the seven days have passed now!"

A sudden pang of grief pierced Najma's heart like a stray bullet, and she found herself clutching her chest in spite of herself.

Seeing her face tighten, Daher asked her, "Is there something wrong?"

"No, son. It's nothing."

On the seventh day they shaved Islibi's head and slaughtered two sheep.

"I thought you'd be so delighted over the birth of your first son that you'd slaughter twenty sheep!"

"Don't people normally slaughter just two? That's the custom, isn't it?"

"It's also the custom for people to name their children when they're seven days old, not hours after they're born!"

"Well, that's the way it happened!"

"Tell me: When are you going to let Nafisa know?"

"I'm not sure news like this would be entirely happy."

Najma was silent. Then she looked up at him and remarked, "There's something going on in your head, Daher."

"Not in my head. If it were in my head, it would be a lot easier. It's going on in my heart."

"And what is your heart saying, Daher?

"It's telling me that this is the last child I'm going to have by Badriya!"

"Would you divorce her after she bore you your first son?"

"I wouldn't divorce her unless she wanted that. But there's something standing between us, Mother, a barrier that's higher and more impassable than the wall of Damascus."

The following night, a giant hand shook Daher's body and a thunderous voice shouted in his ear, "What are you doing here! Haven't you heard Nafisa's news?"

Awaking in a panic, he cried, "What's wrong with Nafisa?"

"What did you say?" asked Badriya drowsily. He didn't reply, and she went back to sleep.

He leapt onto his horse's back, but before he rode away, he found Najma standing in front of him.

"Where are you going at this time of the night?" she wanted to know.

"I'll be gone for a little while."

"So you're going to Nazareth!"

"Rather, I'm going to Nafisa!"

"Are you going to deliver the news to her, or to apologize to her for having had a son?"

"I'm going to see her, Mother. I'm just going to see her."

An hour after sunrise he saw Nazareth bathed in a glow that transformed it into a city of bronze. He goaded his horse, now exhausted from the night's journey, urging him to cover the distance that remained.

When he reached the house, he knocked gently on the gate. Then he knocked again. He hesitated to knock a third time, but had no other choice. As his fist was about to touch the wood, he heard a door open inside.

If he hadn't known that Nafisa was the person living in the house, he wouldn't have recognized her. "Nafisa? Nafisa!"

"Who else would I be?" she asked.

"Are you ill? What's wrong?"

"Nothing!" She reached up and ran her hand over her face as though she wanted to wipe away all the weariness in her features, and rubbed her eyes as though she wanted to polish them like jewels.

"Why did you open the gate yourself? Where is your servant?"

"She's inside, asleep."

"She's asleep when you're in this condition? Where is she?"

"Let her sleep, Sheikh. She was awake with me till dawn."

She reached out and took his horse's reins and stepped aside for Daher to enter the courtyard. Then she followed him with the horse.

"Don't tell me you've come from Tiberias!"

"I've come from Tiberias."

"So you drove your horse all night! Even if you didn't want to have mercy on yourself, you should have had mercy on the poor horse. Why would you make a trip like this?"

"I don't know, Nafisa. A huge hand shook me awake and I heard a voice reprimanding me, so I came."

"Are you going to go on worrying about me like this, Sheikh? Nafisa is no longer a little girl who's afraid of the city. She's grown up, and now it's the city that's afraid of her!" As she tried to laugh, her body was convulsed by a prolonged bout of coughing.

"You're ill, Nafisa. You're ill!"

"I'm just tired, that's all. You know me. Do you remember me ever getting sick before?"

"No, I don't. But you're sick now, Nafisa."

"I'll be honest with you, Sheikh. Tiredness has been trying to get the better of me for days. But I just shoo it away like an obnoxious fly. I'll be all right."

"Let's go in, Nafisa."

"I'll tie the horse and follow you inside. You go in first. Don't worry about me."

"I'll take care of it. You go in."

"Let me do this, Sheikh. I love your horse. Let me whisper in his ear how much I appreciate the fact that he came such a long way, on an even longer night, to bring Daher to me."

She fell silent as though she were trying to remember something. "The moon wasn't out last night, was it, Sheikh?"

"No, it wasn't."

"So let me thank your horse twice! You go in ahead of me."

214

Daher left her and went inside. Weary, he sat watching the sun's rays come in through the window and light up the spacious room. As he waited, he started to doze off. But suddenly a giant hand shook him again and a thunderous voice filled his ears: "Did you come to see Nafisa, or to sleep?"

He wanted to go out to the stable but, remembering her plea, sat back down again.

As the minutes dragged by, the horse neighed twice. The third time, it neighed in terror.

Daher jumped up and rushed out the door, remembering the neigh that had convulsed the house in Arraba on the day the white mare died.

He took off running. Before he reached the stable door, he saw Nafisa on her knees and grasping the horse's right foreleg in an attempt to stand up. As she struggled to rise to her feet, she saw him and smiled at him. She was about to place her hand on the horse's neck when her hand slipped. Like a feather, her body fell without a sound, twisting and turning gently through the air until it settled at the horse's feet.

A Black Light and
Birds without Names

How many memories can two hands hold? How much time? How many laughs and smiles? How many words spoken, nights spent awake, secrets shared, and warmth received?

As if she knew he was going to be looking at her for a long time, Nafisa did her best to appear happy and content. Now that death's arrow had passed through her on its way to the darkness of eternity, the sight of him prompted her to rise above her pain and put herself back together again. When her hand went limp as she clutched the horse's reins, her only hope had been that the smile of contentment she had managed to muster—the only means she had of resisting death—wouldn't fade. She didn't want Daher's last memory of her to be that of a face wrung with pain.

He lifted her head and rested it on his knee. He combed her hair with his fingers and, as he spread it out, it looked like black rays whose lustrous glow framed her fair face in a way he had never seen before.

He looked around for the comb and saw it on top of her wooden chest. He tried to reach it, but couldn't. He tried again, with the same result. It was less than a handspan away from him. Lifting her head, careful not to let it touch the floor, he stretched with his whole body and picked up the comb. Then he placed her head back on his thigh and ran his fingers through her hair again before using the comb.

Every movement of his hand from the roots of the hair to its ends was a journey without end: a journey to an age past and to hopes suspended in the distance. It was a journey back to an incomparable moment of encounter, to a passion whose fulfillment he had longed for so deeply, to a life of perplexity evaporating into thin air, and a verdure that had never flowered to its fullest.

The sun shone intensely outside, and some of its beams stole in and lit up the room. The streets of Nazareth filled with people whose words fluttered inscrutably about him like birds without names.

Everything was over now. Only one thing remained: for him to go on combing her hair forever, to stay at her side forever.

A bell tolled from the Church of the Annunciation, and a muezzin's voice rang out. Nafisa's servant woke in a panic. She looked for her shoes, put them on, and hurried out.

The horse saw her and neighed. She recognized him as the sheikh's horse. She looked over at the door to the large room and saw that it was closed. She stopped, unable to bring herself to approach it and knock.

The horse neighed again. She went over to him and patted him on the neck, then led him to the water trough to drink. Her eyes made their way back over to the closed door. There was no movement. She listened closely. There was no sound.

She fed the horse, her mind on other things.

In the end all she could do was wait, so she sat down in the doorway to her room.

Midway through the afternoon, the horse neighed again. She went over to him and patted him on the neck, led him to the trough to drink, and fed him.

Night fell.

In the darkness that had fallen, Daher couldn't tell whether the comb no longer knew its way through those long tresses, or whether the protrusions that impeded his movement were simply a product of the cruel gloom that was descending stonelike upon their bodies.

In some strange way, Daher sensed that he had spent his whole life in this very situation, and that he would die holding his wife's head in his hands and clinging to her body as the arms of the night stole in to spirit her away to a darkness still crueler and more terrible.

He cried. He cried buckets. His tears were drowning him, sweeping both him and her away.

He hurriedly dried his tears.

The pounding on the door had sounded like rain at first. Then it began growing louder until it turned to thunder, and only then did Daher hear it. He didn't know what to do. How could he leave her alone on the cold floor to go open the door?

The sound of the thunder intensified, and he thought he saw a prolonged flash of lightning illumine her face. Then darkness prevailed once again.

As the thunder roared more loudly than before, he picked her up and went to the door. He turned the key in the lock and opened it, and found himself face to face with his brother Saad. Saad almost said something, but couldn't. He had come hastily from Arraba as soon as the young man sent by Nafisa's servant had reached him.

Daher closed the door again.

The courtyard filled with people. By the fourth day, he realized that death had defeated him: ripping her body to shreds, stealing her fragrance and the delicacy of her hands, and erasing the shadow of her smile that had hovered about the place. He rose to his feet, went to the door, and opened it.

With all the darkness behind him, he said, "Now Death can say that she belongs to him."

He made his way through the crowd of glassy-eyed mourners and left.

His horse neighed when it saw him walking away. The servant girl went over to the horse and untied it, and it followed Daher with heavy steps that bore no resemblance to those of a horse.

A Weaponless Army

After the battle of Jaddin, Daher began searching for a way to learn what his enemies, or those with whom he might find himself at war some day, were doing and thinking.

He called for al-Dankizli and said to him, "I want a unit made up of the best men in the country, a strong unit without swords."

"Strong, and without swords? How is that, Sheikh?"

"What I mean is that I need these men's minds, not their weapons. I want courageous, intelligent men, Ahmad. I also want them to be known to no one but you and me. After you've chosen them, gather them in some secluded location and inform me, because I want to see them myself. I also want a second unit, consisting of the same number of men, that will stay here, and whose function will be to remain in communication with the first unit."

One day, a group of men who took their orders directly from Daher headed out for the various cities to which he had assigned them. By the time they were all in place, there wasn't a single major city in which Daher didn't have spies. They were stationed everywhere from Jerusalem to Damascus: in Gaza, Acre, Haifa, Jaffa, Nablus, Mount Amel, Sidon, Tyre, and Beirut. In each of these cities he stationed two men, one who traveled back and forth between Daher and the city in question, and one who remained where he was.

In this way Daher ensured that he wouldn't wake some morning to find a hostile army arrayed against him without forewarning. He later discovered that this precaution wasn't sufficient, particularly when battles were prolonged. Hence he found himself obliged to devise another strategy.

War by Night, War by Day

D aher awoke in the wee hours of the morning, sweat pouring off his body and his hand swinging in the air as though it held a sword.

Badriya opened her eyes, terrified. "Is everything all right?" she asked.

He didn't reply.

He got dressed hurriedly, wrapped his turban around his head, picked up his sword and his musket, and headed for the door.

"Where are you going at this time of the night?" Badriya asked. By now she had gotten up and was following him out.

He gestured to her to go back to bed. He closed the door behind him and stared into the darkness. Noticing how cold the night air was, he undid his turban and wrapped it around his face before heading for the stable. A horse neighed. He disappeared inside the stable. When he came out again, he saw Badriya, Najma, and Yusuf. Yusuf came up to him and asked him the same question Badriya had: "Where are you going?"

Again he made no reply. He opened the large gate in the wall, and a number of the guards on watch outside jumped on their horses. However, he instructed them to remain in their places. Then he took off in the direction of the city gate. "Who goes there?" cried the guards inside the gate.

"Sheikh Daher. Open the gate."

The guards on top of the wall, more numerous than those inside the gate, jumped on their horses.

"No one's going with me!" Daher shouted.

By this time Yusuf had arrived on horseback.

"There's a problem that only I can solve," Daher told him.

He set out, and when he was several meters from the wall he cried, "Close the gate!"

Then the darkness snatched up his body, and he was gone. Those on the wall watched him for several moments. Then nothing remained but the sound of hoofbeats.

Daher had received a fatal stab. However, it wasn't the first. He'd been having the same dream night after night. He would get up brandishing an unseen sword, look at his chest, run his hands over it, and take a deep breath. His eyes would always fall on the lanterns, and he would see his own flame flickering violently, as though the person who had stabbed him had turned into a gust of wind as he left the room.

He recognized him. He recognized him even though he had only seen him once before.

On the first night, the second night, the third night, the twentieth night, he resisted the urge to get up and follow him. But finally he concluded that unless he got up and went after him, he would never be able to sleep again.

After all those years, it wasn't easy for him to find his way to the grave. His horse stumbled through the thick grasses and shrubs. Nevertheless, given his horse-like feel for the land, he managed to make his way to the lakeshore, where he waded into the water and found the stars refracting, scattering, and fading away on the water's surface.

He stopped the horse and dismounted.

He had a growing sense of danger, and for a moment he thought of drawing his sword. After all, it was night, and he might be overtaken suddenly by some wild beast: a leopard, a wild boar, a wolf, or even a bear, though he hadn't seen a bear since a year earlier in the Jaddin hills.

After a long search, he whispered to himself, "This dead man who's been attacking you every night can't be defeated in the dark, but only in the light of day!"

He drew his sword and planted it in the ground. Its handle danced to and fro in the air, emitting peculiar vibrations. Then he sat down on the lakeshore to wait for sunrise so that he could wage his peculiar war.

Suddenly he found his face flooded with sunlight and his horse snickering nearby. He'd fallen asleep. *How could I have done that?* he wondered. Remembering his sword, he found it next to him, silent and motionless, watching in all directions.

Feeling cold, he drew his cloak more tightly about his body and got up. The sound of oars bringing boats home and the fishermen's muted singing wafted monotonously toward him from a distance.

He watched the fishermen pulling their small boats onto the beach and unloading their baskets and nets. As the sun rose in the sky, he looked around, and realized he was quite a distance from where he was supposed to be. Everything was different: the beach, the trees, the orchards. He got on his horse and, his back to the lake, looked in the three landward directions. Then he prodded his horse, which broke into a run, and kept going until he reached the huge boulder that he had sat on so often, sometimes contemplating the sky and sometimes the horizon.

He flung himself down on it and stared at the sky.

He got up and walked along, following the tracks that time had erased from the soil, but not from his memory. Then a scene from the past repeated itself:

Suddenly he heard a woman's wounded scream. He reined in his horse and came to a sudden halt. He tried to identify the source of the sound, which seemed to be coming from all directions. He prodded his horse and it began going in circles. Seeing that the white mare was hindering the stallion's movement, he loosened her reins from the stallion's saddle and took off in search of the source of the sound. The plea for help grew more intense and more pained, and his consternation deepened.

Ten steps later he stopped. Yusuf was standing in front of him. Daher stared at his hand, and found it empty. "What are you doing here, Sheikh?"

"It's an old story that I had to bring to a close."

"That man?"

"That man."

"Did you come here to make peace with him, or to kill him?"

"I don't know, Yusuf. I don't know."

"And what happened?"

"I killed him again."

"Do you feel better now?"

"I don't know. I'll tell you one of these days."

Atop That Hill

Bishr was a courageous warrior and al-Dankizli was an unrivalled commander, and within the space of three months they were able to form Daher al-Umar's first standing army. The new army consisted of fifteen hundred horsemen who appeared to be far greater in number than they were.

"Once we're ready you'll see us, Sheikh," Ahmad al-Dankizli said to Daher.

Not knowing what the next step would be for the governors of Sidon and Damascus now that he had taken over Jaddin, Daher needed the army to take shape as quickly as possible. At the same time, he didn't want al-Dankizli to be hasty. He wanted a real army, and he realized that the creation of an armed force was a critical process that wasn't likely to be repeated. If his army were defeated in its first battle, it would take Daher back to the zero point.

Money wasn't a problem. On the contrary, Daher and his brothers owned more than enough to fund the undertaking. The share he deducted for himself from the state's taxes before sending them on to Sidon was on the rise, and the family's cotton fields had found a profitable market overseas.

One September afternoon, al-Dankizli arrived at Daher's house in Tiberias. Daher eyed him pensively as he approached, wishing he were his son.

"You come bearing news that we've been anxiously awaiting, Ahmad!"

"Everything is ready, Sheikh Daher, and I'd like you to come with me to see for yourself."

Wanting Daher to see the army at a single glance, al-Dankizli turned and led him up a back road to the top of a hill, at the foot of which lay the spacious Pigeon Valley.

223

When Daher looked down, his heart skipped a beat. The plain below had nearly disappeared beneath the army's formations, while swords and long spears were wielded deftly by horsemen clad in brightly colored uniforms that restored spring to the autumn-tinged expanse. Daher took a deep breath and filled his lungs with the mingled fragrances of thyme, sage, wormwood, saffron, and other wild herbs.

Reaching for his waist, al-Dankizli drew a pistol and fired a single shot into the air. This was the signal that the soldiers below had been patiently awaiting. Suddenly they spread out in all directions, forming squadrons that moved in synchrony toward unseen points. No sooner had they reached these invisible points than they transformed themselves into overlapping circles that continued to come together until their center point consisted of a single horseman who, at a preset moment, raised a fluttering banner.

When the soldiers saw the banner their formations changed once more. Their ranks divided and came together again in four blocs, each of which was shaped like an arrow whose tip was pointing toward the center. The banner disappeared again, whereupon they charged at each other in such a way that each bloc passed through the one facing it and came out the other side. When the horseman raised the banner once again, they scattered in all four directions and vanished, causing the plain to appear empty.

Daher nodded and cast al-Dankizli an admiring glance. But before he could say a word, he heard the sound of hoofbeats approaching from behind. He turned and saw half the army climbing the hill and closing in on its peak. When they reached the top, they rode in circles around Daher, al-Dankizli, Bishr, and Yusuf.

Daher saluted the horsemen with a raised sword. Then he turned toward Bishr and Yusuf, who were visibly moved by the sight. He came up to al-Dankizli, patted him on the shoulder, drew his pistol out of its holster, and gave it to him.

Surprised, al-Dankizli said, "Thank you, Sheikh. You're honoring me for the second time. You honored me the first time when you placed your trust in me by asking me to form this army, and you've honored me a second time by giving me this gift."

"You've done a great deal, Ahmad. And now we'll see where we can go with these brave warriors!"

"Wherever you might command us to go, Sheikh, wouldn't be too far."

The Road to Safad
and the Six Mares

L et's write to him first!" said Daher to al-Dankizli.

The mulish Sheikh Muhammad Nafi' took the letter and rolled it into a ball. He flung it in the messenger's face.

"I'd sooner let him storm this fortress with his army than enter it without a fight as if I were afraid of him! You tell him this: If you want the Safad fortress, you'll have to come get it with your sword. As for Bi'na and Suhmata, I'll never let you near either of them."

Daher's messenger bent down and picked up the letter. After smoothing it out somewhat, he put it in his pocket and left.

"Let's leave him complacent inside his walls for the time being," said al-Dankizli. "We'll clip his wings for him in Bi'na and Suhmata. Then we'll see what he can do!"

"I know Bi'na in a way no one else ever could, Ahmad, and I won't let a drop of blood be shed there. It was there that I lost the first friend I ever had. I lost Sheikh Hussein, who had the loudest, most refreshing laugh that ever came out of a man's heart. So much blood flowed there that all I see is darkness whenever I pass that way. All I can think of is my friend Abbas, his father, his brothers, and the rest of his family with their empty eye sockets!"

"So what can we do?" asked al-Dankizli.

"We'll send its multazim a gift. The best one we can think of. We'll honor him as highly as we possibly can. I want you to choose the kind of gift you yourself would like to receive!"

"I'll deliver the gift myself," said Bishr as he walked with Daher along the lakeshore.

"No, Bishr. A messenger has to get down off his horse and bow in respect before the person he's delivering the message to. And as you know, I never want you to get down off your horse except when you're with me!"

"It's a good thing you let me get off my horse when I'm at home!"

"Your manhood isn't worth anything if you don't treat your wife and children with compassion, Bishr."

"In other words, you're not going to send me to Bi'na this time?"

"I'm going to send you somewhere else—to Sanur."

"And what could Bishr possibly do with the most impregnable fortress between Nablus and Acre?"

"He can look at it, get a feel for it!"

"And why would I want to get a feel for it? I don't know anyone who's been able to go inside it unless he was its sheikh's guest. As for soldiers making it inside, well, it's some fortress, Sheikh. I mean, it's *like this*!" In order to get his point across, Bishr formed an arch with his hands over his head and looked upward, as though Daher weren't familiar with the place he was talking about.

"Even so, go, Bishr. Take a good look at it, then come back to me."

"I don't suppose you're thinking of laying siege to it, Sheikh!"

"Go, Bishr, and when you get back, you tell me what I should do."

"Me, Sheikh?"

Taking a deep breath, Daher stared Bishr in the face and commanded, "Get on your horse, Bishr!"

"Yes, sir."

Bishr took a few steps back, grasped his horse's reins, and jumped onto it.

Daher gestured to him to come forward. He came forward.

"Bishr, I want you to go to Sanur."

"I'm ready, Sheikh!"

"I want you to get a good look at that fortress, then come back and tell me what I'm supposed to do with it."

"Yes, sir. Should I go now?"

"Tomorrow. After all, you have Ghazala, Daher, and Umar. Go spend the night with them, but don't tell anyone where you're going."

"Not even Ghazala?"

"Ghazala! You can tell Ghazala anything, Bishr, just the way I tell my mother Najma everything. In fact, I never feel at peace inside until I've told her."

"I'm the same way, Sheikh. I never feel at peace unless I've shared my secrets with Ghazala."

"Goodbye, Bishr. I'm going to spend some time here, then go home."

When the people of Bi'na saw a small decorated caravan approaching in the distance, they were delighted, and when it had entered the gate, a number of them followed it. The three horsemen leading the caravan were clad in breathtaking attire, the six mares they had brought were decked out like princesses, and two thoroughbred stallions bore items carefully wrapped in colorful fabric with silk ribbons around them.

The gift's arrival came as a complete surprise to the multazim of Bi'na and Suhmata. After all, Daher had conquered Jaddin and secured control over Tiberias, Arraba, and even Deir Hanna and its environs. Not only that, but he now ruled the plain of Bani Amer through his allies Bani Saqr, and had threatened the Safad fortress. Yet in spite of all this, Daher had chosen to send him a present!

The multazim of Bi'na hosted an enormous banquet in their honor as if Daher were there with them. When he served the food, he didn't sit down to eat. Instead he stood on alert, waiting for some signal from them. A short man with fleshy arms, he had a broad mouth that was poised in a continuous smile; a wrinkled, roundish face that looked like a circle with frayed edges; beady eyes; and eyebrows so bushy that they came down to meet his eyelashes.

Daher's messengers were his guests for three days, and as they were preparing to mount their horses, he said, "Here is my gift to Sheikh Daher."

They turned and saw several generously laden camels driven by a well-dressed young man with a handsome face.

On their way back to Tiberias, Daher's men stopped in Arraba at Saad al-Zaydani's behest. They spent a night there, and the following morning Saad gave them a letter to deliver to Daher.

When Daher opened the letter, he was surprised by what it contained: "Now you should request the hand of this multazim's daughter in marriage."

This was the last thing Daher would have expected! He handed the letter to Najma, who read it and handed it back to him without a word.

"You haven't given me your opinion on what Saad says here," Daher said to her.

"The birds in the sky see the branch they're going to land on better than I do."

"That's not an opinion."

"I would have liked to be the one to choose your bride for you. Instead, dear Nafisa did it once, and now it's Saad's turn!"

Bi'na's plain teemed with horsemen displaying their skills. However, Daher's heart was somewhere else: at the graves he had passed on his way into the village, the graves that held his first friend, and that loud, jolly laugh of Sheikh Hussein's that had been swallowed up by darkness.

Before reaching the gate, he lifted his gaze to the top of the wall and saw himself there, running back and forth shouting insults that pierced holes in the governor of Sidon's ears. As he crossed the threshold into the village, he thanked God for giving him the honor of entering the town without having to shed a single drop of blood.

Passersby might easily have seen Daher as a horseman, a traveler, or a guest. Yet none of them saw him as a joyful, expectant groom! Behind him were the faces of Nafisa, Abbas, and Sheikh Hussein, and before him was the unknown face of a girl who was waiting for him and whom he knew nothing about.

"I'd like to have a word with you, Sheikh Daher," said the father of the bride.

"Well, there are no strangers among us now that we're family!"

"It's a word that calls for a bit of privacy."

As they walked together to the far end of his house's upper floor, Daher noticed that in spite of his own short stature, he seemed quite a bit taller than the multazim.

He cast a sweeping glance over the village, searching for the house of the woman who had helped him escape during the siege so many years earlier. When he found it, he smiled, and decided to visit her.

"Now that we're family, Sheikh Daher, I wanted to tell you that I've gotten old, and that I don't have the same get-up-and-go that I did when I was a young man."

"Don't say things like that about yourself. You're more youthful than I am!"

"But it's the truth, Sheikh Daher. So I have a favor to ask of you."

"Just say the word."

"I'm aware, Sheikh Daher, of the things you've been doing. No one, of course, has told me what you're thinking. However, I feel certain that you're this country's hope, both now and in the future, and since you've spread justice in your parts, you'll do the same in all of our villages and towns. I know many men who've worked as multazims and as governors. I've known pashas and I've known viziers, so I know exactly what kind of people they are. And this is why I want you to become multazim over Bi'na and Suhmata!"

"What did you say?"

"I want you to be multazim over these two villages. I'll cede them to you in front of a huge gathering so that they can all be witnesses. Everyone here knows how you defended Bi'na when you were a boy. So they know that you would do everything in your power to defend it now, and that you'll treat its people fairly just as you have the people of Tiberias, Arraba, Hattin, Tabigha, and all the other places you've gone."

Daher heard a woman saying, "I want to see him. I want to see Sheikh Daher!"

Daher jumped up and headed toward the voice. He was sure it must be her. However, he didn't know what she looked like until he saw her. He stood there, trying to recall her face from that distant day. "It's you!"

"Yes, it's me, Sheikh. I'm Amina. So you know my name now!"

Coming up to her, he lifted her hand to kiss it. She quickly withdrew it.

She had aged so much, it was as if Time had taken up residence in her to the exclusion of everyone else.

"I've gotten old. I've aged more than I should. That's what everyone says."

"You're still just the way you were."

"Don't try to fool me, Sheikh! Just a little while ago you were about to kiss my hand as though I were your mother! But since I learned of what you've done in Arraba and Tiberias, I haven't regretted a thing. You know? I'm so overjoyed that death doesn't frighten me any more. Every time I think about you, Sheikh Daher, I feel I still have my whole life ahead of me, and that this old age of mine is nothing but a mask. Now that I've seen you, all I have to do is take it off and fling it to the ground. Don't you feel the same way?"

"Yes, I do, Mother. I feel the same way. But I have one request: that you come back with me to Tiberias."

"Anything but that, Sheikh! How could I leave this house after spending a lifetime here? It talks to me about you every night. Every

229

night it tells me stories about you. It hears your news before anyone else. In fact, it told me a long time ago that you would come and that I would see you. A house like this is one I could never leave, even if it meant seeing you every day."

"Will you at least agree to be my mother, then?"

"What woman wouldn't want Sheikh Daher to be her son?"

"It's agreed, then?"

"It's agreed!"

"In that case, you can't refuse me ever again, and I owe you everything a son owes his mother."

"You've tricked me, Daher!"

"No I haven't, Mother! But now you have to perform a mother's duty to her son: you have to go arrange my wedding with my mother Najma!"

Once the two of them were alone, Daher looked over at the bride. She was the spitting image of her father. He placed his head in his hands for a long time, for so long that he forgot where he'd put it!

Another Gift

Daher asked Ahmad al-Dankizli to prepare another gift like the one he'd chosen for the multazim of Bi'na and Suhmata.

"Whom will we send this one to?" he asked.

"Get it ready," Daher replied, "and bring it to me. Then I'll tell you who it's for."

Three days later the gift was ready. After looking it over carefully, Daher said, "I hope you've presented me in a good light by the gift you've chosen."

"There couldn't be a nicer present in my opinion, Sheikh!"

"Supposing you were the person it was being sent to, would you be pleased?"

"I'd be more than pleased."

"Well, it's for you, Ahmad! Accept it from your sheikh without saying a thing! And two days from now we'll take our next step."

Ahmad al-Dankizli was about to say something. But Daher beat him to it.

"No talking now!" he said.

"One word, at least!"

"I'm the one who gets to speak now. And I want to ask you: What's become of your marriage plans?"

"My marriage? It's even more difficult than before."

"Do you mean to tell me she's refused you again?"

"She's agreed that I can marry anyone else I want!"

"But why? Does that make any sense?"

"She said, 'Do you think I'm crazy enough to give up my position as your beloved by becoming your wife?'"

"But she's being unfair to herself this way!"

"Anyway, that's what happened!"

"But since she's agreed to your marrying someone else, there's no problem any more."

"On the contrary, Sheikh, the problem's bigger than ever. It's hard for somebody to give up the love of his life to marry a woman he might not love at all."

"But he might love her!"

"You've said it yourself, Sheikh: he *might* love her! But it's hard for me to substitute a possibility for a reality!"

Daher's thoughts wandered briefly. Then he took a deep breath that brought him back to himself. Patting al-Dankizli affectionately on the shoulder, he said, "Pardon me, Ahmad. I was about to ruin your life! And I've delayed you. She's waiting for you now. Don't keep her waiting any longer. Go!"

"And what about you, Sheikh? Don't you think you ought to be getting home?"

"Home? My heart doesn't know where that is any more, Ahmad. It's as if I buried it with her in Nazareth."

The Army of Lanterns

O nce again, Safad's sheikh rolled Daher's letter into a ball and flung it in the messenger's face.

"Would you like to send a message back to Sheikh Daher?" the messenger asked.

"We're not in the practice of killing messengers. Otherwise I would have liked to send him your head!"

"You could roll my head, Sheikh Nafi', and it would get there before my horse did. Sheikh Daher isn't far away! If you look through one of the gun loops along the wall, you'll see him."

"What do you mean?"

Daher's messenger walked over to the wall, followed by Sheikh Nafi' and his men.

Daher asked al-Dankizli to display the army's skills the way he had the first time he saw it. The plain that stretched out before the fortress filled suddenly with the harbingers of war. The army disappeared and reappeared as rows of soldiers alternately charged and intermeshed, creating new formations as they went.

This peculiar "war" went on for an entire hour without a drop of blood being shed, and by sunset the army had disappeared as though the earth had swallowed it up. Safad, its houses ascending stair-like toward the peaks of its three hills, observed the scene in amazement, while its fortress stared warily into space like a hawk with trembling wings.

Daher's messenger left the fortress in silence, bearing a silent message, while the fortress's sheikh watched him move away until he vanished beyond the plain.

As for those standing on the wall, their numbers continued to increase by the moment, their eyes wide as saucers.

From time to time a horse's neigh could be heard in the distance, and its echo would reverberate as though a thousand horses were neighing.

The lanterns were lit on the plain surrounding the fortress, a hundred at a time, for a total of one thousand lanterns. Al-Dankizli ordered his brigade commanders to divide their men into groups of fifty and, out of each group, to bring him the soldier whose lantern had gone out first.

The darkness of the night and the silence of the wind seemed to surround the lanterns' flames with a protective barrier that kept them from going out, while Safad's fortress was transformed into a mass of thick gloom.

Three of the soldiers whose lanterns had gone out arrived at Daher's tent and stood outside at the ready.

"And what do you want from these soldiers, Ahmad?" Daher asked him.

"I'm going to send them to the fortress. We plan to open its gates from the inside."

"And where did you hear about this game of the lanterns?"

"After you and your brothers resorted to it as a way of deciding who would become multazim in Tiberias, there wasn't anyone who hadn't heard of it."

"So that's it. Everybody knows about it, then?"

"Yes. By the way, we lit two lanterns on the night before the battle at Jaddin, one in your name and the other in the name of Ahmad al-Hussein. Ahmad al-Hussein's lantern went out, and yours went on burning."

Daher laughed.

"What makes you laugh, Sheikh?"

"It seems the lanterns do tell the truth some of the time!"

As the darkness of the night intensified, the lanterns burned more brightly. Then, shortly before midnight, a soldier came in and announced the arrival of a messenger from the Safad fortress.

"It seems the war is over, Ahmad. However, it didn't end thanks to the lanterns that went out, but thanks to the lanterns that are still burning!"

Daher read the letter that had been sent by Sheikh Muhammad Nafi'.
Then he handed it to Ahmad al-Dankizli.

It wasn't, in fact, so much a letter as it was a document declaring that
Sheikh Muhammad Nafi' would relinquish the position of multazim
over Safad and its environs to Sheikh Daher al-Umar with the expecta-
tion that he would spread justice there and protect it from all aggressors.

Daher sent the messenger back with a letter saluting Sheikh Muhammad Nafi' and promising to work as long as he had life in his veins to rid
Safad of all injustice. In addition, he promised that Sheikh Muhammad
would continue to receive his allotted share of the taxes paid to the state
and that his rights and property would be held inviolable as long as
his work was carried out in a spirit of fairness. He concluded his letter
with the words, "It will be my pleasure to be Safad's guest the day after
tomorrow."

Before Safad's messenger reached the fortress gate, Ahmad al-Dankizli
issued an order for the lanterns to be extinguished, and it was done.

To Daher's surprise, the people of Safad honored him with a warm
reception, complete with song and timbrel:

> O Zaydanis, may death never touch you,
> O lion cubs with the pure hearts!
> When over the barren land you pass,
> Your breath to it verdure imparts!

"As I told you in my letter, Sheikh Muhammad, I won't infringe upon
any of your rights."

"I'm confident of that, Sheikh Daher. The man who opened Safad's
gate with light is bound to make certain that he's remembered there
only for the light he's spread!"

Maybe I'm Just Homesick

The sorrow that wrung Daher's heart over the loss of Nafisa hovered over his head like a dark cloud, and while Badriya's presence made the cloud larger, the presence of the new bride made it thicker.

Striking the ground with his hand, Emir Rashid al-Jabr shouted, "Why does Daher make an alliance with us, then keep us at a distance?" Daher sent him a message in hopes of appeasing him, doubled the money he was paying him, and asked him to prevent his men from raiding caravans and villages, because the one condition he would never back down on was security.

Satisfied, Emir Rashid ordered the raids to stop and brought his brigades back into camp.

"Sheikh Daher, I have a request, and unless you agree to it I won't come into your house or eat your food!" shouted Emir Rashid from outside the diwan.

Hearing the emir's voice, Daher got up and came to see him.

Emir Rashid stood a few steps away from the diwan's outer entrance as though there were a line of fire on the ground that he couldn't overstep. Behind him stood a number of horsemen and a camel laden with an ornamented bridal litter that swayed every time the camel moved.

Daher had never seen a woman as beautiful as Salma, nor encountered anyone more genial. Despite the hardship of life in the Bedouin camps and the moving from place to place, and despite the fact that all the tribe's girls occupied an equal position such that they were all required to work and fetch water, Salma looked like a being from another planet.

He looked up and saw his cloud of sorrow breaking up.

However, he couldn't fail to notice her attempts to avoid looking at him whenever she addressed him. It was as though her eyes concealed some great secret.

He didn't ask her about it, thinking that it might simply be shyness on her part, or that she might be sad because he hadn't touched her yet. Hoping to win her over, he bought a house for her in Nazareth where she could be close to her family's campgrounds, and spent the night with her there.

When, the following morning, the same sadness clouded her features, he knew he would have to wait.

Several months later Salma looked into his eyes for the first time but, to his dismay, all he could see were her tears.

"What's wrong, Salma?" he asked her.

"I don't know, Sheikh. Maybe I'm just homesick!"

The Mare That Turned
into an Arrow

D aher received two letters on the same day. One was from Emir
Rashid asking after him and his new bride. The other was from Emir
Nasif al-Nassar of the Shi'i Matawila tribe in southern Lebanon.

Daher had written to Emir Nasif asking him to cede control over the
villages of Bassa and Yarun. Emir Nasif had replied, "Don't think we're
like the others! Our swords are sharper than yours, and our schemes
more devious. So while you're attacking our neighbors, you'd best
leave us alone. Otherwise, I swear to God, you'll regret it. We've been
oppressed many a time, and many a time we've overcome our oppres-
sors, and when we make a pledge, we're as good as our word. Hence,
you would be well advised to rethink this request."

Daher spread out the letter in front of him and began reading it. But
to his surprise, he didn't feel angry. He'd been observing Emir Nasif's
actions from a distance, and with no little admiration. This was a man
who had been able to do everything Daher had: He had done his utmost
to keep Ottoman governors away from his land and his people. He had
striven to establish a rule of solidarity, working to unify the leaders of
neighboring regions and to prevent the Ottoman state from interfering
in his internal affairs. Thanks to his efforts, tax collection in southern
Lebanon had become quite a different affair from what it was in other
regions because, rather than collecting taxes two or three times a year,
he collected them only once, and when he did so he treated the people
with compassion, taking care not to overburden them.

Daher sent word to Saad, who had restored the fortress at Deir Hanna
and taken up residence there, asking for his help.

In response, Saad went to meet with Emir Nasif and tried to persuade him to relinquish power over the two villages. He refused.

Daher tried to think of some way to avoid a war. And again, he could
think of none better than the giving of a gift. Hence, he sent a gift to the governor of Sidon, asking him to appoint him as multazim over Bassa and Yarun.

When, to Daher's surprise, the governor agreed to his request, he dispatched a force to expel the multazims of the two villages. When news of what had happened reached Emir Nasif, he mobilized a large army, but before it set out, Daher had received news of its imminent advance.

This wasn't the first war Daher had fought against the Matawila. The first war, a short-lived conflict, had taken place in the territory in and around Bassa at a time when Yarun hadn't yet figured in Daher's thinking. During the earlier war the Matawila had unexpectedly managed to capture a mare of Daher's by the name of al-Barisa, one of the few descendants of the white mare that had provided milk for him as an infant.

When Daher learned of the mare's capture, he was beside himself. Desperate to get her back, Daher had sent Emir Nasif a letter telling him that he was prepared to give up his demand for "al-Basisa" in return for al-Barisa. However, the last thing the Matawila were prepared to give up was that exquisite horse, and when they realized how attached Daher was to her, they sent a letter to him saying, "We won't return al-Barisa, and you won't get al-Basisa!"

"She's my sister, for heaven's sake!" he cried.

But instead of attacking them, he withdrew with his army. Then, just when the Matawila thought they would never see him again, he launched a surprise attack and recovered the horse. He instructed Bishr to mount her and not to stop riding until he had reached Deir Hanna. Once he was assured of her well-being, Daher attacked Bassa and secured control over it.

However, this situation wasn't to last for long, and just weeks after his return to Tiberias, the city was attacked by the Matawila, who killed Daher's men and reclaimed the mare.

Daher's second war with the Matawila was the longest his army had ever fought. Known for their valor and strength, the Matawila held out against Daher's forces for a full twelve days, and the plain known as Marj al-Basal, or Onion Meadow, in the vicinity of Tarbikha in the north witnessed such a bloodbath that vultures flocked there from all directions. The birds circled above the battlefield, awaiting the moment when they could claim their share of the carnage. When they grew weary, they alighted hungrily at a distance, waiting for everyone to perish.

Seeing that no one could predict the end of such a war, al-Dankizli approached Daher, saying, "I have a plan that I don't want you to know about, because if you did, you'd reject it! But I promise you: if you'll let me carry it out, we'll be able to bring this war to an end and avoid further bloodshed on both sides."

With a nod Daher said, "If you can put a stop to this war between me and this man I love, I'll be forever in your debt!"

"You say you love him?"

"Yes, I do."

Daher had to exert quite an effort in order to fill the gap left by al-Dankizli and the men who went with him. However, the situation didn't last long, and by sunset that very day, al-Dankizli had returned.

Emir Nasif and Daher received the news at the same time.

The minute he received the news, Emir Nasif left the battlefield ablaze behind him and headed straight for home. The shock was too great to bear. He gave his messenger a letter to deliver to Saad al-Umar. Then, without getting off his horse, he turned to go back to Marj al-Basal.

He had only one thing on his mind: preventing what had happened from leading to events still worse.

Everything in the village was just the way it had been. Nothing had been destroyed or stolen. Not a single person had been killed, even though al-Dankizli had managed without difficulty to surround the town, surprise the men remaining there, and make his way to the home of Emir Nasif.

Clouds of dust appeared in the distance, trying to overtake Emir Nasif's mare as she flew like an arrow. Even before he reached the battlefield he began shouting, "Stop the fighting! Stop the fighting!"

Suddenly everything went still: the clashing of swords and the whizzing of bullets died away, the horses seemed to freeze in place, and the arrows soaring through the air appeared not to know where to go.

Emir Nasif's messenger reached Deir Hanna after midnight.

Saad al-Umar opened the door to find a group of his guards outside. He asked them what had happened.

"A messenger has come from Emir Nasif."

"Couldn't they have waited till morning?"

"It seems to be something that can't be postponed."

"And where is the messenger?"

"He's waiting for you in the diwan."

"I'll follow you."

Al-Dankizli walked in, flanked by two young men. Daher rose and received them cordially. He invited them to sit down, and they responded with the politeness one would expect from those who have been groomed to be emirs.

Daher leaned over and whispered in al-Dankizli's ear, "Is this the only solution you could think of?"

"I wish I could have come up with some alternative, Sheikh. But it wasn't going to be easy to bring a war like this to an end."

Daher patted al-Dankizli on the shoulder. But he appeared care-worn, as though he were carrying the weight of the world on his shoulders. Then he left, following the two boys out.

"You're my guests," Daher said, "and as long as you're here you'll be treated with the dignity and respect I would accord my own family, though I don't expect you to stay long. That's my sincere hope, at least. It isn't my custom to hold my guests captive!"

The older of the two emirs thanked Sheikh Daher, and said nothing more.

Knowing what he did about Daher, Emir Nasif didn't fear for his sons' safety. Still, father that he was, his heart had been pounding out of his chest from the time he received the news of their capture.

When Emir Nasif summoned his army commanders and the men he had placed in charge of his territories, they were sure he was about to make the rashest decision he'd ever made in his life. To their surprise, however, they found him calm and collected. Seeing this, they began attacking Daher and urging him to take action against him.

For his part, he said, "It seems that Sheikh Daher only did what he did because he felt he had no other choice. He'd sent his brother Saad to speak with me. He'd also sent us gifts. But we dismissed him out of hand. Instead of going to war with him, maybe we should have appreciated what this sheikh is doing. After all, everything we've worked to achieve in our territories, he's achieved in his, and the only people he's waged war against are the people we ourselves are at war with. Not only that, but while others persecute us because our doctrines differ from theirs, Sheikh Daher protects everyone without distinction. He works to protect the oppressed and the weak, Christians and Jews."

The other men stared at him in disbelief. But the greatest surprise was what he said next: "We should have realized that by waging war on a man like this, we only wage war on ourselves."

"You would never have said such a thing if he hadn't captured your two sons."

"Their capture might have some bearing on what I just said. But it has no bearing on what I'm about to do!"

Reconciling the two sides wasn't a difficult matter. Saad brought Daher together with Emir Nasif, who now displayed an entirely new attitude. He willingly ceded the position of multazim not only over Bassa and Yarun, but over the entire Matawila region. They agreed that Daher would pay the region's taxes to the governor of Sidon, and in return he promised to protect Emir Nasif and his people from anyone who tried to do them harm, be he the governor of Sidon or anyone else. The two sides also entered into a mutual defense pact.

The two young emirs came forward and, before they rejoined their father, Daher embraced them and issued instructions for their gift to be brought out.

Emir Nasif remained standing where he was, restraining himself from running to meet his sons. When they reached him, he kissed their heads and had them sit down on either side of him. Then he beckoned to one of his men and whispered something in his ear.

The man retreated, and returned shortly with two thoroughbred horses. The emir rose to his feet and presented the horses personally to Daher. The two men embraced. Touched, Daher unsheathed his sword and picked up the copy of the Holy Qur'an on which they had taken their oaths earlier. With his hand on the Qur'an, he swore that he and his men would stand united against anyone who committed aggression against Emir Nasif and his people, and that he would work to ensure that, like Tiberias, Arraba, Jaddin, and the other territories under his control, the Matawila territories would remain free of the Ottoman governors' tyranny. In addition, he announced that in Emir Nasif's honor he would exempt the Matawila territories from a quarter of the taxes they would otherwise have owed the state.

The oath Daher had taken meant more to the emir than the matter of the taxes. He knew that Daher was the only person who could stand up to the pashas and the sheikhs of Nablus who supported them and the state. Consequently, only Daher could protect the Matawila, who had suffered more than their share for their doctrinal beliefs.

What Daher hadn't expected was his brother Saad's angry reaction. No sooner had he bidden Emir Nasif farewell than Saad shouted in his face as though he were still a little boy.

"You've secured control over the Matawila's territory. That I can understand. In fact, I helped you do it! But to make them your allies—do you realize what that means? It means you've declared enmity against all the Sunnis, both here and elsewhere, and challenged the validity of their faith!"

Daher's chest tightened and sparks flew from his eyes.

"After what you just said, Saad, I'm not going to let you say another word! What kind of faith is it that's pained by showing mercy, preventing bloodshed, and preserving people's dignity? What you believe doesn't matter to me. What matters to me is what you do with your belief: Do you build or tear down? Do you wrong others or treat them with fairness? Do you act with loyalty or with perfidy? Do you rob or do you enrich? Do you love or hate? Do you tell the truth or tell lies? Do you liberate or enslave? Do you plant or uproot what's been planted? Do you make people secure or do you release the ogre of fear and let it consume people's hearts? Saad, the people who weave plots against us are Sunnis like us. Those who steal what we've earned by the sweat of our brow and humiliate and subjugate our families are Sunnis like us. You tell me I shouldn't conclude an alliance with Emir Nasif and the people of southern Lebanon. And why? Because we have doctrinal differences! Do Sunnis agree on all points of doctrine? Don't we Sunnis recognize four schools of thought, doctrinally speaking? As long as we all believe in a single Lord, a single prophet, a single direction to turn in prayer, a single Qur'an, and the testimony that 'There is no god but God,' why can't Shi'ism be considered a fifth school of thought, especially now that we all have a single enemy in common? I swear to God, Saad: if two men stood at the door to my heart—a just man who belonged to some religion other than my own, and an unjust Muslim—I'd let the first one in and send the other one away.

"If I thought the way you do, Saad, I wouldn't be Daher al-Umar. I'd make Sunnis belong to one religion and Shia to another. I'd divide

Islam. But God forbid that I should do such a thing. So beware, Saad. As they say, 'Blind faith has evil eyes!'"

Daher took a deep breath, his gaze fixed on Saad's face.

He expected his brother to say something. Instead, he was so taken by surprise that he just stood there in front of Daher, unable to move or speak.

Placing his hand on his shoulder, Daher said, "Hopefully what you said was just a slip of the tongue." Then he left Saad standing there and went his way.

Daher sat watching the lantern flame flicker before him. He waited to see what would happen to it, and just when he felt it was starting to burn more brightly, he dozed off.

At dawn he opened his eyes in a panic. It was as though he had only slept for a minute. Surprised to find the lantern still spreading its light, he got up.

As he looked into the distance, he felt as though he could hear the waves of the sea from the foothills of Tarbikha. He performed the dawn prayer and ate his breakfast at five a.m. the way he did every morning. After lifting his hands and thanking God for His blessings, he asked for his horse to be brought.

While Saad felt himself an outsider, al-Dankizli was pleased with the settlement that had been reached. As for Daher, he sensed that Emir Nasif was the sincerest man he had ever gone to war against, and that the peace treaty they'd concluded was the beginning of a new and different era.

Daher toured the region's flatlands and rolling hills. Then, as he was riding back across the plain to his tent, he came to an abrupt halt. As he patted his horse's neck to calm it, again he imagined hearing the waves of the sea.

He held his breath. The horse grew calmer, and he listened again. Louder than before, it was an extraordinary wave. His horse stepped back with a neigh.

Daher closed his eyes and opened them again.

On that prairie so far from the seashore, he looked down, and what should he find but that the wave had soaked him through and through.

The Going Out of the Sun

One day Daher opened his bedroom window, which overlooked a crowded Nazareth street. Despite the throngs outside, his attention was drawn to a certain young Bedouin, who appeared to be enervated by illness or hardship. The moment he caught sight of Daher, the young man averted his gaze. As he began to walk away, he did his best to appear natural. However, the glance he cast back at Daher's house gave him away.

Daher sifted through his memory in search of that face, but couldn't recall it.

He closed the window and left the house.

The following day as he was eating, Daher found himself drawn to the window. He didn't open it completely, but peeked through the shutters and, as he had expected, he saw the Bedouin there, staring at the house with lackluster eyes as though he were staring into empty space.

He quietly closed the window again.

He looked over at Salma, and found her making circles around herself. He asked her if she was tired or worried.

"No, Sheikh," she replied. "It's nothing." Meanwhile, she became more frantic than ever.

He lay down for a nap after lunch. An hour later he opened his eyes and found her trying to see something through the closed shutters.

He closed his eyes again, wondering what it was that kept that young Bedouin man glued to the wall outside, and Salma glued to the window inside.

He could only think of one thing.

He cleared his throat and turned over to give her a chance to change locations. She moved quickly, and before he opened his eyes she was in the adjoining room.

He got up and went to the window, opened it a crack, and looked out. And as he had expected . . .

245

"Do you need anything from me?" he asked as he left the house.

"No, Sheikh. Thank you," she said.

"If you need anything, I can bring it myself, or I can send it with your servant, since I'll be late getting back this evening."

"All I need is your safe return, Sheikh."

The uneasiness in her voice continued to unsettle him.

He passed the small shed in the center of the front yard on his way to the stable, and she followed him. He looked at her. She had the most innocent face he had ever seen. However, the disquiet in her eyes was so intense it was stirring up the dust under her feet.

When Daher opened the door, the young man turned toward the house. However, Daher was careful not to glance in his direction.

He prodded his horse and rode away.

He made several circuits around Nazareth. He gazed at the Church of the Annunciation in the light of the sunset. It looked the color of bronze, just as it had on the day he'd arrived in Nazareth years before, the day Nafisa died. His heart shrank within him, and he was shaken by the peculiar thought that the sun wasn't just setting, but was about to go out altogether.

He turned to go back to the house.

He looked over at the spot where the young man had been, and didn't see him. He took a deep breath, uttering a prayer for protection.

He gently pushed the gate open and went in. Seeing Daher, the servant ran up to him, took the horse's reins, and led it to the stable.

He cast a glance toward the house. Everything was still, the windows and doors shut tightly against the bitter cold that roamed the earth with its sharpened spears.

When he reached the door, he heard an unfamiliar voice. He listened more closely. A man's voice was coming from inside. A pang went through his heart. He reached out to push the door open. Then he thought better of it and withdrew his hand. His eyes on the door, he retreated to the shed, ascended the four steps that led inside, and sat down.

The servant came out of the stable and saw him sitting in the shed. "Shall I tell my lady that you've arrived, Sheikh?"

"No. You go in, and I'll call you if I need you."

"Wouldn't you like a blanket, Sheikh? It's cold out here!"

"Thank you, but as I said, I'll call you if I need you."

Night fell, and he could no longer see himself inside the shed.

Suddenly the door to the house opened and Salma came out. She looked around anxiously. As if her fear were a radar that enabled her to see him in the dark, she walked awkwardly over to the shed. "Is that you, Sheikh? Why are you sitting here in the dark?"

"I got tired all of a sudden and had to come home. I thought you were asleep and didn't want to disturb you. I think I've rested enough now, though, so it's time for me to go back and finish my work."

She stood there, motionless as a statue, until the sound of his horse's hooves died away. With broad strides she went back to the house, opened the door, and closed it tightly from the inside. Then she opened it again warily, came out, and closed it behind her. Standing in the doorway, she looked in all directions. After making sure her servant wasn't nearby, she pushed the door open and, hand on the knob, whispered, "Hurry! Hurry!"

With rapid, distraught steps the emaciated young man ran across the courtyard. She went inside and watched him through the crack in the door until he reached the gate. She breathed in, but the air was of no help to her. She fell to her knees, repeating the words, "God kept it hidden! God kept it hidden!"

Once at the gate, the young man found himself face to face with Daher.

He froze. Daher reached out and caught his hand in an iron grip.

"You know me, don't you?"

The words were so dry, they came out with difficulty, wounding his throat and tearing his lips to shreds. "Yes. You're Sheikh Daher al-Umar."

"And where were you just now?"

"In . . . in your house."

Daher led him away from the house, his horse following him in silence, and the street lanterns flickering around them. A gentle breeze blew, and Daher watched the lanterns flicker still more. However, none of them went out, and he took a deep breath as though he wanted to inhale the entire breeze.

Then he said, "Be truthful with me as you would with a brother, confess to me the way a patient would to a physician, or ask for my guidance as if I were your father. If you do, I promise to do my duty by you!"

Caught between his desperation, his fear, his impossible hope, and Daher's iron grip, he said, "Ask me whatever you want."

"What's your name?"

"Ghayth, son of Sheikh Safwan."

"So my bride is your paternal cousin?"

"Yes, sir."

"More than once I've seen you in front of my house, and tonight I found you in her room!"

"I swear to you, Sheikh: you're bighearted enough to pardon, and noble enough to forgive!"

"What's your story, Ghayth?"

"My story is my love for her, Sheikh. Please forgive me for overstepping my bounds! I've loved her for a long time. Our parents know about it, and so do lots of other people. But when Emir Rashid came and asked that she be sent to you as your bride, nobody dared refuse his request. They all kept quiet, and so did I. After all, who would dare refuse the emir? And who would dare refuse you? But from that day on, I've been out of my mind. I started coming here to quench my longing by just looking at her! As for my being in her room, it was pure madness, Sheikh. But I swear to you: All I did was look at her. I didn't touch her, and she didn't touch me!"

Daher exhaled forcefully. He felt the air blowing, the lantern flames shuddering, and the night nearly swallowing them up. As he breathed in, the lanterns began shining again and the night retreated from around them.

"Am I so frightening that no one dares refuse any request I might make, Ghayth?"

"No, but we respect and revere you, Sheikh."

"Thank God. You nearly killed me, Ghayth."

"I'd kill myself before I did that, Sheikh!"

"Are you a trustworthy person, Ghayth?"

"Plant me in the Plain of Bani Amer, and you'll see what a good tree I am!"

"I want you to go home and forget what happened here, Ghayth. Forget all about it. Do you understand?"

"I understand, Sheikh. I understand."

At a point along the southernmost edge of Nazareth, Daher stood watching him, and within moments the darkness of the night that gripped the plain had snatched Ghayth's body away.

Daher asked Salma to sit down across from him. She did so. But her eyes were digging a hole in the floor between them. She reached out to touch his hand, but he withdrew it with a strangely charged calmness. She winced. He sat observing her. She made him think of a little lark in the rain, and if she hadn't been his wife he would have wished she were his daughter.

"I hope everything's all right, Sheikh," she said without lifting her gaze.

"I hope everything's all right, Salma." After a silence, he said, "I left here this evening as your husband, and I've returned as your father."

Her eyes dived deeper into the floor.

"I'm going to give you a chance that few husbands would give their wives. So don't waste it, Salma. Do you love someone from your own people?"

Salma hesitated, digging still deeper into the floor with her gaze.

"Don't waste it, Salma. Don't waste it."

"Yes, Sheikh."

"Yes, what?"

"I love a paternal cousin of mine, not in disloyalty to you, but on account of the years we spent together when we were growing up."

"Would you like the person sitting across from you to be your father, Salma?"

This time Salma dived headfirst into the floor, and it swallowed her up. The scandal closed in on her from all sides and pounded her like a nail, deeper and deeper. Even so, she found the strength to get up and take Daher's feet in her hands to kiss them.

He took hold of her and prevented her.

"No, Salma. You entered my household with dignity, and you'll leave it with dignity. No daughter of Daher's is going to kiss someone's feet, not even her father's!"

"You're my mother, my father, my family. If I had to choose between them and you, I would choose you for your kindness and generosity!"

"No, Salma, you won't have to make that choice. That wouldn't be fair to me, or to them! What I want you to do is send a message to your father tomorrow, asking him to come here. When he arrives, complain to him of my ill temper and the way I berate you day and night. Tell him you'll kill yourself if you have to live another day with me! And when he comes to speak with me, I'll complain to him about how ignorant and careless you are, and how you act like a little girl when you ought to be acting like the mistress of a household. Then I'll divorce you."

"You'll divorce me, Sheikh?"

At that moment Salma lifted her eyes, and all the tears she had been holding back came streaming forth.

Three Steps Back

O n his way to the door Daher stopped in front of the mirror. However, he stood there much longer than he'd intended, so shocked was he at the tired-looking face he saw reflected in the glass. There was a lantern next to the mirror, and another behind it along the far wall. His eyes froze on the flame of the lantern behind him, which was flickering violently and about to go out.

He tried to recall if he had seen that lantern before. *Is it real?* he wondered. *Or is it just a memory of that old lantern of mine?*

He didn't dare turn around. *Do you still believe in that old superstition, even now that Saleh has died?* he thought. *What's wrong with you? Do you think your lantern—or his—is haunting you?*

He closed his eyes and opened them again and, to his surprise, the lantern reflected in the mirror had disappeared. *What does that mean?*

Peering again at the face before him, he reached up and took off his kaffiyeh. With the exception of a few white hairs that were hardly noticeable, nothing about him had changed. If the light from the side lantern hadn't been so bright, he wouldn't even have seen them at that hour of the evening.

He took a deep breath and said to himself, "What do you expect, Daher? You've gotten older, and it's time for some white hair to claim its share of that black mane!"

He closed his eyes, and when he opened them again, he saw his father standing behind him with his long, thick, coal-black hair. Umar al-Zaydani had died without so much as a single gray hair on his head.

Najma had once said to him, "Maybe it was God's mercy to him that he died before seeing all this gray of mine. Don't forget: I'm still twenty years younger than he was when he passed away!"

Islibi was trying to get his father's attention, pushing him toward the door and asking to go with him to the diwan. Daher turned and patted him on the head. "Let's go, then," he replied. "Let's see who gets there first!"

Elated, the eight-year-old took off running, trying to get to the diwan before his father. Daher watched him as he ran. He was the sweetest child he'd ever laid eyes on: so bashful that he wouldn't ask for food in his own house when he was hungry, and so contented that he wouldn't have reached down to pick up a gold piece if he'd seen one in the street. He was a boy who wanted nothing from this world. Daher had often tried to entice him with money, candy, and even with an offer to bring him a baby leopard. But such things meant nothing to Islibi.

There was only one thing that made him happy: to rest his head on his father's thigh, turning it into a pillow. That was where he felt comfortable, and from there he would listen to everything that was being said, casting his eyes back and forth among the men's faces as they spoke.

Badriya, Islibi's mother, had spent one cold year after another in Tiberias, and every year seemed colder than the one before. When at last she decided to go back to live with her family in Nazareth, everyone, including Daher, looked forlornly over at Islibi. They'd grown attached to him, and were sure he would go with his mother. However, when Badriya leaned down to pick him up and set him on the horse's back, he surprised everyone by taking three steps back and saying decisively, "I'm staying with Baba."

Never in his life had Daher's heart pounded the way it did on that day. And never before had he felt as selfish as he did in the face of this delightful surprise. But he retained his composure.

Najma looked at the little boy, and she looked at Daher. Their faces were as dark as a couple of loaves that have fallen into the ashes. She was about to say something, but held her tongue, having decided to let the mother and son resolve the issue on their own.

Again the mother came up to the little boy, who retreated another three steps.

Badriya burst into tears.

"I'm going to stay with Baba. I'm going to stay with Baba!" he said, prepared to retreat ten more steps if she tried to get near him a third time.

She turned to Daher, about to ask him to persuade the little boy to go with her. But she didn't.

"Just let me give you a hug, then. Let me say goodbye to you!"

Islibi scanned the faces of those present until his eyes rested on hers. He took his first step calmly. Then he broke into a run and shot madly in her direction, threw his arms around her, and kissed her on the face and hands.

She felt a renewed hope that the little boy might have gone back on his decision, while Daher's face grew darker.

The little boy pulled gently away from his mother, looked at her, and said, "I'll visit you all the time, Mama!"

Daher couldn't escape the strange feeling that Islibi had been a part of him from time immemorial, that he had been separated from him for nine months in his mother's womb plus a full eight years thereafter, and that now at last he'd come back to be a part of him forever.

The Lonely One's Only Son

N afisa isn't coming back, Daher," Najma said to him. Then she said it again.

"Don't let your only child, Islibi, remain an only child. He needs brothers and sisters."

Najma went back to looking at Daher the way she'd looked at him before he was ten years old. As a little boy he had needed a thousand vigilant eyes to keep watch over him lest he be wounded by a mere breeze, or lest a cloud of sorrow pass through his heart.

"I'm going to find you a wife this time, Daher. I'm the one who's going to choose your bride, and no one else!"

"The only time I married happily was the time I chose my bride for myself, Mother. So let me try again."

"I'll look for someone in Tiberias, and once I've found someone who seems suitable, I'll leave the rest to you."

"I'd rather you looked in Nazareth."

"In Nazareth? Why in Nazareth?"

"A lot of Syrian women live there!"

Najma gave him a long look. She almost said something, but thought better of it.

"I'll look in Nazareth, then!"

When Daher saw Duhqana[16] for the first time, his heart skipped a beat. When she uttered a greeting, it skipped another beat. Her pristine Damascene accent alone was sufficient to open his heart anew. For a moment he saw Nafisa before him. He shook his head, then closed his eyes and opened them again. He still saw her!

"With God's blessings," he said.

"With God's blessings," Najma repeated after him. As for Duhqana, she was incredulous that she would be the wife of Daher al-Umar al-Zay-

---

16 Of Persian origin, the masculine form of the word 'dihqan' (or 'duhqan') was used to refer to a merchant or the governor of a province.

dani. Tears ran down her cheeks, erasing Nafisa's features as they fell.

"You knew just what I wanted, didn't you, Mother?"

After a silence, Najma asked him, "And when will you marry her?"

He looked into the sky. The moon was almost full. Even though night hadn't yet fallen, he saw it peeking out over the eastern horizon with the brightness of a winter sun.

"Three days from now."

"Three days from now!"

"On Thursday."

"On Thursday!"

Nasma's Winds
and Ghosts from the Past

Najma looked around her. The house was in a state of bedlam. But she didn't pine for the quiet days of the past. She sat there looking at her grandchildren with a smile on her face.

"I've filled the house for you with children and wives. Are you happy now?"

"Yes, I am. But is *your* heart at rest?"

Daher didn't reply.

"Your heart will never be at rest, Daher."

"I've tried to set it at rest."

"True, you've tried. But all you've managed to do is relieve yourself of my constant nagging, since I can't keep on telling you to get married again now that I have Islibi, Uthman, Ali, and Sa'id around me!"

Daher stood looking at his sons. Seeing their father, the little boys made a rush for him. The only exception was Islibi, who felt he was too old for such things. Daher squatted and took them all in his arms.

"And Grandma? Doesn't she get a hug? Or she is a stranger in this house?"

Daher let go of them, and they dashed over to hug her too.

"God protect you," she said, repeating herself several times.

"That's enough now! You're going to suffocate your poor grand-mother!"

"Don't you believe it! He's just jealous!"

They hugged her even more tightly. After a while they loosened their grip on her. Ali hopped away, and Sa'id followed him as usual. As for Uthman, he retreated a couple of steps and sat down, staring into his father's face.

Daher and Najma watched as Ali played his favorite game: jumping from one thing to another and trying not to fall. He'd discovered the game near the lake, where he would go leaping from rock to rock, indifferent to the possibility of slipping. Smooth rocks were the best launching pads, in fact, and he would go sailing across them intrepidly, light as

256

a feather while the other boys would take one tumble after another, then come home with bloodied heads or broken arms.

"Why are you looking at me that way, Uthman?" Daher asked.

"I want to ask you a question, Baba."

"Go ahead. I'm all ears!"

"Baba, when are you going to die?"

A cruel silence descended on Daher's and Najma's heads.

"And why do you want me to die?"

"So that I can become multazim in your place."

"But I don't have to die in order for you to become multazim, Uthman! I can stay alive while you become a multazim, too. And I promise to make you one when you grow up."

"But then I'll be a junior multazim, and I want to be a senior multazim!"

"In that case, I'll look for a way to die soon so that you can set your mind at rest!"

Najma listened to the conversation with a knot in her stomach. Daher looked over at her and saw that her face had gone yellow. "He's just a little boy, Mother. He's just a little boy!"

"I wish that were the case. This boy's going to give you trouble, Daher. Lots of trouble."

"Don't worry about me. My lantern's still got plenty of oil left in it!"

"I know that. But there's a lot of wind, Daher. A lot of wind."

Duhqana was so in love with Daher, she would have been prepared to have a baby every day if she could have. In spite of the years that had passed since their wedding day, her eyes still welled up with tears when she looked at him, as if she were seeing him for the first time. Just to be his wife was, to her, a treasure worth the whole world.

Meanwhile, Nafisa's face continued to flit between them like a butterfly that, whenever it was consumed by the flame, rose to new life. No one had ever told Duhqana what was going on in Daher's heart. Even so, she knew that when he embraced her, he was embracing another woman; that when he suddenly forgot her name as he was about to call her, another woman's name was on his lips; and that when he attended her as she gave birth, the woman bearing the child was someone else.

Her sole consolation was the knowledge that this other woman had died! However, she didn't know whether the other woman's specter hovered about her to comfort her, or in preparation to assault her in the end.

"I've always tried to be fair in everything, Mother. But I have to admit that I have no control over my heart. I've also done my best not to be selfish. But when I chose Duhqana, I wasn't really choosing her. I was trying selfishly to get Nafisa back. And from whom? From Lord Death! Not only that, but I was trying to get her back through someone who resembles her but who had no hand in her death. And now I've come to see that Nafisa hasn't come back, and Duhqana has never arrived!"

Najma said nothing. Meanwhile, he grew more and more distant.

It was no ordinary concubine that al-Dankizli chose as a gift for Daher. Nasma was by far the most beautiful woman he had ever seen. She was much more beautiful than Amira, his own concubine. If it hadn't been for the fact that he loved his Amira so much that he'd given up everything for her sake—even the possibility of having children by her—he would have kept Nasma for himself.

"It's hard not to be selfish in the face of charm like this!" he said to himself. However, from the time Daher had embraced him with such kindness, saving his life after the Battle of Jaddin and preserving his dignity as a defeated soldier, his loyalty to him had known no bounds.

It was as if al-Dankizli could see into Daher's heart, even though he had never spoken with him about anything connected to his marriage to Duhqana.

When al-Dankizli came in to see Daher, Nasma close on his heels, it was the first time Daher had ever felt afraid of this man whose loyalty he could never doubt. As Daher gazed at her, al-Dankizli took two steps back. And as he continued to gaze at her, al-Dankizli quietly withdrew.

Not only was Daher dazzled by this Circassian beauty; he was amazed at al-Dankizli's ability to choose the very moment when it would have been impossible for him to refuse such a gift. Daher went on staring at that face for an entire month. Like someone who finds himself in a strange place, he began trying to get his bearings and discern which direction he wanted to go, only to choose some other direction in the end.

The Covenant and
the Steps of the Wind

Daher hadn't needed to go to war in order to enter Nazareth. He had simply come quietly from Arraba, Deir Hanna, Tiberias, and Safad and annexed the surrounding area, extending his influence and protection over it together with the Plain of Bani Amer. The governor of Sidon looked around, and what should he find but that Daher had taken over most of his territory.

At the same time, a conflict was brewing, both in secret and in public, between Daher and Ibrahim Jarrar, lord of the Sanur fortress, over control of the Plain of Bani Amer. Sheikh Jarrar insisted that the plain was part of his territory. Daher disagreed. Hence, with the help of his many supporters, he began cutting off Nablus's trade routes by taking control over Nazareth and the plain.

Never before had Daher had so many enemies, and he knew it. So, realizing it would be impossible to take them all on, he decided to move quickly before he was taken by surprise. He began by consulting al-Dankizli and his military commanders. Al-Dankizli reassured him, saying, "We can mobilize two thousand soldiers in a single night."

After hearing out his advisers, Daher said, "I won't wage a war like this with two thousand soldiers."

"But if we need more than that, we can't sit here waiting for them to come to us."

"All right, then," said Daher, "tomorrow I'll go see my uncles in Nazareth."

He had started referring to the people of Nazareth as "my uncles."

He hardly needed to say a word when he arrived. They'd been expecting him. They realized that if Daher's enemies got the better of him, they would end up where they had started: mute captives to injustice and degradation. The first to join his army were the merchants, artisans, and farmers. With these men and others ranked among his fighters, Daher felt a bit more confident.

He then received a message from al-Dankizli saying, "Our spies tell us that Sheikh Jarrar and his men are marching on the village of Mansiy southwest of Nazareth." Daher replied, telling al-Dankizli that they would meet there.[17] He then sent word to Bani Saqr, urging them to join him on the battlefield.

Daher and his forces headed out for Mansiy at dawn. When he came to the Church of the Annunciation, he stopped his horse, and the Nazarene army stopped behind him. He dismounted and walked toward the church, the sound of his footsteps amplified by the early morning silence. He stood for a while, looking into the sky. Then he took his final step and, to everyone's amazement, knelt in front of the church door. Lifting his soil-covered hands and wiping his face, he said, "Daughter of Imran, whom, besides God, can I trust more than you? If you should grant me victory over my enemies, I will remember your gracious favor toward me till my dying day, and your servant Daher will provide oil for your lantern for all time to come!"

As he rose to his feet, he felt a gentle light passing through his heart and caressing his spirit with hands of mercy.

Before leaving, he paused and cast a glance back at the church, which was clearly visible despite the darkness. He nodded reverently as if to confirm the promise he had made. Then he shouted, "To Mansiy! From Nazareth to victory, God willing!"

Before arriving in Mansiy, Daher noticed a lone horseman atop a small distant hill. The sun rising to his right had transformed him into a black, featureless statue, and had it not been for the swishing of his horse's tail, horse and rider would have formed a silhouette perfect in its stillness.

Daher instructed Bishr and another horseman to investigate the situation. He watched the two of them ride away until they were next to the horseman. Shortly thereafter, Bishr rode back, while the other man stayed on the hill.

"What's going on over there?" Daher asked.

---

17   Mount Nablus—that is, the city of Nablus and the surrounding villages—was the property of the Ottoman sultans. The sheikhs of Mount Nablus would pay five hundred kisas annually to the governor of Damascus, who would send it on directly to Istanbul. Consequently, this was Daher's first battle against the Ottoman state itself, since it was the first armed conflict in which he faced loyal allies of the Ottomans who were staunch defenders of the state's interests.

"He's a Bedouin horseman who has news for you, Sheikh, and he says it's important."

"Have you found out who he is?"

"He said you would recognize him, Sheikh."

"Bring him here, then, and let's find out what his story is."

When the horseman was close enough for his features to be visible, Daher's heart quaked. Before reaching the place where Daher stood, the horseman dismounted and gave a respectful bow.

"What are you doing so far from your people's campground, Ghayth?"

"I need a word with you, Sheikh!"

"Can't you say what you have to say in front of my soldiers?"

"No, Sheikh. It isn't something that can be said in the presence of an army on its way to war."

The two men rode some distance away, and that was when the bombshell dropped.

"Jarrar and Ibn Madhi wrote to Emir Rashid al-Jabr promising to reward him richly if he joined them."

"Did he agree?"

"You'll find the men of Bani Saqr waiting for you on the battlefield, side by side with the armies of Nablus."

Daher looked around for a rock to sit on. He found one and went over to it. However, when he saw his soldiers looking over at him, he thought better of it, and remained on his feet.

"Sit down, Ghayth!" he urged. "You must be tired!"

"I couldn't do that, Sheikh. I couldn't."

"In that case, go back to your family now."

"I don't have any family to go back to now that they've done this to you, Sheikh! I'm staying here beside you."

"No, Ghayth."

"I wouldn't have any peace of mind knowing you were surrounded by enemies. Shall I attack you with my cowardice while they attack you with their swords?"

"Your tribe has aligned itself with my enemies now, Ghayth. But I won't let you turn against them."

"Ever since I learned from you how to live, Sheikh, my only tribe has been the truth."

"And your wife? Don't you realize what would happen to her if they saw you fighting at my side?"

"After the battle, I'll go back to my wife and we'll move to Tiberias."

Turning to Bishr, Daher said, "You're in charge of our helper now, Bishr."

"Please, Sheikh," Ghayth implored, "I want you to treat me the way you would any of your own soldiers. I didn't come here to burden you with having to protect me. I came to add my sword to yours!"

"With God's blessings, men!" shouted Daher, signaling with his sword. Then they all set out.

Daher's army numbered three thousand soldiers. It was an army he could never have imagined would one day be under his command. Nevertheless, fear of what the coming hours would bring had his spirit in an uproar.

Al-Dankizli had studied the battleground down to the last detail, and he had determined that the Daliyat al-Rawha area would be the most suitable place for them to engage the enemy. Daher led his forces out at full speed against Sheikh Jarrar's army. However, he was unable to drive a certain image out of his mind. *What if I found myself face to face with Emir Rashid al-Jabr?* he wondered. *How would I fight him? Would I kill him? Would he kill me?*

The earth shook, auguring a battle that would last for days. The two armies joined in battle. But to the astonishment of Sheikh Ibrahim Jarrar and his men, Daher's forces were routed in less than half an hour! Sheikh Jarrar ordered his men, giddy with victory, in pursuit of the defeated enemy soldiers. This was his chance to do away with Daher and his army once and for all.

The battle turned into a chase, in the course of which Jarrar's men mowed down untold numbers of Daher's soldiers at the rear of the fleeing army. Gunfire resounded and arrows flew, mangling the flesh of their unprotected backs.

The elated cries of Jarrar's men shook the plain, drowning out the hoofbeats of horses charging and fleeing. The pursuing army stormed nonstop through a narrow pass between two hills. However, a surprise awaited them: five hundred horsemen led by al-Dankizli, and five hundred more led by Daher's brother-in-law, Muhammad Ali. At that unexpected, fatal moment, Jarrar's soldiers found themselves in the midst of a masterfully prepared ambush.

The men of Bani Saqr were the first to flee, leaving Jarrar and his army easy targets for Daher's horsemen. Before long, Ibrahim Jarrar met his end at the hands of al-Dankizli. The defeat spread among the ranks of Jarrar's soldiers, who began searching for any means of escape.

The plan dictated that Daher's men should go in pursuit of the defeated army. They chased the surviving soldiers as far as the gates of the Sanur fortress, which Bishr had described to Daher with the words, "It would be easier to put your hand through a piece of granite than to penetrate its walls."

What Daher had wanted had come to pass: all coastal territories were now under his control. However, no one was more overjoyed than the inhabitants of Nazareth and the Plain of Bani Amer, who had seen the tyrannical Jarrar slink back into his cage and lock the door on himself.

At the entrance to the Church of the Annunciation, Daher prostrated himself and uttered a prayer, raising his hands in gratitude to the Virgin Mary. He rose and turned toward those looking on, their eyes filled with tears, and issued the following order: "All the oil this church needs for its lanterns will be brought to it every season. The produce from an olive grove in Kafr Kanna and another in Majdal will be set aside permanently for the Church of the Annunciation."[18]

After jumping back on his horse, Daher circled a couple times. "Where is Ghayth?" he asked.

"Here I am, Sheikh!" Ghayth shouted back as though he'd been expecting the question.

"Thank God you're safe!"

"Thank God for the victory He granted us."

"I need to have a word with you, Ghayth," Daher said. He prodded his horse and rode some distance away from his army, and Ghayth followed.

"What is it, Sheikh?"

"Did anyone you know see you in the battle?"

"No, Sheikh. The men of Bani Saqr are the only ones who know me, and they withdrew before they saw me."

---

18 These two olive groves remain the unalienable property of the Church of the Annunciation to this day.

263

"Thank God. So then, Ghayth, you can go back to your family now."

"That's what I'll do, Sheikh."

"And I want you to forget all about the idea of leaving with your family for Tiberias."

"Why is that, Sheikh?"

"I don't want you to turn your back on your people, even for the sake of your love for me."

"You mean you want me to go home?"

"Yes. And if you think you owe me a debt, you're mistaken. I owed myself a debt, and I repaid it when I returned Salma to you. But if something happened to you when you were with me, I'd be saddled with a debt I could never repay."

"But . . . !"

"You do as I say, Ghayth."

Ghayth dismounted and bowed to Daher in salute, saying, "But I'll be loyal to you wherever you are, Sheikh."

"God be with you, Ghayth. God be with you."

Daher turned his horse and went back to join his men. Ghayth watched the army move out until it disappeared. He mounted his mare and took off after them. But then he brought her to a halt. He spent some time staring, first in one direction, then in another, until all four directions looked alike to him. Then he set out in a fifth direction, not knowing for certain whether it would lead him home.

The sheikhs of the Sanur fortress were shocked by a letter they received from Sulayman Pasha, governor of Damascus. They had written to the governor requesting his support after what had happened in Mansiy, and his reply was: "Conclude a peace treaty with Daher. Then wait until the empire issues a decision concerning him."

Similarly, when the governor of Sidon saw that all Daher had sent him was the taxes owed to the state, and that he had withheld the funds that were usually set aside for him as governor, he sent to Sulayman Pasha requesting permission to wage war on Daher. Imagine, then, the governor's shock when Sulayman Pasha stated, "Wait until a decision concerning him is issued by the empire"!

Daher sensed danger lurking beyond the silence that followed the Battle of Mansiy.

One day as he was walking through Tiberias with al-Dankizli and a number of his army commanders, he stopped in his tracks. Lifting his gaze to the top of the city's wall, he said, "That wall doesn't look high enough to me!"

"Can you see them coming?" al-Dankizli asked.

"I may not see them," Daher replied, "but in a silence as heavy as this, it's difficult not to hear their horses' hoofbeats."

Later, standing atop one of the towers, he said, "A tower from which we can't see anything but Tiberias and the lake is blind."

Several days later, work was begun to turn Tiberias into a fortress.

One Surprise, Two Surprises

One idyllic dawn that promised a pleasant day and a merciful sun, Daher mounted his horse. A number of soldiers jumped up to follow him, but he gestured to them to stay where they were.

They hesitated. He glowered at them, and they knew what that stern look meant.

The time had come for him to see with his own eyes what had become of the seeds he had sown.

He rode north to the end of the lake. Then he turned west. After noon he turned south, and then headed north again along the lake.

A certain deep and captivating joy embraced his spirit as he saw people working in their fields, grazing their livestock, and building their houses in peace. No strange flocks were devouring their crops, no swords were devouring their necks, and for the first time he didn't see anyone being obliged to work with his shotgun or sword at his side.

Whenever he passed a field, a flock, or a waterwheel, he would stop and talk with its owners.

"You ask us how we are, Sheikh? Well, we've forgotten all about those days from hell. They're long gone now!"

When he reached his house shortly before the call to the final evening prayer, he found his brother Yusuf, al-Dankizli, Najma, and his sons waiting for him.

"We were worried about you, Sheikh."

"I might have gone on worrying myself if I hadn't done what I did today."

Daher had received a letter from Paul Mashock, the consul for England and Holland, informing him that he would be arriving in Tiberias in a few days' time. For years Mashock had proved himself to be an honest, trustworthy individual, and never once had he gone back on a promise made to the cotton growers in Tiberias and the surrounding regions. In fact, he had readily paid the taxes the farmers owed the state, and had paid them for their crops even prior to delivery.

Daher had observed all of this with satisfaction, and when he began thinking about what the city walls required, Mashock was the first person who came to mind. Daher felt certain that Mashock was benefiting sufficiently from his trade with Tiberias that he wouldn't easily give it up.

When he arrived in Tiberias one midday, he greeted Daher with a warm embrace.

"How are they now?" Daher asked him, pointing to his knees.

"Nothing's changed. I recover in your warmth here, and get worse again in our cold there!"

"What you need is some time at the Tiberias bathhouse. And it's waiting for you!"

Tiberias had two bathhouses[19] that drew many people from the surrounding area, as well as visiting merchants and foreigners who came in search of a panacea for their aches and pains.

Hoping to relieve the pains ravaging his joints, Mashock spent twenty minutes—the longest his fair, milky skin could tolerate such heat—in the hot mineral water, jumping out when he could bear it no more. Then he washed off with cold water and rested for two hours.

His trips to Tiberias were always the most rewarding of his travels. His visits to the city not only brought him certain profit; they brought him healing as well. When he was there, he never tired of the sweet relaxation that flooded every pore in his body, since he knew it was a necessary prelude to the prolonged business trip that lay ahead.

It was the first time Mashock's stay in Tiberias hadn't been long enough for him to make a second visit to the bathhouse. He cut it short after his evening with Daher, which brought two major surprises. The first surprise came when Daher informed him that the export of cotton would no longer take place through the farmers, but rather through a special council composed of a number of Tiberian merchants, a number of farmers, and Daher himself.

"But Tiberias isn't a state. So how can it do this?"

---

19 One was reserved for women, the other for men. Each sported a large, beautiful swimming pool of white marble through which the water flowed. The pool was topped by a dome supported by marble columns, which allowed steam to escape, and it was surrounded on all sides by small rooms.

"No, Tiberias isn't a state. But why shouldn't its people have the same rights as the subjects of a state?"

Mashock bowed his head. Then he looked up at Daher and saw a peculiar complacency. He thought back on the consular reports he had read about how dangerous Daher was, and about his growing power and influence.

After a lengthy silence, Mashock said, "So be it."

"We'll discuss the new prices then."

"You're making things hard for me, Sheikh. Have you forgotten that we pay the farmers' taxes to the state as well as paying the farmers for their cotton crop? Then we transport the cotton by land, pay customs at the entrance to Acre, and transport it by sea, all of which costs us quite a bit."

"I know that. I also know that despite all this, you make a good profit."

"You're forcing us to think of depending exclusively on cotton from Galilee."

"I'm not forcing you to do that. Besides, I know that even if I pushed you in that direction, you would still need Tiberias's cotton!"

When at last they had reached a satisfactory agreement, Daher dropped his second bombshell, saying, "We don't want money in return for this year's cotton."

"What is it you want, then, Sheikh?"

"Arms. I want arms."

This was when Mashock realized that a new game was afoot on the shores of Lake Tiberias, a game whose outcome he couldn't foresee.

"Arms are a complicated matter, Sheikh."

"And cotton is even more complicated! To some people it might seem quite simple: a farmer plants seeds and harvests a crop. We do a lot to ensure your safe arrival here, and the cotton's safe transport from here. And prior to that, we do even more in order to ensure that every cotton seedling grows and produces. Surely you've noticed how much the situation here has changed since the farmers' living conditions improved. But none of this has come without a price. We've paid for these gains not only with our money, but with our blood."

"Decisions that have to do with money, I can make here. As for arms, they're a matter that goes beyond my authority. Consequently, I'll have to consult about it with the governments of Holland and England."

"As I see it, there's a way we could do things that wouldn't involve either of those governments!"

"What do you mean?"

"I mean our own way, a way that requires no government intervention."

"Let me think about it."

"Remember, friend, that time has a way of slipping away from us!"

Things happened exactly as Daher had anticipated. No sooner had he received a letter from Mashock declining to involve himself in "this dangerous bargain" than he sent for one Joseph Blanc, the French consul in Acre, with whom he signed the agreement that hadn't been signed by Mashock.

As he left Tiberias, Blanc felt he'd been liberated, and that he had liberated the French factories and markets from Mashock's constant control over the prices of the cotton that France needed so badly. As for England, it would have to wait several years before it began manufacturing the cotton gins that were destined to revolutionize the cotton industry.

Daher wondered whether the powers-that-be in Damascus had learned of his deal with Blanc. It wouldn't be long before he knew the answer to his question.

It was a secret to no one that something was being done to the walls of Tiberias. How much less of a secret would it be, then, now that weapons were being mounted on top of them?

Warriors and Sages

T he shell that fell in the midst of Sulayman Pasha's vanguard at noon on Saturday, September 8, 1742 came as a total surprise. Killing fourteen soldiers, it delivered Daher's message with perfect clarity. The soldiers hurriedly gathered up the corpses and retreated six kilometers from the tower.

The people of Tiberias cheered at the sight of the retreating army. As for Daher, who knew that a single shell would never defeat an army of that size, he could see that he had some long days ahead of him. He had prepared himself for a confrontation. However, he hadn't expected to see Sulayman Pasha himself at the head of his army.

Hayim Abu al-Afiya had received a letter from Damascus informing him that Sulayman Pasha was preparing to besiege Tiberias and instructing him and all the other Jews there to leave the city before the army's arrival. Instead, Abu al-Afiya came straight to Daher and showed him the letter. It was Daher who had allowed him and other Jews to emigrate from Izmir to Tiberias, enabling them to find gainful employment and to build houses, shops, and playing fields. He had even built an elegant synagogue, a lovely bathhouse, and a sesame-oil press for the immigrant Jewish community.

Daher was baffled. Tiberias fell within the vilayet of Sidon, so if anyone had wanted to march on Tiberias, it would have been the governor of Sidon. Abu al-Afiya insisted that the letter was correct. But in order to make certain, he sent a letter to Damascus asking for more information.

Daher summoned al-Dankizli and asked him why Tiberias's spies in Damascus hadn't been aware of such a major development. Al-Dankizli suggested that they send out additional spies, reminding him that it would take an extensive espionage network to keep abreast of everything happening in such a large city. Daher agreed to the suggestion. Meanwhile, Abu al-Afiya received a letter from two friends of his, Hayim Farihi and Yusuf Lushati, confirming what had been stated in the first letter.

Still full of doubt, Daher forbade the people of the villages surrounding Tiberias to come to the city for refuge when they heard the news. However, he moved quickly to set in large stores of foodstuffs and arms.

Daher knew Sulayman Pasha had registered a complaint about him with the authorities in Istanbul. He had accused Daher of robbing the state treasury by withholding three thousand kisas that he had collected in taxes from Mount Nablus in previous years. However, Daher had sent an explanation to Istanbul stating that he had spent the money on his army—as attested by the elders of Sanur—to protect his territories from external aggression, thereby ensuring that the empire would continue to receive the taxes they owed it.

Yet none of this had been of any avail. After all, the governor was his rival.

Following the battle of Mansiy, Daher had doubled his efforts to establish security throughout the lands under his control, and had waged war on everyone who robbed caravans. He had also worked to rein in the greed of the tribal chiefs and elders and to deliver the villages and towns from the tyranny of their multazims. When a major crisis erupted in Nazareth (the land of his "uncles") between the Franciscans and the Greek Orthodox, he promptly put an end to the dispute by issuing a ruling on places of worship, which led one monk to dub him "King of Galilee."

It pained Daher to know that Sulayman Pasha had succeeded in winning Muhammad Ali, his sister Shamma's husband, over to his side, thereby ensuring his support for the siege of Tiberias. Daher was thus beleaguered by the empire, Bani Saqr, the leading men of Nablus, and the forces led by his brother-in-law, who had become increasingly uneasy about Daher's growing influence.

The only thing that gave hope to Daher and the people of Tiberias was his brother Saad's promise to come from Deir Hanna and level a blow at the besieging forces if Daher should call on him.

"This is the really difficult war," Daher said to al-Dankizli.

"Is it difficult because we're surrounded and outnumbered?"

"It's difficult because any mistake we make toward achieving victory is bound to turn our victory into defeat!"

"I don't understand."

"We're faced with all sorts of potential dilemmas, Ahmad. If Sulayman Pasha, who represents the sultan, is killed, the consequences will be unbearable, since the empire would never forgive us. If, on the other hand, we're defeated, we'll be goners!"

"Then we're walking a tightrope, Sheikh!"

"This is a battle that calls for a seasoned sage more than a brave commander. So let's do our best to be not only warriors, but sages."

Night and Fear

Sulayman Pasha failed to comprehend how Daher could dare to turn everyone around him into an enemy, including even Bani Saqr, who had once stood with him. What, he wondered, would drive a man to fight the whole world?

The people of Tiberias, who rejoiced over the first volley Daher's forces had shot, knew that the battle had yet to begin. However, they had confidence in the walls that surrounded them, and in the sizable army Daher had mustered.

That night, which was as opaque as the mind of a foe, Daher went around the city checking its walls. Najma insisted on accompanying him. She walked alongside him light as a feather, and if he hadn't heard her speak he would never have known she was there. When midnight approached, she said, "You have to get some sleep, Sheikh."

"Really? So do you want to stay up and keep watch in my place?"

"Why not? Don't you think Najma would be up to guarding Tiberias on a night like this?"

"She'd be up to guarding the whole world!"

"So, then, go to sleep, Sheikh."

"I don't think I'll be able to sleep until they're gone."

"We've got a long night ahead of us, then."

"I wonder whether time will be on their side or on ours."

"It's as if you doubt our ability to fight this war, Sheikh."

"This is the first time I've been surrounded since the siege of Bi'na. Anything would be easier to bear than seeing the people of Tiberias go out there with white scarves around their necks! I won't let the scene at Bi'na repeat itself. Ever since that day I've felt those gouged-out eyes staring at me. To this day I still wonder: was it right for me to escape the way I did, leaving everybody behind and letting the people of Bi'na suffer my share of the defeat?"

"You had to leave there in order to be able to fight them here, Sheikh! If you weren't here, who would be fighting them now? Their obsequious hangers-on? The multazims who are prepared to sell their villages and cities to preserve their own interests? Who, Sheikh? Who could avenge Bi'na and those gouged-out eyes if you weren't here today?"

"There would surely have been someone else."

"No, Sheikh. If you weren't here, no one else would have taken your place. Look around you. Years and years have passed since what happened in Bi'na. How many men have rolled up their sleeves and gone out to avenge those poor people?"

"Are you trying to keep me from feeling guilty for not dying?"

"No, I'm urging you forward because you're alive!"

"These things will never stop robbing me of sleep, Mother."

"And I wouldn't have it any other way, Sheikh. I hate people who just accept everything complacently as if it were meant to be."

The first night of the siege seemed no different from any other: little by little the city fell silent and the houses went dark, until nothing could be seen but the street lanterns, and nothing could be heard but the howling of wolves and the baying of stray dogs in the distance.

Daher said to Najma, "You go to sleep."

Before she could reply, a cannon shell exploded and shook the city.

"Now the battle's begun!"

He took her by the hand and walked her down the steps along the inside of the wall. By the time they reached the bottom, the lamplighters had set about extinguishing the lanterns as Daher had instructed them to.

Night descended heavily upon the city. Nothing remained but the sounds of cannon shells exploding and sprays of flame from a street here or a wall there.

"Spend your night awake along with them. This town has been dreaming for too long!" snarled Sulayman Pasha, who stood tracking the cannon shells from the moment they were fired to the moment they exploded. He had done everything necessary to ensure that he would come away with Daher's head: he'd amassed a huge army, mobilized Daher's enemies against him, and come equipped with enough cannons to reduce Tiberias to rubble.

When the dawn call to prayer sounded from the mosques of Tiberias, it bore an altogether new meaning. The words "Allahu akbar!"—"God is greater!"—addressed a single individual in the distance who took arrogant pride in his own power, reminding him that God was greater than he was, and greater than the expert soldiers and commanders who had turned Tiberias and its inhabitants into a firing range.

Some soldiers were uncertain as to whether they should continue bombarding the city or wait until the call to prayer had finished.

Sensing their hesitancy, one of the commanders shouted, "Fire!"

One of them shouted back angrily, "I'm not going to shoot at a plea being lifted to God!"

Silence reigned once more as the voices of many soldiers intoned, "La ilaha illa Allah! There is no god but God!" Their chanting sent shudders through the stones in the city wall, the gate, the rooftops, and the roosters, which no longer knew whether to crow or to keep quiet!

Once the call to prayer had finished, the commanders shouted again: "Fire!"

More than one voice penetrated the darkness: "They're praying now!"

Fearful of losing half his army before the battle had even begun, Sulayman Pasha ordered the firing to stop. From inside Tiberias, where columns of smoke were rising and eddies of dust swirled upward, Daher could sense what was happening from the silence that had suddenly descended.

"Put the cannons back in place!" ordered Sulayman Pasha.

The soldiers brought the mules they had tied some distance away and pulled the cannons back to their earlier positions.

Sulayman Pasha had discovered that night was the best time for positioning his cannons near the city walls. After moving them as quietly as possible until Tiberias was within shooting range, they resumed their offensive.

The next morning Tiberias inspected herself, and was amazed at what she found.

Throughout the long night of shelling, every household had felt sure they must be the sole survivors. But when they came out in the morning, they couldn't believe their eyes. The city was still itself, and still standing! A number of shops and walls had been damaged, but not a single house had been razed.

Despite the thick dust that obscured the scent of the lake and the grasses that covered its shores, people saw a miracle taking place before their very eyes.

People set about their daily routines just as Daher had instructed them to in a speech he had delivered from the back of his horse in the market the day before. "Life will proceed normally," he said. "We're going to buy and sell, cook and bake. We'll go fishing, too, since they can't blockade us from the lake, and if weddings have been planned, they'll be celebrated at their scheduled times. We're not going to let them control our lives just because they have more cannons than we do!"

After checking on conditions in the city, he headed for home. As he approached the house, he saw his son Ali hopping about on the walls followed by Sa'id, who was running alongside him on the ground. He smiled to see that fear hadn't gotten the better of the children.

Eleven Messages

After three straight nights of shelling, Daher said, "We're going out to them."

"How can we go out to them when our gates are sealed, Sheikh?" al-Dankizli wanted to know.

"We'll go out through the broadest gate we have: the lake! Gather our best fishing boats. Then come back here."

The plan was simple: "Let them advance however they please, but we'll surprise them from the rear. That's where they're the most vulnerable because they're sure they're not in danger."

In a darkness illumined by the lake's silvery waters, twenty boats launched quietly before the call to the final evening prayer, the end of which had become the cue for the nightly assault to begin. The boats headed slightly east until they disappeared from view. Then they headed north. Despite their distance from the shore, the men could hear the call to prayer and see the city grow gradually darker until it vanished in preparation for another night of bombardment.

In every boat there was a fisherman—the boat's owner—who served as guide to the soldiers with him. Given their intimate knowledge of the lake and its shores, the fishermen were assigned the task of choosing the safest points at which to land, and waiting for Daher's men until they returned.

Daher had sent out two hundred of his best soldiers. They were led by al-Dankizli himself, who insisted on being directly involved in this particular battle, since only in this way would he be able to ascertain the size of the enemy force.

Before they had covered half the distance to their destination, shells began raining down on Tiberias. The men's hearts quaked as they thought of their children, wives, mothers, and fathers under that hellish fire.

"Faster, faster!" al-Dankizli ordered.

The oars dug powerfully into the water's surface, then rose into the air before descending to plunge into its surface once again.

Along the distant shore one could see tall grasses that seemed stiller than they ought to be. One kilometer from the rear of Sulayman Pasha's army, the men disembarked without a sound.

Al-Dankizli was determined to see the mission succeed. He realized that its success depended on keeping it a complete secret from the enemy army. In order to ensure his men's safe return and their ability to carry out attacks on subsequent nights, he would have to lead the enemy to believe that the assault had come from the land and that it had nothing to do with the lakeshore.

He circled around the unsuspecting tents until he reached the north-western side of the camp, and from there he watched the army.

The cannon blasts drowned out the sound of the men's footsteps as they scurried over the trembling earth. After stealing through vineyards and fig and lemon orchards, they walked along the low stone walls that surrounded them. Then they hid themselves and waited.

As they became able to hear soldiers' conversations, the sound of the waves on the lake faded out, with nothing remaining but a few familiar scents that sought in vain to break through the gunpowder's overpowering stench.

It was difficult to tell which was louder: the sound of the cannons nearby, or the sound of the shells exploding in the distance.

At ten o'clock on that night punctuated by flashes of artillery fire, al-Dankizli and his men launched an easy strike on the unsuspecting guards. The sound of their movements drowned out by explosions, they advanced toward the tents. Sweeping through the tents with swords, spears, and arrows, they reached a point from which they could see Sulayman Pasha's mansion-like triple-domed pavilion. Each of the two hundred men then shot an arrow at the pavilion and its guards. The arrows were released simultaneously, creating what sounded like the whizzing of a projectile that knows just how to reach its target. As planned, the men withdrew before the arrows had fallen on the other side, and thus had no need to fire a single shot.

From inside his pavilion, Sulayman Pasha saw its walls' thick fabric sprout claws like a wild beast springing upon its prey. Emerging from the tent's roof and its northwest side, the claws were sharp and menacing, and some fell at his feet. He and those with him stepped back, expecting another attack. However, none came.

Another attack would have been sufficient to kill everyone inside.

Sulayman Pasha waited for several moments that seemed to last an eternity, his eyes scanning every inch of the pavilion's walls and ceiling.

Even the cannon blasts couldn't have swallowed up the sound of his heartbeats. He realized that what had happened was a message addressed to him that said: "We're much closer to you than you are to Tiberias!"

At that moment he realized he had entered a war that only he could put an end to.

Blood oozed out through holes in the tents, which had collapsed on top of those inside, and dead bodies lay scattered all over the camp.

A squad was quickly formed to go after the attackers. However, it returned several hours later without having found a trace of them. It set out the following morning and searched the area again, leaving no stone unturned. At last, after sighting footprints in some of the nearby vineyards, they seized their owners and brought them in shackles to Sulayman Pasha's pavilion.

Less than two hours later, one of Sulayman Pasha's soldiers approached the gate of Tiberias with a mule in tow and bearing a white flag. When he reached the wall, he dismounted and removed a large sack from the mule's back. A rope was let down from the top of the wall. The soldier secured the sack to the rope and turned to leave as it was hoisted up.

The sack was so heavy that several people were required to lift it over the wall. When it reached the edge, they gave one last heave and brought it down into the broad stone corridor that ran along the inside of the upper wall. Before they opened it, they realized what it contained, and their hearts trembled.

Daher stood staring at eleven severed heads. As he looked into their gaping, sightless eyes, he realized the magnitude of the mistake he had made, a mistake that had turned suddenly into a sin, by not allowing all the peasants in the surrounding villages to take refuge inside the city walls.

The White Dog's Leap

A l-Dankizli's next mission was entirely different.

Over the course of ten nights, Daher's army set out across the lake in three different directions, their sole task being either to bring the peasants from the surrounding villages to Tiberias, or to take them to Arraba, Deir Hanna, Ibillin, Safad, and Nazareth.

It promised to be no easy undertaking now that Sulayman Pasha's army had become more vigilant by night. He had sent out small groups of soldiers to patrol the area twenty-four hours a day.

Tabigha, located directly behind the besieging army, was the first village to be evacuated. Daher's men had been instructed to take its residents to Arraba. One day Daher sent a messenger to Miqdad, multazim of Tabigha, telling him to prepare the villagers to leave, yet without telling him the reason or where the people might go.

Daher's soldiers arrived at two o'clock in the morning. Everything in the village was eerily quiet, like a bomb inside a cannon. The silence forced them to be all the more cautious, since anything could happen: Sulayman Pasha might learn of the plan and lay an ambush for them, or they might leave the village only to encounter the besieging army. They were terrified at the thought that a baby might cry, a horse might neigh, a donkey might bray, or footsteps might waken the night and alert the enemy to their presence.

They muzzled the horses, mules, and donkeys and tied thick pieces of cloth securely around their hooves. The children presented a more complex challenge. Daher's messenger had instructed Miqdad to have the women of the village nurse their babies well, and not to let them sleep a wink all that day. Miqdad found this request rather odd. After all, he wondered, why would Sheikh Daher be concerned about young children's naps and mealtimes when he was busy thinking about how to ward off a besieging army? As for the older children, he asked that they sleep as long they could in the afternoon, even if they didn't want to.

When he arrived in Tabigha that night with Daher's army, the messenger asked Miqdad if he had carried out Daher's instructions. "To the letter," he replied. "Everyone's waiting for you. And now, where are we going?"

"To Arraba and Deir Hanna."

"To Arraba and Deir Hanna? In the dead of night?"

"Don't worry about a thing. Sheikh Saad al-Umar has made preparations to receive you until this war is over."

Miqdad was the tallest person between Lake Tiberias and the Acre Sea. In fact, it was said that he was the only person in the world who could see what was inside a city while standing outside its walls! From the time he was ten years old, never once had he needed to put his foot in the stirrup in order to mount his horse. To his dismay, his feet were constantly bumping up against rocks and plants, so they were always covered with scratches and gashes. But what dismayed him even more was having to carry on a conversation with a short man. Looking down made him dizzy. After discovering this, he began talking to short people with his eyes fixed on the horizon, but never mentioned the matter to anyone.

The arrival of Daher's messenger nearly exposed this secret of his. Daher had made a point of sending a man by the name of Tha'lab—"Fox"—a short, wiry man who took pride in his ability to slip in and out of places with ease and to keep himself out of sight whether it was night or day.

Miqdad couldn't see Tha'lab as he approached, and before he knew it, the little man was standing at his feet. When he began to speak, Miqdad started with fright, and found himself obliged to look down in order to see him. His head started to spin, but he managed to regain his balance by looking into the distance.

Irritated to see that Miqdad wasn't looking at him, Tha'lab shouted, "I'm right here!"

"I know you're there! What do you want?" Miqdad replied, continuing to stare into the distance.

"Talk to me. I want you to talk to me!"

"Don't you hear me?"

Tha'lab looked up at the towering figure before him. For the first time in his life, he started to feel dizzy himself. He looked down again. "I do hear you. But why don't you look at me?"

"What do you want?"

"I want you to look at me when you speak to me. Don't you know who I am?"

"No, I don't. Who are you?"

"I'm Tha'lab!"

"Welcome," Miqdad said, still looking into the distance.

"If you think you can belittle me, then I'll have you know that I am the messenger of Sheikh Daher al-Umar!"

"Daher's messenger?" Miqdad asked. He looked down, and the earth started spinning again.

Miqdad reached out and ran his hand over the top of the wall. Then he slid into a sitting position in the dirt.

"Are we going to sit here?" Tha'lab asked in surprise. "Doesn't the village have a diwan where we can talk?"

"Do you want to talk to me in the diwan? You can go there ahead of me, then."

Miqdad called out at the top of his lungs. A number of men gathered. "Take our guest to the diwan," he instructed them. "I'll follow you there shortly."

What surprised Daher's army was the condition Miqdad stipulated for leaving. "I'm not going anywhere if Tha'lab is going to be our escort!"

"He's the best guide we have. Didn't you know that?"

"If it's a matter of having a guide, I'm the best guide you'll find between Tiberias and Acre!"

"But Sheikh Daher left instructions for Tha'lab to escort us!"

"Anything Sheikh Daher says, I'm willing to do. But I beg you to send this man back." They sat there staring at each other in awkward silence.

A few moments later, Miqdad said, "I'm sure Sheikh Daher will need him more there than we do here."

"So be it," replied the army commander. "Go back to Tiberias, Tha'lab. Maybe Sheikh Daher really does need you more there!"

They worked quickly to ready the caravan: a caravan of silence filled with the fearful clamor of little hearts and big hearts alike. When the caravan moved out, a number of dogs ran after it. The people tried to drive them back home, but the dogs howled and whined. Regretful, the people went back for them.

Everyone who owned a dog was responsible for muzzling it well. The dogs resisted. In the end, however, they relented. They seemed to realize that this was the only way they would be allowed to come along.

Then they were on their way.

Sulayman Pasha's fury at the city of Tiberias had mounted, and in the distance they could see shells raining relentlessly down on it. As those in the caravan listened to the thunder of death and watched the mad flashes that accompanied it, every one of them felt a special gratitude to Daher for what he had done.

As they made their way farther from the city, they felt safer with every step they took. But suddenly something changed. Sensing something peculiar, the dogs tried to bark. They tore in vain at the muzzles with their claws, whining miserably and emitting muffled throaty rasps, but to no avail.

By this time they had stopped behind the caravan while the caravan continued on its way. To make matters worse, no one noticed their frenzy in that all-encompassing darkness.

Looking into each other's eyes, the dogs made a rush in the opposite direction as though they wanted to go back to Tabigha. At that same moment, Miqdad noticed that his dog wasn't with him. He looked for him, but he was gone. As he turned and stared wide-eyed into the distance, he caught a glimpse of his dog, which was white. If only the travelers had noticed his color and smeared him with ashes from a stove or an oven! The dog was running, and he saw him fly through the air and lunge at a mass of darkness. Then he remained suspended in midair, writhing. As a frightened horse's neigh rang out behind them, Miqdad realized what was happening, and Daher's army rushed back.

That night witnessed a minor battle in which the besieging army's entire patrol was wiped out. No one in the caravan, whose members outnumbered the soldiers by ten times at least, had been harmed.

Sadly, all of the dogs were killed. Without the use of their fangs, they hadn't been able to keep death at bay. Miqdad wept bitterly over his white dog, his only comfort being that the night's pitch darkness veiled his tears. He insisted on taking his dog's body with him, whereas the other dogs' owners did nothing but remove their muzzles. They knew that muzzling the dogs had been the only way to protect themselves and their other animals. Even so, they were smitten with guilt.

The call to prayer rang out from distant places. They felt it coming from all directions, from above, from below.

As the sounds of the explosions died away, tongues of fire rose above a now-distant Tiberias. Meanwhile, the caravan continued on its way amid the September night's chill, which deepened as they ascended into the hills.

By the time they reached Arraba, threads of sunlight had begun illumining the plains and the hills, and the air was redolent with the mingled fragrances of wild plants and tree leaves that had fallen on autumn's doorstep. As the earth lit up, they saw a large gathering of men and women waiting for them on the outskirts of the town.

The Wall of Dust
and the Hornet's Nest

S ulayman Pasha waited for the cannons to go off. He didn't hear
anything. He waited some more, but the silence only grew more
deafening.

He came out of his pavilion and mounted his horse. Sensing his
anger, the servants, Mamluks, and slaves scattered.

"Why hasn't the shelling begun?" he roared.

The soldiers, who hadn't moved their cannons into place near Tiberias as they had on previous nights, remained silent.

He repeated his question, and as he did so he smelled dust. He
sneezed violently. Then he kept sneezing—a second time, a third time,
a fourth—until he'd forgotten all about his question.

Taking advantage of the silence that had followed Sulayman Pasha's
last sneeze, one of the artillery commanders replied, "We've run out of
ammunition, my lord."

"You have no ammunition left?"

"That's correct, my lord."

"And where has your ammunition gone?"

"To Tiberias, my lord."

"Nothing is left?"

"No, my lord. Nothing!"

The smell of dust came back more powerfully than before. Sulayman
Pasha covered his face with his kerchief, suppressing another sneeze. Before
setting off, he shouted, "Let the commanders follow me—all of them!"

"Why didn't you inform me about this!" he bellowed.

"We were about to. However, we were occupied today with a group
of men we caught smuggling arms to Daher."

"How could they smuggle arms into a city that we're blockading?"

"We're interrogating them, my lord, and everything will become clear."

"And when will things become clear? You say you caught them
during the day. Hasn't anything become clear yet?"

The commander made no reply.

"I want results by morning, or else!"

"Yes, my lord."

Before the other men had left the pavilion, he smelled dust again. However, he muffled his sneeze until they were gone.

After muffling another violent sneeze with his kerchief, Sulayman Pasha barked an order to one of his servants to bring his concubine, Rihab. The servant hurried away. Despite the darkness of the night, he passed adroitly over the tent pegs and ropes as though he could see them. Rihab's tent was some distance away from the pasha's pavilion. He preferred it to be this way, since the distance, however short it happened to be, intensified his longing for her. The mere anticipation of her arrival would set up a storm of passionate desire that was an exquisite pleasure in and of itself.

He heard a whistling sound and lifted his head. It was coming from the top of the pavilion. It died out, then began again, louder than before.

He thought he saw the western side of the pavilion shaking. He looked in its direction and saw it whipping to and fro. He thought it strange that there would be so much wind on an otherwise calm night. As he was about to call his servants to ask them about it, the pavilion shook violently, and the whistling sound came in through the arrow holes.

He looked up again and saw the tent walls billowing and swaying.

For a moment he thought of leaving. However, he knew that, by comparison with all the other tents in the camp, Rihab's included, the pavilion was the securest structure around.

A few minutes later, a powerful gust of wind blew the pavilion door open. He shut his eyes to protect them from the wind and dust. Rugs scattered every which way, and a small table toppled over on top of his gilded velvet chair. The chair wobbled slightly, then collapsed, and his waterpipe broke. Noticing that the sides of his loose-fitting tunic were flapping in the wind like wings, he smoothed it down with his hands.

One of the guards managed to close the door again quickly, but by that time everything was a shambles, and the wind had brought in dry tree leaves, small branches, and an enormous amount of dust.

The whistling grew louder again from the roof of the pavilion. Outside, the area around the pavilion had turned into a wall of dust so thick that no artillery in the world could have penetrated it.

Rihab came in, her hair looking like a bird's nest, and her head covering gone with the wind. She was a pitiful sight. Sulayman Pasha looked away from her. At that moment, she was the ugliest concubine he'd ever seen in his life, and if he hadn't known for a fact that she was otherwise, he would have sent her away. The desire that had been racking his body was suddenly extinguished, and nothing remained but the whistling, which was growing louder and louder and coming from all directions. He realized he would have to get out of the pavilion, which was now more dangerous than a hornet's nest.

He headed eastward toward Rihab's tent, with Rihab stumbling along behind him. Everything had turned to dust: the air, the tents, the horses and mules struggling to get away, and the overturned carriages. Some tents had blown away, while soldiers had managed to hold others down, clinging to their ropes and driving their pegs more deeply into the ground.

When Sulayman Pasha went into Rihab's tent and saw her close the door behind her, he was tempted again to send her out. She was in far worse shape than she had been before. To his dismay, however, he discovered that he was in no better shape than she was. So he kept quiet. Seeing the state the tent was in, he feared that a single word from him might prompt the wind to blow them both away. The tent quaked more and more violently, but remained in place.

More than thirty soldiers were standing outside Rihab's tent, holding on to its ropes with all their might to keep it from flying away along with the others. Not wanting to draw his attention to their presence, and fearing he might be asleep, they had refrained from driving additional tent pegs, since this would have been sure to wake him up, and would have unleashed a storm of reprimands for not setting up the tent properly in the first place.

Recovering from the effects of the sudden tempest, Rihab managed to take a bath and spruce herself up again. Seeing her coming toward him, his mood suddenly changed. He turned up the blanket and gestured for her to slip in next to him.

As conditions worsened outside, the soldiers suddenly found themselves caught between two storms: one around them, and one inside them. At first all they'd been able to think of was holding on to the ropes. But as the minutes passed, they were all taken captive by a single thought: What if they lost hold of the tent and it flew into the air, leaving Sulayman Pasha and his concubine stark naked?

With this thought, their hands relaxed around the ropes!

The Deadly Message
and the Houses' Moan

With the arrival of the ammunition Sulayman Pasha had requested from Haifa, Acre, and Damascus, Tiberias was transmuted into a cloud of dust. As though he were confident that this final onslaught would kill off everyone in the city, he prepared the ladders that would be needed to scale the walls. However, he preferred not to have the army approach until the entire population was dead and he could smell their rotting corpses from where he was.

By the fourth day after the shelling had stopped, the cloud had dissipated.

Once again the people came out of their houses, every family certain that they were the sole survivors. However, although part of the market had been destroyed, there had been surprisingly little loss of life.

One warm evening in late September, a small squad from Sulayman Pasha's army advanced with the ladders, confident that they wouldn't need them. When they got closer, they were surprised to find that the cloud of dust still lingered. When they were a few hundred meters from the city gate, they still couldn't see a thing. They kept approaching until they were only a hundred meters away, at which point they would either have to advance the rest of the way, or turn back.

Then a shot rang out, and a bullet lodged in a soldier's head.

"I got him," announced Jurays from the top of the wall.

Daher patted him on the shoulder and looked over at Bishr. Bishr aimed, but the remaining soldiers had disappeared behind a low stone wall. He peered out with Bedouin eyes that could detect the slightest movement in the distance. A few moments later he fired.

"Did you hit any of them?" Daher asked.

"There were ten of them before Jurays killed one of them. So let's see how many of them run away."

Behind the low stone wall the soldiers sat counting the hours they had left to live. They realized that trying to withdraw in broad daylight would make them easy targets, so they decided to go on hiding until after sundown.

"They aren't going to advance any farther, and they aren't going to withdraw. So let's go out after them! We might be able to take some of them captive. The last thing they'd expect now is for us to fight them outside the walls," said Yusuf.

"I'll be the first to go out to meet them," said Bishr.

"And I'll go with you!" said Jurays.

Daher turned to a silent al-Dankizli.

"What do you think?" he asked him.

"Nobody's going out after them," said al-Dankizli.

"This is our chance to grab them!" said Jurays.

"Rather, it's their chance to get even," replied Daher. "You'll be completely exposed. One man alive in here is worth more to us than ten dead enemy soldiers out there. They can bring others to take their place, but we can't."

Before the men parted ways, a peculiar message arrived from the governor of Sidon via the lake. The messenger approached, surrounded by a number of Daher's soldiers.

"Speak," Daher said to him.

"I have to speak with you alone, Sheikh," the man said. "You're the only person who's allowed to hear the message I've brought you."

"Follow me, then."

Daher took a few steps away while his soldiers subjected the man to a thorough search.

He had nothing on him, since they had taken his weapon from him during an earlier search.

"I'm listening."

Daher looked out at the lake, where he saw hundreds of dead fish floating on the surface of the water, and some that had washed up on shore.

He turned to face the governor's messenger.

"Say what you have to say. No one can hear us here."

It was a brief message, as if the governor of Sidon didn't want to waste any time. "My lord has sent to you, saying, 'Stand firm against Sulayman Pasha, and wait for the opportunity to go out against him. You have nothing to fear if you should kill him. I will stand behind you.

289

I shall write to the sultan telling him that you killed him in self-defense.'"

"Is that all your lord has to say?"

"Yes, Sheikh. Not a word less, and not a word more."

Daher turned his gaze back to the waves of lifeless fish that washed back and forth between the lake and the shore. The gentle westerly wind was a particular blessing during those days, since it carried the stench of the fish away toward the lake's eastern shore.

"Do you have a message you want me to take back to my lord the governor?" the messenger asked.

"You'll spend the night here and depart tomorrow evening. The well-being of the governor's messenger is of great importance to us. But I want to ask you: What do people outside expect in relation to Tiberias? What are they saying?"

The messenger hesitated.

"Tell me the truth. You're my guest, after all."

"To be honest, Sheikh, a lot of people are angry. They're saying, 'How can we let a city like Tiberias be bombed to destruction while we look on? It's the first time anything like this has happened!'"

"So these are the things people are saying! What do other people have to say? Tell me the truth."

The messenger hesitated again.

"Say what you have to say. If I didn't want to hear the truth, I wouldn't have asked you."

"They're saying that Tiberias is bound to fall sooner or later to the governor of Damascus, since they know how powerful he is. After all, he's backed by the empire and the sultan, whereas Tiberias is backed by no one but itself!"

"But it hasn't fallen, as you can see."

"I'll tell you honestly, Sheikh: Some people say these things with regret, since they can't do anything. Others speak this way because they want things to be over quickly so that they won't have to go on worrying about what's happening here! From Sidon to Damascus, all people are talking about is Tiberias and what it's going through. It worries them, just as it worries the empire."

"And do you think that killing Sulayman Pasha would bring all that to an end?"

"Pardon me, Sheikh. I can't put myself in the middle, between a message I've brought you and a decision that only you can make!"

"Very well. You've said enough."

Daher said nothing about the message he'd received from the governor of Sidon. Instead, he went through the streets helping people: removing heaps of rocks blocking the roads, repairing broken doors, restocking stores that had been damaged, passing out candy to children busily picking up bomb fragments, and warning them not to go near any unexploded shells. In short, he kept on doing the same things he'd been doing since the beginning of the siege.

Despite the harsh conditions they had endured for weeks on end, things remained essentially unchanged for the people of Tiberias. In keeping with Daher's instructions, prices had remained the same and people lacked no essential commodities, while the lake continued to provide a steady supply of food despite all the fish that had been killed by falling shells.

Speaking to al-Dankizli in private, Daher asked him to instruct their spies in Damascus to spread reports about how Tiberias was standing strong despite all the gunfire it had endured, and to talk about how, if it weren't for the shame of defeat, Sulayman Pasha would have come home. Pleased with the idea, al-Dankizli sent for a number of men in Damascus and instructed them to do as Daher had said, and to make a point of expressing sympathy for the desperate, defeated governor so as to enhance their credibility.

"When those soldiers who tried to reach the walls come back with two of their number missing, all hell's going to break loose," al-Dankizli predicted. Daher agreed.

Daher issued orders for the city's lanterns not to be lit at all that night.

They had lost numerous lanterns due to the shelling. Consequently, they had begun keeping them lit until right before the call to the final evening prayer, then having the lamplighters gather them in for fear that they might be destroyed.

"The soldiers came back after losing two of their men," one of the army commanders informed Sulayman Pasha.

"We've still got plenty of time ahead of us. As for Tiberias, let its time run out. How long will it be before the pilgrimage caravan sets out?"

"Two months, my lord."

"In two months we could occupy twenty cities like Tiberias, couldn't we?"

"Absolutely, my lord!"

"I want you to shell any place we have reason to believe Daher might be. Also, I want you to attack the heart of the city. The walls don't concern me now. We'll just be wasting our shells on them. I don't want it to be said that when Sulayman Pasha entered Tiberias, he killed his captives. Rather, when I go in, I want to see all of them already dead. Seven days from now send in a small brigade, and we'll see whether there's anyone left to fire at our soldiers!"

It was hell all over again.

There was already very little left of Daher's house, which had been virtually destroyed. At the beginning of the siege, anticipating the destruction, he had moved his family to a house next to the southern wall. Nevertheless, Najma had gone on visiting the old house at least twice a day.

"Are you still worried about the house?" Daher said. "They've demolished it completely, and you've seen it with your own eyes, Mother! It's enough for you to worry about the children."

"The children are safe. As for the house, I do worry about it. I'm afraid they'll demolish it even more completely, Sheikh!"

"How could they demolish it any more completely than they already have, Mother?"

"There are still a lot of things we need under the rubble."

"I'll bring you whatever you need. Just tell me what it is."

"You won't be able to bring what I need."

"So what is it that you want, Mother?"

"I like to check the house to see if it needs anything from me. I hear it moaning all night long."

"Mother!"

"No, I'm not crazy, Daher," she replied quickly. "I'm really not!" And she left.

One day Jurays came up to Daher and said bashfully, "You know, Sheikh? They're depriving me, my wife, and my children of the chance

292

to celebrate our wedding anniversary today."

"How's that? The whole reason we're fighting them is to keep them from depriving us of the things we love!"

"But I wanted to invite you to come, Sheikh. Considering all you've done for us, our celebration won't mean anything unless you're there."

"And who said I wouldn't be?"

"This war, Sheikh!"

"This war can't keep us from loving each other. I'll be at your house tonight!"

Seated in Jurays's house, Daher pondered the tiny abode illumined by a colorful lantern which, Daher would learn later, was only lit on this particular occasion. Before him were Jurays's three children, who sat gazing happily at the lantern as though the war were a thousand miles away.

Both Jurays and his wife, who went scurrying in and out of the room as though she wanted to get things over with as quickly as possible, were visibly ill at ease.

"Everything's all right, sister," Daher reassured her. "Why are you in such a hurry?"

"How can I not be in a hurry, Sheikh, when war is at our doorstep?"

"Forget the war for a little while. Don't give them the victory by letting them steal this lovely moment from us!"

She disappeared momentarily. Then she rushed back in with five glasses of lemonade as though she hadn't heard a word Daher said.

She handed one to Daher, and one to each of her children. Then she took off her wedding ring. As she was about to place the ring in the fifth glass, Daher stopped her, saying, "You don't usually put the rings into a glass of lemonade, do you?"

"Well, no," Jurays replied diffidently.

"So then, bring your wine glass, and do what you always do! I didn't come to your house today to prevent you from doing what your religion allows. Bring your wine, and leave the lemonade for me and the children!"

"But it wouldn't be proper to do that with you here, Sheikh!" Jurays's wife protested.

"What wouldn't be proper would be for my presence to ruin this lovely ritual, which, I hear, is observed by many couples on this sort of occasion."

With timid, hesitant steps, Jurays's wife got up and left the room. She was gone for such a long time, Daher began to think she wasn't coming back. At last, however, she reappeared, in her hand a glass containing just enough wine to cover its bottom.

Setting the glass down before her, she removed her ring, wiped it with a damp cloth, and placed it inside the glass. Jurays did the same. Then he lifted the glass and, looking at his children, said, "May the Lord shower you with love as He has showered your mother and me. And may happiness flow into your hearts with every sip of this wine, which embraces my heart, your mother's heart, and the sacred pact we've made to love one another, sacrifice for one another, care for one another, and be faithful to one another."

Then he took a sip.

Jurays passed the glass to his wife, who also took a sip. Then the children and Daher drank their glasses of lemonade. Jurays's wife took her ring out of the glass, dried it off, and placed it back on her left ring finger. Then she handed the glass to her husband, who did as she had done.

As Daher and Jurays walked side by side back to the city walls, Jurays exclaimed, "I think I feel stronger now, Sheikh, ready to die for the sake of preserving a moment like this!"

"On the contrary, you'll live many years for the sake of moments like this."

The Cry That Took Cover in Darkness

The people of Tiberias had discovered that the safest houses were those located directly up against the city walls. Hence, they kept as close to the walls as they could, and from there watched their homes vanish before their very eyes.

One night at midnight, someone began shouting so loudly that his voice drowned out the sounds of exploding shells and collapsing buildings. The unidentified voice cried, "They want Daher and the Zaydanis! So why should we have to die? Where is Saad's army, the army we've heard about but have never seen?"

The words rocked the earth beneath Daher's feet. He turned and saw his brother Yusuf, al-Dankizli, the judge, and Bishr all staring at him.

"Shall we find him and bring him to you, Sheikh?"

"Who?"

"The person who shouted a little while ago."

"No, don't do that."

"But he's calling on people to rebel, Sheikh!" said al-Dankizli.

Daher said nothing at first. He looked over at them, though all he could see was the whites of their eyes.

"Are people so afraid of me that they feel they can only say what they really think in the dark?"

No one replied.

"This cry wasn't his cry alone," Daher continued. "So let's see what we can do. Do you think Najma is asleep?"

"Who could sleep on a night like this, Sheikh? She must be sitting at home waiting for us," said Yusuf. "But what would you want from Najma at this time of night?"

"You'll know in the morning."

Sulayman Pasha's anxiety had mounted to the point where, unable to bear getting close to anyone, he ordered his concubine sent back to Damascus.

He replaced his arrow-torn pavilion with a sturdier one. When they had finished setting it up, he took a bow and shot an arrow at it. The arrow bounced off, leaving nothing but a tiny indentation. Then he took a spear and stabbed it, with the same result. When he grabbed a rifle from one of his officers and aimed it at the tent, everyone was sure the pasha had lost his mind. At the last moment, however, remembering that there was still no such thing as a bulletproof pavilion, he lowered the rifle and handed it back to its owner.

"In my opinion, you should make peace with the man!" declared his advisor, Uthman Pasha.

"Make peace with who?"

"With Daher, Pasha! Time is running out, and the weather is changing. Before long winter will be upon us, and the pilgrimage caravan will set out."

"Is that what you really think, Uthman, or are you just parroting the sultan's wishes?"

"With all due respect for the sultan, my lord, I don't think time is on our side!"

"I'm going to ask for fifteen more days to complete the mission I've come to carry out. Never before has Sulayman Pasha turned back in defeat. Besides, who would be defeating me in this case? Tiberias—a puny little town that's hardly the size of a neighborhood in Damascus!"

"Very well, my lord. Let us do everything we can before the fifteen days have passed."

Sulayman Pasha was incredulous when he was told that a messenger from Daher had arrived. Putting on the air of a strong man who would never back down, he refused to meet with him.

"Tell him that the pasha has only one demand: that you open the gates of Tiberias and come out with your kerchiefs around your necks!"

"But he's sent his mother, my lord!" Uthman Pasha said to him.

"His mother?"

"Yes, his mother. As you know, my lord, it's people's custom to send the mother of the emir or sheikh, or some other woman close to him, to conduct negotiations as an expression of humility and goodwill toward the other party, which in this case is us!"

"What do you think I should do, Uthman?"

"I think you should meet with her, my lord. This may ease the awkward position we find ourselves in. After all, we've been at a stalemate for more than two months."

"Bring her in, then."

"She's at the door, my lord."

As a gift for Sulayman Pasha, Daher chose a fine thoroughbred horse that would have fetched a price as high as a thousand piasters. Then he sent it with Najma, instructing her to sit with the governor and find out what his demands were. Nothing would send a clearer message than his response to the gift. If he refused it, it would mean that he wasn't willing to reach an understanding with them. If he did accept it, it would mean that a settlement was possible.

Daher stood contemplating her on the back of the horse.

"Why are you looking at me that way?" she asked him.

"You know what, Mother? I'm going to tell you something, and I hope you won't be angry with me."

"I think I know what it is before you say it. I can see it in your eyes."

"What is it, then?"

"Say it, and if it's what I'm thinking, I'll tell you!"

"I think you need a better, stronger horse than that one. What do you say?"

"Me? Why would I need another horse? Do you think I'm going to live to be fifty?"

Daher laughed. He knew she was about to turn sixty.

"Why are you laughing?"

Sulayman Pasha looked thoughtfully at the messenger, a woman of medium stature with radiant eyes. She was so self-assured you would have thought she was already the victor. Or so it seemed to him. This impression on his part was reinforced by the thoroughbred horse whose reins were held by the strapping young men who stood behind her.

When his eyes fell on her feet, he was taken aback. She was barefoot, as usual. He wondered what this might mean. Was it a kind of entreaty? Or was it, perhaps, an expression of disdain for him? He didn't know.

Realizing what he was thinking, Najma said, "I'm always this way, Pasha. I've never worn a pair of shoes in my life, not even on my wedding day! Sheikh Daher asked me to put on some shoes before coming to see you but I refused, since I'm of the belief that no one should force a free person to do what makes her uncomfortable!"

"Have a seat," Sulayman Pasha said, gesturing to a chair next to him.

"If you'll allow me, Pasha, I'll sit on this rug. I've never liked to be too far from the earth!"

"Be my guest."

As Najma sat down, Sulayman Pasha began thinking about everything she said. She was clearly a shrewd woman, and he could see that Daher hadn't sent her for nothing.

"This is Sheikh Daher's gift to you," she said, pointing to the horse behind her without looking back at it.

Sulayman Pasha looked at the horse again. More impressed with it than ever, he settled the matter within himself. "I accept the gift!" he said.

"Wonderful," Najma replied. "That means there's good to follow."

"I have only one demand: that you open the gates of Tiberias and come out with your kerchiefs around your necks!"

"You should remember, Pasha, that Your Excellency hasn't triumphed, and that we haven't been defeated."

"On the contrary, you were defeated from the moment I arrived here!"

"I've come here today, Pasha, to avoid further bloodshed on both our side and yours, and my hope is that you will strive with me toward this end."

"You needn't worry about our blood. I've got the whole land of Syria behind me, and I can call out a hundred more soldiers for every one that dies!"

"I know that, Pasha. All of us know that! We also know that when we lose someone in Tiberias, it is difficult for us to replace that person even with one other, still less a hundred. However, we grieve over every soul we lose just as you grieve over every one you lose, Pasha, even if you can call out a hundred others to replace him!"

"Do you mean to say you care more about my soldiers' lives than I do?"

"Your soldiers are human just as we are, Pasha. So it's only right that I should worry about them."

"What are your demands?"

"Our demand is that you withdraw with your army, in return for which we will pay all the taxes we owe the state."

"As for my demand, it's that you open the city gates and surrender, and that I be allowed to take Daher with me to Damascus. I've made a vow to do precisely that before I end my term as governor."

"So you intend to take my son to be executed there the way his brother Saleh was?"

"That's my demand!"

Najma bowed her head. When she looked up again, she fixed her eyes on his until he was forced to shift his gaze to her feet.

"Allow us to be on our way, Pasha," she said.

"Goodbye."

Najma rose, patted the horse's back as if in farewell, and departed, followed by the young men who had been waiting for her outside.

Sulayman Pasha watched her walk away barefoot, expecting at any moment to see her trip over a rock or get a thorn in her foot. But nothing of the sort happened. She proceeded as calmly and steadily as if she were strolling down a sandy beach. When she came up to the horse that had brought her, she placed her right foot in the stirrup. Before mounting, she looked back at Sulayman Pasha, who was staring at her. Her foot remained in the stirrup for several seconds until, realizing that he was supposed to look away, he averted his gaze, and she was on her way.

"They say she's the woman who reared Daher after his mother died," remarked Sulayman Pasha.

"Yes, my lord. She, and a certain thoroughbred horse," Uthman replied.

"What?"

"We have to know our enemy well if we want to defeat him, my lord. So I'm going to tell you Daher's story from the beginning."

"All right, but make it quick!"

When Uthman Pasha started relating Daher's story, Sulayman Pasha forgot that it was about his enemy. "So what happened after that?" he asked, urging him on.

As Uthman Pasha went into more and more detail, he was surprised to hear the same question again. "What happened after that?"

"You seem to be enjoying his story, Pasha!"

Catching himself, Sulayman Pasha said quickly, "That's enough. That's enough!"

"But there's another part to the story, my lord."

"I said that was enough!"

The people of Tiberias rejoiced when they saw Najma and her party returning without the horse they'd taken to present to Sulayman Pasha. In fact, some of them were about to congratulate each other on her successful mission.

"She was the best messenger Daher could have sent to Sulayman Pasha!" one of them exclaimed.

"Now you say so!" retorted another. "This morning you asked me, 'Couldn't Daher find anybody but that old woman to send?'"

Shouts

A stony solemnity was etched on people's faces.

With everyone's eyes upon him, Daher stood on one of the steps that led up to the top of the wall. He looked left, right, and front, trying to gather them all into his gaze.

All the people of Tiberias had become a single heart, a single ear.

Daher asked Najma to come up and stand beside him. She hesitated, and he repeated his request. So she came up and joined him, scanning the faces in the crowd, and periodically casting a glance over at Daher. She was her usual strong, immovable self.

Addressing those gathered, Daher began: "Last night I heard someone shouting, 'They want Daher and the Zaydanis. So why should we have to die?' So I sent my mother Najma to see Sulayman Pasha today. I sent her to convey Tiberias's demands to him and to hear his demands. I sent him the woman closest to my heart as an expression of humility, and in the hope that he would hear the message we all want him to hear. He wants the empire's taxes, of course. My mother told him that he would receive the empire's taxes in full, everything to which it's entitled. However, he demanded that you come out in abject surrender, with your kerchiefs around your necks: that you defeat Tiberias with your own hands by opening the gates that his army hasn't been able to reach.

"The state is entitled to collect taxes. However, it has no right to humiliate people, dragging their dignity through the mud. The dignity God has given us isn't state property. Our freedom isn't state property. The spirits being wrested from the bodies of our children for the past two months aren't state property. As for those who believe that their dignity, their freedom, and even their lives belong to the state, I won't keep them here by force. I'll open the gates of Tiberias for them myself, and they're welcome to go live as slaves wherever they wish."

He heard someone shout, "Where's your brother Saad's army?"

Another shouted, "Go out with your army against the governor, Daher, and kill him!"

"That isn't the way I think," replied Daher. "I take a longer view of things. There are only two situations in which I would ask my brother Saad to dispatch his army here. First, if the governor of Sidon brought his army to Tiberias, I would ask Saad to advance and launch a surprise attack on Sulayman Pasha in his camp, since then people would say that it was the governor of Sidon who had attacked the governor of Damascus because the latter had attacked Tiberias, which is located in the vilayet of Sidon. This is what I hope will happen, in fact, because I don't want it to be said that Sheikh Daher rose up against the sultan's representative, the leader of the pilgrimage to Mecca, and killed him. If I did such a thing, I would cause the pilgrimage caravan to be delayed, and give people reason to call me a murderer.

"The second situation in which I would ask Saad to intervene is one that I'll do my utmost never to allow to materialize. If, God forbid, Sulayman Pasha managed to breach the city walls so that there was no longer any other way to keep his forces at bay, then, and only then, would I call on my brother Saad to come to our rescue.

"Brothers, sisters, family: As you know, we haven't lost this war yet, and we still lack nothing. We're as strong today as we were yesterday. Our men are strong, and our walls are impregnable. So why should we go out against the governor and kill him? We would be capable of doing so. However, if we did, I would bear responsibility for his death, and I would implicate you in that responsibility. Then all of us together would be under the sultan's curse. All I hope to do is to preserve my country and protect my people. I want the governor to leave and spare us the harm he wants to do us. So keep up your guard, and wage a war of defense. Kill anyone who comes near the walls, but avoid killing anyone for any other reason.

"It has come to my hearing, sisters and brothers, that according to some people, these things are happening to us because Daher refuses to be anything less than a hero! The worst idea anyone ever had was to be a war hero. There are a thousand other ways to be a true hero. This war was imposed on us, and we aren't fighting in order to be heroes. Rather, we're fighting in order to be human. God Almighty has honored human beings, saying, 'Now, indeed, We have conferred dignity on the children of Adam.' All we want is to be human. My dream is for you all to be heroes after this siege is over. Heroism means building your country in safety, planting your trees in safety, and not being afraid for your children because they are free from danger. Every man will be a hero when he can roam the streets however he pleases without anyone harassing him, insulting his dignity, stealing his children's daily bread, or encroaching on his freedom. I dream of the day when a woman can walk alone through the city or the countryside and be honored and respected by all in the knowledge that she is a heroine, flanked by the spirits of hundreds of heroines and heroes. I want every one of my people, from Lake Tiberias to the Sea of Acre, to be a fearless hero. True heroism means for you to be so safe that no other kind of heroism is required.

"Sisters, brothers, children of mine: if I believed that it would grant you the dream I've just spoken to you about, I would take my head in my hands and deliver it personally to Sulayman Pasha. However, as every one of you knows, and as every city and village that has ever been besieged before us knows, someone who demands one head will end up demanding them all. Is there anyone here who would be willing to offer the head of his mother, his daughter, his son, his brother, his sister, or his wife to Sulayman Pasha?"

"Not in a million years!"

"Not in a million years!" came the reply in successive shouts as people's hearts were filled with renewed strength. From the back of his horse Bishr waved his sword, and Najma patted her son on the back, saying, "May God grant you victory."

Hidden Equations

The governor regrets what he's done to you," stated the messenger, "but he's too proud to ask you for a peace agreement. Therefore, we request that you send your mother to speak with him again. We promise to support her in her negotiations with him, and we feel certain that this time she won't return empty-handed.

"Sulayman Pasha doesn't want to leave Tiberias without having achieved anything," the messenger continued. "He's tired, just as you are, and he senses what's going on in the minds of his commanders and their soldiers. They're all weary of the situation. Tiberias hasn't fallen, and they can't go on besieging it forever!"

After hearing the messenger out, Daher and al-Dankizli stepped aside. "What do you think?" Daher asked him.

"I think you and I are in agreement, Sheikh. Let's try again."

"All right. That is, if Najma agrees to go back!"

When Daher reached the tiny abode where they'd taken refuge next to the northern wall, he saw his son Ali hopping along the wall like a little monkey. He was about to call out to him, but was afraid his call might distract him, causing him to lose his footing and fall. So he watched him in silence, thinking back on the days he himself had once spent on Bi'na's city wall.

When Najma saw him, she asked, "Do you want me to go now, or tomorrow?"

"Where?"

"To Sulayman Pasha's camp."

"Who told you I wanted you to go there?"

"These bare feet of mine, which Sulayman Pasha stared at while I was staring him in the eye!"

"So you knew he would ask for you?"

"Sulayman Pasha is desperate, Daher. He built quite a cage for you, but then discovered that he was trapped inside it too!"

"You'll go, then?"

"Of course I will. But for my sake, please don't make me take a gift like the one you sent me with the first time! When the governor took that horse but refused to make peace, he showed that he wasn't worth even a horseshoe."

"Leave the gift to me. I'll choose it myself, Mother."

"I don't think you'll be able to. You're so generous by nature, you couldn't bear to hear people say, 'Look what a miserable gift Daher sent!' I'm going to choose your gift to him myself this time, Sheikh!"

Najma walked the streets in search of a present. She decided to go to a horse dealer, since horses were considered the best gifts for all occasions.

Pointing to a white stallion, she asked, "Is that horse for sale?"

"No. You can't take it, since feeding it has become a burden."

"Are there people besides you who can't feed their horses?"

"Lots. But we can't talk about how hard it is to feed horses when we're worrying about how to feed ourselves."

"So our horses are hungry?"

"More than hungry."

"Back to what we were saying before: If we weren't under siege, how much would a horse like this be worth?"

"In normal times it would be worth five hundred piasters."

"That's too much!"

"I'll give it to you for three hundred. No, two hundred."

"What concerns me isn't how much you'll sell it for now. What I want to know is its original value."

"To be honest, Madame Najma, I don't understand what you're after!"

"That's all right. And that red horse in the corner? How much would it cost in normal times?"

"Two hundred. But I'll sell it to you for . . ."

"That's too much," she interrupted. "And that speckled one?"

"In normal times, I'd be happy to get a hundred piasters for it."

"Now you're starting to get my drift. Here," she said, handing him the money. "Hand me its reins!"

"What is this, Mother? I swear to God, if Sulayman Pasha gave me a horse like that, I'd go out and fight him in his camp!"

"Didn't I tell you you were generous by nature?"

"And how much did that thing cost?"

"A hundred piasters."

"A hundred piasters, Mother?"

"You seem to be forgetting the value of the person who's going to take it there: your own mother! You seem to forget that by sending me to him, you're showing a respect for him that he ought to thank God for a thousand times over!"

"No, I haven't forgotten that."

"But you *have* forgotten, Daher!"

"I swear I haven't, Mother!"

"Frankly, even this horse is too good for him!"

Daher smiled.

"You agree to send it, then?"

"Of course, Mother. By God, if I sent a hen with you, it would become worth three thousand piasters."

"Are you telling me I'm only worth three thousand piasters, Sheikh?" she asked with a laugh.

"You know I wouldn't sell you for all the world, Mother! You're priceless to me!"

When Sulayman Pasha saw Najma approaching on horseback followed by that speckled horse, his chest tightened. He turned and went inside his tent. When she reached the camp, one of his guards came forward and informed him of her arrival.

"Let her wait for a while!" Sulayman Pasha told the guard.

Najma stayed on her horse, alternately watching the camp and gazing back at Tiberias. Her wait dragged on, and she felt as though a long time had passed since her feet had touched the ground, which distressed her. Nevertheless, she made up her mind not to dismount until he came out.

Her feet began to hurt, as though they were trapped inside a colony of hungry ants. She tried busying her mind with other things, but the ants didn't go away. When she looked down at the ground, she felt it beckoning to her. She lifted her eyes and gazed at the cloudy sky, which augured rain.

Still, no one invited her in.

Finally she couldn't bear it any longer. Should she get down and rub her feet in the dirt for a moment, then get back on the horse? Or should she head back to Tiberias, come what may? Without giving it more thought, she lifted her left leg and brought it down to the ground, rubbed her foot in the dirt, and quickly mounted the horse again as the guards looked on in bewilderment.

As for her other foot, it was still in the ant house.

Najma thought about how much of her life had passed. She did numerous calculations, beginning from the day Umar al-Zaydani had passed away, to their move to Arraba and their return from there, up to the present moment. She finished adding up the years in her head. Annoyed by the outcome, she subtracted ten years and smiled, proud of herself for being able to ride a horse that even teenage girls wouldn't have dared go near.

Then a voice broke her train of thought: "Please come in. The pasha is waiting for you."

She dismounted, doing her best to conceal her impatience to get off the horse. When at last she had her feet on the ground, she rubbed them into the dirt with such fervor, she looked as though she were furiously crushing some creature that no one else could see. The soldiers gave her another bewildered stare, trying to comprehend something that was comprehensible to no one but her.

The air began returning to her lungs and, her eyes glistening with satisfaction, she went in.

Sulayman Pasha welcomed her and invited her to sit down. She looked where he was pointing, but didn't find the brightly colored rug she had sat on the first time. She understood: as the horse is, so shall the rug be!

She apologized, saying, "I've been sitting on a horse for so long, I would prefer not to sit down."

"As you wish."

"I've come again as Sheikh Daher's messenger, and I'm hopeful that we can reach the agreement we failed to reach on my previous visit."

"I've thought at length about your first proposal, namely, that I withdraw and take the taxes you owe the empire. However, that isn't enough for me. Such a proposal might be satisfactory to the empire, but it isn't satisfactory to me."

"But you're the sultan's representative here, Pasha!"

"That's correct. However, I'm also an individual, and I have my own demands."

"And what are your demands?"

"For Daher to pay all the taxes he owes the empire, including taxes from years past, and for him to tear down one side of the tower!"

"And what will the pasha gain from our tearing down one side of the tower?"

"I'll at least have achieved part of what I promised myself!"

"I'll convey your request to Sheikh Daher, and we'll see. Please allow me to be on my way, since I can't go on standing much longer."

Sulayman Pasha remained seated until he heard the sound of her horse's hoofbeats dying away. Then he rose to his feet in a fury, opened the pavilion door, and gave the scrawny horse a swift kick that sent it flying across the prairie in an attempt to catch up with Najma.

From atop the wall they saw Najma approaching, followed in the distance by a terror-stricken speckled horse.

"I won't remove a single stone from that tower," Daher declared. "That tower is to me what a sail is to a ship. What's more," he added, "if at this point he asked me to put out a single lantern in return for withdrawing from here, I wouldn't do it. I've already conceded more than he deserves by letting him go back to Damascus with some of his dignity intact. But now he's gone too far, and he's not getting a thing more from me."

Breaking the long silence that followed, Najma said, "I'm going back to the house."

The lanterns were lit again, and in spite of the fog that descended, immersing the lake in a luminous grayness, Tiberias glimmered like a stately ship anchored along the shore.

Different Winds Begin to Blow

The shelling came to a halt, and there descended a strange calm to which the city wasn't accustomed. In fact, the people of Tiberias had almost forgotten how they used to live before the siege began.

Five days later, the calm was broken by a development that no one would ever have expected: the shells began coming from the direction of the lake! They didn't believe it until they ascended the wall and saw two large gunboats in the water.

"How could it be?" they wondered. But they had no answer to their question.

After long thought, Sulayman Pasha realized that there were two cards he had yet to play. The first was to besiege Tiberias from the direction of the lake. When he ordered two boats brought from Sidon, the governor of Sidon dragged his feet. Eventually he sent them, chuckling at the hilarious novelty of transporting two boats overland to Tiberias. Nevertheless, the camels that had been pressed into service for the occasion—"the ships of the desert"—managed to deliver "the ships of the water" to the lakeshore over a long flat road, and without their suffering any damage to speak of.

As for the second card, Sulayman Pasha had kept it well out of his enemy's sight, intending to bring it out as his final, deadly surprise.

The Splintered Night
and the Elusive Target

W here do you think the boats might be sleeping, Ahmad?"
"On the lake, of course, Sheikh."
"Not in Sulayman Pasha's pavilion, then?"
"Is this a test, Sheikh?"
"No, it isn't. But I'm amazed at how these boats' arrival has terrified people."
"What are you thinking, Sheikh?"
"These two boats are only good for a single day, and that day is over, Ahmad."
"Leave it to me, then."
"When morning comes, I don't want to see them on the lake."
"You won't see them at all."

At midnight the sky filled with thick clouds, permeating the air with the smell of rain. The surface of the lake began to ripple, and before long those living along the western wall could hear waves breaking in the dead of the night.

The same boats that had robbed Sulayman Pasha of sleep numerous times before set out once again, their oars breaking the water's surface as they plied at full speed toward their target.

Venturing out into the northern waters was far less dangerous than it could have been thanks to the fishermen's intimate familiarity with their lake's every detail. This time, however, they were aiming for a target whose location they didn't know for certain. Surmising that the two boats would be stationed near the enemy camp, al-Dankizli headed in that direction at the head of a force consisting of the fifteen largest boats in Tiberias.

The fog was so thick that they expected at any moment to run into one or both of the enemy vessels. This was their only fear. They felt their way along the lakeshore with their oars, and with their hands they explored the cold air around their boats. They found nothing.

Many thought of turning back, wondering whether Sulayman Pasha might have taken his boats back to camp with him, or perhaps not have brought them from Sidon to begin with! However, al-Dankizli decided to try another location: the eastern side of the lake.

It wasn't going to be easy. They would have to cross the lake at its widest point, which would take them nearly two hours. However, they knew that destroying the two boats was the best gift they could possibly offer to the people of Tiberias the following morning, and the cruelest possible blow to Sulayman Pasha.

The men looked around for some sign of Tiberias, but the city had vanished. Given the modest size of their boats, the lake was too large for them to cross in a reasonable time, especially in the thick fog. They kept rowing for what seemed like an eternity until, suddenly, what they had all feared happened: one of their boats collided with one of Sulayman Pasha's ships.

They stopped rowing and held their breath. The fisherman guiding the small vessel couldn't retreat, so it froze in place, as did the hearts of those in it.

They expected to hear a commotion, shouting, and shots that would rip them to shreds. But they didn't. It was nearly four o'clock in the morning, so time was on their side, as exhaustion, complacency, and the fog had made the eyes of Sulayman Pasha's mariners heavy.

Less than a minute later they heard steps approaching along the ship's deck. A ghostlike figure, possibly the guard, came into view. He knelt and peered with difficulty into the water in search of something. The figure was no more than four or five meters from those holding their breath in the small boat. However, the blackness of the water and the huge shadow cast by the boat itself prevented him from seeing anything, while he, given his location on deck, was an ideal target at such close range.

An arrow whizzed through the air, over the heads of the men crouching in the small boat and into the body of the unsuspecting guard. The night was so still that even the passing of an arrow through the body of a ghost sounded as harsh and discordant as a shell exploding in the darkness.

The body tottered, emitting a moan that sounded like a scream that never made its way to its throat. Then it fell into the water, producing a deafening clap that those in the small boat would rather not have heard.

Knowing he had no time to lose, al-Dankizli lit the torch in his hand, and the other men lit theirs. Torches flickered in their hands as oars clapped furiously through the water toward the enemy vessel. It was larger than they had imagined it would be. Nevertheless, they had prepared themselves for this moment.

What worried them now was that they had yet to sight the second enemy boat.

As the small boats retreated, flaming bundles of gunpowder went flying in the direction of the ship. Just then Jurays spotted the other ship's shadow and ordered those with him to head toward it as fast as they could. They hesitated. "Come on now! There's no time!" he shouted.

When they were twenty meters from the first ship, it exploded. The fog dissipated and the fragmented remains of the night fell onto the lake's surface, lighting it up like thousands of lanterns. In no time the second ship's deck filled with soldiers. The smaller boat, only meters away, was now the easiest, clearest imaginable target in the light of the flames consuming the other vessel. Realizing that time was of the essence, al-Dankizli ordered his men to fire. Bodies reeled, and some soldiers fell into the water, while others got down on their stomachs and began shooting.

Little did the enemy soldiers know that the distance between them would allow those in the small boat to throw their bundles of gunpowder all the more easily at their target. The bundles flew through the air and landed on the ship's deck. Seeing that within moments they would be fuel for the fire, the soldiers on board began flinging themselves into the water. However, the explosion was of sufficient magnitude to destroy everything in the immediate vicinity.

Once again, a night in shreds was strewn over the water.

Sulayman Pasha awoke in terror to the sound of the explosions. He was sure Daher must have stormed the camp. However, when he got to the door of his pavilion, he realized that the explosions were far away.

The soldiers in the camp tried to discern what was happening in the distance. All they could make out were faint flashes obscured by the fog. However, the explosions rang out like thunder. Certain now of what had happened, Sulayman Pasha cursed and fumed, swearing that Tiberias's fate would be crueler than that of his two ships.

The Secret of the Days to Come

At first it seemed to everyone like a huge, incredible lie.

"Our spies in Sulayman Pasha's camp are confident of it," Daher told al-Dankizli.

"But that's impossible! He's about to leave the camp!"

"This may be his last shot."

Shortly after sundown, people looking out over the walls saw a towering figure emerging confidently from the lake onto the shore. The guards drew their weapons and aimed their arrows and shotguns at the body, which was still out of shooting range. Meanwhile, pandemonium broke loose in the city.

"What's going on?" Daher asked.

"The city's being attacked by giants!" replied a boy as he fled.

Daher looked at the top of the wall, where everyone was preparing to fire their weapons. Then he went leaping up the stairs to join them. Looking out toward the lake, he saw the giant coming gradually into view.

"That's Miqdad!" Daher shouted. "Lower your weapons!"

"Miqdad? Who's that?" whispered a number of men to each other, convinced that Daher must be in cahoots with evil spirits.

"Miqdad is multazim of Tabigha. Don't worry. He's one of us!"

The closer he came to shore, the taller he got, and when at last he placed his foot on land, he was the tallest creature Daher's men had ever laid eyes on.

"It really *is* Miqdad!" said some men who knew him.

"Has he always been this tall, or has he grown?"

People gathered around him, looking up toward where his head was. For a fleeting moment, Miqdad glanced down at a little boy who was crying and clinging to his mother. The earth started to spin and he almost fell over. However, he got his bearings again and sat down, saying he was tired.

As news spread of the giant's arrival in Tiberias, people came flocking to see him, especially those who had heard about him but had never met him. Daher looked on contentedly at the scene. It was the first time he had seen people this happy since the siege began.

After the final evening prayer Daher took Miqdad aside. The shelling had stopped completely since the destruction of the two ships. However, the lull didn't fool them.

"What brings you here? You could easily have been killed. You're the clearest target around, Miqdad!"

"What brings me here is a big secret, Sheikh."

"And we've gathered to hear what you have to say."

"Sulayman Pasha wants to enter the city from under the wall, Sheikh."

"Do you mean he wants to make a breach in it?"

"No, Sheikh. He's begun digging an underground tunnel. Some people are saying he wants to enter Tiberias. Others are saying he intends to destroy it by planting gunpowder under it and blowing it up!"

"Who told you this, Miqdad?"

"People who love you, Sheikh. There are many people who love you, even in Sulayman Pasha's camp. They know what you mean to me, and when I got the news I thought: I'm the only person I can trust this secret with. So I came."

"How can I ever thank you, Miqdad?" Daher asked him.

"You can thank me, Sheikh, by making sure they turn back in defeat, God willing!"

Leaning toward Miqdad, Daher whispered, "Have you heard any news about your concubine?"

"No, I haven't, Sheikh. But every time I stand up and look around, I realize that there isn't anything or anybody in the world that I want to see the way I want to see her!"

"Don't worry, Miqdad. We'll find her. Don't worry!" Then, in everyone's hearing, he said, "My brother Yusuf will take you to his house to get some sleep. I'm sure you need it."

"But . . ."

"You need rest, Miqdad. Or don't you trust my men to guard you while you sleep?"

"How could I not trust them, Sheikh?"

"Go get some rest, then!"

Clouds were gathering outside, but not a drop of rain fell. Tiberias needed rain to fill its people's wells, and to make life in Sulayman Pasha's camp more difficult.

The idea al-Dankizli proposed was even wilder than Sulayman Pasha's. "There's only one solution," he said. "We'll have to dig a tunnel around the side of the city where they're digging theirs so that before they reach the wall, they'll find our soldiers inside the tunnel waiting for them!"

No one spoke. "Here's the city wall," al-Dankizli explained as he traced a diagram in the dirt. He drew a line leading toward the wall, saying, "This is their tunnel." Then he drew another line parallel to the city wall, "And this is the tunnel we're going to dig, and where we'll fight them."

"We'll have to start right away," said Daher.

"We'll have to start right away," others echoed.

The only thing no one knew for certain was how long ago Sulayman Pasha had ordered the digging to begin. They'd been racing against the clock aboveground, and now they would have to race against the clock underground, and in the dark.

After working night and day for seventy-two hours, they had a tunnel that was at least fifty paces long. They had begun from the center of the wall facing Sulayman Pasha's camp, and dug outward in both directions.

Standing in the center of the tunnel, Daher said, "We want it higher and wider. We won't be able to fight them in this cramped space."

The last month of the siege coincided with the month of Ramadan, and God's blessing was on Tiberias. People seemed more self-denying, and the thirst and lack of food seemed like a part of the fast rather than an outcome of the siege.

One more week, and the month would be over. After long thought, Daher had concluded that Sulayman Pasha wouldn't be able to spend the winter on the outskirts of Tiberias. What he had achieved, he had achieved, and come what may, he would have no choice but to lead the pilgrimage caravan. He now had one week for his final attempt to reach the heart of Tiberias.

Daher looked skyward and saw the clouds growing thicker and darker. Thunder came from somewhere in the distance, reminding him and the townspeople of the long nights of shelling.

But not a drop of rain fell.

Three nights before Eid al-Fitr, the holiday that marks the end of the fasting month of Ramadan, everything changed. The people of Tiberias panicked at first, but once they realized what was happening, they took to the streets rejoicing. Lightning and thunder shook the earth, and rain poured down in torrents the likes of which they had never seen before. It was as though the sky had been saving up its clouds for a storm such as this.

It had yet to occur to anyone that the rains that had been pouring down nonstop for two days had washed out Sulayman Pasha's underground tunnel and drowned all his soldiers there.

All night long the rivers of heaven poured forth until all the townspeople's wells were filled to overflowing. The next morning a timid sun shone through the clouds, and by evening they were able to see Shawwal's new moon.

The morning of Eid al-Fitr, a messenger arrived from Sulayman Pasha offering peace.

"No," replied Daher. "I won't humiliate myself any more than I have already. I won't send anyone to speak to him!"

The messenger assured him that things would be different this time, since the soldiers had grown weary of fighting, and the caravan that carried pilgrims every year from Damascus to Mecca was about to set out. Consequently, he explained, the governor would be willing to accept terms he hadn't been willing to accept before.

"Send your brother Yusuf to negotiate with him," proposed the messenger.

"Shall I send Yusuf so that Sulayman Pasha can take him prisoner? If he can't bring him into Tiberias, he'll take him to Damascus and hang him there so that he can tell everyone that he defeated Daher. That, I will never allow!"

In the end, however, Daher did agree to send Yusuf, provided that Sulayman Pasha send his military commander as surety for Yusuf's safe return.

Escorted by two boys driving ten camels, Yusuf ascended the hill toward Sulayman Pasha's pavilion, expecting the worst. However, like Daher and Sulayman Pasha, he was convinced of the necessity of putting an end to the siege.

Sulayman Pasha was surprised by Daher's gift. Uthman Pasha leaned over and whispered in his superior's ear, "Have you noticed how humble and magnanimous this sheikh is? Even though he realizes we've failed in our mission, he sends us one gift after another. Never in my life have I encountered anyone so generous, resourceful, kindhearted, and intelligent!"

Sulayman Pasha looked daggers at Uthman, who, realizing his faux pas, corrected himself, saying, "Your Excellency, of course, outdoes him by far!"

The negotiations were concluded more quickly than Yusuf had expected, since Sulayman Pasha's demands had shrunk to the size of his withered ego.

"I agree to withdraw from Tiberias on condition that it pay all the taxes it owes the empire."

"Sheikh Daher no longer agrees to this condition," Yusuf replied. "That was his offer in the beginning. But now that Tiberias has suffered so much damage, he needs this money in order to rebuild it."

"Is this what he instructed you to tell us?"

"Yes, it is."

Sulayman Pasha bowed his head, then looked up again. "In that case, I only have one demand remaining: that he remove two rows of stones from the tower."

"He won't object to this. However, he will only do so once your army is three days' march from Tiberias."

"I need some guarantee that he'll make good on his promise."

"If you want me to be the guarantee, I'll go with you to Damascus. When you reach Damascus, release me, and Daher will release the military commander you'll be leaving in Tiberias."

"I don't want you as the guarantee. I want one of his sons."

"I'm sure he'll agree to this. His sons are no dearer to him than his brothers, just as his brothers are no dearer to him than his sons."

"It's agreed, then. However, he should remember that I'll be coming back next year with an army that he won't be able to hold out against for a single hour!"

"Let's carry out what we've agreed on now. As for what happens next year, that's in the realm of the unknown, Pasha."

Daher stood examining his five sons, who were lined up in front of him: Islibi, Uthman, Ali, Sa'id, and Ahmad, and his three-year-old daughter Aliya, who insinuated herself among them with a frown on her face.

He studied their faces as though he were seeing them for the first time. Then he studied them all over again.

"You know exactly which one you're going to choose, Daher. So don't waste any more time!" Najma said to him.

"And you? Do you know?"

"Let them leave now. You didn't need to stand them up like this as if you were looking for the right one to send!"

With a sorrowful smile he signaled to the boys to go, and they scattered. However, Aliya went on standing at attention in imitation of her brothers. He beckoned to her. She came up to him and he took her affectionately into his arms.

"Is it his fault that he looks like me? Is it his fault that he has the dignified bearing of a prince, the bravery of a knight, and the peripheral vision of a horse?"

"No, Daher, none of that is his fault. But everyone who sees this young man will understand the reason behind Tiberias's strength and invincibility, and this is what you and all of Tiberias need."

Winds of the Future

On the morning of Saturday, October 1, 1742, Sulayman Pasha's army set out on its return journey to Damascus. The road leading to Damascus was lined with huge crowds. However, what they had come out to see was not the governor and his army, but rather Ali son of Daher al-Umar, the boy people had dubbed "son of the leopard," the boy whose father had vanquished the greatest of the sultan's governors and sent him home in defeat after a siege that had lasted no fewer than eighty-two days.

As Sulayman Pasha looked back at Tiberias, it seemed so distant that he wondered how he had made it all the way there. Nevertheless, he swore before his army's commanders not to rest until he had destroyed the city and everyone in it and returned to Damascus with Daher's head for everyone to see.

He cast a glance at the young boy and found him seated firmly on his horse, as self-assured as a prince.

He'll get tired in the end and collapse headfirst onto the horse's back, Sulayman Pasha thought. When this didn't happen, he was so infuriated that he had an almost irresistible urge to slap the boy or kick him off his horse and make him grovel in the dirt. Maybe that would teach him some humility!

He glared at Ali the entire way, and it was nothing short of a miracle that he managed to keep his rage in check. But once they found themselves at the Damascus gate, everything changed.

Paradise between
Two Seas

In less than a year,
the foreigners residing in Acre saw a new sun rising
and experienced a confidence and peace of mind
they'd never known before.
Knowing what great profits one can earn in a city
being newly built up, Greeks and Cypriots poured in.
The city's walls rose higher, its streets broadened,
its harbor expanded, and merchants built themselves
an ever-growing number of spacious new houses.
Every day the city received a thousand
merchandise-laden camels that would return
whence they had come, laden
with still more merchandise.
Opening its gates to traders from
Russia, Italy, France, and Malta,
the city was filled with cotton and wool textiles,
sugar, weapons, paper, and glassware,
and the ships that had brought these goods
would sail away laden with cotton, linen,
wool, soap, wheat,
oil, and sesame.

A Powerful Forearm, a Weary Heart

After Sulayman Pasha's army had withdrawn empty-handed, Daher sent a message to his brother-in-law, Muhammad Ali, saying, "I'm going to forget everything that's happened and we can make a new start. You were blinded by greed and ambition, thinking that Tiberias would be yours and that you would become its multazim. As you've seen, however, even the sword of Sulayman Pasha, the most powerful of the sultan's governors, broke to pieces on its walls. So spare your own sword, Muhammad. Be satisfied with Damun, Shafa'amr,[20] and the lands that extend as far as the village of Sheikh Brayk, and I promise you'll remain multazim over them as long as I live."

Waving Daher's letter in his wife's face, Muhammad Ali said with a smirk, "Your brother's threatening me, Shamma! Your brother's threatening me!"

"My brother isn't threatening you, Muhammad. He's making you a promise."

"Is he promising me what's already mine? That's worse than a threat!"

"If I were you, Muhammad, I'd write back to him. After all, he's your cousin, my brother, and our children's uncle."

"Rather, I'm the husband of his sister, and the father of our children!"

When Muhammad Ali received a message from Sulayman Pasha informing him that he was coming to besiege Tiberias again, he replied saying that he would be waiting for him in the village of Lubiya not far from Tiberias. He gathered his soldiers, and one sweltering dawn in late

---

20 The name of this village has been attributed to the Muslim commander Amr ibn al-As, who is said to have been ill when he passed through it. The story goes that when the commander drank from a spring in the village referred to as Ayn Afiya (Healing Spring)—which exists to this day—he recovered from his illness. His soldiers shouted, "Shafa Amr!"—"Amr has been healed!"—and thus the village's name.

August a year after the infamous blockade, he left home. Before he'd gone far, he stopped his horse and, turning to face Shamma, cast her a mocking smile.

How she had hoped he wouldn't turn around. But he did. How she had hoped he would hold his peace. But instead, he flung that sinister smile in her face. As she watched him ride away, the distance between them seemed greater than all the desert expanses on earth.

She went inside and hurriedly began gathering her things. "Where are we going?" her children asked.

"To your uncle's house. To Tiberias. Maybe your father doesn't realize yet whom he's going to be besieging there! He wants to be a hero. So let him be one if he can. But it will have to be over against his wife and children!"

News had reached Tiberias of the colossal army marching its way, since every village it passed on its way from Damascus had sent Daher a messenger to warn him. Hundreds of messengers began descending on the city, all bringing the same piece of news, and all exhausted by the journey. But they weren't willing to let the Damascus army reach the gates before they did.

Shamma arrived, too, her sorrow-laden eyes bearing the most burdensome news of all. All she said was, "I want a sword and a pistol." Once she had them in hand, she took her headscarf and wound it around her forehead. Then she lifted her skirt, tucked it into her sash, and headed for the wall.

As Najma watched her walk away, she whispered, "Lord, what kind of test are you putting this poor girl's heart to?"

The messengers talked about new weapons from Istanbul of a sort they had never seen before. They talked about seeing enough cedar planks to build an entire fleet, and about soldiers beyond number.

As he listened to all this, al-Dankizli looked back and forth between Daher, Bishr, and the other commanders.

"Would you like to say something, Ahmad?"

"Nothing, Sheikh. Nothing."

"All right, then. Let's get ready to meet them."

Daher watched Ahmad al-Dankizli and the others depart. Then he turned and saw Najma standing on the upper balcony of their rebuilt mansion. He went up to join her.

"Is there something you wanted to say, Mother?"

"Yes. Take off your shoes and follow me."

"Now?"

"Now, Sheikh. There's nothing you need more today than to have this earth's strength inside you."

He took off his shoes and descended the stairs toward the courtyard.

"Don't talk. Forget everything but the feeling of the soil under your feet."

Najma began walking beside him. In a few moments she had disappeared, and with her, the whole universe. Nothing remained but his feet and the soil. In less than half an hour, his feet had disappeared, and with them the soil. But the feeling of the soil remained.

His mother nudged him and said, "Let's go back now."

By this time they'd reached the lakeshore. Coming out of his trance, he looked around and saw hundreds of women and men walking barefoot along with him and his mother.

He wanted to speak, but Najma gestured to him to keep quiet.

Then they went back to the house.

Before Sulayman Pasha's forces reached Tiberias, word arrived that he was ill.

For a moment Daher suspected that it was a trick. The only thing he trusted was the instinct that told him to wait.

So he waited.

He had been careful not to make the same mistakes he had made during the first siege. He had invited the farmers in surrounding villages to join him in Tiberias. He had fortified the city and raised its towers. As for arms, they presented no problem now that he was able to obtain them in return for Tiberias's cotton crop.

Reports continued to come in morning and evening. But suddenly they took an unexpected turn: "Sulayman Pasha is dying!"

"Dying?"

By the fourth day the reports had reached their climax: "Sulayman Pasha is dead!"

"Dead?"

Daher's men themselves, who had stolen out of the city across the lake, confirmed reports that Sulayman Pasha's army had begun withdrawing and was heading back to Damascus. Before he could carry out his promise to himself and his soldiers to return to Damascus with Daher's head, the governor's intestines had burst.

Daher ordered his men to pursue the withdrawing soldiers and loot them for all they were worth. One blazing summer midday the gates of Tiberias opened, and within an hour they had overtaken the withdrawing army. The battle had been decided by the governor's death even before it was decided by the pursuing army's swords. Sulayman Pasha's soldiers scattered, and in the ensuing chaos they were mowed down almost effortlessly.

The fleeing forces began ridding themselves of whatever weapons or gear were weighing them down. As for the cannons, they began throwing them into wells and rolling them into ravines to prevent Daher from taking them. However, Daher's army advanced on them so quickly that they weren't able to dispose of them all in time.

Daher's army returned to Tiberias with enough weapons to establish a new army. And with that, everything changed.

That year was the most productive Tiberias had ever known. Daher gathered the multazims in the mansion and instructed them to collect only one-fifth rather than one-fourth of the crops in state taxes. When some of them objected, he replied firmly, "If the peasants thrive, the earth thrives. We should be happy to see them wealthy."

The only heart that was still weighed down with sorrow was Shamma's. Tiberias had been victorious, but for her personally, everything was as bleak as ever. Everyone had expected her to lay down her sword and pistol and untie the scarf knotted tightly around her head. But she didn't.

Without a word, she would get up in the morning, ascend the wall, and wait for her battle to begin.

Those Cruel Memories

Now that all the roads between Tiberias and Acre were passable, Daher mounted his horse and set out toward the city accompanied by a number of his soldiers. He spent his first night in Acre at Khan al-Ifranj, a caravansary frequented by foreigners.

The next day as he was touring the city, he suddenly found himself face to face with Muhammad Ali. The encounter came as a shock to him: *Here he is—your sister's husband and the late Sulayman Pasha's ally—standing right in front of you, Daher. And you're within easy range of his pistol!* He gestured to his men to surround Muhammad Ali. None of the Frenchmen or other foreigners standing nearby made a move to intervene, realizing that whatever was happening had nothing to do with them.

Daher goaded his horse. It set out, then retreated. Then it set out, and retreated again. It was as though the horse, at that moment, embodied the thoughts to which Daher had become prey. When at last it stopped hesitating, he shouted to his soldiers, "To Tiberias!"

The last thing he had expected was to find himself face to face with Muhammad Ali. He had hoped dearly never to see him again after the knife he had plunged deep in his back, first by allying himself with Sulayman Pasha in return for a false promise and surrounding Tiberias with his soldiers' lances, and then by what he had done to Bishr!

If Shamma hadn't left her husband in Damun and come to Tiberias, would you have dared do what you did, Daher? After all, his children are your nieces and nephews!

All the way back to Tiberias, Daher struggled to tame his rage. He succeeded to a fair extent. However, the rage returned with a vengeance. He gazed into the boundless sky, and all he could see was emptiness.

He could have forgiven Muhammad Ali for everything—everything, that is, but the deaths of Bishr, Ghazala, and little Umar and Daher.

One day Ghazala had surprised Bishr with an unexpected request. She said, "We've left our Bedouin campgrounds to come live in Tiberias. And although I hadn't expected to, I love it here now! I've seen Lake Tiberias, and I don't want to die before seeing the Sea of Acre."

"So you want to go to Acre?"

"And why not, cousin? After all, the whole land is safe now, and caravans from Tiberias go there all the time. So don't deprive us of the chance to see the big sea!"

Bishr discussed the matter with Daher, who said to him, "The Sea of Acre is different from the Sea of Galilee, as some people refer to Lake Tiberias. So take them there, and the sooner the better. Nobody can say he's really lived until he's seen the sea!"

When Bishr told him that they would be leaving with the first caravan, Daher replied, "No, you'll go tomorrow or day after tomorrow with a squad of our soldiers."

They set out toward Acre, and when they were half an hour west of Saffuriya, they happened upon a squad led by Muhammad Ali. Bishr started to greet them, but before he could get the words out of his mouth, Muhammad Ali had drawn his sword and charged at him.

Not knowing who his attacker was, Bishr shouted, "I'm Bishr, from Sheikh Daher's army!" But the sword kept coming at top speed. Bishr ducked behind his mare, and hanging onto her right stirrup, he shouted to his men to get away with Ghazala and his two sons.

Muhammad Ali spun and charged again. By this time Bishr was back on his horse and had galloped away. The arrows followed him and those with him, ripping into their bodies. Bishr turned again to attack, only to find his wife and sons screaming. He looked back and found them riddled with arrows. Out of his mind with rage, he kept charging. However, he and his escorts were met by another storm of arrows, a number of which struck Bishr in his chest and abdomen.

Some of Bishr's men managed quickly to withdraw. However, he went on charging as though he were backed by all the armies in the world.

Bishr's mare fell, but he got up again and advanced, sword in hand. The arrows rained down anew, plunging into his body and coming out his back. He looked behind him and saw his family, now lifeless corpses. He tried to crawl over to them, but a new wave of arrows came his way. He raised his head, only to find Muhammad Ali ordering still another attack. The arrows soared high, making their way with difficulty into his already riddled frame.

"Let's see how many tears Daher will shed over these porcupines!" Muhammad Ali said with a sneer as he looked over at the strewn corpses.

A few hours later, Daher arrived with some of the surviving soldiers. Looking out over the broad plain to which his soldiers pointed, all he saw was a gathering of eagles and vultures that were screeching and fighting, alternately rushing at the corpses and retreating. He jumped off his horse and went running toward them. The birds fluttered away, leaving him alone with four huge, motionless porcupines.

His heart quaking, he came closer and saw faces and fingers caked with dry blood. When he heard the other men's footsteps behind him, he raised his hands parallel with his head, his palms spread, and they quietly stepped away.

After what seemed like an eternity, he knelt down and began pulling the arrows out of Bishr's body. He did the same for Ghazala and little Umar and Daher. Seeing him stealing their prey, the birds' screeching rose to a crescendo. Some of them alit some distance away, flapping their wings and shrieking without daring to come any closer.

Bishr's body had been completely dismembered. Daher knelt down to pick him up to the sound of the birds' screams and the frenzied flapping of their wings.

Giving them a wild-eyed stare, he stood up again, and they all went stone still. Then, in a strange moment, Daher stepped back, leaving the four corpses where they were. As he retreated he eyed the birds of prey, which commenced a wary approach.

When he'd gotten about a hundred meters away, he felt his right heel bump up against a rock. He stopped and sat down without taking his eyes off the eagles and vultures, which had begun hurriedly devouring the bodies.

One of his men came up to him and whispered, "The birds are eating them, Sheikh!"

Daher raised his hand and gestured for him to sit down beside him.

Half an hour later, another came up and said, "We've got to take them and bury them, Sheikh." Again he raised his hand and gestured to the soldier to sit down.

By the time an hour had passed, all of his men were sitting and staring with him in the same direction.

"It's a shame for us to let them do this, Sheikh! It's really a shame!"

Daher turned in the direction of the voice and said in a half whisper, "And what makes it a shame?"

"We should take them back to Tiberias to bury them."

"Do you want to return them to the dust?"

"Aren't they made from dust like all the rest of God's creatures? And aren't they meant to return to the dust?"

"Leave them be," Daher said. "Let them soar for a while with these eagles and vultures. Maybe they'll catch a glimpse of the ocean they'd hoped to see. Don't be in such a hurry to cast them into the darkness. They'll live in the bodies of these birds for now, and die with them later on this or that summit." Then he hid his face.

The sun went down. Then it rose again. When he took his hands off his eyes, nothing remained of the bodies but some bones.

He stood up and walked over to them. He spread his cloak on the ground and gently placed their remains on top of it. He tied the edges of the cloak into a knot and took it tenderly in his arms as though he were carrying a newborn child. Then he walked, followed by his men, all the way back to Tiberias.

The distance between Acre and the shore of Lake Tiberias that day felt to Daher like the greatest distance he had ever traveled in his life. The farther he went, the longer the road seemed to get. One minute he would be thinking of killing Muhammad Ali on the road, and the next minute of imprisoning him. One minute Shamma and her children would appear in his mind's eye, and the next minute he would see the bones of Bishr, Ghazala, and their two sons. The sound of Sulayman Pasha's cannons rang in his ears, his head filled with the cruel darkness that had closed in on Tiberias and the hearts of its people.

But the road did end at last, like all roads leading to a known destination.

Looking over at his soldiers, he said, "I don't want to see him. I don't want anybody to see him. All of you just forget that he exists among us!"

On the morning of their arrival back in Tiberias, Daher saw his sister heading out as usual for the top of the city walls. She cast him a weary look. He was about to say something to her, but at the last moment changed his mind.

When they gathered that evening, Daher said, "Today we annexed Shafa'amr, Damun, and the surrounding areas to our territory." And he said nothing more.

The next morning he got up early as usual and had his usual breakfast. But the question he couldn't get off his mind was: *What will Shamma do when she wakes up?* He waited for quite a while. As the sun rose in the sky, he was sure she must have left without his seeing her. He got up and headed for the place where she slept in the mansion. Before he got there Najma appeared. She gestured to him from a distance to stay where he was. He stopped. Then she came up to him and, taking him by the hand, said, "Leave her be. She's sleeping."

Life . . . If One Might Call It That

G one was the time when Daher was afraid of the Ottoman governors. What he feared now was seeing them removed! As'ad Pasha, who succeeded his paternal uncle Sulayman and whose governorship over Damascus would last fourteen years—a feat no governor before him had ever achieved—was careful to avoid any friction with Daher's army.

One day as he sat watching the caravans of camels laden with cotton, wheat, sesame, and dried fish headed for Acre, Daher remarked to al-Dankizli, "Just think of it, Ahmad: all these camels are ours!"

"Of course they are, Sheikh!"

"Do you know what we need now?"

"I don't know, Sheikh. Trade is no longer in the hands of foreigners, and conditions are safe throughout our region, thank God."

"But we need more than just control over trade, Ahmad. We need the big sea. We need a place from which we can see the world, and the world can see us."

"You're thinking about Acre, aren't you, Sheikh?"

"It's all I've been thinking about for years. When we took over Safad, Jaddin, Nazareth, and other cities, I wasn't thinking about these cities and their fortresses. I was thinking about Acre."

"But Acre is quite important to the governor of Sidon. It's important to the empire, too."

"I know that, Ahmad. But we haven't come all this way and fought all these battles for our rights and the rights of the people, only to be turned back at Acre's tumbledown gates! The empire has ports from Jaffa to Tyre to Beirut, and we won't be able to accomplish anything if we stay here at the edge of this lake, in a city surrounded by mountains on every side."

Acre's multazim had a force of no more than a hundred soldiers who kept order in the city and collected taxes. However, the multazim and his forces were captives within Acre's decaying walls, which could protect no one. They dared not venture outside the city, where the Bedouins, and particularly Bani Saqr, lay in wait for them just as they lay in wait for others.

Hence, their life, if one might call it that, had been taken prisoner, and the fertile plains that stretched from Haifa to Ra's al-Naqura had turned into a marshy, disease-blighted wasteland.

One moonlit night Daher summoned the judge, the mufti, and the imam. Once they'd gathered, he dictated a letter to the imam addressed to the multazim of Acre informing him that he would have to leave the city. He wrote another letter to the city's people saying: "Whoever stays will only have himself to blame!"

One morning soon thereafter, one of Daher's messengers set out for Acre, while another set out for Sidon to request its governor's permission to take over the position of multazim in Acre once it had been evacuated. Daher promised the governor that he would pay all the money due him, populate and develop the city, and establish security there as he had done in Tiberias and elsewhere.

As Daher watched his messenger to Sidon ride away, Najma said to him, "It's as though you already know what answer you'll receive from the governor!"

"Or you might say: this is a message I don't expect an answer to!"

No sooner had the messenger disappeared over the western hills than Daher shouted, "To Acre!" Within minutes, three thousand soldiers began gathering as though the earth had magically opened up and brought them forth.

The Sun and the Pelicans' Wings

Daher squeezed Islibi's hand. Then Islibi gave his father a long embrace, before stepping back to let his brothers Uthman, Ahmad, Ali, and Sa'id do the same.

"You'll be responsible for Tiberias, Islibi," Daher told him. "Be sure to make it more productive and more just, and safer than it was before."

"You'll go on being its sheikh and multazim wherever you are, Father."

"Go with God."

He turned to Najma and asked, "Are you ready?"

"I'm ready. But it tires me to think that I won't be going to Acre on foot."

"That means you're still strong, thanks be to God, and that you need a groom!"

"Me, Sheikh? And why a groom? Whoever hears you talking that way will think I'm going to live to be sixty!"

Daher laughed. He laughed so hard he cried.

"You laugh? Lord, let there be a good reason!"

"There's nothing better than having a groom."

"Is that so? Well, if you go on talking that way, I'll stay in Tiberias!"

Before he could stop laughing, he glimpsed a boy making his way toward him with a bundle in his hand. Najma saw him, but averted her gaze as though she hadn't noticed.

Daher's heart began pounding wildly, which perplexed him. It perplexed him to see that his heart was still capable of making such a commotion inside him. As he took the small bundle, his eyes met Yusuf's. Remembering the bundle Daher had left in his safekeeping years before, Yusuf[21] waited for the boy to hand it over the way he had the earlier one. But he didn't.

---

21 Yusuf al-Umar went after this to Acre. From Acre he went to the coastal village of Ibillin, where he settled. A pious, sensible, and judicious man, Yusuf set about constructing mosques and other buildings. It was Yusuf who constructed the Tiberias mosque in 1743, and in 1767 the mosque of Ibillin, where he was buried. He is reported to have said, "People are winds, so get your lantern away from them before they blow!"

After retreating some distance, the boy stopped to watch Daher from behind the horses. Daher placed the bundle in his right saddlebag so he wouldn't be able to smell it. Nevertheless, some fragrance, or the shadow of a fragrance, managed to escape, and it was different from the one he remembered. Had he forgotten the way the earlier bundle had smelled? Can one forget a fragrance the way one forgets a face? Can the nose go blind the way the eye can?

He prodded his horse so unexpectedly that the horse jumped before it set out.

Then he brought it to a halt and, looking over at Najma, said, "Let's be on our way with God's blessing."

When they were half an hour's journey from Tiberias, she whispered to him, "Your horse looks tired out to me, Sheikh. Might he be carrying an extra person that I can't see because of my poor eyesight?"

It was late summer, and the bogs and huge piles of residue produced by the soap factories surrounding Acre filled the air with a stifling odor. As the city's dilapidated walls came into view, it looked as though it had just endured a bloody war even though Daher hadn't had to fire a single shot in order to bring it under his control.

"The smell is unbearable. I know that," he said to Najma as if in apology.

"It will go away!"

"And the bogs . . ."

"They'll dry up!" Najma said, not letting him finish his sentence.

"And those dilapidated walls . . ."

"They'll be rebuilt!"

"And it's such a small city!"

"It will grow! Do you think I would have come with you if you hadn't promised me all these things?" she remonstrated. Then she stopped her horse and looked at him.

"It's as if you're afraid, Sheikh!"

"Yes, Mother, I am. I wouldn't be the brave Daher you know if I were afraid to admit that I'm afraid! What I have in mind is so huge that I can't help but be afraid for it even before it comes to be."

He smiled in an attempt to ward off the emotions churning inside him. "Besides, you're going to suffer along with us. You could have stayed in Tiberias until we rebuilt Acre."

"I would never have been willing to do that, Sheikh. Do you know what makes me so attached to Tiberias?"

"What's that, Mother?"

"The fact that I saw it grow in your care just the way I saw you grow in my care. There's nothing sweeter than remembering your children when they were little, or your city when it was small! I've thought a lot about this lately, Sheikh. There have been moments when I was about to say to you, 'I'm not leaving Tiberias!' But then I'd think: never again will I get to see you as a little boy growing up, but I can see a little city grow up at your hands. Now that I've grown old, Daher, and no longer have the chance to watch children growing up and going away, the sight of a city growing up gives me a new kind of solace."

"I swear, Mother, I don't know where you get such wisdom!"

"As I've told you: you've got to walk barefoot in order to understand the earth and yourself better. But you don't always do as I say."

"How can you say that, Mother? Could I have become what I am today if it weren't for my walking barefoot beside you?"

"No, you couldn't have. But you've replaced your bare feet with shoes! Can a person replace life with the skin of a dead animal?"

"I promise I'll walk barefoot with you again as soon as we dry up these bogs and raise these walls."

"Do you think I'm going to wait that long? You've got to get a feel for this city today the way you got a feel for Tiberias yesterday, so that you can remember it better after it grows up. Many people walk over this earth, but she doesn't feel them because they've never felt her, and sooner or later she's going to cast them off. I know that you and the earth have felt each other. Even so, you need to get closer to her."

"I promise you, then: tomorrow morning after the dawn prayer we'll go walking barefoot in the sand along the seashore."

"You know, Sheikh, there's only one thing I hold against my father, may God rest his soul. It's that when he named me Najma—Star—he distanced me from the earth, and since the time when I understood what my name meant, I've done everything I could to shorten the distance between the earth and me."

The seagulls' cries rose to a crescendo, their wings filling the air, while the sun looked like a little boy trying in vain to hide behind their wings.

As they passed through Acre's gate, they saw the magnificent red disk disappear into the sea.

It wasn't only the heavy air weighing on his chest, the heat that wasn't extinguished by the waves of the sea, and the mosquitoes buzzing in the dark like mischievous little sprites that stole sleep from Daher's eyes.

He fumbled in the dark for his shoes until he found them, and slipped them on his feet. Then, like someone who's suddenly remembered something precious and long forgotten, he came back, took his shoes off, and went out again, taking care not to disturb those who were sleeping.

His soldiers filled the place. He wished Bishr could have been there. He deserved to see with his own eyes what he had achieved with his blood!

Once at the shore, he climbed onto some large rocks and sat down next to the sea. There was nothing standing between him and the wind coming from afar. A gentle, moist wind, it had traversed the sea without knowing that there was a pair of lungs waiting hungrily for it on this shore.

The sea roared. His feet sank deeper and deeper into the sandy beach. His body wasn't there any more. He could no longer feel it. He'd turned into nothing but a long string of memories.

To the sound of Najma's voice he opened his eyes. "There you go again, Sheikh, getting out here before I do to be alone with the sea!"

He turned. Najma was coming toward him. Behind her stood a high wall. Behind her stood the new Acre.

A Beautiful Woman in
a Spacious Land

I t's been a long time since anyone came to us with a complaint,
Ahmad."

"That's reason to be thankful, Sheikh. All the roads are safe
now, and no one dares try to harm others any more," Ahmad replied.

"But my mind still isn't completely at rest."

"Why's that, Sheikh?"

"I want you to bring me one of the prettiest girls in the region."

"One of the prettiest girls? Why, Sheikh?"

"No, I've changed my mind. I want you to bring me the prettiest girl
in all of Galilee!"

"And what do you want from her?"

"Just bring her, Ahmad, and if anyone asks you why you're summoning her, say that the Sheikh wants her in connection with a matter
of great importance."

Ahmad al-Dankizli left Daher's mansion perplexed, wondering what
was going on in the sheikh's head: *Does he want to marry? If so, this isn't the
way people go about it in these parts!*

Two days later a pretty girl arrived escorted by her brothers, who
hadn't agreed to let her come alone even if it was the sheikh himself who
had asked for her.

When the girl arrived, Daher asked Najma to take her inside while
he sat and talked with her brothers.

When she came out again, she'd practically disappeared beneath an
array of gold bracelets and necklaces. Everyone stared at her with an
amazement that would have flooded Acre and its seashore.

"Listen, child, I've called you to undertake a very important task.
And believe me, if I had a daughter as pretty as you are, I would have
sent her in your place. So, are you willing to do something that, if I had
a daughter like you, she would have done herself?"

"I am, Sheikh."

"I want you to leave this mansion and walk the length and breadth of Galilee all alone."

"All alone, Sheikh?"

"Yes."

"Wearing all this jewelry?"

"Yes."

"And then what do I do?"

"Then you come back here."

Seeing the girl's hesitation, Daher reassured her, saying, "If I thought the least harm would come to you, I wouldn't be sending you. There's something I want to confirm, and I won't be able to do that unless I send you on this journey."

She looked over at her brothers, who nodded in agreement.

The girl traveled over hill and dale, leaving the main roads and passing through fields, villages, and towns.

Four days later she returned, weary, to see Daher.

Daher asked Najma to take care of her, so she took her and handed her over to a number of women who worked at the mansion. When they had finished, Najma came and decked her out with all the bracelets and necklaces she had worn on her journey. "Is he going to send me out again?" the girl asked in alarm.

"Don't worry. He's not going to do that!"

When she came out, Daher was reminded that physical exhaustion is nothing but so much dead skin that, once it's sloughed off, leaves one glowing again.

"How was your trip, child?"

"A bit tiring, that's all, Sheikh."

"Did anyone disturb you in any way?"

The pretty girl thought for a while. Then she said, "No, Sheikh. But someone, when he saw that I was alone, asked me where I was going."

"Did anyone else say anything to you?"

"A man of the Bani Saqr tribe. When I told him you'd sent me, he muttered something under his breath, then went away."

Looking at his horsemen, Daher said, "I want you to bring those two men here."

His horsemen left in haste, and within moments she saw them coming back, shoving a couple of men ahead of them. As it turned out,

Daher's men had followed her at a distance, taking care not to let her see them.

"Are these the two men you told me about?" Daher asked her.

The girl looked at them incredulously. "Yes," she said, nodding.

Daher ordered the men taken away, and they disappeared again.

"May I go back to my family now, Sheikh?"

"Yes, but this time you'll go on horseback, and my men will escort you. I promised your brothers that I'd deliver you safely to your door."

The girl stood up and began taking off the jewelry she was wearing.

"What are you doing?" Daher asked her.

"I'm returning it, Sheikh."

"Who are you going to return it to when it belongs to you?"

"To me?"

The following morning two gallows were set up at the Acre gate. Those coming in and out looked at them uncomprehendingly. After the noon prayer, the two men were brought and hanged.

"Let it be known to all," proclaimed Daher, "that this is the recompense that can be expected by anyone who dares to waylay any woman, man, or caravan in this region!"

Acre and the Sea

Daher watched the soldiers who filled the streets with their presence, and the people's eyes with wonder. Many Bedouin men had joined his army after he began pursuing them and preventing them from reaching the roads and villages, leaving them little freedom of movement on the plains. His first task had been to get them away from the city so that he could work on drying up the bogs and removing the noxious piles of waste left by the soap industry. Once he'd done this, he announced that he would welcome any Bedouin man who wished to join his army, and that he would pardon all those guilty of robbery and murder.

When death had come to seem more merciful than staying in the desert pursued by Daher's forces, a group of gaunt Bedouin men arrived warily to see him. To their surprise, Daher welcomed them personally and made certain that they were given the best possible treatment. Within a few weeks, people could see them walking up and down the streets of Acre fitted out with modern rifles and pistols and freshly laundered military uniforms.

They themselves could hardly believe the transformation they'd undergone!

No message had arrived from the governor of Sidon, whose hands were tied because Damascus was turning a blind eye to what Daher was doing. Those in power in Damascus were no longer concerned about anything but what was happening within Damascus itself.[22]

---

22 Devoting his attention solely to his own vilayet, As'ad Pasha, the new governor of Damascus, constructed stately buildings unrivalled anywhere in the Near East, among them the renowned Azm Palace built in 1751. He imposed obedience and order within his soldiers' ranks, putting a stop to their assaults on his subjects. He was lenient as a lender and granted loans on which he took only 6 percent interest. The defeat and death of his uncle Sulayman in the course of his campaign against Tiberias may have been among the reasons for As'ad Pasha's reluctance to make another attempt at reining Daher in.

Hence, Daher gathered the town notables and asked them to write another letter to the governor of Sidon. In the letter, they asserted that only Daher would be able to impose order and protect their city from Bedouin marauders and the Maltese pirates who had been spreading terror up and down the coast, particularly in Acre.

But before their letter reached the governor, they received news of his death. The messenger returned with the letter on the very next day, whereupon Daher set about to complete everything as quickly as possible: the fortress, inside of which he built a mansion for his personal residence, and the city walls with their imposing gates.

Acre received daily reports on the struggle over the governorship of Sidon. The situation went on for long months until at last news arrived that Ahmad Agha had commenced his duties as governor of the city. But by this time Daher had accomplished everything he had hoped to.[23]

Within the year, the foreigners residing in Acre saw a new sun rising and experienced a confidence and peace of mind they had never known before. Knowing what great profits one can earn in a city being newly built up, Greeks and Cypriots poured in. The city's walls rose higher, its streets broadened, its harbor expanded, and merchants built themselves an ever-growing number of spacious new houses. Every day the city received a thousand merchandise-laden camels that would return whence they had come laden with still more merchandise. Opening its gates to traders from Russia, Italy, France, and Malta, the city was filled with cotton and wool textiles, sugar, weapons, paper, and glassware, and the ships that had brought these goods would sail away laden with cotton, linen, wool, soap, wheat, oil, and sesame.

One day as Daher was walking through a marketplace in Acre, he heard two men shouting at each other, so he headed in their direction. Before he reached them, he heard one of them say, "You'll regret it if you don't pay what you owe me!"

The other replied, "If Acre were afraid of the sea's roar, she wouldn't be sitting on the shore!"

---

23   Upon visiting Acre, Swedish traveler and naturalist Fredrik Hasselquist made a comment to the effect that the sultan himself would have taken long years to raise all the buildings Daher had constructed in this short period of time.

The man's words made Daher smile. However, he quickly put on a straight face again.

The two men saw him coming and stepped away from each other.

"Are you arguing here, in Acre?" he asked.

"Pardon us, Sheikh," they said in unison.

"Come with me, and let's see what the dispute is about."

He walked ahead of them, his heart filled with an exhilaration he hadn't felt for years.

When they reached the town hall, each of them told Daher his side of the story. Nodding, Daher said to the second man, "Your friend is right: you should pay him what you owe him. Do you have the amount he's asking for?"

"No, I don't, Sheikh."

"In that case, I'll pay him out of my own pocket now, and you pay me back later."

Daher reached for his belt and produced a bag filled with coins. He untied the bag and gave the first man what the second man owed him, saying, "You're free to go now." The man got up to leave, hardly able to believe his eyes. When the second man got up to leave, Daher asked him, "Where are you going?"

The man replied, "I've got to get to work so that I can pay you back, Sheikh! You might have enough to repay that man at once, but I want to repay what I owe you before you have to come asking for it!"

"Who told you you owed me anything?"

"The jingling of the coins in that man's pocket!"

"No. You don't owe me a thing. You'd repaid whatever you owed me even before I put the money in that man's hand."

"How is that, Sheikh?"

"You said something I liked!"

"What good thing could possibly be said during an argument?"

"You said something nice about Acre and its not being afraid of the sea. Say it again!"

The man stood there trying to recall what he'd said. Then he repeated hesitantly, "If Acre were afraid of the sea's roar, she wouldn't be sitting on the shore!"

"That's it. But I want to hear you say it with more force."

So the man said again, "If Acre were afraid of the sea's roar, she wouldn't be sitting on the shore!"

"Be on your way now, and there's only one thing I want from you. Whenever an occasion arises during conversations with people you know, I want you to repeat what you said just now."

A few days later Daher heard the saying on the lips of a woman, then on the lips of a little boy, then on the lips of a man. The words differed somewhat, but the meaning hadn't changed.

When al-Dankizli got to Daher's house, he was told, "The sheikh has gone ahead of you to the top of the wall."

Even from a distance Daher would have recognized him in a crowd. He went on watching him until he reached the top of the wall. By the time al-Dankizli arrived, he was panting.

"What is this, Ahmad? Are you really panting, or am I imagining things?"

"I'm afraid so, Sheikh."

"Are you all right?"

"If I were, I wouldn't be out of breath. But you're still as strong as ever, Sheikh!"

"Who, me? I've got a different problem, Ahmad. I pant when I go down stairs, but when I go up them, I don't feel a thing!"

Al-Dankizli laughed. "So what's new, Sheikh? You've been that way as long as I've known you!"

"You're just saying that to make me feel good, Ahmad. But that's all right. I'll test you on something other than climbing stairs. Now, look over there."

"Where?"

"There, to the south. Can you see Haifa from here?"

"Even a hawk in flight couldn't see it from here through this haze, Sheikh."

"But I can, Ahmad, as strange as it seems."

Tough Questions

Never had Daher been as attached to a child as he was to Jahjah, his son Uthman's little boy.

"How long has it been since Jahjah came to see me, Uthman?"

"I don't know, Sheikh."

"Well then, let's get going. Times have changed, it seems, and elders are the ones who have to come pay their respects to their juniors!"

Daher stopped in front of a shop, and Uthman got ready to go in after him. But Daher said to him, "This is between me and your children!"

Daher bought some sweets that he knew his grandsons liked, and that brought back memories of his days in Damascus.

Acre was so crowded that evening that there was hardly any room between one camel and the next. Daher watched with amazement as his son weaved in and out among the great beasts. His son Ali's favorite thing was swords, Islibi's was sitting and listening to his father, Ahmad's was peace and quiet, and Sa'id's was catching fish from the sea, which were different from those in Lake Tiberias. As for Uthman, his favorite thing had always been walking at top speed between camels' legs. At first Daher had been convinced that his son would get his ribs crushed one day. But it had never happened. Consequently, he didn't worry about him any more. He was born a dodger, and a smooth talker, too.

As for Jahjah, he was a different sort of little boy who never stopped asking questions. All the way to Uthman's house, Daher wondered what his grandson would ask him.

The minute he saw his grandfather come through the gate, he ran out to him. Hopping like a big grasshopper, he flung himself into his arms and wrapped himself around his neck.

Daher came in and sat down, and before he'd had a chance to ask his grandson how he was, Jahjah said, "Today's Tuesday, isn't it, Grandpa?"

"That's right."

"So Tuesday is today, right, Grandpa?"

"That's right!"

"But when I asked Baba about it yesterday, he said it was tomorrow! And if I ask him about it tomorrow, he'll tell me it was yesterday. So which one is right, Grandpa?"

Daher bowed his head, and when he looked up again he was smiling.

"It looks like you know the answer, Grandpa!"

"As a matter of fact," Daher said, "they're all correct. Tuesday can be today, or yesterday, or tomorrow."

"No, Grandpa. It can't be three different things!"

"But it can, because Tuesday is like you!"

"How can Tuesday be like me, Grandpa? Am I Tuesday?"

"No, you're Jahjah, aren't you?"

"Yes, I'm Jahjah."

"We agree, then. Today you're a boy. But what will you be when you get a little bigger?"

"I'll be a young man."

"And when you grow up some more?"

"I'll be an old man, like you, Grandpa!"

"Am I an old man? So be it! But now tell me, Jahjah: What's your name when you're a boy?"

"Jahjah."

"What will your name be when you're a young man?"

"Jahjah."

"And what will it be when you're an old man like me?"

"It will still be Jahjah!"

"So then, you're the boy, the young man, and the old man, too. Isn't that right?"

"That's right."

"And in the same way, Tuesday is yesterday, today, and tomorrow."

"So Grandpa, am I yesterday or today now?"

"You're . . . now you've confused me. If we look at you as Tuesday, you're the today that hasn't ended."

"That doesn't make sense, Grandpa. If I'm today now, then what was I yesterday if I'm still here today?"

"You were yesterday's today, and now you're tomorrow. You're yesterday's tomorrow, Jahjah!"

Jahjah started turning the answer over in his head, alternately squinting his eyes and raising his eyebrows.

"Who taught him all this?" Daher asked, looking over at his mother.

"You know," she said, "he's been asking questions ever since he started to talk. When we first came to Acre, he stood in front of the window one day and asked me, 'What's this?' 'It's a window,' I told him. 'Why isn't it called a bee?' he wanted to know. 'Because it's a window,' I said. 'Well,' he said, 'I'm going to call it a fish'! And he stuck to his guns until, in the end, if I wanted him to close the window I had to say, 'Close the fish,' since, if I didn't, he wouldn't budge!"

As soon as he left Uthman's house, the smile vanished from Daher's face. He remembered his son Ali, and how he'd come back from Damascus hardened after the time he'd spent with Sulayman Pasha. The love and affection Daher had showered him with had rolled off him like rain off a granite boulder. He had asked him about what had happened there. In the beginning Ali wouldn't answer at all. Then, after he'd gotten a bit older, he'd learned to evade the question by changing the subject.

One day many years earlier, Sulayman Pasha had glanced over at Ali before they reached the Damascus gate. He was sitting straight and tall as though he'd just mounted the horse a few moments earlier. *Is that boy going to ride into Damascus with his head held high while I ride in with mine bowed?* With that thought, he suddenly exploded. Turning his horse, he charged toward Ali at top speed. Then he gave him a swift kick, with which he vented all his bitterness and rage. Ali fell to the ground, and the soldiers burst out laughing. Despite excruciating pain, Ali got up, dusted off his clothes, and wiped away the blood that was flowing copiously onto his face and forcing his right eye closed. Then he closed his left eye, and with his bloodied right eye glared at Sulayman Pasha and swore: "I'll kill you for what you just did!" Then Sulayman Pasha tried to kick him again. This time, however, Ali retreated quickly enough to avoid getting hurt.

Suppressing his scream with all the strength he had in him, Ali looked fiercely ahead as though he were seeing his image in the mirror and swore: *That's the last time you'll let anyone mock you, Ali!*

The Frozen Paradise and the "Holy" Flight

Hussein Pasha went to great lengths to ensure that he entered Damascus as no governor before him had ever done. After a long wait and arduous effort, he was at last to succeed As'ad Pasha as governor of Damascus. He had paid a hefty sum for the position. In fact, he'd paid nearly every piaster he owned. And just when he had been about to despair, Ahmad Agha, the chief chamberlain in Istanbul, had said to him, "Congratulations!"

One fine Thursday morning, drums rolled announcing his arrival in a magnificent procession of horsemen and foot soldiers bristling with ornamented arms and decked out in their finest military garb. Hardly had dawn broken the following day when notables of every color and stripe began flocking to the mansion to pay their respects. Upon their arrival, they were met by angry crowds, who pelted them with stones and chased them away with curses and insults: "Go back to where you came from, you hypocrites! All you do is help the rulers oppress people!"

Seeing that he would have to act quickly, Hussein Pasha issued an order to lower commodity prices. The price of bread went back down to its previous level of three masriyas a loaf, and other prices were likewise restored to what they had been before. However, they promptly soared again, surpassing even their previous highs. This was followed by a deadly March frost that burned away every last bud on the trees and every seedling in the fields.

The weather grew more moderate again, but then another frost hit. Before they knew it, all their fields, farms, and orchards were dying, and the Ghouta looked like a frozen, lifeless paradise. Then, as winter was about to make its final departure, waves of a different sort swept in: waves of blood that shook Damascus and robbed her eyes of sleep. A man was murdered in the city square, and three people were found in the Baramika quarter with their throats slit. A few days later, the Moroccan soldiers serving in the governor's army went on a rampage. They attacked the pasha's mansion, shot ten people dead, and set fire to a number of shops, and the bodies of two women whose throats had been slit were discovered on a hill near the Bab al-Saghir cemetery.

Hussein Pasha managed with difficulty to bring things under control. However, he knew that the best means of ensuring his survival would be to marshal a force large enough to do away with Daher, since it would divert the attention of the people of Damascus elsewhere. "I'll wipe him out!" He said it as though he were completing a statement begun by Sulayman Pasha before death snatched him away on the outskirts of Tiberias.

Before he could carry out his threat, however, it came time for the annual pilgrimage caravan to set out from Damascus to Mecca. The caravan was thus transformed into a lifeline, and the journey from Damascus to Mecca became a kind of "holy" flight.

Hussein Pasha kicked the ground, raising a small dust storm. His army commanders watched him in stunned silence.

With his runty frame, sunken eyes, and bulbous fingers, Hussein Pasha resembled a rolling bomb. Whenever it came in contact with anything, it exploded. Then it would go on rolling, exploding over and over as it went.

As his army commanders stood looking on, he hopped onto his horse like some strange creature and set out. Then he shouted at the top of his lungs, "I won't pay a single piaster to those highway-robber Bedouins!"

He cast a glance at the caravan, which consisted of sixty thousand pilgrims and soldiers, and the sight of it filled him with a hubris that inflated him to at least ten times his normal size. Never was there hubris more confident of its rightness than the hubris of ignorance!

After hearing what the governor had said to their messengers, the men of Bani Saqr, Bani Inza, Bani Atiya, Bani Uqayl, Bani Sardiya, and their allies looked on in silence at the passing caravan as though it had nothing to do with them.

Turning to leave, they quickly disappeared behind the dunes illumined by the glow of the gentle April sun, as though they would never return.

Smiling, Hussein Pasha turned to some of his army commanders who had warned him of the consequences of not paying the Bedouins the protection money due them.

"I knew they wouldn't have the guts to face Syria's army," he gloated. "And now you've seen it with your own eyes!"

However, none of the pilgrims or soldiers felt reassured by the peculiar ease with which the caravan had been allowed to pass.

One evening Daher received news of Hussein Pasha's refusal to pay the protection money due the Bedouins, and he realized that he would need to act quickly to fortify Acre and Haifa.

When he was alone with Najma, he said to her, "Thank God you didn't travel with that caravan!"

Najma had prepared everything for the long journey of a lifetime to Mecca. However, when she learned that Hussein Pasha was now governor of Damascus and heard about his threats against Daher, she reconsidered everything. To Daher's surprise, she'd even begun discouraging others she knew from traveling with Hussein Pasha.

Some had heeded her words, while others suspected that she was only speaking this way on account of Hussein Pasha's attitude toward her son.

"It's good you didn't go," Daher repeated.

"Are you sensing what I am, Sheikh?"

"I would have been really worried about you."

"But my heart still isn't at rest. For some reason I'm worried about that whole caravan. You might think it strange, Sheikh, but I'm even worried about Hussein Pasha! I realize he's your enemy. But whatever happens to him might happen to all the pilgrims."

The days dragged by, as the situation augured an outcome that no one would ever have hoped for.

Harsh months ensued during which the earth bade farewell to a short-lived spring and a parched, breathless summer.

Hussein Pasha was fully confident on his way back, certain that he was subduing the Bedouin tribes and reordering relations with them "in the only language they understand: the language of force." Then he would take his next step: to get rid of Daher! In so doing, or so his thinking went, he would be able to rule Syria for twenty-eight years, twice as long as it had been ruled by As'ad Pasha, *that "soft" governor who cared about nothing but amassing wealth and building palaces, even if he happened to see a highway robber riding his mother! What on earth would have made that good-for-nothing sit back and let Daher take over Haifa, Tira, Tantura, and other towns under Damascus's jurisdiction?*

Eyeing the horizon, Hussein Pasha saw something dark and obscure, something that didn't belong to the desert. His heart pounded, but he regained his composure. He looked at those around him and saw them peering at the long wall that blocked their path and closed off the horizon.

Knowing it would take some time to halt a caravan miles long, he ordered the caravan to stop.

He was about to send one of his soldiers to investigate the situation when he saw what looked like a huge cloak fluttering in the distance and coming his way.

Again his heart pounded. It took him some time to realize that the huge cloak was, in fact, ten black cloaks fluttering abreast. Soon thereafter, ten dark, lean, stern-looking men with hawklike eyes, parched hands, and dusty beards were standing before him.

Contrary to their usual custom, they uttered no greeting of peace. One said, "We didn't want to waylay you before you'd reached the house of God, even though you'd violated your covenant with us. But things are different now, since your return journey doesn't oblige us to be charitable toward you. Pay what you owe and be on your way. That's all we ask. We don't want to see a drop of blood shed on this land."

"What we gave you on our way to Mecca, we'll give you on our way back to Damascus," said Hussein Pasha.

The Bedouin's spokesman kept a long silence. Then he said, "If I were you, I'd think things through again. You're far from Damascus and you're far from Mecca. The only thing you're close to is this." As he finished speaking, he patted his sword and turned to leave.

Hussein Pasha watched them ride away until their cloaks merged again into one.

The Bedouin had chosen the ideal place to wage their battle: an open expanse where they could rip the caravan to shreds with the greatest of ease. There wasn't a stone in sight, or a wall, or a tree, or even a small dune. The dunes on either side of the caravan's path were some distance away, and the sun in the sky portended an inferno.

"Prepare yourselves!" cried Hussein Pasha.

When the news finally reached those at the end of the caravan, some decided that their best hope of survival lay in heading back where they had come from: toward Mecca.

Without voicing what was in their minds, they simply looked into each others' eyes and set out. To their shocked surprise, however, what was ahead of the caravan was behind it as well, and they beat a quick retreat.

Until that moment the Bedouin had simply been people wanting to remind Hussein Pasha of a commitment the pilgrimage caravans had been honoring since the days of the Abbasid caliphate: to pay them in return for safe passage through their territory. In his arrogant conceit, Hussein Pasha had breached the age-old covenant, and they were coming from all directions to warn him to think twice.

Once again, however, he refused to pay, and when he sent them a messenger to inform them of his decision, they killed him on the spot.

In a single moment the world grew dark, and a storm of madness was unleashed. Blowing up from all four directions, it sent masses of humanity scattering like grains of sand, searching in vain for a camel or a horse to hide behind as arrows flew in all directions and swords and spears tore deep into every body in their path. The desert filled with blood-choked lungs, mangled body parts, and dying horses and camels.

The attackers didn't let the caravan catch its breath, and every storm that blew in was followed by another. It seemed that the one thing that had been plucked out of the earth forever was mercy, and several hours later the assault was still as forceful as if it had begun only moments before.

Hussein Pasha looked for something to protect him, but found nothing.

As midafternoon approached, some of the travelers realized that a number of the terror-stricken camels and horses had managed to break through the wall of hell. They followed them, only to have the desert itself close in on them from every side.

With difficulty, some of the soldiers and commanders achieved near-miraculous escapes. With them, Hussein Pasha rode away on a powerful horse toward a point he couldn't see, and without looking back for so much as a moment.

As the sun inclined toward the western horizon, everything became clear: death was everywhere and women's wails filled the twilight, whose redness had merged with the redness of the blood-drenched sand.

The sun set, and everything grew still.

The attackers moved some distance away and lit fires that surrounded the caravan like a noose. The sounds of laughter charged with victory rang out, and from time to time they would hear the screams of one of the women or girls who had been taken off alone by the attackers. Their victory celebration went on till morning, and at daybreak their wind blew again.

Everyone in the caravan was captive to a crushing terror, as they could see that they were alone, with no one to protect them.

The attackers stripped every surviving man and woman, and tens of thousands stood naked as though humanity had yet to discover clothing. Then, in a frenzy of terror, one of the women had an insane idea. She poured water—water! life!—onto the ground. With the resulting mud she began plastering her body, covering her chest and the area between her thighs, and many other women did the same.

However, this did them no good, as the attackers began searching for everything lightweight and of potential value in the bundles of clothing and the saddlebags of the dying camels. When they saw someone swallowing a ring, they split his gut, and they did the same with anyone else whose stomach appeared suspiciously large. Then they turned their attention to the women, searching their vaginas and anuses through the dry mud for anything that glittered.

When they departed at last, they were sure they hadn't left behind anything worth keeping. They had seized everything: the money, the camels, the merchandise, the beautiful and semi-beautiful women, the mahmal, and the weapons that had belonged to the annihilated army.

Everything suddenly fell still. The few survivors looked around them and saw nothing but the desert sands standing in mute witness.

That night, their second night, the odors of blood and flesh were carried away on the wind, and hungry-eyed hyenas, wolves, snakes, scorpions, and the like flocked to the site from all directions.

After a long day of wandering, Hussein Pasha and those still with him found their way to a road leading to Gaza, the city where he had been born and which was home to his family and relatives.

When white standards arrived in Damascus, weighed down with the ignominy of defeat, the entire city burst into tears: its people, its stones, its river, its walls, its fortresses, its gates.

The soldiers delivered six letters to the multazim, the governor's deputy. One of them was from Hussein Pasha, asking him to go out to help the caravan. He ignored the letter, certain that no one could do anything for a caravan so far from Damascus. Noting the multazim's failure to act, people rushed at the governor's mansion, pelting it with rocks, curses, and insults. When they despaired of any response, they called on others to help them gather up pack animals, food, and clothing and go out to aid the survivors. So many people left Damascus it looked like a ghost town.

Fourteen days later the rescue caravans arrived, but it was too late.

The country was in an uproar as people called for the beheading of Hussein Pasha and anyone else who had had a hand in the tragedy. The empire went in search of a scapegoat whose blood could appease the masses. The only candidate near at hand was Ahmad Agha, the chief chamberlain, who had fought for long years, with money and influence, to have Hussein Pasha appointed governor.[24]

On the morning of November 27, 1757, the day when the Prophet Muhammad's birthday was celebrated, Ahmad Agha was beheaded in Istanbul. His head was put on display next to the words, written in bold lettering:

This is the recompense of the man who caused the pilgrims to perish.

---

24 Governors under the Ottoman Empire would obtain their posts either through bribery or by buying them at auction in Istanbul, where the position in question would go to the highest bidder. Other positions, such as that of the daftardar, were similarly obtained. The first half of the eighteenth century saw more than forty governors come and go. These governors would milk their subjects dry with taxes, which they collected through coercion, exploitation, and fraud to compensate for what they had paid in order to win the post.

Meanwhile, the empire commenced a search for Hussein Pasha, granting whoever found him the right to chop off his head. Hussein Pasha wrote to the sultan informing him that Daher al-Umar, who was in rebellion against the empire, and former governor As'ad Pasha, who wanted revenge on the empire for removing him, had incited the Bedouin to loot the caravan.[25]

The empire wasn't convinced by such accusations. However, it needed them in order to thin out its populations of governors and pashas so that it could appoint others in their places and seize their wealth. After locating As'ad Pasha without difficulty, the empire had him beheaded. His head was then taken to Istanbul, together with all his property, which Uthman Pasha al-Kurji,[26] the new governor of Damascus, accessed by all means at his disposal, including threats and torture.

As for Daher, the empire left it to Uthman Pasha al-Kurji to choose the best means of getting rid of him.

---

25 After a lengthy investigation, the Ottoman caliph pardoned Hussein Pasha and the empire appointed him governor of Mar'ash in the Taurus Mountains, but he was murdered not long after. As for the mahmal, it was recovered by Umar al-Mahamid, sheikh of Houran, who paid the Bedouin 170 piasters for its return. It was transported back to Damascus on the back of a camel draped with Umar al-Mahamid's green inner robe.
26 Originally a Mamluk of As'ad Pasha al-Azm, Uthman had been favored by As'ad Pasha for his intelligence. When As'ad Pasha was killed in 1758 and the state impounded his wealth, Uthman was asked, in his capacity as someone who had been close to As'ad Pasha, to provide a list of all his property. When the list Uthman provided turned out to correspond exactly with the list made by the state, he was dubbed "the Truthful One." According to some accounts, Uthman betrayed his benefactor and disclosed his property for his own personal gain.

Acre's Aroma Hunter

He was sitting at home one day when suddenly he jumped as though a snake had bitten him.

"It's time for lunch!" he cried.

His wife looked at him and shook her head.

"Shall I get the food ready for you?" she asked grudgingly.

"What have you cooked?"

"A little rice with yoghurt and broad beans."

"I'm going out! When you get hungry, you have some, and leave the rest for supper."

He got up, gathered his tattered robe around him, and left.

The searing June day's cloying humidity and the crowds of market-goers, camels, and hawkers that filled the streets would have been sufficient reason not to go out. However, the midday hours, like the early morning and evening hours, were times he couldn't possibly spend at home.

With lackluster eyes and wizened mien, Ibrahim al-Sabbagh was the leanest person in Acre, and his protruding ribs were one of the main reasons his clothes wore out so fast. The bones in his face were strangely delicate, while the skin around his eyes was so dry and brittle they looked as though they were about to roll out of their sockets.

Al-Sabbagh quickly surveyed the broad thoroughfare that led to Acre's landward entrance, known as al-Siba' Gate, and his body was charged with an extraordinary energy that made up for the fact that he'd left the house more than an hour late.

Ten steps later, he relieved his eyes of the task of searching and let his nose take over. He stopped at the door to the first shop he came to and called out a greeting. The shop's owner, Jurays—who, after swearing never to live in a city that didn't have Daher as its multazim, had followed him to Acre—tried hurriedly to hide the food.

"Rice, yoghurt, and broad beans—is that what you'd call a meal, Jurays? It'll kill you, ruin your stomach, man! Where's the meat?"

"This is the best thing in the house, Doctor!"

"You've got to eat well, man, if you want to work well and think right. And you know the rest—I mean, if you want to be up to your manly duties at the end of the day!"

He fell silent for a while as though he were trying to remember something.

"Ah, talking about your food made me forget something important. How much do you owe me now?"

"Fifty-seven piasters."

"Don't be late in getting that to me. You'll only make things worse for yourself!"

"I know. It'll turn into sixty-seven piasters if I don't pay by the end of the month."

"I've been thinking of telling Sheikh Daher about this debt of yours. He could pay me, and you could pay him back. What do you say?" al-Sabbagh asked.[27]

"What are you saying, Doctor? That would just leave me in greater debt to Sheikh Daher, who's already been more than generous to me! Let's forget about it for now and enjoy God's blessings. Have a seat! Have a seat!" Jurays urged.

Al-Sabbagh hurriedly sat down and began eating as though he were in a race.

"Don't you worry that food like this might be bad for your stomach, Doctor?"

"Of course I do. But I don't like to let you eat alone! Food we eat alone never tastes good! Besides, when demons see somebody eating by himself, they come and share his food with him without his knowing it!"

"I really believe that, Doctor! But I don't think food loses its taste completely just because we eat by ourselves!"

---

27 Daher had instituted a number of arrangements to make people's lives easier and more orderly. If a merchant sold goods on credit and the buyer lacked the money to pay for them, Daher would pay on the buyer's behalf and, when he was able, the buyer would return the money to Daher. In this way, Daher had put a stop to usury, extortion, and the forcible imposition of taxes. He had instructed governors to grant interest-free loans to any peasant too poor to farm his land, and forbidden them to take any money beyond what people owed in taxes to the empire. He had announced that anyone found taking a bribe, even if it amounted to no more than a piaster, would be hung up by his feet, and he had warned the governors that if any wayfarer in their respective territories was robbed and the thief wasn't identified, the governor himself would be required to restore to the victim whatever money had been stolen.

"You should give that some more thought one of these days when you're eating by yourself!"

"Actually, Doctor, I've never had a chance to do that!"

"God's spared you that unpleasant experience, then!"

Jurays began digging into his food, stuffing a new bite into his mouth with all five fingers before he'd swallowed the one before it.

"Why are you eating so fast, man? You're not giving your stomach a chance to breathe!"

"It's been a long time since I worried about my stomach, Doctor."

The food that originally had been intended for someone else began disappearing. But, as always happened, there was one bite left on the plate. Al-Sabbagh sat looking at it, but, as usual, didn't touch it. He was careful to exercise self-restraint at this point, since leaving that last bite made him feel as though he were able to resist his impulses and desires. In fact, it made him feel morally superior!

Jurays had a different way of looking at that last bite. He saw it on the plate and said, "Praise God!"—thereby announcing that he'd had his fill. Then he sat back in his chair and patted his stomach the way he would pat the back of a fattened sheep.

Al-Sabbagh felt as though Jurays had punched him in the gut.

It occurred to him to say, "It's a shame to throw it away, man. Food is such a blessing!" Then, before Jurays had a chance to comment, he planned to snatch it off the plate. Instead, however, Jurays picked up the plate with lightning speed, saying, "Here, kitty kitty! Here, kitty kitty!"

A cat suddenly appeared as though she'd been waiting for years. He put the plate on the floor, and she devoured what was on it. When she finished eating, she started licking the plate.

"How can you let her eat off the same plate you and your family eat from, man?"

"Didn't God create her just the way He created us, and dogs too?"

"What do you mean?"

"Every morning and every evening we leave something on our plates for our dog, too."

"So your dog eats off your plates too?"

"I told you that a long time ago, Doctor! Even though you warned me against it, I've never gotten sick, thanks be to God, and neither has anyone in my family!"

"For you to let your cat do this, I can understand. But the dog?"

"My dear doctor! I'd rather share my food with goodhearted creatures like these than with demons. Wouldn't you?"

As though another snake had bitten him, Ibrahim al-Sabbagh jumped up and headed outside. Before he got to the door, he reached out and took a piece of candy. He looked back and saw Jurays eyeing him.

"A piece of candy is a good way to change the taste in your mouth. You should try it!" he said as he left.

But instead of putting it in his mouth, he slipped it into his pocket.

As he walked down the street, al-Sabbagh scanned the faces of passersby and patted his stomach, thinking about how empty it was. Suddenly he smelled the aroma of meat wafting in his direction. Seeing the boy who was carrying it, he turned quickly and asked him, "Who are you, boy?"

"I work in Muhammad's fabric shop."

"You'd better hurry, or your boss's meat will get cold. He must be starving!"

The boy nodded and rushed off. Al-Sabbagh followed him at close range, taking care not to lose track of him in Acre's crowded streets.

The Rider Who Raced
His Own Horse

S ensing something amiss, Islibi declined to participate.

What his brother Uthman had said was an unthinkable breach of bounds, which Daher had received with an equally unthinkable magnanimity and composure.

Uthman had told his father, "Don't you think it's time you took a rest, Sheikh? We've grown up now and you can depend on us. As you can see, each of us has been able to manage the region you've placed under his charge in the way you had hoped!"

Daher stood up and walked to the end of the mansion's wonderful garden. From the time he'd seen the gardens in Damascus he'd wished he had one of his own. Once he did have a garden of his own, he began to suspect that the only reason he had wanted one was that such gardens were a symbol of another era.

He picked five red roses. Then he came back and handed one of them to each of his sons.

They were all there: Islibi, Uthman, Ali, Sa'id, and Ahmad.

Pondering the red rose in his hand, Uthman said, "So it seems you agree with what I'm saying, Sheikh."

"No, it doesn't, Uthman. It's true, of course, that each of you has handled his responsibilities well. However, my experience tells me that the first years of a person's service do nothing to change him. Multazims and governors only begin to change after they've spent a long time in their posts, and I need to wait and see how much you yourselves are going to change!"

"But we're your sons, Sheikh, and we deserve a share of what's yours."

"You've always thought this way, Uthman. Do you remember the day you asked me when I was going to die? When I asked you why you wanted to know, you said, 'So that I can become multazim'!"

Embarrassed, Uthman replied, "Yes, I remember that, Sheikh. You remind me of it all the time. But I was a little boy then."

"And are you an adult now, Uthman?"

Daher left the question hanging. It was a difficult question, and one that he didn't need an answer to. He walked again to the end of the garden. He lingered in front of a white jasmine vine, filled his lungs with its fragrance, and walked back.

They looked at him for a long time. Then he said, "The way you look at things is truly strange! Do you think I annexed Acre, Haifa, Nazareth, and other cities so that I could pass them out to my sons?"

"Who would you pass them out to, then?" Ali asked.

"It's as if you still don't know what the Sheikh is thinking," countered Islibi.

"So, what *is* he thinking?" asked Uthman.

Daher cast Islibi an approving look.

"Don't tell us he's going to turn them over to the people!" Ali exclaimed.

"How could I turn them over to the people when they already belong to the people?" Daher asked him. "Are you asking me to take them away from the people and give them to you? This land is theirs, and will remain theirs. But people needed certain things to be provided for them. Hadn't you noticed that, Ali? The farmers' land only became theirs when we provided them with safety. The merchants' caravans only became theirs when we purged the roads of thieves and raiders. Similarly, boat owners only took possession of their boats and the sea when we turned Malta's pirates into guests who accepted the terms of our hospitality, and who now turn their arms over to our soldiers before entering the city. As for those who want to engage in commerce, we provide them with everything they want. Do you think the people who've come to Acre from all over—from Beirut, Sidon, Tyre, and Damascus to France, Greece, Cyprus, Sicily, and elsewhere—have come here just to make a profit? They've come looking for a roof they can sleep under without fear, and a place where they can attend their churches, synagogues, and mosque in peace."

"So then, Sheikh, you're building a state! Have you been doing this without our knowing about it?"

"No, I've been building it before your very eyes, Ali, but you haven't seen it. All you and Uthman can see in front of you is an obstacle: this old man!"

"So," interjected Ali, oblivious to Daher's observation, "why don't you choose one of us to be your heir? After all, only God knows how long any of us is going to live. Or let us choose! Don't you think I deserve to be your heir? I'm the one you sent as a hostage with Sulayman Pasha after the siege of Tiberias. And I'm the one who was made a laughingstock when

Sulayman Pasha started kicking me in front of the Damascus gate."

"So you've been angry with me ever since that day."

"More than angry. That was the first insult I'd ever received in my life. It was also the last, and I'll never forget it as long as I live!"

"Others were dying during those days, Ali. And you blame me for a few drops of blood you shed?"

"Rather, for having my dignity trampled in the dust."

"And will you reclaim your dignity if I put you in my place?" Daher asked with a sardonic smile. Then he added, "Do you think this country is a plot of land, or a palace, or a flock of sheep that I own and can pass down to you and your brothers as an inheritance?"

"Who does own it, then? Don't you rule it?" Uthman asked.

"It's as if you haven't heard a word I'm saying! This country doesn't belong to me, Uthman. All I've done is strengthen its people, calm their fears, and help them reclaim their lost dignity. Now you come and ask me to choose someone to inherit all this. Do you want me to bequeath you their strength, courage, and dignity? Things like this aren't passed down from one person to another, Uthman. You have to have your own strength and courage so you won't covet someone else's, and your own dignity so you won't trample on the dignity of others. You're servants to these people, nothing more. If it should come to my knowledge that any of you has tried to be more than this and raised himself above the people by so much as a stone that he's placed unpretentiously under his feet, he'll have no one but himself to blame for the consequences."

Daher took a deep breath, his fair face flushed, and his fearsome, piercing glance stinging them like a whip.

Focusing his gaze on Uthman again, he turned into a tiger. "You seem to be in a hurry for me to die, Uthman!" Daher shouted in his face.

"Me? Who said that, Father?"

"I can see it. Your eyes give you away. Your eyes say what you can't say with your lips: 'How long is this old man going to keep hanging on? Has Death forgotten about him?' Do you want to be my enemy, Uthman?"

Uthman began trembling. "Me? No, Sheikh! Who would dare oppose you?"

All his father's enemies and the fates they had met suddenly flashed through Uthman's mind. Every governor and vizier who had opposed his father had been either deposed or killed. After observing this pattern, he'd been careful to call his negative feelings toward his father any-

363

thing but enmity! At the same time, he anticipated fearfully the way the conflicts between his father, the Ottoman governors, and others would end, and was waiting for the day when the tide would turn.

Uthman wondered whether his brothers had seen what he had seen but hadn't dared to speak about it, even among themselves.

Daher leaned his back against the wall. With his fair-skinned, flushed face, his thick eyebrows, and his long white beard, he looked like a saint.

"I won't give you more than I've already given you, Uthman," he said. "You've gone too far, and my patience has run out."

"I was only joking with you, Sheikh."

"So you were joking when you said it was time for me to take a rest?"

Daher sensed that he needed to dissipate the dark cloud that had settled over the mansion. They were, after all, his sons, and he couldn't do without them. Besides, conversations of this sort couldn't go on forever.

"You know what, Uthman? This old man's changed his mind about some things. What would you say if he gave you what you wanted provided that you beat him at something?" Daher asked him with a smile.

"Beat you in what, Sheikh?"

"In a race! We'll take our horses to the seashore and race them."

"How could I ever win a race with you, Sheikh? Your horse is a lot stronger than mine!"

"So you do think you could beat me, but that the problem is the horse? Let's all go down to the seashore. Once we're there, I'll give you my horse and you let me ride yours. Whoever is faster than I am will have whatever he wants. What do you say?"

He scanned his other sons' faces, waiting for them to respond.

Islibi refused to be part of the race, and so did Sa'id and Ahmad. However, Ali surprised them by saying, "If you're giving your horse to Uthman, you've decided to give him everything, since the rest of us will lose!"

Daher struck his forehead with the fingertips of his right hand. "Now why hadn't I thought of that, Ali?" he said. "But don't worry. I've got a solution: First Uthman and I will race. If I win, I race you on your horse, and you take my horse the way he did. What do you say?"

"But after racing against Uthman, your horse would be too exhausted, Sheikh!"

"And why didn't I think of that either?" Daher exclaimed, striking his forehead again. Then he fell silent for a little while.

"You know, Ali?" Daher said. "I like the fact that you think of every-thing, but I assure you: there's a simple solution. Uthman and I will race today, and if I win I'll race you tomorrow. You'll take my horse, which by that time will have had a good rest, and I'll take yours. What do you think?"

"And if Uthman wins?"

"I didn't want to hear you casting doubt on this old man's abilities, Ali. But there's a solution to that problem too! If Uthman wins, you race with him the next day, each of you on his own horse, and whichever of you wins, I'll give whatever he wants."

Islibi listened to the conversation with his head in his hands, and when he looked up, he found the sheikh staring at him.

Uthman patted the neck of his father's horse. The horse neighed and turned its head toward Daher as if to ask him what was going on. Daher came up to it, ran his palms over its face, and caressed its forehead.

The horse calmed down.

"Do you see that lemon tree? We'll race to there. Each of us has to pick at least one of its leaves and bring it back to where we're standing."

Each of them mounted the other's horse. Daher's horse looked over at him again, but Daher avoided letting their eyes meet. Ahmad gave the signal, and they were off.

Ali, Islibi, Ahmad, and Sa'id watched them ride away. Within min-utes, Uthman was a considerable distance ahead of his father.

Ali's heart started to pound violently, and he exchanged quick, meaningful glances with his brothers. Islibi turned his back to the others and stared in the opposite direction as Uthman continued in the lead.

"It seems you don't want to see the sheikh lose, Islibi!" Ali remarked.

"There's no need for you to wait for an answer you know beforehand to a question that should never have been asked in the first place, Ali!"

"What do you mean?" Ali asked.

"You've got two eyes to see with," Islibi retorted. "So don't tell me you want me to tell you what you see, Ali!"

In the distance, Uthman leaned over and grabbed a handful of tree leaves before turning to come back. Meanwhile, Daher was still quite some distance from the tree. When he finally reached it, he leaned over, picked some leaves, and turned around.

However, the sheikh who had completed the first lap wasn't the same one who was completing the second.

With a body that was suddenly larger than life, he wasn't the sheikh they knew, and Uthman's horse beneath him looked like a fairy-tale creature from the land of the jinn. The horse beneath him was flying, its hooves not touching the ground. As for the sheikh's horse, it was the only one sending the dust flying as its hooves alternately sank into the ground and rose into the air.

Given his tremendous forward thrust, it was inevitable that the sheikh would finally come up next to his son, and he did just that.

Uthman expected his father to look over at him, to cast him a meaningful glance. But he didn't. He just kept charging ahead as though he were racing no one but himself.

As the sheikh approached the place where his sons stood waiting, he kept coming full speed, and they scattered to give him space. As for Islibi, he stayed where he was, although the wind produced by the horse's passing nearly bowled him over. Looking up, he watched his father ride farther and farther away until he disappeared.

Uthman got down from his father's horse, regretful that he'd gotten himself into a hot spot he could have done without. He tried to say something, then stopped. When he finally managed to get a few awkward words out, he said, "Who would have thought that a man his age could do something like that?"

"He knows horses better than you do," replied Islibi without turning around. "He knows them better than any of us, brother. So we should think twice before we offend a man that our horses recognize in a way they don't recognize us!"

The sun began floating on the face of the water, creating a river of refulgent, shimmering light atop the sea.

As Daher's sons stood waiting for him to reappear, they suddenly heard a horse neighing behind them. They turned in alarm, wondering how it was that they hadn't heard any hoofbeats. It was then that they knew he must really have been flying, since they saw no cloud of dust behind him.[28]

---

28 In *Travels through Syria and Egypt*, historian Constantin-François Volney tells us that the cause behind the conflict between Daher and his sons was his refusal to name one of them his heir.

The Unseen Wound

Daher was about to mount his horse to go out when he felt strangely dizzy. He grabbed hold of the saddle, struggling to remain upright. Islibi saw his father from one of the windows overlooking the mansion's courtyard, and wondered what to make of it.

He waited.

The moments dragged by. Daher's hand trembled slightly, and with it his entire body. His eyes clouded over. Suddenly he collapsed on the ground.

Islibi rushed out to his father like a storm wind. Turning him over on his back, he checked his pulse, and found that it was weak.

The soldiers who had been waiting for Daher at the gate gathered around him. Duhqana arrived, and when she saw Daher she muffled a scream.

"One of you go and call his physician, Sulayman!" shouted Islibi.

Some of the soldiers took off to bring the doctor while Islibi had the rest of them carry Daher inside.

While Islibi walked around in circles like a chicken with its head cut off, Sulayman al-Sawwan was inside attempting to determine the cause of the illness.

He came out and asked whether the sheikh had drunk or eaten anything unusual. The answer came readily: "No."

Half an hour later he came out again, his face ashen and his eyes red. "Had the sheikh complained of pain anywhere, either this morning or yesterday?"

Again came the answer: "No."

"There was nothing wrong with him," Islibi added. "He even raced my brother Uthman yesterday, and won!"

The doctor disappeared inside and checked Daher's pulse. He could hardly feel it. He brought a mirror up to his nose, and when he saw no sign of air coming out of his nostrils, he became alarmed.

367

Najma arrived, agitated. "What's happened to my boy?"

No one said a word.

"What's going on in this house that I don't know about?" she demanded.

"Nothing, Grandma. Believe me!"

"No, there's something big going on, Ahmad. Is my boy Daher all right?"

"He's fine, Grandma. He's fine!"

She headed for the room where Daher and the doctor were.

Islibi tried to block her path, but she pushed him aside, moving past Duhqana, Sa'id, and Daher's vizier, Yusuf al-Sallal.

She shoved the door open and burst into the room. The doctor was taken aback. But before he could open his mouth, she leaned over Daher and caressed his hand.

The night before, Daher had mounted his horse and gone back to the mansion, leaving his sons behind on the seashore. Once there, he headed for his favorite couch, which sat next to a large window on the west side of the mansion. From there he could get some fresh air and let his eyes roam far and wide over the dark waters.

When Jum'a served him his dinner, he didn't see it. He ate, but didn't know he had eaten until he saw the empty dishes on the table in front of him.

He went to sleep, though he didn't know how.

He got up the next morning, again without knowing how.

As he left his room after hearing the dawn call to prayer, the waves of the sea were lapping at the city walls with a powerful, monotonous rhythm. He performed his ritual ablution and prayed.

Afterward he walked up to the balcony overlooking the mansion's eastern courtyard. As he rested his hands on its low wall, he was surprised to find that Uthman's and Ali's horses were both gone. He could imagine why Uthman might have left the house. However, he didn't understand why Ali would have done the same. Only one thought came to mind: *All his life Ali has acted as though nobody could be his equal. He's so brave and strong, he deserves to be proud of himself!*[29] *But did he suspect that I might win my race with him, and did he feel it necessary to leave in order to avoid being defeated in front of his brothers by this old man who doesn't want to slow down? Or*

---

29   Ali even refused to marry off his daughters, lest they be controlled by their husbands!

368

. . . ? Or does he think that even his father isn't good enough to be his equal? In other words, is he too proud to race me?

At that moment Daher felt a stab go through him. He let forth a loud moan, then looked around, fearful that someone might have heard it. No one was there.

He tried to identify the spot where he had felt the stabbing pain. Strangely, he wasn't able to, as though his body didn't belong to him.

With difficulty he walked back inside. When Jum'a brought him his breakfast, he didn't touch it.

Then the unseen spear struck again.

He called out to Jum'a to take the food away. But Jum'a didn't come.

And what about Uthman? Might you have been too hard on him, Sheikh? I know that as his father, you might not be able to answer a question like this. Or, if you did answer it, you'd say that you were too hard on him.

But would you answer it differently in your capacity as "the king of Galilee" (as a certain priest in Nazareth once dubbed you)?

As a matter of fact, you weren't too hard on him, whether as a father or as a ruler of this country. You've given him a great deal and you've been very patient with him. How many times have you pretended not to see what he was doing, or kept silent about what you saw? How many times have you overlooked his greed and his insane desire for you to disappear from the face of the earth? But in the end you had no choice but to teach him a lesson, small though it was. You had to beat him in that race in the hope that he might realize what kind of a person he is, and what kind of a person you are!

"Bon appétit!" Jum'a said when he came back. Then he saw that Daher hadn't touched his food. "Haven't you eaten yet, Sheikh?" he asked.

"I've got no appetite, Jum'a. Take the food away!"

Before Jum'a disappeared through the wide diwan door, the spear struck again. This third time, Daher's right hand shot to the place where he felt the pain: between his kidney and his lower abdomen.

The sun came up and he remembered that he had to go out, as he had a lot of work waiting for him at the administrative office.

Yusuf al-Sallal was one of Daher's closest associates. Their business ties went back to Daher's days in Tiberias, and in the course of their dealings over many years, al-Sallal had proved himself a trustworthy partner and friend. Never once had he hesitated to offer Daher financial help if he needed it, and he had generously provided the seeds needed by

369

farmers in Tiberias and the surrounding region. Hence, when Daher established himself in Acre and was faced with the need to manage a full-fledged state, al-Sallal was the first person who came to mind for the post of vizier.[30]

Yusuf was an educated, intelligent, trueborn Arab. Hence, although many claimed that he had overrun Daher's administrative offices and councils with his fellow Catholics, Daher paid no attention to such prattle. When the complaints reached a crisis point, Daher gathered the leading men of Acre and issued a statement that cut short all further debate: "These administrative offices and councils were established to serve all the people of this country. So if I hear of a man who is said to have demonstrated knowledge, expertise, and integrity in serving others, I'll seek him out personally, on foot if I have to, be he Muslim, Christian, or Jew. Since people have come here and chosen to live side by side with the residents of Acre, we have no choice but to embrace these newcomers and grant them the same freedoms we grant our own. God is my witness, as are you, that never once have I stood opposed to the construction of a church, a synagogue, or a mosque. And never, as long as I live, will I allow anyone in this land to subject those who have fled from injustice in Sidon, Jerusalem, Nablus, Beirut, or anywhere else to the kind of unjust treatment they've left behind."

Unbeknownst to Daher, however, a covert war had been raging between Yusuf al-Sallal and his physician, Sulayman al-Sawwan. It had begun when the vizier discovered that Daher accepted without question whatever his physician had to say about other people. Things had come to a head when someone disclosed privately to al-Sallal that Daher's physician was telling him things about al-Sallal himself.

---

30 Daher established an administrative office that concerned itself with adjustment of state taxes and the collection of local taxes, customs duties, and tourist fees paid by pilgrims coming from abroad to visit the holy places. Needing someone to rule on people's problems and disputes in keeping with Islamic law, he appointed Sheikh Abd al-Halim al-Shuwayki as mufti and Sheikh Muhammad Effendi as judge. He divided his army into an infantry division, under the command of Ahmad al-Dankizli, and a commando division. In addition to the troops led by his sons, he had reserve forces composed of a combination of men from his own territories, members of the Matawila tribe, and other allies. In times of affliction Daher would turn to these forces, which numbered in the tens of thousands.

That evening al-Sawwan came out of Daher's room for the fifth time. At his wits' end, and terrified that Daher might die under his care, he was willing to entertain any solution others might suggest.

"We'll bring al-Sabbagh!" announced al-Sallal.

"Bring whoever you want. Just move!" bellowed Najma.

Al-Sawwan had never thought he would see the day when someone suggested bringing Ibrahim al-Sabbagh to treat Daher without al-Sawwan's raising any objection! He looked over at al-Sallal, and the two men exchanged a meaningful glance.

"Let's look for al-Sabbagh, then," said al-Sawwan. So desperate was he to escape from everything, he would have gone out to help in the search himself if duty hadn't required him to remain on the premises.

A sudden darkness descended over Acre, and the lamplighters began racing with the clock to light the street lanterns.

The problem that now faced those attending to Daher was: where would they find Ibrahim al-Sabbagh, or "the teacher" as most people called him?

Two Nights in One

As they had expected, he wasn't at home. Nevertheless, it came as a surprise to them when his wife said, "Could he possibly be here at a time like this?" Noticing that the people who were asking for him this time were soldiers, she called out after them as they left, "Has he done something? It must be serious if you're coming for him at this time of night!"

"No, but we need him in connection with an important matter," replied one of the soldiers.

"If you need him in connection with an important matter, then why are you leaving? Let one of you stay here, since there's one thing he can't do without in this house, namely, sleep!"

The soldiers held a hurried consultation. Then one of them came walking slowly back. Al-Sabbagh's wife closed the door and the soldier rested his back against it as though he were afraid al-Sabbagh might come in the house without his seeing him.

There ensued a playful race of soldiers and shadows against the walls. As the flames of the street lanterns danced nervously along the sides of the road, they would erase a patch of darkness from one of the walls, only to have a soldier's shadow rush in and bring it back.

Ibrahim al-Sabbagh walked down the streets with his eyes closed. As he went, he cursed the day lanterns were invented and, even more, the person who had had the idea of bringing them out of the houses and hanging them in the streets! Light robbed his olfactory nerves of at least half their keenness, standing like a wall between his nose and the smells around him.

During the nocturnal hours he would never have intruded on anyone who didn't owe him money. After all, it was one thing to walk into an open shop in broad daylight, and quite another to knock on someone's door at night.

During the day all that mattered to him was the quality of the food he managed to get. Consequently, he wouldn't hesitate to go looking for a second breakfast or lunch somewhere else if he hadn't enjoyed the food he'd eaten the first time. At night, however, he had more modest expectations, and was content just to find something edible without regard for its quality.

He closed his eyes and walked, moving his head sometimes to the right, sometimes to the left, and if he ran into someone, he would curse the light for being so dim that even a man with his eyes open couldn't see properly!

When he picked up a scent he would stop and spend a few moments trying to determine what type of food he was smelling. If the aroma was to his liking and if it was coming out of the house of someone who owed him money, he would knock on the door without delay. If, on the other hand, it was coming from the house of someone who wasn't in his debt, he would linger for a while to enjoy the smell for as long as he could before moving on, cursing the affluence people had started enjoying since Daher came along!

About to despair of finding anything to eat, he started thinking about how far it was to his house. He was sure he'd keel over halfway there unless he had something to answer the call of his poor stomach. He scanned his surroundings and decided to try another street. By this time he had reached the seaward gate, having left the Hanging Mosque behind him. He walked northward along the wall until he came to Khan al-Ifranj. He went down a number of streets and alleyways and, with the Khan to his right, he circled around it until he saw what was known as "Daher's Market"[31] with its towering arches. He thought of turning back and heading west, but the hour had grown too late. He turned in the direction of Daher's mansion, and in the distance could see the tip of the treasury tower protruding above it. The streets and alleyways in the low-lying area near the mansion were lined with the houses of merchants and other well-to-do residents who had never let him down.

A raucous medley of voices came from inside the fortress, and lights made their way through the darkness, their bright glow obliterating the night. He decided it wasn't worth his time to go on occupying himself with Daher's fortress and its lights. *But on second thought: Might there be some big banquet I didn't know about?*

---

31 It later came to be known as the White Market.

He stopped, aimed his nose like a cannon at the fortress, and waited. "Nothing!" he exclaimed aloud.

So he started moving again, and within moments he'd lost his bearings. However, he didn't care any more where he had his feet planted. All he cared about was his stomach. Soon thereafter, as he approached the Khan al-Shuna Gate, he was bowled over by a fragrance that left him drunk. He glanced right and left, and when he saw the gate he knew he had arrived.

He walked toward the smell. As he approached its source, he was pleased to discover that it was coming from the house of al-Hallaj Abd al-Hamid al-Ghazzi. Some years earlier, al-Hallaj had left Gaza City, the place of his birth, in search of someone who could teach him to play the lute, but he'd ended up learning to operate a cotton gin instead.

Al-Sabbagh knocked on the door once, then twice. When no one answered, he started to suspect he'd come to the wrong house and that everyone inside was fast asleep. However, he wasn't one to give up easily, especially now that his stomach's call had turned into a wail. When at last the door opened, he saw a sullen face that looked all the more sullen in the dark.

Wasting no time, he explained, "I only came at this late hour because I need the money I lent you!"

The man nearly fell over. "Now, teacher? How could I get your money to you in the middle of the night?"

Al-Sabbagh just stood there, oblivious to everything but the powerful aroma wafting toward him over al-Hallaj's shoulders.

"I realize you don't have any money to give me now, and that I may have come at an inconvenient time. But do you have to leave me standing out in the street?"

"Oh my goodness! Pardon me, teacher! It's just that your request caught me off guard. Come in! Come in!"

"We've got company!" the man shouted. After an apprehensive silence, the household began bustling with activity again.

Hardly had al-Sabbagh taken a seat when al-Hallaj said to him, "We were just about to have dinner. Won't you have a bite with us?"

"I've had dinner, actually. But . . . if you insist!"

The man disappeared, and al-Sabbagh busied himself looking around at all the things in the spacious room. His attention was drawn in particular to a small copper pitcher on the windowsill.

The man returned shortly carrying a straw tray on which he appeared to have placed all the food in the house.

Al-Sabbagh waited for al-Hallaj to invite him to begin eating, and he didn't disappoint. The invitation meant the world to him, since without it he might have died of starvation!

He ate. He ate a lot. And he didn't forget to say, "By God, your food is so good, I feel as though I haven't eaten for days!"

Al-Hallaj smiled and encouraged him to eat still more. As for al-Sabbagh, he couldn't help but comply when he caught sight of a roast chicken that must have come out of the oven only moments earlier.

When at last he finished, he rested his back against the wall and took a breath. However, he couldn't get a chestful of air because his stomach now took up half the space allotted to his lungs.

Meanwhile, the soldiers outside were breathless from hours of asking about him.

In the end he had no choice but to leave his host's house, so he excused himself. Al-Hallaj clung to him, saying, "The night's still young, teacher!"

"Well, I'm not young any more, as you can see, and it's a long way home."

Getting up heavily, he reached for the copper pitcher and turned it over admiringly in his hands. "I didn't think they still made pitchers this nice!" he remarked.

"They don't, in fact. But I'd be delighted if you'd accept it as a gift!"

"No, I couldn't do that. It must mean a lot to you!"

"As long as it's with you, it won't have left my house!"

"I swear to God, you're embarrassing me!" al-Sabbagh stammered.

"There's no need to be embarrassed. You'd honor me by accepting it."

"Well, thank you. Thank you very much!"

This was one of al-Sabbagh's incurable habits. It pleased him no end to acquire some rare object of value and beauty, and he wouldn't think of leaving a place without taking something he liked. But if al-Sabbagh's ears had been as sharp as his nose, he would have heard all the unpleasant things that were said in al-Hallaj's house the minute the door closed behind him.

When he glimpsed a soldier leaning against his front door, he was terror-stricken at the thought that he might have to offer him supper. The
minute the soldier saw him, he came running toward him, and al-Sabbagh's heart sank. Little did he know that veritable mountains were
about to land upon his shoulders!

The Breeze Passing Through

D aher's body lay motionless on the bed.

Al-Sabbagh reached out and felt his pulse.

A different person now, he shouted, "You took your time calling me!"

His words struck terror in everyone's hearts. Sulayman al-Sawwan, Daher's physician, took a couple of steps back as though al-Sabbagh were about to slap him. As for Daher's vizier, Yusuf al-Sallal, he felt miserably inadequate in the face of this difficult test.

"I need my bag. I'll have to go get it," al-Sabbagh said.

"We'll bring it to you," Sa'id told him, his legs barely holding him up.

"But would you know what medicines to put in it if you went by yourself?"

Sa'id made no reply.

"Get a horse ready for me right away!"

"All the horses are ready," replied a chorus of voices.

He headed outside, looking daggers at them and muttering to himself, "Now they come to me? The patient is the sheikh and they come to me now!"

He mounted the horse with difficulty, despite assistance from Islibi. He prodded the horse and it started to move. Islibi gestured to a number of soldiers to escort al-Sabbagh, but after they had ridden some distance behind him, he said, "Go on back. I'll escort him myself."

Al-Sabbagh was at least five years younger than Daher, but the time he had spent on foot hadn't given him the kind of strength Daher had acquired by riding on horseback. Al-Sabbagh was riding the horse at his own usual pace—a walking pace—and if Islibi hadn't noticed how fragile the man was, he would have given the horse a good slap. As things were, however, he was afraid al-Sabbagh might fall and break his neck just when they needed him most.

By the time five minutes had passed, Islibi couldn't stand it any longer. Coming up next to al-Sabbagh, he whisked him off the back of his horse, positioned him in front of him on his own horse, and took off, leaving al-Sabbagh's mount behind.

"You're going to kill us, son!" cried a terrified al-Sabbagh.

"Rather, you and I are going to kill the sheikh if we go to your house at this pace! Now show me the way. Where do you live?"

The horse flew down the streets like the wind, and every time they passed a street lantern, its flame would flicker and nearly go out. Hundreds of lanterns had begun sputtering, and if at that moment Islibi had remembered everything he'd been told about the night of lanterns in Tiberias, he would have ridden more carefully.

Al-Sabbagh pointed, crying, "This is my house! This is my house!" and Islibi came to a sudden halt.

The horse's front hooves plunged into the dust of the street like a couple of plows. The dust mingled with the night, causing a peculiar hue to emerge in the light of the lantern that hung in front of the house. Islibi had never seen a color like it before.

Hardly had al-Sabbagh gone inside when Islibi began pounding on the door, urging him to hurry. His wife came out, wrapped in a black scarf, and pleaded, "Go easy on him, son. He's an old man!"

Before she turned to go in, al-Sabbagh reappeared. He passed Islibi and headed for the horse. Seeing al-Sabbagh trying without success to get on the horse's back, Islibi asked him to hand him his bag before trying to mount, but he just held on to it all the more tightly.

In the end Islibi managed to help him onto the horse, and jumped on behind him. The horse took off running again. When they reached the street by which they had come, Islibi's heart sank. In fact, he nearly burst into tears. All but one or two of the street lanterns had gone out. The street was dark, so lifeless and still that the sound of the horse's hoofbeats could have drowned out the sound of the sea.

But they didn't have far to go.

Those awaiting their arrival began clearing the corridor, glued to the walls on either side to let the doctor through. When at last he reached the door to the room where Daher lay, he cast those inside a sweeping glance and barked, "Everyone out!"

They were surprised at the ease with which they obeyed him. Even Najma found herself backing out before she thought to ask, "And why do I have to leave too?" She was followed out by the vizier.

Daher's physician, Sulayman al-Sawwan, clutched the bed frame with rigid fingers as though the bed were about to fly away, carrying the sheikh into the darkness of no return.

"You too!" al-Sabbagh said to him.

"Me what?"

"You leave too! You've done all you can do." As al-Sabbagh spoke, his hands were fumbling in his bag, his fingers charged with new life.

Al-Sawwan loosened his grip on the bedpost, but his feet didn't take him away.

"Get him out of here!" shouted al-Sabbagh.

Islibi took al-Sawwan by the hand and led him away. When al-Sawwan reached the door, he was sure it was the last time he would ever cross the mansion's threshold.

"Close the door!" al-Sabbagh shouted.

Before they closed it, he added, "And I don't want anybody standing outside. I don't want anyone in the hallway!"

The corridor began emptying as bodies slipped away like water soaking into sand.

The mansion and the courtyard were blanketed in silence. The horses became so still that their heavy breathing could no longer be heard, and the sea seemed to have retreated miles from the shore. Time weighed on everyone's chests like a huge millstone, crushing them without mercy.

The dawn call to prayer sounded in Daher's mosque (the "Hanging" Mosque). Half an hour later, those waiting outside saw al-Sabbagh's figure approaching, exhausted. Before he reached them, his legs gave out and he collapsed next to the gate.

Duhqana screamed, and Najma hurriedly reached out and clapped her hand over her mouth.

Islibi reached al-Sabbagh in four huge strides.

"Has something happened, God forbid?"

"I'm fine! Just get me to a bed somewhere! I need to sleep."

Islibi bent down and picked him up. Al-Sabbagh was as light as a little boy, so the dawn breeze passing through at that moment nearly plucked him out of Islibi's arms.

Islibi laid him on the bed inside. Before leaving the room, he heard al-Sabbagh whisper, "Wake me up in a couple of hours so that I can check on the sheikh!"

Al-Sabbagh's Night

Daher opened his eyes feebly and closed them again. Then, as though he'd seen something long forgotten, he opened his eyes once more to help himself recall it.

Three lanterns illumined the room with the dimness required by someone about to depart, or by someone traveling through the night on the back of the half-death commonly referred to as sleep.

Someone who's sleeping is half dead. Isn't that what they say? So how would one describe a sick person who's asleep? Further, how would one describe the sick person who, when he awakens, finds himself surrounded by this sort of gloom? In a stillness this deep, wouldn't the mere opening or closing of his eyelids be sufficient to extinguish the lanterns around him?

But he wasn't there any more. He'd gone elsewhere.

He was standing alone, half-naked, being pelted with prickly objects. The objects would fall to the ground, but their barbs implanted themselves deep in his flesh.

A long time passed before he realized that he was being pelted with scores of porcupines: spiny spheres that concealed some of the most gentle, kindhearted, intelligent beings in existence.

A female voice came running toward him from a distance. The voice reached him, but not the person it belonged to. He was sure it must be his mother, Najma. She said to him, "There's no need for you to see him, Daher. There's no need for you to see him. He's turned into a porcupine."

"A human being can't turn into a porcupine!" he screamed.

She swore to him that this was what had happened, and that those who had seen it hadn't believed their eyes.

Then Najma's voice disappeared, and she herself came into view. He waited for her to say something, but she remained silent. "Where did your voice go?" he asked her.

Then a sudden stabbing pain struck again. He screamed, but she didn't hear him. "Where did *my* voice go?" he asked her.

He saw her come up and squeeze his hand as though she wanted to console him. He turned and saw that she really was squeezing his hand, but that his hand wasn't there. He wished she would squeeze the other hand and that it would actually be there.

He looked at where she'd been standing, but didn't see her. He thought about his feet, but didn't dare look down. He ran his hand over his head, his beard, his neck, his chest. The stab came again. He screamed. But Najma didn't hear him. How could she not have heard him?

He walked down the hall and stopped in front of a mother-of-pearl wardrobe. He opened it and found Nafisa waiting for him inside. "Why didn't you open the door for me? I knocked again and again. Didn't you hear me?"

She stepped toward him, placing one foot on the floor. But when she placed the other foot on the floor, she disappeared.

He looked around, but saw no one. Meanwhile, the lanterns kept sputtering and sputtering. He looked up and found Abbas clinging to the ceiling.

"What are you doing up there?" Daher asked him.

"Nothing. I'm just waiting for you. Why are you taking so long?"

"Come down. Come down here. What do you say we go to the lake?"

"No, you come up here. I can't come down!"

Daher jumped up and touched the robe of the person dangling from the ceiling. He jumped again and caught hold of his feet. When he let go of them, he saw that they were the feet of his brother Saleh.

"How could you have thought I was Abbas?" Saleh asked him with a grin.

"Because you *were* Abbas!"

"But I'm Saleh!"

Daher looked for a chair to place under the feet dangling in space. Not finding one, he dragged the bed over with difficulty. But when he looked up again, Saleh was gone.

Then a voice came from a distance. It came from in front of him, from behind him, and from either side. He felt a hand patting his shoulder, and turned. It was a woman whose face was half young, half old and wizened. She had her hair in two braids, one black and the other white. As he tried to recall where he'd seen her before, she said, "Have you forgotten me? I'm the girl you rescued beside the lake: Haniya! I've come to thank you, and to tell you that I'm still lily-white, and that my dignity has been preserved untainted just as you left it."

"Who is this elderly woman who's come with you?" Daher asked her, pointing to the other half of her face.

"I thought you'd recognize her!" she said, and began to cry. As for the elderly half, it was saddened, but didn't cry. A withered hand reached out and grasped the young hand on the other side, saying, "I told you he wouldn't recognize you. Didn't I tell you? Come, let's be going. We're late. Night fell on the lake more than two hours ago, and I don't want to lose you. Do you understand? I'll walk ahead of you so that no matter how dark the night is, you'll see this white braid of mine!"

The body moved away sideways, the old half heading east and the young half west. The white braid danced in the darkness until it reached Tiberias without his losing sight of it.

He tried to remember where he was. "I'm in Acre," he said. Then he woke up.

He opened his eyes but didn't see anything. The light was bright, and as harsh as the darkness.

"Good morning!" said Islibi when he saw Daher sit up in bed.

"Good morning! It seems Jum'a's forgotten to bring me my breakfast today!"

"I'll bring it myself."

Suddenly Daher remembered the stabbing pains, the voices that came, and the people who didn't. He remembered the young-old woman and the porcupines that were thrown at his naked body.

"Have I been sick, Islibi?"

"Very sick, Father."

"Could you bring me my food, or . . . ?"

"Yes, I can, Father. I can."

Daher heard Islibi's footsteps running down the hallway, but didn't know what to make of it.

When Islibi got to the other part of the mansion, everyone was there: Najma, Ahmad, Sa'id, and Duhqana. He told them that the sheikh had regained consciousness and had asked for his breakfast. When he saw them all about to go see Daher, he said, "Leave him alone for now."

"How can I leave him alone?" exclaimed Najma, who took off running down the long hallway.

In the mansion diwan, al-Sallal and al-Dankizli sat in silence watching al-Sabbagh sleep. "How is the sheikh?" asked al-Dankizli.

"He's fine," replied al-Sallal. "He's woken up and asked for his breakfast."

"Thank God! Thank God!"

Just then al-Sabbagh stirred and whispered, "He's woken up? Thank God!"

He rested his back against the wall for a bit, studying the other two men's faces. Before getting up, he reached out for his bag as if he had put it there himself. Picking it up, he announced, "I'm going home now."

"Don't you want to see him and make sure he's recovered completely?" Islibi asked him.

"Didn't you say he'd regained consciousness?"

"Yes."

"Well then, my work is done!"

Islibi reached into his pocket. Before he could take the money out, al-Sabbagh said, "Please. Leave it in your pocket! Do you expect me to take money for treating the sheikh?"

Islibi let the coins fall back to the bottom of his pocket. Then he walked al-Sabbagh to the mansion gate and asked the soldiers stationed there to take him home.

"That won't be necessary!" he said. "I want to walk a little!"

"Will you be back to see him in the afternoon, or in the evening?" Islibi asked him.

"There won't be any need for that. Didn't you say he'd woken up?"

Al-Sabbagh stood surveying the busy street outside the mansion gate and wondering if he should go home, put his bag away, and come back, or wander through the markets for a while, then go home and sleep till noon. But before long, an aroma wafted past his nose and decided the matter.

A Final Conversation
with the Angel

As soon as he recovered, Daher secluded himself with the new bundle that had arrived, and which he had done his utmost not to open.

What baffled him was that, unlike the earlier braid, which had been thick and black, this one was wispy and lighter in color. He studied its chestnut hue and ran his index finger over it ever so gently, fearful of doing it harm.

Seeing him on horseback surrounded by a squad of soldiers, Najma asked him, "Where are you off to?"

"To Tiberias. I want to see Islibi!"

Najma nodded knowingly. On the night of his illness, she was the one who had received the bundle from one of their servants.

He embraced Islibi, and before sitting down he said, "I want to see Tiberias!" News of his arrival had spread, and when he went to the door, he was surprised to find the courtyard filled with people. He greeted them and, after speaking with them briefly, came back inside.

A few hours later he left the mansion through the back door. From there he made his way to the lemon orchard. The house in its center was noticeably larger than before, and now had two stories. He entered its large gate and came up to the door. The trees filled the air with a perfume too sweet for words. He knocked on the door and waited. Then he knocked again. Soon a young girl no more than four years old came to the door. Before he noticed her features, his attention was drawn to an empty space where a second braid had once dangled.

"Mama!" the little girl called. There appeared a pretty woman in her mid-thirties who bore a striking resemblance to Haniya on that long-ago day.

She surprised him by saying, "Sheikh Daher?"

He nodded. "But you couldn't be Haniya!"

384

"No, Sheikh. Haniya is my mother!"

Bringing the braid out of his pocket, he asked, "Does this belong to your little girl?"

"Yes, it does, Sheikh. She sent it to you on my mother's instructions."

"You don't owe it to me to keep sending these precious braids."

"It's something my mother vowed to do as long as she lived, and something she's told us to continue doing after she dies. So please don't let it anger you, Sheikh. You can't imagine how beautiful it makes us feel to send you our braids! If you'd like to discuss the matter with my mother, she's right here."

Before Daher could reply, she called, "Mother!"

Like an angel clad in white, a woman appeared in the doorway. Delicate as a breeze, she was so old and fragile that she'd nearly turned back into a child.

Daher stood dazzled before her, as though she were purity itself.

"You've done us a great honor by visiting us, Sheikh," she said.

"May your household be blessed, sister! I was just telling your daughter—"

"I heard you, Sheikh. I also heard what she said to you! Far be it from you, of all people, to rob us of the innocence that you yourself bestowed on us! Allow us to grow in perfection by what we send you of ourselves!"

Daher leaned down and kissed the little girl's head. As he stood back up, he found Haniya beaming with approval. Smiling back at her, he said again, "But please, don't send . . ."

Without finishing what he'd begun to say, he turned to leave. As he did so, the young woman's voice rang in his heart: "You can't imagine how beautiful it makes us feel to send you our braids!"

Kneading Water

T he vizier has arrived," announced the guard standing at the door to Daher's mansion.

"Bring him in."

In a few moments, al-Sabbagh was crossing the threshold clad in his usual tattered raiment, looking wretched as a beggar.

Daher looked at him and shook his head.

"Believe me, Sheikh, I know exactly what you're about to say! But what's wrong with my clothes? Isn't it better for a person to be humble rather than pretentious, and to keep his appearance simple rather than showing off what he has? Look at the people who come crying and complaining to you. When they see the way your vizier is dressed, they'll be ashamed of the fancy clothes they're wearing! And when they compare their physical condition to mine, they'll be ashamed of the good health they enjoy!"

"This is precisely why I want you to change your appearance and take better care of yourself, Ibrahim. Whoever sees you will stop in the middle of his complaint!"

"And what harm would there be in that, Sheikh? This would be to your benefit, wouldn't it?"

"To my benefit? Actually, I can't see how it would be to my benefit. But one thing I'm sure of is that it would do them harm!"

"But Sheikh, didn't your noble Prophet say, 'God will not look upon one who trails his robe in vain conceit'?"

"Yes, he did, upon him be peace. He also said, 'God loves to see the evidence of His blessings on His servant'!"

"And aren't these clothes a blessing?"

"No doubt they are! After all, without them you'd be stark naked!"

"See, you've said it yourself! I just hope you won't worry about this, Sheikh. Think of your mother, Madame Najma. She goes everywhere barefoot, doesn't she? Does this detract one iota from her stature? These clothes of mine that aren't to your liking are just another side of her barefootedness!"

"Yes, Ibrahim, she does go barefoot. If she wore tattered shoes like yours, you could compare your clothes to them. But you haven't changed these clothes of yours since the day I met you! As for Madame Najma, she at least washes her feet five times a day!"

"And who told you I never wash this robe, Sheikh?"

"Well, you may care enough about it to wash it once every month or two. If you washed it five times a day, I wouldn't open my mouth!"

"But if I did that, Sheikh, I'd never leave my house! Or I'd have to come see you naked!"

"Anything but that!" Daher chuckled.

"So are you convinced now?"

"And who wouldn't be convinced by an argument like that? In any case, let's get back to the matter at hand. Did you bring the money?"

"Five thousand piasters in full, Sheikh. Here it is."

"I'll have the money back to you in two months' time."

"I don't like to hear you set a deadline for returning it to me, Sheikh, as if I were worried about it! I'm not!"

"I understand. But I want you to live for at least two more months, and now I know you will, since I'm sure you aren't going to die as long as I or anyone else owes you money!"

"Believe me, Sheikh, I've met a lot of people, but nobody has ever understood me the way you do!"

"You understand me, too, Ibrahim. You know what I'm thinking, and you never hesitate to do anything I need you to."

"Really, Sheikh?"

"Did you think I appointed you my vizier for some other reason? Did you think, for example, that you'd become my vizier because you're so humble and unpretentious?"

Whatever satisfaction al-Sallal had taken in getting rid of Daher's doctor, Sulayman al-Sawwan, vanished when he discovered what a formidable man he was now up against.[32]

---

32 Sensing that new, unpleasant winds were about to blow, al-Sallal decided he would have to get away. He suspected that Daher's fledgling state was in danger due to Uthman Pasha's hostility toward him; he had also observed the beginning of al-Sabbagh's rise to prominence and Daher's differences with his sons. So he gathered his money and his possessions into a couple of boats and fled. When Daher learned of the matter, he arrested and imprisoned al-Sallal. Before long, however, he had him released.

Al-Sallal was familiar with al-Sabbagh. Who in Acre and its environs wasn't? After all, he was the most miserly rich man the region had ever known, and had now become its most renowned physician since Sheikh Daher had recovered under his care.

"What gift shall I give you, Ibrahim? I'm so indebted to you that even if I return all this money, I'll still owe you more than I can say!"

"The best gift you can give me, today or any day, Sheikh, is to let me see you in good health!"

"So how is it that they say that there's nothing you love more than money?"

"I don't suppose you actually believe them, do you, Sheikh? It's nothing but envy. And you know what they say about envy: 'How perfectly envy puts things to rights—the envious soul is the first one it smites!'"

"In any case, aren't you ever going to tell me what was wrong with me?"

"Since it's over and done with, I don't suppose it matters any more."

"Never mind the illness itself, then. I'll just ask you what medicine you used."

"There's no need to know the name of a medicine that's cured a nameless disease!"

Daher laughed and said, "By God, you're the most generous person I've ever known and the most miserly, the kindest and the craftiest, the most miserable-looking and the most knowledgeable!"

"I'd best be on my way, Sheikh. I'm afraid that after hearing all these nice things about myself, I'm going to donate to your treasury all the money I just brought you!"

The Arrival of the French Ship

A t dawn on May 10, 1761, the residents of Haifa woke to the sounds of cannon shells. The city was quaking, and the cries of the seagulls fleeing toward the land boded ill. Chaos spread throughout the city, but no one knew what to do.

The days of peace and security the city had enjoyed scattered like flocks of terrified birds, and New Haifa, with its freshly built walls and houses, seemed an easy prey to the bombs' roar.

The sea that morning was strangely placid and gray. As the ship advanced, its crew was certain they had chosen just the right moment to carry out Uthman Pasha's orders: to seize control of the garrison town in a surprise attack and reannex it to Damascus. However, news of the attack had preceded their arrival, and the entire plan fell to pieces as cannon shells began raining down on the approaching ship.

Caught off guard by the intensity of the attack, the ship tried to retreat. But no retreat was possible. As the vessel went up in flames, its sailors leapt into the water and sought refuge on land, only to be met by Daher's soldiers, whose muskets and arrows were sweeping the shore without mercy.

The sands were strewn with corpses as flames shot into the sky, hastening the sunrise.

It came as no surprise that Uthman Pasha had sent a ship to attack the city. What came as a surprise—indeed, a shock—was the ship's nationality. "How dare the French ally themselves with Uthman Pasha al-Kurji after all I've done for them!" Daher fumed.

The flames that had consumed the French ship in Haifa's harbor now spread until they had engulfed every French inn, shop, and establishment in Acre. Daher showed no mercy, and made no exceptions. Even those to whom he had personal ties found themselves in the raging furnace.

Even so, it would never have occurred to anyone in Acre's French community to leave the city, which had become such a lucrative source of profit that every day spent there promised more profit to come. Daher knew the French sore spot, and all he had to do was press on it a little harder.

He stopped all French ships that were about to set sail and seized their cargo, announcing that he would pay for all undelivered merchandise. At the same time, he left Acre's port open to everyone who wished to leave.

"Let's see how their textile factories will get along now," he mused aloud. Then he issued a definitive order: "From now on, France will get none of our cotton!"

Those were dark days for Acre's French residents, who realized that in order not to exacerbate their losses, they would have to move quickly. They sent word to their ambassador in Istanbul demanding that he do something to restore things to the way they had been before. However, this proved impossible. The French ambassador had been informed by the Ottomans' foreign minister that the sultan would no longer brook Daher's rebellion and expanding influence, that it had become a matter of great urgency to subdue him, and that Acre's French community would have to be patient and endure a little longer.

Uthman Pasha al-Kurji was delirious with rage. He realized what a mistake he had made, and that he should have learned a lesson from the defeats Daher had inflicted on the previous governors of Damascus. The sultan had granted him the decree he had always dreamed of, which would clear the way for him to do away with Daher. However, he could see now that sending a ship to occupy Haifa was the stupidest decision he had ever made.

He had fallen flat on his face at the gates of Haifa. Hence, it was clear that he should have sent a hundred ships to demolish Haifa and bring Acre down on Daher's head.

At that dark moment, Uthman Pasha had a brilliant idea: to destroy Daher's fortress from within.

A Piece of Paper with
a Thousand Sides

Saad al-Umar refused to meet with Uthman Pasha al-Kurji in
Damascus, as he hadn't forgotten the hanging of his brother Saleh
in its square. At the same time, he was sure Uthman Pasha would
never agree to meet him in Deir Hanna.

After a lengthy exchange of messages, the two men agreed to meet
in the village of Fiq on the outskirts of Tiberias. Even then, however,
Saad's heart wasn't at rest. He was so riddled with doubts, in fact, that
he nearly sent his men after Uthman Pasha's messenger to tell him he
had changed his mind. His men stood waiting for him to settle the matter. First he dismissed them. Then he called them back. Then he dismissed them again.

However, Saad's bitterness toward Daher had become greater than
his fear for his own life. He thought: *I've stood by him and supported him since
he was a boy. I've even fought alongside him. But in spite of everything, he doesn't give
me a thought! It's as if he thinks Deir Hanna and Arraba are too much for this old
brother of his to handle! Like all the rest, he gives his sons preference over his brothers,
even though he and they share the same father!*

Little did Saad know that not far away, in Shafa'amr, the winds had
already begun to blow in his favor.

One pleasant sunny morning perfumed by almond blossoms and
wildflowers, a young wet nurse came stumbling out of Uthman al-Daher's mansion. Blinded by her tears, every time she ran into something
she would cry all the louder, until at last she reached home. When her
husband learned of her anguish, he came running. However, her tongue
couldn't bear her words the way her legs had borne her home from
Uthman's mansion. She just kept crying, as though crying were the only
thing human beings had been made to do.

As news of the incident spread, people began flocking to the woman's house, shaken by her story. For some time she remained dissolved

in tears, unable to speak. But at last one day she managed to vanquish the sea of tears that had swept her away.

All she said was: "Uthman al-Daher tried to rape me!"

Her words sent shock waves through the entire country, especially since everyone knew that with Daher at the helm, the days when a man could violate a woman with impunity were long gone.

His eyes fixed on the floor, Uthman stood before Daher, prepared for the worst. Daher held his sword in a powerful grip, with a thousand reasons to have off with his head. The girl on the shore of Lake Tiberias stood trembling before him, crying out for him to protect her honor as her attacker's blood dripped off the hilt of his sword onto his fist.

Najma stood a few steps away, likewise prepared for the worst. At last, unable to bear any more, she turned to leave. On her way to the door she raised her hand and, without saying a word, passed it gently over Daher's right shoulder. Then she kept going as though she wanted to disappear.

Daher signaled to his men, and they came forward. Before stepping away, he said, "Hang him."

A shudder went through Uthman's body as though it were already dangling from the gallows, while the word Daher had uttered with such despairing faintness reached every ear in the mansion.

The guards hesitated, so Daher repeated himself with the same despairing faintness: "Hang him."

Once again the words echoed powerfully through all the rooms in the mansion. However, no one dared leave.

The rope was cast over the crossbeam of the mansion gate. It fell to the other side, and one of the guards took hold of it and knotted it.

When he felt certain that the gallows were ready, Daher turned and looked behind him.

They dragged Uthman, limp as a rag, toward the gallows. They secured the rope around his neck. Then, as they were about to lift him onto the back of a horse, Daher said, "He doesn't deserve to be brought on horseback. Use something else—a table, a chair, a donkey, whatever."

They turned to look for something else on which to lift him. Just then, Uthman's son Jahjah arrived. Seeing the rope around his father's neck, he leapt off his horse even before bringing it to a halt. Then he rushed up to his grandfather and began kissing his feet.

"For God's sake, Grandpa," he pleaded, "don't hang him!"

His body trembling, Daher leaned down quickly and lifted his grandson up.

"Stand up!" he shouted in his face. "You weren't born to throw yourself at anybody's feet!"

Then he pushed him away. As Jahjah wept in silence, Daher watched his tears fall into the dirt.

The guards brought a chair and lifted Uthman onto it. He offered so little resistance, one would have thought they were about to hang someone else, or that he wasn't aware that he was the one about to die. When Jahjah saw his father on the chair and the guards pulling the rope toward them, he fainted.

Daher quickly bent down and ran his hand over his grandson's chest to make sure he was all right. Then he picked him up and said to the guards, "Don't bring him down off the chair. Let him stay there until that woman comes. She's the only person in the world who can remove the rope from his neck. Send someone to bring her here. From this moment on, she's the one to decide whether he lives or dies."

When the woman got there the next morning, Uthman was close to death. His neck was raw after a night spent with a rope around it. Whenever he dozed off, his neck had gone limp, causing the rope to cut into his flesh.

Daher made a point of not staying after the woman arrived. Instead, he left her with two guards to decide of her own accord what it was that she wanted. She stood there all morning, not knowing what to do. But when the noon call to prayer sounded, she looked at the two guards and said, "I've forgiven him!"

Then she turned to leave.

Daher was sitting with Jahjah in the mansion diwan when Uthman came in, looking half dead.

"That honorable woman has granted you a new life. However, this is the last time anyone will be able to give you another chance like this," Daher said to him. Then, in a statement that Uthman would only understand many years hence, he added, "I'll let you go your way now. But never again will I wrong my enemies!"

Uthman came to the woman's house to thank her as Daher had instructed him. He knocked on her door two or three times, but no one answered. Incensed at the thought that she was insulting him by leaving him outside, for a moment he forgot what she had done for him and lunged at the door to force it open. Daher's men took hold of him and led him away.

Many days passed, and the night of terror continued to tighten around his neck. However, he kept puzzling over the veiled threat his father had made: *What had the old man meant when he said, "Never again will I wrong my enemies"?*

The story made the rounds of the country several times over, and when it reached Saad's ears, he decided the time had come to act.

Saad's meeting with the governor, Uthman Pasha al-Kurji, wasn't comfortable for him. From the time the meeting began, he couldn't shake a feeling deep down that he was a traitor. Like a man who had decided to become a murderer, he was more afraid of doing the killing than his first victim was of being killed.

However, the governor appeared confident and even convincing as he assured Saad that he was the best person to oppose Daher. After all, he explained, the state was fond of him, and never once had a single drop of blood been shed between them, even when Sulayman Pasha's forces had besieged Tiberias for eighty-two days. Besides, the governor told Saad, he would be the best person to run affairs after Daher was gone.

On his way back from Fiq, Saad stopped in Deir Hanna just long enough to drink some water before continuing his journey. He had in mind a particular person who, if he could win him over, would ensure his ability to get rid of Daher once and for all. When he reached Shafa'amr, he realized that his nephew Uthman had been waiting for him. People had been circulating the details of what had happened, and added plenty more of their own. They even made jokes about how badly Uthman had been humiliated. Hence, it required little effort on Saad's part to persuade Uthman to join him. In fact, it seemed to him that Uthman would have been prepared to march on Acre and kill his father at that very instant if given the chance.

Urging Uthman to bide his time, Saad asked him to think of a third person who would be willing to work with them, someone with close ties to Daher. He mentioned Daher's sons Ahmad, Sa'id, and Ali. Uthman ruled out Ahmad and Sa'id, whom he described as a couple of spoiled "daddy's boys." When Ali's name came up, Uthman said, "I'm sure he'd be willing to join us. But the minute we beat the old man, he'll turn on us. I can just see it now!"

After his father, there was no one Uthman feared the way he feared Ali. He continued, saying, "We need a man we can bring under our wing, not one who thinks his wings are larger and stronger than ours."

Saad bowed his head for a long time. When he lifted it again, Uthman was surprised to see how wizened he looked, and he wondered: *Am I out of my mind to be putting myself in league with this old man?* Then he remembered that "this old man" was now in league with the governor of Damascus! Another thought that energized him was that it would be easy to get rid of Saad later on.

In the womb of the first plot, a second had begun to grow, and in the womb of the second, still another had been conceived.

Studying Uthman, Saad thought: *His description of his brother Ali is the only astute thing I've ever heard come out of his mouth. Apart from that, he's never shown the least sign of intelligence. He's always been rash and harebrained, with no self-control in relation to women or money. And there's nothing easier to get rid of than a fool like that! Once we've finished I'll send him a pretty concubine, or maybe just an ordinary-looking one, and by the time he's finished his first night with her, she'll have slipped him enough poison to kill him twenty times over!*

"You must be thinking about something grand," Uthman said to him.

"What?"

"I said: you must be thinking about something grand."

"How did you know?"

"Because your bread's been sitting over the fire for half an hour, Uncle. I can see the smoke rising even in the dark!"

"You know, Uthman," Saad replied with a chuckle, "no matter how badly people might think of you, no one could deny that you're a great poet!"

"Thank you, Uncle," replied Uthman, who seemed embarrassed by his uncle's unexpected praise.

Uthman was known for his poems, which were widely memorized, although he wasn't the only one of Daher's sons who composed poetry.

"Karim al-Ayyub al-Zaydani!" Saad said suddenly.

"What?"

"The only person we could ask to join us is Karim al-Ayyub al-Zaydani, your sister Aliya's husband. There have never been any problems between him and Daher."

"But he's my brother-in-law. Besides, why would he be willing to go in with us on something like this? I don't think he'd agree."

"Believe me, he will. I happen to know that he harbors some resentment toward Daher. He says, 'Daher appoints his sons as governors over different parts of the country, but all he sees in me is a foot soldier to guard his fortress gates!'"

"I've never heard him say anything like that, Uncle."

"Well, I have."

"But if that's the case, he couldn't possibly mean it. He lacks nothing!"

"Hens eat and drink, and roosters crow and strut around the governor's yard. But they'll never be more than what they are. The difference between chickens and human beings, Uthman, is that human beings realize the state they're in, and they aren't content with their lot!"

"You're scaring me, Uncle! But test him out if you want to. Just remember that this was your idea, not mine, and that you might pay for it with your head."

"Don't worry, Uthman. I've known Karim all his life, and he'll be ready to kiss my hands for thinking of him in connection with a matter of this importance!"

Holding the letter from Saad al-Umar in his hands, Karim turned it over and over as though it had a thousand sides. All Saad was asking him to do was to find some excuse to leave Acre, then come see him in Deir Hanna, making certain that Daher knew nothing about the meeting. But as he looked at the letter, he had a growing sense that its every word concealed a secret of some sort.

"I haven't seen Karim for a couple of days," Daher remarked. "Does anyone know where he's gone?"

"I hear he's gone to Nazareth to take care of some business there."

"So he's gone to Nazareth!" Daher replied lightheartedly. "Well, he must have some good reason for making the trip." However, he seemed troubled.

Ribs and Stones

ajma watched him with expert eyes, the way a hawk, fixed in the sky like a little cloud not budged by the wind, observes every movement on the ground.

"I see you're worried about something, Sheikh."

"The incident connected with that French ship has muddled everything and I've got to find a solution, since the cotton season will be upon us in just a few months."

"So is that what's worrying you?"

"What could possibly worry me more, Mother? As you know, cotton is a huge part of this country's trade and the life of the people here."[33]

"The cotton season is still months away, and we can leave the solution to God!" She fell silent for a while. Then she added, "Why don't you and I go to Haifa? I think its people need to see you after what happened. Besides, I'm anxious to see the city. It's still in its infancy, and maybe the two of us can take it by the hand and bring it down to the sea."

"I've been thinking of going there."

"Besides, there's something you need now more than anything else."

"And what's that, Mother?"

"I'll tell you when we get to Haifa!"

Daher didn't sleep that night. After walking around the mansion, he went up to the top of the fortress, where the sea breeze nearly bowled him over. He wished he had wings that could carry him to the shore or that, in a single leap, he could traverse the three or four hundred meters that stood between him and the waves. He sat looking at the lamplit

---

33 Cotton manufacturing in England began with the "red cotton" imported from Acre and Sidon. Cotton was also grown in Leda and Ramla, as well as, of course, in Tiberias. The cotton grown in Galilee was famed for its excellent quality and was known in Europe as "cotton d'Arcy." The volume of cotton exported via Acre's port in 1750 came to 3,742 metric tons.

city, but the intensity of the darkness over the sea drew him inexorably into its depths.

Whenever he came to this spot, no matter how burdensome his worries, the sound of the sea's waves would wash them all away. This time, however, his mind and his heart hung suspended on the hoofbeats of Karim al-Ayyub's mare as it rode away.

When he went into his room in the wee hours of the morning, all he could see were the lanterns that flickered as the sea breeze swept past them. Their flames sputtered, until suddenly there was nothing but darkness. Had he stayed awake all night staring at the lanterns, hoping their flames would glow bright again? He didn't know. However, he knew one thing: he hadn't acquiesced to their going out.

"To Haifa, then!" he said to Najma with a smile as soon as the sun had risen.

Daher spent the first half of his day making the rounds of New Haifa with al-Dankizli and a number of his soldiers. The city smelled fresh, like the waves of the sea in the early morning, and a calm had enveloped it now that it was safe from the pirate attacks that had plagued Old Haifa.

They mounted its walls, and a deep blue spread out before them into infinity. Daher leaned over to al-Dankizli and said, "You've done so much for this country, Ahmad, but you've never asked me for a thing!"

"What would I ask you for, Sheikh?"

"Well, you might ask me to appoint you governor in return for your loyalty and selfless service to this country."

"But I'm commander of your army!"

"And doesn't my army commander hanker for anything? Wouldn't he aspire to be governor over Nazareth or Haifa, for example?"

"No, Sheikh. From the day I met you you've treated me like a leader, and that's enough for me. When I aspire to more than that, it will be time for you to get rid of me as fast as you can, since it would mean my allegiance to you had weakened. Besides, does a bird aspire to be anything but a bird?"

"You're remarkable, Ahmad," Daher said, studying him. Then he added, "You've expressed some of the loveliest sentiments I've heard in a long time. But I'd like to ask you a question, and I hope you won't take it as undue interference between the bird and its wings. I hear you've divorced your wife. Is this true?"

"It's true, Sheikh. Maybe she was never really my wife."

"Didn't you marry her officially, in keeping with Islamic law?"

"I did, Sheikh. But is that enough? As you know, I married her under duress. When Amira started getting older, she said to me, 'You have to marry someone, if not to take care of you, then to take care of me!' You know all this, Sheikh."

"Yes, I do. What I don't know, and what no one else knows, is why you divorced your wife."

"I haven't wanted to talk about it because I feel I might have been unfair to her."

"I don't understand a thing. Could you explain, even just a little?"

"One night I was staying with Amira. She was sick. Suddenly somebody started pounding on the gate outside. I could hear it from inside even before the guards opened it. Nobody could prevent her from coming in, of course, since she was my wife. When she got to Amira's room, she started pounding on her door even more violently. 'Where are you?' she screamed. 'I'm your wife, am I not? Don't I deserve for you to be in my house, not in the house of that old concubine of yours?' I swear I'd been fair to her, Sheikh, as I'd always spent an equal number of nights with each of them. I knew she was jealous of Amira, but I didn't know she had it in her to act this way. What she did really disturbed me, Sheikh. If Amira hadn't been sick, maybe I wouldn't have been so upset. I don't mean to go on too long about it with you. In any case, I opened the door, and before I knew it I found myself asking her, 'Who are you?' 'You don't even know me?' she asked. 'I'm your wife!' 'My wife?' I said. 'Yes,' she told me, 'I'm your wife!' Then I said to her, 'You're divorced, then!' And I closed the door."

Al-Dankizli fell silent and looked into the distance.

"So that's the story?" Daher asked.

"That's the story I've kept from everyone, Sheikh. I've even kept it from you, I'm sorry to say!"

"It's all right, Ahmad. It's all right. What you've just told me reminds me of what happened to the multazim of Tabigha. When, long years after she'd been kidnapped, we finally found his concubine for him in Sidon, she hardly retained any of the beauty that had led people to call her Badr al-Budur—'full moon of full moons.' She'd done everything she could to make herself odious to the tax collector who had kidnapped her. She'd neglected herself so that he wouldn't come near her, and she

399

looked wan and old. She looked so bad that for a moment I thought of not taking her back to Miqdad for fear of shattering the dream he'd held on to for so long. He used to come around from time to time to remind me of my promise to him. In any case, when he finally saw her again, he came running up to her as though nothing about her had changed. He kept thanking me over and over again, till I started to doubt his sanity! But then I remembered that this is what love is all about. If it isn't blind and mad, it isn't love!"

Daher's mind wandered, and he walked off as though his thoughts had carried his body away with them.

Al-Dankizli glanced over at Daher and, seeing something amiss, mustered the courage to ask, "Is that sadness I see in your eyes, Sheikh?"

"Terrible sadness. But I still don't know what's causing it!"

"If I could lift the burden off your chest, you know I would."

"There are stones that, if you don't lift them off your chest by yourself, will crush your ribs even more badly if someone else tries to do it for you."

Gazing at Mount Carmel, Najma remarked, "A mountain that magnificent deserves to have people swear by it! Did you see Haifa today?"

"Yes, I did, Mother. It's growing bigger and more beautiful. As the days go by, it's becoming just what I'd hoped it would be."

Najma stood looking out at the sea, her left hand screening her eyes from the sun. "But you haven't seen all of it yet, Sheikh."

"If I remember correctly, I *have* seen all of it."

"You won't see it all until you climb Mount Carmel with me!"

"So you want to climb Mount Carmel? Are you able?"

With a laugh she asked, "And do you think I came here to do anything else?"

"That sounds like a serious laugh!"

"It is. But I need somebody to come with me."

"And of course I'm the only one who could do that!"

"Take off your shoes and follow me."

Before he had a chance to reply, she got up and, walking away, said, "You need to climb it now more than ever before, Sheikh."

Looking around him in disbelief, Daher whispered to himself, "Is she going to climb the mountain at her age?"

"I heard that!" she said. "So you aren't going to let me climb it by myself, are you?"

It was trying at first, as he hadn't gone barefoot anywhere but in the sand along the seashore for quite a long time. Rocks and stubble gashed his feet, and he thought of stopping for a while to catch his breath. As for Najma, she went floating like a feather among the pines and oaks, and if he hadn't seen her, he wouldn't have heard her footsteps.

"Instead of climbing the mountain, you're tiring me out, Sheikh!"

Daher realized that this was precisely what he was doing.

"Climb the mountain, Sheikh! Climb it the way a man like you ought to climb a mountain! Make it feel as though there's a horse, or even another mountain, climbing it. When we get back to Acre, I want to see Mount Carmel inside of you. Forget about me and cast aside everything that might come between you and the mountain under you. Gone are the days when all you needed was the exuberance of a horse. What you need now is the strength of a mountain!"

A few minutes later, Najma and the trees began turning into shadows before his very eyes. The rocks and dry grasses beneath his feet no longer existed. He dove into the mountain, and the mountain into him. Then he rose aloft as though on wings, and the mountain with him.

They passed al-Khadir's Shrine at a distance of a hundred meters, but didn't see it. They passed the dome of the Mar Elias Church, and didn't see it either.

Near the mountaintop the wind died down and became like a gigantic hand that rocked him gently to and fro. Had he been walking with his eyes closed? He couldn't remember. But he was sure he'd opened them when he felt the wind. A few steps away, he saw Najma sitting on a rock, waiting for him.

He wanted to say something, but she stopped him by placing her finger over her lips. He sat right up against her. It had been a long time since he'd sat so close to her.

As the sun began to set, his white beard turned a brilliant henna-like orange. He looked at her and whispered, "Let's go back down the mountain now."

"Rather, let's go up it again on our way back!"

So they did.

Half of the Crime

The ground had been laid, and now all they needed was for him to come.

Karim al-Ayyub, whose delicate features, hazel eyes, and tall stature were reminiscent of a Frenchman's, sat in stunned silence as Saad explained, in Uthman's presence, what he and Uthman were thinking. He did his best to appear noncommittal, alternately answering their questions and asking questions of his own. He realized that his life was in their hands, since, given the nature of the secret being divulged, none of them could walk out the door unless he had made the secret his own.

"But I'm his son-in-law, Sheikh Saad!"

"Pardon me for alarming you. Rest assured that, however dear he is to you, he's that much dearer to us! He is my brother, after all, and Uthman's father! Even so, there are certain things that have to be decided not on the basis of family ties, but on the basis of people's best interests. As you've seen yourself, Damascus sent a French ship to attack him with the sultan's blessing. So you might wake up one of these days to find a French fleet and an Ottoman fleet besieging Acre together. And when that happens—assuming the city's people survive—you won't have any place to raise your children! You know, son, that we can only save this country by restoring its allegiance to the sultan. I tell you—and the governor of Damascus himself would agree—that Daher is finished. So we have no choice but to move quickly, since otherwise we'll be victims of his long years of rebellion. When the empire's army arrives, it isn't going to ask who was with Daher and who was against him!"

"And Sheikh Uthman? What does he say?"

Looking Karim in the eye, Uthman said, "Why do you ask me what I think, Karim, when you already know the answer? You know that I was frank with the old man when nobody else dared to be. You also know what his response was. He could have spared us and himself the situation we're in now if he'd just listened to me. Can you imagine how it pains me to be thinking the things I'm thinking now, Karim? As my uncle Saad just said, he *is* my father, after all! But things can't go on this way. If we don't do something, we'll have nowhere to go for refuge. Even the shores of Tiberias, if they're kind enough to receive us, will receive us not as multazims, but as beggars!"

"Let me give it some thought, then," said Karim.

"We didn't call you here to think," replied Saad, "but to make a decision. Of course, since you're like a son to us, we'll give you till morning to think things over, and we hope that by sunrise you will have made your decision. And now I'd like to have a word with Uthman."

Saad got up to leave and was followed by Uthman. As they were on their way out, Karim asked them, "What will I gain by joining you?"

Saad turned and eyed him briefly. "Do you think we'd overlook something as important as that?" he replied. "You'll have control over Acre! We'll persuade the governor of Damascus to appoint you governor over Haifa as well. All I want is Deir Hanna, Arraba, and the surrounding countryside, which I already have. As they say, 'A little that endures is better than an abundance that passes away'! As for Uthman, all he's asking for is Shafa'amr and the nearby villages, which Daher has refused to give him. I'd also like to alert you to an important point: don't think that, because we're contenting ourselves with so little, we're indifferent to our own interests. There are two things which, if we lose them, will mean that nothing else will be of any use to us: the heads on our shoulders! So remember, Karim, that of the three of us, you have the most to gain, since you'll keep your head, and on top of that, Acre and Haifa will be yours! So what do you say?"

"Let me think it over!"

"As you wish."

Before Saad and Uthman turned again to leave, Karim asked a second question: "And what will be asked of me in return?"

After exchanging a glance with Uthman, Saad bowed his head briefly. Then he said, "To assassinate Daher! You're the one who can get close enough to him to do it."

"Assassinate Daher?"

"Unless you consider his head more precious than yours, not to mention Acre and Haifa."

Karim bowed his head. Then he looked up again and said, "Let me think it over!"

"So be it," Saad replied. He hesitated slightly as he turned to leave, expecting to hear a third question. However, none was forthcoming. So he walked to the door, followed by Uthman.

He was about to open the door when he turned and said, "You must have another question—the hardest question of all—that you're hesitating to ask!"

"True. I do have one more question. And if I hear a clear answer to it, I'll inform you of my decision right now."

Saad walked back toward Karim, while Uthman stood with his back against the door.

"What guarantee do I have that you'll do what you've promised?"

"God is my witness," replied Saad.

"God is my witness," echoed Uthman.

"This is something you'll be asked about before God on Judgment Day. But I need a way to hold you accountable in this world if you don't do what you've said!"

"You know, Karim, that promises of this nature can't be put in writing," Saad said. Then he walked back to where he had been sitting.

"I can't do something like this without a written statement that's been signed by the two of you, and by witnesses I trust!"

"Do you know what it would mean to write down a pledge of this nature?" Uthman interjected. "We'd be gambling with our heads! I won't agree to this."

"Let's consider the matter finished, then, since I know your secret as well as you two know mine," said Karim, hoping to open a door of escape for himself.

"Let's think of some other solution that would satisfy you, Karim."

"The only thing I'll accept is a written pledge that I could present later to the governor of Damascus or someone else!"

"I won't sign any pledge," Uthman insisted.

"No, Uthman, we're going to grant him the pledge he's requested!" said Saad. "Since we know we're going to keep our word, why shouldn't we give it to him?"

"And I want witnesses!"

"You're making things impossible and exposing us from the very start!" said Uthman heatedly.

But Saad said, "I accept. Whom do you want as witnesses?"

Uthman turned to go. However, as he was opening the door, Saad asked him not to leave until they had reached an agreement. He came back in and closed the door.

"Sheikh Rashid al-Jabr, emir of the Bani Saqr tribe," said Karim.

"So be it," said Saad without hesitation. And he added, "Emir Rashid suffers more than we do from Daher's tyranny!"

"But Sheikh Uthman hasn't agreed yet."

Saad looked over at Uthman, who was drawing imaginary circles on the floor with his left foot.

"Let's settle it now, Uthman," said Saad.

"I'm warning you, Uncle. You yourself said a little while ago that promises of this nature can't be put in writing!"

"If we can't trust Karim, we can't trust anyone. I won't trust you, and you won't trust me. So let's shake on it."

The Second Half of the Crime

L ate one night a messenger from Daher arrived at the house of his son Uthman. When Uthman opened the door, he was surprised to find the messenger and the soldiers with him. They instructed him to get dressed quickly, since his father had sent for him.

Uthman tried to dodge the situation, but he could see that his efforts would get him nowhere, since the soldiers stood prepared to transport him to Acre kicking and screaming if they had to.

He went inside to get dressed. He glanced at the window, then went over and opened it, wishing he could jump out. As the dawn breeze blew in, the lantern flame flickered and its shadow danced on the wall. After informing his wife that he would be going to see the sheikh, he closed the window and came out.

Escape was impossible with the soldiers surrounding him on all sides. Only one thing worried him: the thought that Karim might have betrayed him and Saad.

On the way to Acre, he asked the soldiers whether the sheikh had told them to bring anyone else. To his surprise, no one replied. They acted as though they hadn't even heard the question.

Anxiety mounted, gripping him like a vise, and before long he began sweating profusely, his perspiration as thick as mud.

How he wished it weren't such a long way to Acre. And how he wished his uncle Saad hadn't given Karim that written pledge! *If Karim hasn't betrayed us, then maybe the paper has fallen into Daher's hands. After all, the old man can still sense a storm coming before anybody else.*

He nearly asked about Karim. Then he remembered how they'd pretended not to hear his first question. After giving it some more thought, he thanked his lucky stars that he hadn't asked, since if Karim had fallen into the old man's clutches, he would have incriminated himself with such a question.

Two hours after sunrise they passed along the outskirts of Damun, which was full of life: the sounds of shepherds' flutes crisscrossed the air, and farmers' singing filled the fields.

Leaving the village behind, they ascended a hill, and he was surprised to find that in spite of all his inner turmoil he was still able to pick up the fragrances that burst forth whenever a horse stepped on wild thyme or chamomile. In the distance he saw a fig sapling with leaves greener and larger than any he had ever seen. And he wondered: *How can this kind of greenery flourish on top of a hill?* He looked under the tree, thinking there might be a spring or a brook flowing nearby. But he saw none.

He heard a group of boys laughing happily in the distance. Before long, the small procession came alongside them. In their hands they held some partridges that were struggling in vain to escape from their grip. The boys hailed them, wishing them God's peace, a peace he needed badly!

Daher hesitated when Uthman reached out to shake his hand. His hesitation was unmistakable. In the end, however, he responded with the warmth of a tiny, distant star. Uthman's terror mounted, and the sweat began pouring off his body more thickly and profusely than ever. Seeing Uthman's discomfort, Daher realized that he would need to be friendlier toward his son if he wanted to achieve his purpose.

"You need a bath! I don't know which would be better for you, though—a cold one or a hot one!" said Daher.

Uthman could find no explanation for what his father had said.

"I'll see you in an hour! Or do you need longer than that?"

"An hour will be enough," Uthman replied. He had only one wish: to know what had happened!

In the bathroom, once he had his clothes off, he started thinking: *If he wanted to kill me, he would have killed me already! And if he knew something, he wouldn't have received me so kindly. But who can be sure what's going on in that old man's head?* He wished he could get a glimpse of Karim al-Ayyub, if even from a distance, so that he could reassure himself at least that everything was going according to plan.

He finished bathing quickly, and no sooner had he opened the bathroom door than he found himself face to face with Karim al-Ayyub. He was so startled he took a couple of steps back.

"What are you doing here?" Karim asked in alarm.

"Rather, you tell me: Does the old man know what happened between us?"

"How would he? If he hasn't found out from you or Saad, he's not going to find out from me!"

It was a whispered conversation, heavy with foreboding.

"Don't do anything relating to what we agreed on until I tell you to. Understood?" Uthman hissed.

"Understood!" Karim replied. "I'm going now. But I tell you: be sure the old man doesn't dupe you about anything!" Then he scurried away.

Uthman looked this way and that to make sure no one had seen or heard anything. Then he went back in the bathroom and closed the door. The steam-laden air did him no good, and his lungs could hardly take anything in. About to suffocate, he opened the door again and came out.

When Daher saw him he said, "A bath after a trip is a pleasure that shouldn't be cut short!" Then he invited him to sit down across from him.

They talked about everything: about Jahjah and his brothers, about Uthman's brother Ali and whether he ever saw him, and about many other things. Daher told him about the attack by the French ship as though he were telling him a secret. He even asked him his opinion of the incident and what he thought he should do. Then he spent the rest of the time talking about horses and climbing Mount Carmel with Najma.

After hearing the call to prayer, they got up and prayed together. Then they had lunch with Najma. After they had finished their meal, Daher said to him, "You deprived yourself of a real bath! As for your afternoon nap, you've got to enjoy it properly. You must be exhausted!"

Uthman tossed and turned, trying in vain to sleep.

He stared up at the high window, which brought in wind that passed out of the room through a window in the opposite wall. Somehow or other, the moisture-laden air that blew in was born anew as it passed between the two windows, and left the room fresh and light.

Overcome at last with weariness, he dozed off, only to be wakened by a loud rap on the door: "The sheikh is waiting for you in the diwan!" announced Jum'a, who turned forthwith and went back to where he had come from.

Daher instructed Jum'a to close the diwan door and make sure no one came near it.

Uthman's heart was racing so violently, he began massaging his chest in an attempt to calm it.

"Are you in pain?" Daher inquired. "I see you pressing on your chest. Shall I call my doctor?"

"No, there won't be any need for that," replied Uthman, taking his hands off his chest.

Daher took a deep breath, his eyes fixed on his son's face. "You realize, Uthman, that I've called for you concerning a matter of great importance!"

Uthman nodded. He tried to swallow, but his throat was too dry.

"I'll get right to the point, Uthman. It's come to my knowledge that my brother Saad has met with the governor of Damascus in Fiq, and that they've drawn up a plan to get rid of me. Have you heard about this?"

"No, Sheikh. If I had, I would have come to you right away about it!"

"I'm sure you would have. That's why I wanted to talk to you in particular, since your uncle Saad places a lot of trust in you."

"Do you want me to find out all the details from him?"

"I want you for something that goes far beyond that. As you know, your father is aware of what goes on both in Istanbul and in Damascus. How much more, then, would he be aware of what goes on in your uncle Saad's head!"

Daher took another deep breath and said, "Haven't you always dreamed of having control over Shafa'amr? Well, I'll give it to you in return for what I'm asking you to do."

"You give the orders, Sheikh, and I'll carry them out, whether you give me Shafa'amr or not!"

"So we've agreed, then!"

"On what?"

"I'll tell you everything tomorrow morning before you leave for Deir Hanna!"

Never in his life had Uthman seen a lantern like the one in his uncle Saad's diwan. It was suspended from a metal arm fixed to the wall, and its oil supply came from a barrel that was invisible to Uthman. The wick passed through a long tube like the hose of a narghile and disappeared on the other side of the wall.

"What's that?" he asked his uncle.

"It's my new lantern!" Saad replied. "I got it yesterday." He was so excited about his new acquisition that he took Uthman by the hand and led him over to it. Then he asked him to blow on it as hard as he could. Uthman hesitated, but Saad insisted. So he blew.

"Harder!" Saad told him. Uthman blew harder, but the flame was unfazed. The glass ball that housed the flame, ornamented with orange, purple, and red filigree, was entirely closed off to his breath, although there were small openings in its top that he couldn't see.

"Even a storm wind couldn't put out a lantern like this!" Saad boasted. He explained to Uthman that he'd had it brought from Istanbul, and that it was the first inextinguishable lantern the craftsman had ever made.

"Inextinguishable? How can that be?" asked Uthman.

Saad took him by the hand again and led him behind the wall. There, Uthman was surprised to find that the lantern's wick rested in a barrel filled with oil and covered with a tight lid, and that the wick was coiled inside it like an endless white adder.

"What's this, Uncle?"

"As I told you, this is my inextinguishable lantern, with a wick that has no end and oil that never runs out, since I always make sure to keep the barrel full!"

After a long conversation about the lantern, in the course of which Uthman did his best to keep marveling at it and at the way it was made, the two men turned to the subject of Karim al-Ayyub and whether he would keep his end of the bargain. Uthman reassured Saad, saying, "In return for Acre and Haifa he'd kill the sultan himself!" And he tried to laugh.

"Even so, my mind won't be at rest until I see Daher's head with my own two eyes!"

"You'll see it, Uncle. You'll see it! You should remember that when Karim put that agreement in his pocket, he was already more than halfway to the mark."

"I hope so, Uthman. After all, you know that old man. Even the governors of Damascus haven't been able to defeat him!"

"I know, Uncle. But as the saying goes, 'To defeat the cautious man, approach him from the place where he feels safe.'"

"We'll wait. But I don't want the wait to go on too long!"

"Nor would you want our plan to fail, Uncle. Karim has to choose the right time to do what he's going to do. The slightest mistake could bring him down, and if he falls, God forbid, we fall with him!"

"I think we'd better go to bed. The days are going to drag by as we wait for the happy news!"

"Yes, let's do that."

Saad got up and spread out his mattress, and so did Uthman. Suddenly Saad remembered that he hadn't dimmed the lantern.

"Where are you going?" Uthman asked.

"We won't be able to sleep in this bright light!"

"But be careful not to let it go out completely, Uncle."

"And how could it? Didn't I tell you it was inextinguishable?"

It was the custom in those days for a host to sleep in the same room as his guest so that he could meet any need that might arise. Thus they found themselves under the same roof.

Within half an hour Saad's snores could be heard. Uthman lifted his head and looked around the room as if to make sure he was the only one there. Then, on his hands and knees, he made his way over to where his uncle lay sleeping.

He stood up and straddled his uncle. Then he knelt down slowly over his neck. The moment he had his hands around it, he began squeezing with all his might.

Saad tried to push Uthman off, only to discover that his hands were pinned to the mattress beneath his nephew's knees. His eyes bulged, and the force of the surprise alone would have been enough to kill him. Uthman's hands sank more and more deeply into his uncle's feeble neck, as though he wanted to break it with his bare hands.

More than half an hour passed before Uthman got up off his uncle's body and went back to his own mattress.

Forty Days and a Truthful Pledge

T he next morning found Uthman weeping and wailing, embracing his uncle and pointing to a dead adder in the corner of the room. No one suspected a thing, since everyone knew how close the two men had been.

Uthman closed the door and called for Daher.

When Daher arrived, Uthman told him everything. Daher went into the room by himself, uncovered Saad's face, and quickly covered it up again.

On the fortieth day after Saad's death, the last of those who had come to offer their condolences left to go back to their villages and towns. It was the first time such a large wake had been held since Umar al-Zaydani's passing, and Daher had insisted on it.

With Karim next to him, Daher stood on the mansion balcony that overlooked the sea. "You know, Karim, those were the hardest forty days of my entire life."

"I know, Sheikh. I know!"

"I would have liked to appoint you governor over Haifa. But I gave you something far more precious a long time ago: my daughter. Besides, I don't want Uthman to know that I've given you what the two of them had promised you."

"All I want is your well-being, Sheikh."

Karim thought back on the night he'd received Uthman's letter. He'd thought: *Is this a test from Sheikh Daher?*

For two nights he'd turned the question over in his mind. Then he saw Sheikh Daher meeting in the mansion with a number of French merchants who had come to ask him to let them resume business in the city, assuring him that they'd had no hand in their government's collusion against him with the Ottoman sultan. When Daher saw Karim, he cast him a fleeting glance that convinced him with even greater certainty that the letter had been written with his knowledge and that it was nothing but a test. After all, the sheikh had become suspicious of friend and foe alike—including his own sons!

The letter writhed in Daher's hands like a huge snake. It had been a long time since anything had frightened him so badly. But he got hold of himself. When he heard Karim say, "I hope to God this isn't a test from you," Daher patted his shoulder with a powerful hand.

"I might test everyone I know, since I know that the world out there is testing them too, enticing them in hundreds of different directions. As for you, Karim, I don't need to test you. Do you know why? Because my own daughter and her heart stand between us, and that's a wall I couldn't breach even if my life depended on it. Go see my brother Saad and hear what he has to say. Find out everything he's thinking, and I hope to God that good will come of it!"

"But before I go, I want to assure you that I'll never break a promise I've made you. I would never break my wife's heart by betraying her father, or break my children's hearts by betraying their grandfather."

"Thank you, Karim. Thank you!" Then, to his surprise, Daher found himself asking Karim to assure him once again: "I'd like to hear it one more time, Karim, not for fear of what might happen, but just maybe out of a desire to hear a truthful pledge that comes from the heart in these dark days!"

So Karim repeated his oath. Patting him affectionately on the shoulder, Daher said, "Now choose a suitable time and excuse for your absence."

Tears over the Enemy's Demise

Daher reached into his pocket and took out the document in which Saad and Uthman had promised Karim Acre and Haifa. As he pondered it, his gaze settled on a single name: Emir Rashid al-Jabr. Of all the things he'd endured in his relations with Bani Saqr, nothing pained him the way it did to know that they had incited his own son Uthman, his brother Saad, and his son-in-law Karim to murder him.

He would see Bani Saqr's men patrolling the mansion with their spears and swords and riding their horses from gate to gate. And when he dozed off, he could almost feel them gathered around his bed.

Determined to ensure that no one doubted Karim, he began waiting for a chance to teach them a lesson. Meanwhile, Uthman appeared willing to do anything to please his father in hopes of winning Shafa'amr.

Daher wrote to Emir Rashid al-Jabr, telling him to restrain his men and to keep the agreement they had made not to attack either individuals or caravans. He noted that such incidents were on the rise, and that he had no intention of letting them pass in silence.

Emir Rashid al-Jabr was incensed over Saad's death. If they had succeeded in getting rid of Daher, they would have been freed from his iron-fisted rule. They would have gone back to being the kings of the Plain of Bani Amer and the surrounding regions. Once again they would have controlled everything, free to impose their conditions on everyone who came and went, not to mention those who lived there.

Emir Rashid thought a hundred times before going to offer Daher condolences on Saad's death, and when he did go, he had to keep all such feelings well hidden. When, ten days after the wake had begun, Emir Rashid finally arrived to pay his respects, Daher treated him as though he'd been the first to arrive. He went out of his way to have the emir sit next to him like an honored guest.

Emir Rashid and Uthman exchanged fleeting glances, but it was clear that Uthman had chosen his place at his father's side. As for Karim, he made a point not to look at either of them. He looked so grief-stricken, you would have thought Saad's demise had been the death of everything beautiful in his life.

Yet even as Emir Rashid sat at Daher's side, the men of Bani Saqr went on assaulting people just as they had been.

A few weeks after the wake had ended, a man came from Nazareth to Acre complaining that as he was traveling to Damascus, men from Bani Saqr had waylaid him and robbed him of two mules laden with merchandise.

Daher asked the man to sit down. Then straightaway he wrote a letter to Emir Rashid al-Jabr telling him to return the two mules to their owner along with the goods they had been carrying. In keeping with the practice of the governors of his day, Daher would stamp the back of his letters next to his signature if he was pleased, but if he placed the stamp on the front, it meant he was angry.

Daher reread the letter while those around him, foremost among them the owner of the two mules, waited to see where he would place the stamp. He set the piece of paper face up on the ground in front of him and stamped it. However, rather than removing the stamp immediately, he held it down so that, when he lifted his hand at last, the piece of paper clung to the stamp. Then he calmly released it and handed it to the owner of the two mules.

Emir Rashid clutched the folded letter, his eyes searching for Daher's stamp on the back. When he didn't see it, he tossed it to one of his men, who read Daher's orders to Bani Saqr to return the two mules and the stolen goods: "Time and time again I have written to you asking you to keep to your bounds, but you have yet to do what I ask! The man standing before you came to us after being robbed on the open road. As soon as this missive of mine reaches you, you are to determine which of your men committed the robbery. Then you are to send the offender to us and restore the stolen goods to their owner."

"He has the audacity to threaten me over a couple of mules?" Emir Rashid fumed. Then, looking at the man who had brought the letter, he asked, "Can you identify the man you say robbed you?"

"No," the man replied.

"Well, if you can't identify him, then neither can I!"

Wadi al-Milh—the Valley of Salt—south of Acre was blanketed with soldiers. Daher's rage had reached a point where he wasn't willing to allow Bani Saqr's power to grow again.

Yet, packed though it was, the place was a lonesome one. Through the crowds Daher glimpsed Jahjah on a powerful black steed. Prodding his horse as though he'd been bitten by a snake, he rushed over to his son Uthman and shouted, "How could you let Jahjah come?"

"I—I didn't, Sheikh. But you know him. He loves you so much, he must have followed you here."

"Well, he's going back to where he came from right now. Do you hear me? Right now!"

Jahjah, now fourteen years old, loved nothing more than to be by his grandfather's side.

Uthman took off toward his son. Then Daher took up his position again: a spearhead at the vanguard of his army.

Bani Saqr's army was as large and well equipped as Daher's, and they realized that the sky wasn't large enough to hold both Daher's sun and theirs.

On that morning saturated with the odor of horses and with the steam that rose hot from their lungs, the gates of hell suddenly opened, and there ensued a battle that lasted until noon, though it might well have gone on for days.

Karim maneuvered his way through the narrow corridors of the hellish fracas until he found himself face to face with Emir Rashid, who was caught off guard not only by his opponent's strength, but by the indignant rage in the eyes of yesterday's ally.

Karim charged, and the emir, once he had gathered his wits, tried to meet the attack with equal force. They clashed at length until, in a fleeting instant, Karim managed to forge a path of death into the emir's chest. The emir reeled.

"That's for betraying the sheikh!" shrieked Karim. He withdrew his sword and stabbed him again, screaming, "And that's for thinking you could turn me into a traitor! And that's for . . ." As he spoke, the emir fell off his horse. Karim turned and kept fighting, and as he did so, he finished his sentence: ". . . and that's for thinking you could put a price on a free man's heart!"

Suddenly Daher's soldiers began shouting, "Emir Rashid is dead! Emir Rashid is dead!"

One of the soldiers rode up to Daher shouting gleefully, "Have you heard the good news, Sheikh Daher? Emir Rashid is dead! Emir Rashid is dead!"

Daher was engaged in hand-to-hand combat and, on hearing the news, his hand froze in midair. So great was the shock of hearing of his commander's death that Daher's opponent was likewise paralyzed. Otherwise, he could easily have dealt Daher a fatal blow.

The soldier rushed up to Daher, continuing to shout, "Good news, Sheikh Daher! Bani Saqr's emir is dead!"

When Daher had pulled himself together, he shouted at the soldier, "Get out of here! Go! Rashid al-Jabr isn't a man whose death you rejoice over! Get out of my face or I'll kill you!" Stunned, the soldier advanced a few steps, then froze in his tracks as other soldiers came rushing up to him from all sides.

Bani Saqr's men began retreating and Daher's soldiers went after them, though after some distance, they quit their pursuit.

As Daher witnessed his sorrowful victory before those huge throngs of soldiers, he recalled, in moments, the long road he had traveled with this emir for whom no place remained but the belly of the earth. Little did Daher know that a sorrow far more bitter lurked nearby, searching for a breach through which to take possession of both heart and mind.

The Horses with the
Silent Hoofbeats

The army was halfway back to Acre when Uthman came up to his father and said, "Have you seen Jahjah?"

Daher was dumbstruck.

Voices went up in the army's vanguard, center and rear: "Has anyone seen Jahjah?"

The question repeated itself thousands of times on the lips of commanders and soldiers alike until they discovered that all of them were shouting.

There descended a silence so thick that even the horses' hooves made no sound as they made their way forward. As Daher turned his horse and began heading back to Wadi al-Milh, he passed before the soldiers like a ghost, as though his body had vaporized and nothing remained on the horse but his empty clothes.

The entire army turned around behind him. On what seemed like an endless journey back, the soldiers felt as if the army that had been victorious just hours earlier was nothing but a defeated band straggling brokenly back to a country that would refuse to welcome it home.

They looked for Jahjah's horse, but didn't find it. If they had found the horse, it would have meant something. They searched the areas around the battlefield, under trees and bushes, behind low stone walls, and in the tall dry grasses. They even looked among the bodies of Bani Saqr's slain. Nothing.

"We're not going back until he's found!" announced Daher.

Evening fell, but all they had gained from their search was the blackness of the night, which had cast them into a vast, thick fog.

The following morning, which Daher had awaited more anxiously than any morning in his entire life, Uthman said to him, "Maybe he went home!"

"Did you tell him to go back to Acre?"

"I told him to wait for us behind that hill over there."

So they headed home, hoping against hope that Jahjah was already back in Acre.

But when they reached the city, he wasn't there.

The world turned darker for Daher, and by evening everything looked coal-black.

He considered the possibility that Jahjah had been taken captive, though he thought it unlikely that anyone would come to him and say, "We have Jahjah! What will you give us for him?"

I'd give the world for him!

No one came, no one asked, and the direction from which light might have come turned into a wall that stretched from earth to heaven.

The third day was the cruelest. Even so, straining beneath the weight of an unbearable despair, Daher struggled to keep hope's fragile flame burning.

That evening a man on horseback was seen approaching in the distance. When he was a thousand steps away from the landward gate known as the Lions' Gate, he stopped as though he had turned into a pillar of salt.

The soldiers who were about to shut the gate waited for the man to approach. After all, what man would come to a city only to sleep outside its gates on the back of his horse?

As news of the mysterious figure spread, many of Acre's inhabitants ascended the walls to see the horseman, who by now was being swallowed up by the darkness.

Al-Dankizli had been pacing back and forth near the city gate. Sensing the seriousness of the matter, he instructed a number of soldiers to investigate the situation and find out why the man was standing there in such a peculiar way. The soldiers charged away on horseback, but when they came near the man, they, like him, froze in place.

"What on earth is going on out there?" al-Dankizli wondered aloud.

He quickly ordered another group of soldiers out. They too froze in place.

Grabbing the reins of a soldier's horse, al-Dankizli jumped on its back.

The distance he had to cover in order to reach the men-turned-statues was greater than he'd expected. When he reached them at last, he passed among them until he was face to face with the unidentified horseman, who was holding Jahjah's body in his arms.

Mastering his emotions, al-Dankizli's shouted, "Go prepare the people to receive the sheikh's beloved!" Then he turned his horse, his eyes welling up with tears.

After going a few steps, he sensed that the man hadn't budged. "Follow me," he said to him kindheartedly.

"I can't, sir. I can't. I can't go in to see the sheikh carrying this precious piece of his heart in my arms!"

Al-Dankizli came up to the man and gently took Jahjah's body. Then once again he started back toward the city, and the man followed.

When they reached the city gate, a river of grief poured forth.

Daher took his grandson into his arms and carried him to the mansion diwan. Once inside the room, he turned and closed the door with his foot.

Brokenhearted, he bent over him, weeping hot tears.

"Today's Tuesday, isn't it, Grandpa?"

"That's right."

"So, Tuesday is today, right, Grandpa?"

"That's right!"

"But when I asked Baba about it yesterday, he said it was tomorrow! And if I ask him about it tomorrow, he'll tell me it was yesterday. So which one is right, Grandpa?"

Daher bowed his head, and when he looked up again, he was smiling.

"It looks like you know the answer, Grandpa!"

"As a matter of fact," Daher said, "they're all correct. Tuesday can be today or yesterday or tomorrow."

"No, Grandpa. It can't be three different things!"

"But it can, because Tuesday is like you!"

"How can Tuesday be like me, Grandpa? Am I Tuesday?"

"No, you're Jahjah, aren't you?"

"Yes, I'm Jahjah."

"We agree, then. Today you're a boy. But what will you be when you get a little bigger?"

"I'll be a young man."

"And when you grow up some more?"

"I'll be an old man, like you, Grandpa!"

"Am I an old man? So be it! But now tell me, Jahjah: What's your name when you're a boy?"

420

"Jahjah."

"What will your name be when you're a young man?"

"Jahjah."

"And what will it be when you're an old man like me?"

"It will still be Jahjah!"

"So then, you're the boy, the young man, and the old man too. Isn't that right?"

"That's right."

"And in the same way, Tuesday is yesterday, today, and tomorrow."

"So, Grandpa, am I yesterday or today now?"

"You're . . . now you've confused me. If we look at you as Tuesday, you're the today that hasn't ended."

"That doesn't make sense, Grandpa. If I'm today now, then what was I yesterday if I'm still here today?"

"You were yesterday's today, and now you're tomorrow. You're yesterday's tomorrow, Jahjah!"

When Jahjah saw the defeat of Emir Rashid's men, he shouted for joy. Then his horse bolted and took off running after Bani Saqr's horses. He tried to restrain his mount, but to no avail. He tried again, but by this time the horse was like a boulder rolling down a hill, and he had no power to stop it.

Seeing a lone rider speeding after them on a black horse gone mad, the men of Bani Saqr stopped, and with little effort they managed to kill both the rider and his mount even before he had reached them. Then, overwhelmed with the horror of having lost their leader, they ran their spears through his lungs, oblivious to the innocence of his features.

Then they left him in a pool of blood.

As that cruel night of theirs wore on, Bani Saqr were still trying to grasp the fact that their leader was dead and would never return, when suddenly the earth shook beneath their tents. They might have expected anything in the world but what they were about to see. In a swirl of madness, Daher's army surrounded their tents, destroying everything in its path and killing everything that moved. It was a storm of death beyond description, as though hell itself had descended suddenly upon their heads.

421

They fled, searching desperately for a place that no longer existed. Their horses went running in all directions as the screams of their women and children rang out in vain. When at last everything was quiet again, no one but the slain of all ages remained in the camp. The survivors had all fled.

His clothes spattered with blood, Daher looked around and saw a sight he would never in his life have wanted to lay eyes on, and a terrifying, heavy silence descended upon him. He turned to leave with eyes that he would be unable to close for countless nights, a mouth out of which words no longer came, and ears so distant that no sound could reach them.

It had been a victory bitterer than the bitterest defeat. This, the only thought he could think, sank its talons into his chest and gripped his heart like the fangs of an adder.

Blood, the Spear, and
the Mysterious Guest

The mansion went dark, and the slightest movement by a family member or servant made an unbearable racket.

People flocked from all over the country to offer their condolences on Jahjah's death, while men clad in black on horses draped in black twirled about with lowered swords in a mournful dance.

When the last day of the wake had ended, Daher repaired to his diwan in the mansion and shut the door. Najma sat alone outside the closed door, doing her best to keep any new sorrows from assailing him. She sat guarding a fallen fortress that stood naked of all its defenses. Not once did it occur to her to go in, because her heart, like his, was awash in a sorrow as frigid as winter, as hot as blood.

For six entire days his door didn't open. When, on the seventh day, she heard the creaking of wood behind her, she turned and saw Daher standing there: gaunt, weak, and bareheaded, with a face so drawn that his cheeks nearly cleaved one to the other. Behind him a strange darkness filled the room to overflowing.

With difficulty he came over and stood briefly beside her, and with difficulty managed to sit down. Najma stared at the floor, unable to look at him again. It would have killed her to have it confirmed that what she'd seen moments earlier was real, so she buried her eyes in the floor.

She heard a rattling in his throat as he took a breath, and it seemed he wanted to say something. But he didn't. Half an hour later, she heard the same rattling, and when he spoke, his voice was as feeble as his trembling legs.

"Human beings are the vilest beasts God ever created," he said, "and the vilest beast human beings ever created is war!" Then he fell silent.

She lifted her gaze and looked at him, but didn't dare reach out to squeeze his hand.

The survivors of the Bani Saqr tribe gathered up what remained of their tattered lives and moved to the outskirts of Nazareth.

Emir Rashid al-Jabr's death had left a gaping hole in their lives. However, a situation like this couldn't go on forever. One evening Watfa', Emir Qa'dan's mother, strode over to the slain emir's tent with a spear in her hand. When she was a few steps away from its door, she planted the spear in the ground. Then she proceeded inside, where Bani Saqr's emirs and sheikhs were gathered.

"I won't leave until you've chosen someone from among you to be our new leader," she announced.

The men exchanged glances, knowing that the woman who stood before them was someone whose command even the Emir Rashid wouldn't have dared disobey.

"I see you have nothing to say! I've waited patiently for one of you to plant the spear that was broken with Emir Rashid's death. But now my patience has run out, and I'm not budging until I see that you've chosen a new emir for us."

"But Emir Rashid's blood hasn't even dried yet!"

"And it's in the name of Emir Rashid that I command you to do this!"

Shamefaced, they began discussing the matter among themselves.

"Since you've gotten started, I'll leave for an hour. Then I'll be back to hear your decision." All eyes were upon her as she turned to leave.

When she returned, she found her son, Emir Qa'dan, seated at the center of the gathering.

She nodded and said, "I trust you've made the right choice." Then she left, certain that a decision to declare war on Daher would soon follow.

It would have come as no surprise to Daher had they decided to declare war. But what robbed him of sleep was the question: *How much more blood will be shed in the next war?*

Seeing a rider approaching in the distance, Watfa' secured her scarf around her head. She shook some dirt and straw out of her robe and stood up to await his arrival. The sun behind him had turned him and his horse into what looked like a black statue that, apart from its movement toward her and the shadow that preceded it, seemed devoid of life.

He rode up to her and greeted her, and she invited him into her tent.

"Who might the rider be?" she asked him.

"You know me, Watfa'."

"And who are you?"

"Daher. Daher al-Umar," he said as he uncovered his face.

"You kill our emir, our old and our young, and then come here alone?"

"Is that how you welcome a guest, Watfa'?"

"Welcome, Daher. Welcome!"

"And won't you say, 'Welcome, my son?' Or do you think Emir Qa'dan is more chivalrous than I am?"

"Emir Qa'dan couldn't hold a candle to you! I swear to God, I've never met anyone who would have the audacity to do what you're doing right now, and I don't think I ever will!"

"May you be granted a long, healthy life, Mother."

As they sat talking, she would interrupt the conversation now and then to ask, "And how is your mother Najma?"

"She's well, Mother. She's well. May God grant both of you the finest of health!"

"God is gracious, Daher. He's given the two of us the health and long lives we deserve, and more. But whatever God gives of these things, you take away with your endless wars!"

Daher was about to reply when suddenly his gaze froze. The figure of Emir Qa'dan had darkened the door, and he too had frozen in shocked surprise.

"Come in, son. It's Sheikh Daher al-Umar, my guest. Won't you welcome your mother's guest?"

The emir stammered a bit before finding his tongue. "Welcome, Sheikh Daher!"

Daher and Emir Qa'dan spent the whole night talking. After hours of alternately remonstrating with each other and reminiscing about the old days, each of them apologized for the harm he had done the other, and at some point in the wee hours of the morning, Emir Qa'dan promised Daher that there would be no more wars between them.

Then Daher said. "I want you to give me your word that you'll never support Uthman or any of my other sons against me."

He gave him his word.

On his way back to Acre, Daher felt the burden that had so enervated his spirit and body become gradually lighter. All he could think of now was the hope that had blossomed out of Emir Qa'dan's promise: "From this day forth you'll fight no more wars with Bani Saqr!"

But if he could have discerned the direction from which the winds of war would blow next, he would have felt no lighter at all.

Impossibilities on the
Road to Istanbul

D amascus—from the peak of whose great mountain one could reach up and pluck the moon out of the sky, look out over the paradise of its fertile plain, and forget all the world's troubles— wasn't itself any more. When its governor, Uthman Pasha al-Kurji, received a letter from the sultan forbidding him to attack Daher, he was beside himself.

"When are they going to see this man's real intentions?"

"Pasha," his daftardar replied, "what we hear is that before annexing any city or village, Daher prepares the way in Istanbul first. What comes later is the easy part!"

"Could the sultan possibly be that naive?"

"Of course not, Pasha! That's why he gave us the chance to attack Haifa from the sea, as you'll recall. But our luck was bad!"

"So, can anyone explain to me what's happening now?"

"What we always forget, as I was saying, is that Daher has allies among the sultan's senior officials. They persuade the sultan of the sincerity of Daher's intentions, citing the fact that he pays every piaster he owes in state taxes, and then some."

"We'll have to drive a wedge between him and the sultan, then."

"Do you think we haven't tried to do precisely that, Pasha? But the sultan's response is in your hand."

Uthman glared at the letter he was holding and nearly flung it to the ground. However, seeing that all eyes were on him, he realized that the news of his throwing the letter down would reach the sultan before the letter hit the floor.

"You've got to advise me," he said to the daftardar and the others gathered about him. "Haifa belongs to Damascus, but Daher snatched it right out of my hands, which have been tied by all these instructions from the sultan. At first he claimed that he wanted to get rid of the highway robbers on the Acre–Haifa road, though I don't doubt for a moment that he invented those robbers himself. Then he said he'd

426

protect the city from pirates—the very pirates who now go parading through Acre in broad daylight as if it belonged to them. When the sultan sent him some cannons to protect Haifa, he claimed they weren't powerful enough to do the job. Then he set them up on Acre's walls! He built New Haifa to secure control over Mount Carmel and the roads leading to and from Palestine, to guarantee the safety of his soldiers, protect his north–south trade routes, and link the Palestinian coast from as far south as Caesarea to the Plain of Bani Amer and Safad in the north."

"The sour grapes we're eating now were placed in our mouths by that spineless governor As'ad Pasha. If it weren't for him, neither Haifa nor Acre would be under Daher's control now. Then that crazy Hussein Pasha came along."

"I've told you I don't want to look behind me!" Uthman Pasha bellowed. "You're dragging me back to a time that's over and done with. What I want is for the sultan to understand, some way or other, that the only reason Daher built up Haifa was to ensure that, if push came to shove, it would be beyond the reach of the sultan's own cannons! He razed old Haifa and built a new city. Then he surrounded it with a wall and three towers on its landward side, and another huge tower fitted out with cannons overlooking the bay. When he did all that, he had something more than just Haifa in mind!"

"More than just Haifa, Pasha?" the daftardar asked.

"Yes, more than just Haifa. I don't think the sultanate has ever dealt with a fox like him!"

"Isn't it true, Pasha, that he named that cannon tower 'the tower of peace'?" queried the daftardar. The governor ignored his question.

Uthman walked to the door that led out of the spacious hall.

Everyone present exchanged glances, wondering what would have prompted him to withdraw from the conversation before they'd reached a conclusion. Before leaving, he turned and said, "I'll dismiss all of you, and I mean *all* of you, if you don't find me a solution!"

Then he stalked out.

Daher had, indeed, built up a base of devoted senior officials whom he honored and feted whenever they came to visit the holy places: from the Armenian merchant Ya'qub Agha, bosom friend of Qazlar Pasha, the sultan's head butler,[34] to Sulayman Agha, the salahdar, or royal arms keeper,[35] who, before his fortunes changed, became Daher's friend following the death of Ya'qub.

"How old is Sulayman Agha's son?" Daher asked.

"He's twelve years old. Why do you ask, Sheikh?"

"At that age, there's nothing like a thoroughbred horse to steal a boy's heart away! I want you to send the agha the nicest gift you can find, and send the best horse you can find to his son."

"What good would the agha do us now that he's in exile in Cyprus?"

"Pray to God he'll still be in Cyprus when you get there!"

Sulayman Agha was delighted with the gifts Daher had sent him, and his only son was ecstatic over the thoroughbred horse.

"That's strange," said Sulayman Agha. "You know, Daher is the only person who's sent me a gift since I was exiled here. When you're on the throne, you're everyone's master, but the minute you step down from it, nobody knows you any more. Not even your dogs! So how can I return this kindness of Sheikh Daher's?"

"The sheikh sent you a letter also," his messenger said, handing it to Sulayman Agha.

He opened the letter and began reading. As he read, he nodded, exclaiming over and over. The letter said, "I have a request to make of you: that you stop Uthman Pasha al-Kurji from waging war on me, and that you thwart his malicious attempts to deprive me of Haifa, which is my territory's lifeline. . . ."

Sulayman Agha turned to the messenger and said, "The sheikh must realize that I'm in exile here! So how can he ask me to keep the governor of Damascus at bay when I can barely shoo away a fly buzzing around my nose out here on this island?"

---

34 "Qazlar" was the title given in Ottoman times to the individual who oversaw the harem in the sultan's palace (the chief eunuch). Responsible also for the upbringing and education of the crown prince, the qazlar became especially powerful as the authority of the empire began to wane, ranking a close third after the sultan and his mother. It bears noting that as many as five thousand people lived in the sultan's palace, 1,200 of whom were employed in the royal kitchens alone.

35 The salahdar oversaw all affairs relating to armament, including the royal arms depots.

Sulayman began thinking about the letter from Daher, who was now more than seventy-five years old: *Do you suppose he's going senile? Has he forgotten that I'm in exile? But if that were the case, they would have told him they were going to send me his gift without actually doing so, knowing that he would forget all about it!*

Four days later a messenger from the sultan arrived with a royal decree. Sulayman Agha took it in his hand, certain that it must contain orders for him to be exiled somewhere even farther away. But when he opened it, what should he find but that the sultan was restoring him to his former position as royal arms keeper and requesting his immediate presence in Istanbul.

Aboard the ship bound for Istanbul, Sulayman Agha couldn't help wondering: *Did Sheikh Daher have a hand in what's happening to me? Has he acquired this much influence through the men who surround the sultan even when some thought his power had waned since the death of his friend Ya'qub?*

And when he got to Istanbul, the questions were still coming.

The Thorny Paths to Haifa

On the morning of Tuesday, June 7, 1766, al-Qubji Mas'ud Bey[36] arrived in Damascus bearing a royal decree. The temperature had been on the rise since the first day of the month, and by the seventh day people thought the entire city would go up in flames.

Nothing quenches the thirst of dry grass like fire. Several fires broke out in a certain orchard, and the flames quickly spread to neighboring orchards and fields. Landowners rushed to put out the flames, while those whose orchards and fields had been spared stood guard over them, expecting a conflagration at any moment. Some of them grew faint from the heat, and every minute or so people would rush over to help someone who had fallen unconscious.

A day before his arrival, Mas'ud Bey had sent a messenger ahead of him so that Uthman Pasha al-Kurji could prepare to receive him in a manner befitting the governor's allegiance to his sultan. Amid rising clouds of smoke, Mas'ud Bey made his way with difficulty toward the Damascus gate, where the city's daftardar, mufti, and judge stood waiting for him with the vilayet's military commander. The procession then made its way to Uthman Pasha's mansion, where Mas'ud would be staying as his guest.

The sultan's envoy asked to be left alone for a while so that he could bathe and take a nap before meeting with the governor. Two hours later, the governor inquired about him and was told, "He's still asleep." After three more hours had gone by, he asked again, only to be told that he was still sleeping.

"Wake him up!" he ordered.

Uthman Pasha knew it was a long way from Istanbul. First there had been a long sea journey to Beirut, while the trip from Beirut to Damascus in that infernal heat couldn't have been easy. However, he knew he wouldn't be able to sleep himself until he knew what was in that royal

---

36 Qubji Mas'ud Bey was the Ottoman sultan's special envoy, who was sent to the various vilayets on missions of particular importance or confidentiality.

decree! It was a decree he had long awaited, all the while dreaming of one thing: a command to wage war on Daher.

When he took the letter in his hand, Uthman Pasha al-Kurji tried to feign nonchalance. In fact, he deliberately set it aside and began asking Mas'ud Bey about the details of his trip and the news from Istanbul. However, when he asked, "And how are things with the esteemed arms keeper, Sulayman Agha?" he was slightly unnerved by the reply he received.

"Things have fared so well with him, I thought his news would have reached you before I did. He's now the person closest to the sultan himself!"

Uthman Pasha now felt as though he had read the decree even before opening it. After all, Mas'ud's reply had summed it up perfectly.

Unable to let the sultan's decree wait a moment longer, Uthman Pasha calmly reached over, picked it up, and opened it. Within moments everyone in the room could read it in his countenance. His features clouded over in a way they had never seen before. He looked like someone who was about to receive a slap in the face, and whose station in life left him no choice but to receive it with his hands pressed to his sides. At last he lifted his head with difficulty and looked at the sultan's envoy.

"So, is the sultan telling me to appeal to the law to settle the dispute between me and Daher?"

"If that is what the decree says, then yes."

"Does this mean I'll be expected to sit across from Daher and accept him as my equal? Is the majestic Ottoman Empire too weak to go to war against him?"

"Uthman Pasha! The majestic Ottoman Empire is quite capable of going to war against him. However, it is not willing to lose its prestige in the event that he should be victorious! You know how many governors of Damascus, yourself included, have been defeated by this man. You also know, as we do, that Daher, who now holds sway over most of Palestine, has formed a sizable army and won over powerful states by virtue of their shared economic and political ties. Every state that has a consular officer in Beirut, Sidon, and even Damascus also has one in Acre to manage the affairs of his country's nationals and his government's relations with Daher."

"Well then, the Ottoman Empire shouldn't have waited until things came to this!"

"And who says it waited, Pasha? Ever since he became multazim over Tiberias it's been trying to do away with him. It gave you permission to wage war on him too, as you know full well! But whenever it managed to place him under siege in this city or that, he grew stronger, and before we knew it, he'd established a foothold elsewhere. As you can see, the entire region from Lake Tiberias to the Acre Sea is under his control, and no one can resist him any more."

The envoy suddenly fell silent as though he'd remembered something important. Then he said, "I should add that I'll be delivering Daher a decree like the one I brought to you. This conflict between Damascus and Acre has gone on much too long!"

When he read the decree, Daher was no less furious than Uthman Pasha had been. He knew that Haifa, Tira, and Tantura would be as threatened by whatever ruling was handed down as they would have been by the outbreak of war.

Squeezing Daher's hand, Ibrahim al-Sabbagh said, "Don't worry, Sheikh. The truth will prevail, and it will be on your side!"

Uthman Pasha had lost all hope, convinced that having to sit across from Daher would be a defeat greater than any ruling that might be issued in Daher's favor.

"You'll be my legal defense!" he said to the sultan's envoy.

"Me, Pasha?" exclaimed Mas'ud Bey.

"Yes, you. Could I possibly find anyone better?"

This was the only well-placed blow Uthman Pasha felt he could level against the state. In this way he would be throwing everything back on the Ottoman Empire's shoulders. He hoped the empire would be the victor. If it were defeated, however, it alone, and not he, would be vanquished. After all, the decree was the sultan's decree, and Mas'ud Bey was the sultan's envoy. He thought: *If they don't want me to wage war on Daher and put him in his place, then let them wrest Haifa from him themselves, if they're able! Of course, it could be that they're able, but aren't willing!*

Uthman Pasha's heart sank, and he felt it being rent in two: *By persuading the sultan to issue this decree, might Sulayman Agha have arranged things in such a way that Haifa would go to Daher? And might I have prepared the way for this very thing by asking Mas'ud Bey to be my legal representative?*

But it was too late. Mas'ud Bey had already left Damascus, and was now on board a ship that would take him from Sidon to Acre.

Acre's legal experts, judge, and mufti gathered with Mas'ud Bey and the legal advisors who had accompanied him from Damascus, and the session was convened. Mas'ud Bey announced that, in keeping with a letter he had brought with him, he would be Uthman Pasha's representative. Everyone examined the letter and nodded in approval.

As the discussion ramified and arguments followed one on the other, everyone was amazed at Mas'ud Bey's skilled argumentation. Daher talked about how Damascus had neglected Haifa, leaving it an easy prey for pirates and highway robbers. He talked about how unsafe Haifa's people had been and how, were it not for their vulnerability, he would never have thought of annexing the city to Acre.

Mas'ud Bey rejoined, "If the governors and multazims appealed to arguments like this, the sultan would have lost even more of the lands to which he lays rightful claim! It's as if you wanted to take every poor man's children away from him because he didn't have enough to feed them!"

"Well," asked Ibrahim al-Sabbagh, "should he leave them to starve under the care of someone who has no basis for keeping them other than the fact that he is their father?"

Turning to al-Sabbagh, Mas'ud Bey roared, "This is a royal council and a court of law, and I am Qubji Pasha Sultan, representative of the governor of Damascus! As for you, you're a Christian who has no right even to be present at such a venerable gathering. Yet you have the audacity to respond to me? You will leave this very instant!"

Mas'ud Bey's face was flushed with rage, the three large moles near the right side of his mouth had turned black, and his upper lip, which he couldn't close properly in the first place, had curled strangely upward. His harsh words rained down like hailstones on the petrified al-Sabbagh's head. Having suffered a bitter affront to his dignity, al-Sabbagh composed himself and rose to leave. But before he got to the door Daher shouted, "Where are you going? Wait!"

Al-Sabbagh stopped, certain that he was enduring the cruelest moments of his life. Little did he know that moments far crueler awaited him. The hall fell silent as everyone exchanged glances, not knowing what to expect. However, Daher promptly settled the matter.

433

"Mas'ud Bey," he said, "you may be Uthman Pasha's representative, but Ibrahim al-Sabbagh is mine! Whatever applies to my representative applies to me as well, and of this, all those present here today are witnesses."

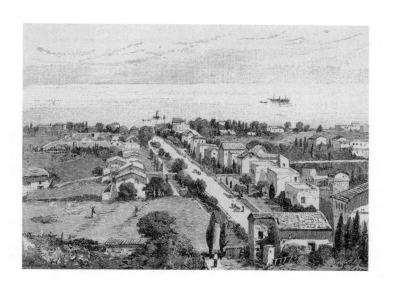

Torment in Paradise

One day, Daher received a letter from
Uthman Pasha al-Misri, governor of Damascus,
informing him that he didn't intend to wage war
on him the way previous governors had done,
since he was certain that Uthman Pasha al-Kurji's attacks on him
in previous years had been the cause of all the
other wars that had afflicted the region.
Hardly had Daher folded up the governor's letter
when another arrived from the
Ottoman Empire's prime minister who,
after conveying his warmest greetings
and wishing him long life and health,
urged Daher to
forget all that was past.

This was the first letter Daher had ever received
from the prime minister.
All he had received in the past were letters from governors
breathing dire threats!
Looking around him,
Daher found that everything he had hoped for
had come to pass.
His rule now extended over all of southern Palestine, as well as
Acre, Jaffa, Haifa, Galilee, the regions of Irbid and Ajloun,
parts of Syria and Houran, and Sidon.
Tyre was in the hands of his allies the Matawila,
and Beirut was in the hands of his friends the Shihabis.
All that remained to the Ottoman Empire was the port of Tripoli in
the north. However, he realized that,
given the Ottomans' approval of those
who stood opposed to him,
he had no reason for complacence.
The Ottomans then took things a step further
by issuing him a royal pardon.
The decree was delivered by a royal messenger
who entered Acre in the grandest, most festive procession
the city had ever seen.
It was then that Daher's fear began to mount,
and for good reason!

The Day the Black Tents Blew In

The people of Shafaʿamr were in an uproar when they learned of Daher's intention to appoint his son Uthman as their governor. The news descended on their heads like a thunderbolt. His reputation had preceded him, while the stench of his depravity had spread throughout the land.

A number of elders from Shafaʿamr came secretly to Acre and met with Daher, saying, "We would sooner die than have Uthman among us!"[37]

Daher assured them that he would deter anyone who thought of treating them unjustly, his own son included.

In the beginning, Uthman and Daher's other sons paid the state taxes they owed. However, given their opulent lifestyles and their proneness to act like spoiled princes, they began dragging their feet as time passed. And as if that weren't enough, they began levying heavier and heavier taxes, causing people greater and greater misery. They'd begun modeling themselves on the governors of Damascus and Sidon, who would raise taxes whenever they pleased just to line their own pockets.

When, eventually, Daher's sons started refusing outright to pay taxes to the empire, Daher sent an ultimatum to Ali in Safad, Saʿid in Saffuriya, Ahmad in Deir Hanna, and Uthman in Shafaʿamr. But it fell on deaf ears.

Of all Daher's sons, Uthman was the angriest of all over his father's ultimatum. Shafaʿamr was the portal to his most cherished dream, since from there he could be the first to reach Acre if the old man were to pass away suddenly. Uthman was on the lookout for the moment when he could take control of the entire country from his well-built, well-fortified mansion.[38]

---

37 During Daher's rule, he arranged for the Druze and Christians of Shafaʿamr to divide the public lands among themselves. Having heard about the security, stability, and tolerance its people enjoyed, scores of Christian families from Syria had come to the city as well.

38 The lower story of the mansion-fortress housed stables for horses, while the upper

As for Islibi, who had responsibility for Tiberias, he was running the city's affairs as though Daher had never left: paying whatever taxes he owed and working assiduously to develop the city and its agriculture.

One morning Daher prepared a large convoy laden with gifts and sent it to Bani Saqr's camping grounds. With the convoy he sent a request. Thanks, perhaps, to a combination of their awareness that their wars with Daher needed to come to an end and their deep-seated raiding instinct, Daher had no difficulty persuading them to go out to teach his sons a lesson.

The following morning Daher's sons awoke in Shafa'amr, Saffuriya, and Safad to find themselves hemmed in from all sides by black tents. They were surrounded so completely that no one could come in or out. Any soldier sent out to investigate the situation was promptly shot down by Bani Saqr's men, who knew they had been sent out solely to wage war on Daher's sons, and that dialogue with them was Daher's province alone.

The surrounding plains closed in around them, then their city walls, then their houses, until they felt as though even their clothes were too small. They had to find a solution—someone to mediate for them with their father. And, as usual, they knew of no one better for the task than Islibi.

With white flags fluttering, a number of men left Safad and headed south for Shafa'amr. Then they turned eastward and made their way to Saffuriya accompanied by some of Bani Saqr's men. Ali had sent messages to his brothers Uthman and Sa'id, telling them to conclude a peace agreement with their father.

---

story housed Uthman's personal residence, the door to which bore an inscription containing the following verses, believed to have been composed by Uthman himself:

> Ponder this dwelling where beauty abounds,
> Where the lion crouches in the halo round the moon,
> and where many will return time and time again.

> Built by Uthman, doer of good to whom dominion has been given,
> its date of construction can be
> discerned easily in "the abode of felicity."

Before long, Islibi found three letters in his hand, all pleading with him to use his good offices with their father to end Bani Saqr's blockade.

The three of them woke one morning expecting the worst. To their surprise, however, they found Bani Saqr departing. They then received a message from Islibi telling them that he had done his part, and that now they would have to do theirs. Daher's sons wasted no time carrying out the agreement, which was all that Daher had wanted.

The Wind Trap

W e've been so intent on looking north that we've failed to see what's to our south," Daher said to his vizier, Ibrahim al-Sabbagh.

"Are you referring to Egypt, Sheikh?"

"I'm referring to Egypt, and to what's happening there. Its people have achieved what we haven't yet: independence from the Ottoman Empire."

"But our situation here is different, Sheikh."

"I know that, Ibrahim. Our proximity to Damascus and Istanbul is a curse that can only be removed by one thing!"

"And what is that, Sheikh?"

"I'll let you know when the time comes."

Daher peered southward, daunted by the vastness of the areas and distances he was contemplating: "It's a long way to Gaza, and a longer way from Gaza to Alexandria, and from there to Cairo."

It was midday and the air was calm. He looked out at Mount Carmel, his mind occupied by the thought of climbing it again with Najma: *Do you think I could still do it after all these years?* he wondered.

"Do I have your permission to build a church in Acre?" al-Sabbagh asked him.

Daher's thoughts had wandered so far that al-Sabbagh had to repeat himself: "Do I have your permission to build a church in Acre?"

"What?" said Daher with a start. "Do you need my permission to build a place of worship? Go and build it!"

"I knew what your answer would be, but I still wanted to ask!"

"So it seems your soap factory is doing well?"

"It's doing quite well, thanks be to God."

"And your business?"

"My business? What can I say? I've been so busy attending to other people's affairs, it's seen a bit of a downturn."

"But you're still making a profit, aren't you?"

"Thank God!"

"Thank God for what? Don't we thank God for good fortune and bad fortune alike?"

"Thank God for my good fortune."

Al-Sabbagh fell silent for a moment. Then he said, "And there's something else, Sheikh. As you know, a good number of Maronites have settled in Nazareth, since they know they're safer there than anywhere else. Well, they've sent me a letter asking if you would allow them to build a church there. So, what do you say?"

"When we get back to Acre, I'll write them with instructions for a piece of land to be set aside for it."

Suddenly interrupting himself, he said, "But why should we wait until we get back to Acre? Write to them right now, saying, 'We hereby grant our Maronite brethren in Nazareth permission to summon a cleric to serve their local community, and to have their own church building.'"

Three days after he and al-Sabbagh had returned from Haifa, Daher received word that his sons Ali and Sa'id had rebelled again, and that they were both demanding additional territories to rule.

Adamant in his refusal, Daher wrote to them saying, "In order for people to live with dignity I waged war on my enemies. In order for people to enjoy their right to safety and to raise their children without fear, I waged war on my enemies. In order to make the roads free of danger, I waged war on my enemies. In order to prevent anyone from being robbed of his fields, his merchandise, his business, his tent, or his home, I waged war on my enemies. Now you leave me no choice but to wage war on you for doing the same things my enemies have done. And out of fairness to my enemies, I *will* wage war on you! I won't let it be said that Daher went to war with his enemies for the injustices they had committed, but lowered his sword when his sons committed the same crimes! I will wage war on you as long as you stand between me and any aim that my enemies have sought to prevent me from achieving!"

Daher reached Saffuriya to find that Sa'id had fled to his brother Ali's fortress in Safad. He went after him, steering clear of the deep valleys and thick forests teeming with bears, leopards, and hyenas. News of the army Daher had marshaled, said to be equipped with new types of cannons and muskets rumored never to have been used in warfare before, struck terror in their hearts.

Wasting no time, al-Dankizli set up the cannons and aimed them at the fortress. At the sight of them, Ali, the bravest knight in the land, was terrified for the first time in his life. Al-Dankizli raised his hand in a signal for the bombardment to begin. However, Daher stopped him.

"Let's give them one last chance!" He then sent them a message demanding that they surrender.

A terror of sorts stirred in Daher's heart and nearly unhinged him when he remembered the faces of Ali's sons, al-Hasan and al-Hussein. Jahjah's face flashed through his mind as well.

Daher thought back on the day when he had marched out against Ali, and the only force Ali had had with which to meet his father's army had consisted of his two sons. After decking them out in their finest attire, he'd placed white kerchiefs around their necks and sent them out to his father. At the sight of the two little boys, which opened up a flood of painful memories, Daher tore the two kerchiefs to shreds and took them into his arms. Then he sent word to his son, saying, "The next time I see any of you coming out unarmed with a white kerchief around his neck, I swear to God I'll kill you with my own two hands!"

Daher waited for his messenger to return with a reply. At last, just before sundown, they saw him approaching. When he arrived, he handed Daher Ali's message, which read, "Didn't you once tell me, Father, that you'd kill me yourself if you ever saw me come out unarmed, with a white kerchief around my neck, in surrender to my enemy? I assure you: I'll never surrender again!"

At that, Daher looked over at al-Dankizli and said, "Safad is yours to do with as you please."

Safad was no easy city. Daher remembered the day he had entered it with lanterns, and as he watched the cannon shells flying overhead, then landing in the city and igniting wildfires, he wished dearly he could have entered it the same way again.

The following evening, a messenger arrived from Istanbul with a letter for Daher. His spies had learned that Uthman Pasha al-Kurji was on his way from Damascus. He had spread word that he was making an annual tax-collecting tour, when in fact his intention was to march on Acre.

Daher had no doubt about the soundness of the report. He knew that Uthman Pasha, who had lost his legal bid for Haifa, would never admit defeat, and had been bound to make a move to take the city back sooner or later. He ordered the shelling to stop, and his army retreated from view. Then he began writing a letter to his sons. In it he asked them to prepare dinner for three, since he wanted to apprise them of a matter of great importance.

Ali and Sa'id had never expected Safad actually to be shelled, thinking all along that their father was bluffing. And once the shelling began, they had despaired of finding a way to escape his siege. Hence, his letter took them entirely by surprise.

Ali felt certain that the most powerful message he could send Daher was his two sons. However, he had used them before, and he suspected that if he sent them again, Daher would take them and write to him, saying, "You'll never see them again. I'm not willing to let them live under the care of a man who has no compunctions about humiliating them whenever he's in a bind!"

Ali's men retreated from the walls and the city gate opened wide. Then al-Hussein rode out on a white horse bearing a spoken message for his grandfather. Daher mounted his horse and rode alongside al-Hussein until the two of them disappeared behind the city walls.

Neither al-Dankizli nor Karim al-Ayyub had agreed with Daher's decision to go alone. However, he had assured them: "If you came with me, whom would they have to reckon with if they thought about doing something shameful? Nothing will happen to me when the two of you are out here!"

Ali reached out to shake his father's hand, fearful that the gesture wouldn't be reciprocated. To his astonishment, however, Daher pulled him forward and wrapped him in an embrace. He did the same with Sa'id. Then he sat down, even before Ali had invited him to have a seat.

They ate in silence. When they'd finished, Daher said, "I've received a letter from Istanbul in which my friends tell me that the truce I was granted by the sultan after the legal ruling awarding Haifa to us was nothing but a ruse. In fact, he's issued a decree calling for me and all my sons to be killed, and for our heads to be brought to him. The task has been assigned to Uthman Pasha, who is on his way here as I speak. He claims that the forces with him are simply coming as part of the tax-collecting tour led by the governor of Damascus every year. So his plan is to take us by surprise."

When they met several hours later in the military camp, they disagreed over how to confront an army of this size, knowing that the entire military force of Damascus was coming out against them.

"If we attacked Uthman Pasha with an army the size of his, it would backfire," said Ali. "Since he claims that he's simply coming out on his annual tax-collecting tour, it would be said that we were the ones who had violated the truce."

"But we can't afford to wait until the winds are blowing our houses down!" Karim objected.

"If we sit here waiting for them, we doom ourselves to perish," said al-Dankizli. Turning to Daher, he said, "We haven't heard your opinion, Sheikh."

"You'll hear it. But I want to hear what everyone else has to say first."

After a lengthy debate, Ali al-Daher said, "I'm asking the sheikh to assign me the task of taking them on singlehandedly. All I need is five hundred of our best soldiers."

Ali's request seemed like pure madness. They were being approached by what was said to be the largest, best-equipped army Damascus had ever mobilized, yet he was asking to be allowed to go out to meet it with a mere five hundred men!

"So be it," Daher replied. "Choose your men, and do what you need to do."

Ali's plan was simple: to advance by night and hide by day until they reached a place where Uthman Pasha's army was encamped on its way to Acre. The last thing Uthman Pasha would ever have expected would be for his camp to be attacked when his men were asleep.

Swift and deadly came the assault by Ali and his soldiers. Panic-stricken, the Turkish soldiers began shouting and firing at each other. Their alarm intensified when one of the soldiers shouted, "Ali al-Daher is attacking you! Ali al-Daher is attacking you!"[39] Then he pointed to a horseman who was leaping from horseback to tent roof to horseback, mowing down everything in his path like the scythe of Fate.

---

39 In *Travels through Syria and Egypt*, Constantin-François Volney tells us that the mere mention of Ali al-Daher's name had a more devastating effect on the Turkish soldiers than his sword did.

On that night rent by screams and gunfire, Ali had no difficulty making his way to the tent of the governor, Uthman Pasha al-Kurji, who had run for his life, leaving both his soldiers and his weapons behind. Once inside the tent, Ali easily located the royal decree his father had spoken of. He looted the governor's dagger and all of his arms: swords, spears, muskets, and artillery. He was about to take the governor's large, sumptuous water pipe, whose metal base was ornamented with three golden lions. But, suddenly recalling his father's dislike for smokers, he kicked it over and left.

A Meeting of Ways

Following his defeat at the hands of Ali al-Daher, Uthman Pasha al-Kurji found himself and his vilayet on the verge of bankruptcy. Hence, he levied new taxes. When people refused to pay them, he called up his forces, not to collect the taxes, but to loot and pillage every city that had refused to pay them. After sweeping through the cities and villages nearest to Damascus, his forces besieged and pillaged Ramla. He marched on Gaza, and when its scholars defied him, he had them buried alive. He then marched on Hebron with the same intent. Upon receiving news of an uprising in Jaffa, he sent out a force to crush it. And so it went. The people of southern Palestine, including the foreigners among them—and the French in particular—found themselves obliged to flee north to Acre, where they would be under Daher's protection.

In view of such developments, Daher realized that he would need another powerful ally in addition to the Matawila and the Shihabis, and he could think of no one more fitting than Ali Bey al-Kabir in Egypt.[40]

As Daher looked for an auspicious way to initiate cooperation with Ali Bey, his minister Ibrahim al-Sabbagh said to him, "I think you'll find

---

40 Born around 1728 CE, Ali Bey (originally named Yusuf ibn Dawud) was a Circassian Mamluk who at the age of thirteen fell into the hands of thieves. After being sold into slavery in Cairo, he changed hands a number of times until he came to work for Ibrahim Bey, chief of the country at that time. When he was eighteen, he was granted manumission by Ibrahim Bey and allowed to marry. In recognition of the extraordinary courage he had demonstrated, Ibrahim Bey appointed him sanjak, and then to the twenty-four-member sanjak council. After Ibrahim Bey was killed, Ali Bey exacted revenge for his master's death, and had a hand in virtually every plot thereafter that aimed to promote, demote, or kill other Mamluks. He masterminded the conspiracy to kill Ridwan Bey, Ibrahim Bey's successor. In 1764, Ali Bey himself became chief of the country and overseer of the pilgrimage caravan to Mecca. At that point he cut off relations with Istanbul, dismissing the Ottoman governor and minting a new coin bearing his own name. In the spring of 1770, he launched an attack on the Hijaz by land and sea, capturing Mecca, Jeddah, and the entire Red Sea coast. He was dubbed Sultan of Egypt and Overlord of Bahrain, and sermons were preached in his name in the mosques.

it in this letter!" He spread before Daher a missive signed by Mikhail Fakhr, Egypt's chief administrative officer.

Daher's features lit up more with every word he read, and when he finished, he looked up at al-Sabbagh with a huge grin on his face. "I can hardly believe my eyes!" he said.

Acre had been receiving reports on Ali Bey al-Kabir's revolt against the sultanate and his refusal to continue paying tribute to the Ottoman Empire, and Daher was gratified to know that he wasn't the only one swimming against the tide.

Shaking his head worriedly, al-Sabbagh said, "You know, Sheikh, the situation in Egypt may be too much for us to handle. No governor, sanjak, or national leader dares turn his back to anyone, since there's always a dagger ready to sink into his vitals!" Then he asked shrewdly, "Do you think you could turn your back to them some day? Whatever they do, they always intend the opposite of what they appear to!"

"No, I couldn't. And I wouldn't. But I need them, Ibrahim!"

"You do as you see fit, Sheikh."

The letter contained a request from Ali Bey to purchase some shields.

"So then," said al-Sabbagh, "if you're inclined to sell some shields, give me some to send to him."

"Slow down, Ibrahim. You're getting ahead of yourself! I want you to write to Mikhail telling him that Sheikh Daher has the shields they want, but that, since he isn't an arms dealer, he would prefer not to sell them to them. Rather, he would be pleased if Ali Bey would accept them as a gift."

In a lavish sitting room furnished with brightly colored cushions and mats, Ali Bey sat listening as his chief administrative officer read the letter from Daher's minister. A rose-colored jewel set into his large turban glittered on his forehead, and he was clad in a long blue robe that opened at the front and a loose white sirwal.

The same scene then repeated itself: his features lit up more with every word he heard, he grinned from ear to ear, and his wispy moustache looked as though it were about to turn into a pair of wings and soar away with him.

"You know, Mikhail," said Ali Bey, "the world is a strange place. We write asking to buy a few shields, and we end up with an ally worth more

than ten thousand shields! Write back to Sheikh Daher and tell him that
I've accepted his gift."

Al-Sabbagh prepared the shields as well as a number of fine horses. He
sent the shields by sea, and the horses overland. On Daher's behalf he
wrote to Ali Bey: "I was quite pleased to learn that you would accept these
seventy-five shields as my gift to you. Allow me also to say how delighted
I am to hear of your victories, with the help of God Almighty, over all
who oppose you. My only request of Your Excellency is that you kindly
allow the person who has delivered the gift to recruit a number of Egypt's
Moroccan fighters, whom we need to ward off an anticipated assault on
our country by Uthman Pasha al-Kurji, governor of Damascus."

The mere mention of Uthman Pasha al-Kurji's name was enough to
rekindle the flames of a hatred that had long seethed in Ali Bey's breast.
His antipathy toward Uthman had begun with their very first encounter
in Mecca, where Ali Bey had been leading the pilgrimage caravan from
Egypt and Uthman Pasha the caravan from Syria. Then, just when
it seemed that the two men's mutual loathing had reached its apex, a
number of Mamluks opposed to Ali Bey fled to Damascus, and Uthman
Pasha refused to send them back, which brought the enmity to the boil-
ing point. However, since he had taken the reins of power in Egypt, Ali
Bey had viewed Damascus as a necessary extension to his own territory,
and everything that had transpired between the two men served as the
perfect pretext for aggression against Uthman Pasha.[41]

"I have received what you sent with the greatest appreciation and affection," Ali Bey replied. "Moreover, I'm aware of the troubles you face
with Uthman Pasha. Hence, your messenger is hereby granted permission to recruit however many Moroccan soldiers he needs to fight by
your side. I will be sending an expeditionary force to your region headed
by my military commander Isma'il Bey, whom I have instructed to obey

---

41   In a letter to the French authorities, the French consul in Sidon once wrote, "There
is a widespread, but groundless, notion that the things being done by Ali Bey and Daher al-Umar are a result of a shared personal antipathy for Uthman Pasha al-Kurji. In
point of fact, the actions of these two rebels are guided by a broader vision, since each
of them takes the same hostile stance toward any pasha who attempts to place obstacles
in the way of his aspirations for independence."

your every command. I want you to know that from this day onward I look upon you as my father, and whoever is your enemy is my enemy!"

As Daher and al-Sabbagh strolled along Acre's beach, al-Sabbagh noticed Daher's bare feet and said, "I'm thinking of walking barefoot like you, Sheikh!"

"Actually," Daher quipped, "that's the very thing I wouldn't want you to do!"

"Why's that?"

"Because I don't want to give you an excuse to be more tightfisted than you already are!"

"Do you really think I'm tightfisted, Sheikh?"

"Does it require any proof?"

"It's just that I love money and appreciate its value. That's all!"

Daher smiled as he watched a wave roll in.

"Let's talk about something else, Ibrahim. This is a subject you wouldn't be honest about even with yourself!"

"In that case, let me ask you a question, Sheikh. Were you afraid I might lose to Mas'ud Bey when I argued our claim to Haifa before the legal council?"

"If you answer my question, I will have answered yours."

"And what is your question, Sheikh?"

"My question is: How did you manage to defeat Mas'ud Bey?"

"It's quite simple, Sheikh: Argumentation is a matter of intelligence, and intelligence is the ability to answer the question your opponent asks you in such a way that you deprive him of the chance to formulate another question!"

A Storm of Beauty and
Phantoms of the Departed

The death of Amira, al-Dankizli's concubine, was the cruelest blow Fate had ever dealt him. It filled his life with a bitterness that settled in his heart, then spread to his limbs, and even to the tips of his fingers and toes. During the wake he went invisible. Then he went into seclusion. Recalling Nafisa's death, Daher could feel al-Dankizli's grief, so he left him alone to wrestle with his sorrows.

When Daher received news that Isma'il Bey had set out from Egypt to reinforce his army in Acre, he couldn't bring himself to share the happy news with al-Dankizli. Just as he feared the plots being hatched from afar, he now feared appearing too overjoyed in al-Dankizli's presence.

On the fourteenth day of al-Dankizli's seclusion, he got up like a soldier who's been called to war. After bathing, he trimmed his moustache and his beard, and called the barber to finish the job. He didn't want anyone to see what a pathetic state he had been in.

However, something he couldn't hide was his alarming thinness. It was as though a knife had passed over his body and sliced off whole layers of flesh. Nor could he conceal his lackluster gaze, his eyes now devoid of the joyful gleam with which Amira had once filled them.

Daher knew that in everyone's heart there dwells the phantom of someone absent, someone lost. He knew there was a type of woman that a man might forget the moment she turned her back. There was a type he might forget within a few days, or months. There was a type he might forget on account of a second woman, a third woman, or a fourth. There was the type a man might forget, not because of someone who had come after her but because of someone who had preceded her. There was a type that could come and rearrange a man's heart completely as though she were the first woman he had ever known. Yet there was also that one woman who, once she had taken up residence in a man's heart, would look on in derision at all other women, none of whom could do more than pass through it as a stranger.

Daher's situation differed little from al-Dankizli's, and perhaps it was this that prompted him to move quickly in search of a woman who could occupy even a tiny fraction of the space that had been occupied by Amira. He sent word to a friend of his in Istanbul, asking him to find the most beautiful concubine he had ever laid eyes on and send her to him as fast as he could. When none arrived, he sent his friend another letter, to which the reply came: "Believe me, Sheikh, I've asked to be shown the most beautiful concubine anyone has ever laid eyes on. But whenever I choose one, I come across another who's even more beautiful. So what am I to do?"

"Open your eyes wider," Daher wrote back. "But be quick about it!"

At midday on August 27, 1770, the boat Daher had been awaiting arrived at last. On board the vessel was a young Georgian woman[42] of indescribable beauty. News of her beauty spread like wildfire throughout Acre and the surrounding territories. The news also reached al-Dankizli, who was curious about just one thing: why Daher hadn't spoken to him about her. In the end he thought: *Maybe she came as an unexpected gift to the sheikh.*

Daher asked his wife Duhqana, who had grown unexpectedly elderly and frail, to take care of the girl. However, he said nothing of what he had in mind. Daher's Circassian concubine—the only one ever to enter their household—had died many years earlier. Seemingly resigned to the presence of a new one, Duhqana instructed her maids to do everything they could to make the young girl comfortable. What pained her wasn't the thought of the girl being in Daher's arms, but the realization that she herself was slipping out of life's arms.

Duhqana asked her what her name was. "Patricia," she replied.

"Why such a difficult name?" Duhqana wondered aloud. Then she dubbed her "Aisha."

Duhqana expected the sheikh to ask about the girl, but he didn't.

"Has Sheikh Daher seen you?" Duhqana asked her. Aisha shook her head.

Even more puzzled now, Duhqana waited. But the most puzzling thing of all was that she herself had begun taking pleasure in Aisha's company. In fact, she'd grown to love her, finding in her a gentleness and grace that she never wanted to see leave the mansion.

---

42 Present-day Georgia, in the Caucasus Mountains.

With red hair, huge, demure, intelligent eyes, a sunny smile that she hid like a bashful little girl, a body as delicate as a breeze, and a moderate height like that of a thoroughbred mare, Aisha had turned the mansion into a little paradise that caused everyone who saw her to forget the beauty of the flowers that filled the garden.

One evening, Duhqana asked her maids to bring an extra bed into her room. When it was time to sleep, she took Aisha by the hand and brought her into her bedroom. Surprised, Aisha held back. However, Duhqana gave her an encouraging smile, and she relented. She brought her over to the bed, pulled back a light cotton blanket made from a white and yellow daisy print, and invited her to lie down. For a second time Aisha hesitated. At last, in response to a tender gesture of Duhqana's hand, she accepted the invitation. After Aisha lay down, Duhqana covered her with the blanket and went back to her own bed.

That night Duhqana slept more peacefully than she had in years. As for Aisha, she wept for joy, muffling her sobs with delicate hands that hadn't been made to still such storms.

The storm that had blown in with Aisha's arrival was stirred up anew. This time, however, it consisted in a rumor to the effect that the beautiful concubine was intended to be the sheikh's gift to al-Dankizli. The truth of the rumor, which had reached al-Dankizli as well, was evidenced by the fact that the sheikh had yet to see her, still less come near her. Angered, al-Dankizli felt that Daher's love for him had become unbearably cruel. After all, by bringing him this concubine, he seemed to be trying to erase the memory of a woman whom Daher knew full well to be unforgettable!

It had been a long time since Amira's death and a long time since Aisha's arrival, and as al-Dankizli grew more sullen by the day, Daher began looking for the right moment to present her to him.

Duhqana had begun feeling that it wasn't time for her to die after all. Meanwhile, al-Dankizli was surprised to find himself becoming interested in Aisha's news. The situation came to a head when he found himself thinking about her one night. He got angry. He cursed. He felt guilty. Nevertheless, the one undeniable fact was that he couldn't sleep a wink.

Suddenly the wind changed course, as reports arriving from Damascus and Egypt augured a different future. There was nothing al-Dankizli needed more than a war. Nothing else would allow him to forget that he was torn between two women, one of whom was enveloped in the past, and one of whom the future had yet to reveal.

A Triumph . . . Like a Tear

Coincidences write the endings to many a story, and in ways one could never have imagined. This, at any rate, was how Ibrahim al-Sabbagh felt as he recalled all the events that had taken place: intersecting, yet somehow not connecting.

Damascus had caught wind of the fact that Isma'il Bey was on his way to fight beside Daher in Acre.

Al-Sabbagh drew a line on the ground representing the progress of Isma'il Bey's forces northward from Egypt, through Gaza, to Ramla. Then he drew another line showing Uthman Pasha al-Kurji's intended route from Damascus to Jaffa, where he planned to meet the approaching Egyptian forces in order to block their advance to Acre. Still another line showed the route to be followed by Bani Saqr's men, now in league with Uthman Pasha, to cut Daher's forces off between Acre and Ramla and thereby prevent them from entering the war alongside the Egyptians.

Daher sent out a military force under the command of his son Uthman. However, when he reached the Maqta' River[43] crossing, Uthman realized that Bani Saqr's men were waiting for him there, and retreated in fright to Acre.

Furious, Daher marched out with a force of his own to wage war on the men of Bani Saqr and force his way through to Ramla. When he got there, however, he found none of Bani Saqr's men, who had withdrawn as soon as they learned that Uthman's forces had fled in terror back to Acre. When Daher and his forces reached the crossing and didn't find Bani Saqr, they continued on their way safely to Ramla.

Casting a glance at the Egyptian forces, Daher was dazzled by their fine organization, their uniforms, and their weapons. The finest of expeditionary campaigns, it consisted of several hundred horsemen fully fitted

---

43 With headwaters flowing out of Mount Faqqu'a northeast of Jenin and Mount Sinai southeast of Nazareth, the Maqta' River snaked through the Plain of Bani Amer and emptied into the Mediterranean Sea north of Haifa.

out with tents, ammunition, powder magazines, carts, camel-borne water-skins, kitchenware, drums, and pipes.

That evening as Daher was meeting with Isma'il Bey—who struck Daher as the gutless, devious type who would ally himself with anyone who issued him an order—a messenger from Uthman Pasha arrived with a letter. In it the governor threatened Isma'il Bey with a crushing defeat and informed him that he would set up camp the following day on Tall al-Fakhar just outside Acre before entering the city to deal Daher the death blow.

The last thing the governor had expected was to receive a response from Daher himself, saying, "I've come to Ramla to spare you the trouble of going all the way to Acre!"

When the governor received the letter Daher had sent him from Ramla, he knew the battle had already been decided in favor of Daher and Isma'il Bey. Hence, he began withdrawing from Jaffa at midnight.

Once they had received news of Uthman Pasha's withdrawal, Daher and Isma'il Bey set out in pursuit of Uthman Pasha and his army, undaunted by the three-hour journey from Ramla to Jaffa. Determined not to allow the governor to escape, Daher had decided to go after him no matter the cost, while the mild late-November weather promised to work in his favor. There thus began the greatest chase scene the country had witnessed for many a year.

Uthman Pasha had set out at top speed and was traveling day and night without a thought for rest or sleep. However, when he reached the village of Qaqun near Tulkarm, he began hearing and seeing the vanguards of the pursuing armies. Looking around in search of some refuge, he decided that his best hope of reaching safety lay in continuing on his way back to Syria. As he went, he began ridding himself of everything that might weigh him down. The cannons being the heaviest of his weapons, he pushed some of them into wells, and abandoned others where they were.

The battle might have ended with a matchless victory, a victory unstained by a single drop of blood. However, hardly had his army stopped pursuing the governor when Daher, now eighty years old, fell ill.

The harsh, night-long bout of illness he had endured in Acre years earlier had been a picnic by comparison with the fever that ravaged him now, finding him an easy prey after eighty years of victories, joys, sorrows, strength, and weakness.

As for Isma'il Bey, he was panic-stricken: a stranger in an unfamiliar land whose newfound ally was fighting a losing battle with a foe that had yet to be defeated: death itself. For some time Isma'il resisted going into Daher's tent, lest he weaken at the sight of him. However, duty prevailed.

On an evening that would have been the ideal time to celebrate the easiest, sweetest victory they could have dared hope for, a black cloud descended over the hearts of everyone encamped on that plain. Isma'il was far from Egypt, and Daher's army was in the heart of territory controlled by the pashas and beys of Nablus, who professed a fierce loyalty to Damascus and its governors.

After the final evening prayer, a number of Daher's men led by Karim al-Ayyub set out hastily on a northwesterly journey to Acre that, short as the distance was, promised to be long and grueling. They reached the city shortly before dawn with a mission that was both highly specific and fraught with danger. Al-Dankizli had given them explicit instructions not to let anyone know what had happened to the sheikh, their only purpose being to bring Daher's minister and physician, Ibrahim al-Sabbagh, back with them.

Ibrahim woke to the sound of gentle knocks on his door. He opened it cautiously to find one of his servants, who informed him that someone had brought him an urgent message from Sheikh Daher. When the men Daher had sent came in, they insisted on speaking with Ibrahim in private. Hence, he sent the servants and the guards out and shut the door.

Less than ten minutes later al-Sabbagh was mounting his horse with difficulty and setting out with them on a lengthy journey. Traveling down the coast, they passed through Haifa, Tira, Atlit, and Tantura. When they were south of Caesarea, they turned eastward and headed for Qaqun, which they reached by midday.

When at last they reached their destination, al-Sabbagh couldn't dismount. His emaciated body worn down by the years, he was so overcome with exhaustion that they had to lift him off the horse. But the moment he saw Daher sprawled out like a corpse resigned to its fate, his body revived somewhat. In fact, his body and spirit were always rejuvenated when he found himself at a patient's bedside. He rolled up his sleeves, about to wage a second battle with death on Daher's behalf.

It was al-Sabbagh's opinion that Daher couldn't be treated in the tent where he lay. Besides, it would be unthinkable for them to stay in Qaqun now that Daher had lost all awareness of those around him. If news of his condition got out, they were certain to be surrounded.

After doing a hurried review of the places Daher could be taken, al-Sabbagh decided that the best location would be Nazareth, since Daher had a mansion there, and since it was much closer than Acre. So, after placing him in a covered wagon fitted out with a bed, the army set out for Nazareth the following morning.

After the fears that had so overwhelmed both him and his soldiers, Isma'il Bey felt at ease in Nazareth. However, his fear for Daher remained unabated. Four days later, Daher's condition remained unchanged despite all of al-Sabbagh's efforts. He realized he was in a race not only with death, but with time as well, and that the best way to guarantee Daher's safety and well-being would be to get him back to Acre as soon as possible.

The Woes of Love and War

O n the way to Acre al-Dankizli thought: *You might be able to treat the woes of war with love, but can you treat the woes of love with war? What's been happening to you?*

As Daher's bed lurched back and forth inside the wagon, an entire era lurched with him, and al-Dankizli lurched beside him, wondering where his ship would set down anchor if some harm came to Daher.

Once this era ends, you'll be stripped of everything you have. Amira is gone, never to return, Daher is gradually slipping away, and before long he'll be gone too!

He knew he was the first person Daher's sons would get rid of. He had never been close to any of them, and he knew they hated him, especially Ali, Uthman, and Sa'id. Hadn't he laid siege to them, chased them down, and waged war on them on Daher's behalf? So what was he to do? *Shall I seek out Islibi's protection in Tiberias and live out my days quietly on the lakeshore?*

Every question he asked opened a door to worse fears.

It's time you got out of here, Ahmad. You've been loyal to Daher throughout his lifetime, but what would it mean for you to be loyal to him when he dies? To die by his side? That wouldn't be loyalty. It would be annihilation! He's given you a great deal. You don't deny that. But what's the use of this "great deal" if it vanishes the moment he's gone? I'm sure the first thing Uthman will do once his father is dead is to seize everything he ever gave you. Then he'll arrest you, throw you into a lightless dungeon, and throw away the key—that is, unless he kills you, mutilates your corpse, and drags it through the streets of Acre as an example to everyone else!

But Ahmad, the sheikh still thinks of you in a way he hasn't thought of even his own sons! Think of the way he stood by you when Amira died. And if it's true that he's brought that beautiful Georgian concubine who's the talk of the town as a gift for you, then it means he thinks of you even more than he thinks of himself, more than he thinks of any of his men or even his own sons. So don't jump to such negative conclusions! Forget all those black thoughts that slip into your hands like pickaxes to dig the sheikh's grave before the time comes!

Karim al-Ayyub came up to him and said, "Since we left Nazareth, I've felt that when I look at you, I don't see you!"

"What do you mean, Karim?"

"It's as if you're somewhere else, somewhere far away!"

"You're right. The sheikh's illness has been hard on me. I've never seen him so frail!"

"I have a feeling that even though the sheikh's flame is flickering at the moment in the wind of this fever, it will shine brightly again. It isn't time for it to go out yet. He's still got lots of oil left in that lantern of his, believe me! As the days go by, you'll see."

"That's what we're all hoping, Karim. Yet we can't help but worry about him when we see him suspended this way between life and death."

"We do worry about him. But that doesn't mean we should dig his grave for him with our fears and anxieties!"

Daher was following their conversation from inside the tent, and Ibrahim al-Sabbagh was standing next to him.

"Are things really that bad, Ibrahim?"

"What's bad about them? By defeating Uthman Pasha, you've managed to annex Jaffa, whose multazim ran away to save his skin. You've also annexed Ramla, Gaza, and the entire Palestinian coast all the way down to the Egyptian border!"

"I mean, things relating to my health."

"Your health? Based on what I just heard Karim say, that lantern of yours is still full of oil! But how do *you* feel?"

"I feel better, and I'll go on feeling that way, God willing. But you know, Ibrahim, it would be hard for me to die now. I know our life spans are in God's hands, but I don't think it would be fitting for me to die of a fever, just like that, especially now that I've lived three times longer than Tarafa ibn al-Abd!"

"The poet Tarafa?"

"It's a story that goes way back. I'll tell it to you sometime."

"I want to hear it down to the last detail! But right now I've got to ask you to obey me and get some rest."

Daher began to cough. When he caught his breath he said, "When we get to Acre, I want you to stop the wagon at Tall al-Fakhar and have them bring me my horse. I'm not entering the city gate in bed!"

"But Sheikh . . ."

"In return for promising to bring me my horse, I'll do what you ask and sleep until we get there. Agreed?"

"Agreed!"

"Now, I have one last request to make before I go to sleep: I want you to lift the edge of the wagon cover so that I can see out. Whenever I pass through this area, I like to stop for a long time and look around."

It was one of the most beautiful areas between Nazareth and Acre.[44]

Daher rode into Acre on horseback at the head of the two victorious armies. He couldn't have allowed himself to do otherwise. He'd thought: *Are you going to enter the capital with a defeated body after a marvelous victory like that?*

But no sooner had he reached the mansion than he felt the knife stabs of the fever lacerating his body anew. More than one hand reached out to help him. However, with a single look he pushed them all away. Najma looked over at al-Dankizli. Misunderstanding what her look meant, he said, "Shall I help the sheikh?"

She shook her head as if to say no. Then she came up to him and asked him a strange question: "Do you have something to say about the oil left in the sheikh's lantern?"

He started with alarm. "Who, me? No, no!" Then he stopped in his tracks as Daher continued on his way to his room, followed by Najma, Duhqana, al-Sabbagh, and Karim al-Ayyub.

Winter approached with cold and storms. The sea raged, lightning struck the earth with flaming swords, and the sky poured down rain more copious than they had seen for many a year.

But there was nothing better than rain for extinguishing the flames of war. When rain fell, armies vanished, which was the very thing Daher needed most in his time of infirmity.

---

44 On page 210 of *Rihlat fi al-Urdun wa-Filastin*, Sulayman al-Musa quotes travel writer William H. Dickson as having described the area as follows: "Everything grows here. Every hill is a vineyard, every valley a field of grain, the rays of the sun mingling with refreshing rains! At every turn one encounters sights reminiscent of those found in Germany, Italy, and Spain. The hills garbed in grapevines laden with white and purple fruits bring to mind what one might see in the Rhine Valley. In short, it is a place that will transport the European back to his homeland!"

On the first day of the new year, Najma woke to find him standing at her head. "Are you still asleep? Come with me! I'm so hungry I could eat a bear. Where's Jum'a?"

"Sit down, Sheikh. Sit down. I'll prepare the food for you myself this time!"

"What, doesn't Jum'a do it?"

Najma hesitated. However, realizing he would have to know eventually, she replied, "Jum'a died, Sheikh. He died!"

"Why didn't you all tell me? And how did he die? He was the picture of health the day I got back to Acre!"

"He was murdered, Sheikh. A few days after you got home, we found him dead in his room."

"But who would stand to gain from killing Jum'a?"

"That's what we don't know. Your doctor says he was forced to take poison. That's why, ever since that day, I haven't let anyone else prepare your food."

Holding his head in his tired hands, Daher began recalling the faces of all the people who came in and out of the mansion, and to his dismay the only face that remained in his mind's eye was that of his son Uthman.

Raging Seas

The waves that pounded Acre's shores in February of that year were the highest the city had ever seen. Roaring like a monster in chains, the sea rushed toward the city with all its might, and it was said that if it hadn't been for its high walls, the water would have swallowed up everything in it.

It wasn't the sea alone that was raging with such violence. Many an inward storm was raging as well.

Uthman al-Daher had disappeared. Reports arrived saying that he had sought refuge in the Druze Mountains. When he received a letter from his father demanding his return to Acre, he wrote back saying, "How can I show you my face after the way I came back in disgrace from the river crossing?"

Shaking his head, Daher mused, "He wants to conceal his shamelessness by claiming to be ashamed of himself!"

As for al-Dankizli, time had given him a new lease on life with Daher's recovery, and the color had returned to his cheeks.

"We'll go out to check on affairs in Acre today," Daher said to him. Glancing at Daher as they walked side by side, al-Dankizli thought: *Whoever sees him would swear he isn't a day over sixty!*

"You know, Ahmad, I feel as though I was sick for forty years, not just forty days!"

The word "forty" swept al-Dankizli's heart away to another place and time—to the day they had first met. However, Daher brought him back to the present when he said, "I've got a surprise for you!"

When al-Dankizli didn't ask what it was, Daher took offense at his seeming indifference. Little did he know that in a few hours' time he would be thanking his lucky stars that al-Dankizli hadn't asked!

When they reached the Krayyim Bridge, Daher looked behind him and saw his fortress in a way he had never seen it before. Its stones were robed in a new, different hue, and the sound of life filled the air with an extraordinary ruckus as though the entire city had turned into a marketplace. They came down from the tower and walked along the wall until they came to the broad street leading to Khan al-Ifranj. After circling the caravansary, they headed north to the market. On their way there, Daher stopped and pondered a spacious plot of land before him. "I think we should build a new caravansary here beside the landward gate," he commented.

"If you ask my opinion, Sheikh, I think we should build one on the plot next to the seaward gate, since merchants and sailors often need that sort of accommodation."

"If that's what you think, then we could build one in each of the two locations!"

They made the rounds of the marketplace, which, as soon as the vendors and market goers saw Daher among them, turned into a festival grounds, with every shopkeeper shaking his hand and inviting him inside. As always, he made a special point of visiting Jurays.

"How are you, Jurays? And how is your family?"

"We're well, Sheikh, thanks be to God."

Sidling up to Daher, Jurays whispered, "We'd be delighted if you came to our house, Sheikh. This Sunday my wife and I will have been married for fifty years!"

"I'll be there!" Daher whispered back to a beaming Jurays.

From the marketplace, Daher and al-Dankizli headed back to the fortress. Gazing up at the morning sky, Daher was sure he couldn't have chosen a better day for a tour like this.

Suddenly he halted on a side street, where people were pushing and shoving for a chance to kiss a certain man's hands in hopes of receiving a blessing. The man was standing in the street stark naked. His presence seemed to have made people oblivious to everything around them, and several men passed Daher with blissful looks on their faces.

"What's going on over there?" Daher asked one of the men.

"That's a saint, Sheikh!"

Daher gestured to his soldiers to bring the naked man and follow him. Then he turned to go back to the mansion. When he got there, he called for his minister, Ibrahim al-Sabbagh, the judge, the imam, and a number of the city's notables. Once they had all gathered, he called for the naked man to be brought before them.

The man came in, full of himself and seemingly heedless of everything. As he was about to sit down, Daher asked him to remain standing. The man appeared a bit muddled, which he attempted to conceal by reciting some verses from the Qur'an.

Gesturing for him to stop, Daher said, "You know the Qur'an quite well. Or am I mistaken?"

"That's right, Sheikh. I know it well."

"I'm relieved to hear that, since I had wanted to ask you something, but wasn't sure whether I ought to."

"Ask whatever you'd like, Sheikh."

"I'd like you to tell me, if you would: In which chapter of the Qur'an or saying of the Prophet are we told that God Almighty permits people to walk through the marketplace with their private parts showing?"

The judge intervened here, saying, "I'll answer you for him, Sheikh! There's no such allowance in either the Qur'an or the sayings of the Prophet. However, you're addressing your question to a majdhub—a saint who's so absorbed in the divine presence that he's lost his senses!"

Leaning over to the judge, Daher whispered, "Does a person like this know what happened yesterday or what might happen tomorrow?"

"No, Sheikh," the judge replied.

"We're in agreement, then."

Daher stood up. Then, with lightning speed he drew his sword, grabbed the man by his shoulder, and pulled him forcefully toward him. "I swear to God, man, if you don't answer me truthfully, I'll cut off your head! Now tell me: What day was yesterday?"

"Thursday!"

"And what day will tomorrow be?"

"Saturday."

Turning to the judge, Daher asked, "Would a majdhub know these things?"

"No," said the judge, shaking his head.

"Why do you demean yourself this way?" Daher asked the naked man.

"I do it out of need, Sheikh. I swear to God, if I weren't needy, I wouldn't do this!"

"Take him and give him something to cover himself with. But don't let him leave. I need to have a few more words with him."

The naked man stumbled away.

465

"It seems to me, Ibrahim, that the alms we distribute to the people aren't solving their problems."

"What do you think we should do, Sheikh?"

"I want you to send someone out to take a census of the poor in Acre, Muslims and Christians alike. Their names should be taken down, and at the end of every month they should be given whatever amount they need. Then any of them seen begging will be flogged. As for this man, give him what he needs to live until the end of the month, and inform him of the instructions I just issued."

Daher had been planning to present al-Dankizli with his gift later that day.

As al-Dankizli left the mansion, Daher asked him, "Can I visit you this evening?"

"My house is your house, Sheikh. You're welcome any time."

Unseen Streams

A l-Dankizli stared into the mirror and saw another man, someone other than himself. He wished he could take his sword, stab him a thousand times, and be rid of him once and for all.

How you've changed, Ahmad! Are you the one standing here? Or are you the one lurking there in the mirror? One minute all you care about is to be free of Daher, and the next minute there's nothing you want more than to be by his side! One minute you cling to Amira's memory as though you were holding her hand in bed and refusing to let her be away from you for a single moment, and the next minute you're so carried away by rumors about a certain concubine that she's all you can think about! So where are you? Do you want to stand with Daher, or to get away from him? Do you want to be true to Amira, or will you forget her the minute some other woman comes along? And if the latter, then why were you faithful to her all those years?

He looked around. His large house stood empty. Gone were the high beds covered with crimson, yellow, and purple spreads, the tables and chairs, the carpets, the copperware, and the ceramic vases large and small brought from India, Istanbul, China, and elsewhere. To his dismay, he noticed that even the walls had lost their distinctiveness now that the designs that once ornamented them had been erased and the swords that had once hung on them had disappeared. Even the arches over the doorways had begun to sag.

He shook his head as if he thought he might be dreaming. But nothing changed.

Seated on an oaken chaise lounge whose back was ornamented with delicate palm trees, birds, and the gracefully shaped glasses decorated with Arabic calligraphy, Daher asked one of his servants to call his wife Duhqana. His mood was mellow, one of the mellowest he'd experienced in years. He turned toward the window, resting his left hand on the edge of the couch. The sea was calm, and the breeze flowed in through the western window toward the open door behind him like an unseen stream.

He filled his chest to capacity with the biggest breath he could take in. Then he held the air in his lungs for as long as he could before letting it out again. Just as he was about to take another deep breath, he heard the sound of footsteps. He turned and saw Duhqana standing in the doorway. He patted the seat, inviting her to sit next to him.

When she sat down, he was surprised to see her looking despondent. "I've never seen you so sad before!" he exclaimed. "It's as if you still didn't know that I'm not sick any more!"

"I do know that, Sheikh, and nothing could make me happier!"

"But all I can see in your face is sadness."

"It's because I know what's on your mind. Tell me honestly: aren't you thinking of sending Aisha to al-Dankizli today?"

"How did you know that?"

"Sheikh, if I have any place in your heart, I beg you to keep her in this house. I can't do without her any more!"

"But that won't be possible, Duhqana."

"Look at me, Sheikh. Never in my life have I asked you for anything. Try to remember a single time when I've asked you for anything I wanted. Don't break my heart now that I'm making my first and last request of you!"

Daher bowed his head and turned back toward the sea.

"Besides, Sheikh, you have to see her. I swear to God, you're more worthy of her than anyone else!"

"Do you want her to be mine, Duhqana?"

"Let her become your concubine, Sheikh, if that's what it will take to keep her here!" Suddenly she called out, "Come in, Aisha!"

Aisha was standing outside the door in the long corridor, waiting for Duhqana's signal.

Before she came in, Daher's heart fluttered. He realized that his wife was putting him to a test whose outcome she must have known beforehand. When Aisha came through the door, a line of poetry by Abd al-Khal al-Dimashqi flashed through his mind, and for a moment it nearly leapt to his tongue:

Is your body made from drops of rain, or is it purer still?
Indeed, one's eyes could almost drink it in!

Captivated by her beauty, Daher's eyes froze on her face. Turning to him, Duhqana said, "Don't break my heart by sending her away unless she herself wants to leave!"

"What?"

"I said, 'Don't break my heart by sending her away unless she herself wants to leave.'"

"I didn't bring her here in order for her to say what she does or doesn't want."

"Sheikh, you're a God-fearing man. And we know that you only took control over Acre, Haifa, Nazareth, and other cities for one reason: to preserve people's dignity, to protect their rights, and to prevent them from being enslaved."

"You're killing me with these words of yours, Duhqana. After all I've done, I don't need someone to remind me of what I've lived my entire life for as though I'd forgotten!"

"It's up to you then, Sheikh. I've said all I have to say."

Daher lifted his gaze and looked at Aisha again. He studied her from head to toe, and to his amazement his heart began pounding in a way it hadn't done for a very long time.

"And what will I say to al-Dankizli now that I've told him I'll be visiting him this evening? I even told him about a present I was going to bring him!"

"You could give him the whole world, Sheikh, as far as I'm concerned. But when it comes to Aisha . . ."

"I understand! I understand!" he interrupted, turning away from the angelic face across the room and staring back at the sea.

Duhqana waited for him to say something. However, he wasn't just looking at the sea. He was riding it to some distant destination. When he'd returned from his imaginary journey, he turned back toward Aisha and asked her, "Do you want to stay in this house, Aisha?"

"That all I want!"

"That's all?" He shook his head, trying to fathom the distance between his promise to al-Dankizli and his entangled emotions. "You may go now!"

Daher watched her as she turned to leave. She made him think of an enchanted gazelle out of a fairy tale. As though it were following her, a gentle breeze blew in the window toward the door, causing locks of her hair to float out in front of her before settling back over her shoulders.

At that moment Daher realized that he wasn't looking at a beautiful woman, but at beauty itself.

One of al-Dankizli's guards came to speak to him, and found him standing in front of the mirror.

"Sire," he said, "Sheikh Daher is coming to visit you, and we've been informed that he'll arrive shortly."

Al-Dankizli nodded. "I'm coming," he replied as he cast a final glance at the man cowering inside the mirror.

When he moved, the man in the mirror moved too, and as he started to walk away, he suddenly turned, gripped by the sense that the other man was following him.

When he reached the gate, he took a deep breath and stood there waiting.

Within moments he saw Daher approaching. But to his bewildered surprise, no one was with him but his guards on horseback.

His heart sank. When he looked into Daher's face, he felt as though the man had grown ten years younger since noon, and if he hadn't known better he would have sworn he wasn't a day over fifty! His heart—the same heart that had rejoiced that morning when he saw Daher looking only sixty—sank even more. As for Daher, he was doing his best to master his conflicting emotions. As he might have expected, he felt both joyful and sorrowful, strong and weak, loyal and traitorous. But what he hadn't expected was the sudden feeling that he was at least thirty years shy of eighty.

He took al-Dankizli aside and, without further ado, told him everything that had happened. He related to him how Duhqana had told him that she couldn't bear to part with Aisha, and how she'd begged him not to send her away. He talked about how this was the first request she had ever made of him, so that . . .

"It's all right, Sheikh," al-Dankizli interrupted. "After all, she *is* the mother of your children. Besides, I can't imagine having another woman in my house after Amira. Have you forgotten that I married on her account, and then divorced on her account?"

"I haven't forgotten. But you have the right to know what happened, Ahmad."

"And now I do know, Sheikh. So I'm telling you again: now that Amira is gone, no other woman would ever enter this house, even if she came as a gift from you!"

"So, you would have embarrassed me by refusing to accept her?"

"Al-Dankizli would rather die than refuse a gift from you!"

"You're confusing me, Ahmad!"

"Just as you would have confused me if you'd brought her!"

Al-Dankizli's features remained steady as though he were facing a skilled opponent on a battlefield. However, it was no secret to Daher that whatever words al-Dankizli might be uttering, his feelings were another matter entirely. When people are determined to appear stronger than they really are, their weakness becomes all the more apparent.

At that moment Daher sensed that he'd let al-Dankizli down. But it was too late to go back on his decision.

The Sleeping Child

If young love can kill you, there's no elixir more magical or life-giving than love in old age! This, at any rate, was what Daher found himself thinking as he recalled Aisha's face, a face he had seen but once.

Lord! Imagine what that face might do for me if I could feast my eyes on it morning and night!

Daher wasn't such an old man, either in his own eyes or in others'. He could still stay in the saddle for twenty hours at a stretch, and though his sons had all lost half their teeth, he hadn't lost a single one of his, which may have been why he loved to smile so much.

All this notwithstanding, he couldn't erase the enormous age difference between himself and Aisha when he imagined her in his arms. It was a difference that loomed large in his mind, refusing to be confined to the dark corners to which it had been relegated. He realized that it wasn't considered shameful for an elderly man to marry a young girl, or for a young concubine to be nestled under an old man's blankets. Even so, he tried to suppress his longing to see her again. Whenever desire pushed him a step in her direction, something would prompt him to take a step back.

Things might have gone on this way indefinitely. However, beauty is a force to be reckoned with, and nothing on earth can match its sway.

Again he resisted.

As Duhqana watched him, she saw in him a peculiar mixture of old age and youth. A certain unmistakable spring could be seen in his step, and roses she had never seen before had bloomed in his cheeks.

Duhqana was so grateful to Daher she would have done anything for him. As for Aisha, who had once lived in constant fear of being sent away never to return, she now flitted from one room of the mansion to another like a butterfly that delighted the hearts of everyone who saw her. Within a week of her arrival, everyone felt as though she'd lived in the mansion since the day it was built—nay, as though the mansion existed for her sake alone!

Surrounded by Jurays's wife, children, and grandchildren, Daher sat contemplating Jurays's lovely stone house with its arched doorways and the colorful lantern that turned its walls into works of art.

"So why do you keep us waiting for the party to begin?" Daher wanted to know.

"Because we don't want you to leave our house, Sheikh!"

"Let's get started."

Jurays's wife left the room, and came back carrying a tray filled with glasses of orange juice and a single large glass of wine.

She served the orange juice to Daher and her grandchildren. Then, setting the glass of wine before her, she removed her ring, wiped it with a damp cloth, and placed it inside the glass. Jurays did the same. He lifted the glass and, looking at his sons, daughters, and grandchildren, said, "May the Lord shower you with love as He has showered your mother and me. And may happiness flow into your hearts with every sip of this wine, which embraces my heart, your mother's heart, and the sacred pact we've made to love one another, sacrifice for one another, care for one another, and be faithful to one another."

Then he took a sip.

Jurays passed the glass to his wife, who also took a sip. The glass made the rounds of their sons and daughters until, at last, it returned empty to their mother. She took her ring out of the glass, dried it off, and placed it back on her left ring finger. Then she handed the glass to her husband, who did as she had done.

The whole house had turned into a holy sanctuary.

Daher, more touched by the event this time than he had been on any of the previous occasions, took his glass of orange juice and sipped it unhurriedly, taking in their faces and their children's smiles with his gaze.

Suddenly he said, "I almost forgot your present!" He reached into his cloak and pulled it out.

Najma came in and found him sitting on his chaise lounge. There was a nip in the air, but the window was wide open and the sound of the sea was so powerful you would have thought it was inside the room.

She came and sat down beside him, and only then did he see her.

"I didn't hear you come in."

473

"How would you, with me barefoot and the sea roaring in your ear?"

"You know what, Mother? If I were in Haifa, I'd climb Mount Carmel right now!"

"But unless they told me your father was coming back tomorrow—a miracle that isn't going to happen—I wouldn't climb it with you!"

"There's something you want to say, and I think I know what it is."

They heard steps approaching and turned toward the door. It was Duhqana. She stepped into the room. Then suddenly she looked behind her and took a step back. She disappeared for a moment, and when she reappeared she was nudging Aisha gently forward, saying, "Don't be shy. It's Sheikh Daher!"

Once again Daher found himself under the sway of that overpowering beauty. He tried to avert his gaze, but some strange force prevented him. He found himself staring at her, incredulous that such beauty existed on earth. The lanterns that hung on the walls of the room began shining more and more brightly. In so doing they exposed his secret, which went quickly in search of a place to hide. However, the only place it found was those captivating honey-colored eyes. He found refuge nowhere but in the very thing from which he was trying to escape.

Najma got up quietly and left the room, and Duhqana followed her, as if they didn't want to wake a sleeping child. When at last he managed to take his eyes off Aisha, Daher discovered that they were gone. His secret had been more obvious than he realized!

Aisha took three steps toward him and sat down on a brocaded rug. It was one of a number of rugs that Isma'il Bey had brought from Egypt as gifts for Daher. He sat there gazing at her for an hour or more, unable to say a word. He had discovered to his astonishment that love is the sultan of sultans, and that the heart is nothing but a small boat that's cast its crew overboard and surrendered itself to the crashing waves.

Long ago, before there were people on earth, virtues and vices roamed the world together. One day, to relieve their boredom, Madness suggested that they play a game. He called it hide-and-go-seek. You know it, right? . . .

The call to the final evening prayer, coming from the Hanging Mosque, filled the air, and only then did Daher realize that Heaven was extending him a helping hand.

"Go now and get some rest, Aisha," he said to her.

Like a little girl whose feelings have been hurt, she rose and headed for the door. As she was about to leave, she turned and said sweetly, "Hope you good night, Sheikh!"

He smiled at her. "And a good night to you, Aisha."

After praying the final evening prayer, Daher dismissed his guards. Then he went alone to the seashore, took off his shoes, and tucked the edge of his robe into his sash. The air was cold and the wetness of the sand bothered him at first. Within a few minutes, however, he'd forgotten about it. When he reached that state where he couldn't remember whether he had feet or not, everything changed, and he was flooded with a peculiar but delightful sense that, like the sea, the wind, the sand, and the dawn, Aisha had taken up permanent residence inside him.

From that moment onward, Daher knew that all he wanted was for Aisha to be in his life. She could be a wife, a daughter, a concubine—it made no difference. She could be whatever she wanted to be, like a bird on a windowsill that fills the house with its song, yet without relinquishing its freedom.

Shortly before dawn he came back to the mansion and found Najma awake.

"I expected you to follow me down to the shore."

"That would have been difficult. On this particular night, the shore wouldn't have been divisible by two!"

"You know, Mother, there are things that take hold of you not with their own hands, but with the hands of Destiny! I'm going to sleep for a while, and later in the morning we'll have breakfast together."

Najma nodded, noticing that Daher had changed his breakfast time for the first time in his life.

Later that morning they gathered around a low table for breakfast. Duhqana looked around. "Where's Aisha?" she asked. "Why isn't she here yet?"

They called her.

Duhqana quickly made room for Aisha between herself and her husband. Not long afterward she began surreptitiously moving closer to Aisha and nudging her in Daher's direction.

When Aisha came in contact with him, a delicious rush went through him. After they'd begun eating, Karim al-Ayyub came in with a letter for Daher. He took it and read it. Suddenly he got up and asked Karim to follow him.

A Thick Trail of Blood

Daher didn't know whether the letter Karim brought had come at the best time or the worst. He was about to tell him, "Go, and I'll follow you." But instead he said, with some effort, "We'll go together!"

"Where?"

"To al-Dankizli's house."

"To al-Dankizli's house?" Karim asked, surprised.

"Yes! That's where we'll meet. Send for Isma'il Bey and our minister, Ibrahim al-Sabbagh, and have them follow us there."

Daher's arrival at al-Dankizli's house that morning came as a surprise. Daher embraced him. Then, in an attempt to overcome the awkwardness of the moment, he said, "I couldn't think of a better place than your house for this particular meeting!"

Al-Dankizli looked strangely wan, and when he saw Isma'il Bey approaching, he knew that the moments to come would bring even more surprises.

"I wanted the meeting to be here, since it's the best place to discuss our next step. As Isma'il Bey knows, this letter is from Ali Bey, who is sending a force under command of his minister and his son, Muhammad Abu al-Dhahab. The plan is then for all of us together to march on Damascus."

The mere mention of Damascus was enough to spark everyone's attention.

"Damascus?" al-Dankizli asked, not believing his ears.

"Yes," Daher replied. "Our only real problem is the army made up of the aghas and beys of Nablus.[45] The minute it receives news that the Egyptian army is approaching, Damascus will mobilize them the way it did the multazim of Jaffa to intercept Isma'il Bey's forces in Ramla."

---

45 The Ottoman state had dubbed the Nablus-based al-Nimr and al-Tuqan clans "aghas" and "beys," respectively.

"But the Nablus army is powerful, Sheikh."

"I know that, Ahmad. That's why, if we aren't able to reach Nablus, Abu al-Dhahab won't be able to get here, and if Abu al-Dhahab can't get here we won't get to Damascus."

"But . . . Damascus?" Ahmad asked again.

"We've been more than patient. We've endured and resisted the empire's assaults on us for long enough, and the time has come for us to turn the tables once and for all by breaking the power of the governors of Damascus."

When Daher woke, he found Aisha waiting for him with that smile of hers, which was so huge a sun could have passed through it. It was as if she hadn't slept a wink.

"What got you up so early, Aisha?"

"I don't like you go without I see you, Sheikh. And I make your breakfasts!"

"You?"

"Me, Sheikh. Or Sheikh think my food like my words, not good?"

"If your food is like your words, then it's the best food in the world. But I'll pray first."

When Daher came back after praying, he found her where she had been before.

Aisha set the food before him, the same food he had every morning. Then she stood nearby, waiting anxiously to see whether he would like it or not.

"Why are you standing? Have a seat!" He patted the cushion, inviting her to sit down.

She hesitated slightly, and he patted the cushion again. Before she sat down, he said to her, "Sit there, across from me! I like that bright face to be right in front of me. Beauty inspires victory!"

She sat down.

"Why aren't you eating?" he asked.

She looked behind her as though she thought he must be talking to someone else. When she found no one there, she asked, "Me, Sheikh? Me?"

"Yes, you, Aisha. You!"

She reached out hesitantly, and as she placed the first bite in her mouth, Daher leaned back against the wall, looking at her and saying, "Praise be to You for Your wonders, O Lord!"

Ibrahim Agha al-Nimr, multazim of Jerusalem, arrived unexpectedly to see Qasim al-Nimr, multazim of Nablus, with news of Daher al-Umar's approach. In no time, huge numbers of forces were called up to defend the city and repair its walls and gates. The Nimr family was assigned the task of defending the city's eastern section, and the Tuqan family its western section. By the time Daher arrived, the city was ringed by twelve thousand muskets.

Daher reached the foot of Mount Ebal in early April. Because of the cannons and other heavy equipment he had brought with him, it had been a grueling journey whose hardships weren't alleviated even by the spring flowers that blanketed the plains and mountains. He sent a message to the townspeople, who were now at the mercy of his cannons, saying that unless they surrendered Mustafa Bey Tuqan, who had intercepted Isma'il Bey in Ramla, he would bombard the city until he had brought it down on their heads. He knew he was asking for the impossible.

Nevertheless, the response wasn't long in coming. Before sundown that day, he was approached by Ahmad Bey Tuqan, Mustafa's brother. He was laden with gifts, his only request being that Daher send a delegation to negotiate. Daher agreed with a readiness that amazed Isma'il Bey, al-Dankizli, and the other army commanders.

As he watched Ahmad Bey Tuqan going back to the city, he said to them, "What you can achieve through peace, don't go to war over!" And they appeared satisfied.

Having seen with their own eyes the army that stood poised to attack the city, the people of Nablus were delighted over Daher's willingness to negotiate, and no sooner had the sun set than lanterns began illumining the balconies that they'd been accustomed to see darkened.

"Would he really send a delegation to negotiate when he has forces like those at his disposal?" they wondered. Nevertheless, the people's misgivings vanished when they saw a group of horsemen approaching the city gate.

Daher chose Karim al-Ayyub and Sheikh Nasif, chief of the Matawila, to head a delegation that would be escorted by sixty horsemen.

When the city gates opened, the delegation was surprised to find Nablus's armed men lined up in four long rows, from the city's eastern gate to the eastern caravansary, and from the caravansary gate to the door of Mustafa Bey Tuqan's house. In the house's spacious courtyard and on its roof stood more than a thousand men armed with muskets.

Nonetheless, the reception they were given was heartfelt and warm.

Karim realized that this show of strength was a message from Nablus that no messenger could possibly have conveyed, since those to whom it was addressed could only receive it by viewing the spectacle with their own eyes. However, he wasn't shaken, and after they had eaten lunch in the garden with the aghas, the beys, and the city's notables, he rose readily to his feet and informed them of Daher's conditions.

"Sheikh Daher's first condition is that Nablus turn over its arms," Karim announced. "And his second condition is that Ahmad Bey and Mustafa Bey come out to meet him so that he can clothe them with animal pelts. He intends to appoint the former multazim over Jerusalem, and the latter multazim over Nablus." It was the prevailing custom for the governor to appoint a new multazim by placing an animal pelt around him, and for the multazim to reciprocate by presenting a gift to the governor.

"We'll never hand over our arms," Mustafa Bey retorted. "And we won't go out to receive Daher's blessing and be appointed multazims on orders from Acre. We were appointed by Damascus!"

"Besides," added Ahmad Bey Tuqan, "who's to guarantee that he would actually appoint us? Or that we'd come back to Nablus alive after meeting with him?"

On their way back to their camp at Karm al-Qadi, Karim and the horsemen with him had to pass once again in front of ominous-looking gun barrels. However, hope of an agreement hadn't been lost entirely, since the Nablusites promised to study the matter and send him a response that evening.

"They're just stalling for time," Daher remarked. "But I'll wait, since it would be a shame for anyone to die on a beautiful day like this."

Sundown's approach had garbed Nablus in a copper hue. The color of the grass and the wildflowers had changed and, with the almond, pomegranate, and fig trees that filled its valley, the city looked like an earthly paradise nestled between Mount Ebal and Mount Gerizim.

In the distance several riders could be seen approaching. At their head was Ahmad Tuqan, flanked by two thoroughbred horses he had brought as a gift. Daher cast a quick glance at the two horses and thanked him. Then he fell silent.

Ahmad Bey Tuqan realized that the time had come for him to speak. He repeated every word that had been spoken to Karim. Then he added, "We haven't reached any further agreement, Sheikh. And we informed your messenger of this."

Daher replied, "Why do you come to tell me something I already know? Do you want me to bring Nablus down on your heads? That's what I'll do!"

Feeling as though he had walked into a trap, Ahmad Tuqan bowed his head in thought. When he looked up again, he said, "This isn't what any of us would want, Sheikh. Let me speak with them one more time, and I promise to bring my brother Mustafa to you. All we want is to be like your own family!"

No sooner had Ahmad Tuqan reached the city gate than he turned his horse, giving a signal to charge. The attack came as no surprise, however, since everyone in Daher's camp could see Nablus as clearly as the back of his hand.

The battle was over quickly, and by nightfall the attackers had fortified themselves in the city again.

"That's the last time we let them come out to us," Daher said.

The sun opened its eyes the next morning to a full-blown assault on the city gate. However, those defending it were able to repel the attackers. The men of Nablus cheered at the sight of Daher's retreat. His forces regrouped and attacked again, and by the time the sun had closed its eyes that evening, Daher had launched seven attacks, yet without being able to enter the city.

As calm returned to the valley and the foothills on either side, everyone anticipated the next storm. But none came. Daher appeared to be planning to place the city under siege. Instead, however, he moved his cannons in secret to the village of Rafidiya. Under their hellish fire his vanguard horsemen charged toward the city. They kept advancing until they reached the walls of the Hadra Mosque and the surrounding orchards.

There's no better place for a pitched battle than a graveyard, and amid the tombstones of Zarikiya—Nablus's western cemetery—death could read its name clearly, having been engraved by swords and muskets on the bodies of so many. Shortly before midday, Daher ordered his soldiers to retreat to Karm al-Qadi.

Attackers and defenders alike then regrouped and counted their dead, to find that they had suffered significant losses.

When Daher's messenger approached the city gate again in the late afternoon, the gate swung quickly open. Daher had requested that they send a legal expert to negotiate with him, so the men of Nablus had gathered for a hurried consultation. Sheikh Lutfi, who enjoyed the affection of beys, aghas, and commoners alike, came out to Daher's camp and, after lengthy negotiations that lasted until midnight, the two sides reached a truce agreement according to which Daher would withdraw his forces in return for a promise from the men of Nablus not to attack or pursue either him or his allies.

As Daher set out in late April on the return journey to Acre, he was dismayed to find that spring had already turned to a summer blaze, and that a scorching sun had robbed the month of its usual balmy verdure.

Uthman al-Daher had been following events from a distance. As soon as he was assured that his father had reached Acre, he jumped on his horse and headed for Nablus, where he was received hospitably by Mustafa Tuqan and declared his indignation over everything his father was doing.

The following April's flowers had yet to bloom when news arrived that Nablus had risen up again. However, much had changed since the previous spring, which was linked to the present one by a thick trail of blood.

On Wars and States of the Heart

As Daher crossed the mansion threshold, he thought: *There's no better reason to end a war than to come home alive to a beloved woman!*

Then, to both Najma's and Duhqana's surprise, the first question he asked was, "Where is Aisha?"

The two women were about to exchange catty glances. However, Duhqana was feeling too frail for such things.

"Are you feeling all right?" Daher asked her.

"I couldn't be better now that you're home safe!"

Throughout the journey to Nablus and back, he wondered: *What if the soldiers could read what's in this heart of mine?* He tensed up. Then he smiled as he thought of another way to word the question: *Or what if I could read what's in the hearts of these soldiers and their commanders?*

As Daher looked out over his troops, he glimpsed hearts illumined by the presence of a woman, hearts anxious to be reunited with a woman, and hearts darkened from having had to part with a woman. As for the men whose hearts were empty, their heads were so devoid of light that he couldn't even see them.

It made him happy to realize that both his heart and his head were illumined by a butterfly whose translucent glow was as bright as a thousand lanterns.

"There you go thinking about lanterns again! Did your lantern really go out that day long ago? Or was it hiding its light, saving it up so that you could see all you've seen and experience all you've experienced?"

"Who knows?"

"Do you want her because you love her? Or do you want her because you'd like to see the world reward you with her? After all, you're proud of what you've accomplished in your life thus far, aren't you? Don't deny it! Or is that, in spite of all the years you've lived and the years you have left—of which there aren't many—you want to reward yourself with her? Don't deny it! Or is it that you want her to be the sweet farewell that you feel a greater and greater need for with every sun that sets?"

"You ask questions like this because you want to drive away the answers that you know. Isn't that so?"

"Who knows?"

"If that's the case, then leave it to her to decide what she wants rather than imposing what you want."

"But in spite of all the freedom you've given her to decide, she isn't really free, Daher! And perhaps you've only given her this freedom so that she can choose you! Isn't that so?"

"Who knows?"

"You're everything now, Daher: a thousand states in one, and one state spread out over a thousand. Do you think she's thought about your return? Do you think she's been waiting for you the way Najma and Duhqana have been?"

"Who knows?"

"Get away from her, Daher. All these questions are nothing but an excuse to get close to her. Isn't that so?"

"Who knows?"

"Let's turn the question around and ask: What if she ran away from you? What if she tried to avoid you? Would it anger you?"

". . ."

"I see you've gone quiet!"

"That's because she's come! Don't you see her?"

"What presents does a man bring his family when he comes home from battle?" Najma asked him when he apologized for not having brought her anything. Then she added, "What present could be better than for you to come back to us alive and victorious, Sheikh?"

"Well, Mother, sometimes that isn't enough!"

Aisha walked in.

"Do you suppose she's become bolder, or more bashful?"

"Who knows?"

"How are you, Aisha?"

"Fine, Sheikh, thanks be to God. I hope you're fine as well!"

"Your language is getting better fast, Aisha," he said, and smiled.

"She's rehearsed what she just said nearly a thousand times!" Duhqana told him.

"Is that right, Aisha?"

"Sheikh, right!"

Daher laughed with all his heart.

They expected him to eat and go to sleep. Instead, he told his guards to get ready to go out, because he had a yen to tour Acre.

When he returned less than two hours later, the sun had begun to set, and there was a slight dampness in the air.

He spent the rest of his evening reading correspondence that had been grouped into three piles: most important, important, and less important.

When he was about to doze off, Aisha came running in, frightened. She told him her mistress wasn't well.

Understanding the fear in her eyes more easily than her words, he got up quickly and followed her.

"Are you all right, Duhqana? What's wrong?" he asked her.

"I was close to death a few days ago, but I didn't want to die when you were away, Sheikh!"

"But you were just fine all day. What's happened?"

"I wasn't really fine, Sheikh. I was just trying to seem that way. I didn't want to spoil your homecoming by being sick."

"Go get al-Sabbagh right away," he said to his servants.

"No, Sheikh. There's no need for that. I've lived long enough!"

"What can I say to that, Duhqana? Should I die, then, because I'm older than you?"

"No, you should live, Sheikh. You should live! And my dying wish is for you to take care of Aisha. Since she came into this household, she's been the best possible companion to me, and I know you wouldn't find a better companion for yourself, either!"

Najma rushed in and came over to Duhqana's bedside. The moment their eyes met, Duhqana smiled and said, "I was afraid I wouldn't see you again!"

Then she closed her eyes.

Duhqana wasn't the type of woman who could have filled Nafisa's shoes. Of course, all of Daher's other wives put together couldn't have performed such a feat! However, Duhqana was good-hearted—so good-hearted that never once had she evinced the slightest intention to usurp Nafisa's throne. On the contrary, she had always acted as though she'd lost the battle before it had begun. When Daher realized this, he tried to give her more, to protect her more. She, however, clung to the firebrand of her defeat as though it were her only victory! And in this, perhaps, lay her only cruelty toward him.

Aisha had disappeared. She had stopped showing her face.

A few days after the wake was over, Najma came in unexpectedly to see Daher.

A stream of air flowed in through the window, trying in vain to reach the open door as though it were spent from crossing the sea. Daher sat there, struggling to take even a passing handful of air into his lungs.

He sat up straight and looked at her. "What is it, Mother?"

"It's Aisha. She refuses to leave Duhqana's bedside. It's been days since she's eaten or drunk anything."

"Speak to her, Mother. Speak to her."

"Do you think I haven't? She's dying. Everyone in the mansion has tried to dissuade her from what she's doing to herself. Everyone but you, that is! But I don't think she would refuse any request you might make of her if you went and comforted her."

"Am I supposed to comfort her over the loss of my own wife, Mother?"

"Rather, you'll be comforting your wife by taking care of the charge she left you!"

"Do you suppose you came back from the war to bid farewell to Duhqana, or to see Aisha again?"

"Who knows?"

The Road to Damascus

There wasn't a city or village that didn't feel the earth tremble as thousands of horsemen and soldiers headed north under the command of Muhammad Abu al-Dhahab, "Father of Gold."[46] On orders from Ali Bey al-Kabir, he had come to place himself under Daher's command.

When news of the advance reached Nablus, Uthman spun about like a one-winged wasp, at a loss as to what to do. All doors seemed to be shutting in his face, and the old man was growing even stronger. However, the door he had thought was closed forever suddenly swung wide open with the arrival of a letter from his father summoning him back to Acre as soon as possible. He was afraid at first. However, the letter was reassuring in its tone.

With Uthman's arrival in Acre, the five brothers were reunited. Daher appointed his sons, al-Dankizli, and Karim al-Ayyub as unit commanders. His son Ali was given command over three thousand horsemen, and an additional force under the command of Nasif al-Nassar had also come to support him. Once all was in order, Daher sent his army out to meet Abu al-Dhahab's forces in Gaza.

When the two armies came together in Gaza, Daher's men were dazzled at the sight of the Egyptian forces. Abu al-Dhahab's army consisted of five thousand horsemen, each escorted by two lower-ranking soldiers; fifteen hundred infantrymen; two thousand servants; hundreds of stewards whose sole function was to supply food and drink; artisans; and merchants. These were followed by caravans of camels, mules, and donkeys, all bearing supplies, ammunition, cannons, and tents.

---

46 Muhammad Abu al-Dhahab, originally Abdullah al-Khaznadar al-Jarkasi, was purchased by Ali Bey al-Kabir in the early 1760s and, after Ali Bey became ruler of Egypt, was named commander of the Egyptian forces. He came to be known as Abu al-Dhahab, "Father of Gold," because, when he acquired the rank of sanjak, he distributed gifts of gold, and became known for his custom of scattering gold coins among the people when he rode down the streets on the way to his home. He is reported to have said, "I am the Father of Gold, since gold is the only thing I take in my hands!"

However, given Daher's decision to remain in Acre, the first encounter between the two allied military commanders turned out to be the first battle! Muhammad Abu al-Dhahab sat awaiting the arrival of Daher's commanders in a velvet pavilion that looked more like a mobile mansion than a tent. Lined with red satin, its pillars and pegs were made of gold-plated brass, and its floor was spread with a yellow carpet decorated with large tree leaves of red and indigo.

As soon as Daher's sons, al-Dankizli, Karim, and Nasif arrived, he invited them to meet with him. Their sweat had hardly dried from the journey, and it was no secret to any of them that Muhammad al-Dhahab was already at work to define the pecking order in his favor.

Ali hesitated to go, and Sa'id and Uthman were of the same mind: "Since he's come here to be under our father's authority, he should wait until we've set up our own pavilions and can invite him to meet with us!"

"And will you invite him to five different pavilions, or to only one of the five, and let it go at that?" asked al-Dankizli.

"We'll invite him to mine," Ali replied.

Anticipating what Uthman was about to say, Karim commented, "I think we should go meet with the man in his pavilion. After all, he's come to support us, and it wouldn't be fitting for us to treat him like a hireling!"

"Whoever wants to go can go," retorted Uthman. "As for me, I still think other people should come to see the sheikh's sons rather than expecting the sheikh's sons to come see them!"

March's gray clouds hung motionless in the sky as though they had been pinned in place with spears. The sea would roll one wave forward and two waves back, and the beach had filled with countless seagulls looking for scraps of food.

Al-Dankizli, al-Ayyub, and Nasif al-Nassar took Islibi and Ahmad aside. Al-Dankizli said, "If they insist on acting this way, I doubt if we'll ever leave Gaza!" He demanded that Islibi speak with them and persuade them to meet with Muhammad Abu al-Dhahab lest he conclude that Daher's army was nothing but factions engaged in internecine squabbling.

Their attempts to reason with Ali and Uthman came to naught. As for Sa'id, they knew it would be useless to speak with him, since he was sure to adopt whatever position his brother Ali did. Hence, Islibi had no choice but to go with the others, leaving to fate the matter of whether his three brothers met with Muhammad al-Dhahab.

Before they saw his face, they glimpsed the blue jewel nestled in the center of his turban. Radiant as a star, it seemed to have sprouted wings and be ready to take off in flight. Clad in silk undergarments, a long kaftan with billowing sleeves[47] whose front was covered with huge gold-embroidered mountain goats' horns that looked as though they'd sprouted from his chest, and armed with a sword that hung from his waist in a gold scabbard adorned with precious stones and inscriptions, he was a veritable king.

He shook their hands with a warmth that astonished them, smiling the entire time, and invited them to sit down. However, the fears that had been voiced by Ali, Uthman, and Sa'id began materializing before their very eyes. After they had taken their seats, he continued speaking to them for several moments from a standing position. He clapped his hands and two servants appeared, carrying a red velvet chair that resembled a throne. They set it down on a raised wooden dais covered with a carpet and colorful cushions, and withdrew. It was the same chair on which, later, he would sit reveling in the sight of seven thousand severed heads.

When at last he sat down, he had defined his position as commander of the army. Still grinning, he said, "I've been told that Sheikh Uthman, Sheikh Ali, and Sheikh Sa'id are with you!"

"Yes, they are," replied Islibi, "but they're a bit tired!"

"Tired?" he asked with a cunning laugh. "How interesting! Are you sure they'll be able to endure the trip to Damascus?"

The four men who had met with Abu al-Dhahab left his pavilion in stunned silence without even bidding each other farewell, and headed back to their own tents. Consequently, Ali, Uthman, and Sa'id asked no questions about what had transpired between them.

"I warned you," Uthman told them.

But when he turned to hear their reply, Ali and Sa'id were already gone.

Like a bride and groom marrying against their wills, Daher's sons forced wan smiles as the army set out, banners aflutter, to the sound of ululations, songs, and prayers for victory. Their way to Damascus was paved

---

47   Long, billowing sleeves were a sign of a leader's rank and prestige.

perfectly by people's talk about the army's strength, and every village and city it reached turned into a festival grounds.

In a race with the clock, Uthman Pasha al-Kurji rushed back to Damascus from Mecca at the head of the pilgrimage caravan, and by a miracle he managed to reach the city before Daher's army arrived. After meeting with the governors of Aleppo, Tripoli, and Kilis, who had been summoned to Damascus's defense by the Ottoman Empire, he quickly fortified the city, anticipating the advancing force's arrival at any moment.

On June 3, the Egyptian army and Daher's forces reached Thaghrat Kawkab southwest of Damascus, but before they could catch their breath, the forces marshaled by the governors in alliance with Uthman Pasha came out and attacked them. Within a mere two hours, the three governors had fled, leaving Uthman Pasha and his son Muhammad stranded alone on the blood-drenched Dariya Plain. However, Uthman Pasha held out, knowing that losing Damascus would mean losing everything.

The sun set and rose again, set and rose again. Just as the two armies had concluded that the battle was doomed to last until they had wiped each other out, Ali al-Daher launched a lightning attack, and before he knew it, Uthman Pasha found himself fighting inside Damascus. Nothing could have frightened Uthman's men more than Ali al-Daher, who went leaping from one horse's back to another as if they were nothing but stairs or low stone walls. Oblivious to whether their riders were his own soldiers or enemy combatants, he harvested heads in a terrifying fury.

The crushing onslaught opened the way for the rest of the attacking forces to advance easily as far as the Maydan quarter.

Now that he was sure Muhammad Abu al-Dhahab knew what kind of a man he was dealing with, Ali felt the time had come to introduce himself. That evening, with the stench of death and smoke hovering in the air, with terror filling the city's marketplaces, streets, and alleyways, and with nothing left to Damascus but the soldiers who had shut themselves inside the fortress, Ali al-Daher headed for Muhammad Abu al-Dhahab's pavilion with Sa'id close on his heels. Shoving the guards arrogantly aside, he walked up to Muhammad Abu al-Dhahab and sat down beside him. Then, without so much as a greeting or handshake, he took a number of cushions that lay near Muhammad al-Dhahab and placed them under his right elbow.

Swallowing the insult despite being surrounded by his military commanders, Abu al-Dhahab turned welcomingly toward Ali and reached out to shake his hand. His arm remained suspended in midair for a few moments in search of a hand to shake. Seeing what was happening, Sa'id felt so uneasy that he nearly reached out to rescue the situation by shaking the man's hand himself, but was afraid of arousing Ali's ire if he did so. Then, just as Muhammad Abu al-Dhahab was about to withdraw his hand, Ali reached out and shook it. Ali gripped his hand so hard that Abu al-Dhahab felt as though he were wrestling him rather than shaking hands. Even so, Sa'id heaved a sigh of relief.

Abu al-Dhahab ran his reddened hand over his goatee. Then, with tense fingers, he began rubbing the emerald-and-sapphire-inlaid golden eagle that hung from a pendant around his neck.

The moonlight did nothing to mitigate the blackness of that Damascus night. The streets went dark, the Umayyad Mosque's minarets disappeared, and there was no trace of either Uthman Pasha al-Kurji or those who had fought with him. The city's scholars, judges, and merchants shut themselves in their houses, waiting to see what the following day would bring.

No one could predict what the dawn would reveal.

Friday's sun peeked out hesitantly like a little girl leaving home for the first time. However, Muhammad Abu al-Dhahab settled matters quickly by sending the city's scholars a decree he had received from Ali Bey al-Kabir. In it he demanded that they surrender the city to him. Otherwise, he would have no choice but to set it on fire. It read as follows:

This illustrious decree was issued by the royal administrative office of Cairo—may its eminent standing be guarded by the Almighty, and may its renown and glorious exploits endure—by orders of him whom the Most Gracious and Beneficent has bestowed upon the people of this age, whose bounty and goodness have spread abroad among the people of the land, and who has set himself against the despotic and tyrannical: the prince of princes, the greatest of the great, formerly Emir of the Sacred Pilgrimage, and presently Sovereign of Egypt.

His Excellency extends greetings of peace, blessings, and prayers for abundance and well-being to the distinguished scholars, jurists, judges, and muftis of the law brought by the illustrious Prophet of Islam; to those in positions of leadership and authority; and to elite and commoner alike throughout the land of Syria and its capital, Damascus. May God honor them with the light of reason and wisdom and protect them from injustice and darkness. As you men of knowledge and discernment well know, the nation of Islam cannot rest on a foundation of error nor condone its perpetuation. Moreover, you well know the injustices perpetrated and the ignorance spread by Uthman Pasha in your land: waylaying pilgrims and visitors and delivering them into the hands of wicked, godless men, overstepping the bounds of religion, and doing what ill befits a nation submitted to God Almighty.

When news of these matters reached our ears, we set about to put a stop to his wicked deeds. You, no doubt, have no intention to succor the unjust—may they be kept far from you one and all. Therefore, be diligent to remove evil from your midst, and to foster that which brings joy and gladness. Do not permit him to remain in your land and among your people. May goodness prevail, and may afflictions be alleviated by the help of Him who directs the course of the cosmos. May peace be upon you.

It was no easy task for Damascus to gather its scholars when it had yet to gather its dead. However, the contents of the decree that had arrived from Ali Bey spread even more quickly than the rumors of Uthman Pasha al-Kurji's flight with his son.

Headwinds

Daher, who was keeping abreast of his sons' news, had heard about the dispute that had arisen over the meeting with Muhammad Abu al-Dhahab. Before his forces reached Damascus, he received reports to the effect that his sons Ali and Uthman had yet to go to the trouble of meeting the man, and his anxiety began to mount. He gathered the leading men of Acre, including the mufti, the judge, his minister Ibrahim al-Sabbagh, and the garrison commander, and informed them that he would be leaving Acre in their care and traveling to Damascus. None of them was in favor of his decision.

"What will you do there, Sheikh?" asked al-Sabbagh. "The army has reached Damascus, and the battles will have already begun. Besides, it's too great a distance for you to travel with a small company of soldiers. Bani Saqr have turned on us again, and the treaty with the Nablusites is so flimsy it wouldn't support a mosquito's weight! So all you can really do is wait, and content yourself with sending messages to your sons."

As al-Sabbagh spoke, Daher was trying to sketch out a route to Damascus that would enable him to bypass the territory of the Nablusites and their allies and the regions where Bani Saqr were active. He managed to draw one up, though he couldn't guarantee the absence of danger.

Bound to remain in Acre, Daher awaited news that would dispel his fears. He knew that the battle raging over Damascus was the greatest he had ever waged, and that if he won, it would achieve true independence for Palestine and beyond. He hadn't lost sight of Jerusalem. However, he knew that as soon as Damascus fell, the battle over Jerusalem, like the battles over all the other cities in Uthman Pasha al-Kurji's vilayet, would come to an end.

On Monday morning, news of the victory arrived. Gunshots were fired in the air, and cannons were fired in salute. The streets of Acre were filled with wedding processions that made their way from the landward gate to the seaward gate, and when night fell, singing, drums, and pipes could still be heard.

Meanwhile, that same night in Damascus, other winds had begun to blow, scattering all that had been gathered in.

The scholars and leading men of Damascus came to Abu al-Dhahab's pavilion to welcome him and acknowledge the city's surrender. After honoring them, he proceeded with them to the governor's mansion. Once he had settled there, he issued a decree granting safety to everyone in the city.

Knowing that his victory would be incomplete as long as the fortress held out against him, Abu al-Dhahab assigned a number of scholars to speak with those who had barricaded themselves inside. When the besieged soldiers refused to surrender, he had no choice but to shell the fortress, certain that the siege would be a long one. To his surprise, however, the fortress didn't hold out. After a long afternoon, and a longer night of shelling, the next morning brought the heartening news that the fortress had surrendered. As soon as the besieging forces saw the Prophet's banner—the flag that accompanied the caravan that bore pilgrims to Mecca—being raised over its walls, they halted their bombardment.

As for Uthman Pasha and his son, they had escaped in the chaos that attended the fighting and fled to Hamah, where Uthman Pasha had begun gathering the remnants of his defeated army.

After a long night of celebrations, the scholars and leading men of Damascus and its army commanders began leaving the mansion. Among them were Daher's sons, all of whom had attended the celebration, with the exception of Ali and Uthman.

Isma'il Bey was about to leave also when Muhammad Abu al-Dhahab said to him, "I need to have a word with you!"

Isma'il came back and sat down.

Abu al-Dhahab looked around him, and for the first time felt he was actually seeing the mansion, whose beauty had been concealed by the large numbers of people. He was captivated by everything he laid eyes on: the decorative woodwork that covered the walls, the ornate windows, the rugs, the copperware, the enormous flower vases that were taller than he was, and the refined, sumptuous air that permeated everything, clothing it with its own special magic.

Isma'il observed him in silence, and as their eyes met, Abu al-Dhahab said to him, "I was watching you tonight, and I noticed that you seem to be the only person who isn't happy about the victory we won! Why is that?"

"Me, sire?"

"Well, yes, unless there's someone else in this room that I don't know about!"

"There are things I know that I'm not at liberty to speak of, sire!"

"As long as we're alone, you can speak freely. I badly need to listen to a loyal man like you."

"It's come to my knowledge that the Ottoman authorities are angry, and their anger might affect Egypt unless things go back to the way they were before."

"I know they're angry. How could they be otherwise now that we've plucked Damascus out of their hands?"

"But they're going to make a move against us back in Egypt. And when that happens, nothing we've done here will be of any use to us. As you can see, Daher's sons despise us. Every time I remember the way Ali al-Daher came in and sat down beside you without showing you the proper respect, I nearly lose my mind! They're strong, stiff-necked folks that the Ottoman Empire hasn't been able to do anything with for more than fifty years! Do you remember how Ali went jumping over those horses like a flying genie, cutting off soldiers' heads as he went?"

"Don't worry, Isma'il. You're blowing things out of proportion. Daher al-Umar will meet the same end that the Arab chieftain Hammam met at our hands.[48] Do these Arabs think that we're going to bend our necks to them again? Gone are the days when the Mamluks were their slaves. You can see for yourself the glories Egypt has achieved, and who rules it now."

---

48 The Arab chieftain Hammam (1709–69) challenged the Mamluks' authority by founding an Arab state in Upper Egypt. He fought against Ali Bey and Muhammad Abu al-Dhahab and defeated them in a number of battles. During the last of these, however, Muhammad Abu al-Dhahab sent a message to Hammam's cousin and military commander, promising to place him in power over Upper Egypt if he would assist them in getting rid of Hammam. In response, Hammam's cousin and commander allowed himself to be defeated. When Hammam learned of the defeat and the Mamluks' advance, he left his capital city of Farshut and died three days later, crushed and heartsick. With Hammam's death, the state of Upper Egypt passed out of existence as if it had never been.

"I see all this, sire. I really do. But we're in Daher al-Umar's territory now, not in Egypt. A foreigner is in a position of weakness, and the farther he is from his own land, the weaker he becomes. We're like a palm tree that's been brought from Egypt to Syria, and no matter how quickly we replant it, we can't guarantee that it will survive!"

"You're forgetting that not only have we planted the palm tree, but it's borne fruit—the fruit of this victory!"

"All this is true, sire. But the tree is still on foreign soil. It may be that the fruit we're seeing now was there in embryo in its homeland, but only became visible here."

Their conversation took many a turn, going on until after midnight. As it drew to a close, Isma'il Bey said craftily, "Sire, the Ottomans aren't angry with you. They're angry with Ali Bey! After all, he's the ruler of Egypt, and he's the one who ordered his army to come here. He's also the one who's made an alliance with the Russians, to whom Daher al-Umar has opened the ports of Acre, Haifa, and Jaffa. Daher is supplying them with whatever they need at the very time when they are embroiled in a fierce, protracted war against the Ottomans. And as you know, the Russians are enemies of the Muslims and of religion itself!"

Isma'il Bey fell silent, seeming hesitant again.

"You still haven't said all you have to say, Isma'il."

"Perhaps I haven't, sire."

"Well, I don't want you to leave here until you've spit it out!"

"If you were given the choice between being governor of Egypt or Damascus, which would you choose, sire?"

"What are you getting at, Isma'il?"

On the eighth night after the fall of Damascus to Daher's forces, a messenger sent by Uthman Pasha al-Kurji arrived from Hamah under cover of darkness. As if Muhammad Abu al-Dhahab's thoughts weren't confused enough already after his talk with Isma'il Bey, the shrewd messenger from Uthman Pasha assured him that the Ottoman Empire would lend him its support and give him Egypt if he were to leave Damascus. In so doing, he planted terror in Abu al-Dhahab's heart, causing him to rethink all his plans.

No longer knowing what to expect, he didn't sleep that night. Had he been told the truth? Or was it part of a skillfully woven plot that would end with his being disposed of for his treachery?

The sun rose, and nothing had happened.

He hurriedly sent for the scholars and leading men of Damascus. Some of them had yet to arrive when he began addressing those present, "The reason we came to Syria was to fight Uthman Pasha. If it weren't for his presence among you, we would not have fought you. Nor would we have attacked the fortress where we believed him to be hiding. Now that we have ascertained that he has left the city, things have changed. We have no designs on your city, nor do we wish to do you any harm. After all, it belongs to our illustrious sovereign, Sultan Mustafa Khan, may God uphold his caliphate till the end of time, and we hope our soldiers have inflicted no harm on any of Syria's inhabitants!"

Hardly able to believe their ears, those in attendance searched for neutral words with which to bid farewell to Abu al-Dhahab's army.

Meanwhile, Daher's sons were beside themselves. When Ali al-Daher, Sheikh Nasif al-Nassar, and al-Dankizli came to confirm the news with Abu al-Dhahab, he received them brusquely. Then he brought the meeting to an abrupt end with the words, "Whoever of you wants to keep me from going back to Cairo will have to fight me, if he can!"

Seeing that they'd been left in the lurch, those in Daher's camp had no choice but to do as Abu al-Dhahab's army had done. So they took down their tents, hurriedly gathered up their provisions and equipment, and headed south in disarray like a defeated army.

Daher's Day

A t last Daher found himself face to face with Uthman Pasha al-Kurji. Feeling as though time had granted him justice at last by placing the old man in his path, Uthman Pasha lunged at Daher like a lance charged with the accumulated hatred of the years.

Yet it wasn't Daher alone who was fighting, working to dodge the approaching blade. His horse, fighting with him, had circled around and positioned itself behind Uthman Pasha's mount. Daher aimed a powerful, swift blow, but Uthman Pasha swerved to dodge it, and the sword sliced the air with a loud whiz.

At last the two had met, not on the walls of Acre as Uthman had envisioned in revenge for what had happened to Damascus, but on the shore of Hula Lake, where Daher had intercepted him. As Uthman Pasha turned again, Daher felt that he wasn't fighting a governor, but a seasoned knight. Then they both charged at once. Their swords met, sending sparks flying, and the force of the collision sent both tumbling off their horses.

On the sandy beach awash in blood they fell, each still holding his sword. Uthman Pasha got up and rushed furiously at Daher, who still lay in the sand. However, Daher was closer to Uthman's feet than Uthman's sword was to Daher's chest. As Daher swung at Uthman's feet, he leapt into the air to dodge the blow, then stumbled and fell.

In a flash, Daher got to his feet, and once again found himself face to face with Uthman.

"So, let's see what more you can do, old man!" Uthman taunted him. Then he attacked him again. Daher reeled, but the blade didn't touch him.

"I might as well be fighting a dead man! Can't you hold yourself steady, old man, so that I'll have something to be proud of when I take your head back to Damascus?"

His eyes fixed on Uthman, Daher took off his right shoe and threw it to one side. Then he did the same with the left. He closed his eyes, and from a distance Najma's voice came to him, saying: *"Many people walk over this earth, but she doesn't feel them because they've never felt her, and sooner or later she's going to cast them off. I know that you and the earth have felt each other. Even so, you need to get closer to her."*

Amazed to see Daher, an eighty-two-year-old man, standing in front of him as though he were surrendering his neck of his own free will, Uthman Pasha rushed at him. As Uthman came toward him, Daher began to feel the earth seeping into him—with her soil, her trees, her roaring seas, her broad plains, her mountaintops. Then he opened his eyes, and at that instant Uthman realized to his dismay what kind of a foe he was up against.

Suddenly Daher began twirling around him, leveling and receiving blows with an ease that robbed Uthman Pasha of his senses. He spun about with the composure and steadiness of someone shooing away a fly. Then, sensing that the moment was right, he rushed at Uthman. Uthman began retreating, his back to the lake, and the water closed over him as Daher came at him with his sword time and time again.

Realizing that he was about to drown, Uthman Pasha began to flail, causing his sword to slip out of his grasp. He wanted to scream. He was dying. Meanwhile, an entire army was advancing along the shore, driving Uthman Pasha's army to a watery death.

As Daher looked on, a number of Uthman Pasha's soldiers gathered around him to shield him from oncoming arrows and help him out to the center of the lake.

Daher turned and found everyone staring at him: Sheikh Nasif al-Nassar and his sons Uthman, Ali, Islibi, Ahmad, and Sa'id.

Ali came up to him and said, "This was your day, Sheikh!"

Daher looked at him, his face glowing with a satisfied smile. He walked over to the spot where he had taken off his shoes and bent to pick them up. When one of his soldiers rushed over to help him, Daher stopped him with his sword and picked them up himself.

"Aren't you going to put your shoes back on, Sheikh?" al-Dankizli asked him.

Hardly had Daher recovered from his last battle when, together with Sheikh Nasif al-Nassar, who was still with him in Acre, he received reports that the Ottoman Empire had ordered Emir Yusuf al-Shihabi to march on Mount Amel. The Ottomans were intent on teaching the

Matawila a lesson after the defeat suffered by the governor of Damascus. In response, Daher sent word to Emir Yusuf, promising that all the state taxes owed by Mount Amel would be paid in full, and asking him to wait until he could come settle the matter himself.

After tearing up Daher's letter in a rage, Emir Yusuf marched with his army to the village of Kafr al-Rumman and set fire to it. Then he continued on his way to Nabatea.

Daher looked at his son Ali, not needing to say a word. Ali stood up with Sheikh Nasif, and together they pledged: "Victory or death!" Then they were off, racing against the clock at the head of five hundred horsemen, who took Emir Yusuf's army by surprise and tore it to shreds.

A crushing victory, it prepared the way for another, equally swift, conquest. Daher's army pursued the routed forces in the direction of Sidon. Before they arrived, reports that Emir Yusuf had been defeated and that Daher's army was close on his heels reached the city, and the soldiers there fled.

It was announced in Daher's name that Sidon had been captured. Several days later, Ali and Sheikh Nasif al-Nassar met with the French consul in the city bearing a letter from Daher reassuring him that French interests there would be protected. Before the two men departed, Daher issued an order appointing Ahmad al-Dankizli the city's governor.

Daher knew that after two critical battles that had effectively destroyed the Ottoman Empire's prestige, as well as the prestige and influence of its allies, he would have to clip Damascus's wings completely. Seeing no better way to do this than to close the city off from the region to the south by taking control of Irbid and Ajloun, he dispatched his sons Ahmad and Sa'id at the head of a force that would take over the two cities' affairs. Then he dispatched his son Ali at the head of another force to take over affairs in Houran, where they confiscated all the governor's wealth and all the money owed in taxes to the Ottoman Empire.

By virtue of this cruel blow, the lines between Damascus and the south were severed, and Damascus turned into a ghost town, with no one buying or selling, and no one able to travel in or out.

Winds of Tribute

Following Muhammad Abu al-Dhahab's humiliating and suspicious retreat from Damascus, Daher returned to Acre feeling he had put the country's affairs in order again.

When Najma saw him barefoot, she smiled.

"So you finally did it!" she said before he'd gotten off his horse.

"I didn't do it by myself. You were there with me on the shore of Hula Lake!"

He saw Aisha dart joyfully toward him from the door of the mansion, fluttering like a butterfly as usual. As he watched her approach, he felt the air lifting him off the horse's back. He held on to the saddle, certain that if he didn't, he would sprout wings right in front of the people of Acre, who had come one and all to receive him.

So, what no one had ever expected had finally come to pass: those who had heard about Aisha had now seen her with their own eyes, and became heralds of her beauty wherever they went.

For weeks after Daher's recapture of Sidon, which sent tremors through the Ottoman Empire, cannons fired in salute and the nights were filled with singing and celebration. So by the time Qubji Pasha Sultan arrived in Acre, intervening events had rendered meaningless the message he bore from the Sublime Porte.

One hot day Daher was in the mansion, reclining on the chaise lounge with his feet up on the armrest and letting a current of cool air sweep over him, when suddenly he glimpsed the royal envoy peering at him through the window.

The moment he saw him, Daher knew what was going through the man's mind. Summoning a member of his retinue who knew Turkish well, he asked him to go out to the envoy and say, "I'm not as you suppose me to be! You must think that, now that I've defeated Uthman Pasha al-Kurji and taken over Sidon, I've become arrogant, and that is why I sit this way with my feet in the air. By the grave of my father

Umar, that isn't the case! It's simply that I'm weary from riding, and suffer from hemorrhoids! I didn't get off my horse for twelve hours, and I'm only seated this way in order to relieve the pain!"

Daher watched al-Qubji as he listened to the man who'd been sent out to speak with him. He saw him look inside and shake his head in seeming wonderment.

"What did he say to you?" Daher asked the man when he came back.

"Well, what he said was, 'Amazing! How does this man know what's going on in people's minds?'"

Al-Dankizli was delighted over Sidon. By this time he had gotten wind of what people were saying about the beauty of Daher's concubine, and he thought: *Might Sidon be his attempt to conciliate me after keeping her for himself?*

He tried to put the thought out of his mind, but without success. He tried again. Standing in front of the mirror, which may well have been the same mirror previous governors of Sidon had stood in front of, he thought: *Do you want to cause yourself more torment, Ahmad? Do you want to get attached to her, only to have death, or some enemy, snatch her away from you? Be thankful that somebody else will have to suffer over her!*

What you want is for Daher to suffer, then! Do you hate him now because he relieved you of your suffering by snatching it away from you? Or because he snatched away a dream more wonderful than any you'd seen even in your sleep? Has love come and swept you off your feet again? Take it easy, Ahmad. You haven't even seen her, and you're doing this to yourself. What would you do if you had seen her, then?

The Siege of the Seven Pashas

Y ou'll go back to Syria and do everything Daher asks of you!"
Ali Bey said to his Mamluk and adopted son, Abu al-Dhahab.
"I won't go back if it means seeing Daher and his sons
again!"

After a silence, Ali Bey smiled cunningly and said, "It's up to you.
After all, you're my son, and I would never stand with Daher and his sons
against you!"

It was at that moment that Abu al-Dhahab saw a conspiracy beginning to unfold.

It would have been difficult to assassinate Abu al-Dhahab when he was
surrounded by so many influential, loyal Mamluks. Nevertheless, in an
attempt to make things still easier for himself, Abu al-Dhahab wrote to
the Sublime Porte accusing Ali Bey of being the one who had incited
him to go to Damascus. He also reminded the Ottoman authorities of
Ali Bey's alliance with "the infidel Russians, his aim being to do away
with the religion of the Prophet and force people to convert to Christi-
anity!"

Abu al-Dhahab's coming and goings were being reported regularly
to Ali Bey, who one night nearly had him surrounded and arrested.
With the help of his own spies, however, Abu al-Dhahab managed to
escape.

Since being sent by Catherine II to attack the Turkish coast, the Russian fleet had become king of the Mediterranean. Ali Bey contacted the
fleet's commander, Count Alexei Orlov, asking him to supply him with
arms in his war against the Ottoman Empire. In reply, Orlov wrote saying, "We shall be in your service against our common foe."

As the Russian ships were headed for Alexandria laden with arms
and ammunition, Ali Bey sent out a force headed by Isma'il Bey to
get rid of Abu al-Dhahab, who had fled for refuge to Upper Egypt.

Isma'il Bey, Abu al-Dhahab's companion on the campaign to Syria, went as directed to Upper Egypt. However, instead of waging war on Abu al-Dhahab, he embraced him and joined forces with him. Then the two men made their way back to Cairo at the head of a single army.

The battle that took place on Egypt's Masateb Plain lasted only a few hours, and led to Ali Bey's defeat. Only hours later, in the midst of a festive atmosphere, Muhammad Abu al-Dhahab declared his allegiance to the sultan and pledged to pay all the taxes Egypt owed to the Ottoman treasury. When, on that dark night in late April, Ali Bey looked around, injured by defeat and pained over his son's betrayal, he could think of only one person who would open his doors to him: Daher al-Umar.

The journey to Acre wasn't easy. After hearing of his approach, the Nablusites waylaid Ali Bey on the outskirts of Jaffa, intending to kill him and prevent him and his men from joining Daher's forces. However, Daher moved out quickly and routed them, rescuing Ali Bey from death's clutches. He then escorted him to Haifa, and he and his men encamped at the city gates.

As the month of March drew to a close, giving way to signs of a blazing summer, Daher sat in Ali Bey's tent, looking over at the ally he was meeting for the first time.

By the time the Russian ships arrived in Alexandria, Ali Bey had departed Egypt, so they followed him to Acre and dropped anchor in its port.[49] From that time onward many things would change. Despite being engrossed in preparing to return to reclaim Egypt, Ali Bey and his Mamluks fought successive wars at Daher's side. With the support they received from Russia's ships, they navigated the sea as easily as they did the land, as no ship could move about in the region without a special permit signed by Daher al-Umar.

Everything seemed to be in a race with time, and the days and months had turned into a roaring stream. Hardly had Uthman Pasha al-Kurji and his younger son Darwish been removed following the Battle of Hula than the Ottomans appointed Muhammad Pasha al-Azm governor of

---

49 Daher made shrewd use of the periods during which the Ottoman Empire was embroiled in foreign conflicts, foremost among them its wars with Russia, to secure control over new cities and regions.

Damascus, and by the time the latter had returned from leading the pilgrimage caravan to Mecca, Uthman Pasha al-Misri had been appointed as his successor.

The Sublime Porte had grown increasingly disoriented in the face of Daher's power. However, this wasn't to last long. Istanbul issued one order to the new governor of Damascus to advance on Sidon and take it back, and another to the leaders of Nablus and Tripoli to help him. War missives crisscrossed the land, etching the features of an unsettling time to which neither the Ottoman Empire nor Daher was well disposed any longer.

The empire appointed Mustafa Bey Tuqan governor of Nablus, Gaza, and Ramla, granting him the title of pasha, while appeasing the Nimr family by appointing Ibrahim Agha, to whom it also granted the title of pasha, governor of Jerusalem. As a result, Daher and his ally Ali Bey found themselves firmly hemmed in from both north and south.

With Sidon enervated from eight days under siege by seven pashas headed by the governor of Damascus, al-Dankizli could see no solution but to surrender. However, just as he was preparing to do so, the Russian fleet arrived unexpectedly in the city's port, and those besieging the city fled under a barrage of shells from the ships.

In the Hara suburb on the outskirts of Sidon, al-Dankizli finished what the ships had begun by launching a massive offensive on the pashas and the governor, who retreated without stopping until they reached Damascus. Daher then destroyed the Ottoman ships at anchor in the port of Beirut, certain that their destruction was the only way to ensure that the battle over Sidon was truly finished.

However, no sooner had the north come under his control than the southern front burst into flames again, auguring the direst of consequences.

The Sword and the Dagger

O ne night in the spring of 1773, Ali Bey paid Daher an unexpected visit in his mansion. Daher could sense that something
momentous lay behind his coming.

With his fair, round face and long, gangly arms, Ali Bey looked
like a sailboat lost at sea. Daher waited for him to speak. However, he
remained silent, fiddling so violently with his huge goatee you would
have thought he wanted to pull it out. Daher asked the members of his
entourage who were present to leave the two of them alone for a while.

Ali Bey was consumed with a single thought, a thought that had
revived memories of the Egypt he had lost and reminded him how long
he had been living in exile in Palestine.

"I've decided to go back to Egypt, Sheikh," he announced at last,
"and you deserve to be the first to know."

"I thank you, Ali. But we hadn't agreed on this!"

"Many things have changed in Egypt since I came here, Sheikh, and
there's no better time to go back than now."

"I'm not objecting to your return," Daher clarified. "I'm only objecting to the timing of it. At present I won't be able to supply you with the
number of soldiers you'll need. Spring is around the corner, and our
crops will need to be tended and harvested. All I ask is that you wait
until we've gathered in the grain."

"I'd like to stay until then, Sheikh, but I won't be able to!"

Taking a deep breath, Daher said, "Allow me to call my minister,
Ibrahim al-Sabbagh. Perhaps he'll have something to say on the matter.
After all, two opinions are better than one, and three are better than
two!"

"Very well, Sheikh."

As they sat waiting, you could have heard a pin drop in the spacious
diwan. Each of them wandered far with his thoughts, making calculations and trying to predict the outcomes.

When al-Sabbagh arrived at last, he greeted the other two men, only to find them in worlds of their own. He greeted them a second time, more loudly, and they woke from their reveries.

Ibrahim listened in silence as Daher told him what was on Ali Bey's mind and informed him of the latter's decision to return to Egypt. But he took so long to reply that they began to think he didn't want to speak. At last he opened his mouth and they waited for something to come out. But instead, he closed it again.

"What is this, Ibrahim?" Daher exclaimed. "Don't you have anything to say?"

"Yes, I do, Sheikh. I do! I was just hesitating."

"Speak up!"

"In my opinion, this isn't the time to be going there."

Al-Sabbagh went on to repeat what Daher had said about the crops and the harvest. Then he added, "And don't forget, Ali Bey, that Alexei Orlov has agreed to send you a cavalry detachment, fully outfitted, to escort you to Egypt, and I don't think it's arrived."

"Honestly speaking," Ali Bey replied, "I have something much more powerful to fall back on than the Russian detachment!"

With a flick of his hand, he took a letter out of his pocket and handed it to Daher, who handed it in turn to al-Sabbagh. Al-Sabbagh unfolded the letter and began reading it, nodding as he went.

"Let us hear what it says, Ibrahim."

The letter contained a pledge by the sanjaks of Egypt to support Ali Bey and fight by his side if he should think of returning to Egypt. The letter's signatories urged him to return as quickly as possible, stressing the fact that the sanjaks of Egypt had never before been in such agreement over a matter of such importance. They reassured him, saying, "Once you reach Salihiya,[50] we'll all break ranks with Abu al-Dhahab and join your army."

Al-Sabbagh folded up the letter and handed it back to the sheikh, who began waving it back and forth as though it were a small paper fan.

"And are you sure that the individuals who signed this letter are being truthful with you?" Daher asked him.

"They're my men, Sheikh. I know them as well as I know myself!"

"But I smell a rat, Ali!"

---

50 The historic city of Salihiya is located in the Eastern Governorate to the west of Ismailiya.

"How could there be anything unsavory involved here when all of them agreed to sign the letter?"

"What do you think, Ibrahim?"

"I agree with you, Sheikh."

"Listen, Ali. I won't argue with you over the loyalty of your men, since you know them better than I do. However, my opinion hasn't changed. We'll wait three months and equip a strong army. By the end of the three months, the Russian cavalry will have arrived, and you can go to Egypt in a position of strength. If, once you're there, it becomes apparent that your men have betrayed you, you won't meet with any harm. If, on the other hand, you find that they were telling you the truth, you'll be that much stronger."

"Sheikh, I know these sanjaks better than anyone else, and my heart tells me that what they've written is the truth. This is my chance to enter Egypt before the pilgrimage caravan returns, since those in the caravan are against me, whereas those who are in Egypt are for me! So, as you can see, I've got no time to lose."

Ali Bey fell silent for a little while. Then he said, "As you're aware, Sheikh, my deputy, Rizq, can predict the future using sand. He's also assured me that according to all the stars, my journey will be successful and I'll win a decisive victory!"

Daher nodded, recalling an entire age past. "One day long ago," he said, "the lanterns told my brothers what the sand and the stars have told that deputy of yours! Look, Ali: In the first letter you ever wrote me, you told me I was like a father to you. So allow me to speak to you as I would to my own son. You can't base a grand scheme like this on a letter that's worth no more than its own weight! And worse still, you're willing to listen to the nonsense your deputy Rizq is feeding you! I swear to God, if you erased all the words written on this paper, it would have more weight than what this man is telling you!"

Daher waited for Ali Bey to speak. But he said nothing. It was then that Daher knew he had already made up his mind, and that he'd come not to ask for his opinion, but simply to inform him of his decision.

At last Ali Bey said, "All I ask is that you provide me with a squad of soldiers to escort my Mamluks to Egypt, and that you lend me the money I'll need for the journey."

"You've got it, Ali. You've got it. As for the military squad, I'll choose my best men and send them out under the command of my son Islibi and my son-in-law Karim al-Ayyub to show you that I mean what I say. As for the money, you'll take as much as you need and more. But let me arrange that with my minister, Ibrahim al-Sabbagh."

Daher took al-Sabbagh aside and said, "You know better than I do how our financial affairs are these days. The wars we've fought over the years have emptied our coffers. But I can't say this to Ali Bey. After all, he's been a faithful ally ever since we met him, and has never hesitated to lend us a helping hand when we needed it. Isn't there some way we can help him?"

"I'd offer him my life if you asked me to, Sheikh. But you're well aware of my financial situation. Nevertheless, for your sake I'll do whatever it takes to get him what he needs. I can take out a loan. But what worries me, Sheikh, is how I'll be able to return the money later to the people I borrowed it from."

"Leave that to me. I'll be your collateral. Is that good enough for you?"

"But I won't take the money unless I can write you a promissory note!" Ali Bey insisted.

"Ali, I'm sending with you my son and my son-in-law, both of whom are precious to me. Do you really think I need you to write me a promissory note if your friendship means that much to me? All I want is to hear good news about you once you get to Egypt. And to reassure myself, I'm going to load a Russian ship with arms, supplies, and ammunition and have it waiting for you on the Egyptian coast when you get there."

A military force was hastily made ready under the command of Islibi and Karim. In the meantime, Ali Bey went to the judge of Acre without Daher's knowledge and drafted a promissory note binding him to repay the amount he had borrowed from Daher. In it, he specified that he would mortgage his sword, which was known as "Yusuf's sword," and his dagger, which was valued at 200,000 francs at a time when an ordinary dagger was worth no more than 9,000 francs. He pledged to repay what he owed as soon as he arrived in Egypt, in return for redeeming the sword and the dagger.

Ali Bey was met at the Acre gate by a large farewell gathering, while those coming in and out of the city stopped to see the army that was

508

going to reclaim Egypt, an army that numbered only fifteen hundred soldiers!

Daher embraced Ali Bey, and tried to say something. But the only thing that came out was a heartfelt, "I'll be waiting to hear your happy news in the days to come."

He embraced Karim and Islibi. Then he watched them until they disappeared over the horizon.

Daher's sadness intensified when, several days later, the Russian detachment arrived without finding the person who had requested it.

All the Winds That Had Gathered

The winds changed direction all at once.

The arms-laden ship that Daher had sent to Egypt to precede Ali Bey's arrival there was intercepted opposite Jaffa. As soon as Mustafa Bey Tuqan learned of it, he sent word to Jaffa asking that the Russian sailors who had been captured be sent to him in Nablus.

Before the captives reached Nablus, Mustafa Bey had made his decision. Viewing them as a gift from heaven, he ordered them beheaded at once. In so doing, he would be killing several birds with one stone. He would please Uthman Pasha al-Misri, governor of Damascus. He would place Daher in an unenviable position vis-à-vis his Russian allies. He would deprive Daher's ally, Ali Bey, of the cannons and ammunition he needed in Egypt. And he would win the favor of Muhammad Abu al-Dhahab.

These achievements would have been enough to send even a mountain soaring!

One midday, as Daher was meeting with a number of Acre's senior administrative officials, a member of his entourage came and stood hesitantly at the door.

Seeing him, Daher gestured for him to come forward.

"What is it?" Daher asked.

"I have news I'd rather not be bringing you, Sheikh."

"Has harm come to Ali Bey, Islibi, or Karim, God forbid?"

"No, Sheikh. It has to do with the ship you sent to Egypt."

As Daher listened in silence, he felt swords piercing him from all sides. His wiry frame tensed and his large eyes flickered with rage. He said, "Didn't the Nablusites understand what it meant the first time I withdrew from their city? Are they betraying the pact we made? So help me God, I won't get down off my horse until I've watered it from Ayn al-Sitt!"

510

He set off on horseback at the head of a formidable army. He sent no warning or messenger ahead of him with an offer to negotiate, and called for no new pact, which he knew for certain they would violate.

When he arrived, he found the people of Nablus in an uproar over what Mustafa Bey Tuqan had done to the captives. The uprising was backed by the courageous Musa al-Tamimi, the city's most powerful judge, who harbored no affection for the beys, and who had stirred the people up against the murder of the captives as a violation of Islamic law.

As Daher swept through the city, Mustafa Bey Tuqan's defenses collapsed in the face of the onslaught, leaving Mustafa and his brother Ahmad no choice but to run for their lives. Daher pressed on until he reached Ayn al-Sitt, "the Lady's Spring," in the heart of Nablus. He watered his horse there, then departed the city, having now taken control of all southern Syria.

Daher wasn't happy about what had transpired. He took no satisfaction in either the lightning-paced victory to which he had been swept or the deafening silence that had swallowed up news of Ali Bey's return to Egypt with Islibi and Karim.

Something was worrying him, making his life miserable. Try as he might to banish all the black thoughts, they refused to leave him, and he no longer took joy in anything. He was troubled over having allowed Ali Bey to go back, and over having sent his son and son-in-law to Egypt simply to show Ali what a loyal friend he was.

Shortly before reaching Salihiya, Ali Bey made sure his army was ready and checked on Islibi and Karim. It was a hot day in early May. He looked up and saw vultures, eagles, and crows filling the sky, obscuring the sun in a way he had never seen before. He didn't know whether to take it as a good omen or a bad one. Whichever the case, he knew that, having come this far, there was no way to go but forward.

In the distance, on the outskirts of Salihiya, he saw clouds of dust that bespoke the approach of horses, and again he didn't know whether to feel joy or dread! However, the time for caution was past, and he had no choice but to press on.

When the approaching horses rushed at his army, he didn't know whether to attack them or to wait on the assumption that their riders were coming to join him. However, it took only moments for the matter to become clear.

The attack came swift as lightning. Despite all the dust obscuring the horizon, he could see Murad Bey rushing at him in a mad fury. As they clashed, Ali Bey was amazed at Murad Bey's stubborn determination, especially in view of the fact that he had been the first to sign the letter pledging him the sanjaks' allegiance.

As the two men dueled, Muhammad Abu al-Dhahab's twelve-thousand-man force closed in on Ali Bey's rapidly dwindling army. Terrified steeds fled the battlefield, leaving behind their slain riders, one of whom was Islibi.

Ali Bey tried to dodge the blows. However, he knew that he had fallen into a well-laid trap of Abu al-Dhahab's making. He tried to retreat, only to have his way blocked by the corpses that covered the ground. So he charged again. But before he reached Murad Bey, he received a sword blow that knocked him off his horse. As he went flying through the air, he had only one hope: that the blow he had received would be the one from which he would never rise again. Yet even the smallest of wishes find themselves strangers and alone on the battlefield. He never even touched the ground, which was carpeted with dead bodies.

Murad Bey, who leapt off his horse and grabbed him, was by far the happiest man on that battlefield, not because he had had the honor of capturing Ali Bey, but because he was awaited by a prize far more tantalizing!

Murad Bey came shoving Ali Bey toward a sumptuous pavilion that stood behind the army's encampment. When he saw them approaching, Abu al-Dhahab ran out to them weeping. He took Ali Bey's hand and began kissing it, with the words, "What have they done to you, Father?"

He alternately embraced him and kissed his head, expressing his sorrow over what had befallen him.

On the evening of May 8, Ali Bey was in his home in Azbakiya, still suffering badly from his wounds, and physicians streamed in and out, doing their utmost to ensure his recovery. That same evening, Abu al-Dhahab summoned the doctor who had come to treat Ali Bey and said to him, "When you go in to see my father, apply this medicine to his wounds. I've heard it's the very best!"

The doctor nodded, knowing he had no choice but to obey, and an hour later, the sound of wailing filled the Darb al-Haqq quarter where Ali Bey's house was located.

The minute he heard the news, Murad Bey rushed to Abu al-Dhahab's palace. Surrounded by his men and smirking like a drunken peacock, Abu al-Dhahab said to him, "Why do you come to me? Go get what I promised you!"

"Shall I go get Ali Bey's wife right now?" he asked.

"Of course: right now! Aren't you in love with her, and didn't I promise her to you if you brought him back here to me? She's no one's wife any more, so go now, before I change my mind!"

As Murad Bey went running out, Abu al-Dhahab's voice followed him: "Hurry up, or I'll beat you to her!"

As the huge hall reeled with the intoxication of victory to the sound of the sanjaks' raucous laughter, Abu al-Dhahab capped a long series of events with the words, "Let's think about tomorrow now. Or is there anyone here who'd like to write to Ali Bey in his grave, assuring him of his loyalty?"

And the laughter vanished like water poured onto desert sands.

The Night and Najma's Lanterns

Acre stood on tiptoe, looking southward in anticipation of news about Ali Bey and the force that had traveled with him to Egypt. It was ill prepared for the reports that reached it several days after the battle at Salihiya: that Ali Bey had been taken captive, Islibi had been killed, and Karim al-Ayyub had disappeared.

Sorrow filled every household, and Acre turned into one big wake. The most sorrowful of all, however, was al-Sabbagh, because he'd lost his money! If wakes were held for lost money, he would have held one himself. However, knowing that this would have lost him that much more, he just retreated to a dark corner of his house every night after coming back from Daher's mansion, dreaming that Daher hadn't forgotten that he had guaranteed his loan to Ali Bey.

After receiving news of the battle, Daher's daughter Aliya came and stood before him in silence. She didn't ask him a thing. The next day she did the same thing. And so it went with the passing of the days, with her unable to ask and him unable to give her an answer.

Daher recalled an image of Aliya as a little girl who, even though she was still only seven years old, would slip out to the lake on "girls' Thursday" to wash her hair in water saturated with starlight and the scent of flower blossoms. He remembered how, delighted with her mischievousness and wanting to make her happy, he would pretend not to see her slip out with the other girls. He remembered how, when she was twelve years old, she had seen nineteen-year-old Karim al-Ayyub while he was visiting Tiberias with his father. Jumping into the air, she'd cried, "That's my husband!" in front of everyone. When she was seventeen, Karim had married her, and never in his life had Daher seen a girl as happy with her groom as Aliya had been with Karim.

Najma, now faced with some of the blackest days of her life, secluded herself in her room, and there was no sign of Aisha anywhere in the house. Daher also sat alone, like a solitary king in a dreary mansion that seemed to receive nothing but unhappy news. By the fifteenth day of the wake, the silence had grown all the more ruthless as he fought off all the questions he knew people must be asking in their hearts.

Suddenly, a lone horseman on the verge of death emerged from the darkness of the road. As people looked on in disbelief, he came closer and dismounted. Only then did Daher realize who he was. At once brokenhearted and overjoyed, Daher went up to him with uncertain steps. Then he held the horseman in a powerful embrace until he collapsed from exhaustion.

Karim's return was nothing less than a miracle. No one from the slaughtered army had made his way back before him, and no one would make it back after him.

That night Najma came out of her room, and Aisha followed.

Embracing Najma as though he were still consoling her, he took Aisha's hand and said, "Forgive me, Aisha. All these wars have made me forget something I shouldn't have forgotten: you're free now."

Looking up at him, she said something he had never heard the likes of before: "In your house, Sheikh, no one could be anything but free!"

"You can go wherever you wish, Aisha."

"If there were a household that freedom loved more than it loves this one, I'd go there!"

"Who taught you to speak so well, Aisha?"

"My mother, Madame Najma!"

Daher spent that entire night, a night torn between joy lost and joy restored, sitting in the garden with Najma. If he hadn't been with her, Najma felt sure she would have spent the night talking to herself.

"You know, Mother?" Daher said. "Even though it was so long ago, the 'night of the lanterns' still comes back to haunt me sometimes. That lantern of mine that went out is still burning! Even so, I feel it dim a little whenever I see a lantern I love go out. My father's lantern went out so that I could have a lantern. The lanterns of Abbas, Sheikh Hussein, my brothers Saleh and Saad, Nafisa, Bishr, Jahjah, Islibi, even Emir Rashid Jabr—don't be surprised if I mention him too—have all gone out, and every time one of their lanterns went out, part of mine went out with it. It's as if the lantern that went out that day wasn't really mine. It was somebody else's. As for my lantern, it's all these lanterns that have gone out, one after another."

"But I'm still alive, Daher. Am I not part of that lantern too?"

"You're its light and its oil, Mother!"

"And don't forget your sons, Sheikh!"

"My sons! Ever since they grew up, all I've seen them do is send one wind after another to put out what's left of my lantern's light! The only exception was Islibi, God bless him. I can't understand why they want so badly for me to disappear into the darkness. Sometimes I wonder: is it because they were born to different mothers that they can't seem to stand united with me? Is that why they send so much wind my way?"

"Don't forget, Sheikh, that there are lanterns that never go out. And yours is one of them. After all you've done, do you really think anyone could put out your light? It's true, of course, that no one would yet dare to sit down and record all the great things you've accomplished. Everyone's too afraid of the Ottoman Empire, which is itself afraid of nothing more than paper and ink! But in another year, or ten years, or fifty years, or one hundred years, things will be different, and your lantern and all these other people's lanterns will start shining again all at once! I don't know how to read the future in the sand or the stars—though I am a star!—but believe me, Sheikh, when I tell you that all these things are going to happen."

"Are you trying to make me feel better, Mother?"

"No, Sheikh. When I say things like this, I'm reassuring the days ahead of what's going to come."

The dawn call to prayer sounded from the Hanging Mosque.

"We'll pray," said Najma, "and then I'll take you for a walk along the seashore. I might need it more than you do. If I tell you why, will you promise not to be hard on yourself, Sheikh?"

"Tell me, Mother."

"Because you forgot that all those lanterns that went out were my lanterns too!"

Daher reached out and squeezed her hand.

"There are lanterns that are watching you without your realizing it!" As she spoke, she handed him a bundle whose contents had become so familiar to him that he knew what it contained before he opened it. As he touched it, he heard a voice saying, "You can't imagine, Sheikh, how beautiful it makes us feel to send you our braids!"

And he looked around to see where the voice had come from.

The Head's Mine,
the Country's Yours!

O ne day Daher received a letter from Uthman Pasha al-Misri, governor of Damascus, informing him that he had no intention of waging war on him the way previous governors had done, since he was certain that Uthman Pasha al-Kurji's attacks on him in previous years had been the cause of all the other wars that had afflicted the region. Hardly had Daher folded up the governor's letter when another arrived from the Ottoman Empire's prime minister who, after conveying his warmest greetings and wishing him long life and health, urged Daher to forget all that was past.

This was the first letter Daher had ever received from the prime minister. All he had received in the past were letters from governors breathing dire threats!

Looking around him, Daher found that everything he had hoped for had come to pass. His rule now extended over all of southern Palestine, as well as Acre, Jaffa, Haifa, Galilee, the regions of Irbid and Ajloun, parts of Syria and Houran, and Sidon. Tyre was in the hands of his allies the Matawila, and Beirut was in the hands of his friends the Shihabis. All that remained to the Ottoman state was the port of Tripoli in the north. However, he realized that, given the Ottoman Empire's approval of those who stood opposed to him, he had no reason for complacence.

The Ottomans then took things a step further by issuing him a royal pardon. The decree was delivered by a royal messenger who entered Acre in the grandest, most festive procession the city had ever seen. It was then that Daher's fear began to mount, and for good reason.

The prime minister's messenger came bearing a letter for Abu al-Dhahab as well. After reading it, Abu al-Dhahab set it down in front of him on an oaken table decorated with stars, squares, and overlapping diamonds. Then he picked it up and read it again while the messenger waited for him to say something. But instead of speaking, he read it a third time.

In the letter the prime minister assured Abu al-Dhahab of his affection for him and his concern for his well-being, warning him of what was happening behind his back. The letter read, "The sultan has granted Daher a royal pardon, and before long he will be urging him to march on Cairo and send your head to Istanbul! Be that as it may, the Ottoman Empire isn't pleased with Daher. What he did to you and its governors is no small matter, and if you make a move before he does, the empire will support you."

Abu al-Dhahab thought quickly, and without consulting anyone, decided to march on Acre. During the days following, which provided too little time to prepare for the campaign while also maintaining secrecy, Abu al-Dhahab accomplished a great deal.

He could think of no one better to lead the campaign than a certain wily Englishman by the name of Robinson. Wasting no time, Robinson equipped the campaign, reinforced it with engineers, musketeers, and cannoneers, and sent ammunition and equipment by sea to Jaffa. Among the pieces he sent was a large cannon that he had cast the year before. Then the army set out across Sinai, headed by Muhammad Abu al-Dhahab himself.

Meanwhile, the war of letters continued, and everyone realized that it could do the impossible. Muhammad Abu al-Dhahab wrote to Ali al-Daher saying, "Let's forget what happened between us during our Damascus campaign! I'm coming to Acre and, God is my witness, I have no designs on your country, but I have a score to settle with your father, who offered support and protection to my enemy, Ali Bey. He even equipped him and sent him to wage war on me! All I want for myself is Daher's head. As for the country, it's yours! However, if you don't join me, then as soon as I've finished with Daher I'll come out against you, too. So make your choice!"

When news of the campaign reached Daher, he equipped a thousand-man force with bronze cannons with wooden bases, and sent them out under Karim al-Ayyub's command to intercept Abu al-Dhahab's army in Gaza. Karim's force traveled night and day and, to his immense relief, they managed to reach Gaza and fortify themselves there before Abu al-Dhahab's army arrived.

However, when the force Daher had promised to send to join him under Sa'id's command failed to appear, Karim's anxiety began to mount. When Ali learned of the force's departure for Gaza, he had sent word to his brother Sa'id telling him to turn back and join him rather than Karim. Taking the letter as an order, Sa'id had joined Ali instead. Reports poured into Gaza about the magnitude of the advancing army. So, backed as he was by nothing but his modest company of soldiers, Karim withdrew from Gaza and repaired to well-fortified Jaffa.

Facing no resistance in either Gaza or Ramla, the approaching army continued easily on its way to Jaffa. When it reached Jaffa on April 1, Muhammad Abu al-Dhahab's army was in no urgent need to go to battle, and decided instead to indulge in some relaxation amid the city's orange, mulberry, and pomegranate trees, next to the waterwheels on its rivers, and on the shore of its sea, which was the most placid Abu al-Dhahab had ever seen. Meanwhile, the ships that had arrived before them waited for a signal from Abu al-Dhahab to begin unloading the cannons and other equipment.

In an elevated spot among the orange groves two hundred meters from Jaffa's walls, Abu al-Dhahab set up eight of his cannons and ordered the shelling of the city to begin. Meanwhile, he spent night after night in his royal pavilion, enjoying himself as though he'd never left his mansion in Cairo. He'd come accompanied by the finest musicians, singers, and dancers, and concubines as well. Like Abu al-Dhahab, Robinson and the sanjaks with him were certain Jaffa would fall within two or three days at the most.

Certain that he was fighting his last battle alone against the most formidable army he had ever seen, Karim al-Ayyub stationed his soldiers by turns on the city walls, with some of them fighting while others rested. The most he hoped to do was to make Abu al-Dhahab's victory as difficult as possible. To this end, Karim's men stood fighting night after night with their muskets, swords, and arrows, and with bronze cannons whose shells fell short of their targets.

As for Daher, the only way he could see to rescue Jaffa, Haifa, Acre, and the rest of the country was to go out personally to his allies and ask them to join him. However, his efforts came to naught. To his dismay, he found that his son Ali had already drawn them over to his side after warning them of the dire consequences of joining Daher.

"We're dealing here with an eighty-five-year-old man. Do you want to ally yourselves with an old bag of bones? You know how strong I am and what I'm capable of. Not only that, but my brother Sa'id has joined me. As for Uthman, if he isn't with me, he won't be with the old man either. The Ottomans are fed up with him, and they'll give me the entire country as soon as they have his head. They've even sent sixty thousand soldiers out against him. So what more do you want?"

These were the things Ali al-Daher would say to every emir, sheikh, and governor he met.

However, by the time Abu al-Dhahab's siege of Jaffa entered its third week, his pavilion had become still as a tomb, and all signs of merriment had vanished. Doubting the efficacy of the campaign and seeing the siege bogged down in a hopeless quagmire, he dismissed Robinson. He thought: *If this small town can hold out against me for three weeks, then how many weeks will Haifa hold out, and then Acre, and then . . . ?*

Abu al-Dhahab asked Ali to come meet him in Jaffa. But Ali didn't come. After all, the number of steps any given party was willing to take in this war was determined not by promises, but by fear. Ali sent his son al-Hussein to see Abu al-Dhahab with a gift of eight horses. Abu al-Dhahab accepted the gift, welcomed the boy al-Hussein, and sent him back laden with additional gifts for himself and his father.

Then, on the forty-eighth day of the siege, Abu al-Dhahab decided on a change of course. He sent someone to the city gate bearing a white flag. The gate was opened for the standard-bearer, and he went in. The letter borne by the messenger called upon the people of the city to surrender in return for their lives.

Rejecting the proposal, Karim told the messenger, "This city, which has stood up to you all this time, isn't going to come crawling out to you in surrender."

That night the shelling came to a complete halt, allowing the townsfolk the soundest sleep they'd enjoyed since the siege began. However, they slumbered beneath a blanket of dread.

To Karim's surprise, the city gate opened the following day and the Moroccan horsemen rode out toward Abu al-Dhahab's camp. Then, before he could close the gates again, the besieging army began pouring into the city in huge waves, in the face of which his men's muskets and bronze cannons were of no use at all.

The city guards, who had despaired of help arriving from the north, had been bribed with 14,000 piasters, and Jaffa fell in less than two hours.

The first thing Abu al-Dhahab's soldiers did was to assure the townspeople of their safety, declaring their families and their property inviolable. Reassured, the people of the city remained in their houses. As the occupation entered its second day, Abu al-Dhahab's army continued its search for fleeing and wounded soldiers, foremost among them Karim al-Ayyub, who had gone on fighting until the very end.

Before noon, a number of Abu al-Dhahab's soldiers went through the city calling on people to gather outside the city gate. When they did so, however, they were shocked to find the soldiers lining them up in a long row and binding them with ropes and chains. Meanwhile, a number of the soldiers brought out a red velvet chair. Abu al-Dhahab seated himself on the chair, flanked by rows of cannons that had been similarly draped in red velvet in celebration of his victory.

He lifted his hand and brought it down, whereupon heads began flying in all directions, until every man of the city lay dead. All alike had been considered enemy combatants: Muslim, Christian, and Jew, learned and ignorant, young and old, wounded and captive. Only the women and children were spared and taken prisoner. However, the scene of death would only be complete with the issuance of his next command, which his soldiers hastened to carry out by building several towers of severed heads. It wasn't a difficult task to perform, with seven thousand heads lying about, their eyes open in a vain attempt to see what was happening after it was too late.

Before Abu al-Dhahab went to Acre, Karim was found wounded in someone's house, but instead of having him killed, Abu al-Dhahab gave orders for him to be taken to Ramla and treated there.

While Abu al-Dhahab was en route to Acre, Ali al-Daher reached the city at the head of a large army composed of his own forces and those of Daher's former allies. He sent word to his father to leave the city, saying, "I don't want to see your severed head at Abu al-Dhahab's feet! You are my father, after all, and I wouldn't want to see that happen to you!"

Alone now, and trailed by sixty thousand soldiers supported by his own sons, Daher had no choice but to do as Ali had said, yet without knowing who might open his doors to receive him. As Daher was departing the city with Najma, Aisha, al-Sabbagh, and everyone else he feared would be objects of Abu al-Dhahab's reprisal, Ali seized control of the city and began looting everything in it, including even Khan al-Ifranj and the French community's property.

The end, however, was far from complete.

The Sword, Terror,
and Luxurious Cages

A s news of the massacre in Jaffa spread, terror struck, sending
people fleeing from their villages and towns to the mountains
and fields. Even the major cities were brought to their knees,
and before long their streets lay deserted from Haifa to Beirut.

The sword of terror had no need to prove its strength. Even so,
its edge was sharpened by Ali al-Daher's departure from Acre after
the arrival of a messenger from Abu al-Dhahab. The messenger had
brought him a letter whose few words were tantamount to a command:
"You would be well advised to leave Acre at once. Otherwise, I'll bring
it down over your head. This city has one master: the person now coming to take it over!"

Abu al-Dhahab's army spread out from the village of Samiriya to
the al-Na'amin River near Damun, thereby sealing the city off from any
help that might reach it by land. Several days later he decided to take a
tour of Acre. When he arrived, he found nothing but the winds blowing
in from the sea and bouncing off the city's walls and houses, whose owners had shut them up tight, taken their keys, and left.

He spent a few hours there. However, he couldn't be truly happy,
despite his broad grins and cutting remarks about the city that wasn't
"afraid of the sea." With a loud cackle he said, "What they didn't realize
was that it was afraid of the land!" As he spoke, he turned to those with
him and realized that they hadn't heard the saying before.

Thinking about his entry into Acre, Abu al-Dhahab didn't know
whether it could properly be called a victory. After all, he had found it
empty, since terror had entered it before him. He'd even found it without Ali al-Daher, his betrayal of whom had likewise preceded him there.
At the very least, he was glad he hadn't been obliged to place it under
siege the way he had Jaffa.

When he reached the door of the mansion, he raised his hand in a
signal to his soldiers to loot the city. And when he returned to his pavilion, he ordered his ships to go to Sidon and occupy it. He also sent a

messenger to Ali al-Daher in Deir Hanna telling him to come meet him, his sole intention being to kill him.

When Ali failed to respond, two forces moved out, one to occupy Deir Hanna and the other to occupy Safad. Once this had been accomplished, anarchy reigned throughout Galilee, where everyone was now free game to be robbed, murdered, and taken captive with impunity.

Meanwhile, in Sidon, al-Dankizli was reordering his life all over again. He could see that nothing remained of Daher and his sons, who were being plucked out of the land one by one, sometimes by fear, sometimes by the sword.

As death prowled Palestine's highways and byways from south to north, reports of Abu al-Dhahab's triumphs were spawning celebrations in Istanbul and Cairo. For three days straight, the streets of Cairo's Bulaq district and its environs—indeed, all of Egypt—had been festooned with banners and filled with raucous processions, song, and dance. But it wouldn't be long before all the merriment came to an abrupt halt.

It appeared that all Abu al-Dhahab needed was time, and he had decided not to waste it. He sent a messenger to the Sublime Porte demanding that he be appointed emir over the vilayet of Syria, and the response was immediate. As a sign of its goodwill, the empire granted Abu al-Dhahab's messenger the rank of vizier with the title of pasha. At the same time, however, it dispatched Admiral Hasan Pasha al-Jaza'iri at the head of a naval force to take the country over from Abu al-Dhahab!

Meanwhile, not a word was heard about Daher. Those who were afraid for his life were equally afraid to offer him protection. Nevertheless, the invading army made the rounds of the towns and villages in search of some clue that would spell an opportunity to get rid of him. Meanwhile, al-Dankizli sent word to the ships that had dropped anchor in Sidon's port, telling them he wanted to negotiate with them.

Not yet secure in his triumph, Abu al-Dhahab invited the elders and emirs in the surrounding region to come congratulate him in Acre. None of them dared not come, including Daher's ally Nasif al-Nassar, chief of the Matawila, and Ahmad al-Dankizli, to whom Abu al-Dhahab had written, saying, "Before you negotiate with me, you'll have to congratulate me!" So come he did, leaving Sidon to wallow in its bloody fate.

To their shocked dismay, however, all those who came to offer Abu al-Dhahab their congratulations were placed in detention. Uthman al-Daher had been about to come, and had been sending Abu al-Dhahab one letter after another. He had even gone so far as to shave off most of his beard and turn it into a goatee in imitation of the one Abu al-Dhahab had been sporting the last time he saw him in Damascus. However, when he learned that no one who arrived to see Abu al-Dhahab had been allowed to leave, he contented himself with more letters declaring his goodwill and his willingness to offer Abu al-Dhahab and his army whatever they needed.

As for the well-wishers now trapped inside the luxurious but perpetually dark cages that had been prepared to receive them, they began thinking of a way to make their escape.

The Winds Change Course

Beginnings might best be likened to climbing a mountain. As for endings, they're best likened to rolling down one!

No one could understand what was happening. Not long before, they had seen Abu al-Dhahab sitting high and mighty atop his towers of severed heads. And now there was a rumor, spreading like wildfire, that he was ill! No one dared rejoice, since no one believed that people like him could fall ill. He was bound to rise again, in better health than ever, and continue his march all the way to Beirut, beheading anyone who dared oppose him. After all, Abu al-Dhahab wasn't an old man, so the worst that could happen would be for him to fall ill, then regain his health.

Hence, people fearfully awaited the news of his recovery. Even Daher, when he heard about it, set little store by the man's illness. When he was told that Abu al-Dhahab had come down with a fever, he suspected that although he might have some delirium-induced nightmares and break out in a profuse sweat, he wouldn't see the vacant stares in the towers of death he'd left behind.

Abu al-Dhahab had given Acre's French community a grace period in which to lead him to the places where Ibrahim al-Sabbagh may have hidden his money in return for a promise not to do them harm. Hardly had he settled into his pavilion when he received reports from informers saying that the Christians of Galilee made an annual pilgrimage to a place on Mount Carmel known as the Shrine of the Prophet Elijah, or Mar Elias, and that they had built a church on the site known as the Church of Mar Elias. It was said that they brought the saint votive offerings, and that the shrine was topped by a huge dome.

Furious, Abu al-Dhahab began ranting and raving. "That isn't allowed!" he bellowed. "How could the Christians have a dome in Muslim territory?" Then he issued orders for the dome to be razed.

News spread in and around Acre that a force had been sent out to destroy the church's dome. When the news reached the keeper of the nearby Shrine of al-Khadhir, which was visited by Muslims from all over the country, he rushed to Acre in hopes of seeing Abu al-Dhahab before the damage had been done.

But by the time he reached Acre, hundreds of soldiers had already climbed to the top of the church and gone to work, and the only response people received to their wailing and pleading was the sound of pickaxes, which began descending on the dome all the more violently.

"Please, sir, this place is sacred to Christians, and close to Muslims' hearts as well. The shrine is a place of refuge for the poor and unfortunate. It's also the site of an ancient church. Never have we heard of anyone razing something that had been built by our forefathers. So I beg you, for God's sake: don't do this!"

No sooner had the keeper of the shrine finished speaking than one of Abu al-Dhahab's commanders came in to inform him that the dome had been destroyed. The man bowed his head, struggling to hold back his tears.

"Go on, Sheikh, go on!"

"Is there anything more to say after this, sir? Didn't God Almighty say, 'The matter on which you have asked me to enlighten you has been decided'? Please allow me to go back now, may God grant you length of days!"

Abu al-Dhahab instructed his assistants to honor the shrine's keeper, whereupon they took him to the neighboring tents and began preparing gifts for him as he looked on uncomprehendingly.

When they had finished, he asked, "What is this?"

"They're our master's gift to you!"

"Please thank your master for me. But I only came to prevent a catastrophe, not to receive a gift!"

As the imprisoned well-wishers paced back and forth like caged animals, al-Dankizli said to Nasif al-Nassar, "We could escape!"

"Escape? Where? Wherever we try to hide, we'll meet up with his soldiers."

"Isn't he sick now?"

"Yes, but his soldiers' gun barrels are in perfect health!"

"Don't look into the eyes of their guns. Look into the eyes of the pashas and beys around him! Can't you see they know he's a goner?"

"I don't want to die a fugitive, even if I'm fleeing captivity!"

Meanwhile, in Abu al-Dhahab's pavilion, a similar situation prevailed. Perceptions were governed by fear alone, which had stolen deep into every heart.

Abu al-Dhahab's face alternately tightened and relaxed, his brow drenched in a sweat that gave off an odor like none anyone had ever smelled before. Midway through the seventh night, he sat up in bed, screaming, "Get them out of my sight! I don't want to see them! Get them away from me! How did they get in here? How? Cut off their legs and their hands! Cut off their heads again! Burn them up!"

Then he lunged forward, reeling, forming a ring with his thumbs and forefingers as though he wanted to strangle someone. His physician and the senior officers present backed fearfully out of his way. But before he reached the center of the pavilion, he stopped suddenly and asked, "How did I get here?" Then he fell to the ground like a stone.

"Is he dead?" the physician asked nervously.

"That's what you're supposed to tell us, not what we're supposed to tell you!" Isma'il Bey shouted.

The physician knelt down and checked his pulse. He knew he was dead, but was afraid to say so. He was afraid that in a moment or two he might suddenly come back to life, hear him pronouncing him dead, and order him killed!

"What? Is he dead?"

"Maybe."

Isma'il Bey realized that the physician wasn't the only fearful one under the pavilion's dome that night. In fact, he suspected that what the physician had just said was the most intelligent thing that had ever come out of his mouth.

Coming closer, Isma'il Bey checked his pulse one more time.

"Shut up the pavilion," he ordered. Then he began thinking fast.[51]

---

51   In another account of events, Daher paid one of Abu al-Dhahab's men 5,000 piasters to slip him the poison that killed him. Those who favor this version of the story base it on the following statement attributed to Daher: "It's impossible to live in an age without being affected by its evils. The age you live in is like a river: you have no choice but to wade into it, and if the plague has spread widely enough, it's bound to afflict you. At the same time, your honor requires you to wipe out the plague, then quickly recover your humanity lest your own soul turn into a plague!"

He was certain that if news of Abu al-Dhahab's death was allowed to spread, his army would disintegrate in no time. He also knew it would be impossible to bury him in Palestine after all he had done.

He summoned the senior military commanders and instructed them to get their battalions in order, since they would be returning south, and he confided in some of them concerning Abu al-Dhahab's death.

Of course, such news was too momentous to keep hidden, and before long it had been spread abroad by the escalating chaos. The first to sense it were al-Dankizli and Nasif al-Nassar, and by daybreak they and those with them had fled.

Faced with the question of how to transport Abu al-Dhahab's body from Acre to Egypt, his men decided to disembowel it and embalm it.

On the morning of June 10, 1775, Abu al-Dhahab's army—a giant, headless body—began withdrawing to where it had come from. Its progress slowed somewhat on the outskirts of Ramla, where the wounded Karim al-Ayyub was being held captive. And as though the campaign that had begun by severing seven thousand heads could only reach completion by severing one more, they beheaded Karim.

The Basket of Heads

When Daher learned of Abu al-Dhahab's death, the smile returned to his face. However, he was careful to make certain that the news was true, and not a ruse like the one Ali Bey had fallen for when he decided to return to Salihiya.

That evening, Nasif al-Nassar arrived. He embraced Daher and confirmed that Abu al-Dhahab was dead.

Embracing him in return, Daher whispered, "You were right!"

Even though he knew that the first place Abu al-Dhahab would look for him was among his allies, and among the Matawila in particular, Daher had sought refuge in the village of Hunin in Matawila territory. The situation had become so dire that Nasif al-Nassar was the only man Daher felt he could trust any more, and Sheikh Nasif had taken him in without the slightest hesitation.

"Did anyone see you on your way here, Sheikh?"

"I don't think so. We made a point of coming separately so as not to attract attention."

"That's good. That means I'll have to move fast too in order not to arouse Abu al-Dhahab's suspicion."

"What are you going to do?"

"I'm going to go congratulate him on taking over Jaffa and Acre!"

"What?"

"It's the only way I can protect you, Sheikh."

"They'll write in tomorrow's history books that you betrayed both yourself and me by going there!"

"That's all right, Sheikh. As long as I'm protecting you, they can write whatever they like!"

Looking half her age in the light of the setting sun, Najma glanced up and said with a smile, "Let him go, Sheikh. Let him go!"

Daher turned toward her. She sat serenely stitching a dress as he'd seen her do long before in Tiberias, and later in Acre.

"Why are you mending your own dress?" he asked reproachfully. "Let someone else mend it for you!"

"Daher," she replied, "there are certain things that I don't let others do for me because I like to do them myself. Would you like someone else to do your walking for you just because you're tired, or because he's faster than you?"

Al-Dankizli looked around him in consternation. There were many things he would have to deal with quickly, before either Daher or Ali reached Acre. Ali's arrival would spell immediate death for him, since Ali would never forgive him for having always sided with the sheikh, or for the wars he had waged on Daher's behalf on every fortress in which Ali and his army had taken refuge. But the best way to prove his loyalty to Daher would be to seize control over Acre and turn it over to him again.

After hurriedly gathering a force of a thousand soldiers, al-Dankizli entered the city. Within a couple of days, however, this little army of his had split, with some supporting Daher and others supporting Ali. Before long the city was divided, and the two warring factions had barricaded themselves in opposite sides of the city and begun firing at each other, each side hoping against hope that its own leader would be the first to arrive at the head of an auxiliary force. But when people began excitedly announcing Daher's arrival, Abdullah al-Wawi, leader of the pro-Ali faction, put down his weapon and surrendered on behalf of himself and his soldiers.

Daher arrived in Acre on a blistering June afternoon, ten days after the departure of Abu al-Dhahab's army. But how the city had changed, and what destruction it had endured! It looked as though it had been hit by several earthquakes and hurricanes. If he hadn't seen its walls towering proudly above him the way he had left them, he would have thought he was in the wrong place.

No one was happier to see Daher than al-Dankizli, who for days had been running his hands over his head to make sure it was still attached to his body. Yet, however wonderful it is to have one's head still on one's shoulders, this wasn't the only reason for his joy.

When al-Dankizli saw Daher riding into the city, he went running up to him. Before he had crossed the threshold, he took his hand and kissed it several times. As he did so, Daher felt a stab of sorts, as though blood had come gushing out of the back of his hand, and at that moment all his fears were confirmed.

It was the first time al-Dankizli had ever done such a thing. Daher pushed him gently away, and he took a few steps back. To his surprise, he found Najma staring at him, and he heard her voice coming from a distance: *Do you have something to say about the oil left in the sheikh's lantern?*

He found himself replying unthinkingly, "Who, me? No, no!" And he froze in place. But as he looked away to avoid Najma's glance, he found himself face to face with a beautiful concubine who needed no introduction, and he froze again.

That evening, despite being weary from his time in hiding, Daher gathered all his close associates in Acre, who had reached the city several days before he did.

Al-Dankizli began talking nonstop, while Daher nodded. He talked about Sidon and the siege it had endured, and about his captivity and the way he had been forced against his will to congratulate Abu al-Dhahab. He talked about his escape after Abu al-Dhahab's death, and his decision to regroup the army and enter Acre before Ali al-Daher. When he had finished, Daher was still nodding.

After al-Dankizli had left with the judge and the mufti, al-Sabbagh turned to him and said, "Did you believe a word he said?"

"Of course, Ibrahim, of course! Besides, he's all I have left now!"

As it watched Daher reel under Abu al-Dhahab's blows even after his death, the Ottoman Empire forgot the royal pardon it had granted him. Ali al-Daher, Abu al-Dhahab's ally, was now lying in wait for his father, while Uthman, who had corresponded with Abu al-Dhahab from his mansion in Shafa'amr, had begun corresponding directly with the Ottoman Empire and making it promise after promise.

The empire now decided to put Daher to an impossible test by demanding that he pay the taxes he had refused to pay over the previous seven years. It was fully confident that he would not do so, for the simple reason that he had nothing left.

As for Daher, he quickly set about repairing and fortifying the city and mounting cannons on its walls. He had received word that the empire was mobilizing a huge army to attack Acre by land,[52] and that Hasan Pasha al-Jaza'iri's fleet would soon arrive bearing a single royal command: to behead Daher and all his progeny, and to bring their heads back to Istanbul.

---

52 The empire appointed the governors of Damascus, Jerusalem, and Adana to head this army, along with Ahmad Pasha al-Jazzar, the coastal administrator who, after the battle over Beirut, had refused to surrender to anyone but Daher. Later, however, he betrayed Daher and went to Damascus to join forces with its governor.

Friend and Foe

The storm that was brewing within Acre, from street to street and alleyway to alleyway, was fiercer by far than the August waves that lapped its walls gently from without.

Daher amassed all the weapons and men he could from outside the city as letters went out in haste all over the region, urging his allies to rally to his side. The first to respond was Nasif al-Nassar. As for his sons and everyone else, they acted as though the letters had never arrived.

Daher met with al-Sabbagh, al-Dankizli, Nasif al-Nassar, and Acre's judge and mufti, requesting their counsel.

"We'll offer to pay Hasan Pasha al-Jaza'iri the taxes we owe, and if he refuses the offer we'll be prepared to fight him," said Nasif al-Nassar.

Al-Sabbagh disagreed. "Where will we get the money to pay him when we haven't got a single piaster in our treasury? But if he wants to take Acre by force, he's welcome to try. We have enough cannons to ward off the attack, and soldiers who can prevent him from coming ashore."

"We won't be able to do anything!" al-Dankizli objected. "They've got thirteen large ships, which I saw with my own eyes when they arrived in Sidon. Acre won't be able to hold out against them! What I need is some money to give to Hasan Pasha so that when he returns to Istanbul, he'll have something to appease the Ottoman authorities with!"

"I've told you that our coffers are empty, and you know Hasan Pasha wouldn't accept anything less than two thousand kisas!" al-Sabbagh replied angrily.

Daher sat listening quietly to the debate.

"What do you say, Sheikh?" Nasif al-Nassar asked him.

"I'm listening. Go on!"

"Sheikh, you know you have servants who could come up with this sum," al-Dankizli said to him, looking directly at al-Sabbagh.

"As for me, there isn't a poorer man around! The sheikh knows I lost all I had when I lent Ali Bey money for his campaign to Egypt. When Ali Bey left, my money left with him!" al-Sabbagh retorted.

"That's what you say. But everyone knows that for the past fourteen years you've been amassing a fortune. Who hasn't heard about the way you fleeced Gaza during the war with Abu al-Dhahab and made away with all its grain? Or the way you left Jaffa bleeding and without even the bare necessities?"

"If what you're saying were true, Jaffa wouldn't have been able to go on fighting Abu al-Dhahab for forty-nine entire days when he laid siege to it. Mark my words: Acre will go on fighting for twice that long!"

Certain that tax collection was the least of the Ottomans' worries, Daher asked al-Dankizli to keep quiet, and he stormed out.

Before Daher could send a messenger to Hasan Pasha, Acre woke to find thirteen warships in its waters.

Daher walked up and down the city's towers and walls, ordering his soldiers to fire. They held back at first, and it was only when he shouted at them, his eyes ablaze, that they carried out his command. However, rather than firing directly at the enemy ships, they fired some distance away from them, and the cannon shells fell into the water.

In response, the ships quickly retreated from the range of fire.

On that placid sea and under the blazing August sun, anxiety was mounting. The army the Ottoman authorities had promised to send to besiege Acre by land had yet to arrive, and Hasan Pasha wasn't prepared to fight the battle alone lest it be said, if he were defeated, that this had happened because he wanted the victory for himself!

So he waited.

That night, which was as still as death, Daher came into the mansion and found Najma and Aisha still awake. Without waiting for them to ask what was happening, he said, "If the two of you would like to leave Acre tomorrow, I won't stop you." And he said no more.

Given the nightmarish lesson he'd learned from the Jaffa massacre, he had ordered the evacuation of women, children, and the elderly.

"Even if you were the last person left here, I'd still stay, Sheikh. Do you think a mother could leave her son behind at a time like this?"

Then, as if she knew he was waiting for her to make him smile, even in the dark, she said, "Besides, as you can see, I haven't got much time left. So do you really think I'd live to be seventy?"

"And how about you, Aisha?"

"I won't leave a house where I've lived as a free woman to go to one where I'd live as a slave!"

His heart smiling at Najma's quip, and aching over what Aisha had said, he turned to leave, wishing the two of them a good night.

At last Najma went to sleep, exhausted, and Aisha fell asleep across from her on the other bed. Not long afterward, Najma heard strange voices outside her window. She got up. She went over and tried to waken Aisha, but without success. She shook her a second time, and a third, but couldn't rouse her. Looking out the window, she saw armed soldiers whispering to each other and coming toward the door. In the distance she saw guards lying dead on the ground. Leaving Aisha, she went running down the long corridor to Daher's room. She opened the door and went in. She tried to waken him, but to no avail. Time was running out. The soldiers' voices were approaching, the steps of death were approaching, and Daher was asleep! She shook him a second time, and a third. *How is it that people don't wake up any more?* she wondered in consternation. She looked around, unsure what to do. The only helpers she found in the end were her own two hands. She bent down and slipped them under his lean body. She was certain she wouldn't be able to carry him. However, some mysterious force prompted her to make the attempt. She did and, to her amazement, she lifted him with the greatest of ease and carried him out the door. He was light as a feather in her arms. She went up some steps, then down again, whereupon she came to a door she had never seen before. She pushed on it with her foot and it opened easily. She went inside and closed it again with her foot. She began inching her way forward in the pitch dark until her right foot came up against something, which she soon realized was a chest or a bed. She leaned forward and placed Daher on top of it. No sooner had she straightened up again than she was dazzled by a bright light and found herself surrounded by soldiers.

She screamed so loudly that Aisha started out of her slumber in fright, saying over and over, "Bismillah al-rahman al-rahim, bismillah al-rahman al-rahim!" as she stroked Najma's hair and forehead. It had been a dream.

The next morning, Najma watched Daher leave the mansion on the back of a white horse, surrounded by a number of his soldiers. She hid her face as if to erase what she had seen, and when she looked up again she found that Aisha had come and sat down beside her.

When Daher reached the diwan, he was surprised to find that al-Sabbagh no longer opposed sending some money to appease Hasan Pasha. However, al-Sabbagh insisted on one thing: "We have to collect the money from whoever is able to give, and not burden people with our request. After all, this is wartime. And at times like this when people know that, God forbid, some harm might come to their country, nothing reassures them more than having secure walls around them and some money in their pockets!"

Daher made no objection, and al-Dankizli seemed overjoyed. He even got up and put his arms around al-Sabbagh, apologizing for all the unkind things he had said about him. Daher signaled to al-Sabbagh to return the embrace. Al-Sabbagh nodded. However, in a response that was tepid at best, all he did was raise his arms and pat al-Dankizli limply on the back.

Glowing from head to toe over his encounter with Hasan Pasha, Daher's messenger Hussein Effendi told them that the admiral had accepted their offer, his only caveat being that the sheikh could have thought of some better way to receive his ships than to fire on them with his cannons!

Hussein Effendi concluded by saying, "I promised him I would be back on his ship this evening with what we had promised: one thousand kisas of tax money, and one hundred kisas as a gift for him, as well as all the sheep, poultry, flour, and other provisions his sailors will need for their journey home."

Al-Dankizli rose and said, "I'll deliver it to him myself so that I can get a close look at his weapons and soldiers. This way, if he tricks us by taking the money without keeping his side of the bargain, we'll have a clear idea of his strengths and weaknesses before the battle begins!" Then he reminded Daher of the time, many years earlier, when he had gone out at the head of a force that attacked Sulayman Pasha's army on the shore of Lake Tiberias.

"No, Hussein Effendi will deliver it," al-Sabbagh objected. "What we've collected, we've collected to gain Hasan Pasha's favor, not so that we can spy on him, assuming that we'd actually do such a thing!"

"What do you mean, Sabbagh?" al-Dankizli shouted. He nearly drew his sword, and would have done so if it hadn't been for a stern look from Daher.

"Al-Dankizli will go, Ibrahim. I agree to the idea," Daher said.

Al-Sabbagh made no reply.

As al-Dankizli left the diwan to prepare what had been requested by the admiral, he was about to explode with rage: *How could Hasan Pasha have agreed to this? How?*

Al-Sabbagh eyed al-Dankizli until he was gone. Then he turned to Daher and said, "Al-Dankizli is a traitor, Sheikh, and he's going to ruin everything Hussein Effendi has accomplished!"

"You say that because you hate him, Ibrahim. But I don't doubt his sincerity. He's been like a son to me ever since I met him."

"And suppose he *is* like a son to you? Look at your sons. They've betrayed you and left you in the lurch!"

"My sons might betray me, Ibrahim. But al-Dankizli would never do such a thing!"

Al-Sabbagh turned and found everyone gathered in the room listening in silence to the harsh exchange. Squeezing al-Sabbagh's hand, Daher whispered to him, "Follow me. I need to have a word with you!"

When they'd gotten some distance away from the diwan door, Daher shouted in a whisper, "Do you think I'm such a gullible fool that you need to preach to me in front of all those people, Ibrahim? Don't you know I'm aware of al-Dankizli's betrayals?"

"And how is that, Sheikh?"

"I saw the way the soldiers hesitated to obey my orders! I saw the shells that fell into the water instead of hitting the enemy ships even though they were within firing range! That's how!"

"How is it, then, that you're sending him to meet with Hasan Pasha? I don't understand that, Sheikh!"

"I'm sending him because I want to know when they'll begin their attack."

"And do you expect a traitor to tell you something like that?"

"Yes, I do."

"I don't understand, Sheikh."

"He'll tell me because that's the only way he has of proving his good-will and innocence."

"So you're al-Dankizli?" Hasan Pasha asked as he looked toward Acre from aboard his ship.

538

"Yes, I am, Pasha."

"You sent me a message through a certain captain promising to hand Acre over to me as soon as I arrived. Well, I've arrived, and all I've seen so far is your cannon fire!"

"I'm still holding to my promise, Pasha. As for the shells, you must have noticed that they fell some distance from your ships. I planned it that way. But what I can't understand is why you agreed to accept the money and the offerings Daher sent."

"Sit down, sit down," Hasan Pasha said to al-Dankizli, pointing to a long wooden bench.

So he sat down.

"I don't doubt your loyalty to me, Ahmad. Do you know why? Because this loyalty of yours is the only thing you have to defend yourself with! So don't worry. I just wanted to gain some time. I can't wage a war before the land forces arrive in Acre. But that doesn't matter any more as long as I have you on the inside. Do you see?"

"I see."

"Very well. You may go now."

"And what will I say to Daher?"

"Tell him what you know. Tell him that the attack will begin tomorrow, since Hasan Pasha has gone back on his promise to Hussein Effendi."

"And why should I give him a piece of information as important as that?"

"Because I want him to be assured of your truthfulness, and because I still need you there inside the walls. I want to know how far this passionate loyalty of yours can take us!"

That night, Hasan Pasha stood observing Acre, certain that the morrow would be its last day. Reassured now that al-Dankizli's soldiers belonged to him, he recalled the events of their meeting, and felt the rapture of a victory that would be his alone.

He ordered his ships to advance toward Acre and demolish it. It took him only minutes to reach the position he needed in order to commence the attack, and a moment later the roar of cannon shells could be heard. In a state of shock and terror, Acre descended into chaos.

Surrounded by his trusted men atop the city wall, Daher was waiting for the decisive moment. He gave an order to fire, but instead of obeying, the cannoneers abandoned him, leaving their cannons silent and descending into the city. He went up to a cannon and began readying it to shell the ships, which were hardly more than an arrow's shot away. He fired one shell, then another. His men tried to help him, but the shells fell far from the ships, or directly in front of them, without effect.

"Bring al-Dankizli here!" he shouted.

His cavalrymen took off to carry out his order, but returned without al-Dankizli, unable to do anything but surround Daher to protect him.

The bombardment went on for three days, with Daher scurrying back and forth in vain between one cannon and another. His army now split in half, he divided the men still with him into two groups. One of them fired at the approaching ships, while the other guarded the backs of those on the wall from attacks by al-Dankizli and his men.

In the predawn hours of the third day, al-Dankizli stormed Daher's mansion, his sole purpose being to take Aisha. With friend and foe so thoroughly mingled that it was impossible to distinguish one from the other, the soldiers guarding the mansion fell like dominoes.

He stormed in, breaking down every door he came to until he reached Aisha's room. He found her trembling in Najma's arms. Putting his pistol to Najma's head, he snarled, "Let her go before I kill you!"

"And do you think Daher's mother could be afraid of a traitor?"

Realizing that it wouldn't be easy to carry out the deed while looking at her, he closed his eyes and pulled the trigger, but the bullet didn't come out.

Opening his eyes again, he grabbed Aisha out of her arms and shoved her violently toward his soldiers, who quickly took her out. "Won't you ever die, old woman?" he screamed in Najma's face.

"Not before I see the likes of you meet their end!"

Then he left.

When Najma got up, darkness filled the mansion.

The intruders had snuffed out all the lanterns on their way out, and there was no more sign of their shadows on the walls.

An hour later, shortly before sunrise, one of Daher's soldiers arrived and instructed everyone in the mansion to conceal their faces and follow him, since the sheikh was waiting for them at the landward gate.

Najma moved quickly to round up all the men and women who worked in the house. When they got to the city gate, they found Daher encircled by his horsemen, who were surrounded in turn by al-Dankiz-li's soldiers. A few meters away from Daher, Najma recognized al-Sabbagh, the judge, the mufti, Hussein Effendi, and the elderly Jurays with his wife and family, all of whom had come in disguise. The only exception was Aliya, who had intrepidly left her face exposed as though she were looking for someone to kill her and relieve her from the torment of having lost her husband Karim.

From atop the city walls al-Dankizli's soldiers were shouting, "All those who want to leave the city should get out now before they're slaughtered by Hasan Pasha's navy!"

People surged toward the gate.

"This is your last chance to leave with the others, Sheikh. So get out before you die," al-Dankizli said to Daher.

"I'll leave knowing that if you could kill me, you would, Ahmad," Daher replied.

Then he headed for the gate, followed by Najma and her company, and joined al-Sabbagh and those with him.

On the morning of August 29, 1775, Daher cast a glance back at Acre, which lay in the distance silent as a tomb. Half an hour later, he came up to Najma and squeezed her hand reassuringly. She looked away to hide a couple of tears that were about to fall.

As Daher went about checking on everyone who had left with him, he suddenly stopped and asked a question that no one could answer: "Where's Aisha?"

Without waiting for a response, he turned his horse toward Najma. When she saw him, she knew he had discovered her absence.

Al-Dankizli stood at the city gate, looking northward. He was clutching Aisha, who looked like a lifeless body propped up by an unseen force. His anxiety had been mounting, but suddenly he smiled when he saw a certain white horse galloping madly in his direction. He cocked his musket and waited.

"I'll be the one to kill him, and no one else," he said to his soldiers, who lowered their guns.

Sand went flying in all directions around the horse as it approached like a wave rolling in from the sea. Al-Dankizli aimed, fired, and reloaded his musket. As he did so, Aisha broke loose from his grip and went flying like an arrow toward the sheikh, who reached down to lift her onto the horse. However, the shot that had penetrated his shoulder had robbed him of strength, and he lost his balance. His arm too weak to lift anyone, he tottered, then fell to the ground beside her.

As al-Dankizli ran toward him, Daher looked in his direction and got up. Holding on to Aisha with one hand, he fired with the other, but missed. Then he quickly flung his pistol aside and drew his sword. The sun had risen higher in the sky, tingeing the entire shore red. Najma and a number of cavalrymen were approaching from a distance, but they could see that it was too late.

Al-Dankizli aimed and fired his fatal shot into Daher's heart. But he didn't fall. He remained standing, blood gushing out of his chest and his eyes fixed on al-Dankizli's face—the powerful, penetrating eyes al-Dankizli knew so well. Drawing his sword, al-Dankizli lunged at Daher and, with all the strength he could muster, cut off his head. As the blood streamed out of his body, it turned into the hugest lantern flame under the sun, and began burning more and more brightly.

Al-Dankizli took a final step in Daher's direction. He nudged him with his foot and he fell over, his head lying nearby on the ground with eyes that hadn't lost their luster.

Meanwhile, Aisha took off running toward the shore, intending to throw herself into the sea. Before she reached the water's edge, a shot rang out. Al-Dankizli saw her fall. Turning to the soldier who'd fired the shot, he shrieked, "Why did you kill her?"

"She was trying to escape!"

In response, al-Dankizli grabbed another soldier's pistol and shot the man dead. As he made his way toward Aisha with uncertain steps, he felt as though the sand were about to swallow him up. Suddenly he stopped in his tracks, turned, and went back to where Daher's head lay. He bent down and picked it up. Then he headed for the city gate, his soldiers close behind.

In the distance, Najma got off her horse and planted her feet in the soil. Then, feeling for the first time that this wasn't enough, she bent and planted her hands there as well. She closed her eyes for a long time. Then she took a deep breath as though she were recovering all she had lost, and got up again.

Endings

When Hasan Pasha saw Daher's head in al-Dankizli's hands, he said, "Put it on that chair. I want to look at it."

Al-Dankizli did as Hasan Pasha had told him. Hasan Pasha peered into Daher's eyes, which were as bright as ever. Then he bowed his head in thought.

Fifteen minutes later, he looked up again and asked al-Dankizli, "Are you the one who killed him, or did someone else do it?"

"I killed him myself, Pasha, just as I promised you I would!"

"How many years did you serve the sheikh?"

"More than half my lifetime."

"And before you worked for him, what did you do in your home country?"

"I was a woodcutter, Pasha."

"How much did you earn in that profession?"

"Just enough to get by."

"And how much did you earn working for the sheikh?"

"At least two hundred kisas a year."

"You lived off his generosity all those years, and then you betrayed him?"

The admiral got up, walked over to al-Dankizli, and said, "May God take revenge on me if I don't take revenge on you!"

And with a stroke of the sword swift as lightning, he sent al-Dankizli's head flying.

Hasan Pasha entered the city and allowed his sailors to loot it. When, several days later, Muhammad Pasha al-Azm's army arrived, he was charged with negligence for being more than two weeks late.

Hasan Pasha arrested Ibrahim al-Sabbagh, who had taken refuge in the Jaddin fortress, and subjected him to all manner of torture until he confessed where he had hidden his money. He had stashed some of it in chests in the Franciscan monastery in Acre, some with a number of French merchants, and some in other places such as Sidon. It was said that one of the chests alone was so heavy that it took eight men to carry it. On orders from their government, the French merchants handed over to Hasan Pasha sixty-three thousand bags of gold that had belonged to al-Sabbagh, as well as eighty-two thousand bags of dirhams and assorted rarities and jewelry.

Hasan Pasha returned to Istanbul bearing Daher's head, which had been preserved with embalming fluid, and with Ibrahim al-Sabbagh in shackles.

Hasan Pasha summoned Daher's sons to Acre, promising to do them no harm. All of them came except Ali. He executed Sa'id and imprisoned the others before exiling them to Istanbul.

Ali al-Daher was hunted, and successive wars were waged against him. His sons al-Hasan and al-Hussein were captured and taken to Istanbul. By a masterful ruse, a commander subordinate to Muhammad Pasha al-Azm, governor of Damascus, joined forces with Ali together with his soldiers after publicly declaring himself in rebellion against the governor. One night, the commander and his men attacked and killed Ali, whereupon his head was taken to Istanbul with the heads of three of his followers. When Ali's two sons were summoned, they wept at the sight of the severed head, thereby confirming to the Ottoman authorities that it did, in fact, belong to him. This had been deemed necessary because Ahmad Pasha al-Jazzar, whom the empire had appointed governor of Acre, had denied that the head belonged to Ali in order to spite the governor of Damascus for having gotten to Ali before he did.

Ahmad Pasha al-Jazzar pursued the Matawila, seized their land, and took their women captive. Nasif al-Nassar was killed, and the remaining Matawila relocated to Baalbek.

Najma was seen in numerous places thereafter, until at last she settled in the village of Hadiya.[53]

---

53   Hadiya is the village in which the novel *Time of White Horses* is set.

Glossary

Ayn al-Sitt: Literally "the Lady's Spring," Ayn al-Sitt is one of sixteen springs located in the Palestinian city of Nablus.

Bismillah al-rahman al-rahim: In the name of God, the most merciful, most compassionate.

Daughter of Imran: A reference to the Virgin Mary.

diwan: A gathering place for the men of a family, tribe, or local community.

Eid al-Fitr: The holiday that marks the end of Ramadan, the Muslim month of fasting.

Fatiha: The first chapter of the Qur'an.

The Franciscans and the Greek Orthodox: The Church of the Annunciation (so called because of a tradition that it was built at the spot where, as Mary was going to draw water from a spring, the angel Gabriel announced to her that she would conceive a son by the Holy Spirit) was destroyed by Baybars and his Mamluk army in 1260 CE. Following this, the Franciscans helped to take care of the site on which the church had been built. After being expelled from Nazareth in the fourteenth century, the Franciscans were allowed to return in 1620 CE by Emir Fakhr al-Din, at which time they built a small domed structure to enclose the grotto that is venerated as Mary's home, and that contains the spring around which the church had been constructed. During his governorship over Galilee (1730–75), Daher al-Umar issued a decree granting the local Greek Orthodox (Arab Christian) community control over the site, which had been previously occupied by the Franciscans and the Greek Catholics. In 1750, the local Arab Orthodox community built a new church to the south of the grotto, and it has been administered by them ever since.

Ghouta: An agricultural belt to the south and east of Damascus.

"Its date of construction can be discerned easily in 'the abode of felicity'": The poet has encoded the year in which Uthman's house was built within this line of the verse. Hence, he tells the reader that this date "can be discerned easily" via the phrase, "the abode of felicity." When the numerical values assigned to the individual letters that make up the Arabic phrase translated as "the abode of felicity" *(dar al-sa'ada)* are added up, they come to 1182 AH, or 1768/9 CE, the year in which Uthman's house is said to have been constructed.

kisa: An Ottoman monetary unit equivalent to 500 piasters.

mahmal: A richly decorated litter sent by an Islamic ruler to Mecca at the time of the Hajj, or pilgrimage, as an emblem of his state's independence. Delivered to Mecca in a grand procession escorted by brigades of heavily armed cavalrymen, the litter would contain expensive gifts to be distributed among the people of Mecca, and money that would be used to fund the repair of pilgrimage routes and maintain the facilities connected to the sacred mosques in Mecca and Medina.

masriya: A monetary unit equivalent to about one piaster.

mudd: A dry measure equal to approximately eighteen liters, or half a bushel.

multazim: An employee of the Ottoman Empire whose task was to deliver to the state all taxes owed by a particular village or town. The multazim would collect the money due, whether in cash or in kind, and deduct a certain share for himself. He was also entitled to resort to force if the occasion required it.

rotl: A measure of weight equaling somewhere between 2.5 and 3.2 kilograms.

sanjak: An Ottoman government official, below a governor in rank.

sayyadiya: A dish made with rice, fish, and a variety of spices, including cinnamon, cardamom, ginger, and tamarind.

Shawwal: The lunar month that follows Ramadan.

Shrine of al-Khadhir: Al-Khadhir, "the Green One," is a sage who is mentioned, though not by name, in Qur'an 18:65–82, where he conveys a number of spiritual insights to the Prophet Moses. A shrine dedicated to al-Khadhir is located on Mount Carmel near the Shrine of the Prophet Elijah (Mar Elias). Through the ages, Jews, Christians, Muslims, and Druze have all made pilgrimages to the site, to which special healing powers have been ascribed. During the Mamluk and Ottoman periods, the sacred cave of al-Khadhir was overseen by Muslim families, the last of these being the al-Hasan family. After 1948, the shrine was taken over by Israel's Ministry of Religions, which posted new signs and placed all its inscriptions in Hebrew, obliterating all mention of the site's non-Jewish history and its shared sanctity to Jews, Christians, and Muslims.

sirwal: Also known as Punjabi pants, a sirwal is a pair of trousers with narrow-bottomed legs and a large waist that is pulled in with a drawstring. They sometimes have a low crotch for ease of wear.

Sublime Porte: A metaphorical reference to the central government of the Ottoman Empire, to whose principal state departments in Istanbul one gains access through a majestic-looking gate.

Uncle: A respectful form of address to an older man, not necessarily implying a family relationship.

uqiya: A measure of weight equal to around 300 grams.

vilayet: a province of the Ottoman Empire.

Qur'anic Quotations

"Say: 'O God! Lord of Power and Rule, Thou givest power to whom Thou pleasest, and Thou strippest off power from whom Thou pleasest; Thou endowest with honour whom Thou pleasest, and Thou bringest low whom Thou pleasest. In Thy hand is all good. Verily over all things Thou hast power.'" 3:26, Abdullah Yusuf Ali, *The Qur'an: Text, Translation and Commentary.*

"Now, indeed, We have conferred dignity on the children of Adam." 17:70, Muhammad Asad, *The Message of the Qur'an.*

"The matter on which you have asked me to enlighten you has been decided." 12:41, Muhammad Asad, *The Message of the Qur'an.*

Sources

The contents of this novel are based on a number of books and manuscripts, including:

Abu Diyah, Musa, ed. *Daher al-Umar wa Hukkam Nablus*.
Abu Nahl, Usamah Muhammad. *Al-Hukm al-Iqta'i li-Matawilat Jabal 'Amil fi al-'ahd al-'uthmani*. Research paper. http://www.yatar. net/index.php/2013-08-08-21-41-02/1-2012-03-07-20-37-02/detail/12-2012-03-07-21-01-35?tmpl=component.
Buechlein, Claus. *Qadiman fi al-balad al-Muqaddas: Rihlat ila Filastin Qadima*. Translated by Walid al-Basal. Damascus: Markaz al-Ghad al-'Arabi li-l-Dirasat, 2005.
Burckhardt, John Lewis. *Travels in Nubia*. Translated by Faysal Adib Abu Ghush as *Rihlat fi al-Diyar al-Muqaddasa wa-l-Nubah wa-l-Hijaz*. Amman: Manshurat Wizarat al-Thaqafah al-Urduniyah, 2005.
Clemant, Marilene. *Contes Tziganes*. Translated by Ziyad al-'Awdah. Damascus: Wizarat al-Thaqafah al-Suriyah, 1981.
al-Hallaq, al-Budayri. *Hawadith Dimashq al-Yawmiya*. http://www. al-mostafa.info/data/arabic/depot/gap.php?file=001494-www.al-mostafa.com.pdf.
Hanna, Abdullah. *Harakat al-'amma al-dimashqiya*. Beirut: Dar Ibn Khaldun, 1985.

al-Jabarti, Abd al-Rahman. *'Aja'ib al-athar*. http://www.al-mostafa. info/data/arabic/depot/gap.php?file=m011689.pdf.

al-Muhami, Tawfiq Mu'ammar. *Daher al-Umar*. Nazareth: Manshurat al-Ma'had al-'Ali li-l-Funun wa Bayt al-Kitab, 1996.

al-Musa, Sulayman, trans. *Rihlat fi al-Urdun wa-Filastin*. Amman: Manshurat Da'irat al-Thaqafa wa-l-Funun, 1987.

al-Nimr, Ihsan. *Tarikh Jabal Nablus wa-l-Balqa'*. Nablus: Matba'at Jam'iyat 'Ummal al-Matabi' al-Ta'awuniya, 1975.

Phillipp, Thomas. *Acre: The Rise and Fall of a Palestinian City, 1730 to 1831*. New York: Columbia University Press, 2001.

al-Sabbagh, Abbud. *Al-Rawd al-Zahir fi Tarikh Daher*. Edited by Muhammad Abd al-Karim Mahafiza and 'Isam Mustafa Hazayima. Irbid: Dar al-Kindi, 1999.

al-Sabbagh, Mikhail Niqula. "Tarikh Daher al-Umar." Manuscript.

Shihab, al-Amir Haydar Ahmad. *Tarikh Ahmad Pasha al-Jazzar*. Beirut: Maktabat Antoine, 1955.

Sirhan, Nimr. *Mawsu'at al-fulklur al-filastini*. Self-published. Amman, 1989.

Volney, M.C.F. "Travels through Syria and Egypt." https://archive. org/stream/travelsthroughsy02voln#page/n5/mode/2up.

Modern Arabic Literature

The American University in Cairo Press is the world's leading publisher of Arabic literature in translation.

For a full list of available titles, please go to:

mal.aucpress.com